THE BLACK COMPANY
GLITTERING STONE I

Fantasy Novels by Glen Cook

The Black Company

The First Chronicle:
The Black Company (1984)
Shadows Linger (1984)
The White Rose (1985)
(collected as *The Annals of the Black Company*, 1986)
The Silver Spike (1989)
The South:
Shadow Games (1989)
Dreams of Steel (1990)
Glittering Stone:
Bleak Seasons (1996)
She Is The Darkness (1997)
(collected as *The Black Company: Glittering Stone I*, 2000)
Water Sleeps (1999)
Soldiers Live (2000)
(collected as *The Black Company: Glittering Stone II*, 2000)

The Dread Empire:
The Fire in His Hands (1984)
With Mercy Towards None (1985)

A Shadow of All Night Falling (1979)
October's Baby (1980)
All Darkness Met (1980)

Reap the East Wind (1987)
An Ill Fate Marshalling (1988)

The Garrett Files:
Sweet SilverBlues (1987)
Bitter Gold Hearts (1988)
Cold Copper Tears (1988)
(collected as *The Garrett Files*, 1989)
Old Tin Sorrows (1989)
Dread Brass Shadows (1990)
Red Iron Nights (1991)
Deadly Quicksilver Lies (1994)
Petty Pewter Gods (1995)

The Swordbearer (1982)
The Tower of Fear (1989)

THE BLACK COMPANY
GLITTERING STONE I

Bleak Seasons
She Is the Darkness

GLEN COOK

FANTASY

BLEAK SEASONS Copyright © 1996 by Glen Cook
Publication History: Tor hardcover, April 1996
Tor paperback, January 1997

SHE IS THE DARKNESS Copyright © 1997 by Glen Cook
Publication History: Tor hardcover, September 1997
Tor paperback, June 1998

First SFBC Science Fiction Printing: October 2000

Published by arrangement with:
Tor Books
Tom Doherty Associates, LLC
175 Fifth Avenue
New York, NY 10010

Visit The SFBC online at *http://www.sfbc.com*
Visit Tor online at *http://www.tor.com*

ISBN # 0-7394-1299-X

CONTENTS

Bleak Seasons

*For Trish and Kim, precious friends
of a decade and more.*

Incessant wind sweeps the plain. It mutters across grey pavements that sweep from horizon to horizon. It sings around scattered black pillars, a chorus of ghosts. It tumbles leaves and scatters dust come from afar. It teases the hair of a corpse that has lain undisturbed for a generation, mummifying. Impishly, the gale tosses a leaf into the cadaver's silently screaming mouth, tugs it away again. The wind carries the breath of winter.

Lightning leaps from pillar to ebon pillar like a child skittering from base to base in a game of tag. For a moment there is color on that spectral plain.

The pillars might be mistaken for relics of a fallen city. They are not. They are too few and too randomly placed. Nor has a one ever fallen, though many have been gnawed deeply by the teeth of the hungry wind.

1

. . . FRAGMENTS . . .

. . . just blackened fragments, crumbling between my fingers.

Browned page corners that reveal half a dozen words in a crabbed hand, their context no longer known.

All that remains of two volumes of the Annals. A thousand hours of labor. Four years of history. Gone forever.

Or are they?

I do not want to go back. I do not want to relive the horror. I do not want to reclaim the pain. There is pain too deep to withstand right here, right now. There is no way to recapture the totality of that awfulness, anyway. The mind and heart, safely over to the farther shore, simply refuse to encompass the enormity of the voyage.

And there is no time. There is a war on.

Always there is a war on.

Uncle Doj wants something. Just as well to stop now. Teardrops make the ink run.

He is going to make me drink some strange philtre.

Fragments . . .

. . . all around, fragments of my work, my life, my love and my pain, scattered in this bleak season. . . .

And in the darkness, shards of time.

2

HEY, THERE! WELCOME TO THE CITY OF THE DEAD. DON'T MIND THOSE GUYS staring. Ghosts don't see a lot of strangers—at least of a friendly persuasion. You're right. They do look hungry. That happens during these siege things.

Try not to look too much like a lamb roast.

Think that's a joke? Stay away from the Nar.

Welcome to Dejagore, what the Taglians call this deathtrap. The teeny brown Shadowlanders the Black Company grabbed it from call it Stormgard. People who actually live here always called it Jaicur—even when that was a crime. And who knows what the Nyueng Bao call it. And who cares, eh? They aren't talking and they aren't part of the equation anyway.

That's one of them. That rascal there, no meat on him and a skull face. Everybody around here is some shade of brown but theirs is different. It has a grey cast to it. Almost deathly. You won't mistake a Nyueng Bao for anything else.

Their eyes are like polished coal no fire will ever warm.

That noise?

Sounds like Mogaba, the Nar and the First Legion rooting out Shadowlanders again. Some get inside almost every night. They are like field mice. You just can't get rid of them all.

Found some the other day that had been in hiding since the Company took the city.

How about that smell out there? It was worse before the Shadowlanders started burying the bodies. Maybe a shovel was a little too complicated a machine.

Those long mounds that radiate from the city like spokes have corpses stacked like cordwood inside. Sometimes they didn't pile the dirt on deep enough and the gasses of corruption burst the mounds open. That's when you hope the wind is blowing their way.

You see how positively they are thinking, all the not-yet-filled-trenches they are digging. A lot of the dirt goes into the ramps.

The elephants are the worst. They take forever to rot. They tried burning them once, but all that did was irritate the buzzards. So where they could they just dragged the bodies over and incorporated them into their ramps.

Who? The ugly little guy with the uglier hat? That is One-Eye. You must have been warned about him.

How come One-Eye? On account of the eye patch. Clever, huh?

The other runt is Goblin. You should have been warned about him, too. No? Well, stay out of their way. All the time is best, but especially if they are arguing, and most particularly if they have been drinking. As wizards go they are no earthshakers but they are more than you will be able to handle.

Puny as they are, they are the main reason the Shadowlanders have stayed out there in the country roughing it, leaving the wallowable luxuries of the city to the Taglian troops and Black Company.

No, now pay attention. Goblin is the white one. All right, you're right, he is overdue for his annual bath. Goblin is the one who looks like a toad. One-Eye is the one with the hat and the patch.

The guys in the once-upon-a-time-they-were-white tunics are Taglian soldiers. Every day now every one of them asks himself what damned fool notion made him enroll in the legions.

The folks wearing the colored sheets and unhappy expressions are locals. Jaicuri.

Fancy this. When the Company and the legions swooped down from the north and surprised Stormshadow they hailed the newcomers as liberators. They strew the streets with rose petals and favorite daughters.

Now the only reason they don't stab their liberators in the back is that the alternative is worse. Now they are alive enough to starve and be abused.

Shadowspinner is not famous for kindness and kissing babies.

The kids all over? Those almost happy and fat urchins? Nyueng Bao. All Nyueng Bao.

The Jaicuri nearly stopped making babies after the Shadowmasters came. Most of the few that were born failed to survive the hard times since. The handful still breathing are protected more fiercely than any treasure. You won't find them running naked through the streets, squealing and totally ignoring strangers.

Who are the Nyueng Bao? You never heard of them?

It is a good question. And a hard one to answer.

The Nyueng Bao don't talk to outsiders except through their Speaker but the word is that they are religious pilgrims who were on the homeward leg of a once-in-a-generation hadj who got trapped by circumstance. The Taglian soldiers say they hail from vast river delta swamps west of Taglios. They are a primitive, minuscule minority abhorred by the majority Gunni, Vehdna, and Shadar religions.

The whole Nyueng Bao people makes the pilgrimage. And the whole people got caught right in the deep shit here in Dejagore.

They need to work on their timing. Or they should sharpen their skills at appeasing their gods.

The Black Company cut a deal with the Nyueng Bao. Goblin and their Speaker gobbled for half an hour and it was settled. The Nyueng Bao would ignore the Black Company and Taglians for whom the Company is responsible. The Nyueng Bao would be ignored in turn.

It works. Mostly.

Their men are a sort you don't want to upset. They don't take shit from anybody.

They never start anything—except, according to the Taglians, by being too damned stubborn to do what they are told.

Sounds like One-Eye style reasoning at work there.

Just kick those crows. They're getting too goddamn bold! Think they own the place. . . . Hey! You got one. Grab it! They aren't good eating but they are a sight better than no eating at all.

Shit. Got away. Hell, that happens. Head for the citadel. You get your best look at the layout from up there.

3

THOSE GUYS? THEY ARE COMPANY. NEVER GUESS, HUH? WHITE GUYS DOWN here? The one with the wild hair is Big Bucket. He turned into a pretty fair sergeant. He is just crazy enough. With him are Otto and Hagop. They have been around longer than anybody but Goblin and One-Eye.

Those two have been Old Crew for generations. One-Eye ought to be sneaking up on two hundred.

That bunch is Company, too. Shirking work. The antique lunger is Wheezer. Not much good for anything. How he got through the big brawl no one knows. They say he busted heads with the best of them.

The other two black guys are the Geek and the Freak. No telling why. Nothing wrong with them. Look like a couple of rubbed ebony statues, don't they?

You think these names just come out of a hat? They earn them the hard way. Usually they come out from under One-Eye's hat, really. Yeah, they probably have real names. But they have been called by nicknames so long even they have trouble remembering.

Goblin and One-Eye are the main ones not to forget. And to remember not to put behind you. They do not deal well with temptation.

This is Glimmers Like Dewdrops Street. Nobody knows why. A real mouthful, right? You ought to hear it in Jaicuri. A jawbreaker. This is the route the Company took coming in to snatch the tower. Maybe they will rename it Runs With Blood Street.

Yeah, the Company charged through here in the heart of the night, killing anything that moved, and jammed in there before they had any idea what was happening. With Shapeshifter's help they roared on up the tower where they let him help finish off Stormshadow before they tagged him.

It was an old Company grudge. They owed Shifter from another generation, when Shifter, helping Soulcatcher break the city's resistance, murdered One-Eye's brother Tom-Tom when the Company was in service to the Syndic of Beryl. Croaker, One-Eye and Goblin, Otto and Hagop are the only guys left from those days. Hell, Croaker is gone now. Isn't he? History-worshipping slob is buried out there in one of those mounds. Fertilizing the plain. Mogaba is the Old Man now. Sort of, in his own mind.

Those who form it come and go but the Company is forever. Every brother, great or small, is a snack just not yet snapped up by the devouring maw of time.

Those big black monster men watching the gate are the Nar. They are descendants of the Black Company of centuries ago. Scary beasts, aren't they? Mogaba and a whole herd of his pals joined the Company quest at Gea-Xle. The Old Crew have had no pleasure of them.

You mix the whole crowd up and squeeze them dry, you could not come up with two ounces of sense of humor.

There used to be a lot more of them than there are now but they keep getting themselves killed. They are bone crazy, the whole lot. For them the Company is a religion. Only their Company is not the Black Company of the Old Crew. That becomes more apparent almost by the hour. All Nar stand more than six feet tall. All Nar run like the wind and leap like gazelles. Mogaba chose only the most athletic and warriorly to join the quest for Khatovar. All the Nar are quick as cats and strong as gorillas. All the Nar use their weapons like they were born with them in their hands.

The rest? The ones who call themselves the Old Crew? Yeah. It is true. The Company *is* more than a job. If it was just a job, just selling swords to whoever would pay, the Black Company would not be in this part of the world. There was work aplenty in the north. The world never lacks for potentates who want to bully their subjects or neighbors.

The Company is family for those who belong. The Company is home. The Company is a nation of outcasts, alone and defying the whole world.

Now the Company is trying to complete its cycle of life. It is on a quest in search of its birthplace, fabled Khatovar. But all the world seems determined that Khatovar shall be unattainable, a virgin forever hidden behind a veil of shadow.

The Company is home, sure, but Croaker was the only one who ever went completely misty-eyed over that damned angle. For him the Black Company was a mystery cult—though he never went as far as Mogaba and made it a holy calling.

Watch your step. They still don't have all the mess cleaned out from the last attack. If you couldn't tell by the smell. The Jaicuri don't help much anymore. Maybe it is lack of civic pride.

The Nyueng Bao? They are just here. They stay out of the way. They have this notion that they can stay neutral. They will learn. Shadowspinner is going to teach them. Nobody stays neutral in this world. The best you can do is choose your spot to jump in.

Little out of shape? You will come around. A few weeks running hither and yon, blunting Shadowspinner's probes and hustling out on Mogaba's spoiling raids, will get you as sharp as a Nyueng Bao sword.

You thought sieges were all just laying around relaxing and waiting the other guy out?

Man, this other guy is a foamy-mouth lunatic.

And not just nuts. He is a sorcerer. A major player, though he hasn't shown much here. Before the Old Man got himself offed in the big slugfest that trapped everyone here he hurt Spinner real bad. The old devil just hasn't been himself since. Poor baby.

This is it. Top of the tower. And there is the whole stinking burg, laid out like it is on one of those sand tables Lady always liked.

Oh, yeah. Those rumors have made it here, too. They started with some Shadowlander prisoners. Maybe that *was* Kina up north. Or something. But it could not have been Lady. She died right out there. Fifty guys saw her taken down. Half of them got killed trying to rescue her.

How can you say that? You can't be sure? How many eyewitnesses does it take? She is dead. The Old Man is dead. They're all dead, them what did not get inside before Mogaba sealed the gates.

The whole mob is dead. All but the crowd in here. And they are caught between lunatics. It's a tossup who is crazier, Mogaba or Shadowspinner.

You see it all? That is it. Dejagore enduring the siege of the Shadowmasters. Not real impressive, is it? But every one of those burned areas memorializes a ferocious hand to hand, house to house negotiation with the Shadowlanders.

Fires start easily in Dejagore.

Hell is supposed to be hot, isn't it?

4

. . . WHO I AM, ON THE IMPROBABLY REMOTE CHANCE THAT MY SCRIBBLINGS do survive. I am Murgen, Standardbearer of the Black Company, though I bear the shame of having lost the standard in battle. I am keeping unofficial Annals because Croaker is dead, One-Eye won't, and hardly anyone else can read or write. I was the heir Croaker trained. I will do it even without official sanction.

I will be your guide for a few months or weeks or days, however long it takes the Shadowlanders to force our present predicament to its inevitable end.

Nobody inside these walls is going to get out of this. There are too many of them and too few of us. Our sole advantage is that our commander is as mad as theirs. That makes us unpredictable. Don't add much hope, though.

Mogaba will not give up as long as he personally is capable of hanging onto something with one hand while he throws rocks with the other.

I expect my writings to blow away on a dark wind, never to be touched by another eye. Or they might become the tinder Shadowspinner uses to light the pyre under the last man he murders after taking Dejagore. If anyone does find this, brother, we begin. This is the Book of Murgen, last of the Annals of the Black Company. The long tale winds down.

I will die lost and frightened in a world so alien I cannot understand a tenth of it when I focus all my soul. It is so *old*. Time lies heavily here. Two thousand-year-old traditions underpin incredible absurdities taken completely for granted. Dozens of races and cultures and religions exist in a mix that should be volatile but has persisted so long that conflicts are just reflexive twitches in an ancient body mostly too tired to bother anymore.

Taglios is only one large principality. There are scores more, mostly now in the Shadowlands, all pretty similar.

The major peoples are the Gunni, the Shadar, and the Vehdna, names which define religion, race and culture all at once. The Gunni are the most numerous and widespread. Gunni temples, to a bewilderingly broad pantheon, are so numerous you're seldom out of sight of one.

Physically, Gunni are small and dark but not black like the Nar. Gunni men wear toga-like robes, weather permitting. Their bright mix of colors declare caste, cult, and professional alliances. Women, too, dress brightly, but in several layers of wraparound cloth. They veil their faces if unmarried, though marriages are made early. They wear their dowries as jewelry. Before they go out they illustrate their foreheads with the caste/cult/professional markings of both their husbands and their fathers. I will never decipher those hieroglyphs.

Shadar are paler, like heavily tanned whites from the north. They are big, usually over six feet. They do not shave or pluck their beard, unlike the Gunni. Some sects never cut their hair. Bathing is not forbidden but it is a vice seldom indulged. Shadar all dress in grey and wear turbans to define their status. They eat meat. Gunni do not. I have never seen a Shadar woman. Maybe they find their babies under cabbage leaves.

The Vehdna are the least numerous of the major Taglian ethnic groups. They are as light as the Shadar but smaller, more lightly built, with ferocious features. They share none of the Shadar's spartan values. Their religion forbids almost everything, rules honored in the breach quite often. They like a little color in their costume, though not bright like the Gunni. They wear pantaloons and real shoes. Even the poorest conceal their bodies and wear something atop their heads. Low-caste Gunni wear nothing but loincloths. Married Vehdna women wear only black. You can see nothing but their eyes. Unmarried Vehdna women you don't see at all.

Only the Vehdna believe in an afterlife. And that only for men except for a few female warrior saints and daughters of prophets who had balls big enough to be honorary men.

Nyueng Bao, rarely seen, usually wear loose-fitting long-sleeve pullover shirts and baggy lightweight pants, generally black, men and women alike. Children go naked.

Any city down here is glorious chaos.

It is always a holy day for somebody.

5

FROM THE CITADEL TOWER IT IS OBVIOUS THAT DEJAGORE IS A COMPLETE contrivance. Of course, most walled cities are shaped by the probability that, part of the time, neighboring states will be managed by thugs. Your own city's masters will never be worse than benevolent despots, of course, and their worst ambition will be to heighten the hometown glory.

Until the appearance of the Shadowmasters one short generation ago war was an alien concept throughout this part of the world. It had seen neither armies nor soldiers in all the centuries since the Black Company's departure.

Into this improbable paradise came the Shadowmasters, lords of darkness from the far reaches of the earth who brought with them all the wolves of the old nightmare. Soon inept armies were about. They stalked unprepared kingdoms like great cruel behemoths even the gods could not stay. The dark tide spread. Cities crumbled. A lucky few the Shadowmasters chose to rebuild. The peoples of the newly-founded Shadowlands were given their options: obedience or death.

Jaicur was reborn as Stormgard, seat of the Shadowmaster Stormshadow, she who could bring the winds and thunder howling and bellowing in the darkness. She who had borne the name Stormbringer in another age and place.

First Stormshadow raised a mound forty feet high on top of the ruins of captured Jaicur, at the heart of a plain she had flattened absolutely by slaves and prisoners of war. Earth for the mound came from the ring of hills completely surrounding the plain. With the mound complete and faced on its outer sides with several layers of imported stone, Stormshadow built her new city up top. And that she surrounded with walls another forty feet high. She did not overlook the latest theories about towers for enfilading fire and barbicans to protect her elevated gates.

All the Shadowmasters seemed driven by a paranoid need to make themselves safe in their home places.

Never once in her planning, though, did she take into account the possibility that she might have to resist the onslaught of the Black Company.

I wish we were half as wicked as I talk.

Dejagore has four gates. Each stands at one point of the compass rose. Each is at the end of a paved highway running straight in from the hills. Only the road from the south carries any traffic these days.

Mogaba has sealed three gates, leaving only sally ports which are guarded by his Nar at all times. Mogaba is determined to fight. He is just as determined that not one of our raggedy-ass Taglian legionnaires will run off and not go down with him.

None of us, be we Black Company Old Crew, Nar, Jaicuri, Taglian, Nyueng Bao, or someone else who had the bad luck to get caught here, is going to get out alive. Not unless Shadowspinner and his gang get so bored they go looking for someone else to bully. Right. You've got the eight and ten of swords and to go down you're going to bet your ass on pulling the nine.

Your chances of pulling that nine are better than ours of getting out of here.

The fortified encampment of the Shadowlanders stands south of the city. It is so close we can reach it with our heavy artillery. You can see charred timbers where we tried to burn them out the day of the big battle. We have raided them a few times since then, too, but no longer have the strength to risk.

We can't seem to discourage Shadowspinner, though.

Like most warlords he doesn't let reality get in the way of his doing whatever he wants to do.

The artillery gives them a wake-up five nights out of five, pick a random time. That keeps them cranky and tired and a lot less effective whenever they attack. Trouble is, so much effort keeps us tired and cranky, too. And we have other projects going as well.

Shadowspinner is a puzzle. He is not the first of his kind in Company experience. The heavyweight killers in our past, though, when faced with a situation like this, would have stomped on Dejagore like jumping on an anthill before looking for a real challenge. But here lightweights Goblin and One-Eye can slide around quickly and treacherously enough to parry Spinner's every feeble thrust.

His weakness is a mystery.

Makes you nervous when an enemy doesn't do everything you think he can. And a Shadowspinner doesn't become a top badass being gentle.

One-Eye sees everything in its wickedest light. He says Spinner is slacking because Longshadow has a hold on him and is weakening him deliberately. Your basic old-time power politics with the Company in the middle.

Before we came along the Shadowmasters did find their biggest challenges in fighting one another.

On principle Goblin seldom agrees with One-Eye about anything. He claims Shadowspinner is lulling us while he recovers from wounds that were more serious than we suspected.

My guess is, six of one, half a dozen of the other.

Crows circle the Shadowlander camp. Always they circle. Some come, some go, but a baker's dozen minimum are there all the time. Others haunt us day and night. Wherever I go, whenever, a crow is nearby. Except inside. They don't get inside. We don't let them inside. Those that try end up in somebody's pot.

Croaker had a thing about crows. I think I understand it now. But the bats bother me more.

We don't see the bats as often. The crows get most of them. (These crows are not ashamed to come out at night.) And those that the crows don't get we do, most of the time. Inevitably, though, a few get away. And that isn't good.

They spy for the Shadowmasters. They are the far-ranging eyes of wickedness out here where our enemies cannot always manipulate the living darkness.

Only two Shadowmasters remain. Spinner has problems. They do not have the reach or control they showed back when they could and did run the shadows into the very heart of the Taglian Territories.

They are fading from the stage.

One dreams.

Dreams too easily become nightmares.

6

WHEN YOU LOOK DOWN FROM THE CITADEL YOU HAVE TO WONDER HOW THE Jaicuri manage, all jammed inside Dejagore's walls. Truth is, they don't and never did.

At one time the hills surrounding the plain were covered with farms and orchards and vineyards. After the shadow came enterprises gradually disappeared as the peasant families abandoned the land. And then the anti-shadow, the Black Company, came, ever so hungry after the long sprint south from the victory at Ghoja Ford. And then came the Shadow-lander armies which battered us.

Now the hills bear little but memories of what once was. Vultures never picked bones much cleaner than those hills have been gleaned.

The wisest peasants were those who fled early. Their children will repopulate the land.

Later the stupid ones ran here, inside the false safety of Dejagore's walls. When Mogaba is particularly cranky he drives a few hundred out the gate. They are just mouths crying to be filled. Food must be hus-banded for those willing to die defending the walls.

Locals who fail to contribute, or who demonstrate a weakness for getting sick or seriously injured, go out the gate right behind the peasants.

Shadowspinner won't take any in but those willing to help raise his earthworks and dig his burial trenches. The former means laboring under falls of missiles directed by old friends inside, while the latter means making the bed where you will lie as soon as you are useful no longer.

Hard choices.

Mogaba cannot fathom why his military genius isn't universally hailed.

He doesn't mess with the Nyueng Bao. Not yet. They haven't con-tributed much to Dejagore's defense but they don't sap resources, either. Their babies are getting fat while the rest of us tighten our belts.

You don't see many dogs or cats now. Horses manage only because they are militarily protected, and then only a handful of them. We're going to eat hearty when the last fodder is gone.

Small game like rats and pigeons are becoming scarce. Sometimes you hear the outraged protest of a crow taken by surprise.

The Nyueng Bao are survivors.

They are a race possessed of a single impassive face.

Mogaba does not bother them mainly because when anybody does the whole bunch gets pissed off. And they consider fighting a really seri-ous, holy business.

They stay out of the way when they can but they aren't pacifists. A couple of times the Shadowlanders have regretted trying to push through their part of town.

The Nyueng Bao generated an amazing amount of carnage both times.

Rumor among the Jaicuri says they eat their enemies.

It is true, human bones showing evidence of butchery and cookery have been found. Jaicuri are mainly of the Gunni religion. Gunni are veg-etarians.

I do not believe the Nyueng Bao are responsible, but Ky Dam refuses to deny even the blackest allegation against his people.

Maybe he will accept any canard that makes the Nyueng Bao seem more dangerous. Maybe he wants that kind of talk so fear will build.

Survivors grasp the tools at hand.

I wish they would talk. I'd bet they could tell stories that would curl your toes and straighten your hair.

Ah! Dejagore! Those halcyon days, slouching through hell with a smile on.

How long before all the fun goes out of the town?

7

BONE TIRED, JUST AS I HAD BEEN EVERY NIGHT FOR AS LONG AS I COULD remember, I went to take my turn on the wall. I had no ambition at all and even less energy. Seated in a crenel, I heaped aspersions on the ancestors of all my bitty Shadowlander buddies. I am afraid I lacked creativity but I made up for that with virulence. They were up to something out there. You could hear rattlings and mutterings and see torches moving around. There were all the harbingers of a night without sleep. Couldn't these people be normal and handle their business during regular hours?

It didn't sound like they were more enthusiastic than me. I caught the occasional sharp remark about me or my foredaddies, like this mess was all my fault. I guess they were motivated mainly by their sure knowledge that they would never go home if they didn't recapture Stormgard.

Maybe nobody on either side would get out of this one alive.

A crow called, mocking us all. I didn't bother throwing a rock at it.

It was misty out. A half-hearted drizzle came and went. Lightning stalked beyond the hills to the south. It had been hot and humid all day, then had turned viciously stormy toward evening. Lakes of water stood in the streets. Stormshadow's engineers had not made good drainage a high priority, despite the natural advantages available.

It would not be a good night for attacking tall walls. And not much easier for anyone defending them.

Still, I almost felt sorry for the little buggers down below.

Candles and Red Rudy finished the long climb from the street, groaning. Each carried a heavy leather sack. Candles grumbled, "I'm too old for this shit."

"If it works out we'll all get to get old."

Both men leaned on merlons while they caught their wind. Then they dumped their sacks into the darkness. Somebody down there swore in a Shadowlander dialect. "Serves you right, asshole," Rudy growled back. "Go home. Let me sleep."

All of the Old Crew invested time hauling dirt.

"I know," Candles told me. "I know. But what good is alive if you're too damned tired to give a shit?"

If you read the Annals you know our brothers have said the same thing since the beginning. I shrugged. I could come up with nothing inspirational. Mostly you don't try to justify or motivate, you just go on.

Candles grumbled, "Goblin wants you. We'll cover you here."

In battered Shadowlander Rudy shouted downward, "Yeah, I know your turkey gobble. Fuck you."

I grunted. It was my watch but I could leave if I wanted. Mogaba didn't even pretend to try to control the Old Crew anymore. We did our part. We held our ground. We just would not conform to his ideas of what the Black Company ought to be.

But there was going to be one hell of a showdown if the Shadowmaster and his circus ever hit the road.

"Where is he?"

"Down Three." That he signed in finger speech. We use deaf speech frequently if we talk business out in the open. Bats and crows can't read it. Neither can any of Mogaba's faction.

I grunted again. "Be back."

"Sure."

I descended the steep, slippery stair, muscles aching, anticipating the weight of the sack I would be carrying when I came back.

What could Goblin want? Probably a decision on something trivial. That runt and his monocular sidekick religiously avoid taking on any responsibility.

I run the Old Crew, most of the time, because nobody else wants to bother.

We have established ourselves in an area of tall brick tenements close to the wall, southwest of the north gate, which is the only gate still fully functional. From the first hour of the siege we have been improving our position.

Mogaba thinks in terms of attack. He does not believe a war can be won from behind stone walls. He wants to meet the Shadowlanders on the wall, to throw them back, then to charge outside and stomp them. He launches spoiling raids and nuisance attacks to keep them wobbly. He won't prepare for the possibility that they might get inside the city in significant numbers, although almost every attack puts Shadowlanders on our side of the wall before we can concentrate enough to push them back.

Someday, sometime, things won't go Mogaba's way. Someday Shadowspinner's people are going to grab a gate. Someday we are going to see full scale city war.

That is inevitable.

The Old Crew is ready, Mogaba. Are you?

We will become invisible, Your Arrogance. We have played this game before. We read the Annals. We will be the ghosts who kill.

We hope.

Shadows are the question. Shadows are the problem. What do they know? What will they be able to find?

Those villains have not been called Shadowmasters just because they love the darkness.

8

WITH THE EXCEPTIONS OF THREE HIDDEN DOORS, ALL ENTRANCES TO THE Company's quarters have been bricked up. Likewise every window opening below third-floor levels. Alleys and breezeways are now a maze of deathtraps. The three usable entrances can be reached only by climbing outside stairways subject to missile fire their entire rise. Where we could manage we have fireproofed.

For the Black Company there is no inactivity during the days of siege. Even One-Eye works. When I can find him.

Every man stays too damned busy and too damned tired to dwell upon our situation.

After entering a concealed entrance known only to the brothers of the Old Crew, the crows and bats, the shadows, the Nyueng Bao watchers down the street and any Nar who care to keep track from the north barbican, I trundled down flight after flight of steps. I reached a basement where Big Bucket dozed beside a lonely, fitful little candle. Quiet though I was, he cracked an eyelid. He wasted no breath on a challenge. A ramshackle, twisted wardrobe tilted against the wall behind him, its door hanging crookedly on one damaged hinge. I pulled the door gently and eased inside.

Any outsider force reaching the cellar would find the wardrobe stuffed with desperately meager food stores.

The cabinet fronts a tunnel. Tunnels join all our buildings. Mogaba and anyone else interested might expect as much. If they got down into our cellars a little work would show them what they hoped to find.

That ought to satisfy them.

The tunnel entered another cellar. Several men were asleep there, amidst tremendous clutter and a smell like a bear's den. I moved slowly until recognized.

Had I been an intruder I would not have been the first never to return from the underworld.

Now I entered the real secret places.

New Stormgard rose atop old Jaicur. Little effort was made to demolish the old town. Many of the earlier structures had been in excellent condition.

We have a bewildering maze dug out down where no one ought to think to look. It gets a tad bigger whenever a sack of earth goes to the wall or into one of our other projects. It is no cozy warren, though. It takes willpower to go down into those dank, dark places where the air hardly moves, candles never come wholly to life, and there is at least a chance that any shadow may harbor a screaming death.

And me, I have a thing about being buried alive.

It gets no easier with practice.

Hagop and Otto, Goblin and One-Eye and I went through this before, on the Plain of Fear, where for about five thousand years we lived like badgers in the ground.

"Cletus. Where's Goblin?" Cletus is one of three brothers who serve as our engineers and master artillerymen.

"Around the corner. Next cellar."

Cletus, Loftus and Longinus are geniuses. They figured out how to bring fresh air down the chimneys of existing structures up top, then into the deep tunnels, let it flow slowly through the complex, then send it up other chimneys. Plain engineering, but it seemed like sorcery to me. A flow of breathable air, though slow and never pure, serves us well enough.

It does nothing to lessen the damp and the smell.

I found Goblin. He was holding a candle for Longinus while the latter slapped wet mortar onto freshly scrubbed stonework about eye level. "What's the problem, Goblin?"

"Rained like a bastard up there, eh?"

"Gods swiped a river somewhere and dropped it here. Why?"

"We've got a thousand leaks down here."

"Big problem?"

"Could be later on. There's no drainage. We're as low as we can go unless the Twelve tunnel goes good."

"Sounds like an engineering problem to me."

"It is," Longinus said, smoothing the mortar. "And Clete did anticipate it. We've waterproofed from the start. Trouble is, you can't tell how you're doing until you get a really nasty rain. We're lucky it didn't go on the way it does during the rainy season. Three days of that, we might've gotten flooded out."

"Still sounds like an engineering problem. You can handle it, right?"

Longinus shrugged. "We'll work on it. That's all we can do, Croaker."

Little dig there. Like telling me, let everybody do their own worrying.

"That's why you wanted me?" It seemed a little weak, even for Goblin.

"No. Longo, you don't hear anything." The toad-faced man made a complex gesture with three fingers of his left hand as he said that. Some half-hinted glimmer trailed behind his fingers momentarily. Longinus went back to work like he was deaf.

"It so important you need to cut him out?"

"He talks. He don't mean no harm but he can't help repeating everything he hears."

"And makes it better when he tells it. I know. All right. Tell me."

"Something has happened with the Shadowmaster. He's changed. Me and One-Eye only decided for sure about an hour ago but we think it's been going on for a while. He's just kept us from seeing it."

"What?"

Goblin leaned closer, as though Longinus might yet eavesdrop. "He's gotten well, Murgen. He's just about back to normal. He's been getting his feet under him before he comes down on us with them both at once. We also decided that he is hiding the change more from his buddy Longshadow than he is from us. We don't scare him that much."

I stiffened, recalling strange behavior on the encircling plain, going on right now. "Oh, shit!"

"What?"

"He's going to come tonight. Real soon. They were moving into position when I came down. I thought it was just the usual. . . . We'd better go full alert." I headed out of there with what energy I had, announcing the alert wherever I saw anybody.

9

SHADOWSPINNER DID NOT HURRY. THE COMPANY TOOK ITS POSITIONS ON the wall. The Taglian rabble we led got as ready as they ever get. I sent warning to Mogaba and Speaker Ky Dam. Mogaba is a jerk and a lunatic but not a complete fool. He believes he keeps the job separate from personalities. If Goblin claimed we were in big trouble he would listen.

Alarms sounded everywhere. Shouts of anger at being anticipated rose outside the wall.

The civilian population began to respond. Fear swept the darkened streets. This felt bigger than usual. As always, the old-timers among the Jaicuri recalled the first coming of the Shadowmasters. Back then the enemy first wave consisted of deadly flickers of darkness.

"One-Eye. Any shadows out there?"

"Won't be any of those, Murgen. They have to come up from Shadowcatch. Longshadow would have to be in on it."

"Good." I've seen what the shadows can do, on a small scale. The Jaicuri were right to be scared.

"I promise you some sorcery, though. It's already gathering."

"I love how you can always cheer me up, runt." I surveyed the walls beyond our section. Hard to see much but it looked like any assault would meet a ready defense.

Which meant nothing if Spinner was in good form.

"Murgen!"

"What?"

"Behind you."

I looked.

Ky Dam, Speaker of the Nyueng Bao, accompanied by a son and some grandsons, by gesture asked if he could come up to the battlements. Only the son was armed. He was a squat, emotionless man rumored to be some kind of master swordsman. I nodded. "Welcome aboard."

The Speaker looked like he was about a thousand years older than One-Eye but was spry enough to climb without help. He didn't have a lot of himself to move around. His hair was evenly distributed around his head and face but very little of it remained. It consisted of white wisps. He was covered with liver spots. His skin color had faded. He was more pallid than some of us northerners.

He bowed slightly.

I responded in kind, trying to match his bow exactly. That would indicate an honor between equals, which ought to earn me some good guy points because, although junior in years, I was senior here because he was on Company ground and I was Company top dog.

Clever me, I make every effort to be polite to the Speaker. And I keep reminding the guys to be respectful and protective of all Nyueng Bao, even if provoked. I am trying to encourage the taking of a longer view than is usual with ordinary people.

We have no friends anywhere in these strange lands.

Ky Dam faced the darkened plain. His presence was strong. Many Jaicuri believe he is a sorcerer. Goblin and One-Eye say he *can* be called a wizard in the word's most archaic sense, of wise man.

The old boy drew a breath that seemed to enhance his aura of strength. "It will be different tonight." He spoke mainstream Taglian with no accent.

"Their master has recovered his powers."

The Speaker glanced at me sharply, then at Goblin and One-Eye. "Ah. So."

"Exactly." I've always wanted to do that when some old fart made cryptic noises. I couldn't help myself when the perfect opportunity arrived.

I eyeballed the Speaker's escort. The swordmaster seemed too squat and bulky for his reputation. Such as it was. Not a lot crosses the cultural boundary.

The grandsons looked like most Nyueng Bao men in their prime. Like if they smiled, or showed any emotion whatsoever, they would forfeit their souls. Like they had cactus plugs up their butts, in Goblin's words.

I went on with my work while Ky Dam considered the night. His escort stayed out of my way.

Big Bucket checked in. "All set, boss."

And the Shadowmaster's men sounded like *they* were ready to play. Their horns began calling like bulls in rut. I grumbled, "It won't be long." They could put it off for another twenty years, though. I wouldn't mind. I was in no hurry.

A Taglian messenger stumbled up from the street, fought for breath, croaked out word that Mogaba wanted me.

"On my way. Less than five minutes," I told him. I scanned the darkness. "Hold the fort, Bucket."

"Just what this outfit needs. Another comedian."

"Oh, I'll slay them."

Ky Dam said something. The swordmaster squinted at the night. For half a heartbeat there was a ghostly flicker in the hills. Star? Reflection of a star? No. The night was cool, wet and overcast.

The Speaker said, "There may be more happening than is immediately apparent, Bone Warrior."

"Perhaps." Bone Warrior? "But, unlike Nyueng Bao, we are not warriors. We are soldiers."

The old man got his mind around that quickly. "As you will, Stone Soldier. All may not be as it seems." Was he making these up as he went?

He did not seem pleased by his speculation. He turned, hastened down the stair. His grandsons had trouble keeping up.

"What was that about?" Bucket asked.

"I don't have a clue. I've been summoned by His Holiness, the Prince of the Company." As I stepped to the stair I glanced at One-Eye. The little wizard was staring toward the hills, about where Ky Dam had done the same. He seemed both puzzled and unhappy.

I didn't have time to ask. Nor did I have much inclination.

I had had bad news enough already.

10

MOGABA STANDS SIX FEET FIVE. ANY FAT ON HIM HAS TO BE BETWEEN HIS ears because there isn't an ounce anywhere else. All bone and muscle, he moves like a cat, his slightest twitch pure liquid grace. He works hard to stay hard but not to become overly muscled. He is very dark but a deep mahogany more than an ebony. He glows with conviction, an unshakable inner strength.

He has a ready wit but never smiles. When he does show humor it is entirely surface, for effect, an illusion spun for his audience. He doesn't feel it and probably doesn't understand it. He is as focused as any human being who ever lived. And that focus is the creation and maintenance of Mogaba, greatest warrior who ever lived.

He is almost as good as he wants to be. He might be as good as he thinks he is. I never saw anyone who could match his individual skills.

The other Nar are almost as good, almost as arrogantly self-confident.

Mogaba's self-opinion is his big weakness but I don't think anyone could get him to believe that. He and his reputation stand squarely at the center of his every consideration.

Sadly, self-indulgence and self-admiration aren't always traits that will inspire soldiers to win battles.

There is no love lost between Mogaba and the rest of us. His rigidity split the Company into Old Crew and Nar factions. Mogaba envisions the Black Company as an ages-old holy crusade. Us Old Crew guys see it as a big unhappy family trying to survive in a world that really is out to get us.

The debate would be much more bitter were Shadowspinner not around to snap up the mantle of bigger common enemy.

Many of Mogaba's own people are less than thrilled with the way his mind is working these days.

Something Croaker harped about, from the moment he first set quill to paper, is what might be called matters of form. It is not good form to bicker with your superiors, however wrong they may be and however one-sided their determination of their superiority is. I try to maintain good form.

Croaker quickly elevated Mogaba to third in the Company, after himself and Lady, because of his exceptional talents. But that did not automatically entitle Mogaba to assume command if Croaker and Lady were gone. New Captains are supposed to be elected. In a situation like the one here in Dejagore the custom is to poll the soldiers to see if they think an immediate election is necessary. If they think the old Captain has become mad, senile, dead, incompetent, or otherwise in need of permanent replacement then an election will be held.

I cannot recall any instance in the Annals when the senior candidate was rejected by the soldiers, but if an election were held today a precedent might be set. In a secret ballot even many of the Nar might declare no confidence in Mogaba.

There will be no vote while we are besieged. I will oppose any effort to hold one. Mogaba may be mad and I may not be able to go along with him in areas he considers religious, but only he has the will to control thousands of skittish Taglian legionnaires while keeping the Jaicuri in line. If he should fall his assistant Sindawe would step up, then Ochiba, and only then, maybe, if I can't hide fast enough, me.

Soldiers and civilians both fear Mogaba more than they respect him after all this time besieged. And that troubles me. The Annals demonstrate over and over that fear is the most fertile soil for treachery.

11

MOGABA HOLDS STAFF CONFERENCES IN THE CITADEL. THERE IS A WAR ROOM there, once the toy of the sorceress Stormshadow. Mogaba considers meeting there a great concession to the distances us underlings must hike. He does not like leaving his own part of the action. For that reason I could count on this being short.

He was polite enough, though it was a strained courtesy obvious to all. He said, "I received your message. It was not entirely clear."

"I garbled it intentionally. I didn't want the messenger telling everybody on his way to see you."

"It is not good news, then, I assume." He spoke the Jewel Cities dialect the Company picked up when it was in service to the Syndic of Beryl. Most of us used it only when we did not want the natives to understand what we were saying. Mogaba used it because he did not yet have enough Taglian to get by without interpreters. Even his Jewel Cities dialect was badly accented.

"Definitely not good news," I said. Mogaba's friend Sindawe translated for the Taglian officers present. I continued, "Goblin and One-Eye tell me Shadowspinner is completely healthy again and means tonight to be his big comeback show. So tonight won't be just another raid, it will be a big punchout for the whole works."

A dozen pairs of eyes stared, praying I was making the sort of bad joke Goblin and One-Eye would find hilarious. Mogaba's own eyes were icy. He wanted to make me recant by sheer weight of his gaze.

Mogaba has no use for One-Eye or Goblin. They are one of the big sources of contention between him and the Old Crew. He is sure that real wizards, however puny, have no place among real warriors, who are supposed to rely on their strength, their wit, their will, and even maybe their superior steel—if they have it.

Goblin and One-Eye, besides being wizards, besides being sloppy and undisciplined and rowdy, worst of all fail to agree that Mogaba is the best thing that could have happened to the Black Company.

Mogaba hates Shadowspinner in part because he knows the Shadowmaster will never meet him in a trial by combat that can be sung about down through the ages.

Mogaba wants his place in the Annals. He *lusts* after a major place in the Annals. And he is going to get that, but not the way he wants.

"Do you have a suggestion about how to deal with this threat?" Mogaba showed no emotion, though Shadowspinner getting well meant the date of our executions had been advanced.

I considered suggesting prayer but it was obvious Mogaba was not in the mood. "Afraid not."

"There is nothing in your books?"

He meant the Annals. Croaker tried hard to get him to study them. Croaker was big on looking for, and deferring to, precedent—mainly because he lacked much confidence in his mastery of strategy and leadership. On the other hand, Mogaba lacked no confidence whatsoever. He always had an excuse not to study Company history. Only recently had it occurred to me that he might not read or write. Those are skills considered unmanly in some places. Maybe that was true among the Nar of Gea-Xle, despite the fact that keeping the Annals was a holy duty of our Black Company forebrethren.

The Nar say very little about their beliefs. The rest of us are aware that they consider us heretics, though.

"Very little. The time-honored tactic is to attract the wizard's attention to a secondary target where he will do less damage than he wants. You hold his attention there till he gets tired or until you sneak up and cut his throat. Sneakups aren't practical here. This time Spinner will protect himself better. He might not even come out of his camp if we don't make him."

Mogaba nodded, unsurprised. "Sindawe?"

Sindawe is Mogaba's oldest and closest friend. They go back to early childhood. Sindawe is now Mogaba's second in command and leader of the Taglian First Legion, which is the best of the Taglian formations. And the oldest. Croaker put Mogaba in charge of training when first we arrived in Laglios and the First is the juggernaut Mogaba built.

Sindawe can pass as Mogaba's brother. Sometimes he acts like Mogaba's conscience. Mogaba values his good opinion possibly more than he should.

Sindawe said, "We could try to outrun them. . . . Whoa, Ga! I'm joking."

Mogaba didn't get it. Or if he did he failed to see the humor.

I offered, "Use artillery to distract him, wherever he is. And if we do catch him in range we can hope we get lucky."

We did that during the big battle that ended with us trapped. And it worked. We even got lucky, some, which was why we were alive to be in deep shit now. But we did not come near eliminating Shadowspinner.

"We will include motion in everything," Mogaba decided. "Our artillerymen will shoot and run. Wherever the Shadowmaster attacks directly we will fade away instantly. We will cover with enfilading fire till his attention is drawn elsewhere. We will not look him in the eye."

Mogaba looked me in the eye. He wanted help from Goblin and One-Eye but his pride would not let him ask. He is on record as saying he cannot abide sorcery, that sorcery has no place in the Black Company. It is wicked, dishonorable, the alternative of rogues. The man just cannot lay off the flattery. He spreads that stuff all over those two clowns every time he sees them, too. He has made them some big offers intended to get them to retire from "his" Company.

Help? Ain't it funny how flexible you get when absolute destruction looks you right in the eye?

Sort of flexible. Mogaba never addressed the matter directly.

I did not twist his tail. I never do. And I hope that drives him crazy. I said, "We will all exercise all our talents to their limit. If we don't get through this, our differences don't mean shit."

Mogaba winced. Among the many things a Nar warrior does not do is employ colorful language. Whatever language he uses.

Good thing we were using the Beryl dialect. Our discussion had gone on long enough that the Taglian officers were beginning to doubt Sindawe's bland translations. We tried to show the outside world a single face. It was especially important to deceive our employers. In the tradition of these things they are, likely, already figuring out how to screw us as soon as we save their royal butts.

Counting sworn brothers taken in since our advent in this forsaken end of the world, the Nar and Old Crew factions together total sixty-nine men. Dejagore's main defenders are ten thousand inadequately trained Taglian legionaires, some willing but ineffective former Shadowlander slaves, and some even less effective Jaicuri. Each day snaps our numbers. Old wounds and current diseases thin our ranks as swiftly as enemy attacks. Croaker tried to teach good field hygiene but it has not stuck anywhere outside the Company proper.

Mogaba awarded me a small bow, the way honors are paid in these parts. He would not thank me outright.

Sindawe and Ochiba now had their heads together over some unit reports that had just come in. Sindawe announced, "No time left for talk. They are about to attack." He spoke Taglian. Unlike Mogaba, he made a grand effort to get beyond pidgin. He strove to understand the culture and thinking of the several Taglian peoples—weird though they are.

Mogaba said, "Then let's go to our posts. We don't want to disappoint Shadowspinner." You could see the edge on the man. He was eager. His excitement was almost unreasonable. He reviewed the tactics he wanted used to reduce friendly casualties.

I left without a word. Without being dismissed.

Mogaba knew I did not consider him Captain. We discuss it occasionally. I will not acknowledge him without a formal vote. He does not want an election yet, either, I suspect because he fears his popularity is not what a Captain's should be.

I will not force the issue. I might get elected by the Old Crew faction. And I don't want the job. I am not qualified.

I know my limitations. I am no leader. Hell, I don't even handle these Annals very well. I don't see how Croaker kept them up and did all the other stuff he had to do at the same time.

I ran all the way to my section of wall.

12

SOMETHING HIT ME LIKE A SMALL, SILENT CYCLONE OF DARKNESS THAT dropped out of the night and nowhere. It devoured me, unseen by anyone around. It grabbed hold of my soul and yanked. I went into the darkness thinking, Boy, the Shadowmaster came back in a *huge* way, didn't he?

This was unlike anything I had encountered ever before.

But why come after me? There were few players less significant than I was.

13

I WAS SUMMONED. I COULD NOT RESIST. I FOUGHT, BUT SOON I REALIZED that a strong part of me did not want to win.

I was confused. I had no idea what was happening. I was sleepy. . . . Was all this just because I wasn't getting enough sleep?

A voice called my name. The voice seemed vaguely familiar. "Murgen! Come home, Murgen!" I felt violent motion, probably due to a blow I didn't feel. "Come on, Murgen! You have to fight it."

What?

"He's coming. He's coming back!"

I groaned. A major accomplishment, apparently, because it generated more excitement.

I groaned again. Now I knew who I was but not where I was or why, or who that voice belonged to. "I'm getting up!" I tried to say. Must be some kind of training. "I'm getting up, goddamnit!" And I tried. But my muscles would not lift me.

They were rigid.

Hands pulled on my arms.

A new voice said, "Stand him up. Get him walking."

The original voice said, "We've got to find a way to head these seizures off before they happen."

"I'm open to suggestion."

"You're the doctor."

"It's not a disease, Goblin. You're the sorcerer."

"It ain't sorcery, either, Chief."

"Then what the hell is it?"

"Anyway, it isn't any sorcery like any I ever seen or heard of."

They had me upright now. My knees would not cooperate but these guys would not let me fall down.

I opened an eye. I saw Goblin and the Old Man. But the Old Man was dead. . . . I tried my tongue. "I think I'm back." This time I had it. This time my words were slurred but understandable.

"He is back," Goblin said.

"Keep him moving."

"He ain't drunk, Croaker. He's back. He's aware. He can hang on here. You can hang on here now, can't you, Murgen?"

"Yeah. I'm here. I won't drift away as long as I'm awake." Where was here? I looked around. Oh. There. Again.

"What happened?" the Old Man asked.

"I got pulled into the past again."

"Dejagore?"

"It's always Dejagore. This was the day you came back. The day I met Sarie."

Croaker grunted.

"It hurts less each time. This trip wasn't bad. But you lose a lot besides the pain. I didn't see half the horror I know was there."

"Maybe that's good. Maybe if you can shed all of that you can break out of this."

"I'm not crazy, Croaker. I'm not doing this to myself."

Goblin said, "It's getting harder to pull him back, not easier. This time he wouldn't have made it without us."

My turn to grunt. I could get caught in a cycle of reliving the nadir of my life, over and over.

Goblin had not guessed the worst. I was not back yet. They had dragged me up out of the deeps of yesterday but I was not home. This was my past, too, only this time I was aware of my dislocation. And I knew what evils lurked in my future.

"What was it like?" Goblin stared like that every time. Like some facial tic of mine might be the one clue he needs to unravel the puzzle and rescue me. Croaker leaned against the wall, the way he does, satisfied now that I was talking.

"Same as every other time. Just less painful. Although this time when I started out I wasn't really me. That was different. I was just a disembodied voice, just a viewpoint giving a guide's sort of speech to a faceless visitor."

"Also disembodied?" Croaker asked. This variation had him interested.

"No. There was somebody there. A complete person but he had no face."

Goblin and Croaker exchanged troubled looks. At that time Otto and Hagop were still away. "What sex?" Croaker asked.

"Wasn't clear. It wasn't the Faceless Man, though. I don't think it was anybody from our past. Might just have been something out of my own head. I might have separated me into pieces so I wouldn't have to deal with so much pain in such big blasts."

Goblin shook his head, not buying that. "It ain't you, Murgen. Something is doing this. Besides who, we want to know why and why you. Did you catch any clues? How did it go? Try for specifics. It's teeny details that will give us our handle."

"I was detached completely when it started. I went down into it gradually. Then I *was* the Murgen back then, living it all over again, trying to get it all down in the Annals, unaware of the future at all. You remember going swimming when you were a kid? When somebody would come up out of the water behind you to dunk you? He would jump in the air and put his hand on top of your head, then let his weight push you under? If you were in deep water instead of just going straight down you would sort of curve through the water and lay out flat? This whole thing went like that. Only once I was out flat I couldn't float to the top. I forgot that I have done it all before, almost always the same way, who knows how many times? Maybe if I could remember the future back then I could change the way things went, or maybe at least I could make extra copies of my books so they don't get. . . ."

"What?" Croaker was alert now. Mention the Annals and you have his undivided attention. "What was that?"

Did he realize that I was remembering the future? In this time my volumes of the Annals are still safe.

The fear and the pain swarmed in on me, then. The despair followed. Because despite all those plunges back there, and despite the visits here, I cannot stop anything from happening. No amount of willpower can divert the river from the horrors.

For a moment I could not talk because I had so much to say. Then, obliquely, I managed, "You came here about the Grove of Doom. Right?" I knew this night. I have been through this country often enough to know its terrain well. Here the landscape varies slightly from visit to visit but afterward time becomes the same relentless river.

If I squinted I could almost see the ghosts of other versions playing out alternate dialogs.

Croaker was surprised. "The grove?"

"You want me to take the Company out to the Grove of Doom. Right? It's time for some Deceiver festival. You think Narayan Singh himself might show up for this one. You think there's a good chance to catch him—or to catch *somebody* who knows where he has your baby hidden. Worst chance, you think we'll get the opportunity to kill lots of them and make them hurt more than they already do."

Croaker has been implacable in his resolve to exterminate the Deceivers. More so even than Lady has been, I think, and she was the more deeply insulted of the two. Once upon a time he wanted his legacy to be the completion of the Black Company's historical cycle. He wanted to be captain when the Company returned to Khatovar. He has the dream still but a nightmare shoved it aside. The nightmare demands satisfaction. Until its gossamer thread of terror, pain, cruelty and revenge has been spun, Khatovar is going to remain nothing but an excuse, not a destination.

Croaker eyed me uncertainly. "How could you know about the grove?"

"I came back knowing." Which was true. But the two of us would not give the same meaning to "back."

"You'll take the men out there?"

"I can't not."

Goblin eyed me weirdly, too, now.

I would do it. And I knew how it would go but I could not tell them that. There were two minds inside my head. The one doing this thinking wasn't the one heaving on the running lines and reefing the sails.

"I'm all right now," I told them. And, "I think there *is* a way to keep me from falling back. At least, to keep me from going so far back. But I can't get it out." I would have shared gladly. I did not want to keep stumbling off the edge of time to fall back into those too-real dark dreams of Dejagores past. Not even if I tumbled into a viewpoint almost blind to the horror and cruelty everywhere then.

Croaker started to say something.

I interrupted. "I'll be down for the staff meeting in ten minutes."

I could not tell them anything directly but maybe I could get something out sideways.

But I knew nothing would change. The worst of all horrors was waiting up ahead and I was powerless to avert it.

I'd still do my best in the grove. Just in case this time that would come out differently. If I could remember the future well enough to make the right moves.

You. Whoever you are. Whatever you are. You keep dragging me to the wellsprings of pain. Why do you do that? What do you want? Who are you? What are you?

As always, you give me no answers.

14

THE GODDAMNED WIND HAD TEETH. WE HUDDLED IN OUR BLANKETS, shivering, as unmotivated as guys get without hanging it up. Weren't many of us wanted to be in that haunted grove in the first place.

Yet something I could not quite catch, some elusive emotion deep inside me, told me this was critical, that this had to be done just right. That more than I could imagine hinged upon that.

Unseen trees creaked and cracked. The wind groaned and whined. It was easy to let your imagination get away and brood on the fact that thousands had been tortured and murdered there. You might hear their moans inside the wind, their pleas for mercy ignored even now. You might expect to see broken corpses rising up to demand vengeance on the living.

I faked being a hero. I could not stop shaking, though. I pulled my blanket tighter. That did not help, either.

"Candyass!" One-Eye sneered. Like the little shit wasn't about to have a seizure himself. "That bonehead Goblin don't quit farting around and get his dead ass back here I'm gonna go strip him barebutt and nail him to a chunk of ice."

"That's creative."

"Don't be no wiseass, Kid. I'll . . ."

An especially exuberant gust took off with what he would.

It wasn't just the cold making us shake, though nobody would admit that. It was the place and the mission and the fact that heavy cloud cover robbed us of even the meager comradeship of starlight.

It was goddamned dark. And these Stranglers might now be friends with the man who ran shadows. A little bird said. Actually, a big black bird said.

"We spend too much time in town," I grumbled. One-Eye didn't respond. Thai Dei did, though, with a grunt. But that was a speech for this particular Nyueng Bao.

The wind brought the creak of a stealthy footfall. One-Eye barked, "Goddamnit, Goblin! Quit stomping around. You want the whole damned world to know we're here?" Never mind that Goblin could not be heard five feet away, dancing. One-Eye refuses to be constrained by mundane reason or consistency.

Goblin drifted into place in front of me, squatted. His little yellow teeth chattered. "All set," he murmured. "Whenever you're ready."

"We'd better do it, then. Before I break out in a case of common sense." I grunted as I rose. My knees crackled. My muscles did not want to stretch any more. I swore. I was getting too damned old for this shit, though at thirty-four I was the baby of the bunch. "Move out," I said, loudly enough to be heard by most everyone. You couldn't use hand signals in that darkness.

We were downwind and Goblin had done his stuff. Noise was not a worry.

The men drifted away, mostly so quietly that I had trouble believing I was alone suddenly except for my bodyguard. We moved, too. Thai Dei covered my back. The night didn't bother him. Maybe he has eyes like a cat.

I had plenty of mixed feelings. This was the first time I had run a raid. I was not sure I was over Dejagore enough to handle it. I shied at shadows and remained crazy suspicious of everybody outside the Company, for no reason I could understand. But Croaker insisted, so here I was sneaking around in a dark and evil forest with icicles hanging off my butt, directing the first purely Company op in years. Only it wasn't so purely Company when you considered the fact that all my guys had bodyguards with them.

I got over the self-confidence hurdle just by getting myself moving. Hell, it was too late to stop anything.

I stopped worrying about me and went to work worrying about how we would look after the raid was over. If we blew it we could not blame that on Taglian treachery or factionalism or incompetence, the usual sand in the machine.

I reached the crest of a low ridge. My hands were frozen but my body was wet inside my clothing. Light wavered ahead. The Deceivers, those lucky bastards, had a bonfire to keep them warm. I paused to listen. I heard nothing.

How did the Old Man know the leaders of the Strangler bands would gather for this particular festival? It was downright spooky the way he knew stuff sometimes. Maybe Lady was rubbing off. Maybe he had some magical talent he never mentioned.

I observed, "We're about to find out if Goblin still has that talent."

Thai Dei did not spend a precious grunt. Silence was comment enough.

There were supposed to be thirty to forty top Deceivers over there. We hunt them relentlessly and have done so since Narayan snatched Lady and Croaker's baby. The Old Man has eliminated mercy from the Company vocabulary. And that fits Deceiver philosophy perfectly, though I would bet those guys up ahead would not think that way in a minute.

Goblin still had the knack. The sentries were napping. Still, inevitably, all did not go as planned.

I was fifty feet from the bonfire, sneaking along beside this especially big, ugly shelter when somebody went heeling and toeing out its end like all the devils in Hell were after him. He bent under the weight of a big bundle. That bundle wriggled and whimpered.

"Narayan Singh!" I knew him instantly. "Stop!"

Right, Murgen. Freeze him with your voice.

The rest of the guys recognized him too. A yell went up. We could not believe our luck, though I had been warned that the big prize might be there to grab. Singh was the number one Deceiver, the villain Lady and the Captain want to spend long years killing, an inch at a time.

The bundle had to be their daughter.

I yelled orders. Instead of responding the men did whatever they thought of. Mostly they went after Singh. The racket wakened the rest of the Deceivers. The quickest tried to run.

Luckily, some of the guys stayed on the job.

"You warm now?" Goblin asked. I puffed heartily as I watched Thai Dei shove a skinny blade into the eye of a sleep-befuddled Strangler. Thai Dei doesn't cut throats. He doesn't like the mess.

It was over. "How many did we get? How many got away?" I stared the direction Singh had fled. The silence there was not promising. The guys would have raised a real hoorah had they caught him.

Damn! I was excited for a while there. If only I could have dragged him back to Taglios. . . . If wishes were fishes. "Keep some alive. We'll want somebody to tell us bedtime stories. One-Eye. How the hell did Singh all of a sudden know we were here?"

The runt shrugged. "I don't know. Maybe his goddess goosed him and told him to haul ass."

"Give me a break. Kina didn't have anything to do with it." But I wasn't that sure. Sometimes it is hard to disbelieve.

Thai Dei gestured.

"Right," I said. "Just what I was thinking myself."

One-Eye looked puzzled. Goblin grumbled, "What?" My wizards. Right on top of everything.

"Sometimes I wonder if you guys could find your dicks without a map. The shelter, old-timers. The shelter. Don't it seem like that's an awful lot of shack for one runt killer and a kid barely tall enough to bite you on the kneecap? A bit big even for a living saint and the daughter of a goddess?"

One-Eye developed a nasty grin. "Nobody else came out, did they? Yeah. You want I should start a fire?"

Before I could answer him Goblin squealed. I whirled. A shapeless darkness, visible only because of the bonfire, reared out of the shelter entrance—then I slammed into the ground, felled by Thai Dei. Fire blasted over my head. Lights crackled. Balls of flame darted in from all around.

The killing darkness took on a moth-eaten look. Then it came apart.

That darkness was why so many of us had been shivering before the attack. But we won this round.

I sat up, crooked a finger. "Let's see what we've caught. It ought to be interesting." My guys knocked the shelter apart. Sure enough, they turned up a half dozen wrinkled little old men, brown as chestnuts. "Shadowweavers. Running with the Stranglers. Now isn't that interesting?"

The geezers gobbled their willingness to surrender.

We had run into their kind before. They never were big on personal heroics.

A soldier called Wishbone said, "These Shadowlanders are getting good at this 'I surrender' stuff." He sneered. "Everybody down there must be practicing their handy Taglian phrases."

"Except Longshadow," I reminded. I told Thai Dei, "Thanks."

He shrugged, a gesture foreign to the Nyueng Bao. The world did touch him occasionally. "Sahra would expect it."

And that was very Nyueng Bao. He would blame his actions on his sister's expectations rather than on any notion of duty or obligation or even friendship.

"What are we supposed to do with these guys?" Wishbone asked. "We got any use for them?"

"Save a couple. The oldest and one other. Goblin. You never said how many got away."

"Three. That counts Singh but not the kid. But we're going to get one of them three back on account of he's hiding in the bushes right over there."

"Collect him. I'll give him to the Old Man."

Sarky One-Eye cracked, "Give them a little authority, they turn into field marshals. I remember this kid when he was so green he still had sheep shit between his toes. He didn't know what shoes were for." But the humor wasn't in his eye. Every move I made he watched like a hawk. Like a crow, in fact, although we had no crows hanging around tonight. Whatever experiment Goblin and One-Eye had going in that area was a complete success during this outing.

Goblin suggested, "Ease up, Murgen. We'll get the job done. How about some of you lazy asses toss a couple logs on the fire?" He began to circle the hidden Deceiver in the direction opposite that taken by One-Eye.

They were right. I get too serious under stress. I was a thousand years old already. Surviving Dejagore had not been easy. But all the rest of these guys had come through that, too. They had seen Mogaba's slaughters of innocents. They had suffered the pestilences and plagues. They had seen the cannibalism and human sacrifices, the treacheries and betrayals and all the rest. And they had come away without letting the nightmares rule them.

I have to get a handle on it. I have to get some emotional distance and perspective. But there is something going on inside me that is beyond my control or understanding. Sometimes I feel like there are several of me in there, all mixed up, sometimes sitting behind the real me watching, watching. There may be no chance for me to recover complete sanity and stability.

Goblin came strutting back. He and One-Eye accompanied a man who was not much more than skin and bones. Few Deceivers are in good shape these days. They have no friends anywhere. They are hunted like vermin. Huge bounties ride on their shoulders.

Goblin flashed his toadlike grin. "We've got us a red-hand man here, Murgen. A genuine black rumel guy with the red palm. What do you think of that?"

The thought lightened my heart. The prisoner was truly a top Strangler. The red hand meant that he had been there when Narayan Singh tricked Lady into thinking she was being inducted into the Strangler cult when in fact the Deceivers were really consecrating her unborn child as daughter of their goddess Kina.

But Lady had employed a trick of her own, marking every Strangler there with the red hand that could not be denied later. Nothing they tried would take the color away, short of amputation. And a one-handed Strangler could not manage the rumel, the strangling scarf, that was the tool of the Deceivers' holy trade.

"The Old Man will be pleased." A red-hand man would know what was going on inside his cult.

I crowded closer to the fire. Thai Dei, done helping dispose of redundant shadowweavers, eased in beside me. How much had Dejagore changed him? I could not imagine him ever being anything but dour, taciturn, remorseless and pitiless, even as a toddler.

Goblin, I noted, was doing that thing he did lately where he watched me from the corner of his eye while pretending to do something else. What were he and One-Eye looking for?

The runt held his hands out. "Fire feels good."

15

PARANOIA HAS BECOME OUR WAY OF LIFE. WE HAVE BECOME THE NEW Nyueng Bao. We trust no one. We let no one outside the Black Company know what we are doing until we are sure what the response will be. In particular we prefer keeping the Prahbrindrah Drah and his sister, the Radisha Drah, our employers, way back there in the deep dark shadows.

They are not to be trusted at all, ever, except to serve their own closest interests.

I smuggled my prisoners into the city and hid them in a warehouse near the river, a Company-friendly Shadar fish place possessed of a very distinctive air. My men scattered to their families or someplace where they could drink beer. I was satisfied. With one quick, nasty stab we had decimated the surviving Deceiver leadership. We almost got that fiend Narayan Singh. I got within spitting distance of Croaker's baby. In all honesty I could report that she seemed all right.

Thai Dei knocked the prisoners to their knees, wrinkled his nose.

"You're right," I agreed. "But this place don't stink half as bad as your swamp does." Taglios claims the river delta but the Nyueng Bao disagree.

Thai Dei grunted. He could take a joke as well as the next guy.

He does not look like much. He is a foot shorter than I am. I outweigh him by eighty pounds. And I am far prettier. He has crudely cropped black hair that sticks out in unkempt spikes. Skinny, lantern-jawed, taciturn and surly, Thai Dei is entirely unappetizing. But he does his job. A Shadar fishmonger brought the Captain to us. Croaker *was* getting old. We were going to have to call him Boss or Chief or something. You cannot call the Captain the Old Man once he's really old, can you?

He was dressed like a Shadar cavalryman, all turban, beard and plain grey clothing. He eyed Thai Dei coolly. He did not have a Nyueng Bao bodyguard himself. He loathed the idea despite his having to disguise himself whenever he wanted to walk the streets alone. Bodyguards are not traditional. Croaker is stubborn about Company traditions.

Hell, the Shadowmaster's officers all employ bodyguards. Some have several. They could not survive without them.

Thai Dei reflected Croaker's gaze impassively, unimpressed by the presence of the great dictator. He might say, "He is one man. I am one man. We begin even."

Croaker examined my prizes. "Tell it."

I told it. "But I missed Narayan. I was this close. That bastard has a guardian angel. There's no way he should have slipped Goblin's sleep spell. We chased him for two days but even Goblin and One-Eye couldn't hang onto his track forever."

"He had help. Maybe from his guardian demon. Maybe from his new buddy the Shadowmaster, too."

"How come they went back to the grove? How did you know they would be there?"

I thought he would say a big black bird told him.

They are less numerous these days but the crows still follow him everywhere. He talks to them. Sometimes they talk to him, too. So he says.

"They had to come someday, Murgen. They are slaves to their religion."

But why *this* particular Festival of Lights? How did you know?

I did not press. You don't press Croaker. He has grown cranky and secretive in his old age. In his own Annals he did not always tell the whole truth about personal things, his age especially.

He kicked the shadowweaver. "One of Longshadow's pet spook doctors. You'd think he wouldn't have enough left to waste them anymore."

"I don't reckon he expected us to jump them."

Croaker tried to smile. He produced a nasty, sarcastic sneer instead. "He's got lots of surprises coming." He kicked the Deceiver. "Let's don't hide them. Let's take them to the Palace. What's the matter?"

Ice had blasted my back, like I was out on the wind of the Grove of Doom again. I didn't know why but I had a grim sense of foreboding.

"I don't know. You're the boss. Anything special you want in the Annals?"

"You're the Annalist now, Murgen. You write what you have to write. I can always bitch." Unlikely. I send everything over but I don't think much gets read. He asked, "What was special about the raid?"

"It was colder than a well-digger's ass out there."

"And that walking sack of camel snot Narayan Singh got away from us again. So that's what you write. Him and his kind are going to get back into our story before we're done. When we're roasting him, I hope. Did you see her? Was she all right?"

"All I saw really was a bundle that Singh carried. I think it was her."

"Had to be. He never lets her out of his sight." He pretended he did not care. "Bring them to the Palace." That chill hit me again. "I'll make sure the guards know you're coming."

Thai Dei and I exchanged looks. This might get tough. People in the streets would recognize the prisoners. And the prisoners might have friends. And for sure they did have enemies by the thousand. They might not survive the trip. Or we might not.

The Old Man said, "Tell your wife I said hello and I hope she likes the new apartment."

"Sure." I shivered. Thai Dei frowned at me.

Croaker produced a sheaf of papers rolled into a tube. "This came in from Lady while you were gone. It's for the Annals."

"Someone must have died."

He grinned. "Bang it around and fit it in. But don't polish it so much she gets all righteous again. I can't stand it when she flays me with my own arguments."

"I learned the first time."

"One-Eye says he thinks he knows where he left his papers from when he thought he was going to have to keep the Annals."

"I've heard that one before."

Croaker grinned again, then ducked out.

16

FOUR HUNDRED MEN AND FIVE ELEPHANTS SWARMED AROUND AN INCOMPLETE stockade. The nearest friendly outpost lay a hard day's march northward. Shovels gnawed the earth. Hammers pounded. Elephants swung timbers off wagons and helped set them upright. Only the oxen stood around, lazing in their harnesses.

This nameless post was barely a day old, the newest point in the relentless Taglian leapfrog into the Shadowlands. Only its watchtower was complete. The lookout there scanned the southern horizon intently. There was an electric urgency in the air, a heaviness like the smell of old death, a premonition.

The soldiers were all veterans. Not a one considered fleeing his nerves. Each had developed the habit and expectation of victory.

The sentinel began to gaze fixedly. "Captain!"

A man distinct for his coloring dropped a shovel, looked up. His true name was Cato Dahlia. The Black Company called him Big Bucket. Wanted for common theft in his home city, he had become advisor-commander of a battalion of Taglian border rangers. He was a hardass leader with a reputation for getting his jobs done and bringing his people back alive.

Bucket scrambled onto the observation platform, puffing. "What have you got?"

The lookout pointed. Bucket squinted. "Help me out here, son. These eyes ain't what they used to be." He could see nothing but the low humped backs of the Loghra Hills. Scattered clouds hung above those.

"Watch."

Bucket trusted his soldiers. He selected them carefully. He watched.

One small cloud hung lower than the others, dragging a slanting shadow. This rogue thunderhead did not travel the same direction as the rest of its family.

"Headed right for us?"

"Looks like it, sir."

Bucket relied on his intuition. It had served him well during this war without major battles. And intuition told him that cloud was dangerous.

He descended, spread word to expect an attack. The men of the construction company, although not combat soldiers, did not want to withdraw. Sometimes Bucket's reputation worked against him. His rangers had prospered, freebooting across the frontier. Others wanted a share.

Bucket compromised. He sent one platoon north with the animals, which were too valuable to risk. The other workers stayed. They overturned their wagons in the gaps in the stockade.

The cloud advanced steadily. Nothing could be seen inside its shadow and tail of falling rain. A chill ran before it. The Taglian soldiers shivered and pranced to keep warm.

Two hundred yards beyond the ditch, teams of two men shivered in covered, concealed pits lighted by special candles. One man maintained a watch.

Rain and darkness arrived. Behind the initial few yards of downpour the rain slackened to a drizzle. Men appeared. They looked old and sad, ragged and pale, vacant and hopeless, hunched against the chill. They looked as though they had spent their entire lives in the rain. They bore their rusting weapons without spirit. They could have been an army raised from the dead.

Their line passed the pits. Behind them came horsemen of the same sort, advancing like zombies. Next came massed infantry. Then came the elephants.

The men in the pits spied the elephants. They used crossbows to speed poisoned shafts. The elephants wore no belly armor. The poison caused intense pain. The maddened beasts rampaged through their own formations. The Shadowlanders had no idea why the animals were enraged.

Little shadows found the pits. They tried to slither inside. Candlelight drove them back. They left a deeper chill and a smell of death behind.

The shadows found a pit where rain had gotten to the candle. They left shrieking, grimacing death in a grave already dug.

Lady encountered the northbound laborers. She questioned them, considered the cloud in the distance. "This may be what we're after," she told her companions. "Ride!" She urged her stallion to a gallop. Foaled in sorcerous stables when she was empress of the north, that giant black outdistanced the rest of her party quickly.

Lady studied the cloud as she galloped. Three similar clouds had been reported near sites where ranger companies had been overrun. This was exactly what she had come to investigate.

It took only minutes to fathom how the raids were managed. Lines of dark power had been laid down long before the Shadowlanders withdrew from this region. The attackers were controlled through those. They would fight without wills of their own while run by those lines.

She could scramble the lines easily now that she sensed them but chose not to do so. Let the attack proceed. These things cost the Shadowlanders more dearly than they cost Taglios.

Longshadow must realize that. So why did he find the exchange worthwhile?

She entered the ranger encampment by leaping her mount over an upturned wagon. She dismounted as an amazed Bucket ran to meet her. He looked like a condemned man granted a last-minute reprieve. "It's the Howler, I think," he said.

"Why?" Lady dragged her gear down from behind her saddle, started changing right there. "What can he hope to accomplish?"

"I think it ain't what they're doing but who they're doing it to that matters, Lieutenant." Though she commanded armies, Lady's Company title remained Lieutenant.

"Who they're doing it to? Yes! Of course." Every unit lost had been led by Company men. Seven brothers had fallen. "They're picking us off." The belief that the Company is invincible is the backbone of Taglian military morale and the black beast of Taglian politics. "That's crafty. Must be Howler's idea. He does love to blindside you."

Bucket helped her with her armor. That was gothically ornate, black and shiny, too pretty to be much use in close combat. But her job was to fight sorcery, not soldiers. Her armor was surfaced by layer upon layer of protective spells.

Rain began to fall as she donned her helmet. Threads of fire snaked along channels etched into the surface of her armor. She followed Bucket up the watchtower.

Rain roared down. Sounds of combat grew louder, nearer. Lady ignored those, extended sorcerous senses in a search for the sorcerer known as the Howler. That ancient and evil being did not betray himself but he was out there somewhere. She could smell him.

Was it possible he had learned to control his screaming?

"I'll catch up with you, you little bastard. Meantime. . . ." She reached down. A fog formed, became dense, slithered between the raindrops, gained color. Pastels swirled, deepened, darkened. Soon the entire storm glowed as though some mad artist had splash-painted it with watercolors.

There were screams inside the storm.

The weather stopped moving. The shrieks of lost soldiers peaked, faded. The Shadowmaster's lines of power, twisting and mutating, had turned lethal.

Lady resumed searching for the Howler. She discovered him stealing southward, flying low and timidly, fleeing the pastel death that had begun eating its way back along the lines of power. She flung a hastily concocted killing spell. It failed. Howler's lead was too great. But he did abandon stealth to run hard. Lady cursed like any line trooper frustrated.

The rain faded away. The Taglian survivors appeared one by one, at first awed by the carnage, then grumbling about all the graves that needed digging. Few Shadowlander survivors were found.

Lady told Bucket, "Tell them to look at the bright side. There will be prize money for the captured animals." The Shadowlander animals, excepting the elephants, had not suffered badly.

Lady glared southward, unforgiving. "Next time, old friend."

17

... FALLING ... AGAIN. ...

Trying to hang on. So tired. When I get tired the present gets slippery.
Fragments.

Not even fragments of today.

The past. Not so long ago.

Freezing my ass off. Failing to catch the great villain Narayan.

Lady at play down south.

Fish stench.

The sleeping man. The screaming Deceiver. Dead men.

Only memories but happier than tonight. There is too much pain
here.

It is my apocalypse.

Slipping.

Can't keep my eyes from closing. The summons is too damned powerful.

*The pillars might be mistaken for relics of a fallen city. They are not. They
are too few and too randomly placed. Nor has a one ever fallen, though
many have been gnawed deeply by the teeth of the hungry winds.*

*In the lightning flares, or in the dawns and sunsets when light steals
beneath the edges of the sky, tiny golden characters blaze upon the faces
of the columns.*

It is immortality of a sort.

After dark the wind dies. After dark silence rules the glittering stone.

18

... SLIDING AWAY. ...

A vast whirlpool pulling me down.

Perhaps a force pushing. Was that a lying promise of an end to pain?
I cannot resist.

All lies. Endless lies.

Brown pages, torn pages stiff with blood. Agony. Hard to ride that anchor through the storm.

19

THERE YOU ARE! WERE YOU LOST? WELCOME BACK. COME! COME! THE great adventure is about to begin. The players are all in place. The engines are wound tight. The spells are collected and ready, in arsenal number. Oh, it will be a grand night of doom.

Look there! Look there. Remember them? Goblin and One-Eye, the wizards? But is that really them? There are two more just like them right over there. And see this. And that. And there. One, two, three Murgens.

No. Definitely not. You can't teach those two to suck eggs. They have been in the fooled-you business since your granny's greatgranny was a stinky little surprise for your however-many-greats grandpa. They have set glamors all over this part of the city. If you are a Shadowlander soldier you won't be able to tell the figments from the real thing till one of them sticks a knife in you.

Look there! Raven and Silent. They have been gone for years. And there. That is the old Captain, dead since Juniper. No, they won't scare any Shadowlanders with who they might be. Not right away. The southerners never heard of them.

What?

You are right. Absolutely right. Nobody here but Otto and Hagop will know them, either. But that doesn't matter. What matters is they can be seen and hardly anyone will know which ones are dangerous and which are illusions.

This is a first trial. A big experiment, saved up special for the night of Shadowspinner's big attack.

Yes. Yes. He did hit hard not that long ago. But he wasn't really going for a knockout then. He would have taken it, but that was really a reconnaissance in force, meant to support planning for this attack.

It is going to be a grand show.

Oh, no, there isn't one ghost anywhere else in Dejagore. Mogaba wouldn't have it. He has no grasp of illusion as a weapon. He has no idea how the Company really worked. He clings to his grand notion of chivalrous warfare, the great deadly game, all honor and set rules. He would settled this mess in a trial by combat between him and any champion the Shadowlanders care to send out.

Oh! Look! That one is interesting. That ugly sucker is Toadkiller Dog. He was a real nasty devil dog. And the Limper! Oh, yes. Brilliant. If the man behind Shadowspinner's mask is anyone the Company has faced before those illusions are provocations he will have to test. He will betray himself.

No, of course the Shadowmasters would not risk an entire kingdom on the outcome of a fight between two men. Their champion might lose.

Yes. Mogaba is naive about some things. He is an arrogant, cruel, unsympathetic general, too.

Ooh. Hear those trumpets. The Company has its own personal bunch of bad guys down front. Let's go to the ramparts and watch from close up.

No. They aren't really bright. Well, you *could* say that if they were bright they wouldn't be in that army in the first place but that wouldn't be fair. Not many of those guys had a choice about signing up. Their only real motivation is their fear of the Shadowmasters.

Sure. No argument. That makes them no less deadly. Hell, a rock can fall out of the sky and kill you.

Yes, this definitely is the big one. Shadowspinner is set to send every man. Maybe shadows have come up from Overlook to help.

Bats! Ha. And crows. Which is chasing which? Duck! Almost got you. They are all over. Never been this many around before.

What is that racket? Oh. Bucket yelling at one of the Murgens to get behind something because he don't want to carry no bodies down no goddamn stairs.

And here comes the first barrage. And if that racket across town means anything the Shadowlanders are hitting hard about where the third and fourth cohorts of the First Legion are stationed. Those are good regiments. They will put up a fight.

20

LIKE A REGULAR HAILSTORM, ISN'T IT? MAKES YOU WONDER WHERE THEY got all the goddamned arrows and javelins for their engines. Just stay under the mantlet, you'll be fine. They aren't good at laying plunging fire onto elevated targets.

If they let up before they attack the Jaicuri will come out and collect the missiles and bring them to the soldiers. The Shadowlanders will get them back business end first.

No, the Jaicuri do not love Mogaba. They don't love the Taglians or the Black Company, either. They wish the whole mob was gone. But they have some dark suspicions about what will happen if Shadowspinner recaptures this burg. So they sort of try to help, but not much. Not yet.

They help some, they figure maybe Mogaba might be less likely to kick them out next time he is in one of his moods.

The sky? Dark as the inside of a priest's heart, isn't it? Oh. Yes. You're right. It isn't an auspicious sort of night. Never is when they attack without benefit of a full moon. It's devil's work for sure, then. Usually it means the Shadowmasters want the darkness so they can run their pets to their best advantage. Or they want everybody terrified that there are shadows to come.

Look at them scurry! Those Jaicuri are motivated tonight. If they become involved in actually fighting it could be closer than Mogaba or Shadowspinner expect.

Whoa! What was that?

Look at that. What the hell is it? That rosy light over the hills.

Here they come. Going to take their whack at breaking the Company.

You don't think so? Maybe you are right. This could be meant to keep the Company pinned while Spinner concentrates somewhere softer.

Look at them down there, though. Like maggots. And no covering fire now.

You're right. The engines will be moving to support the main attack now.

Check that light. It keeps getting brighter. No. Now it's going away. And it doesn't seem like anyone else noticed. That is a little too weird.

Oh. Right again. Must have been a signal to the Shadowlander officers. The racket *is* getting louder, now you mention it.

No, I don't like the sound of it either. The attack had become generalized.

Ho! Look over there! Now we have it there, too. What? The light. Don't you see it? There behind the ramparts?

Yes. I see. You're right again. It is different. This is kind of like the cold light of a full moon tinged with a little blue, isn't it. Yeah. It's kind of misty, too. Sort of like we are seeing it through an autumn haze. There. Now it's so bright you can make out the fighting on the far wall.

Right. Fighting. That means they have a foothold there already. And Mogaba don't have any reserves to send up.

Guess we can bend over and kiss our butts goodbye, friend.

21

DAMN! THE SHIT IS ABOUT TO START FLYING BUT I JUST REALIZED THAT when I started putting these notes together I missed doing the famous formula Croaker always used to open a new volume. So here goes:

In those days the Company was in service to the Prabrindrah Drah of Taglios, a prince whose domains spanned territories more vast than those of many empires. We were participating in the occupation and protection of the recently captured city Dejagore.

And I hope princie and his skag sister the Radisha choke on our memory.

22

THE SHITSTORM ARRIVED. EVERY MAN DEFENDING OUR SECTION OF WALL stayed busy returning some of it to the southerners. The illusory doppelgangers appeared to be hard at work, too. Funny how they could wander around never getting hurt.

"One-Eye! Goblin!" I yelled. "Where the hell are you peckerheads? What the frack is going on over there?" I watched a feeble arrow pass through a Murgen a dozen yards away. "What's that weird light?" Whatever it was, it gave me the feeling that things could get worse than they looked already.

I got no response whatsoever from my favorite wizards.

"Rudy. Flip a flare ball out there. Let's see what's sneaking around." Until recently my now less than favorite wizards had provided spot illumination. "Bucket! Where the hell are Goblin and One-Eye?" Ten minutes ago I had three pairs underfoot, all of them squabbling. Now they were gone and the Shadowlanders were quieter than mice below.

Red Rudy yelled at Loftus and Cletus. One of their engines thumped. A blazing ball arced outward, its only purpose to betray what the enemy was doing in the darkness.

Sparkle piped, "I seen them headed downstairs."

Suckass. "Why?" This was for sure not the time to wander away.

"Uh. . . . They went to talk to Pirmhi and some of them guys from the Horse Brigade."

I shook my head. I would choke them myself. In the middle of a god-damned battle. . . .

The fireball revealed that the Shadowlanders had pulled back from the wall. Spending our missiles was a waste. The southerners were setting up engines capable of throwing grapnels in clusters. That was a stupid way to do business against an eighty-foot wall with veteran soldiers on top, but if they wanted to play it that way we would accommodate them. I was confident that, no matter how many ropes they threw up, we could cut or dislodge their lines before they could climb that high, then, with lungs ready to fall out and arms too heavy to lift, get busy defending their bridgehead while other equally dim types made the same climb carrying a half ton of equipment apiece.

"Goblin!" Goddamnit, I wanted to know what that light was over there.

The Shadowlanders had not scaled the wall there. They had attacked off of earthen ramps. Not a surprise. They had been building the ramps from the beginning. That was just basic siegework, employed since the dawn of time and one reason your thoughtful modern prince builds his stronghold on a crag or headland or island. Naturally, the besieger spans the last dozen feet with a bridge he can yank back if a dangerous counter-attack develops.

The flareball smashed down four hundred yards out. It continued to provide light until the southerners buried it with sand originally intended to extinguish firebombs if we used them. "One-Eye! I'm going to have your wrinkled balls for breakfast!"

I snarled, "Cletus, keep throwing them fireballs. Who's got messenger duty? Feet? Go find Goblin and One-Eye. . . . Never mind. One of them brain-damaged runts just turned up."

One-Eye said, "You rang, milord?"

"Are you sober? Are you ready to get to work now?" He stared at that nasty light across town without me coaching him. I asked, "What is that?" The light seemed more sinister now.

One-Eye raised a hand. "Kid, why not take this gods given opportunity to exercise your least well-honed talent?"

"What?"

"Be patient, dickhead."

The mist or haze or dust started getting thicker. The light grew brighter. Neither happening buoyed my confidence. "Talk to me, old man. This ain't the time for any of your bullshit."

"That haze, that ain't no mist, Murgen. The light ain't shining off it. It's making the light." And the mist and light were drifting toward the city.

"Horse puckey. You can see where there's a light burning in their camp."

"That's something else. There's two things going on at once, Murgen."

"Three things, halfwit." Goblin had arrived, beer breath and all. Presumably all was well at the secret brewery, the arrangements with the cavalry were secure, and he and One-Eye could take time off to help the Black Company defend Dejagore.

Heaven help them if Mogaba discovered what they were doing with grain supposedly set aside for the horses. I wouldn't have a prayer of saving their butts—nor would I offer one.

"What?" One-Eye barked. "Murgen, the man is a walking provocation."

"Watch, bonehead," Goblin countered. "It's already happening."

One-Eye gasped, suddenly astonished, then frightened. Ignorant in the dark arts, it took me longer to catch it.

Shadows snaked through that blazing dust cloud, thin things little more than suggestions but with something flitting back and forth amongst them. I thought both of a weaver's shuttle and of spiders. Whichever, web or net, something was forming inside the blazing dust.

They did call him Shadowspinner.

The glimmering cloud grew larger and brighter. The web grew with it.

"Shit," Goblin muttered. "Now what do we do about this?"

"Exactly what I've been trying to get out of you two clowns for the last five minutes!" I bellowed.

"Well!"

"Maybe you could pay attention over here if you can't do anything about that!" Bucket yelled. "Murgen, those fools have gotten so many ropes up that we can't. . . . Shit!" Another barrage of grapnels fell amongst us. In moments they showed the strain that meant some moron was trying to climb them.

So much for my belief that there was no chance the southerners could scale my wall.

Guys were hard at work with knives and swords and axes. Imaginary people stood around looking fierce. I heard a man grumble that if he had half a brain he would have sharpened his knives. Rudy reminded him, "If you kept your pecker in your pants more you'd have time."

Some Jaicuri women, naturally, inevitably, did what they had to do to survive.

Doing my part, I hacked on ropes but kept turning to check that light and the webs forming inside it.

Goblin howled, creased by a nearly-spent arrow. The cut, on his cheek, was trivial. Arrows have little energy by the time they reach us. He was outraged because fate dared show him the back of her hand at all.

He danced around. Words of power virtually dripped from his mouth in pastel colors. He waved his arms. He foamed at the mouth. He jumped up and down, shrieked, flapped his arms.

His doppelgängers all did the same. It was quite a show.

In all likelihood the gymnastics and yelling had nothing to do with results eventually achieved but I don't mind showmanship as long as he produces. Croaker was right. Showmanship is the biggest part of the game.

Everything hemp within three hundred yards burst into flame. That was a happy eventuality where our relationship with our attackers was concerned but not something likely to wring cries of joy from anyone else, either. Temporary defense works began to fall apart. Our artillery pieces flared and died. They had included lots of rope. Some guys use rope for belts. Some wear sandals made of rope. Hemp is a commonplace everywhere. Some fools like One-Eye even smoke it.

Cletus bellowed, "Goddamn you, Goblin, I'm gonna chop your ass into cat food." The rest of us just pulled our pants up and amused ourselves by dropping masonry bits mined from our cellars onto the cursing tangle of limbs wriggling at the foot of the wall.

One-Eye ignored all that, though he took a moment to smirk at the side effects embarrassing Goblin. Then he began to stare at the glow rising from the enemy camp. And began to stutter.

"Come on, shithead," I growled. "You've played with this stuff for ages. What have we got here?" Not that I wanted to know. That web of shadow woven into the light was now obvious to all but the blind.

"Maybe we might ought to head for the cellar," One-Eye suggested. "I promise you, me and the runt ain't gonna do nothing with that. Bet you even Longshadow would be bugeyed if he was here to see it. The man put a lot of work in, getting that ready. It's going to get real unhealthy around here real soon."

Without investing a quarter of the study time Goblin agreed. "If we seal the doors and use the white candles we can hold out till sunrise."

"This some kind of shadow magic, then?"

"Some kind," Goblin agreed. "Don't ask me to look so close I catch its attention."

"Heaven forbid you should actually take a risk. Can either of you come up with a more practical suggestion?"

"More practical?" One-Eye sputtered.

"We're fighting a battle here."

Goblin said, "We could retire from the soldiering racket. Or we could surrender. Or we could offer to change sides."

"Maybe we could offer up a half-pint human sacrifice to one of Geek and Freak's bloodthirsty gods."

"You know what I really miss about Croaker, Murgen?"

"I'm sure you're going to tell me whether I want to hear it or not."

"Damned straight you are. I miss his sense of humor."

"Wait a minute. His sense of humor? Are you shitting me? What sense of humor? The man . . ."

"He knew none of us were going to get out of this world alive, Murgen. He never took himself completely serious."

"Are you talking about the guy who used to be the Old Man? Croaker? Company Annalist and chief bonesetter in his spare time? Some kind of comedian?"

While we bickered the rest of the world bustled along with its business. Which meant our situation deteriorated by the minute. A human weakness, as old as time, arguing while the house burns down around you.

One-Eye interjected, "You gents go ahead and debate if you want. I'm going to invite the boys downstairs, treat them to a beer and take a turn or two at tonk." He stabbed a crooked black finger earthward.

The gleaming dust with cruel web inside began to arc up over the city. It just might grow enough to net us all.

A vast stillness set in.

Inside the city and out, friend and foe, people of a dozen races and religions all focused upon that shadow web.

Shadowspinner, of course, was totally involved in creating his deadly artifact.

The Shadowlander assault lost impetus as the Shadowmaster's soldiers decided to hunker down and let their boss make their jobs easier.

23

THE WEB OF DARKNESS WOULD SPAN ALL DEJAGORE SOON. "ONE-EYE. GOBlin. You guys have any new ideas?"

"Get religion?" Goblin suggested. "Since you won't let us go den up?"

One-Eye mused, "You might amble over and see if Mogaba will

change his mind about letting us operate his engines." The Taglian crews were ineffective. "We might be able to distract Spinner."

"You did take shadows into account when you spelled the entrances to the underground?" I knew. They had. That was always our biggest concern. But I had to reassure myself. You keep checking on Goblin and One-Eye.

Small groups were returning after long, dangerous journeys through the night, searching for rope that had survived.

"Yeah. For what that's worth. You ready to go down and start starving yet?"

Bad signs followed ill omens. The situation was grim indeed if One-Eye and Goblin could spare no time to quarrel.

A sudden susurrus swept the city and the plain beyond.

A blazing diamond of light rose out of the Shadowlander camp. It spun slowly. A core of darkness centered it. From that, blackness pulsed out into the all-spanning web it anchored.

Nobody was looking at the hills when the pinkish light returned. No one noticed until it flared so brilliantly that it rivalled the brightness here at hand.

It burned behind two bizarre mounted figures. It cast their hideous shadows upon the night itself. Crow shadows circled them. Two huge ravens perched upon the shoulders of the larger figure.

Nobody breathed for a while. Not even Shadowspinner, I'd bet. And I was sure he had no more idea what was happening than I did.

The pink flare faded. A cable of pink reached toward Dejagore, like a snake probing, stretching. As one end neared us the nether end broke loose. That whipped our way too fast for the eye to follow and in an instant screamed into Shadowspinner's bright diamond. Sun-brilliant flash splashed out of that sorcerous construct's far side like suddenly-flung barrels of burning oil.

Immediately the dark web overhead began to shrink back into the remnants of the diamond.

The air vibrated with the Shadowmaster's anger.

"Goblin! One-Eye! Talk to me, boys. Tell me what the hell just happened."

Goblin couldn't talk. One-Eye burbled, "I ain't got the faintest fucking idea, Kid. But we're downwind of one seriously pissed-off Shadowmaster who's probably going to blame you and me for his ulcers."

A tremor disturbed the night, more psychic than physical. I am magically deaf and dumb and blind, except for perceived effects, but I felt it.

One-Eye was right.

The pink light was gone. I saw no more sign of those bizarre riders. Who were they? What? How?

I didn't get a chance to ask.

Little brown fellows carrying torches so they could see where they were running burst out of the Shadowlander camp. That could not bode well for me, my pals, or anyone else inside the wall.

"Poor Spinner," I cracked. "You got to feel for the man."

"Huh?" Sparkle was the only man close enough to hear.

"Don't you hate it when some no-brain vandalizes a work of art?"

Sparkle didn't get it. He shook his head, grabbed a javelin and threw it down at a short person with a torch.

He missed.

Around where those Shadowlanders had gained a foothold on the wall, and on the earthen approach ramps, a big racket began to develop. The Shadowmaster, piqued, had told his boys to get back to work. And don't be so damned gentle anymore.

"Hey, Bubba-do," I shouted at a soldier, "who's got tonight in the pool?"

There is the Black Company for you. We've got a pool on what night the city will fall. I guess the winner gets to die with a smile on his ugly mug.

24

GOBLIN AND ONE-EYE HAD CHOSEN TO STAY CLOSE TO ME. THE REAL Goblin and One-Eye. I checked every few minutes to make sure. Their attention was on the hills, not the excitement across town or any of their own schemes. Strange lights moved out there.

A band of southerners sent out earlier returned at a gallop, half their number missing. They flew as though devils worse than their boss were after them. They dared ride the way they did only because Stormshadow had been obsessive when she leveled the plain and because there was light from the city.

Fires were burning. Only a few so far, but fires.

Sparkle told me, "They're pulling out down below."

I leaned over and looked. Nobody tried to pick me off. Maybe they thought I was another ghost.

Sure enough, the Shadowlanders were going, leaving us all those wonderful grapnels without ropes, for us to dump on our "maybe we can use these someday" pile.

One-Eye said, "Guess we can put up our swords and go back to our tonk games now."

Overlooking the fact that Dejagore was being invaded elsewhere, I observed, "This is the second time you've come out with that silliness. What moron is going to play with you? Can't be anybody that dumb still alive." One-Eye cheats at cards. And he cheats badly. He gets caught every time. Nobody will play with him.

"Hey, Murgen. Listen. I've reformed. Really. Never again will I dishonor my talent to. . . ."

Why listen? He's said it all before, countless times. The first thing we do after we swear a recruit into the Company is warn him not to play cards with One-Eye.

A party of Shadowlanders withdrawn from my sector headed for the hills. They all had torches. It looked like the Shadowmaster himself might be driving them.

"Cletus! Longinus! You guys far enough along that you can drop a barrage on that crowd?" The brothers were repairing their engines as fast as they could. Two were ready, cocked and loaded. Not much of a barrage.

One-Eye asked, "Why do that?"

"Why not? We might get lucky. And can we piss off Shadowspinner more than he already is? He's already vowed to kill us all."

The ballistas thumped. The shafts they hurled did not hit the Shadowmaster. Distractedly, he replied with a spear of energy that dissolved several cubic yards of wall far from any of my guys.

The racket from across town kept getting louder. Some seemed closer than the far wall.

"They're inside," Sparkle said.

"A lot of them," Bucket agreed. "This could get to be a big cleanup job." I liked that positive thinking.

I shrugged. Mogaba liked to keep the cleanups for himself and the Nar and their Taglians.

Fine with me. Mogaba can eat all the pain he can swallow.

I really wanted to take a nap. This long day just kept getting longer. Oh, well. Soon enough I would get to sleep forever.

A short while later I got word that small groups of southerners were in the streets murdering anybody they could catch.

"Sir?"

"Sleepy. What's up, youngster?" Sleepy was a Taglian Shadar we swore into the Company just before I decided to take up this pen. He always looked like he was having trouble keeping his eyes open. He also looked like he was about fourteen years old, which was possible. He was paranoid in the extreme, apparently for good reason. He was a good-looking youth. And pretty boys are fair game amongst Taglian men of all three major religious groups. The Stranglers use their more attractive sons to lure victims to their deaths.

Different land, different customs. You may not like them but you do have to live with them. Sleepy liked our ways better than his own.

"Sir," he said, "the Nar aren't trying to keep the southerners from heading this way. They don't bother them at all anymore after they get through and off the wall as long as they don't head into Mogaba's barracks area."

"Is that deliberate?" Bucket asked.

Someone muttered, "Now ask a stupid question."

"What do you think?" One-Eye snapped. "This is the last straw. If that bigheaded, self-important dick shows his face around here . . ."

"Save it, One-Eye." This was hard to accept. But I could see Mogaba being capable of channeling the enemy our way so as to resolve questions of precedence inside the Company. His morality would allow him to picture it as a brilliant solution to several problems. "Instead of standing around bitching about it how about we do some thinking? Best way to fix Mogaba would be to shove his plan up his ass, no grease."

While the others tried to manage that difficult exercise—thinking—I questioned Sleepy more closely. Unfortunately, he could not add much but the general routes the southerners were using to push deeper into the city.

You couldn't blame the Shadowlanders. Most soldiers of most times jump at the chance to go where resistance is weakest.

Maybe we could use that to pull some into some sort of killing pocket.

I even got a chuckle out of my predicament. "I bet Croaker would have seen this coming a month ago, as paranoid as he was about supposed friends and allies."

A nearby crow squawked agreement.

I should have considered the possibility. I really should have. Far-fetched is not the same as impossible. I should have had something planned.

One-Eye became as serious as ever he gets. "You know what this means? If the kid is right?"

"The Company is at war with itself?"

The little guy waved that off like it was just another annoying gnat of reality. "Suppose Mogaba *is* giving them a golden bridge so they can get rid of us for him? They still have to get through the pilgrims to reach us."

I didn't need to think long to see what he meant. "That asshole. He's going to *make* them kill Shadowlanders in self-defense. He's going to use them up killing his enemies for him."

"Maybe he's a bigger snake than anybody thought," Bucket growled. "It's for sure he's changed a lot since Gea-Xle."

"This ain't right," I muttered, although swords would enter the fight on our side—whether or not they wanted to. Other than a few small skirmishes with lost invaders during past attacks the worst that had happened to the Nyueng Bao was that their pilgrimage had gotten them trapped in the middle of somebody else's war. From the first clash of steel they had worked hard to maintain their neutrality.

Shadowspinner has his spies in the city. He would know the Nyueng Bao had no interest in antagonizing him.

"What do you think they'll do?" Goblin asked. "The Nyueng Bao, I mean." His voice sounded odd. How much beer had he put away?

"How the hell would I know? Depends on how they see things. If they think Mogaba dragged them into it on purpose it might get unhealthy to belong to the Company. Mogaba could see this as a chance to squish us into a crack between a rock and a hard place. I'd better go see their Speaker and let him know what's happening. Bucket. Make up a twenty-man patrol and go looking for southerners. See if Sleepy is right. One-Eye, go with him. Spot for him and cover our guys. Sparkle, you watch things here. Send Sleepy after me if it gets too much to handle."

Nobody argued. When things get tight the guys do become less fractious.

I descended the stairway to the street.

25

I PLAYED THE GAME THE WAY I THOUGHT THE NYUENG BAO WOULD WANT. Ever since childhood I have suspected you get along better if you respect people's ways and wishes regardless of your apparent relative strengths.

That doesn't mean you let people walk on you. It doesn't mean you eat their pain for them. You need to demand respect for yourself, too.

Dejagore's byways are close and fetid. Typical of a fortified city. I went to an obscure intersection where—under normal circumstances—I could expect to be seen by Nyueng Bao watchers. They are a cautious people. They watch all the time. I announced, "I would see the Speaker. Harm is headed his way. I would have him know what I know."

I didn't see anybody. I didn't hear anybody. I expected nothing else. Someone who strolled into my territory would see and hear nothing, either, but death would be nearby.

The only sounds came from fighting several blocks away.

I waited.

Suddenly, in that instant when my attention finally wandered, Ky Dam's son materialized. He made no more noise than a tiptoeing moth. He was a wide, short man of indeterminate age. He carried an unusually long sword but it remained sheathed across his back. He stared at me hard. I stared back. It cost me nothing. He grunted, indicated that I should follow.

We walked no more than eighty yards. He indicated a doorway. "Keep smiling," I told him. I couldn't resist. He was always around some-where, watching. I never saw him smile. I pushed the door inward.

Curtains hung two feet inside. Very weak light slipped through a rent. I closed the door carefully once I understood that I would be entering alone, before I parted the curtains. Wouldn't do to let light splash into the street.

The place turned out to be about as pleasant as you can get in a city.

The Speaker sat on a mat on a dirty floor near the one candle offering light. There were about a dozen people visible, of all ages and sexes. I saw four children, all small, six adults of an age to be their parents, and one old woman of granny age who glowered like she had a special bunk in Hell reserved for me even though she'd never seen me before. I saw nobody who could pass as her husband. Maybe he was the guy outside. Then there was a woman as old as Ky Dam, a fragile flower time-dimin-ished to little more than skin-covered sticks, though an agile intelligence still burned in her eyes. You would get nothing past this woman.

Of material things I saw little but the clothing the people wore, a few ragged blankets, a couple of clay cups and a pot maybe used for cooking. And more swords nearly as long and fine as that carried by the Speaker's son.

In the darkness beyond the candlelight someone groaned. It was the sound of someone delirious.

"Sit," Ky Dam invited. A second mat lay unrolled beside the candle. In the weak light the old man seemed more frail than when he visited the wall.

I sat. Though I wasn't used to it and my tendons weren't supple enough, I tried to cross my legs.

I waited.

Ky Dam would invite me to speak when it was time.

I tried to concentrate on the old man, not the people staring at me, nor the smell of too many folks living in too small a space, of their strange foods, nor even the odor of sickness.

A woman brought tea. How she made it I don't know. I never saw any fire. I didn't think about that at the moment, though, so startled was I. She was beautiful. Even in dirt and rags, incredibly beautiful. I brought the hot tea to my lips and scalded them to shock myself back to business.

I felt sorrow instantly. This one would pay dearly when the southerners took the town.

A small smile touched Ky Dam's lips. I noticed amusement on the face of the old woman, too, and recognized there a similar beauty only externally betrayed by time. They were used to my initial reaction. Maybe it was some kind of test, bringing her out of the shadows. Almost too softly to be heard, the old man said, "She is indeed." Louder, he added, "You are wise beyond your years, Soldier of Darkness."

What was this Soldier of Darkness crap? Every time he addressed me he stuck me with another name.

I tried a formal head bow of acknowledgment. "Thank you for that compliment, Speaker." I hoped he would realize that I was incapable of keeping up with the subtleties of proper manners amongst the Nyueng Bao.

"I sense in you a great anxiety held in check only by chains of will." He sipped tea calmly but eyed me in a way that told me hastiness would be tolerated if I thought it really necessary.

I said, "Great evils stalk the night, Speaker. Unexpected monsters have slipped their leashes."

"So I surmised when you were kind enough to permit me atop your section of wall."

"There is a new beast loose. One I never expected to see." In retrospect I realize we were speaking of two different things. "One I do not know how to handle." I strove to keep my Taglian pronunciations clear. Men conversing in a tongue native to neither sorely tempt the devils of misunderstanding.

He seemed puzzled. "I do not understand you."

I glanced around. Did all his people live like this all the time? They were packed in way tighter than we were. Of course, we could enforce our claims to space with our swords. "Do you know about the Black Company? Do you know our recent history?" Rather than await an answer I sketched our immediate past.

Ky Dam was one of those rare people who listened with every ounce of his being.

I finished. The old man said, "Time has, perhaps, made of you shadows of the Soldiers of Darkness. You have been gone so long and have journeyed so far that you have strayed from your Way completely. Nor are the followers of the warrior prince Mogaba hewing any nearer the true path."

I did not hide my thoughts well. Ky Dam and his woman found me amusing again. "But I am not one of you, Standardbearer. My knowledge has drifted far from the truth as well. Perhaps there is no real truth today because there is no one who knows it anymore."

I didn't have a clue what the hell he was talking about.

"You have wandered long and far, Standardbearer. But you may yet come home again." His expression darkened momentarily. "Though you wish that you had not. Where is your standard, Standardbearer?"

"I don't know. It vanished during the big battle on the plain outside. I jammed its butt into the earth when I decided to put on my Captain's armor in order to pretend that he had not fallen, so the troops would rally, but. . . ."

The old man raised a hand. "I think it may be very close tonight."

I hate this obscurity crap old people and wizards like to perpetrate. I am convinced that they do it only because it gives them a feeling of power. Screw the missing standard. It was not germane, now, tonight. I said, "The Nar chieftain wants to be Captain of the Black Company. He does not approve of the ways of those of us from the far north."

I paused but the old man had dried up. He waited.

I said, "Mogaba is flawless as a warrior but he has shortcomings in some areas of leadership."

Ky Dam then proved to be less than the totally inscrutable and eternally patient old-timer you are led to expect in these situations.

"You came to warn me that he has chosen to lessen his problems by letting southerners do his knifework, Standardbearer?"

"Huh?"

"One of my grandsons was in a position to overhear while Mogaba debated tonight's actions with his lieutenants Ochiba, Sindawe, Ranjalpirindi and Chal Ghanda Ghan. Because Taglian conspirators were present the Nar failed to squabble in their native tongue—though Mogaba showed limited facility with the Taglian."

"Excuse me? Sir?"

"What your honor compels you to report to me, although you only harbor suspicions now, is far worse than you fear. Overruling strong objections by his Nar lieutenants, Mogaba set forth a plan for tonight which will allow southerners who reach the ramparts and do not dally there to have their ways behind the wall. Taglian legionnaires will discourage them from attacking any direction but through our quarter into yours."

"You knew already? That what you're saying? Before I got here you had an actual witness?"

"Thai Dei."

A young man rose. He was an unpleasant-looking skinny little guy who held a toddler in his arms.

Ky Dam said, "He does not speak Taglian well but he understands it good enough. He overheard the plot being hatched. He overheard the arguments of those who found it dishonorable. He saw an angry Mogaba go so far as to continue during the visit of a man believed to be an instrument of the Shadowmasters."

That hit me. It meant that, as of that moment, there existed a tacit agreement between Mogaba and Shadowspinner good until me and mine had been obliterated.

"This is cruel treachery indeed, Speaker."

Ky Dam nodded. Then he told me, "There is more, Stone Soldier. Both Ranjalpirindi and Ghanda Ghan are intimates of the Prahbrindrah Drah. Speaking with the Prince's voice they assured Mogaba that, once the siege has been broken and your band has been eliminated, the Prince will announce his personal support of Mogaba's captaincy of your company. In exchange Mogaba will abandon your previous Captain's quest to become chief warlord of Taglios. With all powers necessary to prosecute the war against the Shadowlands."

"Man, that was some job of eavesdropping." Thai Dei almost smiled.

"And some job of treachery put together by Brother Mogaba."

I could see why Ochiba and Sindawe would argue against it. It was a betrayal almost beyond comprehension.

Mogaba had, indeed, gone through some dark changes since Gea-Xle.

I asked, "What does he have against you people?"

"Nothing. Politically he should be indifferent to us. We have never been a factor in Taglian affairs. But we mean nothing to him in any other way, either. He is eager to spend us like found coin. If the southerners attack you after fighting his forces, then us, huge numbers of his enemies *and* us resource-gulping undesirables will have been eliminated."

"Once I admired this man greatly, Speaker."

"Men change, Standardbearer. And this one more than most. He is an actor and but one wicked purpose impels all his acting."

"Speaker?"

"This Mogaba is the center of, and the reason for, everything that Mogaba does. Mogaba will sacrifice his best friend upon an altar to himself, though probably not even a god could convince the friend that that possibility exists. Mogaba's every wicked order draws another veil off the black blotch devouring his soul. He has changed as the most perfect pomegranate will change when the mold gets inside its skin."

Here we go, talking old-timer sideways again.

"Standardbearer! Though I know of the black danger to my people already I am honored that you believed us worthy of a warning, however pressing your other concerns. That was an act of generosity and friendship. We do not forget those who have extended their hands."

"Thank you. I am pleased by your response." You'd better believe. "And if Mogaba allows you to be attacked . . ."

"The problem is upon us already, Stone Soldier. Southerners are dying right now, only yards away. Once it became evident that we were trapped here we all learned every nuance of the ground upon which we might fight. This is not our swamp but the principles of battle remain the same. We have been prepared for this night for many weeks. It remained to be seen only who would choose to become our enemy."

"Huh?" I could be stupid as a stone when I ran into something cold.

"You should rejoin those who look to you for leadership. Do so secure in the knowledge that you have the friendship of the Nyueng Bao."

"An honor."

"Or curse." The old man chuckled.

"Does that mean your people will actually talk to mine?"

"That might be a little too much." He chuckled again. His wife smiled, too. What a wild joker he was! The man was a laugh riot. He said, "Thai Dei. Go with this man. You may speak if spoken to, but only as my mouth. Bone Warrior. This is my grandson. He will understand you. Send him to me if you have a need to communicate. Do not be frivolous."

"I understand." I tried to get up, embarrassed myself by failing to get my legs untangled. One of the kids laughed. I dared glance around for a reaction from the dream woman who brought the tea, sure I was not fooling Ky Dam. A baby slept in her lap. A toddler dozed under her left arm. She was awake, watching. She looked tired, frightened, confused and determined. About like the rest of us. Whenever that moaning came from the darkness she winced and looked that way. The pain was a part of her.

I bowed myself out. The Nyueng Bao Thai Dei led me back to familiar territory.

26

"I DON'T KNOW," I TOLD GOBLIN WHEN HE ASKED ABOUT MY NYUENG BAO shadow. "He don't talk much." I had not gotten a word out of him yet. "His all-purpose vocabulary seems to be the noncommittal grunt. Anyway, the visit wasn't necessary. The Nyueng Bao know more about the coming shit rain than we do. The old man admits it's all Mogaba's fault and says we're off the hook."

Goblin made as though to look over his shoulder like he was trying to check his own behind.

"Yeah," I agreed. "Strap on your chastity belt. What's happening?" I didn't see Bucket or Sparkle.

"Not much yet. Spinner and his bunch just got to the hills."

And all kinds of excitement broke out out there. A strong pink light cast silhouettes on the night again. Goblin said, "They look exactly like the Lifetaker and Widowmaker costumes Lady made for her and Croaker. Hey! How come you look like you got bit on the ass by a ghost?"

"Because maybe I did. They do look exactly like what you say. Only if you remember I took the Widowmaker armor off Croaker after that arrow got him. I put it on and pretended to be him. And failed because I started too late."

"So?"

"So last week somebody stole the Widowmaker armor. Right out of my quarters while I was laying there asleep. I thought I had it hidden where nobody but me could ever find it. But somebody came in, stepped over me, got it dug out, and got out of there with the load and I never saw or heard a thing. And neither did anybody else." And that was definitely scary.

"Is that why you were asking all those weird questions the other day?" Goblin squeaked. He could sound like a stomped mouse when he was distressed.

"Yeah."

"How come you never said anything?"

"Because whoever took the armor had to use sorcery to get past me. I figured it was one of you guys and I wanted to find out which one so I could cut him off at the ankles before he knew it was coming."

One-Eye came puffing up the stairs. Not bad for a guy two hundred years old. "What gives? How come the grim faces?"

Goblin filled him in.

The little black wizard grumped, "You should have told us, Murgen. We might have picked up a hot trail."

Not likely. The only evidence I had found was one small white feather and a glob of what looked like bird shit. "It don't matter now. I know where the armor is. Out there." I pointed at the hills, which lay beneath what looked like a premature pink dawn. "What did you do?"

"We killed off a bunch of goddamned southerners, that's what we did. Mogaba must be selling them tickets over there. The little suckers are thicker than lice. Anyway, we got out before we used up our luck. Them Nyueng Bao are really going bug fuck." He gave Thai Dei the fish-eye. "Looks like they're trying to make the Shadowlanders want to go chomp on Mogaba's rear. Serve the asshole right, he gets ate up by his own plot. What the hell is going on out there?" He meant the pink-soaked hills.

Goblin replied, "That's something we weren't looking for."

A gout of darkness reared against the pink. Human figures tumbled within it. They flared, burned like bright, brief-lived stars. Moments later an earth tremor rocked the city. I lost my footing briefly.

One-Eye observed, "For once you're right, runt. There's a player in the game we didn't know about."

A pair of crows a few yards off went into hysterics. They jumped into the darkness, kept laughing as they flapped away.

"Surprise, surprise," I muttered. "What with all that booming and crashing and crap in those hills. Come on, guys! Tell me who. The rest even a dummy like me can figure out. So just tell me who."

"We're gonna work on that," One-Eye promised. "Maybe we'd even start now if you went away and left us alone. Come on, runt."

While him and his frog-faced buddy got to work I turned my attention to the excitement still festering inside Dejagore.

Possibly thousands of Shadowlanders had crossed the wall now. A lot of fires were burning. I asked Ky Dam's grandson, "Will the light be trouble for your people?"

He shrugged.

This fellow was no gossip.

27

THERE WAS NO NIGHT NOW. FIRES BURNED EVERYWHERE. THEY BURNED IN the Shadowlander camp, set by Mogaba's beleaguered artillerymen. They burned in the city, set by the Shadowmaster's soldiers. Conflagrations blazed in the hills, hinting of surprise volcanos or powers of a magnitude unseen since the Company went up against the dark lords of Lady's empire. It was too much light for the middle of the night. "How long till dawn? Anybody know?"

"Too long," Bucket grumbled. "You really think anybody is actually worrying about keeping time tonight?"

Way back, centuries earlier in the evening, One-Eye or Goblin or somebody expressed dawn as a goal too remote for hope. The general level of optimism remained that low.

Reports came in, none of them good. Innumerable southern soldiers were inside the city. They had orders to drive toward us, wipe us out, then continue on around inside and atop the wall, the long way, till they got back where they had started. But the Nyueng Bao were not cooperating. Neither were my guys. So the invaders were blundering around doing any damage they could till somebody killed them.

Against the Jaicuri, cowering in their homes hoping to be overlooked despite all their experience with the Shadowmasters, the southerners enjoyed some success.

You could not fault them for not going all out after us. They did not want to get killed either. And Mogaba should not have been surprised when some of the villains he let through turned on him.

Our guys held their positions. The doppelgängers and illusions drove the southerners crazy. They never knew which threat was real. But the big reason our side held up well was that there was no choice. We had nowhere to run.

Shadowspinner was no help to his people. He was out in those hills intent on undoing that mystery personally. Clearly he regretted having made the choice.

Once again a band of riders came flying back, silhouetted by pink light. The Shadowmaster did not appear to be with them. "Goblin! One-Eye! Where the hell are you now, you little shits? Has something happened to Shadowspinner?"

Goblin materialized, his breath heavy with the smell of beer. He and

One-Eye had a few gallons stashed somewhere nearby, then. He dashed my hopes. "The Shadowmaster is alive, Murgen. But maybe he's messed his drawers."

He giggled.

"Oh, shit," I muttered. The little toad had gotten *deep* into the home brew. If One-Eye had, too, I might have one truly interesting rest of the night. It was possible those two would forget everything and pick up the feud they have had going for a hundred years. Last time they got drunk and went after each other they tore up a whole city block in Taglios.

All the while the Speaker's grandson hung back in the shadows and watched like one of those goddamned crows. There were a lot more of those around now.

Old Wheezer came puffing up from the street. He had to take a break before he got to the top. He hacked and coughed and spat blood. He was from the same part of the world as One-Eye. They have nothing else in common except a taste for beer. Wheezer had been to the barrel a few times, too.

He came on up top as I surveyed the city and tried to guess how bad things really were. We were getting very little pressure right then.

Wheezer hacked and wheezed and spat.

A new generation of pink lights erupted at the feet of the hills. They cast two shadows against the sky. There was no doubt they were shadows of Widowmaker and Lifetaker, the dread alter egos Lady created for herself and Croaker so they could scare shit out of Shadowlanders.

"This isn't possible," I told my tame wizards. One-Eye was back. He used one hand to support Wheezer, who seemed to be suffering an asthma attack along with the effects of his tuberculosis. In his other hand One-Eye clutched something polelike wrapped in rags. I continued, "That can't be Croaker and Lady because I saw them go down with my own eyes."

A handful of horsemen drifted toward town. Among them was a blob of darkness that had to be Shadowspinner. He was staying busy. Pink fireflies swarmed around him. He had trouble fending them off.

As though they realized their boss would be in a foul temper when he got back, the southerners' attack suddenly picked up.

"I'm not sure," Goblin mused. He sounded like he had been scared sober. "I can't get *any* sense of the one in the Lifetaker armor. There's a shitload of power there, though."

"Lady had no power left," I reminded him.

"The other one does feel like Croaker."

Couldn't be.

Wheezer finally gasped, "Mogaba . . ."

Several men spat at mention of the name. Everybody had an opinion about our fearless war chief. Listening to them you might have concluded that Mogaba was the most lusted after man in town.

A writhing pink thread reached for Shadowspinner's party. The Shadowmaster batted it away from himself but it slew half his party. Parts of bodies flew in all directions.

"Shee-it!" somebody said, pretty much capturing the popular feeling.

Wheezer barked, "Mogaba . . . wants to know . . . if we can free up . . . a few hundred men to . . . counterattack the enemy who . . . are inside the city."

"How stupid does that bastard think we are?" Sparkle grumbled.

Goblin asked, "Don't that camel's wife know we're on to him?"

"Why should he think we might suspect him? He's got such a tall opinion of his own brain. . . ."

"I think it's funny," Bucket crowed. "He tried to screw us and only ended up with his own ass in a sling. Even better, maybe the only way he can pry it out is to have us do it for him."

I asked Goblin, "What's One-Eye up to?" One-Eye looked like he was praying over one of the ballistas with Loftus. Rags lay scattered around their feet. A gruesome black spear lay in the engine's trough.

"I don't know."

I checked the nearest gate. The Nar there could see us. Mogaba would know I was lying if I claimed we were too beat up to send help. I asked, "Anybody think of a reason we should help Mogaba?" To hold my sector, besides the Old Crew itself, I had six hundred Taglian survivors from Lady's division and an uncertain and changeable number of liberated slaves, former prisoners of war and ambitious Jaicuri.

Everyone replied in the negative. Nobody wanted to help Mogaba. As I approached the engines I asked, "How about if we do it just to save our own butts? If we let Mogaba get stomped we could end up facing the rest of the Shadowlander mob by ourselves." I glanced at the gate. "And those people over there can see everything we do."

Goblin looked, too. He shook his head to lessen the beer buzz. "We'll have to think about that."

"What are you doing, One-Eye?" I was beside him now.

One-Eye indicated the spear proudly. "Little something I've been working on in my spare time."

"It's ugly enough." Nice to know he could do something useful without being told.

He had begun with a black wooden pole and had worked it for a lot of hours. It was covered with incredibly ugly miniature scenes along with writing in an unfamiliar alphabet. Its head was as black as its shaft, darkened iron finely traced with silver runes. There was some color on the shaft, too, although so fine as to be almost invisible.

"Very nice."

"Nice? Sigh. You heathen." He pointed. Loftus looked. So did I.

Shadowspinner's party, sadly depleted, surrounded by swarms of pink sparkles and mocking crows, was getting close.

One-Eye snickered. "This here is my Shadowmaster blaster, bastar'!" He howled. He must have put away a lot of that beer. "Nothing he couldn't stop on a lazy afternoon, but this ain't no lazy afternoon, is it? Loftus shoots, this stick won't be in the air five seconds. That's all the time he'll have to figure out what's coming and what to do to unravel the spells that are there to keep him from turning it. And look how busy that asshole is already. Loftus, my man, get ready to carve you a big victory notch on this thing."

As anybody with any sense does, Loftus ignored One-Eye. He laid his weapon with an artist's care.

One-Eye babbled, "Most of the spells are designed to penetrate his personal protection, counting on him not having time to do anything actively. Because I wanted to concentrate on piercing one point in a passive . . ."

I shut him out. "Goblin. Any chance this will work? The runt's not exactly a heavyweight."

"It's workable, tactically. If he really worked that hard on it. Say One-Eye is an order of magnitude weaker than Shadowspinner. That really only means that it takes him ten times as long to get the same work done."

"An order of magnitude?" So that was One-Eye's problem.

"More like two orders really, probably."

He lost me. And I didn't have time to wring an explanation out of him.

Loftus was satisfied he was leading his target perfectly, he had the range, whatever. "Time," he said.

28

"LOOSE," I SUGGESTED.

The ballista offered its distinctive thump. Silence spread along the wall. The black shaft darted across the night. The occasional spark floated behind it. One-Eye said five seconds of flight. The truth was more like four but they took forever.

There was ample firelight to illuminate the Shadowmaster. Shortly he would disappear behind one of the enfilading towers. He stared back at the hills as he rode. Those bizarre riders out there were on the plain now, daring someone, anyone, to answer their challenge.

I gasped.

Widowmaker carried the Lance. The standard itself was not apparent but that was the lance on which it had ridden from the day the Black Company left Khatovar. Every single Annalist has kept close track—although the reason for doing so has been forgotten.

I focused on Shadowspinner in time to see One-Eye's treasure arrive.

Later Goblin told me Spinner sensed the threat as the missile hit the peak of its arc. Whatever he did then, it was the right thing. Or he was lucky. Or a higher power decreed that this was not his night to die.

The spear changed course by scant inches. Instead of striking Shadowspinner it hit his mount's shoulder. And ripped through the beast as though it was no more substantial than air. The wound glowed red, flickered. The red spread. Shadowspinner bellowed in rage as the animal threw him. He fell in a heap, lay there twitching long enough for One-Eye to start nagging Loftus about hitting him with a barrage of regular shafts, then he scuttled off like a crab to escape the stallion's pounding hooves.

I recognized that animal then. It was one of those magically bred monster horses Lady brought south with the Company, out of her old empire. They vanished during the battle.

The horse screamed and screamed.

A normal animal would have perished in moments.

I stared at those two riders out there. They walked toward the city slowly, offering their challenge. Now I could see that they, too, were mounted on Lady's stallions. I told Goblin, "But I saw them killed."

One-Eye grumbled, "We got to check this boy's eyes."

Goblin said, "I told you before, that's not Lady. You look real close, you can see differences in the armor."

The troops were seeing that. There was a stir among the Taglians.

"And you don't know about the other one? What're they talking about over there?"

"No. It could be the Old Man."

Sparkle went to see why the Taglians were excited.

Shadowspinner's horse collapsed but continued screaming and kicking. Wisps of greenish steam rose from its wound. That continued to grow. The beast's death was a long time coming.

The sorcerer would have died more slowly and gruesomely still had One-Eye's shaft struck home.

Sparkle came to say, "They're all excited because that armor is an exact match for some goddess named Kina in her battle avatar. That's the way she's always portrayed in paintings about her war with the demons."

I had no idea what he was talking about, only that Kina was some sort of death goddess in these parts.

I wondered when the Shadowmaster would snipe back at One-Eye.

"He won't," Goblin assured me. "The moment he gave it attention enough to be effective those two out there would cut his legs off."

I watched Shadowspinner limp out of sight.

His embarrassment spurred his soldiers to increase their efforts again. Somebody would pay for his indignity in pain. Understandably they preferred that we pick up that tab.

Some of them seemed to recognize the Lifetaker armor, too. I heard the name Kina shouted more than once below the wall.

"Thai Dei. Time for a message to your grandfather. I want to bring part of my force through his area so I can help drive the southerners out of the city."

The Nyueng Bao stepped out of the shadows just long enough to listen. He stared at those riders, troubled. Then he grunted, descended to the street and trotted off into the night.

"Listen up, people. We're going to go save our fearless dickhead leader. Bucket . . ."

29

I STEPPED INTO A DARK ALLEYWAY, PLANNING TO SET UP SHOP BEHIND A southern company with Goblin to do his hoodoo on them. And it was like I stepped off the edge of the world, into an abyss without bottom. Like some great psychic flyswatter slapped me down into the void. Goblin barked something in the instant it took to go but I did not understand him.

I had that moment to feel seasick, to be bewildered, to wonder who had ambushed me with what sorcery, and why it seemed to twist me like a wet rag being wrung out.

Had Mogaba taken his treachery to another level?

30

SOMETHING HAD HOLD OF ME. IT PULLED SO VIRULENTLY THERE WAS NO resisting it. I lost track of who I was and where. I knew only that I was asleep and did not want to wake up.

"Murgen!" a far voice called. The pull strengthened. "Murgen, come on! Come home! Fight it, Kid! Fight it!" I fought. But it was that voice I fought. It wanted me to come somewhere that much of me did not want to go. Pain awaited me there.

The pull redoubled as the force dragged at me with inescapable power.

"That did it!" somebody shouted. "We have him back now."

I knew that voice. . . .

It was like coming out of a coma except that I remembered where I had been in every detail. Dejagore. Every little ache, every horror, every fear. But already the sharp edges were going dull. The ties were slipping. I was *here* now.

Here? Which when and where was here? I tried opening my eyes. My lips would not respond. I tried to move. My limbs refused to be troubled.

"He's all here."

"Pull that curtain." I heard heavy cloth being moved. "Will it keep getting harder? I thought we were supposed to be over the worst. That he couldn't recede so far that we would have this much trouble bringing him home."

Oh! That voice belonged to Croaker. The Old Man. Only the Old Man is dead, because I saw him killed. . . . Or did I? Didn't I just leave Widowmaker, alive long past his time?

"Well, he didn't listen. But it can't do anything but get better now. We're around the corner. Over the hump. Unless he *wants* to stay lost."

I got an eye open.

I was in a dark place. I'd never seen it before but it had to be in the Palace at Trogo Taglios. Home. Never have I seen that kind of stone used anywhere else. And there was nothing astonishing about not being able to recognize parts of the Palace. The princes of Taglios all add on a bit during their reigns. Supposedly only the old royal wizard Smoke ever knew his way around the whole place. And Smoke isn't with us anymore. I don't know what happened to him afterward but several years ago he got torn up when a supernatural creature he disagreed with tried to eat him. Handy, because about then was when we discovered that he had been seduced by Longshadow and had gone over to the Shadowmasters.

I was amazed at me. Although I had a headache like the mother of all hangovers my mind, suddenly, was crystal clear.

"He's got an eye open, chief."

"Can you hear me, Murgen?"

I tried my tongue, blurted fluent gibberish.

"You had another one of your spells. We've been trying to bring you back for two days." Croaker sounded put out. Like I was inconveniencing him on purpose? "All right. You know the drill. Let's get him up and walking."

I remembered doing this part several times before. I was less confused now, more able to grasp quickly the distinction between past and present.

They got my feet under me. Goblin got under my right armpit. Croaker wrapped his arm around me from the left, lifted.

I said, "I remember what to do."

They did not understand. Goblin asked, "You got a grip on when you are, Murgen? Ain't going to drift off into the past on us again?"

I nodded. I could communicate that way. Maybe I could use the deaf and dumb speech.

"Dejagore again?" Croaker asked.

I had the connections all made inside. Even plenty I didn't want made. I tried talking again. "Same night. Again. Later on."

"Set him down. He'll be all right now," Croaker said. "Murgen. You get any clues this time? Anything we can latch onto to break you out of this cycle? I need you here. I need you full time."

"Not one damned thing." I paused to catch my breath. I was adapting faster this time. "I don't even know when it hit me. I was just there, suddenly, like a poltergeist or something, with no thoughts of any future at all. Then after a while I was just Murgen with no awareness, no anomalies like I get now."

"Anomalies?"

Startled, I turned. One-Eye had materialized from somewhere. I saw that curtain still stirring. It closed off half the room.

"Huh?"

"What do you mean by anomalies?"

When I concentrated I really didn't know what I meant. I shook my head. "I don't know. It's gotten away from me. When am I?"

Croaker and the wizards dealt a hand of significant looks between them. Croaker asked, "Do you remember the Grove of Doom?"

"Sure. I'm still shivering." A chill did touch me. Then I recalled the key thing. I had no memories of having visited this room before but I should have had them. Because I was still in my yesterdays. I just wasn't as far away as I had been at Dejagore, which was years ago.

Then I tried to remember the future.

I remembered too much. I whimpered.

"Do we need to get him up again?" Goblin asked.

I shook my head. "I'm solid. Let's think. How long between this spell and the last one? How long since we got back from the grove?"

Croaker said, "You got back three days ago. I told you to bring your prisoners to the Palace. You tried. You lost the shadowweaver along the way, in circumstances so questionable I issued orders for all Company people to stay especially alert."

"He was old. He just died of fright," One-Eye said. "Ain't nothing mysterious about that."

My headache was not improving. I had vague recollections of those events but they were not as clear as my memories of other events immediately before previous seizures. "I don't recall much of it."

"The red-hand Deceiver got here all right. We meant to start questioning him that night. But you went back to your apartment, supposedly just walked through the doorway and collapsed. Your mother-in-law, uncle, wife and brother-in-law all agree. Probably the first, last and only time that will happen."

"Probably. The old lady is like One-Eye. She disagrees just to be disagreeable."

"Hey! Kid. . . ."

"Quiet," Croaker told him. "So you just fell down and went rigid. Your wife got hysterical. Your brother-in-law came for me. We took you out of there to ease the stress on your family."

Ease the stress? Those people never heard of the word. Besides, Sarie was the only one of them I considered family.

Goblin said, "Open your mouth, Murgen." He turned my face to the best light and stared down my throat. "No damage in here."

I knew what they thought. Epilepsy. I had considered that myself. I had asked about it of anyone who would listen. But no epileptic I ever heard of got bounced into the past from a seizure. Into a past that was never exactly like the past I had lived already.

"I told you it isn't a disease," Croaker growled. "When you find the answer it will be right there inside your own field and you'll probably feel stupid about not having seen it earlier."

"If there's anything to be found we'll find it," One-Eye promised. Which left me wondering what he had up his sleeve. Then I knew that I had to know already because they were going to tell me pretty soon. But I could not recall that future clearly enough to grasp it.

Sometimes it was spooky being me.

"Was that headless character there again?" Croaker asked.

After figuring out what he meant I said, "Yes. But he was faceless, boss. Not headless. He had a head."

"Might represent the source of the problem," One-Eye suggested. "You ever remember any features, anything at all, tell somebody. Or get it written down right away."

Croaker told me, "I don't want this to happen to anybody else. Can you imagine managing a campaign when your people can fade out on you any minute, for days at a time?"

I felt confident that that would not happen. But I didn't say so because they would press me on it and I did not feel like being poked and prodded. "I need something for a headache. Please. A hangover kind of headache."

"Did you have this headache the other times?" Croaker demanded. "You never mentioned it."

"It was there but not this bad. Just a minor discomfort. A four-beer hangover kind of headache, if it was beer brewed by Willow Swan and Cordy Mather. That mean anything?"

Croaker smiled at the reference to the world's second worst beer. "Between me and Goblin we watched you almost every minute since you got back from the Grove of Doom. It seemed likely that this would keep happening. I didn't want us to miss anything."

And that keyed a serious question. Since while I am in this time I can remember the future occasionally how come I never remember the trips to the past that I am going to make?

And how could they watch me that closely? I never noticed them. And I try to stay alert. You never know when a Deceiver might pop out of a shadow swinging his strangling scarf.

"So what did you get?"

"We didn't see a thing."

"*I* am on the job now, though," One-Eye said, preening.

"Now that really inspires me with confidence."

"Everybody's got to be a wiseass anymore," One-Eye complained. "I remember when young people respected their elders."

"That was in the days when they didn't get a chance to know the old folks very well."

"I have work to do," Croaker said. "One-Eye, stick with Murgen when you can. Keep talking about Dejagore and what's been happening to him. There'll be clues there somewhere. Maybe we don't recognize them yet. If we keep at it something will pop." He left before I could say anything.

Something had passed between Croaker and One-Eye about and

beyond me. And maybe we all had cause to be concerned. This time I could not remember much about where I was. Things seemed to be new, first time, yet some shaking, terrified little creature way back in the night warrens of my mind insisted I was still reliving yesterdays and the worst of those were yet to come.

One-Eye said, "I think we'll just take you home now, Kid. Your wife will have the cure for what ails you."

She might. She was a miracle. Even One-Eye, who seems incapable of offering respect to anyone, treated her and spoke to and of her, as though he considered her an honored lady.

She is, of course. But it is nice to have others confirm that.

"Now that's the first thing you've said that I wanted to hear. Lead on, brother." I didn't know the way.

I cast a backward glance at Smoke and the covered Deceiver. What in the hell?

31

MY IN-LAWS MAKE VERY LITTLE EFFORT TO IMPROVE ANYONE'S OPINION OF Nyueng Bao. Mother Gota, in particular, is a major pain in the ass. The old battleaxe barely tolerates even me and that only because the alternative is to lose her daughter entirely. She is very nasty toward the Old Man.

Still, Sarie and I rated enough for Croaker to insist we swap quarters when her folks showed up last month, in town slumming from their glamorous swamps. But they won't make it back to paradise if Mother Gota doesn't control her lip in the street.

The Old Man never reacts to her constant complaints. He told me, "I've had thirty years of Goblin and One-Eye. One crabby old woman hurting from gout and arthritis is nothing. You did say she's only here for a few weeks, didn't you?"

Right. I did say that. I wondered how those words would taste with soy sauce. Or maybe a lot of curry.

Now that Lady is in the south most of the time, emptying her cornucopia of rage onto the Shadowlands, Croaker has no need for a large apartment. Our old space was little more than a monk's cell. There is just room enough for him, Lady when she visits, and a cradle that was given to Lady by a man named Ram who later died trying to protect her and her baby from Narayan Singh. Ram made that cradle himself. Most likely he died because, like almost every man who spends much time around Lady, he fell for the wrong woman.

Croaker gave me his apartment, all right, but it came with limitations. I could not turn it into the new home of the Nyueng Bao. Sahra and Thai Dei belonged. Mother Gota and Uncle Doj were welcome for visits. And not one freeloading cousin or nephew more.

People who accuse the Captain of using his position to feather his nest ought to take a close look at the nest. The Liberator, Mr. By Golly Military Despot of all the Taglians and their many conquests and dependencies, lives just the way he did back when he was only the Company physician and Annalist.

Also, he moved me to provide me adequate work space. He sets great store by these Annals.

My books are not coming out so good. I don't always get stuff down the best way. In his time, when he was on the mark, Croaker was really good. I can't help comparing my stuff to his.

When he tried to be Captain and Annalist at the same time his work suffered. And Lady's writing strikes me as too direct, too curt, and sometimes mildly self-indulgent. Neither was honest all the time and neither considered trying to be consistent with the other, with their predecessors, or even with their own earlier selves. If you read either one closely and you spot some of their slips, neither will admit any screwup. If Croaker says that it is eight hundred miles from Taglios to Shadowcatch and Lady calls it four hundred, who is correct? Both say they are. Lady says the discrepancy is because they grew up in different places and times where different weights and measures were in use.

What about character? They for sure see with different eyes there. You will never catch Croaker portraying a Willow Swan who is not bitching about something. Lady makes Swan energetic and rattle-mouthed and a lot more mellow. And the difference could be that both Croaker and Lady know Swan's interest in Lady is not brotherly.

And consider how they saw Smoke. You wouldn't think they were writing about the same animal, they looked at that traitor so differently. Then there is Mogaba. And Blade. Both blackhearted traitors, too. There is nothing in Croaker's Annals because he was no longer writing when Blade deserted but in daily life, constantly, he shows you that he hates Blade with a blue-assed passion, on no rational basis. Meantime, he seems almost willing to forgive Mogaba. Lady sees those two the other way around. She would broil Mogaba right in the same pot with Narayan and probably let Blade go.

Blade was another case like Ram and Swan.

I guess you don't need to agree on everything to be lovers.

They wrote differently, too. Croaker mostly kept his Annals as he went along, then went back later to fill in after he heard from other sources. He tended to fictionalize his secondary viewpoints, too, so his Annals are not always absolutely straightforward history.

Lady wrote her entire book after the fact, from memory, while she was laid up waiting to have her baby. Her alternate viewpoint material is mainly secondhand hearsay. I am replacing her more dubious stuff with material I consider more accurate while I am in the process of putting all the confused stuff into a uniform format.

Lady is not always pleased with my efforts, he understated.

My major fault is getting trapped in elaborate digressions. I have trouble leaving things out. I spent some time with the official historians at Taglios's royal library and those guys assured me that the real keys to history are the details. Like the entire course of history can veer sharply because one man gets dinged by a random arrow during a minor skirmish.

My writing room is fifteen feet by twenty-two. That gives me space for all my references, for copies of the old Annals, and for a large trestle table where I work on several projects at once. And there is an acre of floor space left for Thai Dei and Uncle Doj.

While I write and study and revise he and Thai Dei clack away with wooden practice swords or squeal and kick and bounce off the walls. Whenever one of them lands in my space I toss him back. They are amazingly good at what they do—they ought to be with all that practice—but I think they are more likely to hurt each other than any seriously large person, like our Old Crew guys.

I like this job. It beats hell out of being standardbearer—though I am stuck with that, too, still. The standardbearer is always the first guy into a scrape and he always has one hand tied up keeping a bigass pole from falling over.

I worry about not catching details the way Croaker did. And I envy him his naturally sardonic tone. He claims he did good only because he had the time. In those days the Black Company was just a raggedyass gang sneaking around the edge of things and there wasn't much going on. Nowadays we are in the deep shit all the time. I don't like that. Neither does the Captain.

I cannot imagine a man less pleased about having the power that has fallen into his lap, mostly by default. He keeps it and uses it only because he doesn't believe anyone else will take the Company where he is convinced that it has to go.

I managed to get along for several hours without falling down a well into the past. I wasn't feeling badly. Sarie was in an excellent mood despite all her mother could do to ruin our day. I was lost in my work, as comfortable with existence as ever I get.

Somebody came to the door.

Sarie showed the Captain into the apartment. Uncle Doj and Thai Dei continued clacking away. Croaker watched for a minute. "Unusual," he said. He did not sound impressed.

"It's not military," I told him. "It's fencing for loners. Nyueng Bao are big on lone-wolf heroes." Not so the Old Man. His belief that you need brothers to guard your back amounts to a religious conviction.

Nyueng Bao fencing technique consists of brief but intense flurries of attack and defense separated by inactive periods during which the fighters freeze in odd stances, shifting almost imperceptibly as they try to anticipate one another.

Uncle Doj is *very* good.

"I'll grant you, they're graceful, Murgen. Almost like hutsch dancers."

By marrying into Sarie's clan I bought into Nyueng Bao fighting styles. No choice, really. Uncle Doj insisted. I am not terribly interested but I go along to keep the peace. And it is good exercise. "It's all stylized, Captain. Every stance and stroke has its name." Which I consider a weakness. Any fighter that set in his ways ought to be easy meat for an innovator.

On the other hand, I did see Uncle Doj deal with real enemies at Dejagore.

I changed languages. "Uncle, will you permit my Captain to meet Ash Wand?" They had taken the measure of one another long enough.

Ash Wand is Uncle Doj's sword. He calls it his soul. He treats it better than he would any mistress.

Uncle Doj disengaged from Thai Dei, bowed slightly, departed. In moments he was back with a monster sword. It was three feet long. He drew it carefully, presented it to Croaker lying along his left forearm, where the steel would not contact moist or oily skin. He bowed slightly as he did so.

He wanted us to believe he spoke no Taglian. A vain pretense. I knew him back when he was fluent.

Croaker knew something about Nyueng Bao customs. He accepted Ash Wand with proper care and courtesy, as though deeply honored.

Uncle Doj ate that up.

Croaker grasped the two-hand hilt clumsily. On purpose, I suspect. Uncle Doj darted in to demonstrate the proper grip, the way he does with me during every training session. That old boy is spry. He has ten years on Croaker but moves more easily than I do. And he possesses remarkable patience.

"Fine balance," the Captain said in Taglian. It would not surprise me to learn that he had picked up Nyueng Bao, though. He has an easy way with languages. "But this had better be superior steel." Because the blade was thin and narrow.

I told him, "He says it's four hundred years old and will cut plate armor. I guarantee it cuts people just fine. I saw him use it more than once."

"During the siege." Croaker studied the blade near the sword's hilt.

"Yes."

"Hallmark of Dinh Luc Doc."

Eyes suddenly narrow, usually stolid expression shoved aside by surprise, Uncle Doj reclaimed his lover quickly. That Croaker might know something about Nyueng Bao swordsmiths apparently troubled him. Croaker might not be nearly as stupid as foreigners were supposed to be.

Uncle Doj harvested one of his feeble crops of hair, drew it across Ash Wand's edge with predictable results. Croaker observed, "A man could get cut and never know it."

"It happens," I told him. "You wanted something?"

Sarie brought tea. The Old Man accepted even though he doesn't like tea. He watched me watch her, amused. Whenever Sahra is in a room I have trouble paying attention to anything else. She gets more beautiful every time I see her. I cannot believe my luck. I keep being scared that I will wake up.

Cold shivers.

"You have a definite prize there, Murgen." Croaker had told me so before. He approved of Sarie. It was her family that troubled him. "How come you married the whole kaboodle?" For that he shifted to Forsberger. None of the others spoke that northern tongue.

"You had to be there." Which is really all you can say about Dejagore. The Nyueng Bao and Old Crew became alloyed by the living nightmare.

Mother Gota materialized. All four feet ten inches of bile. She glared at the Captain. "Aha! The great man himself!" Her Taglian is an abomination but she refuses to believe that. Those who fail to understand her do so on purpose, to mock her.

She circled Croaker, walking her bowlegged walk. Nearly as wide as she is tall, without being really fat, ugly, waddling that waddle, she looked like a miniature troll. And her own people call her The Troll behind her back. And she has the personality. She could test the patience of a stone.

Thai Dei and Sahra were very late children. I pray my wife will not come to resemble her mother later, in character or physically. Like her grandmother would be fine, though.

Cold in here.

"Why so hard you push my Sahra's man, ho, Mr. So High and Mighty Liberator?" She hawked and spat to one side, the meaning of that no different to Nyueng Bao than anyone else. She rattled faster and faster. The faster she yakked the faster she waddled. "You think maybe he slave be? Warrior not? No time for grandmother to make of me, him always away to do for you?" She hawked and blank spat again.

She was a grandmother all right. But none were mine and none were alive anymore. I didn't remind her. No need attracting her attention.

An hour earlier she had climbed all over me because I was a no good bonehead lackwit layabout who wasted all his time reading and writing. Hardly the sort of thing a grown man does with his time.

Nothing ever satisfies Mother Gota.

Croaker says that is because she hurts all the time.

He pretended he could not fathom her broken Taglian. "Yes, it really is lovely weather. For this time of year. The agricultural specialists tell me we will make two crops this year. Do you think you'll be able to double harvest your rice?"

Hawk and spit, then a lapse into ferocious Nyueng Bao liberally spiced with imaginative epithets, not all of them native to her birth tongue. Mother Gota hates being humored or ignored more than she hates everything else.

Somebody pounded on my door. Sarie was busy doing something somewhere that kept her from being close enough to her mother to become embarrassed. I went. I found One-Eye stinking up the hallway. The little wizard asked, "How you doing, Kid? Here." He shoved a smelly, ragged, grubby bundle of papers into my hands. "The Old Man here?"

"What kind of sorcerer are you if you don't know the answer to that?"

"A lazy sorcerer."

I stepped aside. "What's this mess?" I lifted the bundle.

"Them papers you been after me about. My notes and Annals." He ambled over to the Captain.

I stared down at the mess in my hands. Some of the papers were moldy. Some were waterstained. That was One-Eye. Four years late. I hoped the little rat did not hang around. He would shed lice and fleas. He takes a bath only if he gets drunk and falls in a canal. And that damned hat . . . I am going to burn it someday.

One-Eye whispered to the Captain. The Captain whispered back. Mother Gota tried to eavesdrop. They changed to a language she did not know. She sucked in a bushel of air and went to work.

One-Eye stopped talking and stared at her. This was their first encounter, close up and personal.

He grinned.

She did not faze him. He was two hundred years old. He had had obnoxious down to a fine art generations before Mother Gota was born.

He gave her a thumbs up, sidled over to me grinning like a kid who had stubbed his toe on the pot at the end of the rainbow. In Taglian he asked, "Want to make a formal introduction here, Kid? I love her! She's great! Everything I've ever heard. She's perfect. Give us a kiss here, lover."

Maybe it was because Mother Gota was the only woman in Taglios shorter than him.

That was the only time I ever saw my mother-in-law at a loss for words.

Thai Dei and Uncle Doj seemed taken aback, too.

One-Eye stalked Mother Gota around the room. Finally, she fled.

"Perfect!" One-Eye crowed. "She's absolutely perfect! The woman of my dreams. Are you ready, Captain?"

Was he high on something?

"Yeah." Croaker separated himself from his barely tasted tea. "Murgen, I want you to come with us. It's time to teach you some new tricks."

I started to shake my head. I don't know why. Sarie slipped her arm around me. She was back now, avoiding her mother by being where I was. She felt my reluctance, squeezed my arm. She looked up at me with those gorgeous almond eyes, asking why I was troubled.

"I don't know." I figured we were going to interrogate the red-hand Deceiver. That was not work I would enjoy.

Uncle Doj astonished me by asking, "May I accompany you, husband of my niece?"

"Why?" I blurted.

"I wish to inform my curiosity about what it is you people do." He spoke to me slowly, as though to an idiot. I do suffer from a severe birth defect, by his thinking. I was not born Nyueng Bao.

At least he does not call me Bone Warrior and Stone Soldier anymore.

I never did figure that out.

I translated for the Old Man. He didn't bat an eye. "Sure, Murgen. Why not? But let's get going before we all die of old age."

What the hell? This was the guy who was sure the Nyueng Bao were up to no good.

I looked at the mass of paper One-Eye passed off on me. It smelled of mildew. I would try to make something of it later. If anything could be made of it. Knowing One-Eye it could well be written in a language he no longer remembered.

32

ONE-EYE'S ANNALS WERE AS TERRIBLE AS I EXPECTED. AND THEN SOME. Water, mold, vermin and criminal neglect had left most of his recollections irretrievable. One recent memoir, though, did survive except for a page in the middle which was just plain missing. It will serve to illustrate what One-Eye considers to be an adequate chronicle.

He made up the spellings of most of the place names. I corrected to standard where I could, from the maps, figure out where he had been.

In the fall of our third year in Taglios the Captain decided to send the Khusavir Regiment to Prehbehlbed, where the Prahbrindrah Drah was campaigning against a bevy of minor Shadowlander princes. Me and several Company comrades were told to go along to give the new regiment backbone. The traitor Blade was in the region.

The regiment proceeded through Ranji and Ghoja, Jaicur and Cantile, then Bhakur, Danjil and other recently captured towns until, after two months, we overtook the Prince at Praiphurbed. There half the regiment split off to escort prisoners of war and booty back to the north. The rest of us went west to Asharan, where Blade caught us by surprise and we had to barricade the gates and throw a lot of the natives off the wall because they might be spies. With my talent we were able to hold out even though the green troops were terrified.

In Asharan we found a large store of wine and whiled away the hours of the siege.

After a few weeks Blade's men began to desert because of the cold and hunger and he decided to go away.

It was a very cold winter. We suffered a great deal and often had to threaten the natives to get enough food and firewood. The Prince kept us moving, mostly far from the heavy fighting, because the regiment was not experienced.

In Meldermhai three men and I got drunk and missed marching when the regiment moved out. We had to travel almost a hundred miles counting only upon ourselves in order to catch up. Once we took four horses from a local lord after we stayed over the night in his manor. We took his brandy, too. The noble complained to the Prince and we had to give the horses back.

We spent a week at Forngaw, then the Prince ordered us south to

High Nangel, where we were supposed to join the Fourth Horse in trying to drive Blade's bandits into the Ruderal canyon, but when we got there we found only one old woman in the whole territory and nothing to eat but rotting cabbages, most of which the peasants had buried in the earth before they fled.

Then we went up to Silure by way of Balichore and in the forest there we found a tavern almost like those in the north. While we were drunk an enemy witch sent an attack of poisonous toads against us.

Next day we had to walk several miles through swamps and melting snow and cold mud in a low place where warm water runs out of the earth and keeps everything from freezing. After a few leagues we came to the fortress of Tracil, where a regiment recruited from former Shadowlander soldiers were besieging their Tracili cousins. They had been there a long time so it was difficult to find provisions anywhere nearby, even when we offered to pay.

I worked three days in the field hospital there, where, because of the cold, they treated many cases of frostbite. The cold killed more soldiers than did the enemy.

From Tracil we marched up to Melopil with the Prince's own guards and laid siege to the local king's fortress, which stands on an island in the middle of a lake. The lake was frozen. It was very cold and the ice was very thick and every time we tried to go forward against the enemy their missiles came bouncing over the ice. . . .

. . . Shadowlanders were slaughtered with great vigor along with our men by engines atop the walls until the garrison inside got the gates closed. Then the Howler came up from Shadowcatch on his flying carpet and the magicks flew around like lightning in a thunderstorm and we had to run away. Many were captured by the enemy.

After two weeks passed orders came to march to join the siege at Rani Orthal. On the way we found some wine and that ended in disaster, for the natives stole our packs while we slept.

Forces gathered from all over, on both sides, and I began to fear a major battle. That would draw the Howler to Rani Orthal.

After the city was surrounded the enemy made several attacks on our breastworks and trenches, which resulted in heavy losses for them. After two weeks, when it was starting to show spring, we launched a surprise attack at night which carried the outer works right up to the stone wall. The soldiers killed everybody, so angry were they, and so frightened to be fighting at night. When they reached the top of the wall they threw down everyone, even the women and children.

Then the Howler came up from Shadowcatch and with him a small swarm of shadows and we had to abandon everything we had captured.

The Howler and shadows went away when the sun rose and the Prahbrindrah Drah himself went forward to tell the enemy we were going to attack come evening and this time no mercy would be shown, but the attack never took place because the enemy king decided to throw in his lot with Taglios. The city gates were opened and the town given over to the soldiers for one night but the men were allowed no weapons except their daggers.

The soil in those parts is very poor. The crops are not of a delicate nature. They eat much cabbage and roots, and rye is the common grain.

When we were in garrison at Thruthelwar for a month I befriended the landlord's son, a boy of about eleven, and found him intelligent but ignorant of both religion and of reading and writing. His father reported that the Shadowmasters have banned all religious practice and all education throughout their empire and there were rewards out for books, especially older books, which were burned as soon as they were turned in, and likewise there were rewards for priests who tried to serve their faith, who were also burned as soon as they were turned in. This rule must have pleased Blade very much.

After a month in garrison orders came for the regiment to return to Jaicur, where Lady was gathering an army for a summer campaign in the east. At Jaicur I left the regiment and travelled north to Taglios, where I was received with great joy by my old companions of the Black Company.

The record of that campaign appears to be One-Eye's most careful and detailed. The remaining fragments suggest stories much less coherent.

33

THE CAPTIVE RED-HAND DECEIVER AWAITED US IN A ROOM GUARANTEED proof against sorcerous espionage. One-Eye swore he had woven the spells so well even Lady in her heyday could not have picked through them to eavesdrop.

Croaker grumbled, "What Lady could do back when doesn't concern me. I'm worried about the Shadowmaster now. I'm worried about Soulcatcher now. She's lying low but she is out there and she does want to know everything about everything. I'm worried about the Howler now. He wants a big bite of the Company."

"It's all right," One-Eye insisted. "The Dominator himself couldn't bust in here."

"What do you want to bet that's exactly what Smoke thought about *his* spyproof room?"

I shuddered. So did One-Eye. I had not witnessed Smoke's destruction by the monster that got into his hidden place through a pinhole in his protection, but I had heard. "Whatever became of Smoke?" I asked. The monster had not killed him.

Croaker lifted a finger to his lips. "Right around the corner."

I thought we were going back to the room where Goblin, One-Eye and the Old Man wakened me from my last seizure. I just assumed they had the red-hand Strangler there, behind that curtain. Not so. We arrived at what seemed to be a different place entirely.

And the Deceiver was not alone.

The Radisha Drah, sister of the ruling Prince, the Prahbrindrah Drah, leaned against a wall and stared at the prisoner in a way that suggested she enjoyed a conviction that the Liberator was soft on villains. Small and dark and wrinkled, like most Taglian women who make it past thirty, she was one hard woman, and too bright besides. They say the only time she ever lost her composure was the night Lady killed all the senior members of Taglios's various priesthoods, ending religious resistance to her participation in the war effort as a key player.

There has been a lot less intrigue since that demonstration. Our allies and employers now seem inclined to leave our destruction to us.

If you polled the Taglian nobilities and priesthoods you would find that most of the upper classes believe the Radisha makes the princely decisions. Which is near the truth. Her brother is stronger than is commonly supposed but he prefers to be off soldiering.

Behind the Radisha stood a table. Upon the table lay a man. "Smoke?" I asked.

My question was answered. Smoke was still alive. And still in a coma. He had all the muscle tone of a bowl of lard.

Behind him was the other side of a curtain identical to the one I saw when I awakened. Then this *was* the same room, approached from a different direction.

Strange.

"Smoke," Croaker agreed, and I realized I was being made privy to a major secret.

"But . . ."

"This character said anything interesting?" Croaker asked the Radisha, cutting me off. She must have been amusing herself with the prisoner. And there must be some reason the Captain did not want her paying too much attention to Smoke.

"No. But he will."

The Strangler faked a sneer. A brave man but a fool. He, of all people, would know what torture could do.

Once again I got that spine chill.

"I know. Let's do it, One-Eye. Murgen kept us waiting long enough."

The Annals. He held it off just so I could get it into the Annals.

He did not have to bother. I am not a big torture enthusiast.

One-Eye started humming. He patted the prisoner's cheek. "You're going to have to help me out here, sweetheart. I'll be as kind as you let me. What's this thing you Stranglers got going here in Taglios?" One-Eye looked to the Captain. "When's Goblin coming back, Chief?"

"Get on with it."

One-Eye did something. The Strangler spasmed against his bonds, his scream not much more than a breathless squeak. One-Eye said, "But I found him the perfect woman, Boss. Ain't that right, Kid?" He leered evilly, bent over the Deceiver. That brown raisin of a man wore nothing but a filthy loincloth.

So that was why One-Eye was so excited about Mother Gota. He wanted to use her as a practical joke on Goblin. I should have been angry, I guess, maybe for Sahra's sake, but I could work up no indignation.

That woman begged for abuse.

One-Eye crooned, "You understand your position here, sweetheart? You were with Narayan Singh when we caught you. You have the red hand. Those things tell me you're one of those very special Deceivers that the Captain *really* wants." He indicated Croaker. The word for Captain he used was *jamadar,* which has strong religious connotations to the Deceivers.

Lady got taken in by them but she fixed them by marking their top men permanently with the red hand. That made them stand out in the crowd these days.

One-Eye sucked spit between the stumps of his teeth. Somebody who did not know him might have believed he was thinking. He said, "But I'm a swell guy who hates to see people hurting so I'm gonna give you a chance not to end up like this cockroach over here." He jerked a thumb at Smoke. Fire crackled between the fingers of his other hand. The Strangler screamed the kind of scream that rips your nerves out raw and salts their ends. "You can make this last forever or you can get it over quick. All up to you. Talk to me about what the Deceivers are up to here in Taglios." He leaned closer, whispered, "I can even fix it so you can get away."

The prisoner gaped for a moment. Sweat ran into his eyes, stung him. He tried to shake it away.

"I bet that she'd think that Goblin is just as cute as a bug," One-Eye said. "What do you think, Kid?"

"I think you'd better get on with it," Croaker snapped. He was not happy dealing in torture and had no patience left for the games Goblin and One-Eye play with one another.

"Oh, keep your damned pants on, Chief. This guy ain't going nowhere."

"But his friends are up to something."

I glanced at Uncle Doj to see what the thought of the bickering. His face was stone. Maybe he didn't understand Taglian anymore.

One-Eye barked, "You don't like the way I do my job, fire me and do it yourself." He prodded the prisoner. The Deceiver tensed in anticipation. "You. What's up here in Taglios? Where are Narayan and the Daughter of Night? Help me out here."

I tensed up myself. I felt a big chill. What was it?

The prisoner gulped air. Sweat covered his entire body. He could not win. If he knew anything and talked—as he must eventually—his own kind would show him no mercy later.

"Sufficient unto the day the evil thereof," Croaker told him, sensing his thoughts.

My sympathies all lay with the Old Man. Even if he ever does get his daughter back he won't find what he is looking for. She has been a Deceiver from the day she was born, raised to be the Daughter of Night who will bring on Kina's Year of the Skulls. Hell, they consecrated her to Kina while she was still in the womb. She would be what they wanted her to be. And that would be a darkness to break her parents' hearts.

"Talk to me, sweetheart. Tell me what I need to know." One-Eye tried to keep it one on one, just him and his client. He gave the Strangler a moment to reflect. The rest of us watched without expression, maybe a thimbleful of pity among us. This was a black rumel man. In Strangler terms, generally, that meant he was guilty of more than thirty murders, without remorse—unless he strangled a black rumel man and thus gained acclaim by the most direct route.

Kina is the ultimate Deceiver. She enjoys betraying her own on occasion.

An argument One-Eye did not think to present to our pet Deceiver.

The Strangler screamed again, tried to gurgle something.

"You'll have to speak up," One-Eye told him.

"I can't tell you. I don't know where they are."

I believed him. Narayan Singh was not staying alive by announcing his itineraries in a world where everybody really is out to get him.

"Pity. So just tell us why we have Deceivers here in Taglios, after all this time."

I wondered why he kept going back to that. The Stranglers had not dared to operate in the city for years.

One-Eye and the Old Man must know something. But how?

The prisoner screamed.

The Radisha observed, "The ones we catch are always ignorant."

"Don't matter," Croaker said. "I know exactly where Singh is. Or at least where he'll be when he stops running. As long as he doesn't realize that, I know he'll always be right where I want him."

Uncle Doj's eyebrow twitched. Must be getting exciting for him.

The Radisha glared, frowned, stared. She liked to believe that hers was the only working brain in the Palace. Us Black Company types are just supposed to be hired muscle. You could almost hear the creaks and groans as her mind turned over. How could Croaker know something like that? "Where is he?"

"Right now he's busting his butt trying to join up with Mogaba. Since we can't stop him—because he's moving as fast as any message we could send after him—let's forget him."

I considered offering a word of suggestion about crows. Croaker talks to crows. And crows fly faster than even a Deceiver can run. . . . I was not paid to think and I was not there to talk.

"Forget him?" The Radisha seemed startled.

"Just for the moment. Let's find out what his cronies are up to here."

One-Eye resumed work. I glanced at Uncle Doj, who had stayed out of the way and quiet longer than I had thought possible. He noticed my glance. In Nyueng Bao he asked, "May I question the man?"

"Why?"

"I would test his belief."

"You don't speak Taglian well enough." Little dig there.

"Then translate."

Just for fun, or maybe to nudge Uncle Doj, Croaker said, "I don't mind if he does, Murgen. He can't do any damage." His remark demonstrated clearly his familiarity with Nyueng Bao dialect. There had to be a message in that, meant for Uncle Doj—particularly when taken with his earlier observation about Ash Wand's provenance.

What the hell? I was confused. And getting more than a little paranoid myself. Had I come back to my own world after my most recent seizure?

In Taglian as passable as I recalled him having, Uncle Doj shot quick, amiable questions at the Deceiver. They were questions of the sort most people answer without thought. We learned that the man had a family but his wife had died in childbirth. Then he realized he was being manipulated and controlled his tongue.

Uncle Doj stamped around like a merry troll, chattering, and winkled out much of the prisoner's past but not once did he get any closer to the facts of any new Strangler interest in Taglios the city. Croaker, I noticed, paid more attention to Uncle Doj than he did the prisoner. The Captain, of course, lives in the eye of a tornado of paranoia.

Croaker leaned close to me. In a midnight whisper he said, "You stay when the others leave." He did not tell me why. He went on to say something to One-Eye in a tongue even I did not understand.

He spoke at least twenty languages, he had been with the Company so long. One-Eye probably spoke a bunch more but shared them with nobody but Goblin. One-Eye nodded and continued about his business.

Pretty soon the runt wizard began edging Uncle Doj and the Radisha toward the door. He did it so gently and smoothly that they never complained. Uncle Doj was a guest to begin with and the Radisha did have pressing business elsewhere and One-Eye went about it so unlike his usual abrasive self that he had them thinking it was their own idea. In any event, they left.

Croaker went with them, which helped, but he was back in five minutes. I told him, "Now I've seen everything. There are no wonders left. I can get out of this chicken outfit and go ahead with my plan to start a turnip ranch." Which was only halfway a jest. Whenever the Company stops moving guys begin developing plans. Human nature, I guess.

The turnip is unknown here but I have seen vast tracts of land perfect for cultivating turnips, parsnips and sugar beets. And Otto and Hagop are not far away so seed should be available soon. Maybe they will even bring some potatoes.

Croaker grinned, told One-Eye, "This weasel isn't going to tell us anything we can use."

"You know what it is, Chief? I'll bet you. He's stalling. He's got something he's trying to hold onto just a little while longer. That's what goes through his head every time I hurt him. He thinks he will endure it just one more time. And then just one more time."

"Let him get thirsty for a while." Croaker shoved the Deceiver's chair over against a wall, tossed a piece of ragged linen over him as though he was discarded furniture. "Murgen, listen up. Time is getting tight. Things are going to start happening. I need you in the first rank, healed or not."

"I don't like the sound of that."

He didn't feel like joking. "We've discovered some interesting things about Smoke." Suddenly he was speaking the Jewel Cities dialect, unknown outside the Company here, unless Mogaba was lurking around.

"We stalled because of your lapses and what they might signify, but we have to move on. It's time to take chances. There are some new tricks you need to learn, old dog."

"You trying to scare me?"

"No. This is important. Pay attention. I don't have time to work Smoke anymore. Neither does One-Eye. The arsenal is eating up all his time. And I don't trust anybody else but you to help with this."

"Huh? You're going too fast for me."

"Pay attention. And by that I mean keep your ears and eyes open and your mouth shut. We may not get much time. The Radisha could decide to come back and torment the Deceiver again. She likes that sort of thing." He told One-Eye, "Remind me to see if we can't get Cordy Mather assigned here permanently. She doesn't get underfoot when he's around."

"He's supposed to be back in town soon. If he's not here already."

"That there is my intelligence chief," Croaker told me, pointing at One-Eye and shaking his head. "Blind in one eye and can't see out the other."

I glanced at the cloth-covered villain. He had begun snoring. A good soldier seizing his rest when it was available.

34

HOURS PASSED. CROAKER LEFT, THEN RETURNED. NOW HE SLAPPED ME ON the back. "See how easy it is, Murgen? Ever seen such a big trick that was this simple?"

"Nothing to it," I agreed. "Like falling off a log." Or like falling into a bottomless pit, maybe, which I have had enough involuntary practice doing.

Nothing is ever as simple as somebody tells you it is going to be. I knew this would be no exception when I tried it myself, amazing as it was. "At least now I understand how you got so damned spooky, knowing things you shouldn't."

Croaker laughed. "Go ahead." Showing off his astonishing discovery had put him into a grand mood. "Try it."

I gave him a look he chose to interpret as my not really understanding what he meant. Nothing to it. Like falling off a log. Maybe. Only One-Eye is not a very good teacher.

"Do what One-Eye showed you. Decide what you want to see. Tell Smoke. But be damned careful how you do that. You have to be precise. Precision is everything. Ambiguity is deadly."

"That's the way the magic goes in every story I ever heard, Captain. The ambiguities screw you every time."

"You think so? You might be right." I must have touched a nerve. He became thoughtful suddenly. "Go ahead."

I was reluctant. "This whole thing is too much like what keeps happening to me when I fall down the rabbit hole to Dejagore. Could Smoke be doing that to me somehow?"

Croaker shook his head. "No way. It's not the same. Go ahead. I insist. You're wasting time. Go look at something you always wanted to know about for the Annals. We'll be right here to cover you."

"How about I go look for Otto and Hagop?"

"I know where they are. They just passed the First Cataract. They'll be here in a few days. Try something else." Hagop and Otto had spent the last three years travelling back north with a Taglian delegation and letters from Lady to those she had left behind. Their mission was to learn anything possibly known there about the Shadowmaster, Longshadow. One of the dead Shadowmasters, Stormshadow, had turned out to be a refugee from Lady's old empire, Stormbringer, previously thought dead. And two other big and nasty sorcerers long believed perished also have turned up and remain burrs under our saddles, the Howler and Lady's mad sister, Soulcatcher. And there was Shapeshifter, too, but we took care of him.

That Otto and Hagop managed to survive so incredible a journey was, to me, a major miracle. But Otto and Hagop are blessed.

"I expect they'll have whole new collections of scars to talk about."

Croaker nodded. He seemed a little grim now. I little anxious. Time to get on with my training.

An unexplained tragedy of the past caught my imagination. There had been some grotesque, horrible, senseless killings in a village called Bond that never got connected with anyone or anything, to my recollection. I was sure they had to be important somehow and was baffled that, even today, the slaughter remained unsolved and unresolved.

I gripped Smoke's hand, blanked my mind, spoke careful instructions in a whisper. And away I went, out of my body, so suddenly I almost panicked. For a moment I thought I recalled doing all this before. But I could not remember what was going to happen.

The Old Man was right. This was not the same as my unwanted plunges into my own past. In this nightmare I was aware and in control. I was a disembodied vision racing toward Bond but my mission remained clear in my mind. That was a big distinction. When I floated over Dejagore I lacked identity and control till I merged with my self of the past. Then I forgot the future.

Bond is a hamlet on the south bank of the River Main, facing the

Vehdna-Bota ford. For centuries the Main has been the traditional boundary of the Taglian heartland. The peoples who live below the river share the languages and religions of Taglios but are considered only tributary cousins by the Taglians themselves.

The nonagrarian part of Bond's economy revolved around a small remount station for the military courier post. A minimal garrison of Shadar cavalrymen managed the station and kept watch on ford traffic. Bond was the kind of duty soldiers dream about. There were no officers and very little work. The river was low enough to ford only about three months a year. But the garrison got paid all year round.

Smoke's soul slipped back to that long-ago disaster. I stayed with him, carrying a load of fear despite all of Croaker's reassurances.

It was very dark that night in that Bond gone by. Horror stalked out of the night and those nightmares where men are more often prey than predator. A monster padded through the hamlet, headed toward the army stable. I watched from a place where I could offer no warning.

One solitary soldier had the watch. He was nodding. Neither he nor the horses sensed their danger.

The latch rose inside the stable door. No animal mind knew enough to pull a string. The soldier started awake just in time to see a dark shape with scarlet eyes hurtling toward him.

The monster fed, then padded into the night. It killed again. Screams wakened the garrison. The soldiers seized their arms. The monster, like an oversize black panther, loped to the river, swam to the northern shore.

I knew something now. The killer was a shapeshifter, the acolyte of the sorcerer Shapeshifter, whom we had destroyed the night we captured Dejagore. She got away, trapped in the animal shape.

Why just this one incident in more than four years?

I wanted to follow the panther, to discover what had become of it, but Smoke could not be coaxed to go. The comatose wizard had no will or ego I could detect but, apparently, he did have limits or constraints.

Funny, though. I felt no real emotion until I returned to the reality of the Palace. Then it hit me in a wave, hard, leaving me breathless. I asked, "Is whatever I see out there true?"

"We haven't seen any evidence otherwise." Croaker's caution meant he had reservations. Always suspicious, our Captain. "You look bad. You see something nasty?"

"Very." One-Eye was gone. And the Strangler had fouled himself. I wrinkled my nose. "I can use Smoke to look anywhere?"

"Almost. Some places he can't or won't go. And he can't go back to any time before he went into the coma. You can catch the Annals up now, eyewitness style, if you will. But always remember to be careful about pointing him right."

"Wow." The implications had begun to sink in. "This is worth more than a veteran legion." Now I knew how we had pulled off some really startling coups lately. If you can perch on your enemy's shoulder nothing is going to go his way.

"It's worth a lot more. And that's why you're going to keep your mouth shut even around your dearly beloved."

"Does the Radisha know?"

"No. You, me and One-Eye. Maybe Goblin if One-Eye just had to share it with somebody. And that's the limit. One-Eye found it by accident when he was trying to pull Smoke out of his coma. Smoke has been to Overlook. He's walked around inside. He's actually met Longshadow. We wanted to ask him some questions. We decided they could wait. You don't tell anybody. Understand?"

"There you go being suspicious of my in-laws again."

"I'd cut your throat."

"I get the message, boss. Don't brag it up to my Deceiver drinking buddies. Shit. This could win us the war."

"It won't hurt. As long as it's secret. I have business with the Radisha. Practice using him. Don't worry about working him too hard. You can't." He squeezed my shoulder, left the room with a stride that seemed both determined and fatalistic. Must be facing another budgetary conference. Depending on whether you were the Liberator or the Radisha the military either never had enough or always wanted too much.

So. There was just me and one halfway-dead wizard and one stinky Strangler under a linen rag. I considered using Smoke to find out what Stinky's buddies were up to in Taglios but reasoned that the Captain would not have had him interrogated if Smoke had been able to provide useful answers. Maybe you not only had to be precise in your instructions, you had to have some idea what you were seeking. You could not find your own elbow if you could not guess what directions to give to get you there.

The point? Old Smoke was a miracle but he had major limitations. And most of those would exist right inside our own heads. We would become the beneficiaries or victims of our own imaginations.

What should I go see, then?

I was excited now. I was up for an adventure. So, what the hell? Why not go straight for the biggie? How about taking a peek at the Shadowmaster himself, Longshadow, number one boy on the Black Company shit list?

35

LONGSHADOW COULD HAVE PRANCED RIGHT OUT OF MY FANTASIES. HE WAS A deadly freak. He was tall and thin and twitchy, given to flights of rage and subject to sudden spells resembling malarial shakes. He wore a sort of loose black floor-length chemise that concealed a deathly gauntness. He ate infrequently and then only picked. He could have been a famine victim.

Threads of silver and gold and glistening black, embroidered or woven into his robe, protected him with dozens of static sorceries. At first blush he seemed a hundred times more paranoid than Croaker. But he did have reason. There was just a whole world full of folks who wanted to roast his skinny ass and he had no friends closer than Mogaba and Blade.

The Howler was not a friend. He was an ally.

One of Longshadow's obsessions was the Black Company. I did not understand. The kind of enemies we were should not have troubled him at all. We were no world-killers.

His face, which he kept masked except when he was alone, was skull-like. His waxy, pallid features were frozen in a permanent expression of fear. There was no guessing his birth race. His eyes were a washed-out grey with splotches of pink around the edges but I don't think he was an albino. I exploited Smoke's ability, fluttered about through time to find out all the interesting stuff fast. I did not catch Longshadow completely out of costume once. The man did not bathe. He did not change clothing. He wore gloves all the time.

The last of the four Shadowmasters, now *the* Shadowmaster, he was the unquestioned tyrant of the city Shadowcatch and a demigod within his fortress Overlook. His slightest whim could set a hundred terrors and ten thousand men scrambling to appease him. And still he was a prisoner doing life without hope of parole.

Overlook is, but for one, the southernmost work of Man. I tried pushing past that fortress. Somewhere in the mists beyond Overlook is Khatovar, toward which we have marched for years. Just a glimpse would be marvelous.

Smoke refused to go any farther south.

Smoke had been crazy about Khatovar while he was still healthy. Khatovar was the reason he deserted the Radisha and Prahbrindrah Drah, years ago. His fear of Khatovar must have impressed itself upon his very flesh and soul.

Longshadow's fortress was gargantuan. Overlook dwarfed every human construction I have ever seen, including the Lady's monstrous tower at Charm. Already two decades in the building, Overlook's construction had become the main industry of Shadowcatch—the city that was called Kiaulune before the coming of the Shadowmasters. Kiaulune meant Shadow Gate in the local dialect.

The builders worked day and night. They knew no holidays. Longshadow was determined that his fortress be complete before his enemies overtook him. If he won that race he believed he would become master of the world. No power of heaven or hell or earth ought to be able to reach him inside a finished Overlook. Not even the darkness that brushed him every night with its terror.

Overlook's outer walls reared a hundred or more feet high. Where are you going to find a ladder that tall?

Brass and silver and gold characters shone on the steel plates that sheathed the rude stone of the wall face. Battalions of workmen did nothing but keep those runes polished and gleaming.

I could not read them but I knew they anchored massive defensive spells. Longshadow's spellwork overlaid everything that was part of Overlook, layer upon layer. If he was allowed enough time every exterior surface of the fortress would be hidden beneath and behind impenetrable tangles of sorceries.

Once the sun went down Overlook became a conflagration of light. Bright crystal chambers topped every tower, making the place seem a forest of lighthouses. The crystal domes were places whence Longshadow could observe safe from his terrors. The overpowering lights left no places for shadows to hide.

He feared that which he mastered far more than anything else in the world. Even the Black Company, for him, was a buzzing mosquito of a nuisance.

Even unfinished Overlook daunted me thoroughly. What sort of hubris-driven madmen were we to chart a course that must run through and beyond that stronghold?

But Longshadow had enemies not as easily daunted as I. For some of those no earthly fortress, nor even time itself, meant much. They would devour him now or later, the moment his guard fell.

He had chosen to play for the ultimate stakes in a game where the risks were as grim as the potential winnings were great. It was too late to get out. He would be victor or victim.

Longshadow lived inside the crystal chamber that topped Overlook's tallest central tower. He slept seldom, for fear of the night. He spent hours and hours just staring southward at a plain of glittering stone.

A screech ripped the air over the grim city. The people of Shadowcatch ignored it. If they thought about their master's strange ally at all it was, probably, to hope that a fate would catch up and rob Longshadow of this potent weapon. The inhabitants of Kiaulune were a broken people, spiritless, without hope, worse even than the Jaicuri at their lowest ebb during the siege of Dejagore.

Almost all of them were too young to recall a time when there was not a Shadowmaster there exercising more power over their lives than had their lost gods.

Even Longshadow could not extirpate rumor. Even at the heart of his empire some people had to travel and travelers always carry tales. Some stories are even true. The people of Shadowcatch knew that a doom from the north was coming.

The name of the Black Company lay at the heart of every rumor. That made no one happy. Longshadow was a very devil but many of his people feared his fall would be but the precursor to a far bleaker season.

Man, woman and child, the people of Shadowcatch were privy to the one true secret of the universe: there is always a darker shadow lurking beyond the one whose face you can see.

Longshadow reached out and inflicted pain and fear because he himself was the victim of a thousand terrors.

It was ugly out there. So ugly I wanted to go back somewhere where it was warm and there was someone to hold me and tell me that the dark was not always the lurking place of terror. I wanted my Sarie, my light in the night that rules the world. "Smoke, take me home."

36

CROAKER DID WARN ME. BE PRECISE, HE SAID.

He warned me several times, in fact.

I was ripped this way and dragged that, to and through the place of blood and burning, papers browning, blackening, curling in such slow motion. Blood pooled deep where I lay in my own vomit. The slap of running feet was like the slow booming footfalls of giants.

I heard screams that had no end.

Croaker warned me. I was thoughtless. What he did not tell me, or maybe he did not understand, was that the concept "home" could in one man's mind become defined by emotional pain.

Torn. Shredded. Smoke took me to Taglios only for that minute in the real now that is like the end of all time. I reeled and flung away from there with such revulsion that I threw myself and the hateful shreds and a disoriented Smoke all the way to Hell.

He had no will and no identity so he could not and did not laugh as I floated down into the lake of pain.

Hell has a name. Its name is Dejagore. But Dejagore is only Hell's lesser face.

From the greater Hell I escaped. One more time.

No identity and no will.

The wind blows but nothing moves in the place of glittering stone. Night falls. The wind dies. The plain yields up its heat as shadows waken. Moonlight settles upon the silence of stone.

The plain runs east and west, north and south, without discernible bounds, viewed from within. Though its ends be uncertain it has a definite center. That is an epic structure built of the same stone as the pillars and plain.

Within that fastness nothing moves, either, though at times mists of light shimmer as they leak over from beyond the gates of dream. Shadows linger in corners. And way down inside the core of the place, in the feeblest throb of the heart of darkness, there is life of a sort.

37

NO WILL. NO IDENTITY.

Now no smoke.

Now just pain. So much Smoke drifted away. Now just slavery to the memories.

Now at home in the house of pain.

38

So here we are again. You were missed.

. . . faceless thing that, nevertheless, seems to be smiling, pleased with itself.

It has been a night full of adventures. Has it not? And the fun continues. Look. There. The Black Company and their auxiliaries have begun making life especially unpleasant for Shadowlanders so bold as to have taken up residence inside Dejagore's wall.

See how they use the doppelgangers and imaginary soldiers to lure the southerners into deadly traps, to get them to betray themselves.

Oh. And come back to the wall. This is a small thing but it could become the stuff of epics.

The fighting has all shifted to the east side of the city. Hardly anybody is over there now. A few men to watch from the ramparts is all. And some unenthusiastic Shadowlander scouts down there in the darkness, not really paying attention. Otherwise how could they miss this spidery little figure rappelling down the outside of the wall?

Why on earth would a two-hundred-year-old, fourth-rate sorcerer want to climb down a rope to go where very unfriendly little brown men might decide to dance on his head?

The wounded stallion of mysterious sorcerous breed has stopped screaming. At last. It is dead. Green misty stuff still rises from its death wound. The wound still glows at its edges.

Out there? Yes. Look at them. Two very devils they are, aren't they, cloaked in their pink mists? They don't seem to be coming to devour the city, though, do they?

What is that? The Shadowlanders out there are scattering like the fox is in the henhouse. Their cries are filled with pure terror. Amongst them something dark moves swiftly. Look. It pulled a man down there. Didn't it?

There is so little light now that the focus of battle has shifted. The old man is as black as the heart of the night itself. Think any mortal eye will notice him sneaking around among the dead? Where is he headed? Shadowspinner's dead horse?

Who would expect that? It's the act of a madman.

The creeping darkness is moving toward the dead horse, too. See how its eyes flash red when the fires in the city flare up. Look at that fool, running toward it instead of away. There go his guts. Stupidity can be fatal.

The little black man has vanished because he has stopped moving. There he is. He heard something. There he goes, trotting toward the dead stallion. He wants his spear back. And maybe that does make some crazy sense. He worked hard making it.

He has stopped again, eye huge as he sniffs the night and catches an almost-forgotten odor. At the same moment the deadly darkness catches wind of him.

A pantherine roar of triumph stills hearts all across the plain. The darkness begins moving faster and faster.

The little black man grabs his spear and runs for the wall. Will he make it? Can two stubby, ancient legs carry him there fast enough to escape the death racing toward him?

The thing is huge. And it is filled with joy.

The little man reaches the rope. But he is still eighty feet down from safety. And he is old and winded. He whirls. His timing is perfect. The head of his spear reaches out just as the monster leaps. The beast twists in the air, evading the killing thrust but taking a cruel wound from its snout back through its left ear. It howls. Green mist boils off its redly-glowing wound. The beast loses all interest in the old man, who begins his long climb to the ramparts. That bizarrely carved spear is slung across his back now, held there by a mundane length of cotton string.

No one notices. No one cares. The fighting has gone elsewhere.

39

THE SOUTHERNERS SEEM TO HAVE JUST CLOSED THEIR EYES AND SHOVED their heads into a beehive, don't they?

What? Why so reluctant? Come see. This is amusing.

Everywhere you look the southerners are falling back. Sometimes they are running, sometimes just slinking away through the shadows before death overhauls them.

Look there. Shadowspinner, the king enemy himself, all but crippled, paying no attention to anyone or anything but those two pink-limned archetypes come out of the hills to devour him.

And Mogaba? Watch him be the master tactician. Watch him be the ultimate warrior exploiting the enemy's every weakness—now that there is no chance to accomplish the deviltry that moved him earlier in the evening. See that? No southerner, however great his reputation, dares come near Mogaba. Even their great heroes are like novice children when he steps forward himself.

He is way bigger than life, this Mogaba.

He is the triumphant centerpiece of his own imagined saga.

Something has gone out of the southerners.

They wanted to conquer. They knew they had to conquer because their master Shadowspinner would not tolerate anything less. He has a particular lack of understanding when it comes to failure. His followers are established solidly inside the city. Mild stubbornness will give them success.

But they are on the run.

Something has grabbed hold of them and convinced them that it is not possible for even their souls to survive if they stay inside Dejagore.

40

"YOU ALL RIGHT, MURGEN?"

I shook my head. I felt like a kid who had spun around about twenty times, intentionally trying to make himself dizzy before jumping into some silly competition.

I was in an alley. Runt boy Goblin was beside me, looking extremely concerned. "I'm fine," I told him.

Then I fell to my knees, stuck my hands out to grab the alley walls so I would not spin around anymore. I insisted, "I'm all right."

"Of course you are. Candles. Keep an eye on this dork. He tries to take over, get deaf. He's got too tender a heart."

I tried not to let my ego become engaged. Maybe I *was* too tender, too much a sucker. The world sure isn't kind to the man who tries to be gentle and thoughtful.

Its spin slowed down till I no longer had to hold on.

A scuffle broke out behind us. Someone cursed in a nasal, liquid tongue. Somebody else growled, "This asshole is fast!"

"Whoa whoa whoa!" I yelled. "Let the man alone! Let him come up here."

Candles didn't knock me over the head or contradict me. The short, wide Nyueng Bao guy who had shown me to Ky Dam's hideout marched up to me. The fingers of his right hand rubbed his right cheek. He seemed utterly astonished that somebody had laid a hand on him. His ego suffered again when he spoke in Nyueng Bao and I said, "Sorry, old-timer. No speakee. Gonna got to be Taglian or Groghor with me." In Groghor, which my maternal grandmother spoke because Grandpa captured her from those people, I asked, "What's happening?" I knew maybe twenty words in Groghor, but that was twenty more than anyone else within seven thousand miles.

"The Speaker sends me to lead you to where the invader is most vulnerable. We have watched closely and know."

"Thank you. We appreciate it. Lead on." Shifting languages, I observed, "Marvellous how these guys suddenly talk the lingo when they want something."

Candles grunted.

Goblin, who had sneaked forward for a look around, returned just in time to offer me directions to the same weak point the Nyueng Bao had in mind. The squat man seemed a little surprised we could find our butts with our hands, maybe even a touch disgruntled.

"You got a name, short and wide?" I asked. "If you don't have one you prefer I guarantee you these guys will hang one on you and I promise you won't like it."

"Hear hear," Goblin agreed, chuckling.

"I am Doj. All Nyueng Bao call me Uncle Doj."

"All right, Uncle. You going up there with us? Or did you just come over to direct traffic?" Already Goblin was whispering instructions to the guys creeping up behind us. No doubt he had left a few soft spells of sleepiness or confusion amongst the southerners as he was scouting.

Little discussion was needed. We would drive into their soft spot, kill anything that moved, split them in half, butcher anybody who didn't run away, then we would back away before Mogaba began feeling too confident.

"I will accompany you although that stretches the Speaker's instructions to extremes. You Bone Warriors surprise us continually. I wish to watch you at your work."

I never considered killing people to be my profession but did not care to argue. "You speak Taglian very well, Uncle."

He smiled. "I am forgetful, though, Stone Soldier. I may not remember a word after tonight." Unless the Speaker jogged his memory, I supposed.

Uncle Doj did a great deal more than watch us hack and stab southerners. He turned into a one-man cyclone flailing around with a lightning sword. He was as sudden as the lightning but as graceful as a dancer. Each time he moved another Shadowlander fell.

"Damn," I told Goblin a while later. "Remind me not to get into a quarrel with that character."

"I'll remind you to bring a crossbow and let him have it in the back from thirty feet is what I'll do. After I put a deafness and a stupidity spell on him to even things up a little."

"Don't be surprised if it's me distracting you someday when One-Eye sneaks up and offers you a cactus suppository."

"Speaking of the runt. Tell me. Who's being conspicuously absent without leave lately?"

I sent messages to the various units suggesting that we had done our part to relieve Mogaba's troops. We should all go back to our part of town, patch ourselves up, take naps, like that. I told the Nyueng Bao elder, "Uncle Doj, please inform the Speaker that the Black Company extends its gratitude and friendship. Tell him he is free to call upon that at any time. We will extend ourselves as much as possible."

The short, wide man bowed far enough that his movement had to mean something. I bowed back, almost as deeply. That must have been the right move because he smiled slightly, bowed shallowly for himself, hustled off.

"Runs like a duck," Candles observed.

"I'm glad that duck was on our side, though."

"You can say that again."

"I'm glad that duck . . . Argh!" Candles had me by the throat.

"Somebody help me shut him up."

That was just the start of what became a wild night of blowing off tensions. I got no chance to participate myself but I heard it was a banner night for the Jaicuri whores.

41

"WHERE THE HELL HAVE YOU BEEN?" I SNARLED AT ONE-EYE. "THE COM-pany just fought through its nastiest episode in, oh, just *days,* and you were obviously absent every stinking second." Not that his presence would have made any difference.

One-Eye grinned. My displeasure did not bother him a bit. He had outlived or outstubborned a parade of snotnoses like me. "Shit, Kid, I had to get my Shadowmaster sticker back, didn't I? I've got a lot of work in that thing. . . . What's the matter?"

"Huh?" For a moment I saw a little black louse scuttling across a grey landscape from a height unattainable anywhere in Dejagore, even atop the citadel, where Old Crew guys were not welcome anymore. "Never mind, runt. I'd like to kick your ass but it wouldn't do any good now. So you were out there. What became of Widowmaker and Lifetaker?" While I was arranging a quieter life for our leader those two vanished without a trace.

I wondered how Mogaba would write all this if he was keeping the Annals.

"One-Eye?"

"What?" Now he sounded irritated.

"You want to answer me? What happened to Widowmaker and Lifetaker?"

"You know something, Kid? I don't have the faintest freaking idea. And I don't care. I only had one thing on my mind. I wanted my spear back so I could use it next time that sucker ain't looking. Then I had to worry about dodging a gang of raggedyass Shadowlanders who tried to jump me. They went away somewhere. All right?"

And none of us could fathom that. Because they vanished just when the Shadowlander confidence was rockiest. Shadowspinner had his tail between his legs and his boys could have been broken.

I grumbled, "If that *was* the Old Man and Lady they would've kept coming till they broke the whole show wide open. Wouldn't they?"

I glared at an albino crow perched not twenty feet away. Its head was cocked. It stared at me with malign intelligence.

There were a lot of crows tonight.

Other agendas were being pursued. I was just one pawn caught up in tides of intrigue. But if we were careful the Company need not get swept away.

Mogaba and the Nar and their Taglian troops stayed busy for days. Maybe the Shadowmasters decided to make Mogaba pay for his failure to fulfill his end of the implicit bargain.

Which was just one more example of the way people down here go bugfuck when they are involved with the Black Company.

It could make a guy nervous if he thought about everybody within a thousand miles seeming to wish he'd never been born.

My guys enjoyed Mogaba's situation. And he could not squawk about their attitudes. We gave him exactly what he asked. We saved his ass and set him up so all he had to do was chase a few Shadowlanders out of town.

I had to see him almost every day at staff meetings. Again and again we showed ourselves to the soldiers, pretending to be brothers marching shoulder to shoulder against our evil foe.

Not once was anybody fooled except maybe Mogaba.

I never took it personal. I took a stance I believed the Annalists of the past would approve, just picturing Mogaba as not one of us.

We are the Black Company. We have no friends. All others are the enemy, or at best not to be trusted. That relationship with the world does not require hatred or any other emotion. It requires wariness.

Perhaps our refusal to remonstrate, or even to acknowledge Mogaba's treachery, was the final straw, or perhaps the backbreaker was his awareness that even his Nar compatriots now believed the real Captain might still live. Whatever, the ultimate and perfect warrior drifted across a boundary from beyond which he could not return. And we did not discover the truth until we had paid in treasures of pain.

It took ten days for Dejagore to return to normal—if normal was our state before the great attack. Both sides had suffered terribly. I believed Shadowspinner would now just lick his wounds and let us get hungry for a while.

42

"GOT SOMETHING FOR YOU, KID."

I started awake. "What . . . ?" What happened? I don't drift off that way.

One-Eye had a big shit-eating grin on but it evaporated when he looked at me closer. He darted in, grabbed my chin, turned my head right and left. "You just have one of your spells?"

"Spells?"

"You know what I mean."

Not exactly. I just had their word for the fact that I went spooky sometimes.

"You've got a kind of psychic shimmer. Maybe I caught you just in time."

He and Goblin kept talking about doing experiments to find out what is happening but there never seemed to be time to actually do anything. "What do you have?"

"The work parties broke into the old catacombs this morning."

"Longo told me."

"Everybody's charging around in there, all excited."

"I can imagine. Find any treasure yet?"

One-Eye looked put-upon. For such a blackhearted toad he can manage a truly impressive show of self-righteous injury.

"I take it not."

"We found some books. A whole pile. All sealed up neat and every-thing. Looks like they've been there since the Shadowmasters first came."

"Makes sense since they always burned the books and the priests. You find any priests lurking down there?"

"Not hardly. Look, I got to get back." Before somebody grabbed a treasure out from under him, no doubt. "I got a couple guys lugging them books up for you."

"Gods forfend you should have lifted anything yourself."

"You got a serious attitude problem, Kid. I'm an old man." One-Eye did a fade. He has that knack when he is about to find himself in an inde-fensible position.

A city seldom is buttoned up so tight that no news gets in from outside. Sometimes it seems almost mystical but the word does come through. In Dejagore rumor seldom brought in anything Mogaba wanted to hear.

I was studying the discovered books, so intrigued I was letting duties slide. They were written in Jaicuri but the written form thereof is almost identical to written Taglian.

Goblin stepped in. "You doing all right? No more dizziness?"

"No. You guys worry too much."

"No, we don't. Look, some new rumors are going around. There's sup-posedly a relief column headed our way. Blade, of all people, is in charge."

"Blade? He isn't. . . . He's never run anything bigger than a reduced company. Before we ever got here. Fighting guerrilla style against ama-teurs."

"I don't make them up, I just report them. He did do well."

"So did Willow Swan and Cordy Mather. But that was accident and luck and Shadowlander stupidity more than anything those three actually did. Why on earth is he commanding an army?"

"He's supposedly Lady's second in command. Not much doubt any-more that she survived. She's also pissed off. And putting together a new army."

"Bet Mogaba's jumping for joy. Running around hollering, 'We're saved! We're saved!' "

"You might say he's jumping."

Over the following few days we heard a thousand wild stories. If a tenth were true some really bizarre changes were underway out there in the world.

"You heard the latest?" Goblin asked me one night when I took a rare break from the books to examine that outer world from the wall. "Lady ain't Lady after all. She's the incarnation of some goddess named Kina. A real badass, too, apparently."

"She would be. Thai Dei. You know Kina, don't you? Tell us about her." Thai Dei wasn't allowed into our warrens but he always turned up whenever I came up for air.

He forgot all three words of Taglian he had admitted to knowing. The name of that goddess scrubbed his brain clean.

I said, "That's what happens when you mention Kina to any of these people. I can't even get our prisoners to talk about her. You would think she belonged to the Black Company."

"Must be a real charmer," Bucket opined.

"Oh, she is. She is. There's one." I meant a shooting star. We were keeping count. Also of enemy watchfires. The southerners had scattered in small unit encampments around the plain recently. I guess they were afraid we might sneak away.

"You know something about her, then?" Goblin asked.

"From those books you guys found." The men were bitter. The books and some sealed jars filled with grain were the only treasures they unearthed. The Gunni were the majority religion in Jaicur and the Gunni do not bury their dead. They burn them. The minority Vehdna do bury their dead but do not include any grave goods. Where their dead are bound they have no need of luggage. In paradise everything is provided. In hell, too. "One was a compilation of Gunni myths, in variants from all over. The guy who recorded them was a religious scholar. His book wasn't meant to get out where it might confuse ordinary people."

"I'm confused and there ain't nothing ordinary about me," Bucket observed.

"So what's the scoop, Murgen? How come they won't tell us about this bitch? Whoa! Did you see that one? It exploded."

"All right," I told them. "The Gunni religion is the most common one around here."

"I think we know that, Murgen," Goblin said.

"Just making the point. Most people down here believe in Kina. Even if they're not Gunni, they believe. Here's the story. The Gunni have Lords of Light and Lords of Darkness. They've been doing their lording since the beginning of time."

"Sounds like standard stuff."

"It is. Only the value systems are different from what we knew back home. The balance between darkness and light is more dynamic here, and isn't weighted the same emotionally as our struggle between good and evil. Moreover, Kina is a sort of self-elevated outside agency of decay and corruption that attacks both darkness and light. She was created by the Lords of Light to help defeat a horde of really nasty demons they couldn't handle any other way. She helped by eating the demons. Naturally, she got fat. And apparently wanted dessert because she tried to eat everybody else, too."

"She was stronger than the gods who created her?"

"Guys, I didn't make this stuff up. Don't ask me to rationalize it. Goblin, you've been everywhere. You ever seen a religion that can't be picked to shreds by any nonbeliever with brains enough to tie his own bootlaces?"

Goblin shrugged. "You're as cynical as Croaker was."

"Yeah? Good for me. Anyway, there's a lot of typically murky mythological stuff about mothers and fathers and vicious, hideous, probably incestuous carryings-on amongst the other gods while Kina kept getting stronger. She was real sneaky. That's one of her attributes. Deceit. But then her main creator, or father, tricked her and put a sleep spell on her. She's still snoring away somewhere but she can touch our world through her dreams.

"She's got her worshippers. All Gunni deities do. Big, little, good, bad, indifferent, they all have their temples and priesthoods. I can't find out much about Kina's followers. They're called Deceivers. The soldiers won't talk about them. They flat refuse, like naming Kina might actually waken her. Which, I gather, is the holy mission of her worshippers."

"Too weird for me," Bucket grumbled.

Goblin said, "That explains why Lady scares the shit out of everybody whenever she dresses up. If they really think she's turned into this goddess."

"I figure we should find out everything we can about this Kina."

"Crack plan, Murgen. How? If nobody will talk?"

Yeah. Even the boldest Taglians threatened to get the vapors if I pressed. It was obvious that they were not just terrified of this goddess. They were scared of me, too.

One-Eye brought heartening news. "This stuff about the relief force is gold, boss. Every night now Spinner is sneaking troops out through the hills like he don't think we can see them go if it's dark."

"Could he be giving up the siege?"

"The troops are all headed north. Home ain't north."

I did not offer another alternative. One-Eye would not have come if he was not sure.

Of course, One-Eye being sure never meant that One-Eye was right. He was One-Eye.

I thanked him, sent him to do a small chore, found Goblin and asked him what he thought. The little wizard seemed surprised I would bother. "Did One-Eye stutter or something?"

"No. But he's One-Eye."

Goblin could not contain his big frog grin. That made perfect sense to him.

Nobody relayed the news to Mogaba. I thought it would go easier for everybody if he didn't know. But Mogaba heard rumors, too.

Dejagore was a nightmare town filled with factions only loosely united in defiance of the besiegers. Mogaba's forces were the strongest. The Jaicuri were most numerous. We Old Crew, with our auxiliaries, were less numerous and less powerful. But boy were we strong in our righteousness.

And then there were the Nyueng Bao. The Nyueng Bao remained an enigma.

43

KY DAM'S FAMILY OCCUPIED THE SAME DISMAL, FILTHY, SMOKY, PUNGENT hole until the deluge drove them out. The perquisites of power did not appeal to the Speaker. He had a place to get out of the rain. That was enough.

Maybe that was more than he had had back in the swamp.

He did share with a troop of descendants who stopped bickering only when the outsider came around. And then the children restrained themselves only for a while.

On successive afternoons Ky Dam summoned me to consult on trivial matters. We faced each other over tea served by the beautiful granddaughter while the children quickly lost their awe of me and resumed brawling. We traded information on friends and enemies. That fevered character in the shadows moaned and groaned.

I did not like that. He was dying. But he was taking a long, long time getting it done. Every time he cried out the beautiful one went to him. I ached in sympathy. She was so haggard.

Second visit I said something to indicate sympathy, one of those things you toss off without much thought. Ky Dam's wife, whom I now knew to be named Hong Tray, glanced up from her tea, startled. She said three soft words to Ky Dam.

The old man nodded. "Thank you for your concern, Stone Soldier, but it is misplaced. Danh welcomed a devil into his soul. Now he pays the due."

A burst of rapid, liquid Nyueng Bao erupted from the shadows. A squat old woman waddled into the light. She was bowlegged, ugly as a warthog, in a vicious humor. She barked at me. She was Ky Gota, the

Speaker's daughter and my shadow Thai Dei's mother. She was a dark legend among her own people. I have no idea what she was on about but I got the feeling that she laid all the ills of the world squarely at my feet.

Ky Dam said something gently. It did not get through. Hong Tray repeated his words, more gently, in a whisper. Silence fell instantly. Ky Gota scurried into the shadows.

The Speaker offered, "In all our lives we enjoy successes and failures. My great sorrow is my daughter Gota. She has within her a cancer of agony she cannot conquer. She insists on sharing it with the rest of us." A tiny smile touched his lips. This was self-deprecating humor, meant to inform me that he was speaking metaphorically. "*Her* great failure, the wellspring of heartbreak for all of us, was her hasty choice of Sam Danh Qu as the husband for her daughter." He indicated the beautiful flower. The flower betrayed a blush as she knelt to refill our cups.

There was no doubt that all these people understood Taglian perfectly.

Ky Dam added, "That is the one great error that Gota cannot deny, a culmination of deficiencies that is like a brand. She was widowed young. She arranged the marriage hoping to enjoy her elder years luxuriating on the wealth of the Sams." The Speaker showed me that little smile again, probably sensing my incredulity. Wealth and Nyueng Bao are contradictory concepts.

The old man continued, "Danh was clever. He concealed the fact that he had been disinherited because of his cruelty and wickedness and treachery. Gota was too much in a hurry to investigate harsh rumors. And Danh's evil only grew worse after the nuptials. But that is enough about me and mine. I asked you here because I wish to keep an eye on the character of the leader of the Bone Warriors."

I had to ask. "Why do you call us that? Does it mean anything?"

Ky Dam traded looks with his wife. I sighed. "I get it. It's more of the Black Company claptrap everybody does. You think we're something our predecessors were supposed to have been four hundred years ago, only probably weren't because oral history exaggerates ridiculously. Speaker, listen. The Black Company is just a gang of outcasts. Really. We're plain old mercenary soldiers caught up in circumstances we don't understand and really don't like. We're just passing through. We came this way because our Captain has a bug up his ass about the Company's history. Most of the rest of us couldn't think of anything else we wanted to do more." I told him about Silent and Darling and others who had parted with the brotherhood rather than hazard the long journey south. "I promise you, whatever scares everybody—and I wish somebody would tell me what that is—it would have to involve way more work than I'm willing to put into anything."

The old man eyed, me, glanced at his wife. She said and did nothing but something passed between them. Ky Dam nodded.

Uncle Doj materialized. The Speaker told me, "Perhaps we misjudge you. Even I allow prejudice to guide me at times. There is a chance I will know better when next we speak."

Uncle Doj made a small gesture. Time for me to leave.

44

GOBLIN CAUGHT ME HITTING THE JAICURI BOOKS. "MURGEN!"

I started. "Huh?"

"About goddamn time."

"What? What're you talking about?"

"I been standing here watching you for ten minutes. You never turned a page. You never blinked an eye. I couldn't tell if you was breathing."

I started to make an excuse.

"Won't sell. I had to yell four times and slap you on the back of the head to get your attention."

"So I was thinking." Only I could not recall even one thought.

"Yeah. Right. Mogaba wants your scrawny ass over to the citadel."

"A lot of southerners have sneaked off to meet this relief column," I told Mogaba. "At first I thought they were trying to trick us. Pull back and hit us when we tried to take advantage. But Goblin and One-Eye promise me they've just kept going. There can't be a relief army, though. Where would the soldiers come from? Who would lead them?" Would Mogaba believe that I had not heard the more interesting rumors? He heard more than I did. And Croaker's survival probably figured in a lot of those.

What would he do if the Old Man turned up alive?

I was pretty sure Mogaba thought about that a lot.

I was thanked and told to return to my people with no other comment. I did not find out why he sent for me.

Mogaba did just what I feared. He launched a recon in force, maybe trying to find new weak spots. He employed only his own most trustworthy men. And I was content to sit atop my part of the wall, watching. And wondering why Mogaba was so sure we would desert if we got outside.

I tend to ignore Mogaba here. He was a much greater part of everyday life than I show. He was misery on the hoof. My dislike makes it impossible to write about the man rationally so I discuss him only when I must.

Of all the Nar, in those days, only Sindawe ever made the effort to be civil.

Anyway, Mogaba thought he had a chance to hurt the Shadowmaster but the planners outside were getting the hang of how his head worked. He did not let a lack of success discourage him. There was that about Mogaba. He never became discouraged. No setback ever shook his conviction that he was invincible. If his plans fizzled he just recalculated.

Mogaba's soldiers began to desert without benefit of escape from the city, coming to hide out with friends among our Taglians. They complained that Mogaba was too profligate with soldiers' lives.

Mogaba responded by ordering special rations and preferential access to prostitutes for his most dedicated men.

We found those sealed jars of grain left over from the Shadowmasters' first siege. Whether to share generated considerable debate. One-Eye insisted that Mogaba would not be satisfied just to share. He would want to know all about our find. He would want to see for himself. Did we want him wandering around our warrens?

No.

So what does the little shit do? He turns right around and starts selling fresh-baked bread for twenty times what a loaf cost before the siege.

I found a nice quiet spot for just One-Eye and me, atop the wall on a lazy afternoon. There were fresh rumors of a battle up north but that was not our topic. I asked, "What did you tell me about why we shouldn't let Mogaba share the stores we found?"

"Huh?" This was not the hassle he expected.

"You were extremely persuasive. All that stuff about not letting the man get into our hideout."

He grinned, proud of himself. "So?"

"You stand by what you said?"

"Sure."

"Then what the fuck are you doing selling his men bread when we're not supposed to have no grain to grind for flour?"

He frowned. The connection eluded him. "Making a profit?"

"You really figure Mogaba is so stupid he won't notice that bread? You really figure he won't ask questions?"

"You got too rigid a way of looking at things, Kid."

"You keep up your crap you're really going to think rigid. You get me killed I'm going to haunt your ass forever."

"You probably would. There's times I think you're halfway a haunt already."

"What's that supposed to mean?"

"These spells you have. When you have them it's like there's some-body else looking out from behind your eyes. It's like there's some other soul swirling around you."

"I never noticed." Would I notice?

"If we had us a skilled necromancer or a spirit talker we might be surprised what we found. You wasn't born twins, was you?" His stare was fierce.

A chill stalked my spine. The hairs on my neck stirred. I did feel spooky, sometimes. But he was just trying to change the subject.

Goblin joined us uninvited. "There's something going on with the Shadowlanders, Murgen."

A crow nearby made a sound like laughter.

I asked, "They aren't setting up for another big attack? I thought Mogaba screwed their main ramp."

"I couldn't get close enough to catch any details. Mogaba is staying out where people can see him. But I think there *was* a battle. And I think Shadowspinner's creeps got whipped. We may have friends out there ready to bust us out."

"Calm down. Don't start packing your gear."

One-Eye snickered. "That's the runt all over, counting his chickens when he ain't even stole no eggs yet."

I grumbled, "You remember what we were just discussing? Stupid moves? And you'd dare get down on Goblin?"

Of course he would. That was his great mission.

"What's going on?" Goblin demanded.

Uncle Doj materialized. His presence ended the discussion. That man could be spookier than any shade, he moved so fast and quiet. "Speaker says tell you southerners carrying tools instead of weapons are assem-bling south of the city."

"And what's that over there?" From our perch most of the activity was hidden behind the curve of the wall but it looked like a big engineer-ing party had begun to gather north of the city as well. "You see any pris-oners or slaves out there . . . ? Huh? What's that?"

That was the sparkle of sunlight off metal in the hills. The sparkle repeated itself. People were moving out there, not carefully enough.

Shadowspinner's men had no need to sneak. I told Goblin, "Pass the word. Full alert come sundown."

Uncle Doj considered the hills. "You have good eyes, Bone Warrior."

"Know something, Stubby? I'd a whole lot rather be called Murgen."

The squat man smiled thinly. "As you wish, Murgen. I have come on behalf of the Speaker. He says tell you hard times are coming. He says prepare your hearts and minds."

"Hard times?"

One-Eye laughed. "The party is over, Kid. Now we got to pay for loafing around and getting fat while the houris slithered all over us."

"Keep it in mind next time you're tempted to do some profiteering."

"Huh?"

"You can't eat money, One-Eye."

"Killjoy."

"That's me all over. Tell Wheezer to hike over to the citadel and tell Sindawe the southerners are up to something." Sindawe might be all right. I could talk to him without having to conquer an urge to squeeze his throat. And this would cover me on keeping Mogaba informed.

What would happen if the Shadowmaster just up and walked away, leaving us to sort ourselves out?

Sounded like the smart thing for him to do.

45

WHEEZER BARELY MADE IT TO THE TOP. THEN HE SPENT FIVE MINUTES HACKing and wheezing before he could talk. That old man had no business soldiering at his age. He ought to be off living off his grandchildren. But like the rest of us he had nothing outside the Company. He would die under the deathshead standard. Under what passed for a standard today.

It was sad. Pathetic, even.

Wheezer was an anomaly. Usually the mercenary life is brutal and short, pain and fear and misery only occasionally interrupted by a fleeting moment of pleasure. What keeps you sane is the unfailing comradeship of your brethren. In this company. In lesser bands. . . . But they are not the Black Company.

Croaker and I both put a lot of effort into sustaining that brotherhood. In fact, it looked like time to resurrect Croaker's habit of readings from the Annals so the men would remember that they were part of something more enduring than most kingdoms.

I told Wheezer, "You better take a couple hours off."

He shook his head. He would go on the best he could until he could go on no more. "The Nar lieutenant. Sindawe. Sends greetings. He said . . . we better . . . look out tonight."

"He mention why?"

"He sort of hinted . . . that Mogaba might try . . . some big stunt after . . . dark."

Mogaba was always trying some big stunt. Shadowspinner ought to let him set himself up. One raid too many, at the wrong time, and Mogaba would find out personally why Spinner was called a Shadowmaster.

Wheezer said something in his native tongue. Only One-Eye understood him. Sounded like a question. One-Eye muttered a few clicky syllables in reply. I figured the old man wanted to know if it was all right to talk in front of the Nyueng Bao. One-Eye gave him the go ahead.

Wheezer said, "Sindawe said tell you guys the rumors about a big battle are probably true."

"We owe Sindawe, guys," I said. "That sounds to me like him telling us he won't back Mogaba a hundred percent anymore."

Thai Dei and Uncle Doj sucked up our conversation like Nyueng Bao sponges.

Tension built for hours. With no real evidence we began to feel this night would be critical. Mostly the guys worried about new nastinesses from Mogaba. We didn't expect trouble from the Shadowmaster any time soon.

I kept an eye on the hills.

One-Eye snapped, "There it is!" He shared my anticipations. Pinkish light flared. Lightning crackled around a bizarre rider.

"She's back," somebody said. "Where's the other one?"

I did not see a Widowmaker right away.

Panic swept the plain. The apparition had taken the scattered Shadowlander camps unawares. Sergeants shrieked orders. Messengers galloped around. Soldiers stumbled into one another.

"There he is!" Bucket yelled.

"There who is?"

"Widowmaker." He pointed. "The Old Man."

The Widowmaker figure shimmered back in the hills, larger than life.

Goblin grabbed my arm. I don't know where he came from. "Look over there." He indicated the Shadowlander main camp. We could not see the camp itself but a pale, gangrenous glow rose from its approximate location. The light intensified steadily.

"Spinner wants to play," I observed.

"Yeah. He's sending a big one."

"A big what? Do we need to get our heads down?"

"Wait and see."

I waited. And I saw. A nasty ball of green fire streaked toward the hills. It hit near where Lifetaker first showed herself. Earth flew. Stone burned. All to no avail. Lifetaker was long gone.

"He missed."

"What an eye!"

"Lifetaker didn't play fair. She didn't stand still."

"He made a stupid choice of tools," One-Eye sneered. "You can't expect somebody to just hang around and wait for you."

"Maybe that was his best go. He hasn't been healthy."

I sidled away. In a few minutes Goblin and One-Eye would start bickering.

The confusion on the plain worsened. The southerners were more rattled than seemed reasonable. What I could get from their chatter suggested that they had been caught just starting something big of their own and their disarray left them virtually unable to defend themselves. In hushed tones, too, I heard Kina mentioned.

Lifetaker, who resembled that goddess of corruption, vanished. Maybe she lost interest. She did not reappear. Shadowspinner pasted the hills with any sorcery he could slap together. Other than starting a few brush fires he had no obvious impact.

The fox was in the henyard. Southerners scooted all over, their panic feeding on the panic of others. When one got close my guys took turns sniping. Goblin said, "They keep cussing about their feet getting wet." I heard that, too. It made no sense.

"Holy shit!"

I don't know who said it but I could not have agreed more.

Scores of brilliant white fireballs erupted straight up above the Shadowlander main camp. They obliterated the darkness completely. They seemed a tool of more use to a Shadowmaster's enemies than to the villain himself.

A huge uproar followed.

Uncle Doj vanished. One moment he was beside me, the next a shadow running through the street below, then gone.

One-Eye told me, "This time I'm sure it's Lady."

His tone alerted me. "But what?"

"But the other one ain't the Captain."

Widowmaker had been visible for less than one minute. "Tell me it ain't so," I muttered.

"What?"

"That we got two sets. Each one only half the real thing."

A crow nearby cackled.

I asked, "What kind of sorcery would do that? Split them in two?"

"I wish I could tell you something you want to hear, Kid. But I've got a very bad feeling there's stuff going on we don't even want to know about."

46

ONE-EYE WAS A PROPHET. ALTHOUGH I DID WANT TO KNOW. AND THANKS TO the Nyueng Bao I heard a story.

The light across town faded. The attendant racket subsided. Part of that drifted toward the hills. The rest fell back toward Mogaba's part of town.

The crackle of small sorceries rippled across the plain. The whole expanse glistened silver. "That was a strange one. One-Eye, what say we build a watchtower on top of one of the enfilading towers? That way we could get high enough to see what Mogaba and Spinner are doing."

"You got Nyueng Bao to spy for you over there."

"Suppose I don't ask you to do any work yourself?"

"The idea sounds a lot better already. But I still think the Nyueng Bao could be your eyes, you play it right. You don't need to get as paranoid as Croaker. Just look at what they bring you so you see whose purpose it might serve. Consider what might be missing the same way."

"Sometimes I'm as lazy as you are," I told One-Eye. "Only with me it's mental. That sounds like a lot of thinking. And I'd rather see stuff with my own eyes anyway."

"Just like the Old Man," he grumbled. "You got to read them Annals all the time, how about you read some that was written by somebody besides Croaker? I *was* looking forward to a little relief from his right-eousness."

So we were back to the black-market bread scheme.

Goblin turned up. "Pretty exciting stuff happening over there."

"Yeah? Like what?"

"I got up on the wall over there. For a while. Mogaba's guys weren't worried about getting caught letting me peek. He led this raid in person."

"Just tell us about it," One-Eye grumbled. "You all the time got to flap on about stuff that . . . Awk!" A huge bug landed in One-Eye's mouth. Goblin's smirk hinted that he might have been involved in the insect's errant navigation.

"That Doj character can tell you more than me. Some of his guys snuck out there behind Mogaba's gang."

"Why?"

"I think Mogaba was trying to bushwhack Spinner. But he stumbled into Lady instead."

"You're shitting me."

"When that bunch of flareballs went up? There she was. Her and about fifteen guys. They were right outside the camp gate, practically crawling over Mogaba's mob. Least that's what I heard. I didn't see it myself."

"So where's Uncle Doj?"

"Probably checking in with the Speaker."

Probably. "Yeah? Look, we've got a bunch of deserters from the First. See if some will sneak back to find out more."

"Here comes chunky boy now."

We talked right in front of Thai Dei, like he was deaf. Or like we didn't care squat what he heard.

Uncle Doj brought a couple other Nyueng Bao. They surrounded another chunky boy, this one a wide little Taglian. He seemed more prisoner than companion though no weapons were in evidence.

It amazed me that Uncle Doj could climb to the ramparts without breathing hard. Maybe he used some wild sorcerery that stole Wheezer's breath.

That sounded like something out of the Gunni myth book.

"What have you got, Uncle?" I stared at the squat Taglian. He was indifferent to my gaze.

"An outsider. The Speaker sent Banh and Binh to watch the black men, who wanted to attack the Shadowmaster himself. But they ran into others from the outside pursuing a similar goal. This one left his party and joined those running for the wall when the flares went up. The outsider group may have been betrayed intentionally so this one could become separated in the confusion."

I continued to study the outsider. He was a Gunni, more stockily built than anyone in these parts. Maybe he worked at that. He seemed possessed of a powerful arrogance.

I asked, "Is there anything special about him?" Uncle Doj seemed strongly interested in him, too.

"He bears the mark of Khadi."

That took a moment. Oh. Yeah. In the books from the catacombs. Khadi was an alternate or regional name for Kina. There were quite a few of those. "If you say so. I don't see it myself. Point it out."

Uncle Doj's eyes narrowed. He drew a deep breath, exasperated. "Even now you refuse to reveal yourself, Soldier of Darkness?"

"Even now I don't have any fucking idea what you're raving about. I *am* tired of hearing it." I was developing suspicions, though. "Instead of sputtering and fussing and offering cryptic grumbles why don't you say something I can understand? Pretend I'm what I say I am and can't call down the lightning to part your hair. Who is this guy? Who do you think I am? Come on, Uncle. Talk to me."

"He is a slave of Khadi." Uncle Doj glared at me, daring me not to understand that. He did not want to be more explicit.

That made no sense to me. But I am not a superstitious man. Did he believe his one mouth had the power to raise the she-devil alone? "Kina must be one badass bitch," I told One-Eye. "She's got Uncle drizzling down his leg. You. You got a name?"

"I am Sindhu. I am of the staff of the warrior woman you call Lady. I was sent to observe the situation here." He continued to meet my gaze. His eyes were colder than any lizard's.

"Sounds reasonable enough." If taken with a block of salt. "Lady? This is the Lady who was second in command in the Black Company?"

"That Lady. The goddess has smiled upon her."

I asked Uncle Doj, "Is he a liaison man, then? Between us and Lady?"

"He may tell you so. But he is a spy for the *toog*. He will not speak truth when a lie will do."

"Uncle, old buddy, you and me and the old man need to sit down and try to talk the same language for a while. What do you think?"

Uncle Doj grunted. Which could mean anything. "The *toog* will not speak truth when a lie will do."

Sindhu was amused.

The man struck me as a complete false face. I said, "Goblin, find this guy some place to sleep." I shifted languages. "And don't let him out of your sight."

"I have chores enough already."

"Somebody's sight. All right? I don't like him at all. I don't think I'm going to like him even this much tomorrow morning. He smells like trouble."

One-Eye agreed. "Big trouble."

"Why don't we just chuck his hairy ass off the wall, then?" Goblin can be pragmatic in the extreme.

"Because I want to find out more about him. I think we've crawled right up to the edge of the mystery that has hung us up ever since we got here. Let him run free. We'll play dumb and keep track of every breath he takes." I was sure I could count on the Speaker's help with that.

My two wizards scowled and grumbled. Hard to blame them. They always end up carrying the load.

47

I WAS SNORING HEROICALLY DOWN DEEP IN OUR WARRENS, HAVING GONE TO Nod confident I could sleep in. Tomorrow nobody would have the ambition to get up to any mischief.

I was down there so far and so far out of the way that not five people knew where to find me. I was on a mission to catch up on my sleep. If the end of the world came the guys could celebrate without me.

Somebody shook me.

I refused to believe it. It had to be a bad dream.

"Murgen. Come on. You got to come see this."

No I didn't.

"Murgen!"

I cracked an eyelid. "I'm trying to get some sleep here, Bucket. Go away."

"You ain't got time. You got to come see."

"I got to come see what?"

"You'll see. Come on."

There would be no winning this. He would pester me till I lost my temper, then get his feelings hurt. But the long climb to the sunshine was not an inducement to rise.

"All right. All right." I got up and got myself together.

They didn't need to drag me out but I understood the impulse. Things had changed. Radically.

I stared at the plain, mouth open. Only, what plain? Dejagore was surrounded by a shallow lake that featured the tops of burial mounds as small islands. Each mound boasted its handful of disconsolate animals. "How deep is it?" I asked. And, "There any chance we can catch some of those critters for the pot?" With all that water down there no southerner would be guarding against sorties.

"Right now, five feet," Goblin said. "I had men go down and measure."

"Is it still coming up? Where is it coming from? Where is Shadowspinner?"

Goblin pointed. "I don't know about Spinner, but there's the water. Still coming in."

I have good eyes. I made out the water boiling and foaming as it roared out of the hills. "The old aqueduct came down there, didn't it?" Two major canals had irrigated the hill farms and fed aqueducts to Dejagore before the fighting started. The Company cut those when the southerners were on the inside. Now the city survived on rainwater and the contents of large, deep, very stagnant cisterns we knew nothing about back then.

"Exactly. Clete and his brothers figure they diverted the entire river into the canal. Same thing south of town."

Dejagore sits on a plain below the level of the country beyond the hills. Modest rivers run both west and southeast of the hills.

"I presume the boys are studying the engineering aspects?" I asked.

"Them and three dozen Taglians who had some skills the guys could use."

"Any conclusions yet?"

"Like?"

"Like how high will the water get? Are we going to drown?" If that was Shadowspinner's plan it indicated major changes in his thinking. Before, he wanted Dejagore recovered intact. This seemed a more practical and final answer to his problems, though more destructive of property—which, of course, was more valuable than any number of lives.

"They're trying to figure that out right now."

I grunted. "I take it Spinner pulled out after Lady left."

"No," One-Eye responded. "They hung around to swim. They don't get to a lot of beach parties where they come from."

"Man's not as stupid as we thought," I mused.

"Huh?"

"He floods the plain, even if he don't drown us he locks us up so tight he don't have to use hardly any men to keep us under control. He can chase Lady all he wants. We can't help her and she can't help us. For him it's better than getting reinforcements out of the Shadowlands. Longshadow's soldiers couldn't be trusted behind his back."

Thai Dei showed up. He always turned up soon after I came out, which indicated how closely we were being watched.

Thai Dei was a waste of manpower. He didn't carry many messages. He didn't understand any of our languages well enough to be a good spy for the Speaker. But he was always, always just a few steps away.

There would be a reason. The Speaker would do nothing without consideration. I just did not grasp his view of the world.

The longer I stared at the flood the more questions I came up with that needed answers soon. Most critical? How high would the water rise? How long would it take to do so? The rate of rise would slow down substantially as each vertical foot required more water volume because of the fall back of the hills, evaporation from the larger surface area, and absorption by more covered soil.

I told Goblin and One-Eye, "Dig up every educated man in town and give him to the brothers." I thought about building boats and heightening towers and securing stores. I thought about our vast and wonderful warrens and the likelihood that thousands of manhours would go for naught. I thought about how we would have to prepare ourselves mentally for lots worse if we were going to survive. I thought about Ky Dam and his talk of hard times to come.

Thai Dei stepped over when nobody else was near. "Grandfather would speak with you. Soon, if possible." His manners were impeccable. He did not call me Stone Soldier even once.

The old man must want something badly. "As you wish." I noticed the outsider Sindhu on the battlements off toward the Western gate. I could feel him watching me. "One-Eye."

"What?"

"You don't need to bark. If you want to bark I'll see if I can't have the Shadowmaster turn you into a dog."

One-Eye was startled. "Huh?"

"You guys keeping an eye on our guest?"

"Geek and Freak are taking turns. He ain't done much yet. Wandered around town. Talked to people. Tried visiting with the Taglians, here and over with Mogaba. Ours wouldn't have anything to do with him. The al-Khul Company ran him off with their swords drawn."

"Would anybody talk about him?"

One-Eye shook his head. "It's the same old shit. Maybe even worse. You better make it clear him being here wasn't your idea."

Thai Dei, listening, murmured something that sounded cabalistic. He followed with a gesture resembling that meant to avert the evil eye.

"Hey," One-Eye said. "Something can bother these guys after all."

"I'm going to go listen to their boss talk. You're in charge, but only because everybody else around here is less trustworthy than you."

"Thanks a shitload, Kid. You make a guy feel like he's on top of the world."

"Try to have something left when I get back."

48

THE VERTIGO HIT ME IN THE SAME ALLEYWAY AS BEFORE—JUST YESTERDAY? I remembered it as the darkness closed in. This was more of a sneaking, gentle, enveloping blackness than the thunderbolts that got me before.

My thoughts scrambled but I did recall several minimal episodes since the big blackout, just moments when I was out of my head and I came back as soon as somebody said something.

This one was stronger. Thai Dei's hands closed on my left bicep. He spoke but his words were sounds that had no meaning. The light faded. My knees went watery. Then there was no sensation at all.

There was a place that was brighter than day, although it was daytime. Huge mirrors gathered sunlight and splashed it onto one tall, gaunt individual in black. The gaunt man stood upon a windswept parapet high above a darkening land.

A scream ripped through the air. A dark rectangle slanted toward the tower from high above and far away.

The gaunt figure fitted a stylized mask to its face. Its breathing increased pace, as though it needed more air to face visitors.

Another scream tore the air.

The gaunt man muttered, "Someday . . . !"

The ragged flying carpet settled a short distance away. The masked man remained motionless, glaring at every hint of shadow around the device. The wind tugged at his robe.

Three persons rode the flying carpet. One was a tiny thing bundled in dark, stinking rags crumbling with mildew. He was masked, too, and shook continuously. He could not control the occasional scream. He was the Howler, one of the world's oldest and most wicked sorcerers. The carpet was his creation. The gaunt man hated him.

The gaunt man hated everybody. He had little love for himself. He mastered his hatreds for short periods only, entirely through the implacable exercise of will. He had a powerful will—as long as he was not threatened physically.

The ragball gurgled as it stifled a scream.

Howler's nearest companion was a short, skinny, filthy little man in a ragged loincloth and grubby turban. He was frightened. His name was

Narayan Singh, living saint of the Deceiver cult, alive only because of Howler's intercession.

Longshadow considered Singh less than a flop of buffalo dung. Nevertheless, he had potential as a tool. The reach of his cult was long and lethal.

Singh's opinion of his own new ally was of no supreme elevation, either.

Beyond Singh was a child, a pretty little thing, though filthier than the *jamadar*. She had huge brown eyes. Eyes like the windows of hell. Eyes that knew all evil of old and would revel in it now and forever more.

Those eyes troubled even Longshadow.

They were whirlpools of darkness that pulled, pulled, twisted, hypnotized. . . .

A sudden, sharp pain in my left knee sent wires of agony searing through my flesh. I groaned. I shook my head. The stink of an alleyway penetrated my awareness. I seemed blind. But my eyes, apparently, were adapted to brilliant sunlight. Hands gripped my left arm, pulling, lifting. My vision began to return. I looked up.

A gaunt face looked back, startling me. I retained a legacy of fear from my vision, though what that had been was fading already. I tried to hang on but the pain in my knee and Thai Dei talking shattered my concentration.

"I'm all right," I said. "Just hurt my knee." I tried to stand. When I took a step the knee almost folded. "I'll manage, damn it!" I pushed his hands away.

The vision was gone except for a memory that it had happened.

Had it been the same with my other blackouts? Were there visions that flew away so thoroughly that I could not recall having had them? Did they have any connection with reality? Vaguely, I recalled seeing lots of familiar faces.

I would discuss it with Goblin and One-Eye. They ought to know what to make of it. They picked up a little loose change interpreting dreams.

Thai Dei started gabbling the moment we entered the Speaker's presence. Ky Dam considered me speculatively, his expression deepening oddly as Thai Dei chattered.

The old man appeared to be alone when we walked in but as Thai Dei talked and Ky Dam became unusually attentive other Nyueng Bao came out of the shadows to study me. Hong Tray and Ky Gota were the first. The old woman settled by her husband. Ky Dam said, "I hope you do not mind. Sometimes she is able to part the veil of time."

Gota said nothing. I suspected that that was unusual.

The beautiful woman appeared. She got right onto the tea service business. Tea is a big thing with the Nyueng Bao. Did she serve any other function in the family?

The guy in the shadows wasn't moaning and groaning today. Had he left us?

"Not yet," the Speaker said, reading my glance. "But soon." Again, he sensed a question. "We sustain our share of the marriage vow even though he betrayed his. We will stand before the Judges of Time without stain on our karma."

I had a notion what he meant only because I was studying the Jaicuri scriptures. "You are a good people."

Ky Dam was amused. "Some might argue. We do strive to be an honorable folk."

"I understand." We so strive in the Black Company.

"Excellent."

"I came because Thai Dei said you want to talk."

"I did."

I waited. My gaze kept straying to the woman making tea.

"Standardbearer."

I started. . . . "No," I said softly, unaware that I was speaking aloud. I had not fallen into one of those black fugues. I'd just become distracted momentarily. Couldn't blame a man for that. Not with a woman like that to distract him.

I said, "Thank you, Speaker. For not labelling me with one of those unappealing names you tend to employ."

I could not resist a small smile that told him I knew he wanted something badly enough to keep me in a generous mood.

He nodded in turn, acknowledging my awareness.

Damn. I was turning into an old man myself. Maybe we could sit here grinning and grunting and nodding and arrange the whole future of the world. "Thank you," I said when the pretty woman presented my tea.

That surprised her. She looked me in the eye for a moment, startling me. Her eyes were green. She neither smiled nor acknowledged me in any other way.

"Remarkable," I said, to nobody in particular. "Green eyes." Then I controlled myself and waited while the Speaker sipped some tea before he started circling in on his problem.

He told me, "Green eyes are rare and greatly admired among Nyueng Bao." He took a ritual sip. "Hong Tray may part the veil occasionally but her visions are not always true, or not always fixed. Or they may be visions that have not yet come to pass. She does not see recognizable people so it is hard to determine when the visions might be taking place."

"Uhm?" The woman in question sat with eyes downcast, slowly turning a jade bracelet that hung loose upon her left wrist. Her eyes were green, too.

"She foresaw the flood. We believed that would prove to be a false vision because we could imagine no way so much water could be brought to Jaicur."

"But we're in the middle of a lake now. The world's widest moat. The Shadowlanders won't bother us anymore."

It took the old man a minute to understand that I was not serious. "Oh." He chuckled. Hong Tray looked up and smiled. She had gotten the joke first. "I see. Yes. But it will serve the Shadowmaster, not us. Any attempt to leave will require rafts or boats, easily spotted, which cannot move enough men to force a breakthrough."

The old boy was a general, too.

"You got it." Shadowspinner had found an ingenious solution to his manpower problem. Now he could challenge Lady confident that we would not jump on his back.

"The reason I wished to confer is that in her vision Hong Tray saw the water rise to within ten feet of the battlements."

"That would make seventy feet of water." I glanced at the old woman. She seemed to be studying me in a way that had nothing to do with curiosity. "That's a shitload."

"There is another problem."

"Which is?"

"We tried to calculate how many structures will rise above the waterline."

"Oh-oh. I see." I saw. Dejagore enjoyed a vertically oriented architecture, as walled cities do, but not many buildings overtopped the wall. And most surviving structures, even many that were partially burned, were occupied by someone. There would not be much housing available if the city flooded.

Luckily for us Old Crew our quarter boasted a lot of tall tenements.

"Oh-oh indeed. In this area there are enough such structures to house our few pilgrims. But elsewhere it will go hard for the Jaicuri when the black men and their soldiers finally understand how much space they will need."

"No doubt." I thought a moment. Hell. People could camp out on the wall. Them getting in the way would not be a problem militarily.

Still, whatever we did, life would become pure hell if the water rose that high. "Presents a dilemma, doesn't it?"

"Possibly a larger dilemma than you suspect."

"How so?"

"If preparations are not initiated immediately much that might prove useful will be lost. But if you tell Mogaba this then it is likely the strong will rob the weak and leave them to suffer. There is now no need to exercise restraint because of potential attack."

"I see." Actually, I had foreseen the scramble for stores and high ground. But I did overlook the fact that Shadowspinner extricating himself also freed Mogaba to manage internal frictions in a manner more to his liking. "You have something in mind?"

"I wish to examine the possibility of a temporary alliance. Until Jaicur is relieved."

"Has Hong Tray foreseen that as well?"

"No."

I was surprised by the black despair that collapsed upon me.

"She has seen nothing one way or the other."

I brightened. A very little.

"I am reluctant to undertake such an obligation," Ky Dam confessed. "It was not my idea. It was Sahra's." He indicated the beautiful tea server. "But she trusts you for no reason she will explain and, moreover, her arguments make sense."

Hong Tray wore a bemused expression. There was, in the way she looked at me, a hint that she foresaw much that she did not share.

I shivered.

Ky Dam continued, "*We* have no hope if we assume a traditional Nyueng Bao stance and depend upon ourselves alone. You have little hope if your Mogaba does not feel he needs your arms anymore."

I stared at the beautiful one, though that was bad manners. She blushed. The attraction was so powerful, suddenly, that I gasped. I felt as though I had known her several lifetimes already.

What the . . . ? This did not happen to me. Not anymore, anyway. I was no sixteen-year-old. . . . Hell, I never felt like this when I was sixteen.

My soul was trying to tell me I knew this woman as well as a man ever knew any woman when, in truth, I had only just heard her name spoken for the first time.

There was something else over there, with her. That was more than one lovely daydream. I knew another one just like her, somewhen else. . . .

The darkness came.

It was sudden and absolute and I had no time to decide if I was running away or being pulled down.

49

THERE WAS A LONG, LONG TIME IN THE DREAMLESS DARK. A TIME WITHOUT an I. A time neither warm nor cold, a time with no happiness or fear or pain in a place no tortured soul would want to leave. But a pin pricked a hole in the envelope. The tiniest thread of light found its way in and fell upon an imaginary eye.

Movement.

A rush toward a point, which swelled and became a passageway into a world of time and matter and pain.

I knew who I was. I staggered under the crushing weight of a host of congruent memories surfacing all at once.

A Voice spoke to me but I could not comprehend its words. I floated like gossamer through golden caverns where old men sat beside the way, frozen in time, immortal but unable to move an eyelid. Madmen, they, some were covered with fairy webs of ice as though a thousand winter spiders had spun threads of frozen water. Above, an enchanted forest of icicles grew downward from the cavern ceiling.

Because I had memories of memories within memories I recalled having read words very much like those somewhere in something I did not believe had yet been written.

"Come!"

The power of the call was like the punch of a thunderbolt.

Darkness came. I tumbled away, ceased being *I*. Nevertheless, before I faded from that cavern I sensed a startled presence coming alert and striving to direct its attention my way.

Somehow I had gone somewhere where no mortal was welcome to travel and still come away.

Memory fled. But pain went along on the journey.

50

LIGHT IN THE DARKNESS, AGAIN. I BEGAN TO BE I, THOUGH WITHOUT A name. I shied from the light. The light was not a pleasant place. The pain would be waiting. But something farther beneath my surface turned to the light like a drowning man fighting toward lifesaving air.

I became aware that I was flesh. I felt my muscles, tightened till some were cramped. My throat was painfully dry. I tried to talk. "Speaker . . ." I rasped.

Someone stirred but no one replied.

I was slumped in a chair.

The Nyueng Bao had no furniture in their place, which was little more than an animal den. Had they returned me to my own people?

I forced an eye open.

What the hell? What was this place? A dungeon? A torture chamber? Had Mogaba snatched me? There was a skinny little Taglian over there, tied into a chair just like mine, and another man was strapped onto a table.

That was Smoke, the Taglian royal wizard!

I levered myself up. That hurt. A lot. The prisoner in the chair watched me warily.

"Where am I?" I asked.

His wariness redoubled. His lips pursed. He said nothing. I looked around. I was in a dusty, almost barren chamber—but the nature of the stone answered my question. I was in Taglios. This was the Royal Palace. There is no stone like this stone anywhere else.

How?

Ever seen paint run down a wall? That is what happened to reality. Right in front of my eyes it ran and dribbled and streaked. The man in the chair squeaked. He shook. I have no idea what he thought he saw. But reality drifted away and I was in a grey place, confused, filled with memories of things never experienced or seen. Then the confusion began to sort itself out and the grey washed away and in a short time I was in a room somewhere in the Palace at Trogo Taglios. Smoke lay on his table breathing slowly and shallowly as always. The Deceiver was in his seat. He earned a narrow-eyed glare because of the way he was sweating. What was he up to now?

His eyes bugged. What did he see when he looked at me?

I rose, aware that I had to be recovering from one of my spells. But there was no one here who could have brought me back. Didn't it take Croaker or One-Eye to drag me up out of the depths of darkness?

Hints of memory stirred in the deeps of my mind. I snatched at them, tried desperately to hang on. Something in a cavern. A song of shadow. Waking up once in a past long ago but still only a moment earlier in this time.

I was weak. This business was debilitating. And thirst was becoming a rage within me.

I could do something about that. A pitcher and metal cup stood on the table beside Smoke's head. Beneath the cup I found a scrap of paper torn from a larger sheet. It carried a message in Croaker's tight script. *No time to coddle you now, Murgen. If you wake up on your own drink this water. There is food in the box. One-Eye or I will be back as soon as possible.*

The scrap might have come from a procurement request. The Old Man hates to waste any fragment of blank paper. Paper is too damned dear.

I checked the tin box on the other side of Smoke's head. It was filled with heavy, unleavened cakes of the sort my mother-in-law bakes despite all pleas to desist. In fact, on closer examination, I knew no one else could have baked them. If I survived here I would owe Croaker a swift kick in the slats.

P.S. Check the Strangler's bonds. He nearly got away once already.

So that was what he was doing when I woke up. He wanted to worm out so he could murder me and my pal Smoke and then make a run for it.

I drank from the pitcher. The Deceiver looked at me with a longing you could almost smell. "Want a sip?" I asked. "Just tell me what's going on."

The man was not yet ready to sell his soul for a drink of water.

Soon after I wolfed down one of Mother Gota's sinkers I felt my strength returning. "Let's get you cinched up good and tight," I told my companion. "Wouldn't want you wandering off and getting hurt."

He stared at me in silence while I fixed him up. He didn't need to speak to let me know what was on his mind. I told him, "This is the risk you took when you signed on with the bad guys."

He would not argue but he refused to agree. I was confused. I was the bad guy because I wasn't blazing hot on the effort to bring Kina back into the world. I patted his head. "You could be right, brother. But I hope not. Here." I snatched up the cloth and drew it back over him, where it belonged. Then I drank some more water and ate part of a roll and when I got to feeling frisky I decided to return to my apartment. It was subjective as hell but it was an age since I had seen my wife. In reality it could not have been more than a few hours.

I got lost.

51

OF COURSE I GOT LOST. IT WAS INEVITABLE. THE FUTURE ME WITHIN ME DID not recall anything else but it did remember that I was going to get lost, then find my way to someplace I was not trying to go. That much came to me just after I realized that I did not have a clue how to get back to any familiar part of the Palace. I stopped to take stock.

At that moment I had enough near-current memories of other Murgens from other times that I was ready to trust any memory from any time, though it came with no supporting context whatsoever.

This memory of getting lost carried flavors of the excitement of unexpected discovery and powerful overtones of pain. An echo told me I did not want to find my way again.

Somewhere, while still stubbornly trying to get out, I came upon a gloomy hallway that seemed to smell of old magic. A few yards away a shattered door hung precariously upon a single hinge.

Discovery beckoned.

I went forward unafraid.

One look inside told me I had found Smoke's secret library, the place where the only surviving copies of the first several Annals had been gathered and sealed away so there would be no chance we Black Company types would ever chance upon them.

I wanted to read them so badly. But I had not come to read. I did not have time to sort the wheat from the chaff of a hundred other books. I had to get back to my family.

I strove valiantly but could not get there. Head spinning, I tried to retrace my steps. It looked like I would have to wait with Smoke until One-Eye or the Old Man turned up. They could lead me out the easy way—and maybe tell me why I did not want to go, because that part would not come to mind clearly.

I got back to Smoke easily, with no misturns. I had begun to suspect that there were spells webbed into that part of the Palace, cast so no intruder could find his way around the maze without One-Eye's blessing. It might be that all paths led to the same destination. Or maybe they all led away if you did not start out with Smoke to begin.

That would not surprise me, though I had no idea if One-Eye had the skill and power to manage it. Nor would it surprise me to find out that he did not remember casting the spell in the first place, so had made no provision for me to get around it.

The Deceiver was wiggling when I returned, my step so soft he did not sense my presence immediately. He froze when he did. Give that man credit for determination.

I settled into the empty chair. I waited. Nobody came. It seemed hours passed but probably it was just a few long minutes. I got up and tramped around, back and forth. I tormented the Strangler some but that just made me feel bad, too. I covered him up and sat down again.

I stared at Smoke. I thought about the Black Company and its tribulations. I remembered what Smoke could do.

Why not? Just to kill time? But where to go? What to see? When?

Why not the great enemy again?

It was easy this time. Nothing to it. Like closing my eyes and drifting off into a reverie.

I did not go without some reluctance. I was spending way too much time beyond the normal pale, against my will. Why add to my confusion by going wandering on my own, too?

With almost a snap and pop I found myself adrift outside fortress Overlook. The mad sorcerer Longshadow stood atop one of his tall towers, amidst reflected light, less than ten feet away. I suffered a mild panic. He was looking right at me.

Right through me.

Behind him, stance mocking, was that wretch Narayan Singh, with Croaker's kid, the mortal flesh of Kinda, the Daughter of Night, the One Foretold who would bring on the Deceivers' Year of the Skulls, which will end with the awakening of their goddess. Singh never let the child out of his sight.

Singh was a dangerous tool but Longshadow needed every ally willing to join him.

Quite a few folks seemed willing to sign on against the Black Company.

A figure emerged from a hatchway apparently dark only because of the intensity of the light surrounding the mad wizard. This man was tall, ebony, lithe as a panther. No anger touched me because emotions turn pale in Smoke's domain, although this was Mogaba, the most dangerous of the Shadowlander generals.

I suspect Longshadow appreciated Mogaba less for his abilities than because he could be trusted. Mogaba has nowhere to run. The Company stands astride every road to safety.

I cannot understand why Croaker does not hate Mogaba. Hell, he makes excuses for the man, even feels sorry for him. He takes his feud with Blade much more to heart.

Mogaba said, "Howler brought news. The storm system no longer works."

Longshadow grunted. "I saw. My small shadows remain useful. I recall that I predicted they would catch on quickly. Have you any thoughts on how the woman Senjak could regain her powers when, by the nature of these things, she ought to be at the mercy of anyone who knows her True Name?"

I had a feeling he really wanted to know how Howler could survive a Lady with her powers restored and her old, wicked knowledge intact. Longshadow viewed the world through a lens of paranoia.

I wondered myself. About Lady's powers. Croaker guessed it had something to do with crossing the equator. That did not sound plausible. Neither One-Eye nor Goblin would hazard a guess. Lady herself refused to discuss it. I had no idea what she believed. Nobody pressed. That was not something you did if you wanted to stay friendly with somebody like Lady. She can get real unpleasant if she doesn't like you.

"No ideas," Mogaba said. "It isn't something I understand." There were many things Mogaba did not understand, including any languages native to that region. He communicated with Longshadow using his improved but still flawed Taglian. "Maybe she changed her name."

Could they do that?

I realized the remark was Mogaba's attempt at a joke. But Longshadow did mull it over as though it was possible in some subjective fashion.

The moment passed. Longshadow faced Singh. "Deceiver. Why are you here? What machinations has the Howler involved you in now?"

Mogaba answered for Narayan. "The Black Company jumped them in their holy grove and killed everyone but him and the girl. Your shadowweavers barely had time to call for Howler before they died. Howler found these two hiding a few miles away and got them out only yards ahead of the pursuit."

So. This was only a short while after our raid. And here was a surprise. I believed Narayan had gotten warning from the Shadowmaster. But he had not. So how had he shaken the sleep spell?

Mention of the shadowweavers rocked Longshadow. I thought he would fly into one of his famed foamy-mouthed rages. Those strange little old men were a resource he dared not squander. It took a lifetime to train them. And we have taken care of a bunch of them over the years.

Longshadow sucked in a deep breath, held it, restrained his insanity. "My error. I should not have sent them. Have you any idea how our enemies could appear at a time so propitious to their cause?"

Nobody volunteered the news that we could hover over his shoulder any time the urge hit.

Longshadow observed, "This is not good. Each day they develop new resources. Each day ours dwindle." He glared at Singh. "What are we getting from these Deceivers?"

Mogaba replied. "They spy. Before long they will undertake selected assassinations. The enemy shows no awareness of that program. If their assassinations succeed the results will be of more value that anything but a decisive encounter on the battlefield."

Mogaba invited comment from Singh with his glance but Narayan held his tongue.

Mogaba said, "Unfortunately, the intelligence the Deceivers gather grows less reliable with each report. The enemy have enjoyed considerable success in their efforts to eliminate the cult."

Still no one else spoke.

Mogaba continued, "Lady and Croaker have become very aggressive against spies. I believe that indicates a major move is imminent."

"It's winter," Longshadow said. "And my enemies are in no hurry. They are content to nibble me to death. This so-called Liberator will never be satisfied that he has men and weapons enough."

He was right about that. Croaker never stopped going after more.

The Howler joined the group, stifling a scream as he did so. He husked, "The enemy labor battalions have completed the paved road linking Taglios and Stormgard. A similar road is almost complete from Stormgard to Shadowlight."

Shadowlight lies near the heart of the most populous and prosperous region of the Shadowlands. Shadowspinner had been overlord there. Nominally, the city and its environs still owed allegiance to Longshadow. Yet our soldiers were building a road in the area untroubled.

I wondered why. Croaker's strategic plan did not require it. He had no intention of besieging Shadowlight. That would tie up too many men for far too long.

Mogaba grumbled, "They press us everywhere. No day passes but that we hear of the fall of another town or village. Many places the locals no longer resist at all. And it would be folly to assume that Croaker and Lady will respect the season."

Longshadow turned his dread mask toward Mogaba, who flinched. "Have you done anything to make it difficult to sustain a major campaign, General?"

An army *must* live off the land if it ventures far from home. You cannot carry enough food and fodder to sustain it any length of time.

"Very little." Mogaba didn't show an ounce of contrition. "I have my orders. And our enemies know what those orders are."

"What?" Now Longshadow was testy.

"They expect me to sit still." Mogaba indicated Singh, who nodded agreement reluctantly. "Their strategy assumes that I will defend one fixed point. Because your orders constrain me to do just that they scatter their forces and attack everywhere. Blade cannot blunt their sword alone. The villages will not resist because the people know no help will come. I could defeat the fools in detail, in a short while, if our strategy changed suddenly."

I don't think so, I thought, floating there smug in the knowledge that we had Smoke.

"No!" Longshadow forced his quaking flesh to face southward. He glared at the plain of glittering stone. "We will discuss military matters in private only, General."

Howler delivered a horrible scream edged with mockery. Singh practically dove through the hatchway. His contempt for the Shadowmaster was obvious to everyone but Longshadow himself—though it was likely Longshadow would not have cared. To the Shadowmaster the Strangler was little more than a useful termite. In his mind none of us were much more than pesky insects.

The child left last. She considered Longshadow coldly. Her eyes seemed as old and wicked as time itself. She was a scary little thing for sure.

I wondered what the Old Man thought when he saw her. Or if he even dared look.

Longshadow said, "They don't think I know what I'm doing."

"My soldiers are wasted where they are," Mogaba replied. "They're losing what edge they had."

"You may be right. But to attack in any direction you will have to leave what protection I am able to afford you. Without my lost comrades I cannot reach nearly as far as once I did. Will you risk their sorcery without mine to support you?"

Mogaba grunted. He glared at the glittering plain.

"You believe I am a coward for fearing that, General?"

"I stipulate the danger. I grant the value of your protection. But there is much that I could do anyway. Blade has been allowed to act on a limited scale and has accomplished great things. For certain he has demonstrated repeatedly how these Taglians will collapse if you attack their weaknesses."

"You trust Blade?"

"More than most. Like me, he has nowhere else to run. But I trust no one completely. Our allies least of all. Neither Howler nor the Deceiver joined us out of love for our cause."

"Indeed." Apparently amused, Longshadow seemed to relax. "I must explain, General." Mogaba's surprise told me that this was an extraordinary eventuality. "I do not stay bottled up here because of the plain. I can leave Overlook for short periods. I will if I must. The Shadowgate wards are fresh and strong and reliable and entirely under my control. But if I do venture out I will have to so do by stealth."

Mogaba grunted again.

"The reason I stay here is that there are some less obvious players in this game."

Mogaba frowned. Sounded like a crock to me, too.

"Howler springs from that clan once known as The Ten Who Were Taken."

"I know."

"Stormshadow matriculated from that slave school as well. Another graduate was Senjak's sister. They called her Soulcatcher."

"I believe we've met."

"Yes. She embarrassed you at Stormgard." Actually, that was Lady that time. Wasn't it?

Mogaba nodded. I was surprised. Time seemed to have given him the ability to manage his temper.

"Some years ago circumstances deceived Howler and I. We took Soulcatcher prisoner under the impression that we had captured her sister. She was masquerading as Senjak at the time so the mistake was more her fault than ours. She escaped during some confusion that arose later. Although we did not treat her severely she bears us a unreasonable ill will. She has done us mischief before now and awaits the opportunity to do us major harm."

"You think if you left Overlook she might invite herself inside and forget to leave the door unlocked?"

"Exactly."

Ha! Imagine hijacking that incredible fortress.

Mogaba sighed. "So whether I like it or not it will have to be decided on the Plain of Charandaprash."

"Yes. Will you win?"

"Yes." Mogaba never did lack confidence. "As long as Croaker remains the man I knew, scarred by that streak of softness."

"If?"

"He hides behind a hundred masks. His soft streak may be another of those."

"So this man concerns you despite your desire to discount him."

"We continue to play to his strengths, not to attack his weaknesses. We allow him time to think, to plan, to maneuver, so he does not need to be subtle. His forces advance everywhere. Along the frontier the people are more afraid of the Black Company than of you. For pure viciousness there is nothing to match his war against Singh's kind. The Croaker I remember would have taken prisoners. He would have pardoned Stranglers willing to abandon their religion."

Right, I thought sarcastically. Then I reconsidered. Mogaba might be correct. Croaker *had* been forgiving, once upon a time.

"Maybe Senjak wants the example made."

"Possibly. She is that hard. But her influence doesn't explain Croaker's having spent seven thousand lives trying to get Blade."

What? This was news.

"Blade deserted him."

"I deserted him. And I was Company. Blade was only an adventurer, not a brother. He hasn't come after me that way. With Blade he's fighting a personal war."

The falling out with Blade and Blade's subsequent flight and defection baffled a lot of people, especially his buddies Cordy and Willow. And my name can go to the top of the list. Whispers were that Croaker stumbled onto something real going on between Lady and Blade. Whatever, it was certain that he was as obsessive about Blade as he was about Narayan Singh.

Lady did not interfere in Croaker's vendetta. Neither did she help.

"That troubles you?"

"Croaker confuses me. In some ways he has become dangerously unpredictable. At the same time he becomes more and more the high priest of the Black Company legend, admitting no other gods before his precious Annals."

That was not true. Croaker grew less interested all the time. But allow Mogaba his hyperbole. He wanted to sell something.

Mogaba continued, "I fear he may become so skewed he'll attack in a way so novel we won't recognize it until it's too late."

"As long as he comes. Only disaster awaits him."

"He'll come. But is the overall outcome so certain?" I got the feeling both men nurtured major doubts, but each mostly about the other.

"You circle back upon my constraints. Desist. You fear him?"

"I dread him. More than I dread Lady. Lady is straightforward in her enmity. She comes right at you with everything she has. Croaker is determined to flim-flam you into looking somewhere else while he sticks a knife in your back. He will come at you with everything he has, too, but how will he use it? He is not a man of honor."

Mogaba didn't really mean that Croaker was dishonorable but that he was not a gentleman in the sense that meant so much to Mogaba—who could not be considered a cavalier himself anymore.

Mogaba continued, "He is no longer sane. I do not believe he is sure what he is doing himself. These days he has to face much for which there is no precedent in his Annals."

Wrong again, chappie. After four hundred years there is a precedent for everything in the Annals somewhere. The trick is knowing how to look.

"He has limits, General."

"Of course. Those Taglians are factious and divisive."

"And that could be his undoing. Politically he will have no option but to try his luck at Charandaprash soon. Where we will crush him."

"And if I do? We should consider the possibilities of life unplagued by this disease called the Black Company."

"Oh?"

"Winning one battle will not be enough. If even one of them survives and maintains possession of the Lance of Passion new armies will rise against us. Lady proved that."

"Then you will have the pleasure of crushing them again."

Mogaba wanted to argue but elected not to bark into the wind.

"Once Overlook is complete you can hare off on any adventure you like, with my approval *and* with my total support."

"Adventure?"

"I understand you better than you suppose. You were Gea-Xle's greatest warrior but you could not prove that to yourself. In the Black Company you were overshadowed by your captain and Senjak. It was necessary for you to have command in order to demonstrate your scope and genius. When you did have an opportunity all your efforts were sabotaged and suborned. You came to me because the Black Company would not allow you the opportunity you need."

Mogaba nodded. He did not seem pleased with himself, though. And that surprised me. I had thought him too self-centered to entertain moral doubts.

"Go. Conquer the world, General. I'll enjoy helping you. But you have to crush the Black Company first. You have to stop the Taglians. Because you will have nothing if I fall. Will the Strangler be much help, really?"

"He could be. He talks big about his goddess getting involved but I won't count on that. I've never seen the gods actually take a hand in mortal affairs."

Odd. Mogaba's god was Narayan's goddess, more or less. Had Mogaba lost his faith? Maybe Dejagore had scarred him deeply, too.

"Use them up. Leave none over to turn on us later."

In my imagination the Shadowmaster was always this huge stinking devil incarnate, a colorful lunatic the magnitude of the worst Taken back in the north. But the real Longshadow was just a mean-spirited old man blessed with too much power.

He told Mogaba, "If this becomes the Year of the Skulls I want it to be *our* year. Not theirs."

"Understood. What do you think of the child?"

Longshadow grunted uncomfortably.

"Spooky, right? A thousand years old. Her mother in miniature, only worse. More intense, with a deeper darkness inside."

He could be right. The kid definitely looked weird and evil from my ghost's eye view.

The Shadowmaster mused, "We may have to hurry her into the embrace of her goddess."

Mogaba shrugged. He turned to go. "Anyone else you want to see alone?"

"Howler. Wait!"

"What?"

"Where is the Lance of Passion?"

"Wherever Croaker is, I imagine. Or the Standardbearer. That's still that serpent Murgen, I believe."

I love you too, Mogaba.

"We must take possession. Might that not be a task for the Deceivers? Even destroying the Black Company may not be enough in the long run. And one other thing for the Deceivers. Have them find out why Senjak wants all that bamboo."

"Bamboo?"

Was there an echo?

"She has been stripping the Taglian territories for months. Wherever her soldiers go they loot bamboo."

"That is curious. I will find out." I followed Mogaba for a moment. Once he was clear of the parapet he muttered, "Bamboo. I have to humor a lunatic."

I tried to travel south of Overlook. Smoke went only a short way before he balked. Well.

I would find out sooner than I wanted, I supposed. After we settled Longshadow and Overlook the plain was next on the list of obstacles blocking our path to Khatovar.

52

I RETURNED TO THE CHAMBER WITH SMOKE AND OUR STINKY PET STRANGLER. I was hungry and thirsty but also so excited I shook. I had not uncovered much of resounding import, but, gods! The potential!

I drank from the pitcher, cleared my throat, lifted the corner of the cloth covering the prisoner. "You in there? Want a drink? Want to tell me . . . ?" He was asleep. "Be that way."

So what now? Help had not arrived. I gnawed on one of Mother Gota's stones. That eased my hunger. That was all I wanted at the moment.

What now? Keep going out until somebody came to reclaim me? See Lady? Look for Goblin? Hunt for Blade? How about finding out where Soulcatcher was hiding? She had to be out there somewhere, though we had not stubbed our toes on her lately. No place was free of crows if a member of the Company was around.

Soulcatcher is patient. That is her scariest trait.

It was kid-in-the-candy-shop time.

I decided to look for Soulcatcher. She was the oldest mystery going right now.

Smoke jumped right out, but then he stalled. His soul, or ka, or whatever, became more agitated as I grew more insistent. "All right! She always was more trouble than I want to deal with, anyway. Let's find her goofy sister."

Lady did not intimidate Smoke at all.

I found her in the citadel at Dejagore, in the conference chamber with four men, leaning over a map. The frontier markings on the map lay far south of Dejagore. Earlier boundaries were noted and identified by date.

She needed a new map. Her old one was too busy. She had won too many skirmishes.

Lady is a beauty even fresh from the field. She looks way too young for Croaker although she is far older than One-Eye. One-Eye never mastered any youth sorcery.

Two of Lady's companions were Company men, Gea-Xle Nar anxious to show the world that Mogaba and his traitors were mutants, that their like would not be seen again. I did not buy that. Neither did Lady or the Old Man. We were confident that Mogaba had left somebody behind.

Croaker once told me, "Watch out for somebody to start pointing fingers. That'll be the traitor."

A third man was the Prahbrindrah Drah, the ruling Prince of Taglios. He was about as nondescript, for a Taglian, as a man could be and still be breathing. He put in the last four years learning the arts of war. He commanded a full division now, the right wing of the field army. Lady and the Old Man took pains to entangle him deeply in their war machine so he had a personal stake to maintain there.

The last man was the improbable Willow Swan. When I focused on him Smoke became agitated, which proved to me Smoke's self was partially aware on some plane. He and Swan had gotten on like rats and mice.

These days Swan is the captain of the Royal Guards detachment assigned to Dejagore.

Swan wears his cornsilk hair longer than Lady does her shoulder-length black hair. Sometimes Willow braids his but at the moment it was pulled back into a ponytail. Lady's hair was back in a tail, too. Usually she lets it hang free. She did keep it combed and clean when she could.

A soldier by accident, Swan did not want to be a hero. His Guards existed outside the army and functioned mainly as military police. He and they owed their allegiance directly to the Prince and his sister.

Lady said, "Howler has quit attacking outposts."

"You said he ain't stupid," Swan replied.

"I got too close when I missed him. That scared him off for good."

One of the Nar observed, "Our raids must trouble them."

"They trouble me, Isi. And I authorized them." Lady shivered momentarily.

"They are effective."

"Beyond a doubt."

The Prince asked, "But would the Liberator approve?"

Lady's smile revealed glistening white teeth that were almost too perfect. She had mastered the cosmetic sorceries early. "He doesn't approve. Definitely. But he won't interfere. I'm the one who is here and I'm relying on my own experience."

The Prince asked, "Will Longshadow unleash Mogaba?"

The Nar brigadiers tensed. Mogaba shamed them greatly by letting pride and vanity seduce him away from the ancient ideals of the Nar. Not to mention he was going to be blue-assed hell in a fight.

Swan asked, "You take any prisoners down there?"

"Yes. And what they knew would fit into a thimble with room left for a stork's nest. Nobody responsible down there ever sits around the campfire swapping secrets with the troops."

Swan stared at her while her gaze was directed elsewhere. He saw a woman five and a half feet tall, blue-eyed, 110 perfectly arranged pounds. She was big for this part of the world. She looked like she might turn twenty soon.

That old black magic.

Swan was transparent.

Lady is cold and hard and committed and deadlier than a sword with a will of its own, but these guys just can't seem to help themselves. It started with the Old Man way back but the parade goes on. The fever cost Blade big.

Despite what may have happened with Blade I am convinced that Lady is the Captain's woman absolutely. Whatever happened, Croaker took it to heart. He drove a good man over to the enemy and became something as cold as Lady himself. Half the time, anymore, Croaker is this living wargod so fierce that when he barks even the Prince and the Radisha jump.

Aloud, Lady wondered what Howler's raids were meant to accomplish. Swan blurted Bucket's answer. "He wanted to pick off Black Company guys. That's obvious."

"Isi?" Lady asked. "Is there more?"

One of the Nar replied, "Mogaba wouldn't test himself against lesser men. Longshadow might want to remove those so he can better manipulate Mogaba's obsessions. Or he might be trying to initiate the final battle by being a continuous irritant."

The Prince nodded to himself. Now *he* was watching Lady with that gleam in his eye.

Was it the fatal lure of evil?

"Perhaps he does want to bring Croaker to the front."

How many times over the centuries has Lady stood like that, about to loose fire and sword? She said, "We do need to move this headquarters nearer to the action. The communications lag has become unacceptable. Swan. Hand me that map there."

Swan plucked a map off a sideboard cluttered with mystic paraphernalia. His caution indicated that he found that stuff obscure and wanted it to stay that way.

The map portrayed the far south. A large blank space on its left was labelled Shindai Kus, which was a desert. Beyond the unmapped nether edge of the desert was additional blank space labeled Ocean.

Beginning in the Shindai Kus, running east and curving northward, are mountains generically referred to as the Dandha Presh. They become rougher and rougher as they swerve around to form, eventually, the eastern limits of the Taglian territories. The range changes its local name frequently. It is supposed to be impassable east of the Shindai Kus except through the high pass at Charandaprash.

Longshadow, Shadowcatch and Overlook lie on the far side of the Dandha Presh. Mogaba's army was the cork in the pass bottlenecking the road south. For ages a common subject when officers were not listening was how badly would we get whipped if we took a crack at Mogaba.

A racket apparently arose outside because Swan jumped to the window. "A courier," he announced. I could hear no sound from outside that room. In fact, when I did glance out the window I could see nothing but greyness. Strange.

Lady elbowed Swan aside. "Can't be good news. Get him before he talks too much."

Swan returned quickly. "It's not *too* bad. Seems a really huge mob of Shadar and Vehdna fanatics were chasing Blade and had the bad luck to catch him."

What? That wasn't news. I knew about it. The Shadowmaster knew about it. . . . Of course. Lady did not have a Smoke or a screaming-nut sidekick with a flying carpet. And I had known for just a little while. Maybe it seemed longer because I learned it so far away.

"What are you babbling?" Lady demanded.

"Blade wiped out over five thousand religious goofs who were after him to punish him for his religious excesses." Blade was pretty hard on temples and priests when he had the opportunity.

His religious attitude had a lot to do with his running away, too. He had made thorough, blood-bitter enemies of all Taglian priests long before his falling out with the Old Man. The devout considered his fall from favor a blessing from heaven.

I was confident that the priests secretly looked forward to all of our fates becoming gifts from the angels.

"Five thousand?"

"Maybe more. Maybe up to seven thousand."

"Loose on their own? How could that happen?" Neither the ruling family nor we liked having huge groups of armed men not under our control blundering around righting wrongs. "Out. All of you, out of here. Come back in two hours."

Lady started murmuring the instant she was alone. "That damned Croaker." She grabbed stuff off the sideboard. "He's out of his mind."

I learned that you got damned focused out there with Smoke. Time could rush past if you let yourself become introspective. Fragments of all that was happening to me came to me in no rational order and I almost got lost trying to piece the puzzle together.

Realization, and resulting terror, feeble as it was out there, brought me back to the present in the place I was watching when I lost my concentration. Hours had passed.

Lady was still grumbling about the Old Man. "What's the matter with him? How could he *believe* those damned rumors?"

She was angry. She had managed some mystic scrying of the distant battlefield as it appeared after the event. All that carnage had left her more upset. "Damned fool!" It was the worst disaster for Taglian arms since Dejagore.

From some hidden recess in the sideboard she produced a piece of black cloth. I was startled, despite having studied her Annals closely. That was the silk rumel of a master Strangler. She began exercising with the killing scarf.

Maybe that helped her relax.

She was upset because she had been left out of something. Usually she was the Captain's partner.

Got you a clue, woman, I thought. Lately he is cutting everybody out.

Lady's scarf flashed. She was good. I wondered. Was there still some connection with Kina?

Did Croaker fear there might be?

They were not called Deceivers for nothing.

She calmed herself. She sent for her council. Once they gathered she said, "There were survivors from that battle. Some are still there burying the dead. Catch me a few."

53

CROAKER NEVER CAME TO THE HIDDEN ROOM. NEITHER DID ONE-EYE, NOR even the Radisha to torment our prisoner. Nobody wakened me.

I drifted back there almost without design, perhaps summoned by my body. I had been gone a long time. Longer than the subjective time spent out there. My stretch of introspection must have extended farther than it had seemed.

My stomach was roaring. But Mother Gota's baked rocks were all gone.

The Strangler had gotten the cloth off himself again. He watched me wide-eyed. I got the feeling he had been about to do something that I would regret.

I discovered that he had managed to work one hand free. "You naughty boy." I took a long pull off the pitcher of water, then fixed him up again. Then I tried to decide whether to risk the labyrinth once more, in an effort to get to some of Mother Gota's lethal chow, or to stay and take yet another look at the wide world through Smoke's eyes while I awaited help.

"Water."

"Sorry, pal. I don't think so. Unless maybe you want to tell me what your buddies are up to." My belly grumbled again.

The Strangler did not answer. Weak as he was, his will remained firm. Even ignoring my own presence it seemed somebody should have come to feed him.

It was late. Maybe Mother Gota was asleep and Sarie would handle my meal. She did not cook like she was out for vengeance.

I was at the doorway, trying to make up my mind. Was there some way to mark my passage? Some way to follow footprints in the dust? But there was no light. This part of the Palace was not in regular use. No one maintained any candles or torches. The lamp in the chamber behind me would be the only light available. Unless I waited till daylight, when the sun would steal in through random cracks and tiny windows.

I glanced back at the lamp. It had been burning a long time. No one had been by to fuel it. I ought to see about refilling it before I did anything else.

There was a metallic sound from far, far away, come around a hundred corners and down the rambling halls. It chilled me despite Taglios's natural heat and humidity.

"Water."

"Shut up." I found a beaker of lamp oil, cocked my head while I worked. The metallic sound did not repeat itself.

I had not covered the Strangler again. When I glanced at him I discovered his deathshead face stretched in a grin. It was the grin of Death.

Spilling oil, I flung myself out of there.

I got lost again. Fast.

54

LOST IN THE PALACE WAS NOT A MATTER FOR PANIC SO I DIDN'T. I CONFESS to a certain amount of frustration, though.

You would think my situation vulnerable to the application of common sense. I sure thought so.

One good rule proved to be not to enter any corridor dustier than the one I was using. Another was to avoid apparent shortcuts religiously. They never led anywhere I wanted to go. Most important was, don't yield to emotion or frustration.

The Palace is the only place in the world where you can step through a doorway and end up on a different floor. I found out the hard way. And it was not any sort of elf magic. It came from the place being a conglomeration of ages and ages of add-ons built upon very uneven ground.

My anxiety reached the point where I elected to pursue what seemed the wimp route. I decided to go down to ground level, find one of the Palace's thousand postern doors, which can be opened only from the inside, and get out into the street. Out there I would know where I was. I would walk around to the entrance I used regularly. Then I would be home.

It is really dark in there in the middle of the night. I found that out after I stumbled descending a stair and dropped my lamp.

It broke, of course. And for a while there was a lot of light down below. But soon the fire burned out.

Oh, well. It was a certainty that there would be a door to the street below. The stairwell curved down against an exterior wall. I had leaned out a window to make sure before I ever entered it.

Descending an ancient stair that spirals isn't easy when there are no handrails and you cannot see what you are doing. Nevertheless, I got to the bottom without breaking any bones, although I did slip a couple of times and endured one long spell of vertigo after passing through the smoke from the burned lamp fuel.

Eventually the stair ended. I felt around for a door. As I did so I frowned. What was I doing? Took me a moment to reach back into my head and bring up the answer.

I found the door, felt around for a release. I found an old fashioned wooden latch bar, which was not what I expected at all.

I yanked, pushed. The door swung outward.

Wrong answer to your problem, Murgen.

Within that fastness nothing moves, though at times mists of light shimmer as they leak over from beyond the gates of dream. Shadows linger in corners. And way down inside the core of the place, in the feeblest throb of the heart of darkness, there is life of a sort.

A massive wooden throne stands upon a dais at the heart of a chamber so vast only a sun could light it all. Upon that throne a body sprawls, veiled by shoals of shadow, pinioned by silver knives driven through its feet and hands. Sometimes that body sighs softly in its sleep, impelled by bitter dreams acrawl behind its sightless eyes.

This is survival of a sort.

In the night, when the wind no longer licks through its unglazed windows, nor prances along its untenanted halls, nor whispers to its million creeping shadows, that fortress is filled with the silence of stone.

55

NO WILL.
No identity.
At home in the house of pain.

56

THERE YOU ARE! WHERE HAVE YOU BEEN? WELCOME BACK TO . . . THE house of pain?

57

THE HOUSE OF PAIN.
I went there but do not remember the journey or the visit.
I was on hands and knees on broken pavement. My palms and knees hurt. I lifted a hand. My palm was torn. Blood oozed from a dozen abrasions. My mind was numb. I raised my other hand, began picking out bits of paving brick.
Fifty yards away the side of a building glowed olive, pulsating. A circle of masonry blew outward. Shadows sprang out of the darkness. With weapons bare they scrambled through the hole. Shouts and the clang of metal came from inside.
I got up and wandered that direction, vaguely interested but not sure why, not even thinking definable thoughts.
"Hey!" A shadow at that hole stared at me. I did not yell so that must have been the shadow. "That you, Murgen?"

I kept walking, head spinning. My course curved to the right. I banged into the side of a building. After that I had a sure means of navigation. Like a drunk I steered by keeping one hand on the wall.

"Here he is!" The shadow pointed at me.

"Candles?"

"Yeah. You all right? What did they do to you?"

I had little pains everywhere. I felt like I had been stabbed and cut and burned. "Who? Nobody did anything? . . ." Did they? "Where am I? When?"

"Huh?"

A man leaned through the side of the building. He wore a scarf wrapped around his face. Only his eyes were visible. He studied me momentarily, popped back inside. Somebody in there yelled.

People jumped into the street. Some carried bloody weapons. All were masked. A couple grabbed my arms and took off.

We scurried through darkened streets in a nighted city and no one would answer my panted questions so for a while I had no idea when I was, or where. Then we crossed an open space from which I glimpsed the citadel of Dejagore.

That answered my most immediate questions.

But a new crop sprouted. Why were we outside the Company's part of town? How had I gotten there? Why didn't I have any memories of this? I recalled sitting with Ky Dam, secretly lusting after his granddaughter. . . .

The men accompanying me removed their wraps and masks. They were Company. Plus Uncle Doj and a couple of Nyueng Bao sprites. We ducked into an alleyway that led to Nyueng Bao territory. "Slow down," I gasped. "What's going on?"

"Somebody snatched you," Candles explained. "At first we thought Mogaba did it."

"Huh?"

"Shadowspinner's taken his whole army off after Lady. We could walk away if we wanted. We thought he decided to take a hostage."

I did not believe Spinner was gone. "Uncle Doj. The last thing I remember was sipping tea with the Speaker."

"You began to behave oddly, Stone Soldier."

I growled. He did not apologize.

"The Speaker thought perhaps you had been drinking before you arrived. He instructed Thai Dei to take you home. He was offended. You proved to be such a burden that Thai Dei was unable to defend himself when you were attacked. He was beaten badly but managed to get home with word. Your friends began looking for you as soon as we informed them." His tone suggested that he wondered why they had bothered. "They seem more skilled than they pretend. They pinpointed you quickly. You were not in the citadel, which is where Mogaba would have confined you."

"How did I get clear across town?" I winced. In addition to the other pains I had a hangover-type headache. I had been drugged.

Nobody had an answer for me.

"Is this the same night, Uncle?"

"Yes. But many hours later."

"And it definitely wasn't Mogaba that grabbed me?"

"No. There were no Nar in that place. In fact, soon after you were taken someone attacked Mogaba, too. They may have planned to murder him."

"Jaicuri?" Maybe the locals wanted to get to the heart of the problem.

"Perhaps." He did not sound convinced. Maybe he should have taken prisoners.

"Where's One-Eye?" Only One-Eye could have ripped that hole in the wall back there.

Candles told me, "Covering our backtrail."

"Good." I was near normal now. Which meant I was as confused as ever, I guess. Whoever grabbed me had done some slick work to sneak through Nyueng Bao territory unnoticed.

Uncle Doj divined my thoughts. "We have not determined how the villains managed to ambush you, nor how the others got so close to Mogaba. Those four did pay in blood."

"He killed them?"

"By all reports it was an epic battle, four against one."

"Goody for Mogaba. Even he deserves a little happiness in life." We were approaching the tenement that masqueraded as Company headquarters. I invited everybody in. The boys got a fire going. When One-Eye showed up I suggested he see if he could not scare up some beer, that I had heard there was some floating around and we sure could use a drink.

Grumbling, One-Eye returned to the night. Before long he and Goblin turned up lugging a barrel. "On me," I told everybody. One-Eye made a whining noise.

I stripped down and flopped onto a table. Which is why the fire. To take the edge off the chill. "How do I look, One-Eye?"

His tone was that of a man responding to a stupid question. "Like a guy that's been tortured. You don't know how you ended up in the street?"

"My guess is they heard you coming and tossed me out to distract you while they got away."

"Didn't work. Roll onto your side."

I spotted a face outside the open door. "Come in here. Have a beer with us."

The outsider Sindhu joined us. He accepted a mug but appeared to be very uncomfortable.

I noted how closely Uncle Doj watched him.

58

IT WAS STILL THAT SAME ADVENTUROUS NIGHT. I WAS STILL DISORIENTED, still hurting and definitely still exhausted but here I was wrapping a rope around me so I could rappel down the outside of the wall. "You sure the Nar can't see us from the gate tower?"

"Damn it, Kid, will you just go? You fuss worse than a mother-in-law."

One-Eye might know. He has had several.

I started down. Why did I let Goblin and One-Eye con me into this?

Two Taglian soldiers were waiting when I reached the crude raft. They helped me board. I asked, "How deep is the water?"

"Seven feet," the taller man replied. "We can pole across."

The rope stirred. I held it. Soon the outsider Sindhu dropped onto the raft. Mine was the only help he got. The Taglians wouldn't even acknowledge his existence. I tugged the rope three times hard to let the top end know we were going. "Start poling."

The Taglians were volunteers chosen in part because they were well rested. They were quite happy to be leaving the city—and depressed because they would not get to stay gone.

They considered this crossing an experiment. If we made it over, slipped through the southerners, then got back to Dejagore tomorrow night or the next soon whole fleets would hazard the crossing.

If we got back. If Shadowspinner's men did not intercept us. If we found Lady at all, which the soldiers did not know to be part of the mission. . . .

One-Eye and Goblin browbeat me into looking for Lady. Never mind them injuries, Kid. They ain't shit. Sindhu was along because Ky Dam thought it was a good idea to get him out of Dejagore. Sindhu's opinion had not been asked. The Taglians were supposed to guard me and provide strong backs. Uncle Doj had wanted to come but had failed to convince the Speaker.

The crossing was uneventful. Once we stepped ashore I retrieved a tiny green wooden box from my pocket and released the moth inside. It would fly back to Goblin, its arrival announcing my safe arrival.

I had several more boxes, each a different color and each containing a moth to be released in a particular circumstance.

As we started to move up a ravine Sindhu quietly volunteered to take the point. "I am experienced at this sort of thing," he told me. And I believed him within minutes. He moved very slowly, very carefully, making no sound.

I did all right but not as well. The two Taglians might as well have worn cowbells.

We had not gone far before Sindhu hissed a warning. We froze while grumbling Shadowlanders filed across our track twenty yards uphill. I caught only enough conversation to understand that they prefered a warm blanket to a night patrol through the hills. Surprise. You would think things would be different in somebody else's army.

We encountered another patrol an hour later. It, too, passed without detecting our presence.

We were past the ridgeline when dawn began creeping in from the east, extending visibility to the point where it was too dangerous to keep moving. Sindhu told me, "We must find a place of concealment."

Standard procedure in unfriendly territory. And it was no problem. The ravines out there were choked with brush. A man could disappear underneath easily as long as he remembered not to wear his orange nightshirt.

We disappeared. I started snoring seconds after we went to ground. And I did not go anywhere else, or anywhen.

The smell of smoke wakened me. I sat up. Sindhu rose at almost the same instant. I found a crow studying me from so close I had to cross my eyes to focus on him. The Taglian who was supposed to be keeping watch was sleeping. So much for well-rested. I said nothing. Neither did Sindhu.

In moments my fears were confirmed.

A southern voice called out. Another answered. Crows laughed. Sindhu whispered, "They know we are here?" It sounded like he had trouble believing that.

I lifted a finger, requesting silence. I listened, picked out a few words. "They know somebody is here. They don't know who. They're unhappy because they can't just kill us. The Shadowmaster wants prisoners."

"They aren't trying to lure us out?"

"They don't know any of us can understand some of their dialect." The albino crow in front of me cawed and flapped its way up out of the brush. About twenty others joined it.

"If we cannot evade them we must surrender. We must not fight."
Sindhu was an unhappy young man.

I agreed. I was an unhappy young man myself. The Taglian soldiers
were two more unhappy young men.

We evaded nothing and no one. The crows found our efforts amusing.

59

TIME HAD NO MEANING. THE SHADOWMASTER'S CAMP LAY SOMEWHERE NORTH
of Dejagore. We four were among the earliest prisoners taken but more
soon joined us in our pen. Lots of Mogaba's guys wanted to leave town.

He would have less trouble feeding the ones who stayed behind.

One-Eye and Goblin seemed to hold our part of town together.
Nobody I knew became a prisoner.

I did not send any more moths so they knew I had found trouble
instead of Lady.

Even our guards had no notion how Spinner meant to use us. We
were happier not knowing, probably.

I spent uncounted days in total misery. Piglets in a feed lot live better
than we did. More and more prisoners arrived. The food was inadequate.
After a few meals everybody got the runs. There were no sewage provisions, not even a simple slit trench. They would not let us dig our own.
Maybe they did not want us getting too comfortable.

In fact our life was not much worse than that of the Shadowlander
private soldiers. They had nothing anymore and could expect only nothing. They indulged in a ferocious desertion rate despite the Shadowmaster's reputation. They hated Shadowspinner for putting them into such an
awful state. They took their anger out on us.

I do not know how long we were there. I lost track. I was busy trying
to die from dysentery. I noticed only that there was a sudden absence of
crows one day. I was so used to having crows around that anymore I
noticed them only when they were not there.

I faded in and out. I suffered a bunch of my spells. They were more
frequent now and left me emotionally drained. The shits left me physically drained.

If I could only get some sleep . . .

Sindhu wakened me. I recoiled from his touch. It was astonishingly
cold and seemed vaguely reptilian. I was the only man in the pen he knew

so he wanted to be my pal. I was willing to do without a friend. He offered me a cup of water. It was a rather nice tin cup. Where did he get that? "Drink," he said. "It's clean water." All around us prisoners lay in the mud twitching endlessly in haunted sleep. Some cried out. Sindhu continued, "Something is going to happen."

"What?"

"I felt the breath of the goddess."

For an instant I smelled something that was not the stink of vomit or unwashed bodies or dead men or pools of liquid shit, too.

"Ah," Sindhu whispered. "It's happening now." I looked where he pointed.

The happening something was going on inside the big tent belonging to the Shadowmaster. Lights of strange color flickered and flared. "Maybe he's getting something special ready for somebody." Maybe he had Lady spotted.

Sindhu snorted. He seemed to thrive in these conditions.

The something went on a long time but attracted no attention. I became suspicious. I had Goblin's ward against sleep spells set on me. Oh . . . ? I dragged myself to the compound fence. When nobody smashed me back with the butt of a spear I was sure. The camp was under an enchantment.

Sindhu's water gave me strength quickly and started my brain perking. It occurred to me that if no one was inclined to stop me this might be the perfect time to take leave of the Shadowmaster's hospitality. I started worming my way between the fence rails.

My stomach rumbled in protest. I ignored it. Sindhu grabbed my arm. His grip was iron. He said, "Wait."

I waited. What the hell? That was one of my favorite arms. I didn't want to deprive myself of its company.

The moon began to rise, a big old squashed orange egg in the east. Sindhu continued to restrain me and continued to stare at the big tent.

A shriek drifted down from high above.

"Holy shit," I muttered. "Not him."

Sindhu cursed, too. He was so startled that he let me go. He glared upward.

"That's the Howler," I told him. "Really bad news. Shadowspinner could take advanced cruelty lessons from him."

The side of Spinner's tent opened. Out rushed a bunch of people carrying what proved to be human body parts. I recognized some of them. The people, that is. Who could mistake Willow Swan with his wild yellow mane? Or Lady, who carried a severed head by its mangy hair? And Blade was only a step behind her, his ebony skin shiny in the moonlight.

I did not recognize any of the others.

The sleep spell on the camp, laid rather poorly, unravelled. Southerners jumped up to ask what was happening. Metal clanged and jingled as weapons and mail were located.

One of Lady's companions, a huge Shadar, started bellowing something about bowing down to the true Daughter of Night.

Sindhu chuckled. Nothing bothered him, it seemed. He could take anything.

He was not holding on to me but I no longer had the strength or inclination to go anywhere.

60

THEY PULLED IT OFF, LADY AND HER DAMNFOOL GANG. AUDACITY PAYS. They slipped into the camp, murdered Shadowspinner, and when they got caught they convinced the southerners that it was all fated and they should not go doing anything because of that. I could not be much of a witness to their mass conversion. My bowels overruled my desire to observe. I spent most of my time making a worse mess of myself.

At some point our former guards decided to bring us to Lady's attention in an effort to curry favor.

Blade recognized us as they brought us out of the pen.

Blade looks like he might have been born Nar. Like them he is tall, black and muscular, without an ounce of fat on him. He says little but has a strong presence. His background is shadowy. He ran with Willow Swan and Cordy Mather, who saved him from crocodiles several thousand miles north of Taglios. What everyone knew for sure, what Blade made no effort to hide, was that he hated priests, singly, collectively, and without any prejudice whatsoever where belief system was concerned. Once I thought he was an atheist who hated the whole idea of gods and religion, but after further exposure I decided it was only the retailers of religion he detested. That suggested sharp incidents in his past.

No matter now. Blade took Sindhu and I away from our guards. "Standardbearer, you stink."

"Call out the ladies in waiting. Let them give me a bath." I could not remember my last bath. In Dejagore we did not waste water on trivialities.

Of course, now we could bathe all we wanted—although the water would be unclean.

Blade obtained fresh clothing by the expedient of robbing some southern officers, had us clean up and visit the inadequate field physicians Croaker had tried to train for the Taglian forces. They knew less about stopping the drizzling shits than I did.

It was daylight when Lady saw me. She already knew the prisoners were deserters from the city. She was blunt. "Why did you run out, Murgen?"

"I didn't. We decided somebody had to come find you. I lost the election. . . . Uh." She was in a bleak mood, apparently pretty sick herself. Never mind the humor, Murgen. "One-Eye and Goblin figured I was the only trustworthy guy who had any chance of getting through. They couldn't leave. I didn't make it, though."

"Why did you feel the need to send someone?"

"Mogaba elected himself god. With the water around us, keeping the southerners back, he doesn't need to get along with anybody who doesn't agree."

Sindhu said, "The black men believe they serve the goddess, mistress. But their heresies are grotesque. They have become worse than unbelievers."

I pricked up my ears. Maybe I would learn something about Sindhu's bunch. I had bones to pick with them. I had not yet found any evidence to suggest that it was not them who kidnapped me and took a crack at murdering Mogaba.

Still, I could not imagine why they would bother.

Sindhu and Lady talked. Her questions sounded vaguely doctrinal. Sindhu's replies made no sense.

Once Lady interrupted the interview to be sick. A skinny little gink named Narayan, who kept hanging around, seemed inordinately pleased. I noted that Sindhu showed him considerable deference.

I was not happy. The little I knew of their cult assured me that I did not want them influencing my captains.

The interview ended. Blade's cronies took me away. I got to hang out with Swan and Mather, meaning I had somebody to speak a reasonable language with for a while, but soon I felt like a forgotten man.

"What are we doing?" I asked Swan.

"I don't know. Cordy and I just tag along behind Her Lordship pretending not to be watching her for the Prabrindrah Drah and Radisha."

"Pretending?"

"Ain't much good being a spy if everybody knows it, is there? Anyway, Cordy gets to do all the worrying. He's the one playing pattycake with the Woman."

"You mean that ain't just a vicious rumor? He's really plooking the Radisha?"

"Hard to believe, ain't it? She's got a face like . . . Hey! Cordy! Where's them cards? We got us a pigeon here thinks he can play tonk."

"Thinks? Swan, you're gonna think I invented the game if you get into it with me."

Mather was a nondescript character of average height with ginger hair who stood out only because he was white in a land where nobody but harem girls, kept out of the sun from birth, had fair skin. He asked, "Willow's mouth running away with him again?"

"Maybe. I've made a career of playing tonk. Hell, they boot you out of the Black Company if you don't make journeyman player."

Mather shrugged. "Then you'll twist Willow's head back around straight for him. Here. Deal. I'll see if the mighty general Blade wants to sit in."

Swan grumbled, "That would take him out of sight of Lady." Sounded like some sour grapes there. Mather showed him a smirk that confirmed my guess.

"What *is* it about her?" I asked. "Every damned guy that walks on his hind legs gets near her for five minutes, he starts floating around with his tongue hanging down, banging into things. But I've been around her for years. I can see she's got the right stuff in the right places put together about as good as you could want but I don't think I could get excited even if she didn't used to be the Lady and she wasn't married to the Old Man." Not that that was literally true. They had not even bothered to jump over a sword.

Swan shuffled. "Cut?"

I cut. I always cut. One-Eye taught me that.

Swan asked, "You really don't feel it? Man, she comes around me and my brain goes south. And she's a widow now, so . . ."

"I don't think so."

"What?"

"She ain't no widow. Croaker is still alive."

"Shit. That'd be my luck, too. You want to stack Cordy a hand, make him think he's got a winner, then skunk him?" As soon as I shook my head he wanted to know how come I thought Croaker was alive. I evaded a definitive answer for the few moments it took Mather to return.

"Blade's too busy looking for an angle to use while he's close to the magic. You load me up again, Willow? No? Bullshit. Let's just pick them up and deal them over."

"Ain't this the story of my life?" I grumbled. "Look here." I had two aces, a pair of deuces and a trey. An automatic winner, damned near couldn't be beat. "And that's a true natural, no help."

Swan snickered. "Don't matter. You don't got anything to do anyway."

"You got a point. Why don't you guys come over to Dejagore? I'll buy you a mug of One-Eye's home brew."

"Ha! Competition, huh?" Swan and Mather had gone into the brewing business back when they first came to Taglios. They were out of the racket now, among their reasons the fact that the priests of all the native religions condemned the use of alcohol.

"I doubt it. The only thing good about their brew is it gets you skunked."

"That was the only good thing about the rat piss we made," Mather said. "My dear old daddy the brewmaster rolled over every time we tapped another keg."

"We never laid any beer up," Swan countered. "Soon as it was ripe we skimmed the scum off and poured it down Taglian throats. And don't buy that shit about his daddy, neither. Old Man Mather was a tax assessor who was so dumb he didn't take bribes."

"Shut up and deal." Mather snatched up his cards. "He did brew his own beer. And Swan's old man was a hod carrier."

"But a handsome one, Cordy. And a lover. I inherited his good looks."

"You take after your mother. And if you don't do something about that hair pretty soon you're going to wind up in somebody's harem."

This was a side of these guys I had not seen before. But I had not spent much time loafing with them. They were not Company. I kept my mouth shut and concentrated on my cards and let them tell me about who they used to be before the wanderdust settled on their shoes and set them roving against all odds.

"What about you, Murgen?" Swan asked after he noticed that I was winning more than my share of hands. "Where did you come from?"

I told them about growing up on a farm. There wasn't anything exciting about my life until I decided that farming wasn't what I wanted to do. I joined one of Lady's armies, found out I didn't like the way things were done there, deserted and joined up with the Black Company, which was the only place I could hide with the provost after me.

Mather asked, "You ever regret leaving home?"

"Every goddamned day, Mather. Every goddamned day. It was boring raising potatoes but not one time did I ever did have a spud try to stick a knife in me. I was hardly ever hungry and almost never cold and the landlord was all right. He made sure his tenants had enough before he took his share. He didn't live much better than we did. Oh, and the only magic we ever saw was the kind your wandering conjurers perform at town fairs."

"So why not go home?"

"Can't."

"If you're careful and don't look prosperous and don't go around pissing people off you can travel almost anywhere safely. We did."

"I can't go home because home ain't there no more. A Rebel army came through a couple years after I left." The Company passed through later still, marching from somewhere unpleasant to somewhere where we would be unhappy. The whole country had been turned desert in the name of freedom from the tyranny of the Lady's empire.

61

LADY SENT FOR ME AFTER SIX DAYS. I HAD SHAKEN THE RUNS AND HAD eaten well enough to regain a few of the pounds I lost in the pen. I still looked like a refugee from hell. And I was. I was indeed.

Lady did not look good. Tired, pale, under severe pressure, apparently still fighting the sickness that had her puking the other day. She wasted no time on small talk. "I'm sending you back to Dejagore, Murgen. We're getting disturbing reports about Mogaba."

I nodded. I had heard some of them. Every night more rafts crossed the lake. The deserters and refugees always were astonished to learn that Shadowspinner was dead and Lady controlled his army—though that was evaporating through desertion, too.

Lady was a hard one. My guess was she meant to let the problem posed by Mogaba solve itself—despite what that would cost Taglios and the Black Company.

"Why?" That was not smart. All those Taglians in there had relatives back home. Many were people of place and substance, for it was that sort who had volunteered to defend Taglios.

"I need you to just go back and be yourself. But write things down. Hone your skills. Keep the Company together. Be prepared for anything."

I grunted. That wasn't something I wanted to hear, knowing that the siege could be ended right now.

Lady sensed my reservations. She smiled wanly, made a sudden gesture. "Sleep, Murgen."

I collapsed on the spot.

She was her nasty old self.

My mind would not clear. The Taglians who had helped me leave Dejagore were like zombies. They did not talk and seemed almost blind. "Down!" I muttered. "Patrol coming." They did what I said but like men heavily drugged.

Patrols were few by day. It was easy to elude them. It was not their mission to keep people out, anyway. We reached lakeside without any trouble.

"Rest," I ordered. "Wait for dark." I was not sure why we had crossed the hills by day. I did not recall starting. "Have I been acting real weird?" I asked.

The taller Taglian shook his head slowly, not quite sure. He was more confused than I was.

I said, "I feel like I walked out of a fog a couple hours ago. I remember getting captured. I remember them keeping us in a nasty pen. I know there was a fight or something. But I don't remember how we got away."

"Nor do I, sir," the shorter soldier said. "I do have a very strong feeling that we need to get back to our comrades quickly. But I don't know why."

"How about you?"

The taller man nodded, frowning. He was going to bust a vein trying to remember.

I said, "Maybe Shadowspinner did something to us and let us go. That's worth keeping in mind—especially if you have urges that really surprise you."

After dark we stole along the shoreline till we found a raft, jumped aboard and headed for Dejagore. And discovered immediately that we were going to get nowhere using poles. The water was too deep. We ended up using poles and broken boards as inefficient paddles. It took us half the night to make the crossing. And then, naturally, everything went to hell.

One-Eye was on watch and had been passing the time making love to a keg of beer. He heard water splash and people ask for a hand up and concluded that the evil hordes were upon him, whereupon he flung fireballs hither and yon so any handy archers could plink us.

One-Eye recognized me before more than three or four arrows whizzed past. He yelled for a ceasefire. But the damage had been done. The Nar at the North Gate saw us.

We were far enough away that they should not recognize faces. But the possibility that the Old Crew might have outside contacts would get Mogaba's interest.

"Hey, Kid, good to see you," One-Eye said as I clambered to the top of the wall. "We thought you was dead. We was going to have a funeral in a few more days if we got time. I been stalling it, account of if you was officially dead then I'd have to start keeping the Annals." Generously, he offered me a drink from his very own unwashed for a fortnight mug. I declined the honor. "You all right, Kid?"

"I don't know. Maybe you can tell me." I told him what I could remember.

"You have another spell?"

"If I did these guys had it with me."

"Interesting. Come around and see me about it tomorrow."

"Tomorrow?"

"I'm gonna be off watch in ten minutes and I intend to hit the sack. And you need some sleep yourself."

My pal. Don't know what I would do if I didn't have One-Eye to worry about me.

62

BUCKET WAKENED ME. "ONE OF MOGABA'S GUYS IS HERE, MURGEN. SAYS His Majesty wants to see you."

I groaned. "Does it have to be so bright out there?" I had not bothered to go down into the warrens.

"He's pissed off. We've been pretending you were here but couldn't talk to him. Goblin and One-Eye put doubles of you on the wall sometimes so the Nar could see you."

"And now you have the real Murgen back you want to throw him to the wolf."

"Uh . . . Well . . . He didn't ask for nobody else." Meaning he did not want Goblin or One-Eye. He wanted to stay away from those two.

"Find my bitty buddies and tell them I need them. Now."

The wizards turned up at their own leisure, of course. I told them, "Put me in a litter and lug me over to the citadel. We're going to admit that you've been lying about me but only because I was totally sick. What we were doing on that raft last night was taking baths. You thought it would be cute to pop off a few fireballs while I had my pants down."

One-Eye started to complain but before he could start I growled, "I'm not facing Mogaba without backup. He don't have any reason to be nice anymore."

"He won't be in a good mood," Goblin predicted. "There's been rioting. Food shortages are getting really bad. He won't turn one grain of rice loose. Even his handpicked Taglian sergeants have started to desert."

"It's all falling apart for him," I said. "He was going to take over and show the world wonders but his followers can't match his iron will."

"And we're some kind of philanthropic brotherhood?" One-Eye muttered.

"We never kill nobody who don't ask for it. Come on. Let's do it. And be ready for anything. Both of you."

But first we went up to the battlements, both so I could see this world by daylight and so the Nar at the North Gate could see me looking sick before I presented myself that way.

The water level was just eight feet below the ramparts, higher than Hong Tray's prediction. "Any flooding inside?"

"Mogaba sealed the gates somehow. He has Jaicuri working parties bucket-brigading what seepage there is."

"Good for him. How about down below?"

"There's some seepage in the catacombs. Not a lot. We could keep up by hauling it up in buckets."

I grunted. I stared at Shadowspinner's lake. I saw more corpses than I could count. "Those didn't float up from the mounds, did they?"

Goblin told me, "Mogaba threw people off the wall during the riots. And some might be from rafts that turned over or broke up."

I squinted. I could just make out a mounted patrol beyond the water. A raft with Jaicuri piled high had been caught by daylight. The people aboard were trying to move away from the waiting patrol by paddling with their hands.

Thai Dei turned up so we knew his people were watching. I figured he would want me to visit the Speaker. But he said nothing. I told my bearers, "Take me to his worship."

As we approached I observed, "The citadel looks like something out of a spook story." And it did, with the sky overcast behind it and crows swarming around. Dejagore was a paradise for crows. They were going to get too fat to fly. Maybe we would get fat eating them.

The Nar at the entrance would not let One-Eye and Goblin inside. "So take me home," I told them.

"Wait!"

"Stick it, buddy. I got no need to put up with Mogaba's crap. The Lieutenant is alive. So is the Captain, probably. Mogaba ain't shit nowhere but inside his own head anymore."

"You could have at least argued until we were rested up." One-Eye started shuffling sideways so he could turn and head back down the steps.

Ochiba caught us before we reached street level. He was cast in the same mold as all Nar. His face remained neutral. "Apologies, Standard-bearer. Won't you reconsider?"

"Reconsider what? I don't especially want to see Mogaba. He's been eating magic mushrooms or chewing lucky weed or something. I been shitting my guts out for over a week. I ain't in no shape to play games with no homicidal lunatic."

Something fluttered behind Ochiba's dark eyes. Maybe he agreed. Maybe there was another war going on inside him, a struggle between keeping faith with Gea-Xle's greatest Nar ever and keeping faith with his own humanity.

I was not going to pursue it. Any hint of outside interest would push waverers in the direction of "That's the way it's always been."

That was the top two, then, quietly questioning Mogaba's way. If these guys doubted him things were probably worse than I thought.

"As you wish." Ochiba told the sentries, "Let the litterbearers in."

Nobody missed the significance of who my litterbearers were. It was a pretty direct statement.

I felt comfortably confrontational.

63

WAS MOGABA HAPPY TO SEE GOBLIN AND ONE-EYE, AND THEM LOOKING SO fit? You better believe he wasn't. But he did not pursue his displeasure. He just ticked something on his mental get-even slate. He would make me even more unhappy than he had planned. Later.

"Can you sit up?" he asked, almost like he cared.

"Yeah. I made sure. That's partly why I took so long. That and I wanted to make sure I'd stay rational."

"Oh?"

"I've been suffering severe fevers and dysentery for over a week. Last night they took me out and threw me in the water to cool me down. That worked."

"I see. Come to the table, please."

Goblin and One-Eye helped me into a chair. They put on a fine show.

There were just six people in the conference chamber, us three and Mogaba, Ochiba and Sindawe. Through the window behind Mogaba I saw water and hills. And crows. They squabbled over space on the window sill, though none would come inside. An albino turned an especially baleful pink eye my way.

I suppose we looked too hungry.

For one instant I saw that same room in another time, with Lady and some of the same faces around the same table. Mogaba was not among them. The window behind *them* opened on greyness.

One-Eye pinched my earlobe. "Kid, now ain't the time."

Mogaba watched intently.

"Less recovered than I thought," I explained. I wondered what the vision meant. And vision it was because it was too fully realized for imagination.

Mogaba settled into a chair opposite me. He pretended solicitousness, avoided his usual assertiveness.

"We face numerous grave problems, Standardbearer. They are out there and indifferent to whatever animosities we have developed amongst ourselves."

Goddamn! Was he going to turn reasonable on me?

"They will be there whether or not we want to believe the Lieutenant or Captain survived. We will have to face them because I do not expect to be relieved any time soon."

I would not argue with that.

"We would be better off had Lady not interfered this last time. We are isolated and trapped now because the Shadowmaster was forced to find a solution for managing two fronts."

I nodded. We *were* in a worse situation. On the other hand, we would not have yowling hordes piling over the wall every few nights anymore. Nor would Mogaba be flinging men hither and yon without regard for their lives, just trying to irritate the Southerners into doing something stupid.

Mogaba glanced out the window. We could see two Shadowlander patrols raising dust in the hills. "He can starve us out now."

"Maybe."

Mogaba grimaced but controlled his anger. "Yes?"

"For no rational reason I feel confident that our friends will break us out."

"I must confess that I remain a stranger to that sort of faith. Although I concede the importance of maintaining an optimistic aspect in front of the soldiers."

Was I going to argue? No. He was more right than I could be.

"So, Standardbearer, how do we survive a protracted siege when most of our food stores are exhausted? How do we recover the standard once we do get out of these straits?"

"I don't have any answers. Although I think the standard is in friendly hands already." Why was he interested? Almost every time we talked he asked something about the standard. Did he believe possessing it would legitimize him?

"How so?" He was surprised.

"The Widowmaker that was here the first time carried the real standard."

"You're sure?"

"I know it," I promised.

"Then share your thoughts about food."

"We could try fishing."

Wisecracking was not a good idea with Mogaba. It just made Mogaba angry.

"Ain't no joke," Goblin snapped. "That water comes down here from regular rivers. There's got to be fish."

The little shit wasn't as stupid as he acted sometimes.

Mogaba frowned. "Do we have anyone who knows anything about fishing?" he asked Sindawe.

"I doubt it." They meant among their Taglian soldiers, of course. Nar are warriors, back for a dozen generations. They do not sully themselves doing unheroic work.

I was negligent. I failed to mention that the Nyueng Bao came from country where fishing was, probably, a way of life.

"It's a thought," Mogaba told me. "And there is always baked crow." He glanced back at the window. "But most Taglians won't eat flesh."

"A conundrum," I agreed.

"I will not surrender."

No reply seemed adequate.

"You have no resources either?"

"Less than you," I lied. We still had a little rice from the catacombs. But not much. We were stretching ourselves every way possible, in accordance with hints recorded in the Annals. We did not look like famine victims. Not quite yet.

We looked, I noted, less well fed than did the Nar.

"Suggestions for reducing the number of unproductive mouths?"

"I'm letting my worn-out Taglians and any locals who want build rafts and go. But I don't let them take anything with them."

He controlled his anger again. "That does consume valuable timber. But it is another thought worth consideration."

I studied Sindawe and Ochiba. They remained jet statues. They were not even breathing, it seemed. They expressed no opinions.

Mogaba glared at me. "I feared this meeting would be this nonproductive. You haven't even thrown the Annals in my face."

"The Annals aren't magic. What they say about sieges is plain common-sense stuff. Be stubborn. Ration. Don't support the nonproductive. Control the spread of plague. Don't exhaust your enemy's patience if there is no hope of outlasting him. If surrender is inevitable do it while your enemy is still amenable to terms."

"This enemy never offered."

I wondered about that, although the Shadowmasters did have a tendency to think like gods.

"Thank you, Standardbearer. We will examine our options and keep you informed of what we mean to do."

Goblin and One-Eye helped me ease my chair back. They settled me into the litter. Mogaba said nothing else and I could think of nothing I wanted to tell him. The other Nar just stood there awkwardly and watched us go.

"What was that in aid of?" I asked once we were clear. "I expected yelling and threats."

"He wanted to pick your brains," Goblin said.

"While he made up his mind if he was going to kill you," One-Eye added cheerfully.

"Oh, that's real encouraging."

"He did decide, Murgen. And he didn't pick the option you want to hear. It's time to start being real careful."

We did make it home unharmed.

64

"DON'T BOTHER DRAGGING ME UP THERE TILL WE FIND OUT WHAT UNCLE wants." Goblin and One-Eye were at the foot of steps leading to the battlements. Doj was up top, looking down.

"I wasn't planning to carry your dead ass anywhere anyhow anymore," One-Eye told me. "Far as I'm concerned this exercise was for camouflage."

Uncle Doj started downward.

I stared at the wall. Tiny beads of sweat covered it, but that was because the stone was cooler than the air, not because water had begun seeping through from outside.

The Shadowmasters were good builders.

"Stone Soldier. You are well?"

"Not bad for a guy with the runs. Ready to dance on your grave, Stubby. We got business?"

"The Speaker wishes to see you. Your excursion was not successful?" He moved his head to indicate my trip outside.

"If you call spending two weeks as a guest of the Shadowmaster a success I tore them up, Uncle. Otherwise, all I did was get sick, lose some weight, then have barely enough sense left to run for it when some Taglians hit Shadowspinner's camp with a nuisance raid. That's all right. I can walk that far." Just don't let me fall down any rabbit holes.

I could walk to the Speaker's place easily but why give up the pretense of weakness if it might be useful?

Nothing changed with the Speaker's crew. Except that this time one smell was absent. I noticed that as soon as I stepped inside. I could not identify the missing odor, though.

The Speaker was ready. Hong Tray was in place. The beautiful one had tea brewing.

Ky Dam smiled. "Thai Dei ran ahead." He read my curiosity from my glance and flaring nostrils. "Danh has gone to his judgment. At last. A bleak season has ended for this house."

I could not help myself. I looked at the young woman. I found her looking at me. Her gaze shifted immediately, but not so fast that I did not feel guilty when I returned attention to the Speaker.

The old man missed nothing. Neither did he get excited about something best left ignored. He was wise, was Ky Dam.

I had come to respect that frail oldster a lot.

"The hard times have come, Standardbearer, and will lead to more terrible tomorrows." He reviewed my discussion with Mogaba well enough to convince me that someone had watched us.

"Why tell me this?"

"To support my claim when I tell you we spy on the black men. After your departure they spoke only their native tongue until they sent messengers to the tribunes of the cohorts and other senior Taglians. They are to gather at suppertime."

"Sounds big."

The old man bowed slightly. "I would like you to see something for yourself. You know these men more certainly than do I. You can determine if my suspicions are well-founded."

"You want me to spy on that meeting?"

"Something of the sort." The old man did not tell me the whole story. Not then. He wanted me walking into it cold. "Doj will conduct you."

65

DOJ CONDUCTED ME. THE WAY LED THROUGH CELLARS AS INTRICATELY CON-
nected as ours but less care had been used in the tunneling. The people who
did this just wanted to be able to sneak away. They had had no intention of
hiding. They must have been Jaicuri collaborators in Stormshadow's
administration, acting for her. She would have wanted an emergency exit.

"I'm surprised at you," I told Uncle Doj. "I wouldn't think underground would occur to swamp people. I don't suppose there are a lot of
tunnels in the delta."

"Not many." He smiled.

My guess is they found the escape route through sheer blind luck,
maybe coupled with an informed suspicion about how Stormshadow's
mind worked.

Getting into the citadel, then, was no problem, though it required
some crawling. The architects had not been concerned with Stormshadow's dignity. It was tough for me. I was not yet back to my best.

We came to a small open space beneath a ladder. That rose straight up
into infinity, so far as I could see by the light of one feeble candle. I had a
feeling the candle was a luxury laid on for me, that the Nyueng Bao made
this journey entirely in darkness.

I could not have endured that. I dislike enclosed places intensely
despite having lived in them. Close places, darkness, recurring spells and
visions were not a combination I wanted to tempt.

I did seem more stable lately, I reflected.

I set a hand and foot on the ladder.

Uncle Doj grabbed my wrist, shook his head.

"What? Isn't that the way to the council chamber?" My whisper rattled off like the scurry of mice.

"Not what the Speaker wants you to see." Doj used almost no air
when he whispered. "Come."

There was no crawling now, just a lot of easing along sideways in an
airspace almost too narrow for Uncle. His belly was going to ache from
rubbing against stone.

I learned that there was a lot more to Stormshadow's citadel than I
had seen in the little time I spent there these past few months. Down
below there, beneath the surrounding plazas, were countless unsuspected
storerooms and prison cells, armories and barracks rooms, cisterns and

smithies. I whispered, "They have supplies down here to hold out for years." Meaning the Nar and their favorites, holed up inside the citadel. Stormshadow had laid in a great store against the evil day.

Mogaba had lied to me, just trying to find out how well off we Old Crew were.

Was that what the old man wanted me to know?

Was this why the Nyueng Bao had seemed to prosper while everyone else became gaunt? Were they nibbling at these stores like mice, taking just a little here and there so their predations would go unnoticed?

Uncle Doj beckoned. "Hurry."

Soon I began to hear a distant chanting. "We may not be in time, Bone Warrior. Hurry."

I didn't slug him mostly because the racket would have alerted the singing men.

I knew they were Nar before I saw a thing. I had heard the rhythms and style before, though not these particular lyrics. Always before, though, there had been joy in their work songs and celebrations. This song was cold and grim.

Uncle Doj left the candle, tugged my elbow. We continued to step sideways until, suddenly, we were in an ordinary passageway, not some tight, secret squeeze behind a wall. Nothing concealed the entrance to the hidden ways. That was just a shadowed corner unlikely to entice a closer look.

There was light out there, from candles in sconces widely spaced. The people in charge were frugal despite their wealth.

Uncle Doj placed a finger to his lips. We were near dangerous people who might detect us in an instant. He dropped to his knees and led me right into a large chamber where most of the Nar had gathered. Lighting was nonexistent except down where they were. Doj got behind a pillar. I squatted behind a low, dusty table just inside the doorway. I wished I was as dark as the Nar. My forehead must be shining like a little half moon.

This life hardens you. Too soon you have seen so much that when you encounter another something terrible you don't howl and run in circles, snapping at your tail. But most of us still appreciate horror if horror is there.

Horror was there.

There was an altar. Mogaba and Ochiba were involved in something ceremonial. Above the altar stood a small statue of dark stone, a four-armed woman dancing. I was too far away to make out details but I was pretty sure sure she had vampire fangs and six teats. She might be wearing a necklace of baby skulls. The Nar might give her another name but she was Kina. The worship offered by the Nar was not that described in the Jaicuri scriptures, though.

The Deceivers do not want to spill blood. That is why they are called Stranglers.

The Nar not only spilled blood on behalf of their goddess, they drank it. And it looked like they had been doing so for some time down there. Drained corpses hung to one side. Their latest sacrifice, a hapless Jaicuri, got hoisted up with those soon after I arrived.

The Nar were practical in their religion. After the grim ceremony ended they began butchering one of the bodies.

I got down and crawled out of there. I did not give one rat's ass what Uncle Doj thought.

I have seen a lot with the Company, including tortures and cruelties almost beyond comprehension and inhumanities I do not have the capacity to fathom, but never had I encountered socially-sanctioned cannibalism.

I did not puke or boil over in outrage. That would be silly. I just put distance between me and that till I could speak without worrying about who might overhear. "I have seen enough. Let's get out of here."

Uncle Doj responded with a thin smile and lifted eyebrow.

"I have to relay this. I have to write it down. We may not survive this siege. They will. Word of what they are has to survive, too." He watched me closely. Was he wondering if the rest of us also enjoyed the occasional long-pig roast as well?

Probably.

This sort of thing might go some toward explaining our ambiguous reception in these parts.

Mogaba could not read. If it did not occur to him that the dark side of the Nar was no secret anymore I could leave word in my Annals, to be salvaged by Lady or the Old Man.

"They are all down there," Uncle said. "So we will return by a swifter path." By which he meant we would stroll through regular passageways just like we belonged there.

"What's that noise?" I asked.

Uncle gestured for silence. We stole forward.

We discovered a group of Taglian soldiers bricking up a sallyport we could have used to leave. Why were they doing that? That door could not be broken open from the outside. It still had Stormshadow's spells protecting it.

Uncle pulled me back, headed another direction. Obviously, he knew the citadel quite well. And I had no difficulty imagining him roaming around in there all the time, just for the hell of it. He seemed like that kind of guy.

66

"YOU LOOK LIKE SOMEBODY ATE YOUR FAVORITE PUPPY," GOBLIN TOLD ME. Cracks like that could be heard all the time now that there were no more dogs. There were just two sources of meat left. The Nar exploited both. We restricted ourselves to stupid crows.

I told Goblin and One-Eye what I had seen. Uncle Doj stood behind me, quietly disgruntled because I wanted to see my own people before I visited the Speaker. I was barely halfway through it when One-Eye interrupted. "You got to tell the whole Company this one, Kid." For once he was as serious as a spear through the gut.

And for once Goblin agreed with One-Eye without any big groan and moan about the unfairness of it all. "You need to get this word out exactly the way you want it known to everybody. There's going to be a lot of talk. You don't want anybody building it up worse than it is when they pass it along."

"Get them together, then. While I'm waiting I'm going to skim those Jaicuri books. There may be something else I need to tell them."

"May I join you?" Uncle Doj asked.

"No. Go tell the old man that I'll be there as soon as I can. This is family."

"As you will." He said something to Thai Dei, stalked away.

Bucket interrupted my reading. "Got them together, Murgen. All but Clete. He's off somewhere whoring and even his brothers don't know where to find him."

"All right."

"It something bad? You got that look."

"Yeah."

"It can get worse than it already is?"

"You're going to hear all about it in just a little bit."

In five minutes I got up in front of sixty men and told my tale, marvelling as I did that a band so frail and few could be so feared. More, I marvelled that there were so many of us when, hardly more than two years ago, there were just seven of us pretending to be the Black Company.

"You guys want to keep it down until I'm done?" The news had them excited in a grim way. "Listen up. That is the word. They're making human sacrifices and eating the corpses. But that ain't the whole story.

Ever since they joined us at Gea-Xle they've been hinting and even say-ing right out that us northern guys are heretics. That means they think the whole Company used to do things their way."

That started everybody talking and yelling.

I pounded a mason's hammer on a block of wood. "Shut up, you morons! It *ain't* the way the Company ever was. The Nar never kept any Annals. They would know that if they had. But they can't even read."

I could not be absolutely sure that human sacrifice was never a Com-pany rite. We were missing several early volumes of the Annals and I now suspected strongly that our earliest forebrethren did follow a dark and hungry god with breath so foul and cruel that even oral histories were enough to keep the native people terrified.

Most of the guys did not care about the implications. They were just angry because the Nar were going to make life harder for them.

I told them, "This is one more thing to make trouble between us and them. I want you all to realize that we might have to fight them before we get out of here.

"Tonight I'm bringing back some traditional business that we have let slide since Croaker got to be Captain. We are going to have regular readings from the Annals so you all know what you have become part of. This first reading is from the Book of Kette, this part probably set down by the Annalist Agrip when the Company was in service to the Paingod of Cho'n Delor." Our forebrethren endured a long and bitter siege then, though there had been a lot more of them to suffer. Additionally, I planned readings from books Croaker recorded on the Plain of Fear, when the Company lived underground for so long.

I dismissed the men to supper. "One-Eye. No more groaning when I announce a reading. All right? These guys didn't live through that stuff."

"Cho'n Delor was way before my time, too."

"Then you need to hear about it."

"Kid, I been hearing about it for two hundred years. Every damned Annalist that ever was wallowed in the horrors of Cho'n Delor. I wish I could get my hands on those guys who did the Book of Kette. You know Kette wasn't even the Annalist? He was the . . ."

"Goblin. Grab Otto and Hagop. I want a little confab with the oldest Old Crew."

We five put our heads together, conjured a little something for the meanness. Once we had a scheme I said, "I'll see what the Speaker thinks."

67

KY DAM LISTENED PATIENTLY, AS AN ADULT WILL TO A BRIGHT CHILD WITH an ingenious but impractical idea. He told me, "You are aware this could spark fighting?"

"Sure. But that's inevitable. Doj says Mogaba decided that at our meeting. Goblin and One-Eye agree." So did Hagop and Otto. None of us favored a get-along effort. "There are more of us than there are Nar." But their Taglians way outnumbered ours and there was no way to guess how the Taglians with either group would jump.

The old man turned to Hong Tray. A quizzical expression accentuated the lines at the corners of his eyes.

Ky Sahra knelt beside me, presenting tea. This was a step beyond anything previous. She met my wondering gaze. I don't think I slobbered.

Hong Tray observed without reaction. That made her far calmer than I was. She focused on her husband, nodded. He said, "There will be fighting. Soon. The Jaicuri will revolt."

That was not what I wanted to hear. I asked, "Will they bother your people or mine?" I should not have shoved in. I apologized immediately.

Ky Sahra poured more tea for me, before even she served her grandparents.

Ky Gota manifested like a demon conjured for its serrated tongue. She barked at her daughter in a harsh, lilting gale.

The old man looked up, said one word sharply. Hong Tray supported him with a complete sentence in what I would have to call a sharp whisper. It seemed she could speak no other way.

Ky Gota withdrew. There were well-defined limits and absolute hierarchy inside the Ky family.

I glanced at the beautiful woman. She met my eye again, rocked back and rose. Flushing.

Was something going on? They would not try to manipulate me, would they?

It would not work. No woman, not even this woman, was that special. And Ky Dam had seen enough of me to guess that about me.

If he wanted to manipulate me he would have better luck trading me the straight poop on why the hell everybody pissed blue when the Company got mentioned.

He and the old woman batted whispers back and forth in flurries.

Suddenly, he told me, "We will join you in this enterprise, Standard-bearer. Provisionally. Hong believes that fighting between the Jaicuri and the soldiers of the black men is imminent. It will be fierce but might not touch the rest of us. That would provide sufficient distraction. But I must insist that Doj has the option to end it if it risks calling unfriendly attention to our people."

"Excellent. Of course. Done. Though I would have tried it without you."

Ky Dam permitted himself a small smile, either at my enthusiasm or at the prospect of adding a little more misery to Mogaba's life.

After dark, assuming the riots got started, we were going to steal Mogaba's food stores.

68

IT STARTED LIKE A WELL-REHEARSED PLAY WHERE MOGABA'S CHARACTERS were desperate to please their audience. The rioting, that is. Uncle Doj and I formed work parties to take advantage. We got into the storage chambers without challenge, ten Old Crew and ten Nyueng Bao. We started dragging off sacks of rice and flour, sugar and beans. The riots were nasty from the start. They swamped the whole southern half of Dejagore. Every man Mogaba controlled was out there helping crush the rebellion. And every Jaicuri man and boy seemed to want to get at the Nar, even if they had to exterminate the whole First Legion to reach them.

My people went on the alert, established in strong positions, long before nightfall. Likewise the Nyueng Bao, who had no immediate trouble. We ambushed one mob. A shower of missiles from front, sides, and above swiftly changed their minds.

Mogaba's men had more problems. They were not ready. Worse, they were scattered, often in isolated work parties and patrols.

For a while everybody joked and cracked wise and speculated on Mogaba's first words after the fighting ended and he found his cellars plundered.

I ran into Bucket my second trip back. "Beans," I told him, dropping a huge sack. "The change of diet will do us good."

"It's real bloody out there this time, Murgen. Mogaba has asked for support twice. We told him we couldn't find you."

"Well, keep on not being able. Unless it looks like we would end up worse off if we didn't help."

"That's not likely. He has most of the weapons. His men have been throwing people off the wall by the hundreds, just anybody, whether or not they're rebelling, men, women and children."

"That's Mogaba's way. What about those fires?" There were a few. Whenever there is disorder somebody starts burning things down.

"They're burning themselves out."

"Everything is going fine, then. But keep an eye out."

I went back to my looting happy as the proverbial clam. This might be the end of Mogaba as a royal pain in the ass.

Uncle Doj caught me in the storage chamber later. "Some Taglian soldiers are abandoning their posts for the safety of the citadel. If we continue this raiding we will get caught."

"Yeah. If we don't get spotted Mogaba will blame it on natives who knew about the passageways." This raid was going to cost us our opportunity to spy on any more staff meetings.

It was worth it.

Would I feel the same way tomorrow, when Mogaba began looking for his stores? When I had a full belly?

"There is a small problem, Standardbearer," Uncle Doj said a while later. Each of us staggered under a last sack of rice. We were the last brigands out.

"What's that?"

"News of our success is sure to leak."

"Why? Only a few people know. It's in all their interests to stay clammed."

"Someone talked about what I showed you earlier."

"Huh?"

"The dark ceremonies. Someone talked. The rumors sparked tonight's riots."

"I don't believe that. They were too organized."

"There was an organized cadre, naturally, but this uprising was more widespread. It is also out of control."

"Whatever you say." He had spent his evening with me. He had had no chance to observe any riots.

Before he could respond Thai Dei popped out of the darkness. He gobbled away, becoming too animated for the space. If he killed my candle I was going to choke him. As soon as I found him. "What's happening?"

"The black men are trying to break open the north gate and flood the city."

"They're what?" That would take care of the riots, all right. But not even Mogaba would go that far. Would he?

Uncle Doj and I did our best to run carrying sacks of rice. I bet we looked silly.

69

OTTO. HAGOP. ONE-EYE. GOBLIN. GEEK. FREAK. BUCKET AND CANDLES. You guys come with me. The al-Khul company will help us. Wheezer went to get them. We'll go straight along the battlements. If the Nar get in the way we trample them. If they fight us, we kill them. That understood?"

Not even Goblin or One-Eye tried to lawyer. We were some of the people Mogaba meant to drown.

The Taglians arrived. They were Vehdna by religion and the best Taglians attached to the Company. They were reliable and almost friendly. Of six hundred who had come south from Taglios months ago only about sixty were left.

I explained what was happening, what I wanted to do about it and how they could help. They would overrun anyone trying to open the gate after Goblin and One-Eye softened them up. "Don't hurt anybody unless they just plain force you."

"Why not?" Candles demanded. "They're trying to hurt us."

"Mogaba is. These guys are just following orders. I'll bet you we don't find any Nar there when we get there. And I'll bet you that if they open the gate they get hurt as bad as anybody else. Mogaba doesn't need them anymore."

"Let's just do it," Goblin groused. "Or go back and catch a few beers."

I moved them out.

Maybe my blackouts gave me the gift of prophecy. There were no Nar at the North Gate. The fighting was so brief and desultory it almost did not take place. The Taglians working there fled. Damn! Mogaba would find out who foiled his latest nastiness. I told One-Eye, "This will mean no more pretending we're buddies."

"Yeah. Show me how to sneak into the citadel. I'll put a sleep spell on him, then leave pieces of him all over his crazy temple."

That did not sound like a bad idea.

We had no opportunity to implement it.

Somebody yelled up at me. I peered down into the gloom. It was

Uncle Doj. I had not included any Nyueng Bao in this. I had not seen any need to put them onto Mogaba's bad side, too.

"What?"

He shouted, "This was a diversion! The real flooding will start at . . ."

"Oh, shit! Yeah." Mogaba did know me well enough to anticipate that I might interfere. "Come on!" I snapped. "Everyone!" I hustled down to the street. "Where?" I demanded of Doj.

"East Gate."

Would Mogaba also anticipate me crossing town to spoil his game, amidst the Jaicuri uprising?

He might. He might hope my crew would get trapped and overrun, or badly cut up. There was no guessing what he thought anymore. He was crazy.

One-Eye and Goblin eased us past bands of both Jaicuri and Taglians. We skirmished with the Jaicuri twice, our numbers and sorcery telling quickly. The light of scattered fires set scary shadows dancing everywhere.

What a time for the Shadowmaster to send his monsters out to play.

We encountered barricades erected to protect the soldiers trying to open the gate. This time we faced Nar as well as Taglians. A lot of shouting went back and forth. Some of their Gunni Taglians tried to run away when our Vehdna Taglians convinced them that Mogaba was trying to drown everybody. The Nar cut down several would-be deserters. I told Goblin and One-Eye, "You break up whatever they're doing to open the gate. The rest of you, let's chase them off. Go for the Nar first."

An instant later an arrow found the eye of a Nar named Endibo. Another of the Nar speared the Geek, an incredibly handsome youngster who joined the Company while we were crossing the savannah north of Gea-Xle, several years earlier. One-Eye hung the uncomplimentary name on him. He wore it with pride, refusing to be called anything else.

For the first time in its history, insofar as I was aware, Company brother slew sworn brother in willful combat.

Geek's blood brother Freak slew the Nar responsible for Geek's death but I never learned the Nar's name so I cannot remember him here.

Most of the First Legion Taglians took off then. Many of the al-Khul soldiers did not want to fight, either, although those other Taglians were Gunni. Still, quickly, a genuine small battle had friend hacking at supposed friend.

I happened to glance back and notice that armed Jaicuri had begun to gather to watch. Uncle Doj faced them alone, poised in an odd but apparently relaxed ready stance, long sword vertical.

"Oh, shit!" Goblin shrieked. "Gods damn it! Look out!"

"What?"

"We're too late. It's going to go."

Something began to grind and groan like the hinges of the world breaking loose. The masonry blocking the gateway bulged inward.

The fighting stopped fast. Everybody faced the gate.

A sudden spear of water shot through the bulge.

Every man there took off, Nar and Black Company, Gunni and Vehdna Taglian, Jaicuri and lone Nyueng Bao running side by side, splitting up, heading whatever direction felt safest but everybody always getting away from that gate.

The masonry gave one final, mighty groan. The water roared triumphantly and charged inside.

70

THE WATER THUNDERED THROUGH THE GATE BUT THERE WAS NO EVIDENCE of it yet where I stood. I was in a good mood, considering. While passing the citadel I saw the Nar trying to shuffle their own kind inside without admitting any Taglians. I chuckled. Mogaba was going to bust a vein when he found the water coming in through his cellars.

I now understood why those soldiers had been bricking up. The flood was no spur of the moment plan. Mogaba must have nurtured the idea from the moment that Shadowspinner had used water to isolate Dejagore.

As we parted I told Uncle Doj, "Swim over and see me sometime." Fifteen minutes later I was discussing waterproofing. Our measures had begun the day we started our warrens but not in anticipation of anything like this. Enemies employing smoke and fire had been our real concern.

"Longo, you guys explored every part of those catacombs? They aren't open anywhere?" I was surprised that Stormshadow had not broken into them when she was building the citadel. Maybe she got her location advice from knowledgeable locals.

"I didn't see anything. They were plastered good way back when because they were below the level of the plain. But if you put seventy feet of water out there and thirty in the streets sooner or later it will find a way in. The best we can do really is fight a holding action."

"How about just sealing them off?"

"We could try. But I wouldn't bother until flooding became a threat. We close them off, spring a leak up here, we got no place for the water to drain."

I shrugged. "Is everything that could be damaged up high?" The guys started preparing for the worst back when the plain started flooding. We were not weighed down with a lot of possessions.

"We're all right. We can hold out for a long time yet. We might want to beef up our fortifications a little, though."

"Do what you can." Longo and his brothers always saw a little more that could be done.

71

MOGABA COUNTERATTACKED WHILE THE WATER WAS STILL JUST ANKLE DEEP and the rest of the city was just starting to panic. He used all his Taglians and encouraged cruel behavior. The slaughter was terrible.

I may never discover the truth about the attack on the Nyueng Bao. It has been said that the Taglian tribune Pal Subhir misunderstood his orders. Others, like me, believe Mogaba was responsible, maybe because he suspected the Nyueng Bao of looting his stores.

I know he knew some had been plundered. He found out right away because he sent soldiers down to see if any water was getting inside. By questioning a few Jaicuri prisoners he discovered that no locals were crowing about snatching a ton of food. Too, somebody in my outfit might have shot off his mouth again.

Whatever, Pal Subhir's cohort, with transfer replacements to bring it to full strength, attacked the Nyueng Bao. The tribune cannot testify. He died early. In fact, a lot of Taglians died during the attack. But reinforcements kept turning up, which is why I believe Mogaba engineered the massacre.

I knew nothing about it at first. I had located no listening posts outside our perimeter. I had no way of making sure my people would be secure out there. And where we bordered the Nyueng Bao community there was no reason to doubt that we would receive ample warning.

Thai Dei was, as always, nearby. I had gone to the top of an enfilading tower to stare at the nighted hills and brood. Would help ever come? Lately no news at all came in from outside.

Plenty of people wanted to leave. I could hear some of them out there now, willing to take their chances with the Shadowmaster. Fickle folk. A little hunger and stress and they forgot all about liberty.

"What is that?" Thai Dei astonished me by asking a whole question. I was amazed. I looked where he pointed.

"Looks like a fire."

"That is near grandfather's house. I must go."

More curious than suspicious, I said, "I'll go with you."

He started to argue, shrugged, told me. "Do not suffer any spells. I cannot care for you."

So the Nyueng Bao knew about my blackouts. And apparently suspected they were epileptic. Interesting.

Thai Dei surely learned plenty just standing around with his ears flapping and his jaw tight shut. My guys hardly noticed him anymore.

Nowhere was the water yet deeper than halfway to my knees. But it grabbed my feet when I tried to run. And Thai Dei was in a hurry. He was sure something was wrong. And he was correct.

We ran through that alley where I had stumbled before and had plunged into hell. For a second I thought I had run from Dejagore into another nightmare.

Taglian soldiers were dragging Nyueng Bao women and children and old people out of the buildings and throwing them to soldiers in the street. Those soldiers hacked and slashed. Their faces were distorted with the horror of their actions but they were out of control, far past the point where they could stop. The flicker of firelight made everything seem more hellish and surreal.

I had seen this before. I had seen my own brothers this way, a few times, back in the north. The blood smell takes control and kills the mind and deadens the soul and there is nothing human left.

Thai Dei howled a tortured cry and flung himself toward the building the Ky family occupied, sword wheeling overhead. The place showed no obvious signs of having been invaded. I followed him, my own blade bare, unsure why, though I thought fleetingly of the woman Sahra. Probably my actions were as thoughtless as those of the Taglians.

Taglians got in our way. Thai Dei engaged in some sort of bobbing, weaving dance. Two soldiers fell, their throats spurting. I beat another around with my sword, leaving him a collection of bruises and a lesson about dueling a guy a foot taller and fifty pounds heavier.

Then there were Taglians everywhere, most paying no attention to us. I did not have much trouble defending myself. Those people were smaller and weaker and had a much shorter reach. And what I managed by brute power Thai Dei accomplished through maneuver. Hardly anyone was interested in us by the time we reached the Speaker's door.

I had guessed wrong before. Five or six Taglians had gotten inside. They just were not going to leave again. Not walking.

Thai Dei barked something in Nyueng Bao. A voice replied. I took a wild swing at one last particularly stupid Taglian, spending the rest of the edge of my blade on his helmet. Then I shoved the door shut and barred it. And looked around for something to pile against it. Unfortunately, the Kys were so poor their best furniture consisted of ragged reed mats.

A lamp's flame rose, then another and another. For the first time I saw the entire room the Kys occupied. I saw the mauled corpses of several invaders. They had become focused on exploiting the beautiful woman before they finished everyone else.

Ky Gota was still mutilating the Taglian corpses.

But not all the corpses were Taglian. Not even the majority were Taglian. Only a small percentage were Taglian.

Sahra was holding her children to her chest but neither would ever know fear again. Sahra's eyes were empty.

Thai Dei made a sound like a kitten's whimper. He threw himself onto a woman. The woman lay face downward upon two little ones she had attempted to shield with her body. Her effort had not been in vain. The youngest, less than a year old, was crying.

No Taglians seemed inclined to try the door. I dropped to my knees where I had sat talking to the Speaker so often. It appeared he and Hong Tray had watched death arrive and had engaged it in their places of honor. The old man was stretched out with his head and shoulders in Hong Tray's lap but his lower body remained almost as it had been when he was seated. His wife slumped forward over him.

The racket outside picked up. "Thai Dei!" I yelled. "Get your ass pulled together, man."

What? The old woman was still breathing, making a raspy, bubbly sound. Gently, I lifted her.

She was alive and even aware. Her eyes unglazed. She seemed unsurprised to see me. She smiled. She managed to whisper despite the blood in her throat. "Don't waste time on me. Take Sahra. Take the children." Her wound was a sword thrust that had gone in outside her right breast and downward through her lung. At her age it was a miracle she had lived this long.

She smiled again, whispered, "Be good to her, Standardbearer."

"I will," I promised, not understanding what she meant.

Hong Tray managed a wink and a wince of pain. She leaned forward onto Ky Dam again.

The racket outside increased again. "Thai Dei!" I leapt over the bodies, flung a foot that glanced off Thai Dei's behind. "If you don't get your ass up and get organized we're not going to help anybody." I spotted a couple more kids cowering in the back. One of them had lighted the lamps. Other than Sahra and her mother no adults appeared to have survived. "Sahra!" I snapped. "Get up!" I slapped her. "Round up those kids back there." They were too terrified to trust me even if they knew me. I was still an outsider.

A little yelling was all Thai Dei and his sister needed. Their universe suddenly regained structure and direction, though they could not see its sense. They just needed somebody to get them started.

We found only one more living child and no more surviving adults.

"Thai Dei. Can you keep these kids together if we make a run for the alley?" The Taglians would cease to be a problem if we made it that far. In there one man could hold off a horde till help arrived.

He shook his head. "They are too frightened and too badly hurt."

I was afraid of that. "Then we'll carry them. Can you settle your mother down? She'll need to help. Sahra. Take the baby. I'll carry the girl. On my back. I want my hands free. Tell her to hang on tight but to keep her hands out of my face. If she don't think she can do that let me know now. We'll tie her wrists together."

Sahra nodded. She was past her hysteria. She knelt beside Hong Tray, held the old woman for a moment, then removed her jade bracelet. With a deep sigh and evident reluctance, she slipped the bracelet onto her own left wrist. Then she turned to Ky Gota and began trying to calm her.

Thai Dei talked to the children, translating my instructions. I realized that Sahra never spoke at all, not even in a whisper.

The girl I was going to carry was about six years old. And she did not want to go.

"Tie her on, then, damn it!" I snapped. I had begun to shake. I did not know how much longer I would retain full control. "We're running out of time."

Only the baby was unhurt. A boy of about four looked like he would not make it. He for sure would not if I did not get him to One-Eye in a hurry.

Water splashed and a man shrieked right outside. A body slammed against the door, which creaked and gave a little. Sahra swatted the girl to calm her, fitted her onto my back. I asked, "How about your mother?"

Never mind. The Troll was with us now. She had a two-year-old of indeterminate sex riding her left hip and the business end of a broken spear clutched in her right hand. She was ready for Taglians.

Getting ready actually took less time than it requires to tell it.

Sahra carried the baby. Thai Dei tied the wounded boy onto his back, kept his sword in hand. He and I went to the door. I peeked through cracks between the mutilated timbers. A Taglian soldier lurched past outside. I asked, "You first? Or me? One to lead, one as rearguard."

"Me. From this day forward."

What?

"Back!" I snapped. But he glimpsed the hurtling shape at the same time. He slid to the right as I moved to the left of the doorway. We were out of the way when the door blew inward. We jumped at the intruder, recognized him barely in time.

"Uncle Doj?"

He was a lucky man. The weight of the children we carried had slowed us just enough to allow us time to see who had blown in.

"Go," I told Thai Dei. We did not need to hold a conference.

Thai Dei encountered a pair of Taglians immediately. I jumped out and drove one away. Ky Gota wobbled out behind us. She stuck the tip of her spearhead into the throat of the nearest Taglian. Then she settled the child more comfortably on her hip, turned on the other soldier.

A white crow swooped past, laughing like a troop of monkeys.

The surviving Taglian was not a foolish young man. He headed for the nearest gang of his countrymen.

"Go! Go!" I barked at Thai Dei. "Gota. Sahra. Follow Thai Dei. Uncle! Where are you? We're gonna leave your ass here."

Uncle Doj stepped outside as the Taglian pointed us out to his comrades. "Take the child away, Standardbearer. Ash Wand will be your shield."

He put on an amazing display—though I glimpsed only a few furious moments. That funny little wide man took on the whole mob of Taglians and killed six of them in about as many seconds. The rest took off.

Then we splashed into the alley. We reached safety moments later. In minutes One-Eye was working on the wounded children, albeit not cheerfully. And I was deploying some of the Old Crew, with Goblin, for a limited counterattack.

72

THAT NIGHT WAS THE FINAL WATERSHED. THERE WAS NEVER ANY PRETENSE of friendship with Mogaba again. I had no doubts myself that he would have come after us if the "mistaken" attack on the Nyueng Bao had been a success.

Fighting continued until the water got too deep.

Despite insistence by One-Eye and others that protecting the Nyueng Bao was not our mission I did salvage a third of the pilgrims, about six hundred people. The cost of the attack to Mogaba was bitter. The following morning most of the remaining Taglians found themselves in positions where they had to commit for or against Mogaba.

The Taglians who had been with us from the beginning stuck with us. So did those who had deserted to join us. More came over from Mogaba's side now but not a tenth as many as I expected. Tell the truth, I was disappointed. But Mogaba could make a hell of a speech to the troops when he wanted.

"It's that old-time curse again," Goblin told me. "Even now they're more afraid of yesterday than they are of now."

And the water kept rising.

I took the Nyueng Bao down into our warrens. Uncle Doj was amazed. "We never suspected."

"Good. Then neither do our enemies, whose brilliance is eclipsed by yours." I brought the Old Crew inside, too. We packed people in as comfortably as we could. The warrens were quite spacious for sixty men. Adding six hundred Nyueng Bao did cramp things some.

We had to learn to recognize one another, too. My men had been trained to strike instantly at any unfamiliar face encountered underground.

I went back outside after darkness fell. Thai Dei and Uncle Doj dogged me. I assembled the Taglian officers who had attached themselves to the Old Crew. I told them, "I believe that we have done all we can here. I believe it is time to begin evacuating everyone who wants to get out of this hellhole." I did not know why but was convinced that not much work would be required to evade or outwit the Shadowlander pickets ashore. "I will send one of my wizards to cover you."

They did not buy it. One captain wondered aloud if I intended to drive them into slavery so I could make it easier to feed my own men.

I had not thought this through, had not considered possible difficulties. I had forgotten that many of these men had attached themselves to us only because they believed that that was their best shot at staying alive. "Never mind. If you guys want to stay and die with us we'll be happy to have you. I was just trying to release you from your soldier's oaths so you would have *some* chance."

After dark, too, we let the Nyueng Bao men go back home to look for salvage and survivors and stores. They did not find much. Mogaba's soldiers had been thorough in their own search and the water had risen to cover everything.

Mogaba's men, using makeshift boats and rafts, began attacking Jaicuri-occupied buildings one by one, harvesting stores forced out of hiding by the rising water.

Mogaba had drowned his own supplies.

73

WHEN I WAS SURE NOBODY WOULD NOTICE I PULLED ALL MY BROTHERS inside. We bolted up and locked up and left Dejagore to its misery. We took the Nyueng Bao survivors with us. Excepting a few men who kept watch from lookouts accessible only from inside we withdrew into the deepest, most hidden parts of the warrens, behind booby traps and secret doors and a web of confusion spells scattered by Goblin and One-Eye, who left only the occasional flicker of a doppelganger to mark our passing.

I started out sharing my quarters with eight guests. After just a few hours I told Uncle Doj, "Let's you and me take a walk."

With all those Nyueng Bao down there the air was stuffy and getting riper fast. Light was provided by candles so scattered you could get lost trekking from one to the next.

Uncle Doj was close to being spooked. "I hate it, too," I told him. "It keeps me riding the edge of a scream. But we'll manage. We lived this way for years once."

"No one can live like this. Not for long."

"The Company did, though. It was a terrible place. It was called the Plain of Fear, with good reason. It was filled with weird creatures and every one of them would kill you in a blink. We were hunted constantly by armies led by wizards way worse than Shadowspinner. But we gutted it out. And we came through it. Right here in these tunnels you have five survivors who can tell you about it."

The light was too bad to read him, though that was difficult in broad daylight. I told him, "I'm going to go crazy if all of you stay with me. I need room. Nobody can get around without stepping on somebody right now."

"I understand. But I do not know how to help."

"We have empty rooms. Thai Dei and his baby can have one. You could. Sahra could share one with her mother."

He smiled. "You are open and honest but pay too little attention to Nyueng Bao ways. Many things happened the night you helped Thai Dei rescue this family."

I snorted. "Some rescue."

"You saved all who could be saved."

"What a good boy am I."

"You had neither an obligation nor any cause of honor." In actuality he used honor and obligation in lieu of Nyueng Bao concepts of similar but not identical meaning which include overtones of free-will participation in a divine machination.

"I did what seemed like the right thing."

"Indeed. Without any appeal or obligation. Which caused your current predicament."

"I must be missing something."

"Because you are not Nyueng Bao. Thai Dei will not leave you now. He is the oldest male. He owes you six lives. His baby will not leave him. Sahra will not leave because she must remain under her brother's protection until she marries. And, as you can see, she may be a while getting through the horror. In this city, upon this pilgrimage she never wanted to make, she has lost everything that ever meant anything to her. Except her mother."

"A man might almost think the gods had it in for her," I said, then hoped that did not sound too much like a wisecrack.

"One might. Standardbearer, the only good thing she recalls about that hellnight is you. She will cling to you the way a desperate swimmer will cling to a rock in a rushing stream."

It was time to be careful. A big part of me wished her clinging was more than metaphorical. "How about Ky Gota and those other kids?"

"The children can be adopted into the families of their mothers. Gota, surely, can move." Doj continued muttering under his breath, which was uncharacteristic. Sounded like something about wanting to move her a couple thousand miles. "Though she will not take it well."

"Don't tell me you're less than enchanted with Ky Gota too?"

"No one is enchanted with that ill-tempered lizard."

"And I once thought that you two were married."

He stopped cold, stunned. "You're mad!"

"I changed my mind, didn't I?"

"Hong Tray, old witch, what hast thou wished upon me?"

"What?"

"Talking to myself, Standardbearer. Engaging in the debate I cannot lose. That woman, Hong Tray, my mother's cousin, was a witch. She could see into the future sometimes and if what she saw failed to please her she wanted it changed. And she had some strange ideas about that."

"I trust you know what you're talking about."

He did not get it. "Not entirely. The witch toyed with all our destinies but never explained. Perhaps she was blind to her own fate."

I let myself be distracted. "What will your people do now?"

"We will survive, Standardbearer. Like you Soldiers of Darkness, that is what we do."

"If you really think you owe me for stumbling in there with Thai Dei, tell me what that means. Soldiers of Darkness. Stone Soldier. Bone Warrior. What do they mean?"

"One might almost accept your protestations."

"Look at it this way. If I do know what you're talking about you have nothing to lose by telling me what I already know."

In that light it was hard to tell but I believe Uncle Doj smiled again. For the second time in one day. "Clever," he said. And did not explain a thing.

74

UNCLE DOJ RELIEVED ME OF MOST OF MY GUESTS. I ENDED UP SHARING QUARTERS with Thai Dei and his son To Tan, plus Sahra. Sahra helped with the baby and struggled to put together meals, though the Company kitchen could serve everyone in the warrens. She needed to stay busy. Thai Dei followed me almost everywhere. Both he and Sahra were lethargic and uncommunicative and added up to about half a human being between them.

I began to worry. They belonged to a hardy people accustomed to surviving cruel disasters. They should show some signs of recovery.

I assembled the brains of the outfit: Cletus, Loftus, Longinus, Goblin and One-Eye, Otto and Hagop. "I got some questions, troops."

"He got to be here?" Goblin meant Thai Dei.

"He's all right. Ignore him."

"What kind of questions?" One-Eye demanded.

"So far we haven't had any major health problems in the Company. But there's cholera and typhoid out there, not to mention plenty of the old-fashioned drizzling shits. We all right?"

Goblin muttered something and passed gas loudly.

"Barbarian," One-Eye sneered. "We're all right because we follow Croaker's health rules like they was religious laws. Only we can't make the rules stick much longer. We're almost out of fuel. And these Nyueng Bao. They don't like to bother boiling water and keeping clean and not shitting where they live. We got them going along right now but it ain't going to last."

"It's been overcast and nasty for a few days, I hear. Are we collecting any rainwater?"

"Plenty for us," Loftus told me. "But not enough for us and them, let alone getting any put back into the cisterns."

"I was afraid of that. About the fuel, I mean. You guys know any way to fix rice or beans so you can digest them without cooking them?"

Nobody knew. Longinus suggested, "Maybe soaking them a long time in water might help. My mother did that."

"Damn. I really want us to get through this. But how?"

Goblin seemed to develop a small secret smile at that. Like he had a definite idea. He exchanged glances with One-Eye.

"You guys got something?"

"Not yet," Goblin told me. "There's an experiment we still have to try."

"Get on with it."

"After the meeting. We need you to help."

"Wonderful. All right. Can anyone tell me what the rest of the city thinks about our disappearance?"

Hagop coughed, clearing his throat. He did not say much ordinarily so everybody paused to listen. "I been doing watches in the lookouts. Sometimes you can hear talk. I don't think we done our reputation any good. Also, I don't think we fooled anybody. They don't talk about us much but nobody figures we just cut out. They think we found some way to dig a hole and fill it up with wine, women and food and pulled it in after us and we ain't coming back out again till the rest of them are good and dead."

"Guys, I tried to get the wine, women and banquets but all I could come up with was the hole."

Out of nowhere, Otto said, "The water's going down."

"What?"

"It is, Murgen. It's down five feet already."

"Would flooding the city make that much difference? No? Why's that?"

Goblin and One-Eye exchanged significant looks.

"What?" I demanded.

"After we do our experiment."

"All right. The rest of you guys. You know the problems. Go see if there's anything we can do about them."

75

"TALK TO ME," I TOLD THE RUNT WIZARDS.

Goblin said, "We think something was done to you when you were out there." He jerked his head shoreward.

"What? Get serious! I . . ."

"We are. You were gone a long time. And you changed. How many disappearing spells have you had since you got back?"

I gave it an honest think. "Only one. Maybe. When I was kidnapped. I don't remember anything about it. I'm sure they drugged me. I was drinking tea with the Speaker, then I was in that street where you found me. I have no idea how I got there. I have vague recollections of smelling smoke and going out a door which put me somewhere that I did not expect to be when I got to the other side. I vaguely remember thinking something about being in the house of pain."

"They tortured you."

"They did." I still had the nicks and bruises to prove it. I had no idea what I might have been asked, if anything. I did suspect that Sindhu's pals were behind my abduction and the attempt on Mogaba.

If so, their life sure took an unpleasant turn when the Black Company found them.

"We've been watching you," Goblin said. "And you have been behaving pretty strange sometimes. What we want to do is put you to sleep and see if we can't reach the part of you that was there when things happened."

"I don't get you."

"You don't have to. You just have to cooperate."

"You're sure?"

"We're sure."

He did not sound sure.

I awakened on my own pallet. Not refreshed. Someone was wiping my hot face with a cold, wet cloth. I opened my eyes. In the light of one tiny candle Sahra looked more lovely than ever. She looked better than imagination. She continued to wipe my face.

I had another hangover-type headache. What had they done? I ought at least to get the enjoyment that came before the pain.

To Tan began to fuss. He slept in a basket of evil-smelling rags beneath my writing table. I reached over and took his hand. He stopped crying, content to have human contact. He did not cry for his mother much anymore.

I raised my other hand to take Sahra's. She pushed it back gently. She never spoke. I never did hear her speak, not even to her own children.

I looked around. Thai Dei was gone. Anymore it seemed I had a better chance of shaking my shadow. Thai Dei was there even in the dark.

I started to sit up. Sahra held me down with two fingers. I was too weak to do anything. And my head felt like it doubled in size just rising that foot.

Sahra offered me a hand-carved wooden cup filled with something that smelled so foul my eyes watered. Nyueng Bao swamp medicine. I drank. It tasted worse than it smelled.

She continued to mop my face. I shivered and shook. The pain went away. I began to relax, to feel both energetic and positive. That was good stuff. Maybe they made it smell and taste bad so people would not take it all the time.

We stared at one another a long time, saying nothing but reaching a decision our conscious minds did not entirely recognize at the moment. Hong Tray drifted across my thoughts with a smile and an admonition.

This time I managed a smile when I sat up. Unchallenged. "I have work to do."

Sahra shook her head. She fished under the table for To Tan, dug him out of his basket. He was in desperate need of changing. Sahra tugged my finger.

"I haven't done this in twenty years." Not since I was a kid myself and had baby brothers and sisters and cousins to change. "Stop wiggling, you little turd. You ought to know the drill by now." To Tan looked back at me with serious big eyes, not understanding my words but catching my tone.

We got him cleaned up and clothed again, in rags that would have embarrassed a beggar. I told Sahra, "I'll go kill somebody, get him something better to wear."

She laid a hand lightly on my forearm, restraining me.

"That was a joke, hon. You hang around with me, you're going to hear some dark stuff. I don't mean it literally. I'm going to work now."

I moved into the passageway slowly, my legs watery. Sahra followed, To Tan straddling her left hip. We ran into Bucket right away, looking groggy as he headed for his own pallet. I asked, "You seen Goblin and One-Eye?"

"They went upstairs with their magic junk. To the big lookout."

"Thanks."

Before we walked five feet, Bucket called, "Longo tell you the water is coming up in the catacombs?"

I sighed and shook my head, listened to the half-hearted rumble of my stomach, wondered if anybody had found a way to get some food cooked, wound my way through the maze to the ladders that would take me up to Goblin and One-Eye.

The light of day might do me good. If I had the strength to climb that far. I had not seen the sun for a long time.

76

I WOULD NOT SEE THE SUN FOR A WHILE LONGER.

Sahra handed To Tan up through the trapdoor. He was asleep again. I guess you do sleep a lot when you are a baby starving to death.

It was daytime but a driving rain was falling. Hagop sat astride a chair turned backwards, forearms on the chair's back, staring into the rain morosely. "How long has this been going on?" I asked.

"Day or three."

"We getting any fresh water out of it?"

"About as much as we can being as we're hiding out."

"What're those two doing?" Goblin and One-Eye were on the floor in the middle of the room, crosslegged, farthest from the moisture blowing inside. They did not look up.

"Wizard stuff. Don't bother them. They'll bite your leg off."

One-Eye grumbled, "And somebody's gonna lose a set of ears if he don't stop yakking."

Hagop and I each spent one of our diminishing supply of single-finger salutes. One-Eye did not acknowledge the accolade.

The lookout had a window facing each direction. I went to the biggest.

This rain was not what we called a gullywasher back home but it was strong and steady. I could barely sense the vague loom of the surrounding hills. Nearer at hand I could make out the surface of the water. It was down despite the rain. It was a grey that spoke of sickness.

I saw a Jaicuri raft out there, so loaded with people that it was awash. Men using short boards as paddles labored carefully to drive it toward shore.

I made the rounds of the other windows, studied the city. I was pleased to see our Taglians at their posts the way they had been taught.

"They've been doing it by the numbers," Hagop agreed. "And that gets them left alone."

"By Mogaba?"

"By everybody. The fighting is almost constant."

The streets and alleys were now canals. I saw bodies floating everywhere. The stench was overwhelming. The water level, though, was lower than I had expected. I could see the citadel from the east window. There were Nar up top there, ignoring the weather. They moved around the parapet, studying our part of town.

Hagop noticed me watching them. "They're worried about us. They think we might come sort them out sometime."

"Sure we will."

"They're superstitious about guys like Goblin and One-Eye."

"Which shows you how dangerous a little ignorance can be."

"I heard that," One-Eye grumbled. He and Goblin could have been playing some obscure dice game for all I could tell. I liked it better when they conjured big lights that went around smashing things and burning them up. Destruction I can understand.

Sahra seemed tired of lugging To Tan so I took him. She offered a grateful smile. It lit up the lookout.

One-Eye and Goblin paused to exchange glances amongst themselves and with Hagop.

"What are you guys doing?" I demanded.

"We found out we were right."

"Yeah? That might be a first. You were right about what?"

"About your head having been tampered with."

I shuddered to a sudden chill. That is not something anyone welcomes. "Who did it? How?"

"How we haven't been able to figure out for sure. It might have been managed several ways. Who and what are more interesting, anyway."

"So give."

"Who was Lady. And *what* was knowledge of the fact that she is out there."

"Excuse me?"

"It's a little hard to tell from here, especially when we got tourists and their girlfriends traipsing through the workplace, but it looks like Lady and the Taglians are in charge out there. Their camp is on the other side of the hills, up the north road. The southerners we see patrolling are auxiliaries who report back to Lady."

"Run through that again."

Goblin did so.

I said, "You guys go ahead. I'm just going to sit over here in the corner and think."

77

UNCLE DOJ AND THAI DEI WERE BACK FROM WHEREVER THEY HAD GONE. They scowled at Sahra and me when we returned but neither said a word. Hong Tray still had her hold on the Kys. Thai Dei took his son. The little guy brightened immediately.

Uncle Doj told me, "My people are not mushrooms, Standardbearer. They cannot endure this much longer. You Stone Soldiers have been generous to a fault and have given no provocation but even so there will be trouble eventually. A wounded animal will strike out at even the most loving master."

"We'll be out of here sooner than I planned." I was not in a good mood. I wanted to drag Lady across my lap and paddle her. "I've already given orders to start the process."

"You sound angry."

"I am angry." Lady used me in a political game with Mogaba with never a thought for the Company's welfare. She was no more real Company than he was.

Longo leaned in the doorway. "You get the word about the catacombs flooding, Murgen?"

"Bucket told me. How soon is it going to be a problem?"

"Four or five days. Maybe more. Unless the leak gets a lot worse."

"We'll be gone. Your brothers and One-Eye are up in the big lookout. Go find out what's up."

Longo shrugged and went, grumbling about the climb.

I asked, "Who speaks for the Nyueng Bao now?"

"We have not yet chosen," Uncle Doj replied.

"Could you? Quickly? A Taglian general name of Lanore Bonharj—the guy who's in charge of the freed slaves and friendly Taglians and Jaicuri right now—is going to come by. We'll need somebody Nyueng Bao to join us in planning our evacuation." He started to say something. I rolled on. "It seems that the Shadowmaster isn't a problem anymore, only nobody bothered to tell *us*. Our own so-called friends have been jobbing us for political reasons. We could leave any time—I don't know for how long now."

I put all the blame for our ignorance on Goblin and One-Eye. You can blame a wizard for anything and people will believe you.

Sahra tried to make a meal from what we had. I touched her hand as she passed. She smiled. I told her, "This should be the last time we'll need to do this."

I hoped.

I was wrong.

Everything takes time.

Lanore Bonharj followed me down into the warrens. He was both amazed and appalled. He was high-caste Gunni. It was bad up top but this squalor down below was beyond his imagination. We talked. Uncle Doj spoke for the Nyueng Bao. Bargains were struck, agreements agreed, plans quickly laid. Preparations began in earnest.

78

IN THE DARK OF NIGHT, IN THE RAIN, THE BLACK COMPANY STOLE FORTH, crossed a rickety makeshift bridge to stairs to the battlements, joined the Taglians of the al-Khul company. With Goblin at the point we sneaked along the wall, seized the North Gate and barbican from the Nar and their Taglians. Goblin's sleep spell made that easy. Nobody got hurt. In our gang.

Before the last body splashed into the water outside Goblin and I and the Company cadre headed back to grab the West Gate and its barbican.

With the gates in our hands we could proceed unobserved by Mogaba's men.

Loftus and his brothers got to work inside the central of the three towers between the gates. While the wall itself was stone with a rubble fill the towers were not solid. They had to be hollow to allow crossbowmen inside to pepper the wall faces with missiles. The boys got to work opening a hole to the outside from the floor nearest the present water level.

The Nyueng Bao brought our remaining food stores to the surface. The women would use the last of the Taglians' fuel to cook for everyone. I wanted everybody to build strength. A lot of us were little more than stick figures now.

When the sun rose next morning the Nar atop the citadel saw nothing they had not seen the day before, except less rain. They got no signals from the north or west barbicans but did not seem concerned.

"Aren't many crows around anymore," Goblin noted as daylight began to fade.

"Maybe we ate them all."

Night returned. Everybody went back to work. The hammering and pounding and the collapse of masonry into water had to be audible all over town but nobody could see what we were doing and nothing was evident when the sun rose except that several derelict buildings were missing.

The lake continued its slow fall. The weather continued damp.

The rafts the carpenters were building floated outside, against the wall. Everything capable of offering flotation went into their construction. Even the occasional empty beer barrel.

That afternoon we acquired some useful lumber when Mogaba sent three rafts to the North Gate to find out why his signals were not being answered.

We could not keep the ambush from being seen from the citadel. Mogaba wasted no more men or materials.

Loftus and his brothers said the best raft would be built long and thin so more people could paddle against less front-end water resistance. Working in three feet of water the three brothers and a few skilled Taglians assembled one raft after another, each able to carry ten or more adults. By using everything they could find they built forty-one craft. They guessed that fleet could carry seven hundred people, more than five hundred of whom could be put ashore while the rest brought the rafts back, reloaded them and got under way again before dawn.

So about twelve hundred could get away overnight. Enough to establish a modestly solid beachhead on what we did not know for certain would be a friendly shore.

Problem. The numbers we needed to move undetected were greater than I had guessed. I had my forty Old Crew, more than six hundred Nyueng Bao, and a whole lot more Taglians, freed slaves and Jaicuri volunteers than I had thought.

Lanore Bonharj wanted to move nearly a thousand men and dependents. There was no way to get everyone out in one night.

"Here's what you do," One-Eye said. "You only take one load across the first night. Draw lots for the spots. That way we don't get people climbing over each other and nobody getting out in the panic. Figure the draw so a representative percentage goes from each group. Then nobody bitches. Dump the five hundred and some with orders to build a camp. Have the rafts come back and tie up, then finish up with two trips next night."

"The man is a genius," I said. "You or Goblin will have to go, just in case."

"Shouldn't be necessary."

"Why not?"

"Things aren't that dangerous anymore."

"Then we won't need to dig in. We can send the Nyueng Bao and dependents out first."

"That will go down great."

"Women and children and old people? That will work. I'll bet you. Include the Taglians' dependents. Hold up on the Jaicuri, though, or we'll have the whole damned city lining up. We figure how many that all is, then draw lots for the rest of the positions."

It worked out that thirty Taglians, five Black Company guys and fifteen Nyueng Bao warriors could be sent with the first group. We would have fifty swords on the beach.

Uncle Doj grumbled about the scheme because for one night he would not be able to keep his whole tribe together. "Clever, Soldier of Darkness." We were back to that? "You hold us warriors hostage."

"You want to go, go. There are more of you than there are of us. Take the rafts."

He scowled, his hand called.

"It's one night, Unc. And fifteen warriors will go with them. They'll be drawn by lot so one of them might even be you."

One-Eye and Goblin did not want to leave. "I'm not going over tonight," One-Eye told me.

"Me too neither," Goblin insisted.

They had that weasel look they get when they are dealing off the bottom of the deck. "Why not?" They looked like they could use a straight man.

"It ain't safe out there," One-Eye told me, after Goblin failed to convince me of his altruistic desire to protect the world by blunting Mogaba's wickedness. "That bitch from Juniper. Lisa Daele Bowalk. She's laying for us out there."

"Who?" I heard no bells ringing.

"Lisa Bowalk. From Juniper. Nasty little bitch. Ran with Marron Shed. The corpse runner. Shifter took her as his apprentice after the Company went on the run. She was there when we skragged Shifter. The Old Man let her get away. Well, she's out there, prowling, waiting for a chance to get even. She's already tried a couple times."

"And you never bothered to tell me?" A healthy dose of skepticism is in order any time One-Eye waxes passionate on any subject.

"Wasn't no problem till now."

Why argue? The truth seemed evident. Those two had plunder stashed and did not want to leave it unguarded. Nor did either want the other left with it alone. I told them, "Take your chances with the rest of us."

* * *

Bonharj and Uncle Doj, Goblin and One-Eye all glowered at me. I told them, "I shouldn't have to take a turn."

One-Eye chuckled. "Maybe not. But *you* said we *all* had to take our chances."

I had not yet drawn. Trouble was, the outcome was not in doubt. There was only one stone left in the jar. Five black pebbles had been allocated to the Company and only four had been drawn.

I would go to the mainland with the first wave.

Why did my bitty buddies look so smug? "Pick your rock and pack your shit," Goblin said. They would not have rigged the draw, would they? Nah. Not those two. Paragons of virtue, they were.

"Anybody want to buy this?" I held up the expected black pebble.

"Stuff it, Kid," One-Eye said. "We'll manage without you. Again. What could go wrong in one day, anyway?"

"With you guys in charge?" It did not seem right, me going ashore before the last Black Company brother was out of the city.

"Just get your stuff together and go," Goblin snapped again. "It'll be dark in an hour."

It was still drizzling. Darkness would come early, though not early enough to complete two crossings and get the rafts back unseen. Damn it.

Sahra was burdened down with odds and ends and six pounds of rice and beans. I carried a pack containing a Nyueng Bao tent, blankets, various clutter useful in the field, plus I had To Tan perched on my hip. That kid was the least troublesome baby I ever saw.

Thai Dei had not drawn a black stone.

I meant to enjoy his absence.

We climbed out of the warren, descended steps, crossed to the wall, climbed up, walked the battlements, descended inside the middle tower. And that was about as much exercise as I wanted.

On my raft we were all Nyueng Bao except me and Red Rudy. The Nyueng Bao were patient about waiting their turns. The guys in the tower, operating by feeble lamplight, were patient too. Morale was good.

"Careful," Clete said as I stepped aboard. I accepted children as he started handing them across. "I picked you a good one, boss, but it will lean over if you don't keep the weight balanced. Ma'am." He helped Sahra. She acknowledged his courtesy with a dazzling smile.

"Thanks, Clete. See you tomorrow night."

"Right. Round up some cattle and dancing girls."

"I'll check around."

"Kneel down. You got to keep the center of gravity low so the damned thing don't tip."

I glanced around. We were ready to go.

Six Nyueng Bao men were aboard. They would paddle over. Five would bring the raft back. Other than them, Rudy and I and one gimp Nyueng Bao about fifty were the only adult males aboard. There were fifteen or sixteen kids and half as many women. We were crowded but Nyueng Bao make a light load. I volunteered to help paddle but the men on the job lost their capacity to understand Taglian.

Rudy said, "If they want to be dicks and bust their nuts, no sweat off our asses."

"You're right. But keep it down. We're doing a sneak here."

It turned out the Nyueng Bao were skilled boatmen. Which should have been no surprise considering their origins.

They remained as quiet as falling feathers. And made rapid headway. The rafts immediately ahead had Taglian paddlers who not only made a lot of noise, they were slow. With just a whispered word my paddlers swung right and began passing.

It was not much of a sneak, overall. Paddles splashed. People bumped, grunted, banged around and occasionally managed to collide with other rafts. But those were noises that came off the water every night and tonight the drizzle was deadening some of the racket. And, of course, we were headed straight away from the city. The light inside the opened tower served as a navigational beacon.

My paddle men maybe did not keep the best watch on the light. We drifted way off line and lost it altogether.

Somebody hissed.

Paddles stopped dipping. Even the murmur of the little ones stilled as mothers placed hands over their mouths or pulled lips to teats.

I heard nothing.

We waited.

Sahra rested her hand lightly upon my arm, sharing reassurance.

Then I heard the clumsy paddling. Somebody was farther off course than we were. . . . Only this raft was headed the other way.

It was too early for that.

The sounds grew louder.

The other raft came abreast, so close that it seemed they had to see us despite the darkness and rain.

A voice said something softly, just a few words edged with anger. In the language of Gea-Xle. I had picked up maybe twenty words, none of which I recognized now.

I did not need to know words. I knew the voice.

That was Mogaba.

He had not been spotted leaving during the day. From the north and west barbicans it was possible to watch most of the lake surface.

Which meant that he had been away at least since the previous night. Which, in turn, would explain why there had been no response to our capture of the barbicans.

What business could Mogaba possibly have over there?

The Nar paddled on into darkness. We resumed our journey. I remained lost in thought till the raft ran aground and tossed me forward.

Sahra and I took up To Tan and our burdens and marched ashore. The little guy was sleeping like his aunt's arms were a palace bed.

In moments I discovered that my companions, although utterly ignorant of the Taglian language, expected me to be in charge on this side, too. Uncle Doj's idea, no doubt, and in effect only till he arrived.

"Rudy. Take charge of getting camp set." We had swung back into the general course of the fleet and had made landfall where others joined us in savoring the miracle of life outside Dejagore's walls.

Hanging around in a rainstorm in the middle of the night did not seem much of an improvement to me.

"Let's go, people. We can't just stand here. Start putting up those shelters." We had the tents the Nyueng Bao had carried on pilgrimage. We had blankets, wrapped inside those same tents so they would stay dry. "Somebody collect some brush and get some fires going." Maybe easier said than done in this weather. "Bubba-do. Take some men and set a perimeter. You. Joro? That your name, sergeant?" I was talking to one of the Taglian soldiers. "Get patrols out. Come on! Come on! We don't know that there aren't people over here who want to kill us." But it gets hard to care when you are cold and wet and tired.

I was tired to the point of collapse but I made myself an example. Sahra followed and helped. While I barked at people we took turns caring for the baby. I had visions of some major historical asskicker like Khrombak the Terrible ordering his hordes about while he had a smelly baby tucked into the crook of his arm.

To Tan was a good kid but he always needed changing.

Soon everyone was bustling industriously. Shelters went up. Brush got cut. Small fires took life and spawned others until there were enough to heat water to cook rice. The water we gathered using some tents to collect rain into the pots. It was going to be difficult for any of us to get wetter than we were already.

We even sent several small loads of brush over to the city on returning rafts. Our friends might get to do a little cooking, too.

79

WE HAD KNOWN SO MUCH MISERY FOR SO LONG THAT NIGHT BECAME JUST another sad chore. And in time there was poor shelter, bad food, and feeble warmth for all. But by then it was getting light and the rain was just an occasional sprinkle. Sahra and To Tan and I crept into our tent and bundled up. For a while I was almost happy.

That To Tan was remarkable. He was almost as quiet as Sahra most of the time, though he could get a good fuss going when he wanted. He was content to sleep right then. For the first time in a week his tummy was full.

Mine, too.

I got four hours of perfectly wonderful sleep before disaster interrupted.

First it took the shape of Ky Gota. I had not seen Sahra's mother since Uncle Doj cajoled her out of my quarters. I had not missed her, either.

Because I was asleep I did not witness the part where she ripped open the end of the tent. When I awoke she was spitting and howling in a mix of Nyueng Bao and really bad Taglian. Sahra was sitting up already, her mouth open and tears starting.

To Tan began to cry.

Ky Gota was not immune to baby tears. The soul of a granny did lurk behind all the ill temper. Way behind. She said something to the toddler. Gently!

Rudy hurried up. "You want I should throw this one back in the lake, Murgen?"

"What?"

"She crawled out of the water a while ago. Claimed somebody tried to murder her. Supposedly pushed her off the raft she was riding. Looks to me like maybe she asked for it."

"She probably did." Sahra looked at me in surprise. Despite her tears. "But I got to be nice. She's almost family."

"Man," Rudy said. He walked off shaking his head.

Sahra began gesturing exasperatedly at her mother. To Tan stared at his granny, sucked his thumb. I caught a whiff. "Go to Nana," I whispered. "Show her how good you can walk." He did not understand me but she did and held her arms out.

Near as I could tell To Tan was the only person in the world who cared for Ky Gota. He toddled and his granny forgot all about being wet and cold and cranky.

Sahra looked at me hard. I shrugged, grinned, mouthed, "He needs changing again."

Rudy found me staring at the city. Fresh smoke hung over our part of town. "Bubba-do just ambushed a patrol, Murgen."

"Shit. When they don't report . . ."

"He said they knew we were here. They were sneaking up. That Swan character is with them."

"One-Eye was right, then. Anybody get hurt?"

"Not yet."

"Good. Good. Did they get a look at the camp?" The Nyueng Bao had done a good job of camouflage, considering. You could tell where the camp was but not its extent.

"I think they just saw the smoke. They were real surprised to get jumped according to Bubba-do."

"They see him?"

"Yes."

"Unfortunate. Maybe they didn't recognize him." I shrugged. "Some things can't be helped. I'll deal with them. Hang on." I stomped over to Sahra and her mother. "Hush!" I snapped when the old woman opened her mouth to start. "We have trouble. Who can speak for the Nyueng Bao?" I did not know who else to ask. These strange people did what I said when I told them, if that improved our situation, but they did not talk.

The old woman put the baby down and rose. She squinted. Her eyesight was not good. "Tam Dak!" she barked.

A frail ancient turned. Despite his age he was carrying a huge bundle of brushwood. Ky Gota beckoned imperiously. The oldster headed our way at a high-speed shuffle.

I went to meet him. "Greetings, father. I am the one who dealt with the Speaker." I spoke both loudly and slowly.

"I'm not deaf yet, boy," he replied in Taglian better than mine. "And I know who you are."

"Good. Then I'll get to the point. The soldiers over here have found us. We don't know what their attitude toward your people might be. If they're in a bad temper I can't help much. Your warriors have scouted. Can you disappear?"

He looked at me for a dozen seconds. I looked back. Sahra came to stand beside me. Behind us, To Tan giggled as he played with his grandmother. The old man shifted his look to Sahra. For a moment he seemed to be staring into yesterday. He shivered. His expression grew more inscrutable. "We can."

"Good. Do it while I'm with them." I jerked a thumb uphill. "I'll get word to Doj. He'll find you."

Tam Dak continued to stare coolly. Not inimically at all, just without comprehension. I was not behaving like a proper foreigner.

"Good luck." I returned to Rudy. "Here's the deal. The Nyueng Bao need to take a powder. I'll go with Swan. I'll stall around when I get to his camp. You see that the Nyueng Bao get moved out, then make this mess look like we were setting up for the guys coming over tonight."

The old man overheard every word.

I continued, "As far as anybody around here goes, these people never existed."

"But . . ."

"Do it. And let them have most of the food. We can sponge off Lady's gang." I hoped.

Rudy looked at Sahra. Everybody seemed to think that she was the key. He shrugged. "You're the boss. I guess I don't need to understand. How are you going to explain her?"

"I don't have to." I headed toward where Swan's patrol was surrounded.

Sahra came right along after pausing to grab up To Tan.

"Stay here," I told her. She looked at me blankly, smitten by sudden deafness. I took a few steps. She matched them. "You need to stay with your own people."

A little smile teased her lips. She shook her head.

Hong Tray was not the only witch in this family.

"Ky Gota . . ."

Boom!

"You! Soldier of Darkness! You her ruin, now is not good enough for you? Cruel witch was my mother but . . ." She became incomprehensible but not the least bit quiet. I checked Tam Dak. He remained inscrutable but I would have bet my shot at heaven he wanted to laugh.

"Fuck this. Rudy! Find out what belongs to Sahra and see that it stays in our tent. Come on, woman."

80

"HOLY SHIT," SWAN MURMURED WHEN I STEPPED OUT WHERE HE COULD SEE me. "No wonder you went back."

"Hands off, pretty boy. Ay, Nyueng Bao! If you are out there go see Tam Dak. It's important. Taglians. See Rudy from the Company." I turned back to Swan. "There. We're down to a few snipers. Just in case."

He stopped staring at Sahra. "Sorry. You really stumbled into the sweet shit, didn't you?" He did have the courtesy to make his remarks in Forsberger.

"Yeah. I did. What's going on? I wake up the other day, after my wizards did an experiment on me, and I find out that somebody has been inside my head, messing with my memories. I find out I'm back over there in hell's kitchen hunting rats and fighting cannibals when all the time my so-called friends are sitting around out here not even letting me know the Shadowmaster is dead."

Swan gave me a dumb look. "But . . . You knew that, Murgen. You was over here when we killed the bastard. You was here for a week after that."

"Killed him?"

It began to dawn. "You didn't insist on going back? She said you. . . ."

"No. I didn't. When I found myself headed that way I thought I was escaping from Shadowspinner. I really believed that I hadn't gotten to you people. I think." It got more confused as I tried to figure it out.

Somebody called out something in Nyueng Bao. My troops had not followed orders. Someone else, in Taglian, called, "Can you come up here please, Mr. Murgen?"

I told Swan, "I don't know what's up. You better stand fast. These guys are real touchy."

"I got nothing else to do with my life."

"I mean it. They're paranoid in a big way. If you had spent the last several months in there you'd understand." I clambered up a steep slope to where one Taglian knelt in some scraggly brush with a Nyueng Bao about fifteen years old.

The boy pointed, eager to be the first to deliver bad news.

Fresh smoke rose from Dejagore. From, near as I could tell, the north barbican. It looked like there was fighting there.

A mauve flash told me One-Eye or Goblin was involved.

Mogaba must be trying to recover the barbican.

I spied flickers around the west gate, too.

"Damned Mogaba. Thanks, guys. Nothing we can do about it, though." I hoped One-Eye and Goblin carved Mogaba a new poop chute. "Get on back to camp, will you? There's stuff that's got to get done."

Lady was gone. Blade was in charge and just sitting around collecting refugees from the city, keeping them from reporting back with news about Shadowspinner. He admitted that. "That's what she wants done." He seemed indifferent to Sahra, unlike every other man in camp.

"She's lucky she's not here," I grumbled. "I'd turn her over my knee."

Since there was nothing else going on I sat around with him and Swan and Mather until it started to get dark. Somebody found a puppy for To Tan to play with. When it got late I said, "We'd better get back to our people. They'll be getting nervous."

"No can do, buddy," Mather told me.

Blade agreed. "She said no exceptions."

The warmth went out of the air. I gave each one what I thought of as the Nyueng Bao look. Swan and Mather averted their eyes. Blade took it but with a twitch.

Sahra seemed untroubled. I suppose, after Dejagore, it was hard to imagine a turn for the worse. She even smiled.

"I assume the prison pen is where I left it?" I remembered that part of my previous visit perfectly.

"We will keep you more comfortably," Blade promised.

Mather volunteered, "I'll show you where to bunk."

We were far enough away not to overhear, Swan thought. He told Blade, "You look at her good? That's one spooky woman."

I glanced at Sahra. I assumed she heard, too, but her expression told me nothing.

If Blade answered Swan he spoke more softly.

I continued to study Sahra, wondering what Swan had seen.

81

THE TENT WAS DECENT. IT MUST HAVE BELONGED TO A MIDDLE-GRADE Shadowlander officer. We were not unhonored guests. And the tent came with a man assigned to make us comfortable and bring us our supper. Blade's troops were foraging successfully, it seemed. I ate better than I had for a long time.

"What I want more than anything in the world," I told our man, whose name I never learned, "is a bath." Sahra hit him with a smile guaranteed to melt armor plate. She was enthusiastic about that idea. "I'm so filthy my fleas have lice," I said.

Must have been a real ration of guilt going around at high levels. An hour later several soldiers showed up humping a looted stone horse trough. With them came guys lugging buckets of hot water. I told Sahra, "We must of died and come back as princes."

Our tent was big enough to contain the trough and water with room left over.

Swan turned up. "What do you think of that, eh?"

"If I didn't have friends over there fighting and dying I'd ask for a life sentence."

"Take it easy, Murgen. It'll all work out."

"I know that, Swan. I know that. But some of us aren't going to be happy how it does."

"Yeah, well. Good night."

It was. Beginning with the bath Sahra made it clear her definition of our relationship was exactly what others feared or suspected. She astounded me with her ability to communicate without spoken words, amazed me that in the midst of such unrelenting hell a flower of such beauty could bloom and defy the night.

I slept longer and better than I had for months. Maybe some part of me just resigned and let go.

Water in the face wakened me.

"What?" I cracked an eyelid. And popped upright. Sahra sat up as I did. "To Tan? What're you doing, kiddo?" The little guy was leaning over the edge of the horse trough, spanking the water. He looked at me and grinned, said something in Nyueng Bao baby talk that sounded like "Dada."

"What's going on?"

Sahra shrugged. To Tan said "Dada" again and headed out of the tent.

Things were happening outside. I grabbed my clothes, climbed in, stuck my head outside. "Holy shit! Where the freak did you guys come from?" Thai Dei and Uncle Doj were seated outside. Their swords lay across their laps. Sheathed, thankfully. Gangs of Taglians were coming by to check them out. I guessed they had not been there long nor had they asked permission to enter camp and assume their posts.

Swan and Mather appeared.

Uncle Doj told me, "Only one group made it out again last night. The black men attacked. Many men were injured. Numerous rafts were damaged. But their soldiers did not want to fight and many asked to join Bonharj."

"Who the hell are these guys?" Swan demanded. "How did they get here?"

"The rest of the family. I expect they sneaked. They're good at that. Obviously, your perimeter ain't what it should be."

Blade shouted something from the distance. "Crap," Swan grumbled. "Now what?" He jogged away.

Mather considered Thai Dei and Uncle Doj briefly, shrugged, followed Swan. Uncle Doj said something to Sahra. She nodded. I guess he wanted to know if she was all right.

To Tan climbed around on his father.

Doj told me, "You did well, and more than you were obliged, Standardbearer. Our people are safely away and these men know nothing about them."

"Yeah? Good. What about mine?"

"They would not come out. The wizards want to pursue their vendetta with Mogaba. They might come tonight."

82

THEY DID NOT COME THAT NIGHT. NOR DID THEY COME THE NEXT THOUGH they sent a lot of Taglians and Jaicuri out in place of the Company.

Two mornings later Mather finally let me in on what the excitement had been about when Blade interrupted our discussion over Uncle Doj and Thai Dei. He told me, "Croaker will be here in an hour or two, Murgen. You might put in a good word."

"What?"

It was not an hour and it was not just the Old Man. Croaker was travelling with the Prahbrindrah Drah himself. He looked like he had seen a lot of hard road. I moved toward him in fits and starts, unsure where we stood after all this time.

He jumped down, said, "It *is* me. I'm real."

"But I saw you die."

"No. You saw me get hit. I was still breathing when you cut out."

"Yeah? The shape you was in, there wasn't no way . . ."

"Shouldn't have been, either. It's a long story. We can chew on it over a few beers sometime." He waved. A soldier trotted up. Croaker grabbed his spear, which was almost long enough to be a pike, shoved it at me. "Here. You left this when you ran off to play Widowmaker."

I did not believe it. Not at first. It was the lance for the standard.

"You really need to hug it?"

"It's really it! I was almost sure it was lost." Despite what I had told Mogaba. "You got no idea how guilty I felt. Although I did think I saw it that one time. . . . It's really you?" I looked at him closely. Having seen what illusions One-Eye and Goblin could conjure I was not quite ready to accept the evidence of my own eyes.

"It's me. Really. Alive and in a mood to kick some ass. But that's not what I've got on my mind right now. Where's Lady?"

Poor boy. Blade gave him the bad news. His paramour had left more than a week ago, headed north. They missed each other on the road.

Swan and Mather were impressed by the presence of the Prince, their supposed boss.

Why was he out running around, anyway?

I noticed Croaker had a hard stare for Sindhu, who had stayed behind when Lady left.

The Old Man snapped, "Quit making love to that damned thing, Murgen. I need to catch up. I'm way out of touch. Will somebody take this damned butt-cruncher?"

A soldier grabbed his mount's reins.

"Let's get out of the sun."

"I want to hear your story," I said. "While it's fresh."

"Going to put it into the Annals? You been keeping them up?"

"I tried. Only I had to leave them in the city." I did not like that, either. One-Eye could promise the moon about taking care of them but would he deliver?

"I'll look forward to reading the Book of Murgen. If it's any good you've got the job for life."

Swan said something about Lady planning to write a book of her own when she got time. Croaker flung a stone at a crow. It was the first of those birds I had spotted since the albino in the night. Maybe he brought it with him. I sketched some of what had been happening in Dejagore.

"Guess it hasn't been fun for anybody. Seems Mogaba is the main problem. Better get right after him. How many people are still over there?"

"My guess is him and the Nar have a thousand to fifteen hundred men. I don't know how many people I have. Some come out every night but since I got elected prisoner here I can't keep track. Goblin and One-Eye and most of the Company are still over there." I hoped Uncle Doj and

Thai Dei were using this distraction to get To Tan and Sahra and them-selves on the road.

"Why would they stay?"

"They don't want to leave. They say they want to wait till Lady gets all her powers back. They say something is out here waiting for them."

"Powers back?"

"It's happening," Blade said.

"Hunh. So what are they afraid of, Murgen?"

"Shapeshifter's apprentice. That bitch from Juniper. She almost got One-Eye once already once. . . ." How come I believed the little rat now but had not when he had told me?

I had a momentary vision of One-Eye puffing through the night with fanged death closing in. It was as solid as actual memory.

"I remember her. She was a real piece of work. Marron Shed should have taken care of her when he had the chance."

"Evidently she wants to get even with us for doing Shifter. She may be locked into the forvalaka shape, too. Which would really piss anybody off, I guess. But if you was to ask my personal opinion I think she's only an excuse. They want to stay where they are because otherwise they might have to leave something behind."

"Like what?"

I shrugged. "They're Goblin and One-Eye. They've had months to pilfer and profiteer."

"Tell me about Mogaba."

Now we got down to the grim stuff.

Before the discussion ended even nasty Sindhu condemned the Nar.

"I'll put an end to that. You want to take a message to Mogaba?"

I looked over my shoulder. He could not be asking the guy behind me. There was nobody there. "You shitting me? Not unless it's an order. And maybe not then. Mogaba wants my head. Not to mention my heart and liver for breakfast. Crazy as he is right now he might go after me with you standing right behind me."

"I'll get somebody else."

"Good idea."

"I'll go," Swan volunteered. Then him and Mather got into an argu-ment about that. Evidently Swan had something to prove to himself and Cordy did not believe he needed to bother.

83

MY STATUS IN CAMP CHANGED SHARPLY. SUDDENLY I NEVER WAS A PRISONER, never had been unfree to do whatever served the common good. Only problem was, my tent was cold. All I had left of Sahra and the Nyueng Bao was the jade amulet Sahra had taken from Hong Tray before we had carried the children out of the killing place.

"You done yet?" Croaker demanded, finding me seated in front of my tent, working on the standard.

I showed him what I was doing. "Good enough?"

"Perfect. You ready?"

"Ready as I'll ever get." I touched the jade amulet.

"She pretty special?"

"Very special."

"I want to hear all about her people."

"Someday."

We walked through the hills and down to the shore. A sizable boat was out on the lake already. Blade's soldiers had transported it overland after having failed to work it along the canal from the nearest river to the lake. Croaker and I took up position on a prominent hummock. I displayed the standard. They would be able to see that from the city even if they did not recognize me and the Old Man.

Mogaba wanted to know where the standard was? He could see for himself, now.

While the boat crossed over and returned Croaker and I speculated as to what made both Mogaba and Lady want to be in charge so badly.

"Looks like Swan is getting results. Can you see what's going on?"

"Looks like somebody black getting into the boat."

That somebody turned out to be Sindawe. I told the Old Man, "This guy was always as right with us as having Mogaba for a boss would allow. Ochiba and Isi and some of the others weren't too bad, either. But they wouldn't disobey orders."

Sindawe stepped ashore. Croaker saluted him. He responded uncertainly, looked to me for a clue. I shrugged. He was on his own. I had no idea where this was headed.

Sindawe made sure he was face to face with the real Captain. Once he was satisfied, he suggested, "Let us step out of sight and talk."

The Old Man made a small gesture that told me I should let them talk in complete privacy. They walked around behind the hummock and sat on a rock. They talked for a long time, voices never rising. Sindawe finally rose and walked back to the boat like a man borne down by an incredibly heavy burden.

"What's the story?" I asked Croaker. "He looks like he suddenly added twenty years on top of the wear and tear of the siege."

"Years of the heart, Murgen. Feeling morally compelled to betray somebody who has been your best friend since childhood will do that to you."

"What?"

He would say nothing more. "We're going over there. I'm going to meet Mogaba nose to nose."

I thought of a pile of arguments against. I did not bother. He would not listen. "Not me." I shuddered. My spine was shivering to that chill they say happens when somebody walks over your grave.

Croaker looked at me hard. I drove the butt of the standard into the earth, vigorously, meaning, "Here I stand." He grunted, turned and went down to the boat. The creature Sindhu snaked out of nowhere and joined the party. I wondered how much of Sindawe's and Croaker's conversation he had overheard. Not a word, probably. The Old Man would have used the Jewel Cities dialect.

Once the boat was well out onto the water I sat down beside the standard, clung to the pole and tried to figure out what made it impossible for me to go back over there.

84

I HAD SUFFERED NO BIG SEIZURES FOR A WHILE. I WAS NOT ON GUARD ANYmore. This one began insidiously, like just losing focus and drifting into a lazy daydream. I stared at Dejagore but no longer really saw it, thought of the women who had entered my life and the ancient one who had left it. Already I missed Sahra and so-serious To Tan.

A white crow landed on the crossbar of the standard, cawed down at me. I paid no attention.

I stood at the edge of a shimmering wheatfield. A twisted, broken black stump rose thirty yards from me, in the field's center. Bickering crows surrounded it. The fairy towers of Overlook gleamed in the distance, days' walk away. I recognized them for what they were without understanding how I could know.

Suddenly the crows rose up and wheeled around, flew that direction in an uncrowlike flock. One white crow stayed behind, circling.

The stump shimmered darkly. A glamor faded away.

A woman stood there. She looked very much like Lady but was even more beautiful. She seemed to look right through me. Or at and into me. She smiled wickedly, playfully, seductively, perhaps insanely. In a moment the albino bird settled onto her shoulder.

"You are impossible."

Her smile shattered into shards of laughter.

Unless I was completely, inescapably mad there was only one person this could be. And she died long before I ever joined the Company.

Soulcatcher.

Croaker was there when she went down.

Soulcatcher.

That would explain a lot. That would illuminate a hundred mysteries. But how could that be?

A huge black beast that looked something like an ebony tiger padded past me, from behind, went and settled on its haunches near the woman. There was nothing servile in its manner.

I was frightened. If Soulcatcher was alive and in this end of the world and inclined to meddle she could become the greatest terror around. She was more powerful than Longshadow, Howler or Lady. But, unless she had changed since the old days, she preferred to use her talents in small ways, for spite or her own amusement.

She winked at me. Then she spun around and just seemed to disappear, leaving more laughter rippling in the air behind her. Her laughter became the mirth of the white crow.

The forvalaka became bored with the show, went off into the distance. And I faded.

85

A CROW CAWED OVERHEAD.

A hand shook my shoulder, not gently. "Are you all right, sir? Is there a problem?"

"What?" I was seated on a stone step, clinging to the edge of a massive wooden door. An albino crow paced back and forth on the door's top edge. The man who held my shoulder tried to shoo the bird with his free hand and some pithy curses. He was huge and hairy.

It was the middle of the night. What light there was came from a lantern the man had set upon the cobblestones. It set eyes glowing across the street, at a low level. For an instant I thought I saw something huge and catlike slipping past.

The man was one of the Shadar patrolmen the Liberator had employed to roam the streets after dark, maintaining order and keeping a watch for outsiders of dubious provenance.

Laughter came from the darkness across the way. The patrolman was not doing a good job. I was supposed to be one of the good guys here. She was one of the dubious strangers.

I was in Taglios!

I smelled smoke. The lantern?

No. The odor came from the stairwell behind me.

I recalled dropping a lamp. Recalled a confused cacophony of wheres and whens. "I'm all right. Just had a dizzy spell."

Laughter from across the street.

The Shadow glanced back but otherwise seemed indifferent. He did not want to believe my story. He wanted to find something wrong right here right now. He did not like foreigners. And us northerners were all madmen and drunks. But, unfortunately, we were also very much in favor with the Palace.

I got up. I had to get moving. My mind was clearing. The truth was coming back. I had a desperate need to get to the old familiar entrance to the Palace because I had to get to my apartment in a hurry.

The moon suddenly splashed its light down into the street. It had to be past midnight. I saw the woman watching from across the way. I started to say something to the Shadar but a sharp whistle came from the distance, in the direction the monster had seemed to be moving. Another patrolman needed assistance. He said, "Take care, foreigner." He jogged away.

I ran too, not pausing to take the elementary step of closing the sally door.

I reached my customary entrance. Something was wrong. Cordy Mather's Guards should have been on duty there.

I was unarmed except for a belt knife. I drew it, pretending I was a fierce commando. There was no way Mather's gang would leave an entrance uncovered. You could not bribe those guys to screw up.

I found the sentries in the guard room. They had been strangled.

No need to question the prisoner further, now. But who was the target? The Old Man? Almost certainly. The Radisha? Probably. And anyone else important that they could get.

I fought panic, managed to keep from haring off blindly. Thai Dei and Uncle Doj were up there, anyway.

I stripped the shirt off one dead guard, wrapped my throat. That should afford some protection against a Strangler's scarf. Then I bounded upstairs like a mountain goat who was long out of practice. I reached my own floor so winded I had to lean against the stairwell wall and strain to keep from puking. My legs were jelly.

Alarms banged everywhere now. It was happening as I stood there. I got some wind back, left the stairwell for the corridor—and tripped over a dead man.

He was filthy and undernourished. A blade had laid him open from left shoulder to right hip. His right hand lay ten feet away. It still clutched a black rumel. There was blood everywhere. Some still seeped from the corpse.

I stared at the scarf. The dead man had murdered many times. Now Kina had betrayed him.

Such treachery is one of the goddess's more endearing qualities.

Only Ash Wand could cut that clean and deep.

Another corpse lay near my apartment door. A third lay in the doorway itself, holding the door open.

All the blood was fresh. The corpses still bled. As yet few flies were in evidence.

Knowing I did not want to do so I entered my quarters ready to sink bare teeth into anything that moved.

I smelled something.

I spun and stabbed as someone skinny and brown and unwashed flew at me, hit me, threw me backwards. A black rumel spun around my neck but failed its function because of the shirt wrapping.

I hurtled backward into my worktable. There was a sharp pain in the back of my head. Inside I screamed, "Not again!"

Darkness closed down.

Pain awakened me. My arm was on fire.

My crash into the table had overturned a lamp. My papers, my Annals, were burning. I was burning. I leaped up shrieking, beating my arm, and when I had that extinguished I began jumping around trying to save the papers. I saw nothing else and thought of nothing else. This was my life, going up in smoke. And beyond the smoke there was only the house of pain, only the bleak seasons.

Way, way over there, like down a long, cruel tunnel, I saw Uncle Doj kneeling beside Thai Dei. Between them and me lay three dead men. The floor was invisible beneath their blood. Two of the dead showed Ash

Wand's characteristic precision cuts. The other had fallen to a cross cut
that betrayed a hint of raggedness. The swordsman had been in the grip of
an uncontrolled rage.

Uncle Doj held Thai Dei's head against his chest. Thai Dei's left arm
hung as though broken. His right surrounded To Tan on his lap. The five-
year-old's head was tilted at a bizarre angle. Thai Dei's face was pale. His
mind was not in this world.

Uncle Doj rose, came toward me, stared into my eyes, shook his
head, then stepped close and wrapped powerful arms around me. "They
were too many and too fast."

I collapsed.

This was the present. This was today. This was the new hell where I
did not want to be.

. . . fragments . . .

. . . just blackened fragments, crumbling between my fingers.

Browned page corners that reveal half a dozen words in a crabbed
hand, their context no longer known.

All that remains of two volumes of Annals. A thousand hours of
labor. Four years of history. Gone forever.

Uncle Doj wants something. He is going to make me drink some
strange Nyueng Bao philtre.

Fragments . . .

. . . all around, fragments of my work, my life, my love and my pain,
scattered in this bleak season. . . .

Darkness. And in the darkness, shards of time.

Hey there! Welcome to the city of the dead. . . .

86

THE APARTMENT WAS OVERRUN WITH GUARDS.

What was going on? I was confused. Another fainting spell?

Smoke. Blood. The present. The hard present that breathed pain like
a dragon breathes fire.

I became aware of the Captain's presence. He came from the back of
the apartment shaking his head. He eyed Uncle Doj curiously.

Cordy Mather blew in looking like a man encountering the worst horror show of a long and unhappy lifetime. He went straight to the Old
Man. I heard only ". . . dead men all over the place."

I could not catch Croaker's response.

". . . were after you?"

Croaker shrugged.

"You just moved out last. . . ."

A Guard rushed in. He whispered to Mather. Mather barked, "Listen up! We've still got some live ones out there. Be careful." He and the Old Man moved a little closer. "They're lost in the labyrinth. We'll need One-Eye to find them all."

"The excitement never ends, does it?" Croaker sounded really tired.

To no one special Uncle Doj announced, "They have only just begun to pay." His Taglian was excellent considering he had been unable to speak a word the day before.

Mother Gota came from the back, bent and moving slowly. Typically of Nyueng Bao women dealing with disaster she had brewed tea. This was quite possibly the worst day of her life. It would be a good pot.

The Captain gave Uncle Doj another searching look, then knelt beside me. "What happened here, Murgen?"

"I'm not sure. I walked in in the middle of it. Stabbed a guy. That one. Got thrown across a table. Tripped and fell through a hole in time. Maybe. Woke up on fire." I still had charred pages around me. My arm hurt like hell. "There were dead people all over. I lost it. Next thing I knew it was now."

Croaker caught Mather's eye. He used a rocking motion of his right hand to indicate Uncle Doj.

Cordy Mather asked Uncle for his story. He spoke perfect Nyueng Bao.

It was a night of a thousand surprises.

Uncle Doj said, "These Deceivers were skilled. They gave no warning. I wakened just an instant before two fell upon me." He explained how he had evaded death, breaking a neck and a spine in the process. He described his kills clinically, even critically.

He spoke harshly of both himself and Thai Dei. He was down on himself because he had allowed himself to be tempted into pursuing other Deceivers when they fled. Their flight proved to be a diversion. Thai Dei, who had not been drawn away, received criticism for showing the instant of hesitation that had cost him his broken arm.

"Cheap lesson for him," Croaker observed. Uncle Doj nodded, missing the Captain's sarcasm. He had to face the cruel cost of having allowed himself to be deceived.

There were fourteen corpses in my apartment, not including those of butchered Annals. Twelve had been Deceivers. One had been my wife and one my nephew. Six perished by Ash Wand, three at Thai

Dei's hands. Mother Gota gutted two and I pigstuck one when I walked in.

Grasping my shoulder in what was meant to be a comforting gesture, Uncle Doj said, "A warrior does not slay women or children. That is the work of beasts. When beasts kill men all men are constrained to hunt and destroy them."

"Nice talk," Croaker said. "But the Deceivers never claimed to be warriors." He was not impressed by Uncle's speech.

Neither was Mather. "It's religion, Old Timer. Their Path. They are the priests of death. The sex or age of their sacrifices doesn't mean squat. Their victims all go straight to paradise and never have to take another turn around on the wheel of life, no matter how buggered up their karma was."

Uncle Doj's mood grew blacker by the minute. "I know *tooga*," he muttered. "No more *tooga*." Nobody was revealing any mysteries to him.

Cordy smiled wickedly at the swordmaster. "You guys probably won a high spot on their desirable victim list by killing so many of them. If you're a Deceiver there's big status to be gained by killing somebody who has killed a lot of people."

I heard Mather's blather but it did not register as sense. I muttered, *"Tooga* ain't no crazier than any other religion around here."

That seemed to offend everyone equally.

Good.

Mather turned to fuss at his Guards. They had failed their trust. My own disaster was just one of several. Others were still happening.

Numbly, I said, "You can't defend against this kind of thing, Mather. These guys weren't commandos." I swatted the nearest corpse with the charred sheets I was holding. "They came in here expecting to make it to paradise by midnight. Probably didn't even have an escape plan." In a softer voice, I said, "Captain, you might better check on Smoke."

Croaker frowned like I had given away everything but asked only, "You need anything? Want somebody to stay?" He understood what Sarie meant to me.

"This is where I came from. When I kept falling back. I got family with me, Captain. If I start to go bugfuck in the head they'll cool me down. You really want to help? Fix Thai Dei's arm. Then go do what you got to do."

Croaker nodded. He made a small gesture that in normal times meant "Go!" but which meant a good deal more now. "Narayan Singh is going to wake up some morning and realize that he has reaped the whirlwind. There is no safe place for him anymore."

I rose. Grimly, I set out for my bedroom. Behind me, Thai Dei groaned as Croaker set his arm. The Old Man paid him no other mind. He was busy issuing orders that meant a major intensification of the war.

Uncle Doj followed me.

The reality hurt less than the anticipation had. I indulged in the pointless gesture of removing the rumel from my wife's throat. I stood there with the scarf dangling, staring. This Strangler must have been a true master. Her neck was not broken, nor had her throat been bruised. She looked like she was sleeping. There was no pulse when I touched her, though. "Uncle Doj. Can I be alone?"

"Of course. But drink this first. It will help you to rest." He handed me something that smelled really nasty.

Did we do this already?

He went away. I laid down beside Sarie for the last time. I held her while the medicine began to course through me, calling forth sleep. I thought all the usual thoughts, nurtured the usual hatreds. I thought the unthinkable, that it might be best that this had happened before Sahra learned what it really meant to be Company.

I reminisced the great miracle. Ours was a match that never should have been. A match neither ever regretted for an instant, yet one created by a force so slight as the unspoken whim of an old woman cursed with hysterical, unreliable precognitive visions.

I thought both sanely and crazily—and commenced the process of beatification that is inevitable after any untimely death. I slept. But even in Nod I could not escape the pain. I dreamed cruel dreams I could not reclaim when I awakened. It was almost as if Kina herself were mocking me, telling me that triumph was a costly deception.

Sarie was gone when I awakened, my head throbbing with a medicinal hangover. I stumbled around until I ran into Mother Gota. The old woman was fussing over some tea and talking to herself exactly the way she talked to the rest of the world. "Where is Sahra?" I asked. "Tea. Please. What happened to her?"

Gota looked at me like I was mad. "She is dead." No pulling punches for her.

"I know that. Her body is gone."

"They have taken her home."

"What? Who?" Anger began to rise within me. How dare they . . . ? Who was they?

"Doj. Thai Dei. Her cousins and uncles. They have taken Sahra and To Tan home. I am here to watch over you."

"She was my wife. I . . ."

"She was Nyueng Bao before she was your wife. She is Nyueng Bao now. She will be Nyueng Bao tomorrow. Hong Tray's fantasies cannot change that."

I gained control before I exploded completely. Gota was right, from a Nyueng Bao point of view.

Also, there was not a lot I could do about it right now. Not without coming up with a lot more ambition than I had this morning. All I really wanted to do was sit around feeling sorry for myself.

I went back to our room with my tea. I settled on our bed, picked up the jade amulet that had belonged to Hong Tray. It seemed very warm this morning, more alive than I. I had not worn it for a long time. I slipped it onto my wrist now.

I could work my anger out on Uncle Doj when he got back.

If he came.

87

NOT ONE STRANGLER ATTACK TEAM ACHIEVED ITS TACTICAL OBJECTIVE, BUT even so their raid was successful psychologically. It stunned the city. It shocked the leadership. It generated terror out of all proportion to actual damages.

Croaker grabbed it and turned it around.

Next morning, while most of us were still wrestling with our emotions, he went to the Taglian mob and spoke in his old guise as Liberator. He announced a new and furious era of total, relentless warfare against the Shadowmaster and *tooga* although he divulged few real facts about the Palace raid. That set rumor running wild through the alleys and byways and fueled fresh anger. For years the war had been a long way away, in the old Shadowland, and so had become emotionally remote to most of the people. The Deceiver raid brought the war back home. The old enthusiasm resurfaced.

The Liberator told the crowd that the years of preparation were over. It was time to carry justice to the wicked.

But moving immediately meant a winter campaign. I asked the Old Man if he really intended that.

"Damned straight. More or less. They have their feet up down there. You know that. You've been riding Smoke. I mean, who would be crazy enough to take a crack at the Dandha Presh when the snow is flying?"

Who indeed? "It'll mean some major hardships for the soldiers."

"If an old fart like me can take it they all can take it."

Right. Only some of us can take it better than others. Some of us are obsessed.

Hell. Us Black Company guys have obsessions and hatreds enough for everybody.

Work became my all. I was past the evil time. No longer did I fall back into cruel yesterdays in order to escape crueler todays—that I could detect. But I did not sleep well. Hell still lurked beyond sleep's wall. I lost myself in the Annals, rerecording everything the fire had claimed. I ran away by riding Smoke out into the past, where and when I could, to check my recollections.

One-Eye's arsenal increased its production. The Old Man drove the ruling class crazy trying to get money to pay for everything.

Word of the new stage spread through the Taglian territories as fast as horses could run.

Lady began gathering her forces and training them to deal with the darknesses that had given the Shadowmasters their name.

I became aware that Goblin had dropped out of sight, completely, but that only weeks after the actual event. I feared that he had been murdered. But Croaker did not seem concerned.

One-Eye was fussed. He was desperate to get his sidekick connected with my mother-in-law but he could not unearth a trace of the little toad.

In the night when the wind no longer licks through its unglazed windows, nor prances along its untenanted halls, nor whispers to its million creeping shadows, the fortress is filled with the silence of stone.

Cold cruel dreams stir within the figure pinned to the throne so ancient that bits have given up to dry rot. A gleam from beyond flickers. The figure sighs, drawing in the light, exhaling a balloon of dream that somehow finds its way through the tortuous passages of the fastness and out into the world in search of a receptive mind. Upon the plain itself the shadows swirl like minnows sensing the passing of a huge predator.

The stars wink down in cold irony.

There is always a way.

88

HOUSE OF PAIN?

Mocking laughter.

She is beautiful. Yes. Almost as beautiful as I. But she is not for you.

The woman tucked a child in for the night. Her slightest movement bespoke grace.

I . . . There was an I, suddenly.

NO! Not for you!

She is mine!

Nothing is yours but what I give you. And I give you pain. This is the house of pain.

No! Whatever you are . . .

GO!

89

"OUCH!" I OPENED MY EYES. UNCLE DOJ AND THAI DEI CROUCHED BESIDE me, one to either side, looking concerned. I rolled my head, surprised to see them back so soon.

I was on the floor in my workroom. But I was dressed for bed. "What am I doing here?"

"You walked in your sleep," Doj told me. "Also talked, which alerted us."

"Talked?" I never talk in my sleep. But I do not walk in my sleep, either. "Gods damn it! I was having another spell!" And this time I remembered. Some. "I have to get this down. Right now. Before I lose it." I scrambled across the room. In moments I was scratching away.

And when I was done I realized I did not have a clue about anything. I threw my pen down.

Mother Gota appeared. She carried a pot of tea. She poured for me, then for Doj and Thai Dei. Sahra's death had hurt her deeply. For the moment her normal, contentious character was submerged. She was an automaton.

This had been going on for days.

"What is the trouble?" Uncle Doj asked.

"There's nothing there. I remembered perfectly but can't find a clue toward an explanation."

"Then you must relax. Stop fighting yourself. Thai Dei. Get the practice swords."

I wanted to scream that this was not the time. But this was his answer to all stress. Come to the swords. Pursue the exercise rituals. Parade the stances. To do it right required total concentration. And it always worked, no matter how much I disbelieved.

Even Gota joined us, though she was less adept than I.

90

THE NIGHT THAT I HAD TRIED TO FIND MY WAY BACK FROM SMOKE'S HIDEOUT I had wondered if One-Eye had cast some confusion spells around there. I learned that he had—and had scattered random pockets of confusion all through the disused parts of the Palace so the one critical area would not stand out. He gave me an amulet of charmed woolen strings, several colors twisted together, that I was supposed to wear on my wrist. It would let me pass through the spells no more confused than my usual state.

"Be careful," he told me. "I change these spells every day now that you're working Smoke regular. I don't want nobody stumbling in there while you're out of body. Especially not the Radisha."

That made sense. There was no calculating Smoke's value. No instrument for espionage this valuable had ever existed before. We did not dare risk compromising him.

The Old Man gave me a list of regular checks he wanted made. These included keeping a close watch on Blade. He did not use that information immediately, though. I supposed he was laying back, letting Blade gain confidence. And, occasionally, letting Blade deal with our religious problem children for us, too.

I did not ask but I am sure the policy was coolly deliberate. The priesthoods provided our main political challenges. Made sense to me, too, to use them up keeping Blade from getting too strong.

I had my personal list of investigations, too, some meant to satisfy my own curiosity, most to get straight events that needed to be recorded in the Annals. I spent about ten hours a day just working on the books.

* * *

I rise, write, eat, write, visit Smoke, write, sleep for a little while, then get up and do it all again. I do not sleep long or well because I do not care to tarry in the house of pain.

Uncle Doj has decided not to return to his swamp. Likewise, Mother Gota. They stay out of my way, mostly. But they are always here, always watching. They have expectations.

The new phase of the war is here. They have decided to play a part. They mean the cruelty of the Deceivers to be requited by the cruelty of the Nyueng Bao.

One of the big problems of espionage, I have discovered, is figuring out *where* to look for the information you want. When I need to know something for the Annals I usually have an idea when things happened, where and who was involved. It is a chance to flit off and double-check my memory, which I have found to be astonishingly unreliable.

Apparently none of us really remember anything exactly the way it happened. And often the divergence is proportional to the amount of ego and wishful thinking we have invested.

One-Eye has his ego problems, of course. Maybe they are why he will not let me wander through his arms factory. If it does not have something to do with guarding his ledgers from outside scrutiny. I will spy on him now that he plans to close down soon.

One-Eye carries a lot on his old shoulders. Among the things he does is he acts as a sort of Minister of Armaments. He has a whole fortified section of town where he oversees the manufacture of everything from arrowheads to monster siege engines. Much of his production gets crated up and sent straight to the docks, to be loaded aboard barges and sent downriver to the delta where, via a series of crude canals, the barges are worked over into the Naghir River, which shares the delta. Then they travel up the Naghir and its tributaries to armories near the frontier. I have no doubt that some of the material fails to reach its destination. I expect that One-Eye somehow profits. I hope he has sense enough not to sell to the enemy. Croaker catches him doing that and One-Eye will think that Blade gets treated like a mischievous kid brother.

My first swoop into the arsenal was a quick psychic raid. One-Eye's compound consisted of a gaggle of once dissimilar and unrelated structures now interconnected in a mad maze. All windows and most doors had been bricked up. Men selected for their size, bad tempers and lack of imagination infested the few entrances. They allowed no one in and no one out. The street outside the freight entrance was crowded day and night. Files of wagons and carts, drawn by weary oxen, crept forward to be unloaded and loaded by weary workmen watched banefully by the unimaginative men, who foamed at the mouth if carters and laborers so much as made eye contact. Around and amongst the carts swarmed countless runners carrying long poles from which hung dozens of pails filled with hot food for the workers. The guards checked every pail. They even took turns checking on each other.

Taglios has a richly diverse, complex, and deeply specialized labor economy. Folks will make a living one way or another and other folks will give them room. Near the Palace is a bazaar devoted entirely to grooming services, catering mainly to Palace functionaries. One guy does nothing but trim nose hairs. Right beside him, operating in a space less than four feet wide, with oils and silver tools displayed on a tiny inlaid table, is an old character who will clean the wax from your ears. He does nothing else but retail gossip. This business has been in his family for generations. He is sad because he has no son to inherit. When he goes his family will lose that space in the bazaar.

It is all symptomatic of horrid overpopulation and the desperate difficulty of surviving at the bottom. I would not want to be a Taglian of low caste.

Lucky me, I did not have to check in with One-Eye's thugs. There seemed to be no provision against magical espionage. I darted inside. I guess One-Eye did not worry because Longshadow could no longer send his pets snooping this far. But what about the Howler? He could sneak up on us any time he wanted.

Trying to track Howler was one of my regular duties.

The arsenal workers were doing ordinary things. Making arrowheads. Sharpening them. Making arrows. Fletching them. Building artillery pieces. Attempting to mass produce a light cotton body armor for the ordinary infantryman—who, no doubt, would discard it because it was hot and uncomfortable and a nuisance to lug around.

Only the glassblowers surprised me.

There were two dozen workers in that department and most were employed producing small, thin bottles. A platoon of apprentices tended fires, heated the silicates that became raw glass, carried off trays of bottles once they cooled. Those went to carpenters who placed them into crates with sawdust packing. A few of the crates went aboard big long-haul wagons but most went to the waterfront.

What the devil?

There was a big piece of slate in One-Eye's office. Upon it, in Forsberger, were chalked what appeared to be production targets. Fifty thousand bottles. Three million arrows. Five hundred thousand javelins. Ten thousand cavalry lances. Ten thousand sabers. Eight thousand saddles. One hundred fifty thousand infantry short swords.

Some of those numbers were absurd and there was no way any could be reached by One-Eye's arsenal alone. But production took place all over the Taglian territories—most often in one-man blacksmith shops. One-Eye's main job was to keep track. Which looked to me a lot like letting the fox do bedcheck at the chicken house.

The list also included animals and wagons and lumber by the hundred barge loads, much of which I did understand. But five thousand box kites, ready for assembly, twelve feet by three feet? Each with one thousand feet of string? One hundred thousand yards of silk in bolts six feet tall?

He was not going to get that one.

I went roving to see what else was being readied for Mogaba and his friends.

I saw training camps where commando teams prepared for every imaginable terrain and mission. Down south, Lady pursued her own programs, creating forces prepared to operate offensively on the sorcerous battlefield.

She had scoured the Taglian territories for every person possessed of even the slightest magical talent and had schooled them just enough to make them useful in a program I could not fathom no matter how I poked at it. As Longshadow had noted, she was stripping the Taglian territories of bamboo. That got cut into several standard lengths and had red-hot rods run through to burn out the joints. Lady had the resulting tubes packed with little spongy colored marbles created by her squads of hedge wizards.

Another game of baffle the Shadowmaster? Half of what we were doing was smoke and mirrors meant to confuse the opposition and make them waste resources or commit them in the wrong places. But I was more confused than Longshadow could possibly be.

Lady slept less than did the Captain. Croaker seldom slept more than five hours a night. If sheer drive could conquer Mogaba and the Shadowmaster we were surefire winners.

Both Lady and the Old Man hide so much inside themselves that even after all these years I have no sure grasp of how they think. They share a strong love but seldom demonstrate it. They want to recover their daughter and avenge themselves upon the Deceivers but never speak of the child publicly. Croaker is determined to lead the Company back to mysterious Khatovar, to unearth its origins, but does not talk about that at all anymore.

On the surface it would seem those two live only for the war.

*   *   *

I drifted back to One-Eye's factory. I was reluctant to leave Smoke. I knew if I delayed much longer I would return to find my body exhausted, starved, and extremely thirsty. The smart way to use Smoke was to take short journeys mixed with lots of times out for snacks and drinks. But that was hard to recall out there, especially when there was so much pain waiting back in my own slice of reality.

This time I discovered a room I had overlooked earlier. In it Vehdna workers moved lazily amongst a dozen ceramic tubs. Some carried buckets from which they scooped fluid into the tubs a cup at a time. The fluid came from a vat a man kept stirring when he was not adding water or some white powder.

I saw little remarkable about those tubs. The solution got added at one end. At the other end fluid trickled down a glass tube into a large earthenware jug. Once filled each jug got stopped and carried carefully to storage on shelves well out of the way. Unlike wines, they were shelved upright. Curiously, the lamps in the room burned unusually bright.

I studied one tub, noted that small bubbles kept rising at the end where the workers added the fluid. At the far end, well below the surface, were dozens of short rods caked with a silvery-white substance. On the floor of the tub were several handleless glass cups. Using ceramic tools a gloved worker moved a cup under a rod, scraped stuff off into the cup. Once that settled he used wooden tongs to lift the cup from the tub. He carried it with considerable care but, nevertheless, managed to stumble.

The stuff off the rod blazed fiercely when exposed to the air.

I had to get back to my flesh. I had to eat. Soon enough I would have to pack because real soon all of us would be headed south. The war's next stage was gathering momentum.

91

OTTO AND HAGOP WERE BACK, AFTER INNUMERABLE FRUSTRATING DELAYS on the last river leg, which should have been the easiest part of their journey. They were concealed in the same Shadar waterfront warehouse that I had used to hold the captives from the Grove of Doom. One-Eye collected me from my quarters. He and I and my brown shadow headed for the river.

The Old Man beat us there. He could drop everything when he really wanted. "You all right, Murgen?"

"I'm handling it."

"He's spending too much time with Smoke," One-Eye said.

"That don't sound healthy. Would you look at these guys?" He meant Otto and Hagop, though the others of their expedition were confined to the warehouse, too, and were not enthusiastic about being kept away from their families.

It had been almost three years.

Neither Otto nor Hagop looked much different. I told Hagop, "I'd almost given up on you guys." We shook hands. I shook with Otto, too. "I thought your luck finally ran out."

"We came close, Murgen. We used up a lot."

"So," the Old Man said. "What took so long?"

"Actually, there ain't that much to tell." Hagop looked at Croaker oddly, as though to make sure he was talking to the real Old Man. Croaker was in his Shadar disguise. "We went, we did what we could, we came back." Like a fourteen-thousand-mile round trip was routine? In the Company we do not brag about the big stuff. "We didn't do a lot of sightseeing."

While Hagop talked Otto made a circuit of the doors and windows. He asked, "We need to worry about spies?"

"This is Taglios," Croaker replied. By which he meant that everyone is always watching everyone else, looking for an edge.

"We figured you guys would have then all squared away by now."

"That's a lot of squaring. Shadowlander spies, yeah, they aren't a problem. Lady and Goblin and One-Eye took care of them."

I said, "We still have the priesthoods."

"And we've had a little Deceiver trouble lately."

Something in my face warned Hagop against pursuing that. Not now. "How goes the war, then?"

"Slowly," Croaker told him. "We can talk about that later. You do us any good up there?"

"Not much, to be honest."

"Damn!"

"We did get a bunch of stuff for the Annals. Murgen, you might want to work it in. It's stuff about what other people were doing that will help make better sense of what we did. I figure you could work it in between stuff that Croaker wrote. That way them that comes after us can see both sides. Huhm?"

"Maybe you ought to take over." Sourly.

"Learn me how to read and write. I'm too old for this other shit."

"Might do that," I glanced at Croaker. "Long as you don't edit me."

The Old Man grinned.

Hagop chuckled. "The gods forfend, Murgen. Not me. Hey. I found out all about what happened after we left up there, too. You wouldn't believe the excitement. The Limper came back one more time. Don't worry. It's all settled now. The empire is boring these days."

"Sounds like I wish I was back home."

Croaker asked, "Did you actually get into the Tower?"

"We spent six months there. Mainly getting the runaround at first."

"And?"

"We finally convinced them that Lady was getting her powers back. They got cooperative then. Folks in the Tower these days like not having her around."

"Gee. That'll break her heart," I said.

Hagop grinned. "Yeah. They won't send us any help. Say they don't want to make any new enemies. I think it's mostly because they don't want Lady getting nostalgic for her good old days and heading back north."

Croaker said, "We figured that. There's nothing in this for them but keeping Lady away. What did you get?"

"They opened their records. Lent us translators. Even opened graves when we asked."

"They would have an interest in who was buried there themselves."

"Damned if they didn't. They had to change their linens after we told them who all turned up alive down here. See, they had a major scare when the Limper came back and damned near took them apart."

I said, "That guy had a bigger boner for us than Soulcatcher does." No way did we need to add the Limper to our list of enemies. "What about my turnip seeds?"

Hagop said, "They made sure of Limper this time. Absolutely sure. I got your seeds. Turnips and parsnips and even some seed potatoes—if they haven't spoiled."

Croaker said, "They *would* make sure of Limper." He watched Otto prowl. Otto was restless, uncomfortable. "So they let you poke around and even gave you some help with it. What did you learn?" That had been the point. To see if they knew anything way up north that we could use here.

"Not much. It don't seem likely that Longshadow was ever one of the Taken."

I was confident of that. I was sure he would have betrayed himself to Howler by now if they had been allies in the past. "Those potatoes. Did you get the little kind like I . . ."

Hagop glowered at me, told the Old Man, "There is the remotest chance that he could be the Faceless Man, Moonbiter, or Nightcrawler— although everybody up there was sure those three really did bite the dust. It was just that we couldn't come up with any bodies."

"How about one of the later Taken?" Croaker mused.

"Five actually survived. Journey, Whisper, Blister, Creeper and Learned. But Lady stripped all five of their powers. In front of witnesses."

"But Lady has been getting her powers back," I argued.

"A point. On the other hand, we know the exact day when the Shadowmasters appeared. Even the hour, I gather. All the later Taken were still in business up north. In fact, most of them weren't even Taken yet."

I traded glances with the Old Man. He began pacing. He said, "When Soulcatcher held me captive she told me one of the Shadowmasters who died at Dejagore wasn't ever one of the Taken."

I added, "Neither was Shadowspinner."

Hagop said, "All they could tell us, really, was that they didn't have a clue if Longshadow used to be one of the old mob. The written record supported them."

Croaker kept pacing, narrowly avoided a collision with Otto, but stayed well away from the cluster of unhappy Taglians awaiting his blessing upon their desires to go home. After all this time could they recognize him through his Shadar disguise? Probably.

I was sure he was thinking that this war with the Shadowmasters was no ordinary struggle, that the stakes went far beyond simple survival. He said, "We've taken three of the bastards down. But Longshadow is the worst. He is the craziest. He's working on Overlook day and night. . . ."

"Still?"

"Still. The poor idiot is a living testimonial to the fact that everything takes longer and costs more. Even magic can't get you around that. But he's a lot closer to being finished than he was when you left. And if he does get done before we get him we can bend over and kiss our butts goodbye. It'll be the end of the world. His plan is to pull his hole in behind him and loose the dogs of hell—then come out later and collect up the pieces of whatever is left."

I grumbled, "I've heard this one before." I never took it entirely serious despite the characters involved. But it did sound like Croaker believed Longshadow was capable of doing it. Maybe his adventures with Smoke had shown him something I had missed so far.

So the end of the world was imminent, either at the hands of Kina and her Deceivers or at those of Longshadow. Either way, only the Black Company could prevent the tragedy.

Yeah. Sure.

I wanted to tell Croaker, old buddy, we're only the Black Company. We're just a gang of misfits who can't make it in life except as hired swords. Sure, we got ourselves into an asskicking contest with some bizarro creeps now but there ain't nobody going to care in a hundred years. We are entangled in an affair of honor because of promises we made and stuff like the Stranglers snatching your kid. But don't try to sell anybody on saving the world.

I was scared the Old Man might be developing a case of the big head, like Longshadow, Mogaba, the Howler, Kina, all the devils of our time. One of the Annalist's duties is to remind the Captain that he is not a demigod. But I was out of practice. Hell, I could not deflate Uncle Doj when he got going.

"I need an edge, Hagop," Croaker said. "I need it bad. Tell me you found something. Anything."

"I found Murgen's turnip seeds."

"Damnit. . . ."

"The best suggestion they had was that we might try to trace the survivors of the Circle of Eighteen."

Well. That was interesting.

Croaker stopped pacing. He looked at me as though I might be able to tell him something. I saw his focus fade. He was remembering the Battle at Charm.

The Circle of Eighteen raised huge rebel armies to pull Lady down. The culminating battle at Charm had been the bloodiest in recorded history.

The Circle did not win.

Croaker said, "We killed Harden and Raker. Lady turned Whisper to Taken. That accounts for three."

"A lot more just got lost when we whipped them," I observed. My "we" drew smiles from Otto, Hagop and the Old Man. I was maybe twelve at the time and had not yet even heard of the Black Company.

Hagop said, "We were too damned thorough back then, boss. We went out looking for and flat could not find any Rebel veterans to interrogate. We couldn't even find names for seven of the Eighteen. But there were people at the Tower who were junior officers then who claimed they had witnessed the deaths of all of the Eighteen except one called Trinket, those who became Taken, and one of the ones whose names we couldn't find out."

"Trinket." Croaker resumed pacing. He mused, "I remember Trinket. But just the name. We were at the Stair of Tear. We got word that Trinket was surrounded. In the east. We were busy with Harden. I don't know if I even mentioned it in the Annals."

Ha! A chance to show off. "You did. One sentence. That's it, though. You said Whisper had taken Rust and Trinket was surrounded."

"Whisper. Yes. She'd been Taken only a little while." He had been there to help set up the Taking. "That's one for Lady. She would know if there was anything between those two."

"Trinket was female," Hagop told us. "What's Longshadow?"

Croaker frowned.

I said, "He never gets all the way naked but I'm pretty sure Longshadow is a he. Physically."

The Old Man offered me a daggers look. Damn! But the Taglians were way off in a corner sulking. None of them caught my slip. Hagop was not on the list of three, either, though. I hastened to amend myself. "But Smoke is the only one who ever saw him in the flesh. And he ain't talking."

"He still alive?" Hagop asked.

"Barely," Croaker said. "We keep him alive. Men have come back from comas before. That's it, Hagop? All that time and travel. That's all you got me?"

"That's the way she goes sometimes, boss." He grinned. "Oh. I almost forgot. They did give me a coffin full of papers and stuff that night have belonged to some of the people who *maybe* could have turned into Longshadow—if he was ever one of the Eighteen. The stuff is all packaged and labeled in case some wizard decides he wants to use them."

Croaker's face lit up like a bonfire. "You shithead." Grinning, he yelled, "Otto, send them guys home, why don't you? Bonharj, the rest of you, what the hell are you doing hanging around here? Your people want to see you." He told me, "Guess we ought to ship that stuff down to Lady. She'll know what to do with it."

Otto hustled the Taglians out of the warehouse. They seemed baffled by the Liberator's sudden generosity. Me too.

Hagop said, "Now how about you guys telling what's been happening?"

I said, "A whole lot. But nothing big and dramatic. We keep nibbling them to death."

"Is Mogaba really the head honcho of Longshadow's army?"

"Absolutely. He's one kickass sonofabitch, too, only Longshadow won't let him run loose. He has to mess with us secondhand, mostly, letting Blade do his dirty work."

"Huh? Blade? Like in Blade of Blade and Mather and Swan?"

"Oh. Yeah." I glanced at the Old Man, whose expression had gone stony. "Yeah. Blade defected while you were gone."

"Let's get back to the Palace, Murgen," Croaker said. "We have work to do."

92

CROAKER DID NOT SAY MUCH AS WE WALKED, THOUGH HE DID SNARL AT PEO-
ple who dared stare at the Shadar and his white-devil companion. We
northerners are so few that even after years few of the commoners have
yet seen any of us. And, of course, we have done very little to dispel our
evil reputation.

Some intellectuals inside the priesthoods have argued that the friendship of today's Black Company is as deadly to Taglios as was the enmity
of its remote forbears.

Their complaint may have merit.

We were coming up to the Palace. Croaker kept grumbling to himself, mostly because so little had come of the expedition. That had been
his pet and his expectations had run away with him. He asked, "How long
are your in-laws going to hang around?"

I was not going to make him happy. "For the duration. They want
their slice of Narayan Singh." The Old Man still distrusted Uncle Doj.

"They know about Smoke?"

"Of course not! Damnit . . . !"

"Keep it that way. You find his library again yet?"

I had mentioned having stumbled onto that. "Not yet." Fact was, I
had made no more than a token effort. I had too much else on my mind.

"Try a little harder." He knew. "Don't spend so much time with
Smoke. And I think it might be useful to look at those old Annals before
we head south."

"How come you never looked for the library yourself? You've had
years."

"I heard it got destroyed the night that Smoke got mauled. Now it
looks like that must have happened in some other room. The Radisha
wouldn't mislead me about something like that. Would she? Nah."

We paused while a Vehdna cavalry regiment passed in review outside
the Palace. It had come from upcountry somewhere and was just paying
its respects before taking the field. The robes and turbans of the troopers
were clean and gaudy. Their lances were all brightly pennoned. Their
spearheads gleamed. Their mounts were beautiful, admirably trained and
perfectly groomed.

"Too bad pretty don't win wars," I said. The Black Company is not
pretty.

Croaker grunted. I glanced at him. And surprised what might have been a teardrop in the corner of his eye.

He knew what awaited all those brave young men.

We crossed behind the horsemen, stepping carefully.

One-Eye met us in the hallway outside Croaker's apartment. "What's the word?"

Croaker shook his head. "No magic answers."

"We always get to do it the hard way."

I told him, "I'm supposed to look for that library room I found the other night. You got something to help keep me from getting confused?"

He looked at me like that might be a tall order. "I already gave you something." He indicated the yarn on my wrist.

"That was for *your* spells. There's probably still a bunch of Smoke's left over, too."

The runt thought about that. "Could be. Give me that." His gaze fell on my amulet as I removed the yarn. "Jade?" He held my wrist momentarily.

"I think so. It belonged to Sarie's grandmother, Hong Tray. You never met her. She was the old Speaker's wife."

"You been wearing this all these years and I never noticed?"

"I never wore it till Sarie . . . Until the other night. Sarie wore it sometimes, though, when she wanted to dress up."

"Ah, yes. I recall." He frowned like he was trying to remember something, then shrugged, went off into a shadow and muttered to the yarn for a while. When he returned he said, "That ought to get you through anybody's confusion spells. Except maybe your own."

"What?"

"You had any of your attacks lately?"

"No. Not that I remember." I offered the amendment because I had had them before without being aware of them. Apparently.

"You had any new ideas about what caused them? Or who you kept running into when you went back to Dejagore?"

"I was escaping from the pain of losing Sarie."

One-Eye laid one of his more intense stares upon me, just the way he had whenever he helped fish me out of the past. Evidently he was not convinced.

I asked, "Is it suddenly important again?"

"It never stopped being important, Murgen. There just hasn't been time to pursue it."

Nor was there now.

He said, "We just have to let you take charge of yourself, to watch out and do the right thing in a crunch."

One-Eye being totally serious? That was spooky.

Croaker had lost interest. He was back at his charts and figures. But he did reiterate, "I want to see those books before we hit the road."

I can take a hint, sometimes. "I'm on my way, Boss."

93

I STOPPED IN TO MAKE SURE SMOKE WAS STILL BREATHING. I FED HIM WHILE I was there. Keeping him fed and clean was now my cover for being there should someone like the Radisha ever penetrate One-Eye's network of spells, much augmented since I had begun working with the old wizard. Then I tried to recall the various twists and turns I had taken the night I found Smoke's library. My memories were not clear. That had been a time of stress and a lot had happened since.

I did know it was on this same level. I had not gone downstairs or up. And it was in an area apparently undisturbed since Smoke's own last visit. The dust and cobwebs were heavy and untouched.

It did not take me long to reach desert territory. It was almost as though the deep interior of the Palace became a vast and dusty maze, needing no spells of confusion to protect it.

I found the dead man only minutes after leaving Smoke. I smelled him first, of course, and heard the flies. That told me what would be coming up before I saw anything. Only the who was a mystery until the Strangler appeared at the limit of my lamplight. He had fled here to die of his wounds, trapped by darkness and confusing spells.

I shuddered. That touched my deepest fears, the wellspring of my nightmares, my crushing dread of tight, dark places underground.

I wondered if his fickle goddess had taken delight in his unhappy end.

I moved around the corpse carefully, averting my eyes and pinching my nose. In death he continued to serve Kina's corruption avatar.

Soon afterward I discovered evidence that at least one more Strangler had become entangled in the confusion of the Palace. I nearly stepped in it, being alerted only when my approach startled the attendant flies.

I paused. "Uh-oh." That looked fairly fresh. Maybe there was still a madman in here willing to dance for his goddess.

I started moving much slower and more carefully, one hand at my throat. I started imagining noises. All the ghost stories I ever heard came back to haunt me. Each few steps I paused, turned around completely, searching for the gleam of eyes betrayed by my lamp. Why did I decide to do this alone?

I began to see signs of recent traffic. I knelt, discovered what appeared to be my own previous footprints in the dust. Someone had been through since, armed with a battery of candles. Drops of wax had fallen into the disturbed dust. And somebody had been through after that, possibly crawling, perhaps even eating what wax drops he could find.

I listened to the silence. This deep within the Palace even vermin were scarce. They could only eat each other.

Still cautious, I followed the trails of those who had come after me. My heart thumped like it was about to explode.

I started sneezing. And once I did the sneezes just kept coming. I could hold off for half a minute sometimes, but that only made the next sneeze worse.

Then I started hearing all sorts of sounds. And could not still myself long enough to reassure me that I was imagining these noises, too, or to get a fix on their source if they were genuine.

Maybe it would be better to do this some other time.

Then the broken door loomed out of the darkness. I stopped and studied it. I had a notion it was hanging a little differently. Disturbances in the dust suggested that someone had visited since I had done so myself.

Cautiously, touching nothing, I rounded the door, stepped into the room. "Shit!"

It had been torn apart. Few of the books, bound or scroll, remained on their shelves or in their cubbies. The undisturbed items, where I could decipher titles, were prosaic inventories or tax records or irregular city histories of little interest. I wondered why Smoke would bother with those. Maybe just to hide the good stuff? Maybe because he was fire marshall as well as court wizard?

Whatever, the good stuff was gone. And by that I mean not only any long-missing volumes of the Annals that might have been lying around but also a number of what I had suspected to be magical texts when last I looked in.

"Damn it! Damn it!" I wanted to throw things, to break things, to bounce rocks off villains' heads. Even before I found the single fallen feather I had a good idea of what had happened.

I collected that feather.

On the way back I definitely heard sounds that did not spring from my imagination. I did not bother to investigate. The man tried to follow my light but could not keep up.

94

CROAKER LOOKED UP, PUZZLED, WHEN I LAID THE WHITE FEATHER IN FRONT of him and said, "The books are gone. And there are Deceivers lost in there. At least one dead one and one still alive."

"Gone?" He plucked the feather off the document he was studying.

"Somebody took them."

His distress was apparent only because his hand began to shake. "How?"

"They just walked in off the street and carried them away." I did not for a moment consider the possibility that someone inside the Palace had visited Smoke's books.

He said nothing for a while. "What perfect timing." Another silence. "What's this feather?"

"Maybe a message. Maybe just a lost feather. I found one like it when I discovered that the Widowmaker armor had disappeared from hiding in Dejagore."

"A white feather?"

"From an albino crow." I ran through my catalog of encounters, real and possibly imagined.

His hand shook again. "You never actually met her. But you recognized her? She was here the night the Deceivers struck? And you never said anything?"

"I forgot that. That was the worst night of my life, Captain. That night has twisted everything else around me. . . ."

He gestured for silence. He thought. I stared. He was nothing like the Croaker who had been Company physician and Annalist when I joined up. After a while, he muttered, "That must be it."

"What?"

"The voice you encountered whenever you were pulled back to Dejagore. Think. Was it inconsistent?"

"I don't think I understand."

"Did it seem like it might be different people talking all the time?"

Now I got it. "I don't think so. It did seem to have different attitudes and styles sometimes."

"The bitch. The sneaking bitch. Always playing another game. I won't swear this for sure, Murgen, but I think the root mystery behind you tumbling all over time must have been Soulcatcher playing."

Not a wholly original theory to me. Soulcatcher rated high on my own suspects list. Motive was my big stumbling block. I could not figure a "why Murgen?" for anybody, Soulcatcher included.

"Where is she now?" Croaker asked.

"I don't have the foggiest."

"Can you find out?"

"Smoke balks every time I try to head her way."

Croaker considered that. "Try again."

"You're the boss."

"As long as it suits everybody's convenience. You sure your in-laws won't go home?"

"They're going wherever I go."

"Tell them we'll be on the road befor the end of the week."

"I look forward to that like a case of the piles." I took my white feather and stomped off for a session with the fire marshall.

95

I DID NOT GO STRAIGHT THERE. I STOPPED BY THE APARTMENT, COLLECTED A flask of tea, a gallon of water, a basket of fried chicken and fried fish, rice and some of Mother Gota's special baked rocks. I expected a long session. There were things I wanted to do beyond my expected swift rebuff in a search for Soulcatcher.

Smoke seemed unchanged. As always. I wondered what he would remember if, as sometimes happened, one day he just woke up from his coma. I hear tell people have done that even after being under years longer than Smoke has.

I filled my stomach with water before I left the apartment. I took in more fluid when I reached Smoke. I went to work.

Drifting. Quick check of all the villains. Mogaba and Longshadow, Howler and Narayan Singh and the Daughter of Night were all acceptably located, either at Overlook or Charandaprash. Blade was skirting the Shindai Kus with maybe twelve hundred men, trying to get behind the Prahbrindrah Drah, but the Prince had a screen of light cavalry out far enough to give him plenty of warning.

The man had a knack.

Before I carried out my obligation to look for Soulcatcher I took Smoke back in time to see just how early I could find and spy upon some of the principals. I wanted to see what had happened that night I had been held captive and tortured. I wanted to unveil the details of Mogaba's defection.

I found that I could not go back that far.

I recalled that raft on the lake, Mogaba cursing in the darkness. That had to be it. He should not have been there. What honest mission could have taken him ashore? Had he changed allegiances while still holding Dejagore for the good guys? Was his deal already made when Croaker faced him down? Did he meet the Howler out there, far enough away that Goblin and One-Eye would not detect the sorcerer's flying carpet?

Maybe. And if he had that might explain why even Sindawe and Ochiba were willing to abandon him.

All of us would be dead already and the war long since lost had Longshadow been in a position to seize that moment.

The cold claws of death may have come closer than ever I had suspected.

I wish I could have had eyewitness evidence, though.

Smoke can be tricked. And he can be driven by a sufficiently-determined will.

From the frontiers of past time I raced toward the night of my despair. I did not drive him to the center of its evil, though. Instead, I slowed and drifted into an earlier hour, as the Stranglers first approached the Palace and in best Deceiver form used two of their number, disguised as holy prostitutes of Bashra out to perform their obligated random acts of joy, to get close to the Guards.

But that was not the history I wanted to review. I brought him forward to the moments of my own interlude upon the sallyport steps. I watched myself emerge from the Palace, vacantly settle to the stone. The seizure lasted scarcely a minute, for all the time I spent amongst the horrors of yesteryear.

Now the slick move. The focus upon the woman in the shadows across the way, behind the hairy Shadar. The lock onto her despite Smoke's increasing anxiety and spiritual wriggling.

I never got to know Smoke in full life but, by most accounts, he had been a pure chickenshit, inalterably opposed to anything that might involve even the most minor risk to anyone in the court wizard or fire marshal rackets. Cowardice must have run right down to the foundations of his being because he writhed like a worm on a fishhook the whole time I watched Soulcatcher loot his library.

She had no trouble with confusion spells. She had none with Stranglers, either, though she did encounter a band. They just gaped at her briefly, then decided their best interests ought to lead them elsewhere.

She seemed unaware of my scrutiny, unlike that time in the wheatfield. Could it be that even she was unaware of the secret of Smoke?

Wouldn't that be lovely?

I watched her for a long time, even after she departed the Palace. Smoke resisted every second.

Then I went back and had a drink and a snack before I tackled the more interesting business of tracking Goblin down and, to slake my own curiosity, having a look at the final falling out between Croaker and Blade. I had been unable to find witnesses to the actual explosion.

96

TO TRACK GOBLIN I WENT BACK TO THE LAST TIME I SAW THE RUNT MYSELF, then followed him forward in time.

Soon after having helped me out of one of my plunges into yesterday Goblin walked out of his quarters carrying one modest bag, hiked to the waterfront, boarded a barge manned by trustworthy Taglians who had become professional soldiers, and drifted down the river. Right now—approximately today—he was in the heart of the delta, transferring the barge's cargo, himself and most of the Taglians, to a deep-sea vessel wearing flags and pennons entirely unknown to me. Off on the sodden shore flocks of Nyueng Bao children and a handful of lazy adults watched as though this business of outsiders was the greatest entertainment they had encountered in years. Despite my familiarity with the tribe they all looked inscrutably alien in their native context, more so than they had in Dejagore where we all had been out of place.

For no reason clear to me I had never visited Sahra's world. I just welcomed her into mine and savored the miracle.

Goblin's behavior was less interesting than his whereabouts, which I had now established. So why not see what life was like for the Nyueng Bao? Uncle Doj insisted that the delta was paradise.

Possibly, if you were of the mosquito clan. I swear. The fact that I was a disembodied point of view was all that kept me from being devoured. Goblin was candyass enough to protect himself and his crew with potent spells, augmented by bad smells. But the Nyueng Bao had to deal with bloodsucking buzzards able to carry off small children. I reminded myself that I had seen all the bugs I wanted coming south through One-Eye's home jungle and it was likely that Sarie's people could manage excellently without the presence of Sarie's husband.

I drifted through the area, curious about how she had lived before we met. Hamlet, rice paddies, water buffalo, fishing boats, the same yesterday, last year, last century and tomorrow. Everyone I saw looked like someone I might have met in Dejagore or among the Nyueng Bao serving with the Company now.

What?

I was sweeping along like a darting swallow. I glimpsed a face looking up in a hamlet miles back from the river where Goblin and his crew were sweating their guts out. My heart flipped. For the first time out there with Smoke I enjoyed a really strong emotion. If I had been in my body I would have wept crocodile tears.

Man-eating crocs adorn the delta, too.

I whipped back, around, hunting that face so much like Sahra's that it could have belonged to her twin. Down there somewhere, near that old temple.

No. I guess not. Wishful thinking, Murgen. Plain wishful thinking. Probably just another Nyueng Bao girl newly a woman, endowed with that incredible beauty they have for four or five years between childhood and the steep slope into despair.

I pressed in once more, wanting desperately to find even the simulacrum of Sahra. And, of course, I found nothing. The pain became so great I withdrew from that region entirely and went looking for a place and time where the gods held me in higher favor.

97

I HAD TO FALL BACKWARD IN TIME, TUMBLING SMUGLY TOWARD THE ONE ERA in my life when I was totally happy, when perfection was the order of the universe. I went to the hour that was my pole star, my center, my altar. I went to the moment every man who ever lived dreams of, that one instant when all wishes and fantasies have the potential to come true and you have only to recognize that and grab it within a heartbeat to make your life complete. For me that moment came almost a year after the end of the siege of Dejagore. And I almost wasted it.

Nyueng Bao were almost always a part of my life then. A scant three weeks following Croaker's showdown with Mogaba, and Mogaba's consequent flight, while us survivors were still creeping north toward Taglios, pretending to be triumphant heroes who had liberated a friendly city and rid the world of a bunch of villains, I awakened one morning to find myself under the dubious and permanent protection of Thai Dei. He was no more talkative than ever but in a few words he insisted that he owed me big and he was going to stick to me forever. I thought that was just hyperbole.

Boy, was I thrilled. I was not in a mood to cut his throat so I let him hang on. And he did have a sister I wanted to see a lot more than I wanted to see him, though I never found the nerve to tell him that.

Even so . . .

Back in the city, established in the Palace, in my tiny room with my papers and books and Thai Dei sleeping on a reed mat outside my door, him insisting that To Tan was in good hands with his grandmother, I lived a life of confusion, trying to figure out what had happened to us all and to make sense of Lady's writings. I was not thinking with absolute clarity when I received a gentleman name of Bahn Do Trang, who was a relative of one of the pilgrims of Dejagore. He had a message for me. It was so cryptic it could have qualified as one of the great goofball sybilline pronouncements of all time.

"Eleven hills, over the edge, he kissed her," brother Bahn told me, all splashed up with a huge and un-Nyueng Bao grin. "But the others were not for hire."

To which I offered this countersign, "Six blue birds in a peppermint tree, warbling limericks of apathy."

Death of the grin. "What?"

"That's my line, Pop. You told the guys downstairs you had a critical message for me. Against my better judgment I let you come up here and right away you start spouting nonsense. Tamal!" I yelled at the orderly who assisted me and several others who worked out of rooms nearby. "Show this clown the way to the street."

Do Trang wanted to argue, looked at my sidekick, thought better of making a fuss. Thai Dei watched the old boy closely but did not look like he wanted the honor of flinging him out on his enigmatic ass personally.

Poor Bahn. It must have been important to him. He seemed stricken.

Tamal was a huge Shadar man-bear, all hair and growl and bad breath. He would have liked nothing better than to pummel a Nyueng Bao all the way to the street and thence to the edge of the city. Bahn went without protest.

Less than a week later I received the identical message as a handwritten note that looked like it had been inscribed by a six-year-old. One of

Cordy Mather's Guards brought it up. I read it, told him, "Give the old fool a beating and tell him not to bother me again."

The Guard gave me a funny look. He glanced at Thai Dei, then whispered, "Ain't old, ain't a him, but probably is a fool, Standardbearer. Was I you I'd take the time."

I got it. At last. "I'll just box his ears myself, then. Thai Dei, try to keep the bad guys out. I'll be back in a few minutes."

He did not listen, of course, because he could not bodyguard me from a distance, but I did confuse him long enough to get a headstart. I got down there and got my hands on Sahra before he caught up or got ahead of me. After that he had little say. And my clever lady had brought To Tan to distract him.

Thai Dei did not talk much but that did not make him stupid. He knew he could not win with the cards he held right now.

"Clever," I told Sahra. "I thought I'd never see you again. Hi, kiddo," I said to To Tan, who did not remember me. "Sahra, honey, you gotta promise me. No more of that cryptic stuff like Grandpa Dam. I'm just a simpleminded soldier."

I led Sahra inside and up to my little hole in the wall. For the next three years I marvelled every morning when I wakened to find her beside me and almost every time I saw her during the day. She became the center of my life, my anchor, my rock, my goddess, and every damned one of my brothers envied me almost to the borders of hatred—though Sahra converted them all into devoted friends. She could give Lady lessons on softening the hearts of hard men.

Not till Uncle Doj and Mother Gota came to visit did I find out that Sahra had done more than just defy the customs of the Nyueng Bao. She had ignored the express orders of her tribal elders to come make herself the wife of a Soldier of Darkness. Confident little witch.

Those toothless old men put no value on the wishes of the "witch" Ky Hong Tray.

I think I have a realistic picture of who and what I am so I am amazed that Sahra ever thought as much of me as I thought of her.

98

I SIPPED WATER, ATE, AND REFLECTED THAT THIS WAS ONE TIME WHEN I HAD no trouble leaving Smoke's world. There was no attenuation of the pain if I went out there to see Sarie.

What was I doing here?

There was one mystery yet to be illuminated before I allowed Croaker to drag me off into the next fun phase of our great adventure. I wanted to know what had happened between him and Blade.

Smoke and I zigzagged back and forth through time, quartering the temporal reaches, tacking into the winds of time, following a search pattern, looking for anomalies in the relationship between Blade and my boss. I knew about when the blowup happened so, instead, for the time being, I sought contributory evidence.

You can cover a lot of time fast riding Smoke. It did not take long to establish, beyond a doubt, that Blade's relationship with Lady was never anything but proper, however charged with wishful thinking on his end. Lady never acknowledged Blade's mooneyes—nor those of anyone else. She seemed too accustomed to them to pay them any mind.

So what did happen?

I worried it like a wild dog trying to dig a rodent out of its hole. Smoke was no help at all. There were places, times, angles that he just refused to go see. I tried tricking him several ways, just to find out why he could not or would not go where I wanted him to go. None of that did any good.

Maybe I was baying down the wrong trail.

The actual headbutting had been less than wildly explosive and made only marginal sense when viewed from another point in time. All I could find out that made sense was that Blade and Croaker were sipping some potent home brew before they started getting crazy.

Verbal sniping turned into angry implications which became threats on the Old Man's part. And the beer continued to flow.

I have to say that Croaker was definitely the bad guy. Or fool. He kept on and on while Blade did his best not to let himself be baited.

That only infuriated Croaker. He spouted threats that left Blade no choice but to run.

I backed away, embarrassed for my Captain. I had not thought that he could be such a complete asshole. I did not understand why he was so insecure about Lady. I felt for Blade, deeply, and had to think less of one of my heroes.

Now that I reflected on it, I recalled occasional bestowals of unpleasantries upon Willow Swan that had *not* gotten out of hand. And Croaker had even exchanged cross words with the Prahbrindrah Drah once.

I sensed a pattern. It was not one I wanted to see. But it was obvious if you looked for it.

Croaker was obsessed with his woman. He would alienate anyone who offered her too much attention, however costly that might be.

Shit. Why? She was not Sarie.

We had lost Blade already. I do not have a lot of use for Willow Swan, who is much too pretty and too blond, but I would really hate to have the Company on the wrong side of the Prince just because one man could not be sure of his woman.

More scales fell from my eyes, leaving disappointment behind.

I needed to take this up with the brain trust, the oldest of the old, One-Eye, Otto and Hagop. Goblin was too far away and Lady both too far and disqualified by being too intimately involved. A Captain who thought with his balls instead of his brains could get a lot of people killed.

I do not worship any gods myself, though I guess some are real in their own ways. I have to believe that all of them get regular belly-laughs because one of them was ingenious enough to create human sexuality. Even greed and lust for power do not come close to generating the stupidities that us being male and female do.

But by giving it half a thought I can think of as many glories that spring from the same dichotomy.

Say, Ky Sahra.

Gods, Murgen. You need to get away from this half-dead old man. You are a hired sword. A soldier. You should not be playing philosophical games. Not even with yourself.

99

I POPPED OUT OF CONTACT WITH SMOKE. "IT'S TIME, ONE-EYE. SHE'S GONE."

The little wizard tossed a friendly miniature owl into the darkened hallway. Untouched by confusion spells it headed for that part of town where it imagined it nested. It did not look for any particular human. That was not its mission. But plenty of humans looked for it. When it fluttered past them two dozen Black Company veterans and their Nyueng Bao bodyguards rushed a building that had deserved razing a generation before the Shadowmasters entered this quarter of the world.

I had tracked Soulcatcher back to that building from her raid on Smoke's library. She felt so safe there she was almost contemptuous of security precautions. She had managed to get by undisturbed there for years.

She was going to be one unhappy player when she discovered that she was less in control than she imagined.

I watched, pleased, while Black Company soldiers took the building by the numbers and in a manner so professional that not one Captain ever would have found cause for complaint. The men now even had the knack of getting their jobs done without stumbling over the Nyueng Bao, who were worse than a herd of cats when it came to getting underfoot. You just had to use them like they were your shadows.

Hardly anyone not directly involved noticed my guys. They got inside, spread out, dug deep, found what I wanted, gathered it up and got back out long before Soulcatcher discovered that she had been outmaneuvered.

Otto and Hagop directed the raid. Putting them in charge was my way of bringing them back into the family. Good soldiers they, they carried out my suggestions, not just cleaning out Soulcatcher's hideout but grabbing her favorite white crow. They plucked a couple of his feathers and left them in place of the books, tied together with a strand of hair taken from the head of a much younger Soulcatcher, a long time back, and come south with the plunder brought by Otto and Hagop.

That ought to rattle her.

Maybe I should have let Croaker and Lady in on my scheme. In a way, I was making a statement in their names. But this had become personal. I had a statement to make for Murgen. And there was no time for consultations and conferences.

Smoke and I swooped over the guys as they lugged their plunder toward the Palace. I meant to give the books to Croaker as soon as they arrived. He could do whatever he wanted with them. Which probably meant that they would bounce once and land back in my lap, to be disappeared from the ken of all villains and villainesses—probably no better than I had hidden the Widowmaker armor.

I wondered if I was going to get too intimate with the meaning of hubris. Soulcatcher would know who done her wrong. She was maybe only a year younger than Lady, which left her an ageless amount trickier and nastier than me.

But what did I have to lose? The only thing I ever loved was gone. I could dance with disaster and grin to the end. Soulcatcher could not do anything that would hurt more than losing Sahra had.

Really?

Sometimes you bullshit yourself.

100

AN HOUR BEFORE SUNSET FOUR DAYS BEFORE THE WINTER SOLSTICE, CONsulting neither the convenience of mortal man, nor sorcerer, nor god or goddess, the earth shifted and shook. In Taglios dishes tumbled off shelves, sleepers awakened in confused panic, dogs howled and cracks appeared in old walls whose foundations had been set with incomplete diligence or without forethought for the possibility of earthquake. It was a half-hour sensation.

In Dejagore structures weakened by former high water or hidden structural defects yielded to the relentless seduction of gravity. Farther south the impact was more severe. Beyond the Dandha Presh, where mountains descended upon valleys with ferocious roars of triumph, the quake left epic horror. Kiaulune was devastated. Even Overlook suffered, though the masonry shrugged off the earth's worst. Longshadow was in a panic for hours, until it became obvious that the earth's convulsions had not broken his shadowgates and shadowtraps. Then he began to rage because the destruction and loss of life in Shadowcatch would delay his construction efforts by months. Perhaps even by years.

101

I HAD THE VAGUE FEELING THAT SOMEBODY WAS LOOKING OVER MY SHOULder, though how anybody could get behind me when I was nothing but a floating viewpoint I did not know. The voice was not there but otherwise the feeling of presence was the same as it was during my earliest plunges into the horrors of Dejagore with the taunting spirit that must have been Soulcatcher.

Only a smell accompanied this presence. An odor like. . . .

Like the smell of the dead Strangler I had found in the deeps of the Palace, like the stench that had become so much a part of life in Dejagore that eventually you noticed it only when it was gone. It was the smell of death.

I had felt a full measure of pain in the delta, imagining that I saw Sahra alive among the Nyueng Bao, despite being out in the numb with Smoke. Now I enjoyed a full measure of terror despite being out there.

I began doing what, in flesh, would have been a full turnaround, slowly. I turned a second time and a third and a fourth, each time faster than the last and each time less in control. And each time around, as I faced what I suspected was southward, I glimpsed something vast and dark and, horribly, each time more clearly, till the last time around I saw a black woman as tall as the sky. She was bare-ass naked. She had four arms and six teats and fangs like a vampire. The stench was her breath. Her eyes burned like windows into hell yet looked into my own and held them and spoke to me with a blistering compulsion and promise—a ferocious eroticism beyond anything I had known with Sahra.

I screamed.

I popped out of Smoke's universe.

Smoke had wanted to scream, too. I think he came close to being terrified awake.

One-Eye laughed. "Cold enough, Kid?"

I was soaked. With *very* cold water. "What the hell?"

"You try staying out there forever again, I'll freeze your ass for good."

I began to shake. "Oh, shit, that's cold." I did not tell him what I had seen, why I was shaking really. Probably just my imagination running away with me again, anyway. "You dog turd, what the hell are you trying to do, give me a heart attack or something?"

"No. Just trying to keep you from getting lost. You won't look out for yourself."

"I think I'm lost already, old timer."

The stars wink down in cold irony.

There is always a way.

The wind whines and howls with bitter breath, through fangs of ice. Lightning snarls and barks upon the plain of glittering stone. Rage is a red, near-animate force, as bloated with compassion as a starving serpent. Few shadows frisk among the stellae. Many have been summoned, there or yon.

At its heart the plain is disfigured by the scars of cataclysm. A jagged lightning bolt of a fissure has ripped across the face of the plain. Nowhere is that fissure so wide that a child could not step across but it seems bottomless. Trailers of mist drift forth. Some bear a hint of color when they emerge.

Cracks mar the surface of the great grey stronghold. A tower has collapsed across the fissure. From the fastness comes a deep great slow beat like that of a grumbling world-heart, disturbing the silence of stone.

The wooden throne has shifted sideways. It has tilted a little. The figure nailed thereon has changed its sprawl. Its face is drawn in agony. Its eyelids flutter as though it is about to awaken.

This is immortality of a sort but the price is paid in silver of pain.

And even time may have a stop.

She Is the Darkness

In memoriam
Tracy Zellich, who soldiered on.
Your place in the Annals is assured.

The wind whines and howls with bitter breath. Lightning snarls and barks. Rage is an animate force upon the plain of glittering stone. Even shadows are afraid.

The scars of cataclysm disfigure a plain that has known only an age of dark perfection. A jagged fissure lies like a lightning slash across its face. Nowhere is that fissure so wide that a child could not step across but it seems bottomless. Trailers of mist drift forth. Some bear a hint of color. Any color clashes with the thousand blacks and greys.

At the heart of the plain stands a vast grey stronghold, unknown, older than any written memory. One ancient tower has collapsed across the fissure. From the heart of the fastness comes a great deep slow beat like that of a slumbering world-heart, cracking the olden silence.

Death is eternity. Eternity is stone. Stone is silence.

Stone cannot speak but stone remembers.

1

THE OLD MAN LOOKED UP. HIS QUILL TWITCHED, BETRAYING HIS IRRITATION at being interrupted. "What is it, Murgen?"

"I went for a walk with the ghost. That earth tremor we felt a while ago?"

"What about it? And don't give me none of that around-the-bush crap One-Eye's always handing out. I don't have time for it."

"The farther south you go the worse the destruction is."

The Old Man opened his mouth, closed it to think some before he said anything else.

Croaker, the Old Man, the Captain of the Black Company, the right-now-by-god military dictator of Taglios and all its tributaries, dependencies and protectorates, does not look the part. He is in his middle fifties, possibly closer to sixty. He stands more than six feet tall. He has grown slightly heavy during four years spent mainly in garrison. He has a high forehead with a feeble crop of hair farther back. Lately he has been affecting a beard on his chin. It is grizzled. So is what hair still lurks upon his head. His icy blue eyes are deeply set, giving him a hard, scary look, like some kind of psychopathic killer.

He does not know. Nobody ever told him. Sometimes he is hurt because people back off. He does not understand why.

Mostly it's his eyes. They can be really spooky.

He considers himself just one of the guys. Most of the time.

If he understood it he would use his impact to its limit. His belief in the value of creating illusions in the minds of others borders on religious conviction.

He stood up. "Let's go for a walk, Murgen."

In the Palace it is always best to be moving if you want to keep your conversations your own. The Palace is vast, a honeycomb networked with a labyrinth masking countless secret passageways. I have been mapping those but could not winkle them all out in a lifetime—even if we were not heading south any day.

The point is, there is always a chance our friends will be listening to anything we say.

We have been very successful at driving our *enemies* out beyond arm's reach.

Thai Dei picked us up at the doorway. The Old Man grimaced. He has no personal prejudice against my bodyguard and brother-in-law but he abhors the fact that so many Company brothers have acquired similar companions, none of whom are bound to his direct command. He does not trust the Nyueng Bao. He never has, never will and cannot explain clearly why.

He does understand that he was not there in hell's forge when the bonds were hammered into existence. He will stipulate that. He has done his time in other hells. He was suffering one at that time.

I made a small gesture to Thai Dei. He dropped back a step, symbolically acknowledging our need for privacy rather than actually accepting it. He would hear everything we had to say anyway.

So every word we said would be spoken in the dialect of the Jewel City Beryl, which lies six thousand miles beyond the edge of any world Thai Dei can even imagine.

I wondered why Croaker bothered walking when he was going to use an alien tongue. No Taglian would understand a word. "Tell me," he said.

"I walked with the ghost. I went south. I made the routine checks. I was just following the daily ritual." I understood his desire to walk. Soulcatcher. Soulcatcher understood the Jewel Cities dialects. She would have more trouble eavesdropping if she had to find us first.

"Thought I told you to ease up. You're spending too much time out there. It'll hook you. It's too easy to shake loose from the ache. That's why I don't go anymore."

I masked my pain. "That's not a problem, boss." He would not believe me. He knew just how much Sarie meant to me, how much I missed her. How much I hurt. "I'm handling it. Anyway, what I want you to know is, the farther south you look the worse the damage done by that earthquake gets."

"Am I supposed to be concerned? Dare I hope that you'll tell me the Shadowmaster's house fell in on his head?"

"You can hope all you want but you won't hear it from me. Not now. His faults don't include being a bad architect."

"I had a feeling you wouldn't tell me what I wanted to hear. You're no fun at all that way."

Part of my job as Annalist is to remind my superiors that they are not gods. "It didn't happen this time. Overlook came through almost unscathed. But Kiaulune was destroyed. Thousands were killed. The way disasters go, thousands more will die from hunger, disease and exposure." The heart of winter was fast approaching.

Kiaulune is the southernmost city of men. Its name means Shadow Gate. When he came out of nowhere two decades ago and made himself master of the province, the Shadowmaster Longshadow changed the name to Shadowcatch. Only the peoples of the Shadowlands, who are inclined to avoid the Shadowmaster's displeasure, actually employ names enforced upon them by their enslavement.

"Is that good news?"

"It'll sure slow down construction work on Overlook. Longshadow won't like it but he's going to have to take time out to help his subjects. Otherwise he'll run out of people to do his work for him."

Our parade continued slowly through busy hallways. This part of the Palace had been given over to the war effort completely. Now people were packing. Soon we would be heading south, bound toward a major and possibly final collision with the armies of the Shadowmasters. Most of our forces were in transit already, a slow and difficult process. It takes ages to move large numbers a great distance.

The men in these offices had been laying the groundwork for years.

Croaker asked, "Are you saying we don't need to get in any big hurry?"

"There's no need now. The quake crippled him."

"There wasn't any pressing need before the quake. We could've gotten there before he finished his oversized sand castle."

True. We were starting the campaign now mostly because the Captain and his woman were so thirsty for revenge.

Add the name Murgen to that list. My taste for vengeance was newer and bloodier. My wife was a more recent victim.

Longshadow and Narayan Singh would pay for Sarie's death. Especially Narayan Singh.

You living saint of the Stranglers, your nightwalking companion now hunts you, too.

"Something that hurts him doesn't really change anything at our end."

I agreed. "True. Though it does give us more flexibility."

"Yet it makes sense to jump them while they're stunned. How widespread was the damage? Was it just Kiaulune?"

"There's heavy damage everywhere south of the Dandha Presh. It gets worse as you go farther south. Those people won't have much energy to spend trying to stop an invasion."

"All the more reason to stay on schedule. We'll stomp them while they're down."

The Old Man was bitter and vindictive. Comes with the job, I guess. And because of all the evils done to him.

"You ready to travel?" he asked.

"Personally? Me and my whole household have our preparations made. You name the day and we'll be on the road." My own bitterness leaked through.

I kept telling myself not to let the need for vengeance sink roots too deep. I dared not let it become an obsession.

Croaker pursed his lips, sour for a moment. My household includes not only Thai Dei but Sarie's mother, Ky Gota, and Uncle Doj, who is not really anybody's uncle but is a family attachment nonetheless. Croaker refuses to trust them. But he does not trust anybody who has not been a brother of the Company for years.

Proof was immediate. "Murgen, I want you to add the Radisha to the list of people you check regularly. I'm betting that as soon as we clear the city wall she'll start fixing to break our hearts."

I did not argue. It seemed likely.

All through our history the Black Company has suffered the ingratitude of our employers. Usually those blackguards received ample cause to regret their villainy. This time there was a good chance we could subvert the effort before the Radisha Drah and her brother, the Prahbrindrah Drah, could deal us any major treachery.

Right now the Radisha and Prince have to restrain themselves. As long as Longshadow survives, the Company will remain their lesser fear.

I asked, "You looked at those books yet?"

"Which books?"

He could be exasperating. I snapped, "The books I risked my precious ass to steal back from Soulcatcher the other night. The lost Annals that are supposed to tell us why every damned-fool lord and priest in this end of the world is scared shitless of the Black Company."

"Oh. Those books."

"Yeah. Those . . ." I realized that he was ragging me.

"I haven't had time, Murgen. Although I did find out that we're going to need a translator. They aren't written in modern Taglian."

"I was afraid of that."

"We're taking the ghostwalker south with us."

The sudden shift surprised me. Lately he has been so paranoid he will not mention Smoke, by name or otherwise, for any reason, even in a non-Taglian language.

There is always a crow around somewhere.

I replied. "I assumed we would. The resource is too valuable to leave here."

"We don't want anyone to know if we can help it."

"Uhm?"

"The Radisha already wonders how come we find him so interesting that we'll take care of him and keep him alive. She no longer thinks there's any chance he'll recover. If she puts much thought into it she might start adding things up." He shrugged. "I'll talk to One-Eye. You two can smuggle him out when nobody's looking."

"One more thing to do in my copious spare time."

"Hey. Enjoy it while you can. Soon we'll get to sleep for ages."

He is not a religious man.

2

"I GOT TO DO EVERYTHING," ONE-EYE GRUMBLED. "ANYTHING THAT'S GOT to be done, just stick it on old One-Eye. He'll take care of it."

I sneered. "That's only if you can't find Murgen first."

"I'm too old for this shit, Kid. I ought to be retired."

The little black man had a point. According to the Annals he is about two hundred years old, still alive mostly because of his own clever sorcery. And good luck beyond what any human being deserves.

The two of us were inside a dark circular stairway, lugging a body down on a litter. Smoke did not weigh much but One-Eye made the job a pain in the ass anyway. "You about ready to trade off?" I asked. I had the uphill end. I am more than six feet tall. One-Eye goes five feet if you stand him on a thick book. But he is a stubborn little shit who can never admit that he is wrong.

For some reason One-Eye had it in his head that the downhill end of a litter would be the easy one to handle on a stairway.

"Yeah. I think. When we get down to the next landing."

I grinned in the darkness. That would leave us with just one story to go. Then I grumbled, "I hope that damned Sleepy is on time."

Though barely eighteen Sleepy is a four-year veteran of the Company. He went through the fire of Dejagore with us. He still has a tendency to be late and a little irresponsible but, hell, he is still awful young.

Youth made him the best man to be driving a wagon around Taglios in the middle of the night if you did not want to attract attention. A Vehdna Taglian, he could pass as an apprentice easily. He could not be expected to know what he was doing. Apprentices do what they are told. Their masters seldom feel obliged to explain to them.

The kid would have no clue what he was up to tonight. If he arrived on time he would not guess his part for years. He was supposed to wander off before the wagon acquired its mysterious burden.

One-Eye would take over after we loaded Smoke. He would explain, if he found himself in a position where that became necessary, that the corpse back there was Goblin. No one would know the difference. Smoke had not been seen at all for four years and seldom publicly before that. And Goblin had not been around for a while because the Old Man sent him off on a mission weeks ago.

Anybody running into One-Eye would know who he was right away.

He is the most recognizable member of the Company. His ugly old black hat gives him away even in the dark. It is so damned filthy it glows.

I exaggerate only slightly.

People would believe One-Eye because everyone in Taglios knows the nasty little runt runs with a toad-faced little white wizard called Goblin.

The trick would be to distract them from Smoke's skin color. Or One-Eye could put a glamor on him and make him actually look enough like Goblin to deceive the Taglian eye.

Eventually somebody would discover that Smoke no longer was in the Palace. Probably later. By accident. When somebody stumbled through the network of confusion spells surrounding the room where Smoke had lain hidden for years.

"Somebody" would be the Radisha Drah. She and Uncle Doj are the only people besides me and Croaker and One-Eye who know Smoke is still alive, if unutterably lost in the land of coma.

He is more useful now than he ever was when he was conscious and the secret court wizard.

Smoke had been as thoroughly craven as it is possible for a human to be.

We reached the landing. One-Eye damned near dropped his end of the litter. He was in a hurry to take a break. "Let me know when you're ready," I told him.

"You don't got to go smart-assing me, Kid." He muttered a few words in a dead tongue, which was totally unnecessary and entirely for show. He could have said the same thing in Taglian and have achieved the same result. Which was that a globe of shimmering swamp gas materialized above his ugly hat.

"Did I say anything?"

"You don't got to talk, Kid. You're grinning like a shiteating dog." But he was puffing too hard to keep it up. "Old fart's heavier than he looks, isn't he?"

He was. Maybe because he was all lard after four years asleep, getting his sustenance as soup and gravy and any other sludge I can spoon down him.

He is a mess to take care of. I would let him croak if he was not so damned useful.

The Company wastes no love on this man.

Maybe I like him better unconscious than conscious, though we never butted heads personally. I have heard so many horror stories about his cowardice that I cannot say much in his favor at all. Well, he *was* a modestly effective fire marshal when he was awake. Fire is an enemy Taglios knows far more intimately than any remote Shadowmaster.

If he had not been such a chickenshit and gone over to Longshadow he would not be in the sad shape he is now.

For reasons unclear even to One-Eye, Smoke's comatose spirit is anchored to his flesh very loosely. Making a connection with his ka, which is what they might call it around here, is easy. It takes instructions well. I can connect with him, detach from my flesh and ride him almost anywhere, to see almost anything. Which is why he is so special to us today. Which is why it is so critical to keep everything about him under wraps.

If we succeed in this dark war, victory will come largely because we can "walk with the ghost."

"I'm ready to go," One-Eye said.

"You come back fast for an old fart."

"You keep running your jaw, Kid, you're never gonna get a chance to find out what it's like to be old enough to deserve respect but not to get none from pups like you."

"Don't go picking on me because Goblin ran out on you."

"Where the hell is that stunted mouse turd, anyway?"

I knew. Or thought I knew. I walk with the ghost. One-Eye did not need to know, though, so I did not clue him in. "Lift the damned litter, limberdick."

"I just know you're going to enjoy life as a polecat, Kid."

We hoisted the litter. Smoke made a gurgling sound. Foamy spit dribbled from the corner of his mouth. "Hustle up. I need to get his mouth cleaned out before he drowns himself."

One-Eye saved his breath. We clumped down the stairs. Smoke began making strangling noises. I kicked the door open and went through without looking outside first. We got into the street.

"Put him down," I snapped. "Then cover us while I take care of him." Who knew what might be watching? Taglian nights conceal countless curious eyes. Everyone wants to know what the Black Company is doing. We take it as a given that some of those are people we do not even know yet.

Paranoia is a way of life.

I knelt beside the litter, tipped it a little and turned Smoke's head. It flopped like he had no bones in his neck. Smoke gurgled and hacked some more.

"Hush," One-Eye said.

I looked up. A tall Shadar watchman was headed our way, carrying a lantern. One of the Old Man's innovations, the nighttime foot patrols have crippled enemy espionage efforts. Now our creativity was about to turn around on us.

The turbaned soldier walked past so close his grey pants actually brushed me. But he sensed nothing.

One-Eye is no master sorcerer but he does a hell of a job when he concentrates.

Smoke made that noise again.

The Shadar stopped, looked back. His eyes widened. They were about all that could be seen between his turban and his massive beard. I do not know what he saw but he touched his forehead and swept his fingers in a quick half circle ending over his heart. That was a ward against evil common to all the peoples of Taglios.

He moved on hurriedly.

"What did you do?" I asked.

"Never mind," One-Eye said. "Let's get him loaded." The wagon was waiting right where Sleepy was supposed to leave it. "He's going to report something. He'll have his whole family here in a few minutes."

The watchmen were equipped with whistles. Our man remembered his and started tooting as One-Eye lifted his end of the litter. In seconds another whistle answered.

"He going to keep that shit up?" One-Eye asked.

"I'll lay him on his side. The phlegm should drain off. But you're the guy who knows the medical stuff. If he's coming down with pneumonia you better start working on him now."

"Go teach granny to suck eggs, Kid. Just shove the little bastard in the wagon, then get your ass back through that door."

"Shit. I think I forgot to wedge it open."

"I'd call you a dumb shit but you keep ragging me about stating the obvious. Unh!" He swung his end of the litter into the bed of the wagon. Good boy Sleepy had remembered to leave the tailgate down, exactly as he had been instructed. "I remembered for you."

"You were the last one out anyway." Damn, would I be glad when Goblin came back and One-Eye could get back to feuding with him. I shoved my end of the litter.

One-Eye was scrambling up to the driver's seat already. "Don't forget to get that gate up."

I twisted Smoke's shoulders so his mouth would drain, raised the tailgate and dropped the oak pins into their slots. "You check on him as soon as you're clear."

"Shut up and get out of here."

Whistles were shrieking all around us now. Sounded like every watchman on duty was closing in.

Their interest was going to attract that of others. I ran for the postern door. Steel tires began to rattle on cobblestones behind me.

One-Eye was going to get a chance to test our cover story.

3

IT IS A LONG TRAIL FROM THAT POSTERN TO THE APARTMENT I CALL HOME. On the way I stopped by Croaker's cell to let him know what had happened while we were getting Smoke out of the house. He asked, "You see anything besides the Shadar?"

"No. But the uproar is going to attract attention. If they hear that One-Eye was involved people interested in us will start poking around. They'll be sure something was going on even if One-Eye sells his story to the watchmen."

Croaker grunted. He stared at the papers he had been trying to read. He was bone-tired. "Nothing we can do about it now. Go get some sleep. We're going ourselves in a day or two."

"Uhn." I did not look forward to traveling, especially during wintertime. "I'm not really looking forward to this."

"Hey. I'm older and fatter than you are."

"But you'll be going toward something. Lady is down there."

He grunted unenthusiastically. Any more you had to wonder about his commitment to his woman. Ever since the trouble with Blade. . . . None of my business. "Good night, Murgen."

"Yeah. Same to you, chief." He did not want to be civil, that was fine with me.

I headed for my apartment, though there was nothing for me there but a bed that would give me no rest. With Sarie gone the place was a wasteland of the heart.

I closed the door behind me, looked around like maybe she would jump out laughing and tell me it was all a bad joke. But the joke was not over yet. Mother Gota still had not finished cleaning up the mess left by the Strangler raid. And, pushy though she was, she had not touched anything in my work area, where I was still sorting the burned remains of several of these Annals.

I must have gone drifting with my thoughts. Suddenly I was aware that I was not alone. I got a knife out in half a heartbeat.

I was not in trouble. The three people staring at me belonged by family right. They were my in-laws, Sarie's brother Thai Dei with his arm in a sling, Uncle Doj and Mother Gota. Of the three only the old woman ever said much. And nothing she said was ever anything I wanted to hear. She could find the bad side of anything and complain about it forever.

"What?" I asked.

Uncle Doj countered, "Did you drift away again?" He sounded troubled. "When did you go? Dejagore?"

"It wasn't that. That hasn't happened for a while." All three continued to stare at me like I had something hanging out of my nose. "What?"

Uncle Doj said, "There is something different about you."

"Shit. Goddamned right there is. I lost a wife that meant more to me than—" I clamped down on the rage.

I turned toward the door.

No good. Smoke was in a wagon headed south.

They continued to stare at me.

It was like this every time I came back after going out without letting Thai Dei tag along. They did not like me getting out of their sight.

That and their stares gave me a little shiver of the sort of feeling Croaker got every time he looked at one of the Nyueng Bao.

Sarie being gone left a vacuum bigger than the one that emptied my heart. She had been the soul that made this weird bunch work.

Uncle Doj asked, "Do you wish to walk the Path of the Sword?"

The Path of the Sword, the complex of ritualized exercises associated with his two-handed longsword style of fighting could become almost as restful and free of pain as was walking with the ghost. Although Uncle Doj has been teaching me since I became part of the family, it is still difficult for me to get into the sort of trance the Path requires.

"Not now. Not tonight. I'm tired. Every one of my muscles aches." Yet another way I was going to miss Sarie. That green-eyed angel had been an artist at massaging out the accumulated tensions of the day.

We were speaking Nyueng Bao, which I use fairly well. Now Mother Gota demanded, "What you doing, you, you hide from your own?" in her abominable Taglian. She refuses to believe she does not speak the language like a native.

"Work." Even without the Old Man's paranoia I would have kept Smoke to myself. Hell, I'm taking a huge risk just mentioning him in these pages even though I'm scribbling them in a language hardly anyone down here even speaks, let alone reads.

Soulcatcher is out there somewhere. Our precautions against her discovering Smoke are more elaborate than those keeping the Radisha and the Shadowmaster away.

Catcher was in the Palace not long ago. She stole those Annals that Smoke hid before his disaster. I am pretty sure she did not notice Smoke himself. The network of confusion spells around him is supposedly extremely subtle on its fringes, so that even a player as powerful as Soulcatcher would not notice the misdirection unless she was really focused on finding something like it.

I told them, "I just talked to the Captain. He said the headquarters group will leave tomorrow or the next day. You're still determined to go?"

Uncle Doj nodded. He did not seem emotional when he reminded me, "We too have a debt to repay."

The few material possessions the three shared were packed and piled by the apartment door already. They had been ready to go for days. I was the one who needed to focus and finalize my preparations. I had lied to Croaker when I had said I was ready to travel.

"I'm going to bed now. Don't wake me up for anything but the end of the world."

4

SLEEP IS NOT AN ESCAPE FROM PAIN. IN SLEEP THERE ARE DREAMS. IN SLEEP I go places more horrible than those I walk when I am awake.

In dreams I still go back to Dejagore, to the death and disease, the murder and the cannibalism and the darkness. In dreams Sarie still lives, whatever the horror of the place she walks.

That night my dreams did not restore me to the wonder of Sarie's company.

I remember only one. It came first as a shadow, an all-enveloping malice full of playful cruelty, as though I was sinking into the soul of a spider that enjoyed tormenting its victims. The malice did not take note of me. I passed through to its other side. And there the dream wrenched sideways, twisted, and took on life, though it was a life entirely of black and white and greys.

I was in a place of despair and death. The sky was lead. Bodies rotted around me. The stench was strong enough to drive the buzzards away. The sick vegetation was coated with what looked like thick grasshopper spit. Only one thing moved, a distant flock of mocking crows.

Even amidst my horror and revulsion I felt that the scene was familiar. I tried to hang on to that thought, to pursue it, to sustain my sanity by ferreting out why I would know a place I had never been. I stumbled and tripped across a plain of bones. Pyramids of skulls were my milemarks.

My foot slipped on a baby's skull that spun and went rattling off to the side. I fell. And fell. And then I was in another place.

I am here. I am the dream. I am the way to life.
Sarie was there.

She smiled at me, then she was gone, but I clung to her smile as the only thing capable of letting me keep my head above the waters of a sea of insanity.

I was in that other place. It was a place of golden caverns where old men sat beside the way, frozen in time, alive but unable to move so much as an eyelash. Their insanity slashed the air like a million dueling razors. Some were covered with glittering webs of ice, as though a million fairy silkworms had spun them into cocoons of delicate threads of frozen water. An enchanted forest of icicles hung from the cavern roof.

I tried to dash forward, past the old men, to get out of that place. I ran as you run in dreams, slowly going nowhere.

And then the horror worsened as I realized that I knew some of those mad old men.

I ran harder, into the treacly resistance of animate evil laughter.

I swung wildly at whoever was touching me, flung my hand under my pillow to recover the dagger hidden there. A powerful blow slammed my wrist as it came into the light. A strong voice snapped, "Murgen."

I focused. Uncle Doj stood over me. He looked grave, troubled. Thai Dei stood near the foot of my bed, where he could take me from behind if I jumped up at Doj. Mother Gota stood in the doorway, agitated.

Uncle Doj said, "You were screaming in a language none of us knows. We found you wrestling with the darkness when we arrived."

"I was having a nightmare."

"I know."

"Hunh?"

"That was obvious."

"Sarie was there."

For one instant Mother Gota's face became a mask of rage. She muttered something softly and too quickly for me to follow, but I did catch the name Hong Tray and the word "witch." Sahra's grandmother Hong, long dead, was the only reason her family had accepted our relationship. Hong Tray had given her blessing.

Ky Dam, Sahra's grandfather, also gone now, had claimed his wife possessed the second sight. Perhaps. I had seen her forecasts work out during the siege of Dejagore. Mostly they had been very sybilline, very vague, though.

I had heard Sarie described as a witch, too, on one occasion.

"What is that smell?" I asked. The shakes had left me. Already I could recall details of the nightmare only through determined effort. "There a dead mouse in here?"

Uncle Doj frowned. "This was not one of your journeys through time?"

"No. It was more like a trip to hell."

"Do you wish to walk the Path of the Sword?" The Path was Doj's religion, his main reason for being, it sometimes seemed.

"Not right away. I want to get this down while I still remember it all. It might be important. Some of it seemed familiar." I swung my feet to the floor, aware that I was still being scrutinized intently.

There was a lot more of that now that Sarie was gone.

It was not yet time to make a point of it.

I went to my writing area, settled and got to work. Uncle Doj and Thai Dei found their wooden practice swords and began to loosen up on the other side of the room.

Mother Gota continued to talk to herself as she got busy cleaning up. As long as she was in the mood I even let her help with my mess, offering suggestions from the corner of my mouth just often enough to keep her simmering.

5

THE GREAT DARK RAGGED SQUARE SETTLED SLOWLY THROUGH THE AIR, rocking unpredictably in winter's icy breath. A screech of pain soared up above the complaints of the wind. Twice the tattered carpet tried to set down atop the tower where the Shadowmaster stood waiting. Twice the wind threatened it with disaster. The carpet's master howled again and descended fifty feet to a larger and safer landing area atop Overlook's massive wall.

The Shadowmaster cursed the weather. This winter gloom was almost as bad as night. Here, there, shadows came to life in unpredictable corners. All his labor and genius could not take away every cranny where they might lurk. In his ideal world he would halt the sun itself directly above the fortress where it could sear the heart out of the night and slay the terrors that lurked within.

Longshadow did not go down to meet his henchman the Howler. He would make the deformed little cripple come to him. In conversation he could pretend that they were equals but that was not true. A day would come when the Howler would have to be disposed of altogether. But that time was a long way off yet. Those damnable nuisances from the Black Company had to be buried first. Taglios had to be chastised with fire and shadow. Its priests and princes had to be expunged. Senjak had to be taken and milked of her every dark secret, then she had to be destroyed, utterly and for all time. Her mad, flighty sister Soulcatcher had to be hunted down, murdered, and her flesh thrown to wild dogs.

Longshadow giggled. Much of that he had said aloud. When he was alone he did not mind verbalizing his thoughts.

His list of people to be rid of grew almost daily.

Here were two more now.

The first two faces to rise from the stairwell were those of the Strangler Narayan Singh and the child his Deceivers called the Daughter of Night. Longshadow met her eye only for a moment. He turned to look out over the devastation north of Overlook. A few fires still burned in the ruins.

The child was barely four but her eyes were windows to the very heart of darkness. It seemed almost as if her monster goddess Kina sat behind those hollow pupils.

She was almost as frightening as those living wisps of darkness that, because he could command them, gave him the title Shadowmaster. She was a child only in flesh. The thing inside was ages older and darker than the dirty, skinny little man who served as her guardian.

Narayan Singh had nothing to say. He stood at the edge of the parapet and shuddered in the chill wind. The child joined him. She did not speak, either, but she showed no interest in the ruined city. Her attention was on him.

For half a heartbeat Longshadow feared she could read his mind.

He stirred his long, bony frame toward the stairwell, concerned that Howler was leaving him alone too long with these bizarre creatures. He was startled to find the Nar general Mogaba, his leading commander, coming up the steps behind the little sorcerer, engaged in a vigorous conversation in an unfamiliar tongue.

"Well?"

The Howler was floating in the air, as he often did even when not piloting his carpet. He spun himself around. "The story is the same from here to the Plain of Charandaprash. And east and west as well. The quake spared no one. Though the damage becomes smaller the farther north one travels."

Longshadow turned instantly, stared south. Even in winter's advancing gloom that plain up there seemed to glitter. Now it even seemed to mock him, and for a moment he regretted the impulse that had led him to challenge it so many years ago. He had gained all the power he had dreamed of then—and had not known a moment of peace since.

By its very existence the place beyond Shadowgate taunted him. Root of his power, it was also his bane.

He saw no evidence that the quake had disturbed anything there. The gate, he believed, should be proof against all disasters. Only one tool could open the way from the outside in.

He turned back to find the child smiling, one white tooth showing like a diminutive vampire fang. She combined the scariest effects of both her mothers.

Howler shrieked a shriek he cut short partway through. "The destruction leaves us no choice but to defer the labors of empire till the populace can sustain them once more."

Longshadow raised a bony, gloved hand to his face, to adjust the mask he always wore in company. "What did you say?" He must have heard wrong.

"Consider the city before you, my friend. A city which exists only to build this fortress ever taller and stronger. But those who live there must eat in order to have the strength to work. They must have shelter from the elements, else they weaken and die. They must have some warmth and water that does not lead them to their deaths with dysentery."

"I will not coddle them. Their only purpose is to serve me."

"Which they can't do if they're dead," the black general observed. "The gods have taken a dislike to us lately. This earthquake hurts us more than all the armies of Taglios have in all the years of this war."

That was a hearty exaggeration, Longshadow knew. His three fellow Shadowmasters were dead. Their great armies had perished with them. But he got the message. The situation was grim.

"You came to tell me that?" It was presumptuous of the general to come to Overlook unbidden. But Longshadow forgave him. He had a soft spot in his heart for Mogaba, who seemed much like his own younger self. He indulged the Nar where he would have endured far less from his other captains.

"I came to ask you one more time to reconsider your orders forcing me to remain immobile at Charandaprash. After this disaster, more than ever, I'll need flexibility to buy time."

It was an old, old argument. Longshadow was weary of it. "If you cannot carry out your orders as given, General, without questioning everyone and nagging me continuously, then I'll find someone who will. That fellow Blade comes to mind. He's done wonderful things for us."

Mogaba inclined his head, said nothing. He particularly did not note that Blade's successes came because he *was* allowed exactly the sort of freedom of decision and movement that Mogaba had been petitioning for for almost two years.

Longshadow's outburst was not unexpected. But Mogaba felt obligated to try, for the sake of his soldiers.

The Strangler Singh took a step toward the Shadowmaster. His odor preceded him. Longshadow shrank back. The little man said, "They are moving against us. There is no longer any doubt."

Longshadow did not believe that because he did not want it to be true. "Winter has only just begun." But when he glanced at the Howler the crippled little sorcerer nodded his rag-covered head.

He stifled a shriek stillborn. "It's true. Everywhere I look Taglian forces are on the move. None are large but they are everywhere, following every possible road. Singh's attempt to assassinate their top people seems to have set them off."

Singh's failed attempt, Longshadow did not say aloud. His own espionage resources were feeble now but they had gotten that much back to him. The alliance with the Stranglers was very unpopular and therefore very precarious. The Deceivers were loved no more in the Shadowlands than they were in the Taglian Territories.

Mogaba moved his feet but held the remark eager to force its way past his teeth. Longshadow knew exactly what it was. The general wanted to be allowed to strike the Taglian bands before they could gather into a large force on the Plain of Charandaprash.

"Howler. Find Blade. Tell him to deal with as many of these small forces as he can. General."

"Sir?" Mogaba had to strain to keep his voice neutral.

"You may send some of your cavalry north to harass the enemy. But only some and only cavalry. If I find you interpreting me as having turned you loose you will indeed be turned loose. On the other side of the Shadowgate." It had been a long time since he had sent someone through to watch him die a cruel death. He just had no time for himself anymore. Nor could he open the way these days, without the Lance. The only other key had been stolen long ago by one of his dead colleagues. He did not have the necromantic power to call up their shades and compel the villain to reveal where the thing was buried. "Have I made myself clear?"

"Absolutely." Mogaba stood a hair straighter. The concession was not much but it was something. The terrain north of Charandaprash was not suited to cavalry maneuvers, though, so he would have to use his horsemen as mounted infantry. Still, it was an opportunity. "Thank you, sir."

Longshadow glanced sideways at the child, who almost never spoke. He surprised a look of complete disdain that vanished even as his gaze shifted, disappearing so quickly it seemed nothing more than a flicker of imagination.

The Shadowmaster let his gaze travel on to the plain of glittering stone. Once he had been driven by an obsessive need to learn about that place. Now he just hated it and wished it would go away, but he needed it, too. Without it he would be feeble, no match for the likes of Howler or the woman Soulcatcher, whose madness and enmity were entirely unpredictable. She seemed a complete child of chaos.

"Where is the one called Soulcatcher?" he asked. "Has there been no sign?"

Howler, who had had a report from a skrinsa shadowweaver whose circle directed a colony of spy bats, lied, "Nothing. Though there was something strange that happened in Taglios about the time Jamadar Singh's brothers infiltrated the Palace. Could have been her." A shriek twice as long and piercing as normal ripped itself from the little sorcerer. He began to shake and shudder and spit.

Even the child took a step back.

Nobody offered to help.

6

FOUR DAYS PASSED BEFORE CROAKER WAS READY TO LEAVE TAGLIOS. HE spent most of that time arguing with the Radisha. Their sessions were private. I was not allowed to sit in. The little I heard from Cordy Mather later suggested they had butted heads vigorously. And Cordy had not gotten to hear a tenth of what was said.

I do not think Cordy is real pleased with his role around here anymore. More and more the Radisha treats him the way some powerful men treat their mistresses. He is supposed to be the commander of the Royal Guards and he has done a damned good job there but the more he plooks the Woman the more she seems to think he is just a toy, not to be trusted with anything substantive.

If he had not been feeling irritable about it he would not have mentioned the conflict.

"Same old same old?" I asked. "Expenses?" Over the years Croaker got the Radisha to buy millions of arrows, hundreds of thousands of spears and javelins, tens of thousands of lances and saddles and sabers. He filled warehouses with swords and shields. He acquired mobile artillery accompanied by ammunition caissons. He accumulated dray horses, mule and ox teams by the dozens of hundreds. He had war elephants and work elephants. Lumber enough to raise new cities. A thousand unassembled box kites big enough to lift a man. . . .

"Same old," Mather admitted. He tugged angrily at his tangled brown hair. "He apparently expects this to go bad."

"This?"

"The winter offensive. That's what the squabbling was about. Starting to accumulate replacement stuff now in case this goes bad."

"Hmm." That sounded like the Old Man. He could never make enough preparations. Which was probably why, as the passion of his response to the Strangler raid waned, he seemed ever less eager to throw everything into the fray.

But knowing Croaker the arguments could be a diversion, too. He might just be trying to scare the Radisha into being reluctant to pull any political stunts while he was away.

"He was close to the line."

"What do you mean?"

"There's a point where the Woman just won't argue anymore."

"Oh." Enough said. I understood. If the Old Man went any further he would have to exercise his warlord's powers and place the Princess under arrest. And would that ever stir up a nest of vipers.

"He'd do it," I told Mather. I assumed word would get back to the Woman. "But not over war materiel. I don't think. If the Prahbrindrah Drah and Radisha don't live up to their promises to help the Company get back to Khatovar, though . . . The Captain could turn unpleasant."

Taking us back to the Company's origins in fabled Khatovar had been Croaker's main passion for nearly a decade now. If you pressed him a little, sometimes an almost fanatical determination shimmered behind the usual coterie of masks he presents to the world.

I hoped Cordy would take that message to his bedmate. Also, I was kind of poking an anthill with a stick to see if, in his funk, he would reveal the royal thinking about our quest.

It was not something the Prince and his sister discussed, mostly because the Prahbrindrah Drah had taken a liking to life in the field and just did not see his sister anymore. Walking with the ghost told me nothing.

But Smoke was evidence in his own way. It was his terrified determination to keep the Company away from Khatovar that had led him to defect to the Shadowmaster and thereby put himself into a position where he might be stricken. As Lady noted in her contribution to these Annals, the rulers of Taglios, both religious and lay, have no more love for us than they do for the Shadowmasters. But we have been gentler. And if we vanish from the stage prematurely they will have only a short time to regret our passing.

Longshadow has no use whatsoever for priests. He exterminates them wherever he finds them. Which may be one more reason why Blade deserted to his cause. Mather's old friend has the most pernicious case of priest-hatred I have ever encountered.

"How do you feel about Blade?" I asked. The question would divert Mather from wondering about my agenda.

"I still don't understand. It just doesn't make any sense. Did he catch them doing it?"

"I don't think so." I knew. I had walked with the ghost. Smoke can take me almost anywhere. Even the past, back almost to the very moment when the demon burst in upon him and drove him into hiding in the farthest shadows of his mind. But even after having used Smoke to go observe the actual furious encounter between Blade and the Old Man, alcoholically enhanced, and indeed over Blade's too obvious interest in Lady, I still did not understand. "But I'll tell you, with the Prince and Blade and Willow Swan and about every other guy in town drooling all over themselves every time Lady walks by, I don't know as I blame him for finally blowing up."

"Just about as many guys looked at your wife the same way. She was probably the most beautiful woman any of them ever saw. You didn't blow."

"I think that's a compliment, Cordy. Thanks. For me and Sarie both. You want me to be honest, I think it was more than Lady. I think the Old Man thinks Blade was planted on us somehow."

"Huh?"

"Yeah. But you got to know his background." Cordy was born in my end of the world. He knew the way things were. "He spent years dealing with the Ten Who Were Taken. Those monsters laid out schemes that took decades to unfold."

"And some are still around. Why Blade in particular?"

"Because we don't know anything about him. Except that you dragged him out of an alligator pit. Or something."

"And you do know about me and Willow?"

"Yes." I did not explain that my Company brothers Otto and Hagop had gone all the way back to the empire and, in passing, had rooted around in the pasts of army deserters Cordwood Mather and Willow Swan.

That did not leave Mather feeling comfortable.

Too bad.

It never hurt to have our paranoia worry somebody else so much they behaved themselves.

I glanced at Thai Dei. He was always there. But I never forgot that.

He might be my bodyguard and brother-in-law and might owe me for saving the lives of some of his family and I might even like him fairly well but I never talked about anything substantial in front of him using Taglian or Nyueng Bao unless there was no other choice.

Maybe the Old Man's paranoia was rubbing off on me. Maybe it came from how Thai Dei and Uncle Doj and Mother Gota sometimes seemed almost indifferent to Sahra's murder. They acted as though the death of Thai Dei's son To Tan was ten times more important. . . . They had chosen to stay with me, to take part in the journey south to extract revenge, then seemed to give the matter little more thought. For me Sarie's memory is a holy thing, due its moments every day.

Me thinking about Sarie is not a good thing, though. Every time I do I want to run to Smoke. But Smoke is not there for me now. One-Eye did get him out of town and even with the little wizard unlikely to be in a hurry the ghostwalker was getting farther and farther away.

7

CROAKER SENT WORD THAT HE WANTED TO SEE ME. I WENT TO HIS HOLE IN the wall, started to knock but heard voices inside. I paused, glanced at Thai Dei. He was not big and not handsome and was always so impassive you could not begin to guess what he was thinking. At the moment, though, he did not appear to have heard anything he should not. He just stood there scratching around the splints on his broken arm.

Then there was a raucous outbreak that sounded like crows squabbling.

I pounded on the door.

The noise stopped instantly. "Enter."

I did so in time to see a huge crow flap out the one small window in Croaker's cell. A twin of the first perched atop a coatrack that looked like it had been rescued from the gutter. Croaker did not much care about material things.

"You wanted me?"

"Yeah. Couple of things." He spoke Forsberger from the start. Thai Dei would not get it but Cordy Mather would if he happened to be listening. And so would the crows. "We're going to pull out before sunrise. I've decided. A few of the top priests are starting to think I won't do them the way Lady did, so they're trying to push a little here and there, test the waters. I figure we'd better hit the road before they get me tied up in knots."

That did not sound quite like him. When he made deaf-mute signs as he finished I knew the speech was for other consumption even if it was factual.

Croaker pushed a folded scrap of paper across. "Take care of that before we go. Make sure you don't leave any evidence to tie it to us."

"What?" That did not sound good at all.

"Be ready to move. If you really have to drag the in-laws along have them ready to go, too. I'll send word."

"Your pets tell you anything I need to know?" Like I did not know that they were not his pets at all but spies or messengers from Soul-catcher.

"Not lately. Don't worry about it. You'll be the first to know."

This was one of those points where the paranoia grabbed me. I could not be sure of the actual relationship between Croaker, Soulcatcher and those crows. I had to take him completely on faith at a time when my faith in everything was being tested severely on every hand.

"That's it?"

"That's it. Make sure you've got everything you need. It won't be long."

I opened the scrap of paper by the light of one of the few lamps illuminating the corridor between Croaker's apartment and mine. I made no attempt to keep Thai Dei from seeing it. He is illiterate. Plus the note was written in the formal language of Juniper, as though to a bright six-year-old. Which was lucky for me since I have only a vague familiarity with the language, from documents dating back to the time the Company spent there, before I joined.

Soulcatcher was dead in those days. I suppose that is why Croaker chose to use that language. It was one he felt she was unlikely to know.

The message itself was simple. It instructed me to take the Annals I had recaptured from Soulcatcher, who had stolen them from where Smoke had had them hidden from us, and conceal them in the room where we had kept Smoke hidden.

I wanted to go back and argue. I wanted to keep them with us. But I grasped his reasoning. Soulcatcher and everyone else with an interest in keeping us and those Annals apart would assume that we would keep them close till we could decipher them. Out there in the field we would not have time to worry about protecting them. So we might as well hide them in a place that, right now, only the Radisha knew existed.

"Shit," I said softly, in Taglian. No matter how many languages I learn I always find that word useful. It has pretty much the same meaning in every tongue.

Thai Dei did not ask. Thai Dei almost never does.

Behind me, more than the next lamp away, Croaker came out of his cell with a black blob perched on his shoulder. That meant he was going to see somebody native. He thought the crows intimidated the Taglians.

I told Thai Dei, "This is something I have to handle myself. Go tell Uncle Doj and your mother that we'll be leaving sometime during the night. The Captain has decided."

"You must accompany me partway. I cannot find my way in this great tomb." He sounded like he meant it, too.

Nyueng Bao keep their feelings well hidden but I saw no reason why someone who had grown up in a tropical swamp should feel at home inside an immense pile of stone. Especially since all his past experience with cities and big buildings had been negative in the extreme.

I hurried to get him back into territory he knew well enough to walk alone. I had to get into Croaker's cell fast, before he and his feathered friend returned. That is where we were keeping the books right now. We did not want anyone to know we had them—though Soulcatcher surely suspected if she was aware that they had been stolen from where she had hidden them.

What a convoluted game.

I felt my wrist to make sure I still wore the loop of string that was really an amulet One-Eye had given me so I would be immune to all the spells of confusion and misdirection around the chamber where we kept Smoke.

Even before I collected the books—noting that Croaker had shooed all crows, closed the window and covered it with a curtain—I was thinking how best to conceal them once I had them where Croaker wanted them to go.

It would not be long after we left that the Radisha would start wondering who was taking care of the wizard now. My bet was that she would start looking for him. She was stubborn enough to find her way to the room.

Though she had shown little interest in Smoke lately she had never given up hope of bringing him back. If we enjoyed many successes against the Shadowmaster she would want his help even more.

Everything we did seemed to have potentially unpleasant consequences.

8

WHEN THE OLD MAN DECIDES TO MOVE HE MOVES. IT WAS STILL TOMB-dark when I left the Palace and found him waiting with two of the giant black stallions that had come down from the north with the Black Company. Specially bred during the Lady's heyday, with sorcery instilled into their very bones, they could run forever without getting tired and could outrace any mundane steed. And they were almost as smart as a really stupid human.

Croaker grinned down at my in-laws. They were completely non-plussed by this development. How were they supposed to keep up?

Kind of pissed me off, too. "I'll handle it," I said in Nyueng Bao. I handed Thai Dei my stuff, climbed the monster Croaker had brought for me. It had been a long time since I had ridden one but this one seemed to remember me. It tossed its head and snorted a greeting. "You too, big boy." I took my stuff from Thai Dei.

"Where's the standard?" Croaker demanded.

"In the wagon with One-Eye. Sleepy put it there before—"

"You let it out of your control? You don't ever let it out of your control."

"I was thinking about giving Sleepy the job." Standardbearer was one of the hats I wore. And not one of my favorites. Now that I am Annalist I should be passing it on. Croaker has mentioned that himself on occasion. "Give me your stuff now," I told Thai Dei once I had mine settled in front of me.

Thai Dei's eyes got big as he realized what I intended.

I told Mother Gota and Uncle Doj, "Stay on the stone road all the way and you'll catch up with the army. If you're stopped show the soldiers your papers." Another innovation of the Liberator. More and more people involved in the war effort were being given bits of paper telling who they were and who was responsible for them. Since hardly anybody was literate the effort did not seem worthwhile.

Maybe. But the Old Man always has his reasons. Even when those are simply to confuse.

Croaker realized what I was doing just as I extended my hand to help Thai Dei climb. He opened his mouth to raise hell. I said, "Don't bother. It ain't worth a fight."

Thai Dei looks like a skull with a thin layer of dark leather over it at the best of times. Now he looked as though he had just heard a death sentence pronounced. "It'll be all right," I told him, realizing he had never been on a horse. The Nyueng Bao have water buffalo and a few elephants. They do not ride those, except as children sometimes, helping with the plowing.

He did not want to do it. He really did not. He looked at Uncle Doj. Doj said nothing. It was Thai Dei's call.

Croaker must have started looking smug or something. Thai Dei stared at him for a moment, shuddered all over, then extended his good hand. I pulled. Thai Dei was as hard and tough as they came but he weighed almost nothing.

The horse gave me a look nearly as ugly as the one I had gotten from my boss. The fact that they are capable of a job does not make the beasts eager to do it.

"Whenever you're ready," Croaker said.

"Go."

He headed out. The pace he set was savage. He rode like he could feel no pain. He grumbled and fussed at me to keep up. He grumbled even more after we collected a cavalry escort south of the city. The regular horses had no hope of matching the pace he wanted to set. He had to keep waiting for them to catch up. Usually he was well ahead, surrounded by crows. The birds came and went and when we exchanged words he always knew things like where Blade was, where our troops were, where there was resistance to the Taglian advance and where there was none. He knew that Mogaba had sent cavalry north to blunt our advance.

It was weird. The man just plain knew things he should not. Not without walking with the ghost. And One-Eye was still ahead of us, making much better time than I would have believed possible had we not been trying to catch him.

Croaker got over his snit after the first day. He became social again. Headed for the Ghoja Ford, he asked, "You remember the first time we came here?"

"I remember rain and mud and misery and a hundred Shadowlanders trying to kill us."

"Those were the days, Murgen."

"They were as close to hell as I want to get. And that's said from the viewpoint of a man who's been a whole lot closer."

He chuckled. "So thank me for this nice new road."

"Thank you for the nice new road." The Taglians called it the Rock Road or Stone Road. The first time we traveled it, it had been nothing but a snake of mud.

"You really think Sleepy is right for the standardbearer job?"

"I've been thinking about that. I'm not ready to give it up yet."

"This is the same Murgen who complained that he's always the first guy into every scrape?"

"I said I've been thinking. I find I've got some extra motivation." Our other companions told me I was handling Sarie's loss pretty well. I thought so myself.

Croaker looked back at Thai Dei, who was clinging desperately to a swaybacked dapple mare we had picked up thirty miles back. He was handling his problem moderately well, too, for a guy who could use only one hand.

Croaker told me, "Don't let motivation get in the way of good sense. When all the rest is said and done we're still the Black Company. We get the other guys to do the dying."

"I'm in control. I was a Black Company brother a lot longer than I was Sarie's husband. I learned how to manage my emotions."

He did not seem convinced. And I understood. He was concerned not about me as I existed right now but as I would in a crunch. The survival of the whole Company might hinge on which way one man jumped when the shitstorm hit.

The Captain glanced back. Despite their best efforts our escort had begun to string out. He paid no attention to them. He asked, "Learned anything about your in-laws?"

"Again?" He never let up. And I did not have an answer for him. "How about 'love is blind'?"

"Murgen, you're a damned fool if you really believe that. Maybe you ought to go back and reread the Books of Croaker."

He lost me there. "What's that supposed to mean?"

"I've got me a lady, too. Still alive, granted. We've got plenty tied up in each other. We made us a baby together. Any two fools can do that by accident, of course, but it's usually a benchmark in a relationship. But what we have as man and woman, father and mother, doesn't mean I trust Lady even a little in any but that one way. And she can't trust me. It's the way she's made. It's the life she lived."

"Sarie never had any ambitions, boss. Except maybe to get me to actually go into the farming I'm always talking about so I wouldn't get skragged gloriously in some typically heroic military manner like falling off a horse and drowning while I was crossing a creek during the rainy season."

"Sahra never worried me, Murgen. What bothers me is this uncle who doesn't act like any other Nyueng Bao I've ever seen."

"Hey, he's one old guy who has a thing about swords. He's a priest and his scripture is sharp steel. And he's got a grudge. Just keep him pointed toward the Shadowmaster."

Croaker nodded grimly. "Time will tell." He did grim very well.

We crossed the great stone bridge Lady had ordered built at Ghoja. Crows filled the trees on the southern bank. They squabbled and carried on and seemed to find us highly amusing.

I said, "I worry more about those things."

Croaker did not respond. He did order a halt to rest the animals. So many had gone south ahead of us that there were no well-rested remounts available. Amidst all the saluting and hasty turning out of an honor guard and whatnot, I stared southward and said, "That little clown is making damned good time." I had asked already and had learned that One-Eye was still a day ahead.

"We'll catch him before we get to Dejagore." Croaker eyed me as though he feared the city name would strike me with the impact of some terrible spell. I disappointed him. Thai Dei, who could follow the conversation because we were speaking Taglian, showed no reaction, either, though the siege had been as terrible for his people as for the Company. Nyueng Bao seldom betray any emotion in the presence of outsiders.

I told Thai Dei, "Give your horse to the groom and let's see if we can't find something decent to eat." Living on horseback is not a gourmet's delight.

For the same reason there were no fresh remounts, there were very few delicacies at the Ghoja fortress, but because we belonged to the Liberator's party we were given a newly taken gamecock that was so full of juice and substance my stomach nearly rebelled at taking it in. After eating we got to stay inside, out of the cold, and get some sleep. I should have stuck to Croaker in case his talks with local commanders turned up anything that belonged in the Annals, but after a short interior debate I chose sleep instead. If he heard anything worthwhile the Old Man would tell me. If necessary I could come back with Smoke later.

I dreamed but did not remember the dreams long enough to note them down. They were unpleasant but not overpowering or so terrible Thai Dei had to awaken me.

We were back on the road before sunrise.

We overtook One-Eye passing through the hills that surround Dejagore. When I first glimpsed his wagon and realized it had to be him I started to shudder and had to fight an urge to kick my mount into a faster pace. I wanted to get to Smoke.

Maybe I had more of a problem than I wanted to admit.

I did not show it enough to be noticed, though.

One-Eye never slowed down a bit.

There had been some changes since my days of hell in Dejagore—or Jaicur, as its natives called it, or Stormgard, as it was named while it was the seat of the deceased Shadowmaster Stormshadow. Poor witch, she had been totally unable to guard the Shadowlands against the storm of the Black Company.

The plain outside the city had been drained of all water and cleared of wreckage and corpses, though I thought I could still smell death in the air. Prisoners of war from the Shadowlands still labored on the city walls and inside the city itself. Why seemed problematic. There were almost no Jaicuri left alive.

"Interesting notion, planting the plain in grain," I said, seeing what looked like winter wheat peeping through last year's stubble.

"One of Lady's ideas," Croaker replied. He still watched me as though he expected me to start foaming at the mouth any minute. "Anywhere there is a permanent garrison one of the responsibilities of the soldiers is to raise their own food."

When it came to the logistics of war Lady was more the expert than Croaker. Till we came to Taglios he was never part of anything bigger than the Company. Lady had managed the war-making instruments of a vast empire for decades.

The Old Man simply left most of that stuff to Lady. He would rather lie back scheming his schemes and piling up the tools Lady could use.

The crop notion was not new. Lady had done the same around most of her permanent installations in the north.

You got to go with what works.

Helps keep the neighbors more tractable, too, if you are not stealing their daughters and seed grain.

"You sure you're all right?" Croaker demanded.

We were nearly at the foot of the ramp to the north barbican. One-Eye was no more than a hundred feet ahead now, perfectly aware of our presence, but not slowing down a bit. I guess I was starting to push ahead.

"I've got it under control, Captain. I don't fall off into the past anymore and I hardly ever wake up screaming. I hold it down to a little shaking and sweating."

"Anything starts getting to you, I want to know. I expect to be here a while. You're going to need to be able to take it."

"I won't screw up," I promised.

9

I DID NOT WAIT LONG AFTER THAI DEI AND I TOOK UP QUARTERS IN ONE OF the same buildings we had occupied during the siege. Reconstruction had not reached that part of town yet. Some of the old litter still lay around. "At least they got rid of all the bones," I told Thai Dei.

He grunted, looked around like he expected to see ghosts.

"You be all right here?" I asked. Nyueng Bao do believe in ghosts and spirits and ancestors who follow you around nagging if you have not gotten them buried properly. A lot of Nyueng Bao pilgrims passed over here without benefit of the appropriate ceremonies.

"I must be. I must have everything ready when Doj comes."

That was a major speech for Thai Dei.

Uncle Doj was a priest of some sort. Presumably he would take this opportunity to complete what he had not had time to do four years ago.

"You go ahead. I have things to do." Far places to see. Pain to be given the slip, though I did not admit that directly even to myself.

Thai Dei started to put his few possessions aside.

"No. It's more of that secret Company stuff that I'm expected to do alone."

Thai Dei grunted, almost pleased to have his time be his own.

It always was his but he would not listen when I insisted he did not owe me. If it were not for me he would not have lost his sister and son.

Arguing with a Nyueng Bao is like arguing with water buffalo. You cannot get through and after a while the Nyueng Bao loses interest in listening. Might as well save your energy.

"Wondered how long it would be," One-Eye said when I tracked him down. He had brought the wagon into our old part of town but had not taken Smoke out. He had it backed into a tight alleyway where, I presumed, the wagon would vanish inside camouflaging spells as soon as he dealt with his team.

"Unhitch them animals, Kid, and get them over to the transient stable while I straighten up here."

Arguing with One-Eye gets to be a little like arguing with Nyueng Bao. He goes completely deaf. He did so in this instance. He went about his business exactly as though I was not there. In the interest of efficiency I took care of the animals.

I believe I did a little grumbling about wishing Goblin was back.

That little toad of a wizard Goblin is One-Eye's best friend and worst enemy. He was so hard to find I thought, at first, that I was having trouble getting Smoke to understand what I wanted to do. Then I tried going back to where I had seen him last, in the river delta on the edge of Nyueng Bao country. My plan was to follow him forward in time to where he was now. And that worked just fine till Goblin's ship entered a fog bank and never came out again.

Smoke could not find him.

It took me a while to comprehend that Smoke might have been primed to shy away from what Goblin was doing. Maybe to keep One-Eye from finding out and interfering. It would be just like the little shit to blow a whole operation because he did not think before pulling some nasty practical joke on his friend.

I did some experimenting. Sure enough, Smoke had been given some special instructions. The Old Man had not given up visiting him completely.

Once I knew that, I had little difficulty getting past Croaker's safeguards. I fear One-Eye would have had little more trouble.

I found Goblin standing on a sandy beach far down the uncharted coast of the Shindai Kus, a terrible desert that fills a vast chunk of land between the northern and southern regions of the Shadowlands. The impassable mountains called the Dandha Presh only get shorter out there before they finally wade into the ocean.

Goblin was looking out to sea. A ship rode her anchor inshore. Boats were plunging in the surf. Goblin was yammering a litany of complaints. From the faces of his companions it was safe to guess that they had heard it all before.

What the hell was Goblin doing out there on that bleak coast?

I dropped back in time to listen in from the beginning.

Goblin was tormented by hatreds. So what does the Captain do? He sends nobody else but Goblin himself off to chart the unknown coast. Goblin hated swamps. So naturally the first leg of the journey took him downriver through the delta, which was one huge swamp two hundred miles across, without one decent channel, obviously totally unfit for human habitation because only Nyueng Bao lived there.

Goblin hated sea travel almost as much as One-Eye did. So what did he get after cutting through the swamp, damned near building a canal to manage that? A goddamn ocean with waves taller than any self-respecting tree. He hated deserts. So what did he find after he finally got his little fleet past the end of the swampy coast? Country so barren scorpions and sand fleas could not make a living there. You baked during the day and froze at night and you never got away from the sand. The wind blew it into everything. He had sand in his boots right now. . . .

"I wasn't born for this," Goblin complained. "Nobody deserves this. Me less than most. What did I ever do to the Old Man? All right, so maybe me and One-Eye drink a little and get rowdy sometimes, but so what? It's just youthful high spirits if Sleepy does it."

Naturally he overlooked the fact that when he and One-Eye get drunk they always start squabbling and tend to begin throwing sloppily woven spells around, busting things up far worse than Sleepy ever could.

"A man has to cut loose sometimes, you know what I mean? Nobody ever gets hurt, do they?" That was not an exaggeration, that was an outright fabrication. "Hell, in a world where there was any shred of justice I'd be retired somewhere where the wine is sweet and the girls appreciate a man with experience. I gave the Company the best centuries of my life."

Goblin hated being in charge. That meant having to think and make decisions. And it meant taking responsibility. Goblin hated all those things, too. He just wanted to cruise through life doing only what was necessary to get by while somebody else did the thinking and made the decisions.

Goblin hated hard work, too, and in this desert everybody was going to have to bust ass to stay alive.

I had Smoke take me up high, with the eagles—had any been able to survive out there—to see what had Goblin so excited.

He had not exaggerated about the desert.

Near the coast the Shindai Kus was all golden sand. The surf brought that in from the deep. Continuous gales carried that sand inland, using it to scour the skin off hills that, as they grew up and marched to the east, became the Dandha Presh. On the coast few of the hills stood more than a hundred feet above the sand. None of those showed the least sign of water erosion. It had not rained there for a thousand years.

I started to descend. Goblin and two others were walking inland slowly, testing the surface. Something exploded out of the sand ahead. An impossible something. A monster that could not exist in this world, a devil thing the size of an elephant but with more legs and hair than a tarantula plus some squidlike tentacles and a scorpion's tail thrown in for good measure. It staggered around groggily. Obviously it had lain there a long time, awaiting the footsteps that called it forth.

Goblin's companions fled. The little wizard cursed and said, "Another thing I hate is things that jump up out of the sand." While the monster was still woozy he hit it with some of his best stuff.

Something like a yard wide, a three-legged stained-glass throwing star appeared in his hand. He used it like a throwing star. The monster bellowed in outrage as the star clipped a couple tentacles and several legs off its right side. It tried to charge Goblin, who elected for the better part of valor and hauled ass.

The monster sort of dragged itself around in a big circle, leaving ruts in the golden sand. It lost interest in the men on the beach. For a while it tried to put its severed limbs back on but the graft would not take. Finally, it just sort of shuddered fatalistically and began to dig itself back down into the sand with the limbs it still had.

"And another thing," Goblin complained, "I hate the whole concept of the Shaded Road."

Shaded Road was some secret project kept from me because I had had no need to know. I had overheard the name mentioned once or twice.

"I'm even beginning to wonder how much I like Croaker. This shit is pure insanity. I hope the son of a bitch gets to spend his afterlife in a place like this."

No more need to check up on Goblin. He was fine. Like any good soldier, if he was bitching he was perfectly all right.

I went back to Dejagore.

I came back into myself inside One-Eye's wagon. I was starving and thirsty. Smoke smelled bad. "One-Eye! I have to get something to eat. Where's the transients' mess?"

The little black man stuck his disgusting hat into the wagon. I could barely make out his equally ugly face. It must be getting dark out already.

"For us it's in the citadel."

"Isn't that wonderful. Maybe I won't eat the meat." Mogaba and his cronies, still on our side then, had sat out the siege in the citadel, dining on the occasional hapless citizen of Jaicur.

"Pretend it's chicken, it ain't so bad," One-Eye said, just to turn my stomach. His nose wrinkled. "Smells in here."

"I told you. You'd better get him cleaned up."

He tried out his baleful stare. It did not work. I said, "You have to live with him."

10

I THOUGHT CROAKER WOULD WANT TO CATCH UP WITH LADY. THEY HAD NOT seen one another for a while. But he seemed content to rest at Dejagore, communing with his dark messengers more and more.

The crows troubled those of the Old Crew whose duties tied them to Dejagore. Candles and Wheezer came to me complaining. I told them, "He's the boss. I guess he can like crows if he wants." I studied Wheezer closely, unable to believe his disease had not killed him yet. He coughed almost continuously now.

"It's what the natives think about them," Candles said. "They're bad omens to everybody but Stranglers."

"I have a feeling they'll be really bad omens for anybody who starts complaining about them. Wheezer, you on permanent assignment here?"

The old man hacked his way around an affirmative answer.

"Good. I don't think you ought to be in the field at this time of year."

"What good will it do to leave me back here to die alone?"

"You're going to outlive me, you stubborn old fart."

"I'm part of this thing now. You people all the time tell us about our history and now we got a chance to find the beginning place. . . . I'm going to be there."

I nodded, accepting that. That was his right.

That made me reflect on how different we were from other mercenary bands I have seen. There was almost no bullying or brutality among the men. Historically you would not have gotten in if you were the sort of shit who made himself feel good by causing pain to those around you. And if you did chances were you would not survive long.

The history and culture and brotherhood stuff is laid on early and often and if you survive long enough to give it a chance you usually go for it.

Croaker, of course, was the ultimate disciple of the Company thing. And he was able to sell everyone else. Except Mogaba. And Mogaba's main problem with the brotherhood was that Mogaba was not in charge.

Not really relevant, except to indicate that we are not a band of misfit brutes. We are a sensitive bunch of misfits who try to care about our brothers. Most of the time.

One-Eye appeared and invited himself into the conversation, ignoring Wheezer even though the old lunger was from his own homeland. "Hey, Kid, I just saw the Troll trundling along Glimmers Like Dewdrops Street. You sure you don't know where Goblin is? I got to get those two together."

The Troll is what her own people call Mother Gota behind her back. She is even nastier to them than to us outsiders. We have an excuse. We were not born Nyueng Bao.

I told One-Eye, "They made real good time considering the way she walks." My mother-in-law walks like she is terminally bowlegged and has no joints in her legs, rolling like a fat merchantman in heavy seas.

The little black man slipped a glance sidelong at Thai Dei, who was handy as always when not specifically told to stay away. Thai Dei showed signs of actual emotion. One-Eye was hoping he was not offended to the point where he was going to go flailing around. . . .

I whispered, "Even he calls her the Troll sometimes. But do be more circumspect." Louder, I asked, "What about Uncle Doj?"

"Didn't see him."

"Thai Dei. You'd better find your mother." Uncle Doj would find us. When it suited him.

Everybody watched Thai Dei go. When he was out of earshot I murmured, "I never missed her for an instant." I hoped Thai Dei would find some way to prolong my joy.

One-Eye snickered.

I said, "You ask me, she's the perfect woman for you, not Goblin."

"Bite your tongue, Kid."

"I mean it."

"You got a sick sense of humor. And you got the Old Man aggravated."

"Huh? How?"

"Way he told it, you're a couple days overdue with your standard reports."

"Oh-oh." That was not entirely true but it was close. "I'll get on it right away."

"Still wearing your bracelet?"

"Uh . . ." I got it. "Yeah."

"Good. You'll need it."

Candles and Wheezer had no idea what we were talking about. But Candles did offer a good bit of advice as I departed. "Mind the crows," he told me.

The crows did seem to be interested in me lately. I did not like that, but it did make sense from a viewpoint other than my own. I was very close to Croaker. Soulcatcher would want to keep an eye on me, too.

The old saw applied. Forewarned was forearmed.

I needed to catch up on events since last I had had time to spend with Smoke. I should have been surveying the front instead of checking up on Goblin. Croaker did not want to know about Goblin. Whatever the little shit was doing, it was so secret nobody was supposed to know.

The string on my wrist allowed me to approach One-Eye's wagon without becoming disoriented or distracted, just as it had done in the maze of the Palace. The crows following me, though, began to get confused while we were still a quarter mile away. They lost me.

I wondered if that was all good. That sort of thing was sure to arouse Soulcatcher's curiosity—if she had time free from her other schemes.

I wondered if Smoke's attitude toward Soulcatcher would be different out here, if I could get him to stalk her now that he was away from the Palace. Always, while we were there, his soul stubbornly refused to play along whenever I tried to spy on Lady's mad sister.

I climbed into the wagon and made myself comfortable. It looked as though One-Eye had been doing a little ghostwalking of his own. Food and water were available in large quantities. I have to eat and drink a lot when I go out a lot. Ghostwalking sucks the fluid and energy out of you fast. I can see the trap there. The world Smoke walks is so comforting you could easily forget that you have to come back to eat. You could end up just like Smoke.

After a long drink and a sugar bun I lay down on the smelly mat and closed my eyes, reached out and took hold of Smoke's soul. He seemed vaguely troubled. Usually he is blandly empty. I could find no proximate cause for his discomfort. Maybe One-Eye was not taking care of his physical needs well enough. I had best check. After I ran my circuit.

I went out and watched the Taglian brushfire crackle through feeble Shadowlander defenses. The southerners were still groggy from the earthquake. Many places their collapse was so swift it had no chance to become a rout.

Confused reports began to reach Mogaba at Charandaprash. He relayed them to Longshadow. The Shadowmaster remained convinced that we could not manage a major winter offensive, that this was just another of Croaker's clever attempts to direct attention away from what he was really doing.

Longshadow was getting his reports without help from Howler. The misshapen, tortured little sorcerer seemed to be on vacation. I could not find him.

Narayan Singh and the Daughter of Night were holed up in a Strangler tagalong encampment near Mogaba's main force at Charandaprash. I am not sure why but the child caught my interest. I began to roam back and forth in time, studying her. I grew troubled. I had found something the Old Man needed to know.

His daughter had some way of scrying distant events, though not as intimately as Smoke did. So far nobody, not even Singh, was listening to her, but they would when Narayan realized that all her vague oracles hit their marks.

She seemed to go into a trance each time. I wanted to study that more closely but Smoke rebelled. And this time I am not sure I blamed him. That child had an aura about her that made you shudder and think of tombs and things best left buried even out there in the emotionless space that Smoke walked.

Lady was far to the south of Dejagore, pushing herself and her soldiers. She looked extremely haggard, though hardly showing her age since she makes One-Eye look like a pup. Willow Swan, with the Royal Guards, was in her train, as was the Prahbrindrah Drah, who claimed he had to be there in order to coordinate his efforts with hers. I do not think he fooled anyone but himself. Lady was short enough of temper that she did not put up with any moon-eyed crap from anybody.

Swan was troubled. The Prince was baffled. I eavesdropped on several conversations where they tried to reason out what was bothering Lady. They came up with no ideas and Lady offered no clues herself. Once again she was content to keep the bleakness and pain of her interior world to herself.

I supposed after a life as long as hers, as alone, as tormented when she was the wife of the Dominator, coming out and petitioning the help of lesser beings seemed pointless, though she was one of us maggots herself, now. More or less.

In defiance of all that was known by amateurs and experts alike, her lost powers had been coming back for years. She was not the Lady who had built the empire up north, so strong she kept ten like the Howler on leashes, as hounds to bay before her and do her dark bidding, but she was strong enough to trouble Howler and Longshadow and, I am sure, her sister Soulcatcher.

That was another wedge that had come between Croaker and Lady. The Old Man does not trust the side of her that loves the darkness. She had been too intimate with it for too long.

He fears losing her. I am afraid he is driving her away because he is not dealing with his fears very well.

Lady was becoming the terror of all who resisted her advance, that was certain. That advance was crueler than the earthquake wherever anyone fought back.

I found my Company brethren in the thick of the action everywhere, leading this band or that. Their Nyueng Bao bodyguards stayed busy. Though they were weak after years of being hunted down by Croaker and Lady, the Deceivers were aptly named. Those who remained alive were the most skilled of their kind and they shunned no opportunity to strike at the Company in honor of their goddess.

Though Mogaba had several thousand horsemen moving north they were not yet involved in the fighting. Of Shadowlander forces in the regions being swamped only Blade's bunch had not been caught flatfooted. And Blade, after a couple of brisk—and for him very satisfactory—encounters with regiments raised by Taglian religious leaders, was making little effort to hold any territory. He was falling back toward Charandaprash at a pace just fast enough to make certain our forces did not get behind him.

His whole area of operations was becoming infested with the religious bands. Ever since their falling-out Croaker had been allowing the priests to go after Blade virtually independent of the rest of the military. Blade hated priests and never hid that fact. Working with the Shadowmaster gave him an opportunity to express his hatred fully. In turn, the priesthoods were determined to silence him forever.

The Old Man seemed perfectly happy to allow the priests, who had a strong tradition of intrigue and interference in secular events, to spend their treasure and energy and most devout followers trying to rid him of someone he detested.

As he retreated Blade kept drawing those guys in and destroying them. For a general with no formal training he did a great job of taking advantage of his enemies' blind spots.

All across the south forces from both sides drifted toward the Plain of Charandaprash. The big show would take place there before much longer. Certainly before winter turned.

I came and went with Smoke. Time passed, almost without meaning. The Old Man got us onto the road again. I scarcely noticed. I was too busy with Smoke. Croaker did not like me being in the wagon all the time but there was so much going on so many places that he had to put up with it in order to get the information he wanted. Though his attitude could shift with the breeze.

For a while I pretended to be sick, to give the crows and my in-laws a reason for my being in the wagon all the time. Crows are stupid. They did not catch on. But I think Uncle Doj got the idea there was something up almost before we cleared Dejagore's south gate.

11

I WAS NEVER A BOOZER OR HOPHEAD. IN THIS PART OF THE WORLD ALL THE major religions frown on alcohol so there is not a lot available—though One-Eye never has trouble finding the little there is. If none is around he will make some. All my life addictions scared the shit out of me. When I see a guy whose pain has driven him behind the veil of alcohol or any drug I want to flee the same weakness I fear can be found inside me.

I was becoming addicted to the freedom from pain to be found in the in-between. When I was out there with Smoke the horrors of Dejagore and the agony left behind by Sarie's murder became no more than distant, nagging aches. That weak side of me kept promising that even the far-away aches would fade if Smoke and I just kept working.

I was both happy and completely miserable at the same time. My in-laws were little help. Thai Dei, as ever, said almost nothing. Uncle Doj merely urged me to be strong. "Death and despair are what we endure all our lives. This world is all one of pain and loss illuminated only briefly by moments of happiness and wonder. We must live for those times, not bemoan their passing."

"We must live for revenge," Mother Gota snapped. "You old fool." She was contemptuous as she glared at me. Nor did she spare my feelings. "My mother was a madwoman in her last days. We will be well rid of this weakling."

Being a weakling and not much caring for this world anymore, I did not feel obliged to keep the peace. "I bet that back in the swamp they thank their lucky stars every night that you decided not to come home."

Thai Dei became pure stone as I put him in a spot where his obligations had to butt heads.

Uncle Doj chuckled. He rested a hand on Thai Dei's arm. "A shaft well sped, youngster. Gota, I must remind you that we are here on sufferance. The Stone Soldier accepts us for Sahra's sake. His master does not."

Though I have a pretty good handle on Nyueng Bao these days I knew I had missed some key part of that. I did understand that he was telling her not to piss Croaker off because he might toss them out. And that was something he could perfectly well do. He considered them little more than camp followers. And Croaker hates camp followers. He considers them worse than leeches.

I had to wonder if Uncle Doj was not interested in something more than just revenge for the murders of Sahra and Thai Dei's son To Tan.

I am not certain where we were. I think about eighty miles south of Dejagore and passing over into territories only recently taken into our hands, where our appearance was endured with the same stoicism as the earthquake. Not much cleaning up had gotten done because the Shadowmaster's henchmen had employed the locals in a vain attempt to blunt our advance. Brave fools. Now there was no one to bury them.

Total paranoia hit me there.

I was unaware of the fact because I was in the wagon but we were just making camp. I was out scouting the maneuvers of Mogaba's cavalry and sitting in on his planning session for making our lives much more unpleasant at Charandaprash. I had a sneer in my heart. He would not have a single surprise for us. From having watched Lady and all the special forces she and Croaker had put together I knew we would have plenty for Mogaba.

Bright man, he expected that. He got to know Croaker pretty well before he deserted to the Shadowmaster.

Then the paranoia hit. Smugness evaporated. Had I been in flesh I would have begun to shake as though suddenly thrown into an icy river. I *knew* I was not alone.

I would have panicked except for the dullness of emotion out there. I did do a sort of sudden spin around on the spirit level.

For a second I thought I saw a face, not directed my way.

It was a face out of a collective nightmare, as big as a cow, the color of ripe eggplant. Its smile was all fangs. And it was smiling at whatever it saw.

Its eyes were plates of fire that, at the same time, seemed to be pools of darkness capable of drowning souls.

I withdrew, very carefully at first, but in full flight toward the safety of reality when the face seemed suddenly startled and began to turn. I emerged too terrified to be hungry or thirsty. I was shaking and babbling and making no sense at all. The Old Man was close by. One-Eye had him in the wagon by the time I got myself under control.

"What the hell happened, Murgen? You have some kind of fit? You going to start going away again on me?" He touched me, felt the shakes that still went right down to the heart of me. "One-Eye . . ."

I croaked out, "I just saw Kina. I don't know if she saw me."

Death is eternity. Eternity is stone. Stone is silence. Stone speaketh not but stone doth remember.

Deep within the dark heart of the grey fastness stands a massive throne of worm-eaten wood. This throne has shifted sideways and tilted dramatically. A dark shape sprawls upon the throne, locked in enchanted slumber, nailed down by silver daggers driven through its limbs. Its once vacant face is drawn in agony.

The figure draws a deep breath. Silence yields to a great slow rumbling beat.

This is immortality of a sort but its price is paid in diamonds of pain, in treasure by the bucket.

In the night, when the wind no longer blows and small shadows no longer creep, the fortress reclaims its silence.

Silence is stone. Stone is eternity. Eternity is death.

12

SOUTH OF SHADOWLIGHT, WHICH OFFERED NO RESISTANCE, THE LAND ROSE and became gorsy, stony, and as wrinkled as my mother-in-law's face. Snow lurked wherever sunlight seldom fell. Trees were scattered but of a variety that clung stubbornly to some of its fruit throughout the winter.

That fruit was tough and dry but it grew tastier as we moved farther from civilization and anyplace where we could acquire more palatable foods. The route the Captain insisted we follow was one that had received very little preparation. And there were no navigable waterways up which barges could carry supplies.

We had cattle along. The animals could sustain themselves—poorly—off the vegetation. Those of us willing to eat flesh could gnaw on their stringy meat. But we were just getting started here and already I was convinced that Croaker had made the wrong choice, attacking now.

Those soldiers who were vegetarians suffered terribly.

The morning wind had a real bite. This definitely was no season for travel. We could end up in real trouble if Mogaba held us up for long.

That might be a good strategy for him to pursue. Just hold us at Charandaprash while all our forces came together, with all their camp followers, then continue to hold us there while we exhausted our resources. Then he could slaughter the starving remnants as they tried to flee.

Though he never mentioned it in so many words, part of Croaker's plan was to replenish our army by seizing supplies Mogaba had laid in for his. The Captain very much counted on victory now, soon, however cautiously he talked.

He had put us in a position where there was no other choice.

The region around Shadowlight remained prosperous even after the earthquake but already that was four hard days' march behind us. Our foragers were eating up half what they gathered just bringing it in.

Longshadow remained unconvinced that our advance was for real. He had a distinct problem imagining minds working differently from his own. Mogaba entertained doubts himself though the Deceivers and his own agents kept him informed of all the disasters to the Shadowmaster's cause. Few of the quake-battered towns and cities made more than token attempts to resist. The Captain had chosen his moment well, if emotionally.

Dark grey-indigo mountains spanned the southern horizon. Charandaprash was just days away. The Captain slowed our advance to a very deliberate pace so the soldiers would have more time to hunt and forage. Our part of the army began coming together in larger and larger forces. Mogaba's cavalry did not seem much inclined to skirmish yet. Ahead of us streamers of smoke sometimes rose as fleeing enemy caravans failed to run fast enough to outdistance our own horsemen.

Our headquarters party clung to the road. Always, now, there seemed to be corpses lying beside it. They came in all varieties, few of them being our own people.

Croaker had forced me out of One-Eye's wagon. I was no longer allowed inside while we were moving. So I led the way, mounted atop that giant black stallion, always presenting the Black Company standard. Crows were around constantly. I expect Soulcatcher, wherever she took their reports, was thoroughly amused. The standard was one we had adapted from one she had assigned us decades ago, based upon her own fire-breathing skull of a seal.

Uncle Doj walked beside me. He carried a lance as well as Ash Wand, his holy sword. He had assumed the job of bodyguard while Thai Dei was elsewhere with his mother. We two encountered all the corpses first. "There's another one that looks like a Deceiver," I said, indicating a badly hacked body wearing nothing but a ragged loincloth, despite the weather.

"It is good," Uncle Doj told me. He rolled the corpse over. The man had been run down by someone with an especial dislike for his cult. He had been mutilated badly, mostly while he was still alive.

I did not feel a shred of pity. Men just like him murdered my Sarie.

We encountered nothing but signs of outstanding success. But those did not inspire my confidence in the future.

Roads converged. Forces massed up even more. Every hour we drew nearer Charandaprash, Mogaba and his four badass divisions of well-trained and motivated veterans. Getting closer to soldiers who had been getting ready for us for years. Getting closer to soldiers who were not the clumsy, indifferent militias that had made up most of our opposition so far. The Old Man talked confidently in front of the Taglians, who did not know any better, but I knew he had his doubts.

We would have a numbers advantage but our men had not been drilled until they were automatons. Our men did not fear their officers more than they feared death itself. Our men did not know the price you paid if you stirred the anger of a Shadowmaster. Not in the intimate way the defenders of Charandaprash knew.

Our men had not rehearsed again and again, learning every boulder on the ground where they would be expected to fight.

13

A BREEZE WHIPPED SMOKE AND THE STENCH OF DEATH INTO MY FACE. A soldier shouted. I glanced back. The Captain, wearing the hideous black Widowmaker armor Lady had created for him, was coming up. Ravens surrounded him. For the thousandth time I wondered about his connection with Soulcatcher.

"You sent for me?"

"There's something you ought to see, I think." I had not seen it myself yet, but did know what to expect.

He gestured. "Let's go."

We rode up a small rise. We stopped to look at the bodies of six small brown men far too old to have been soldiers. They lay inside a bowl that had been hollowed out of the hard ground, around a fire that still yielded a puny thread of smoke.

"Where are the men who killed them?"

"They didn't hang around. You don't take chances with these people."

Croaker grunted, not pleased but understanding the thinking of the ordinary soldier. He removed his ugly winged helmet. Crows took the opportunity to perch on his shoulders. He seemed not to notice. "I'd say we've gotten somebody's attention."

I had run into little brown men like these before, years ago when first we had come into the south and more recently in the Deceivers' holy Grove of Doom, where I had ambushed many of their top people. A group of these skrinsa shadowweavers had had the misfortune to be there on behalf of the Shadowmaster.

These men would have been doing the same as those others, using a gaggle of little shadows to spy and run messages. Croaker pointed. Several of the old men had had chunks ripped right out of them. He observed, "Lady did say you shouldn't get in the way of her bamboo toys."

We had overtaken Lady, more or less. She was following a line of advance several miles to our left. If Croaker and she had stolen a kiss they had managed it by magic. Croaker was in too big a hurry to assume complete control of his assembling center corps of two divisions.

He carried a bamboo pole slung across his back. So did I. And so did every other man in the main force, now. Some carried a bundle. "Oh?"

"She'll pitch a fit if this gets to be a habit." Croaker was amused.

"She never was a ground-pounder."

Your average infantryman does not give a rat's ass about the design function of a weapon. He is concerned about staying alive and about getting his job done with the least risk taken. The bamboo doohickeys were meant for combating killer shadows? So fucking what? If using them made taking out nasty little wizards easier, guess what was going to happen?

Pop!

14

WE SIGHTED LAKE TANJI AN HOUR BEFORE NIGHT FELL. THE SUDDEN VIEW was so stunning I stopped dead in my tracks.

The lake was miles across and cold grey. It dwindled away to my right, the direction our road ran. To our left the land was very rugged. Arms of increasingly substantial hills ran down to the water. The Dandha Presh itself seemed to rise directly from the far shore, all greys in the evening light, dark down low and lighter at the peaks, where snowfields sparkled. A playful god had scrawled a thin cloudline across the panorama, halfway up the mountains, so that the peaks rode a magic carpet.

Grey, grey, grey. Right then the whole world seemed grey.

"Impressive," the Captain said.

"Not at all like seeing it through Smoke's eyes."

He frowned at me even though not even a crow was near enough to hear. "Look there."

A village burned along the shore several miles ahead. A ball of blue light streaked out of the conflagration, over the water, narrowly missed a small boat. The men aboard the boat tried to row harder but began to catch crabs and get in one another's way. A swarm of points of light darted at them, not only blue but green, yellow, pink and a stunning shade of violet. A man jumped up and flailed around after a ball hit him in the throat. He fell overboard. His antics rocked the boat dangerously. It shipped water, raised its stern into the air momentarily.

A ball of light zipped through its bottom, leaving a shimmering hole.

Most of the balls missed. Those continued across the lake, slowing gradually. Eventually they just drifted on the breeze and faded away.

The excitement brought a flock of crows fast. They circled overhead. Two big ones dropped onto Croaker's shoulders. The others scattered in pairs.

The boat sank.

It had been bound for an island that was little more than a rock outcrop boasting a dozen scraggly pine trees and some halfhearted brush. A crow that got close suddenly folded up and went ballistic, hit the water and floated without twitching.

Croaker glared. "Murgen. Move down the foreslope, out of the wind. Find a place to dig in for the night. Line troops only on this side of the ridge. I want a double watch kept. I want two battery wagons up, trained on that island."

His shoulder ornaments were agitated now. I did not mention them. He was starting to go spooky—and he did not answer questions anyway.

One of the ravens squawked. Croaker grunted back. He dismounted, grabbed an extra bamboo pole from a nearby soldier, headed downhill. His mount followed the trail he broke.

The soldiers who had begun to gather followed Croaker's example. They formed a skirmish line as they advanced. I could not unsling my own bamboo pole because I was mounted and burdened with the standard. I followed the men on foot. Uncle Doj formed a one-man rearguard.

Two Shadowlander militiamen broke cover suddenly. They stumbled toward the water's edge. Arrows swarmed.

Standing orders were to take no prisoners. The Shadowlanders had been warned. They had been given four years' grace. They had made their choices.

Afterward the soldiers began to settle in groups, finding what shelter they could, starting their cooking fires. More and more came up to the line. Our staff group gathered in the lee of a shattered boulder, everybody grumbling and shivering. Pessimists started talking about the chances of snow.

I planted the standard. Uncle Doj and I got ready to make supper. There were no servants in this army. Servants ate up food soldiers could fix for themselves.

Supper would be rice and dried fruit. Croaker and I would add a few strips of jerked beef. Uncle Doj would add some fish meal to his rice. Many of the soldiers would eat no flesh because of religious proscriptions.

I said, "Maybe we can find out if there are any fish in this lake."

The Old Man looked out there. "Looks like there could be trout." But he did not say anything about maybe catching them.

The battery wagons came up. Each had a bed four feet wide by ten feet long packed with bamboo tubes. They were the ultimate product of Lady's arsenals. The Captain supervised their positioning. He wanted them set just right.

Under this overcast it would not be long before it was dark enough for shadows to prowl.

East of the lake, where Lady's left wing division was advancing through very rugged country, a single point of light shot into the air, sped southward, lost velocity and began to lose altitude slowly. Balls in several colors followed quickly.

The soldiers stirred nervously.

A *whiff* sound came from a nearby wagon. A green fireball streaked out over the lake, its light reflecting off the water. The breeze had died. The lake's surface was growing calm.

I was more nervous than any of the soldiers. I had seen what those stinking little shadowweavers could do. I had seen men scream out their lives while something invisible gnawed at them.

The soldiers had heard the stories. The sentries would stay awake tonight.

The green ball did not dip toward that island. I sighed. Maybe there was no danger after all.

The wagon crews loosed another ball at regular intervals. Not a one dipped toward that island. I regained my confidence. The men began to relax. Eventually I rolled up in my blankets and lay there watching fireballs streak across the sky.

It was a comfort knowing no shadow attack would go undetected.

I listened to the wagon crews lay bets on what color fireball would pop out next. There was no known pattern. They were getting bored. Soon they would be bitching about getting stuck with the duty while everybody else got to sleep.

15

I WAS HAVING A BIZARRE DREAM ABOUT CORDY MATHER AND THE RADISHA when somebody poked me. I groaned, cracked an eyelid. I knew I did not have to stand a watch. I had helped with the cooking. I cursed, pulled my blankets over my head and tried to get back to the Palace, where Mather was arguing with the Radisha about her plans to shaft the Black Company after the Shadowmaster fell. It almost felt like I was actually there rather than dreaming.

"Wake up." Uncle Doj prodded me again.

I tried to cling to the dream. There was more to it. Something nebulous but dangerous about the Radisha. Something that had Mather upset in a major way.

I thought I might be working out something important in my sleep.

"Wake up, Bone Warrior."

That did it. I hated it when Nyueng Bao called me that, never explaining what they meant. I grunted, "What?"

"Trouble is coming."

Thai Dei stepped out of the darkness. He spoke! "One-Eye told me to warn you."

"What're you doing up here?" His arm had not yet healed completely.

I glanced at the Captain. He was awake. He had a bird perched on one shoulder, beak moving at his ear. He eyed Thai Dei and Uncle Doj but said nothing. He clambered to his feet wearily, collected a couple of bamboo poles and trudged around to where he could see the lake. I followed him. Uncle Doj tagged along behind me. It amazed me that a man so short and wide could move so quietly and gracefully.

I saw nothing new out there in the darkness. Occasional flecks of light continued to streak the tapestry of the night. "Like fireflies." There were a million stars. The guys who expected snow were going to be disappointed.

"Hush," Croaker said. He was listening to something. The damned bird on his shoulder?

Where was the other one?

A crimson ball zipped away from one wagon just like scores before it. But when this one neared the island it dipped violently and swerved to the right, scattering the rippling water with ten thousand rubies. At water level the ball became a splash of blood that faded immediately.

There was no reflection off the water anywhere nearby.

"Shadows."

A half-dozen balls streaked out. They defined a river of darkness snaking across the lake. Then balls started flying around over the remnants of the village that had been burning while that boat sank.

The discharges there reached panic level quickly. The Captain ordered, "Swing one of the wagons around. Give them some support down there. And let's see if we can't get a couple more wagons up here fast."

Some individuals were plinking at the village already, for whatever help that would provide. Croaker told the crew of the second wagon, "Cut loose on that island. Everything you've got. Murgen. I want everybody awake and up here. The shitstorm is about to hit."

I ran off to tap-dance on a couple of snorers famous for their bugle calls.

Both wagons cut loose about the same time. Their trigger cranks squealed and rattled as they whirled. Bamboo tubes discharged color in furious series. How many balls could a wagon launch? A shitload.

Cavalry tubes carried fifteen charges. Standard infantry and infantry long carried thirty and forty charges respectively. The hundreds of tubes on each wagon were longer still.

The fireflies went mad. Every single ball launched darted downward after a shadow. Each made its dip nearer shore.

"Lots of shadows," Croaker observed laconically. This was a new thing but a thing we had feared for years. Shadows attacking in waves and a flood instead of sneaking around like spies and assassins.

The Old Man seemed calm. Me, I damned near drizzled down my leg. I ran, but only far enough to get hold of the standard and a bundle of bamboo. I planted the former beside the Old Man, got the business end of a pole pointed southward, found the handgrip trigger mechanism and started turning. Each quarter turn sent another fireball streaking. I told Thai Dei, "Grab you some bamboo, brother. You too, uncle. This isn't going to be anything you can stop with a sword."

Balls were arcing over from the far slope now. There were enough in transit to define the wave of darkness headed our way. Fireballs plunged into that darkness like bright hail, flared, faded. This was the nightmare tide we had dreaded for so long, the hellpower of the Shadowmaster unleashed.

Balls consumed shadows by the thousand. The flood came on. Unlike mortal soldiers those things could do nothing but follow commands. Sorcery compelled them.

My pole went dry. I grabbed another one. Uncle Doj and Thai Dei began to grasp the situation. They found poles and got into the act, though Thai Dei was not very fast one-handed.

The dark tide came off the water and headed upslope. As it drew closer I began to make out individual shadows.

I saw these things first way back when we first came to Taglios, in the days when there were four Shadowmasters and together they could reach a lot farther than could Longshadow now. The skrinsa shadowweavers came north to kill us. They failed. But in their time they used small shadows, few bigger than my fist. I never saw one bigger than a cat.

Some in this flood dwarfed cattle. Those absorbed fireballs with no apparent effect. I saw dozens survive multiple hits.

I muttered, "Maybe Lady wasn't as clever as she thought."

Croaker replied, "Think what it would be like without her cleverness."

We would be dead already.

"Got you."

Closer. Closer. The dark wall was but a hundred yards distant now, the shadows far fewer in number and moving slower but relentless nevertheless.

Now the wagons could not depress their aim low enough to hit the shadows. They shifted their attentions to that island.

Uncle Doj shouted, drew Ash Wand. I have no idea what he thought that would do to the huge clot of darkness racing straight toward us while a swarm of small shadows scurried around it like frightened offspring. No sword held any power against this darkness.

I tried to burn a hole through the clot's heart, poised on the brink of panic.

Death ravened closer and closer.

Balls from the rear began falling around us as little shadows slithered in amongst the rocks.

The screams began.

The dark mass became a bonfire as fireballs hammered it. It slowed, slowed some more, but never stopped coming. It reared like a boar grizzly issuing his challenge. I spun my handgrip hard, yelled some kind of nonsense. That killer slice of hell's breath strained to get at me but could not. It was as though the thing, at the last instant, had encountered some invisible and unbreakable barrier.

The darkness radiated a dank psychic horror I imagined went with the grave, a hunger known only by things undead, an odor of the soul I remembered from too many bad dreams about bone-strewn wastelands and old men bound up in cocoons of spun ice. My terror grew stronger. I yanked at my handgrip long after my pole went dry, long after there was no more reason to crank.

The shadow kept trying to get to me until the barrage of fireballs consumed its last whisper of darkness.

The excitement faded quickly. Only balls launched toward the island found many targets.

The rock outcrop was taking a pounding from Lady's division, too, the troops over there having figured out what was happening. I thought the volume of fire so heavy it might actually consume the island.

Then Croaker ordered fire reduced to precautionary levels. "No sense wasting our tools. We're going to run into this sort of thing again." He stared at me for half a minute. Then he asked, "How did we get surprised like this?" He used that Juniper tongue.

I shrugged. "Don't ask me." I chose Forsberger because I did not know the other well enough. "I was busy carrying the standard." Meaning I was cut off from Smoke most of the time these days for what he considered sufficient reason. He was going to have to count on One-Eye to provide his warnings.

"Shit," he said, without much venom. "Goddamn shit. Don't get clever with—"

A grand shriek rolled across the lake. Lady's troops loosed a furious barrage at something that darted up from the island and raced away southward. Croaker grunted. "The Howler!"

"We got them scared now, boss. The Shadowmaster is sending the big boys out to play."

Croaker showed me a twitch of the lip. Not much. His sense of humor had gone to hell lately. Maybe he lost it when he was Soulcatcher's prisoner. Or maybe when he came back to find out that he was a father but chances were he would never see his kid.

Howler escaped.

We stood down eventually but hardly anyone got any more sleep.

16

DAWN DID COME. IT FOUND OUR DEAD ALREADY BURNED OR BURIED BY SOLDIERS who had been unable to sleep. I did not have to look at one tormented face.

There was no shortage of tormented landscape. It looked as though small lightnings had been on a year-long rampage around the lake. Already some of the more daring troopers were down at the water's edge collecting dead fish.

Of the things that had attacked us there was no trace at all.

Croaker suggested, "You might spend a *little* more time with Smoke." Which, of course, was more than a suggestion, though given reluctantly. He had given up counting on One-Eye for anything but grief.

I glanced around. My in-laws were nowhere in sight. I told him, "One-Eye did send warning."

"It wasn't what I'd call timely. It must have taken Howler and Long-shadow days to set last night up. We should have been ready."

"Maybe not being ready will work out for the best, though."

"Why? How?"

"If we'd ambushed their ambush they would've started wondering how we knew about it. The way it worked out they'll just sit around cussing Lady for thinking ahead."

"You got a point. But I still want a little more warning. Just don't go getting hung up on ghostwalking."

"What about the standard? I don't know where Sleepy is these days and there isn't another sworn brother handy." Nobody who was not Company was going to touch our most holy of relics. The standard—actually, the lance from which the standard hangs—is the only artifact we have which has remained with the Company since its beginnings. The oldest Annals have all been recopied time and time again, undergoing translation after translation.

Croaker told me, "I'll manage it. You get sick and have to ride for a while." He did and I did. Wearing his full Widowmaker armor he became terrible to behold once he took up the standard. A dark aura seemed to envelop him.

Much of that had to do with spells Lady had built into and onto the armor, layer after layer, for years. Even though Widowmaker was pure powerless invention, the vision was supposed to suggest something way beyond the ordinary, was supposed to stir the observer's superstitions. So was the Lifetaker character Lady had created for herself. But hers had grown into its legend. Or had been something more than invention to start.

When Lady donned that armor she resembled one of the avatars of the goddess Kina. Some of her soldiers and more of her enemies half believed that when she donned the Lifetaker garb she became possessed by the dark goddess. I did not like that idea and did not accept it but Lady never discouraged it.

It did touch near a suspicion I have entertained from the time I first read Lady's volume of the Annals.

Could it be possible she was still a tool of that Mother of Night? Maybe unwittingly?

Uncle Doj and Thai Dei scowled suspiciously when I told them I was sick again and was going to ride in One-Eye's wagon for a while. I am sure Uncle Doj now knew Smoke was aboard and wanted to find out why the comatose wizard was important enough for us to carry off to war. He did not press me, though. He remained sensitive to Croaker's scrutiny.

"How you doing, Kid?" One-Eye asked as I clambered aboard. He sounded depressed. Maybe he had a good ass-chewing from the Old Man. Again.

"You missed some big fun last night."

"Not hardly. And I can tell you that I'm too damned old for this crap. Croaker don't get us to Khatovar pretty damned soon I'm gonna drop out and take up leek farming."

"I've got some good turnip seed. And rutabagas. I could use a manager. . . ."

"Work for you? Bullshit. Anyway, I know where I can get me some good ground cheap. Up in the Dhojar Prine. I could take Goblin along and make him lead field hand."

He was just making chin music and we both knew it. I suggested, "You want to run a big operation you're going to need a good woman to help. My mother-in-law would just love to remarry."

Sourly, he told me, "I had it all scoped out to fix Goblin up with her. That would've been my all-time masterpiece. But he had to go and disappear."

"Gods just can't take a fucking joke, can they?"

"No shit. You should get more sleep. You look like you've been up all night. And you're getting a little testy."

Like a demon summoned by the naming of its name Mother Gota came waddling around the side of One-Eye's wagon. One-Eye squeaked in surprise. I gulped air. She was supposed to be a long way back up the road.

But, then, Thai Dei was supposed to be back there recuperating, too.

The old woman was lugging so many weapons she looked like a dwarfish arms merchant. She looked up. Her usual grim scowl was missing. She smiled at One-Eye, showing us her absent teeth.

One-Eye gave me a look of hopeless appeal. "They can't take a joke. Not even a little one, not even once. Don't stress him, Kid. I got the cough fixed but now he ain't taking his soup so good." Ignoring the Nyueng Bao woman, he settled himself on the driver's seat, cracked a whip.

I wasted no time. I made myself comfortable and went ghostwalking.

I like the word "consternation." It sounds like what it means.

There was a shitload of consternation surrounding Mogaba when I arrived. He and his gang had gotten an incoherent report from Howler, who was not exactly in pristine condition when he reached Charandaprash. He and his carpet both had been hit by Lady's marksmen.

An important point was that Howler and the Shadowmaster had cooked up the night's festivities without ever having consulted Mogaba. Mogaba was pissed off, the way generals get whenever their expertise is disdained.

Blade's force had joined Mogaba's. Croaker had talked about trying to cut him off but nothing had developed. There had been no time for planning and launching a strong enough force.

Usually the boss does manage to separate the wishful from the possible, whatever his own feelings.

Upon arriving, Blade took charge of the division forming Mogaba's left flank, meaning he would be head to head with the Prahbrindrah Drah when the field armies collided. It was interesting to note that all the division commanders of the Shadowlander main force, along with the head general himself, were renegades who had gone over from our side.

They were all competent soldiers but I doubted that Longshadow cared. What mattered to him most was that they would be strongly motivated to avoid defeat and capture.

I scurried ahead to Overlook, to be there when Howler reported from the front. It ought to be entertaining. Longshadow turned into a raving, foamy-mouthed madman when things really went wrong.

I had to adjust my position in time only slightly to watch the screaming sorcerer arrive on a carpet that was a herd of holes held together by a handful of threads. It was a wonder it did not fall apart under him.

Longshadow listened to Howler's report. He was angry but he did not fault his ally. Which was odd. He was not one to assume much blame himself. Howler observed, "She was a step ahead this time."

"Did any of our assets survive the skirmish?"

Skirmish?

"No."

"Time to keep the skildirsha behind the Dandha Presh, then. For now we'll use them only for communications and reconnaissance. What of the skrinsa? Any out there?"

"Not living. Not that I transported."

"Excellent."

This was scary. Longshadow always dealt with bad news by turning into a raving lunatic.

The Howler said, "Husband those who still live. Order them to begin teaching their craft to any with the capacity to learn it. If your mighty general fails and the Company breaks through at Charandaprash, shadowweavers will be priceless."

Longshadow grunted, fiddled with his mask. "You knew the woman. Senjak. Does she have the power to break our armies?"

"She would have in olden times. It's possible she may be strong enough now. Unless we go up there to preoccupy her while our troops exterminate hers."

I found it interesting that they believed Lady was in charge, whatever appearance we presented. Possibly that was because Howler had been under her thumb for so long, virtually her slave. He might not be capable of believing her anything less than the master. Too, they seemed unable to recognize the fact that our better motivated troops had beaten theirs regularly without any sorcerous, mystical or divine assistance.

Longshadow asked, "Are there a great many of them coming?"

"Yes. Although they have broken with past practice. Many are camp followers weakened by trying to live off a land already scoured by military foragers."

True. And even the soldiers were less than one hundred percent. However much groundwork we had laid, the last leg of the journey passed through barren country.

"But their force is larger?"

"The combat force is, yes, slightly. But it consists of less disciplined troops. The evidence all says she's made this move out of political expediency. The Taglian priesthoods have recovered from the blow she struck them four years ago. They have started testing her. She's just diverting them. Singh's spies say all the senior Taglians expect this campaign to end in defeat."

"Get some rest. Prepare the other carpet. If I must go up there then I must accept the risk fully. I'll want to arrive there before Mogaba succumbs to the temptation to take the fight to his enemies."

Even now, after natural disaster had stalled construction on Overlook indefinitely, Longshadow was determined to stall for time instead of taking the offensive.

I am no military genius but I have read the available Annals a few times. Nowhere in there did I ever find mention of anybody who won a war sitting on his ass.

Much as I hate the man personally, professionally I can feel sorry for Mogaba. For about fifteen seconds. Before we cut his throat.

17

SMOKE SEEMED UNTROUBLED AND COMFORTABLE AFTER MY VISIT TO OVERlook so I left the ghostworld long enough to fill both our stomachs with food and water. He had fouled himself. One-Eye was uninclined to stop and clean him up so I did the honors while the vehicle creaked and bounced and tossed me around. The thankless chore done, I decided to relieve myself before I suffered a similar embarrassment while I was out.

It had happened before.

I found the whole Ky gang trudging along within rock-throwing distance of the wagon. One-Eye scowled down at me. He did not like having them hang so close. Especially Mother Gota, who kept trying to strike up a conversation. I grinned and headed off into the brush.

Somebody almost mistook me for a Shadowlander straggler but my luck held and I got back to the wagon in one piece. One-Eye bitched, "I'd like to lay my paws on the dickhead who decided this was a road. This damn seat is beating my ass into a paste."

"You could get married, retire, drop out and raise turnips."

"You got a serious attitude problem, Kid. You come on anything interesting?"

"Not really. But I'm going out again. Soon as you stop chattering."

"Goddamn kids. You try to be nice—" The left rear wheel fell into a hole, shaking the entire wagon and shutting him up for as long as it took him to marshall an array of curses to direct at his team. I got myself comfortable with Smoke.

Since the unconscious wizard seemed especially amenable today I decided it might be time to test his limits, to see if I could push him nearer things he had refused to approach in the past.

I started with what lay south of Overlook, after just a glance in to see that nothing new was happening with Howler and Longshadow.

Kiaulune in the aftermath of disaster had no appeal. Overlook, while bright, was a mask for madness and despair. Beyond lay rocky grey slopes almost steep enough to be called an escarpment. A road ran from Kiaulune past Overlook and up the boulder-strewn slope. It was a road that had seen little traffic ever, yet it remained clearly defined. Only a few stubborn, hardy weeds had taken root there. Except for one small slide way up the hill no rocks seemed willing to remain on the road's surface.

I tried to take Smoke in that direction.

I enjoyed no more success than I ever had, which meant I managed to cross half the distance from Overlook to the slide before Smoke refused to go any farther.

Someday the Black Company would go up that road. No one else ever went but we would go. That was the road to Khatovar. That was the road that would lead us to our origins.

From Kiaulune I rode Smoke north in a sweeping search for Soulcatcher, Lady's mad, wicked sister. I found no obvious sign immediately but she was skilled at not being seen. I closed in on the Old Man himself, began using Smoke's ability to move through time as well as space to backtrack the crows that follow the army and hang around him.

I fooled the coward for just a moment. For long enough to carry myself into view of Lady's nemesis.

She was out in the wastes, all alone except for her pets. She was eating, something I had never seen or heard of Soulcatcher doing. She was gorgeous. Gorgeous like only evil can be. For an instant I felt that same twinge I had experienced the first time I saw Sahra.

Thought of Sahra startled me. Out here was my time free of that pain. . . .

The instant I lost my focus Smoke's cowardly soul seemed to sense how near Soulcatcher it was. It pushed away as though repelled. I did not resist. I needed to be away from there, too.

Soulcatcher was a madwoman, bold beyond reason, likely to do almost anything if it amused her. She must be having great fun lately.

If Smoke's visions could be trusted she was less than a mile away right now, here in the middle of the army, undetected, so close she could strike anyone anywhere instantly whenever the urge came upon her. And such urges did.

The Old Man needed to know. . . .

Or did he?

He might, reasoning that crows had a limited endurance.

I went away from there and took Smoke back to the Palace in Taglios. He seemed comfortable with that. We went to the room where he had been hidden so long. Dust was gathering there. The lost Annals were still out of sight where I had concealed them.

In another part of the Palace the Radisha was going about the daily business of ruling an empire, she and all the powerful priests and lords and functionaries going along with the pretense that she was just standing in momentarily for her brother, the Prahbrindrah Drah. As long as everybody agreed not to notice the Prince's extended absence, the engines of state continued to function reasonably well.

In truth, though never stated publicly, the state operated much more efficiently without the Prince present to filter and soften his sister's will.

I found the Woman and buzzed around her like an invisible mosquito, forward and backward in time, sticking my long nose into her every conversation—excepting those she had with Cordy Mather when no one else was around. Much.

I heard enough to know Mather was getting used. But it was use most men willingly endure, at least for a while.

Her conversations with several senior priests were interesting, though never as explicit as I would like. The Radisha had matured in the seldom-friendly environment of the Palace, where a thousand plots great and small were afoot every day, at the best of times, and there were always ears eager to pick up anything you said.

She did not plan to keep her word to the Captain and Company. Surprise, surprise. But she was not yet pursuing any vigorous course of betrayal. Like everyone else she was certain Croaker's winter campaign was either a tactic not directed at the Shadowmaster at all or if pursued genuinely would result in a debacle for Taglian arms. This despite our having seized victory in the face of certain defeat on several occasions earlier.

We just might be able to make her sorry she was not a more ambitious backstabber.

What other avenues needed exploration? Goblin? He could manage without me watching over his shoulder.

Out of curiosity and because I was not yet ready to return to the world, I traced each of my in-laws back for the last few weeks. I learned nothing that would support the Old Man's paranoia. But they were a cautious folk, just three of them out here amongst folk no Nyueng Bao had reason to trust or love. Thai Dei and Uncle Doj said very little about anything, just like they did when I was around. Mother Gota was little different, too. She just complained about different things.

Her opinion of me was not completely flattering. Hardly an hour passed when she failed to take the opportunity to damn her mother for having wished me onto the family Ky.

There were times when I was not too fond of Hong Tray for having wished all her family on me.

What should I see now? I was not ready to go back yet.

Narayan Singh and the Daughter of Night? They were at Charandaprash with Mogaba, collecting the scabby remnants of the Deceiver cult under the Shadowmaster's standard. Not much mischief they could get up to there.

Lady, then. Then I would report to the Captain.

I had not been tracking her but wherever she was I was likely to find somebody the Company needed to watch, like the Prahbrindrah Drah or Willow Swan.

The Prince was not in Lady's camp. He was capable of letting duty overrule wishful thinking. He was with his own division, paying attention to business.

Charandaprash was no longer that far away. Around the lake, over a few hills and valleys, then there we would be, staring across the stony plain at the mouth of the only practical pass through the Dandha Presh.

Swan was close to Lady, of course. He looked worried whether I rolled back through the days or stayed hovering right now. Lady was having problems she would not share with him or anyone else. She looked as though she had been getting no sleep. I knew she slept very little at the best of times. For her to abandon sleep like this now, as we neared our most important confrontation in years—one that could become a defining event in the Company's history—suggested that she had no faith in the future at all.

Running through time did give me a clue or two, though. She was indeed doing without sleep. And whenever she did take a nap she did not rest well. She seemed to be having dreams as ugly as some of mine.

For some reason crows never came close to her. But they were always around, somewhere in the distance, watching.

Lady was not interesting. She did nothing but work. She did not bother to look overwhelmingly beautiful anymore, unlike her sister. Was she, like some women do, going all dowdy because she had herself a man?

She was just fine as far as Willow Swan was concerned. Even after four years of no luck at all he was happy to tag along, using his assignment as commander of royal guards as an excuse to stay near the front.

So what was worth reporting here? That Lady had to get some rest?

Maybe. Exhaustion could impair her judgment at a critical moment.

I started to back away, drifting up and over Lake Tanji, which was pretty damned impressive even from Smoke's point of view.

I shivered in the cold wind. . . .

There was no wind out there with Smoke. There was no warm, no cold, no hunger, no pain. There was just being and sight.

And fear.

For there in the gathering darkness above the lake's southern shore was a dark ghost of a form with many arms and teats and wicked black lips drawn back to reveal a vampire's grin.

You can panic out there. I did.

18

"YOU ALL RIGHT?" ONE-EYE ASKED AS I CAME TO THE FRONT OF THE WAGON. It was dark out. He had turned his team loose to forage nearby, had a fire burning, and was now back on his driver's seat polishing a spear that looked as though it had been carved from ebony, inlaid with silver highlighting a hundred grotesque figures. "You were thrashing around and yelling back there."

"Thanks for coming to see what was wrong."

"The old woman said you do that all the time. Didn't seem worth worrying about."

"Probably wasn't. I just rolled over on your still parts." Not true but I had a feeling he would have some around somewhere. Even during the worst of the siege of Dejagore he and Goblin had managed to produce something they pretended was beer.

He bought it long enough to give himself away. If this damned wagon stayed in one place very long something better used as food or horse fodder would turn into something else stinky but liquid and alcoholic.

"What's the spear for?" I asked. "Haven't seen it out for a while." He had created it for the specific purpose of killing Shadowmasters.

"Talked to some of our brothers who've been with Lady's division. Came by while you were snoring. Big Bucket and Red Rudy. Said they've seen a big black cat a couple three times lately. Figured I ought to be set with my best."

He did not sound concerned but he was. That spear was a masterpiece of his art.

The cat was probably a shapeshifter named Lisa Deale Bowalk who could not shed her animal form because One-Eye had killed her teacher before she learned how. She had tried to get him before. He was confident that she would try again.

"Catch her if you can," I told him. "I got a notion we could use her if we let Lady work on her for a while."

"Right. That'll be the main thing on my mind."

"I'm going to see the Old Man."

"Tell him I want to go home. It's too damned cold out here for an old man like me."

I chuckled, the way I was supposed to. I got down to the ground despite my stiffness and headed the general direction I presumed Croaker would be, based on the size of the fires.

Good thing One-Eye and I made a habit of using old languages. Thai Dei stepped out of the shadows before I had walked twenty feet. He said nothing but he was there guarding my back, wanted or not.

19

THE JOURNEY CONTINUED. WAGONS BROKE DOWN. ANIMALS CAME UP LAME. Men injured themselves. Elephants complained about the weather. So did I. It snowed a couple of times, not blankets of big soft wet flakes but the wind-whipped pellet kind that stings your skin and never amounts to anything but a few traces when it is done.

On the plus side, Mogaba's cavalry never really got in our way. They were no problem as long as our foragers and scouts did not range too far ahead. I guess Mogaba was more interested in knowing where we were than in wasting soldiers trying to stop us before we came to his strong point.

Then one afternoon nobody received the routine order to halt and camp. The soldiers stumbled forward doggedly, cursing the bite of the wind while reminding one another that generals are seldom of sound mind and unbesmirched ancestry. They would not be generals if they were.

I went looking for the Captain.

There he was, his big crows on his shoulders. More circled him, bickering. He was smiling, the one happy fool in the army. The generals' general. "Hey, boss. We going to keep humping it all night?"

"We're less than ten miles from Charanky-whatsit. I think it would be nice to be camped there when Mogaba gets up in the morning."

He lived in his own reality, no doubt about that. Had to be a general. He actually believed he could play with Mogaba's mind.

He had not seen Mogaba at Dejagore. Not enough.

I said, "We'll be so beat he can come over and dance on our heads."

"But he won't. Longshadow has a ball and chain tied to his tail."

"So he kicks ass and lies to his boss later."

"That what you'd do?"

"Uh . . ." I might.

"Longshadow will be here watching him. Go get some sleep. When the sun comes up I want you perched on Mogaba's shoulder." Uncle Doj was only steps away, taking everything in. We were speaking Forsberger but I wondered if that was enough of a security measure.

Those crows were never far away.

What I got from the exchange was that Croaker did have a plan. Sometimes it was hard to believe that.

"I'm not tired right now." I *was* hungry and thirsty, though. Any extended period spent with Smoke leaves me that way. I took advantage of the staff officers' mess.

Messengers began to come and go. Croaker grumbled, "Guess it's time to start telling people what they need to do."

"There's an original concept. After all these years."

"Do we really need another smartass Annalist, Murgen? Get some rest."

He began gathering senior officers for a meeting. I was not invited.

I went back to One-Eye's wagon, where I ate some more, drank a lot of water and then went ghostwalking again.

Me and the fire chief eavesdropped on Croaker and his commanders but I should not have wasted the time. I learned very little. Croaker did all the talking, referring to a detailed map showing everyone where he wanted each unit to light in front of Mogaba. The only real surprise was that he wanted the Prahbrindrah Drah's division stationed in the center while his own two divisions positioned themselves on the right flank—excepting one specially trained combat team he wanted on the extreme left, outside Lady's left flank.

Interesting. Our right wing just happened to face and lap the Shadowlander division Blade had been given to command.

Croaker really wanted Blade.

Narrow-eyed, Lady asked, "Why did you decide to arrange the army this way? We've talked about this for three years. . . ."

Croaker told her, "Because this is where I want you all."

Lady had trouble keeping her temper. In a long life she had not had to do that much.

Croaker smelled the smoke. "When I don't explain to you nobody else finds out what I'm planning, either." He offered some tidbit to one of his crows.

That helped. A little. But the Prahbrindrah Drah and most of the rest had no idea of the significance of Croaker's crows.

I left Smoke, drank again, snacked, made sure the sleeper got some soup. He did not need nearly as much sustenance as I did. Maybe he was sucking on me out there, like some kind of psychic spider.

I slept. I had bad dreams that I recalled only in shards when I awakened. The Radisha was there. Soulcatcher was there. I suppose the old men in the caverns were there, too, though none of that stuck. Somewhere a bleak fortress.

I gave up trying to remember, went out with Smoke to try to see our approach as the enemy would.

Fireballs scattered colored pearls across the night. Torches speckled distant slopes with islands and snakes of light. The Shadowlander commanders watched without remark except when Blade suggested that the Captain was making his force appear more formidable by burning lots of torches.

They were not concerned. A lot of the junior officers expected Longshadow to turn them loose after they stomped us. They saw themselves heading north in early spring, with the whole summer to plunder and punish.

But a few were veterans of armies we had embarrassed in the past. Those men showed us more respect. And betrayed a more intense desire to cause us pain. They did not believe it would be easy but they did believe we would be defeated.

Mogaba himself seemed more taken with his plans for a counterinvasion than he was interested in further preparing to withstand us here.

I did not like it but I saw no real reason to believe they were overconfident.

Still, all those fireballs and torches were heartening.

That vast mass in motion out there had been inspired by the Black Company. And I had no trouble recalling when there were just seven of us, as unprepossessing a bunch of thugs as ever walked the earth. That was barely more than five years ago. Triumph or failure, this campaign would survive as a mighty drumbeat in the Annals.

I went back to my flesh and slept again. When I awakened our vanguards were already approaching the Plain of Charandaprash. Mist had formed in all the low places and gullies.

20

WE STOPPED AMIDST A GRAND HUBBUB. I LEANED OUT OF THE WAGON.

The mists had become an all-enveloping fog. People with torches hustled hither and yon, their torches glowing like witchlights. None came near me. All the forces had come together and now the world was very crowded.

Croaker appeared. I told him, "You look totally beat."

"My ass is banging off my heels." He climbed aboard, checked Smoke, settled down and closed his eyes.

"Well?"

"Uhm?"

"You're here. How come? And what about your goddamned pets? They watching?"

For a moment I thought he had gone to sleep that quickly. He did not answer immediately. But: "I'm hiding out. From the birds, too. One-Eye scared them off." About two minutes later, he added, "I don't like it, Murgen."

"What don't you like?"

"Being Captain. I wish I could've stayed Annalist and physician. There's less pressure."

"You're managing all right."

"Not the way I hear it. I wasn't Captain I wouldn't have any long-term worries, either."

"Hell. And here I thought you were having the time of your life baffling the shit out of everybody."

"All I've ever wanted was to take us home. But they won't let me."

"It's for sure nobody's ever going to open any doors for us. Especially not the Radisha. What to do about us seems to be on her mind a lot lately."

"It ought to be." He smiled. "And I haven't forgotten her." He paused a moment, then said, "You're up on your Annals. What was the bloodiest mess we ever got ourselves into?"

"Right here is my guess. Back in the beginning, four hundred years ago. But that's only by implication in the surviving Annals."

"History may repeat itself." He did not sound thrilled. Not at all. He was not a bloodthirsty man.

Neither am I, despite the hatreds I obsess over here. But my scruples do have blind areas. I do want to see several thousand villains suffer for what happened to Sahra.

Croaker asked, "Do you know of any way to authenticate the lost Annals you took back from Soulcatcher?"

"What?" What a horrible question. It never occurred to me before. "You saying you think they might not be real?"

"I couldn't read them but I could see that they weren't originals. They were copies."

"They might not have told the true story?"

"Smoke believed every word in the ones he had. And oral history supports his view of the Company as the terror of the ages, though there aren't any specifics. But I do have to wonder because there just aren't any contemporary accounts from independent observers."

"Something happened. Even if these books we have now are fabrications. What're you thinking?"

For a moment Croaker seemed tired of fighting. "Murgen, there's something going on that's more than you and me and Lady, the Taglians and the Shadowmasters and all that. Strange things are happening and they don't add up any other way. I started to wonder when you kept falling into the past."

"I think Soulcatcher had something to do with that."

"She may well have. She's got her fingers in everywhere else. But I don't think she's all of it. I think we're all—even Soulcatcher—being manipulated. And I'm even beginning to think that it's been going on for ages. That if we had the true firsts of the missing Annals and could read them we might see ourselves and what's happening in a whole different way."

"Are you talking about the thing Lady goes on about in her book? Kina? Because I've seen her myself, a couple of times, when I was out walking the ghost. Or what I think was her based on myth and what Lady wrote."

"Kina. Yes. Or something that wants us to think it's Kina."

"Wouldn't that be the same thing, as far as we're concerned?"

"Uhm. I think she's having those dreams again."

I thought so myself. "Looked like that to me, too. She's getting pretty haggard."

"I thought a lot about this during the trip down here. Not much to do but think when you're riding all day. My guess is, things have started going too fast for Kina. This is a critter that's used to shaping long, slow shadow plays, manipulations that can take decades to unfold. Maybe even generations in our case. Her big scheme might have begun way back before our forebrethren headed north. But now we're coming home to roost and everything is happening too fast for her. The more she tries to guide events the more hamhanded she gets."

"For instance?"

"Like what she did to Smoke."

"I really figured that was something Soulcatcher did." Although there had been no evidence to pin that on her, either.

"I suppose that's possible, too. It's even possible they were both after him and they got in each other's way."

I recalled what I could of the incident from Lady's book. I decided to stick with my Soulcatcher theory. Deceiver mythology did not credit Kina with that much ability to reach into the mundane world. The whole point of the cult was to bring on a time of such dramatic horror that the walls preventing Kina from touching our world could be ripped down from our side.

I explained that.

Croaker just shrugged. "Listen to this. I'm almost certain there wasn't supposed to be any Black Company left after Dejagore. Except for Lady. She was the only one who was supposed to survive. And her number was supposed to be up when the Stranglers took our baby."

I considered that. "If that guy Ram hadn't fallen for Lady . . ."

"That would've been the end of everything. Kina would've had her Daughter of Night over on this side and the Year of the Skulls beginning to unfold without anyone to interfere."

I looked interested. That was easy. I was. I wanted him to keep going. Before he finished I might actually have some idea why he did everything he did.

He said, "The wild cards messed up Kina's hand."

"Wild cards? You mean Soulcatcher?"

"She's the biggest. But there's Howler and there was Shifter and there's still Shifter's apprentice out there somewhere. All of them not part of the plan."

It was a hypothesis. It was well beyond any thinking I had done. Or in a different direction.

"You be careful, Murgen. Stay in close touch with your feelings. Don't let the ghostwalking seduce you. This thing manipulates us through our emotions."

"Why should I worry? I just write stuff down."

His response was cryptic. "The standardbearer could be more important than the Daughter of Night before this is all over."

"How's that?"

He changed the subject. "You looked for the forvalaka lately?" He meant the shapeshifter trapped in animal form, the apprentice he had mentioned a moment ago.

I thought about it, told him, "I've looked a few times but haven't seen it since I doubled back on the massacre at Vehdna-Bota."

"I see. No hurry but when you get a chance, find out where she is now. We couldn't be so lucky that she's gotten herself killed."

"Oh, she hasn't. One-Eye says she's right out there in the wilds, following us. We were talking about her the other night. He's convinced her only reason for living is to get even with him for killing Shifter before he taught her how to change back."

Croaker chuckled. "Yeah. Poor old boy. One of these days he's going to discover that he isn't the center of the universe. May all our surprises be pleasant ones. And all of Mogaba's surprises real gut-rippers." He chuckled again, wickedly. As he climbed down from the wagon he said, "Almost showtime."

He did see warfare more in terms of showmanship than in those of deadly games.

21

ONCE AGAIN I FLUTTERED AROUND MOGABA'S HEAD. ME, MURGEN, ANGEL of espionage.

Howler and Longshadow had arrived soon after dawn. They believed it would take both their concerted efforts to keep Lady from ripping Mogaba a new poop chute. Lady's powers seemed to swell as she moved farther south.

An idea hit like religious epiphany. I knew the fear that haunted the Captain. He suspected that Lady had regained her powers by making a pact with Kina.

I have suspected that myself, off and on.

The way sorcery works, the way I understood it, her loss of powers during the battle at the Barrowland should have been irreversible. It had to do with some unfathomable mystical gobbledegook about true names. Gunni mythology contained numerous stories about how gods and demons and devils went around hiding their true names in rocks or trees or grains of sand on the beach so their enemies would not be able to glom onto them and gain a hold. The whole business made no sense but that did not keep it from working.

Lady's true name had been named during the final showdown with her husband. She survived but, according to the mystical rules, was now an ordinary mortal. With looks to kill for. What made her interesting to people in her former trade was that she was a living storehouse of wicked lore. She had not lost any of her knowledge, only the ability to employ it.

I was surprised that she had not been a bigger target than she had so far.

Her name had no power over her anymore. Being powerless herself, apparently, she could not take advantage of those true names she knew. Otherwise she would have dealt with the Howler and her sister a long time ago. And she would not give those names away even to One-Eye and Goblin. She would die first.

It takes a strange sort to become a wizard or sorceress.

She had her own agenda still, that was certain. One-Eye or Goblin were not much but some things were like dropping a rock down a well.

From conversations overheard I knew Longshadow would part with three or four thumbs to get hold of what Lady knew.

Funny. Whenever he sent Howler to capture her the scheme machine never quite clicked. You would almost think Howler did not want his senior partner to become any more senior.

Someday I will have to get Lady to explain the whole true names thing in a way that even a dummy like me can understand. Maybe I can get her to explain the whole business of sorcery so that those of us who study these Annals will have at least a vague idea of what is going on.

Knowing will not keep us from crapping our small clothes when we run into sorcery but, still, it would be nice to have a notion what is behind all the deadly lights.

The Shadowlander soldiers were all in place. They gnawed field rations sleepily, hard at work at what soldiers do most. While we all waited I hung around those who spoke languages I could understand. The philoso-phers among them examined the intellects and characters of generals who put their troops into formation and made them stand ready when nothing was going to happen. Nothing. The damned Tals were too damned tired to do anything. They had spent the whole damned night on the move.

"Tal" was a sort of pun. Though short for "Taglian" it also meant "turd" in the Sangel dialects common south of the Dandha Presh.

I felt like I had soldiered with those guys. They spoke my language.

Mogaba had built himself a giant observation tower a safe distance behind the lines. It was wooden. I thought he was going to find it uncom-fortable pretty soon. Longshadow and Howler had joined him up there. The atmosphere was not festive but it was far from grim. Nobody was worried about us.

Longshadow threatened to become cheerful. This battle was the cul-mination of all his planning. When it was over nothing could stop him from making himself master of the world. Except maybe a few allies who did not quite share his ambitions.

I was hurt. A guy likes to be taken seriously. Mogaba had these peo-ple, from top to bottom, believing they were invincible.

In the soldiering business you are often what you think you are.

Confidence generates victory.

Howler did not scream once while I watched. Longshadow did not throw one tantrum.

Much as they fussed about Lady you would think they would be more tense.

22

THE RISING SUN BEGAN BURNING OFF THE MIST—EXCEPT AROUND OUR camp. The wind was a feeble breeze coming from Lady's flank. Fires smoldered there, keeping the camp obscured. The Shadowlanders could see only the camp followers who had been strong-armed into feeding the fires—and four wooden towers now rising above the smoke and mist. They were your basic siege towers, being assembled from precut parts brought up from barges on the Naghir River only with a lot of effort and plenty of good old-fashioned cussing.

I did not understand. What was the point out here? We were not going to be clambering over any castle walls.

Knowing Croaker, the project was under way just to get Mogaba wondering why.

I dove Smoke into the smoke. The activity inside was not what I expected. The soldiers were asleep. Those who were up and about were mostly camp followers. They fed the fires, assembled the towers, smoothed the ground in paths leading toward Mogaba's lines, cursed the moment Croaker was born. They had not followed the army so they could do its work.

The soldiers who drove them to their tasks were not kind. The Old Man was clever enough to have had the work crews assembled according to religion, then managed by soldiers who did not cherish their beliefs.

Some details of Croaker's plan had begun trickling down through the ranks but there was no way anyone could put the pieces together into a whole. He would not let the whole picture get out where a genius could puzzle it out from its fragments.

Now the challenge was to keep the only man who knew what it was alive until . . . Ah, me, Murgen. Where is your Black Company confidence?

It never existed except as show.

Ha. Here was Willow Swan, tall, blond and beautiful, trying harder than I to understand. An intuition might win him points with Lady. But he was grumbling in confusion to his companions.

I found Lady not far away. She was not worried about what was going on. She was focused on business. She had taken station atop a knoll that raised her above the smoke. She stared up the pass, ready if the other side tried something.

I took Smoke back to One-Eye's wagon. Time for breakfast.

"About goddamned time, Kid!" One-Eye complained. "You've got to start taking shorter trips. You're gonna end up getting lost out there."

Everybody kept telling me that. It did not seem to be happening, though, so my share of those fears were fading away. I asked, "Anything interesting happening?"

"There's a war on. Come on. Get out of the way. I need the old fart so I can do my part. Go get some exercise. Eat something. Make him some soup so you can feed him when I'm done."

"You feed him when you're done, bat-breath. You're the man with the job."

"You got a real attitude problem, Kid."

"We about to try something?"

"No. We hiked five hundred goddamn miles in the middle of goddamn winter because they say the brush down here is so goddamn great for cookouts."

"Everybody acts like they're drugged."

"Could be on account of they're drugged. I don't know. Just my opinion. I could be wrong. Get out of my way. I got work to do."

The smoke was awful. And it got worse nearer the front of the army. Scant yards made a huge difference. After my first foray in that direction I decided curiosity could wait. I hung around the wagon. I ate and ate and ate. I used up most of One-Eye's water. Served him right, the way he abused me.

I thought about Sahra. I knew I would be thinking of her a lot now. Danger has a way of making you dwell on the things most important to you.

The proximity of Narayan Singh haunted me, too. The living saint of the Deceivers was less than a mile away, tending his own cookfire while the Daughter of Night looked on dreamily, well bundled against the morning chill and damp.

I started. Damn! That little reverie was almost real.

I got restless waiting to get back to Smoke. I wanted to see if Singh was making breakfast. I needed to get away from all these thoughts about Sarie.

When would the scars form around the pain? When would it stop hurting so much that I had to run away?

I stared into the fire and tried to banish the thoughts. That was like picking at a scab. The harder I tried to think about something else the more I focused on Sarie. Eventually the fire filled my entire horizon and I seemed to see my wife on the other side, rumpled and beautiful and somewhat pallid as she went about the mundane business of cooking rice. It was like I was looking back through time to a moment I had lived before.

I made a noise like a dog strangling and jumped to my feet. Not again! I was over those falls into the past . . . wasn't I?

One-Eye clambered down from the wagon. "All done, Kid. You can have him if you need him but you really ought to give it a break. Ain't nothing going to happen for a while, anyway."

"What're we burning in these fires? I'm having visions or something here."

One-Eye sucked in a couple gallons of air, held his breath a while, then blew it out, shook his head, disappointed. "You're imagining things."

"I never did."

I never did. That was worth thinking about. I glanced around to see who was listening. Mother Gota was at the family cookfire but her Forsberger was not good enough to give her a clue.

She had appointed herself full-time family cook. Which meant that, even with the demands made by my travels with Smoke, I was in no danger of getting fat. She still lugged her personal arsenal. She acted like she knew how to use it those rare times she troubled to practice with Thai Dei and Uncle Doj. She did not talk to me much anymore. I was not the reason she was here. I was an inconvenience and an embarrassment.

She *knew* none of this would have happened if love and Hong Tray had not gotten in the way of common sense and ancient custom.

I was just as happy she stayed out of my way. I had my own feelings to tame. Among them was the conviction that life might have been much better for me had Sarie's mother never come to stay with us. Sahra might even be alive still. Though there was no way I could work that out so that it fit any logic.

Much as Smoke called I decided to endure the pain. I had to get used to it sometime. So why not try walking around the camp again? I could stay away from the worst smoke.

Thai Dei materialized almost as soon as I started moving. "Your sling and splints are gone," I said. "Are you back on the job?"

He nodded.

"Sure it isn't a little soon for that? You could break that arm again if you don't give it time enough to heal."

Thai Dei shrugged. He was tired of being a cripple. That was that. Tough as he was, he was probably right.

"What happened to Uncle Doj?" I had not seen the old boy for a while. If Thai Dei was back Doj might give in to an impulse to go after revenge on his own. His Path of the Sword thinking would find that perfectly reasonable.

Thai Dei shrugged.

He was lucky he did not have to talk for a living. There would be even less of him than there is now.

"Help me out here, brother. I'm going to get real upset if that old man gets himself killed." Uncle Doj was not ancient. He had maybe ten years on the Old Man and was more spry than Croaker.

"He would not do that."

"Glad to hear it. Trouble is, anybody can. While we're at it, remind him to try not being so weird in front of people who don't know us. The Captain didn't survive Dejagore with us."

Thai Dei was positively loquacious all of a sudden. "He lived his own hell." Which was true but not a point I would expect Nyueng Bao to note.

"He sure did. And it twisted him. Same as Dejagore twisted us. He doesn't trust anybody anymore. That's a lonely way to be but he just can't help it. And he especially don't trust people whose beliefs and business and motives are completely opaque to him."

"Uncle?"

"You have to admit that Uncle Doj is odd even by Nyueng Bao standards."

Thai Dei grunted, conceding the point privately.

"He makes the Captain very nervous." And the Captain was a very powerful man.

"I understand."

"I hope so." Ordinarily even Doj has to pry words out of Thai Dei so I felt rewarded. He remained talkative. I learned a good deal about his childhood with Sahra, which was pretty unremarkable. He believed there was a curse on their family. His father had died when he and Sahra were children. His wife My had drowned when their son To Tan was only a few months old, early in the pilgrimage that had brought the Nyueng Bao into Dejagore just in time for the siege. Sahra had married Sam Danh Qu, who had put her through several years of hell before he died of that fever in the early days of the siege. Then the children had all died, Sahra's under the swords of Mogaba's men in Dejagore, To Tan during the Strangler raid that had ended with my wife dead and Thai Dei's arm broken.

Evidently nobody in this family ever died of old age. This dying family. Mother Gota would bear no more children. Thai Dei had the capacity to become a father again but I did not expect that to happen. I expected Thai Dei to get killed avenging his sister and son.

Thai Dei stopped being communicative when To Tan's name came up.

The army lined up so: Lady's division to the left, the Prince's in the center, the Captain's two to the right, stacked one behind the other. All our cavalry assembled in the gap between the front and trailing divisions.

Why? The reserve division belongs behind the center. That has been customary since the dawn of time.

And why did Croaker station all his specially trained units behind or beyond Lady's division?

Either the Old Man thought he could dive Mogaba berserk trying to winkle out the answers or he was letting his hatred for Blade and his paranoia define his tactics.

And why were the camp followers, voluntarily or otherwise, being gathered together right on the front line? Croaker hated camp followers. That he had not run them off weeks ago was a wonder to all who knew him.

I could not find Uncle Doj. Still.

23

I FELT IT BEGIN BEFORE ANY GROWL OF DRUM OR SNARL OF TRUMPET. I RAN for the wagon, leaping rocks and fires in the mist.

I had Smoke take me up where Mogaba watched from his high tower, sensed uncertainty immediately. He knew Croaker. He knew that half what the Old Man did would be done to mess with his mind. But which half?

The knowing itself would cause a hesitation at every point of decision.

I loathed Mogaba the traitor but admired Mogaba the man. He was tall, handsome, intelligent. Just like me. But he was the perfect warrior, too.

He had no company but couriers and the two big wazoos. And they were doing a great imitation of two guys sleeping. Their strategy was to wait for Lady to make a move so one could grab her while the other one blindsided her.

Mogaba's platform provided a less than perfect view though probably the best attainable. A portion of his left flank was masked by a jumble of boulders while to his right a steep knee of stone concealed his flank there along with a portion of the Taglian left wing.

I took Smoke up amongst the crows for a vulture's-eye view. The smoke was thinning out. People were stumbling uphill, unable to make an orderly advance over the rocky ground.

Now I understood why the troops had been issued calthrops.

Calthrops are like large kids' jacks, only the tips are sharp and sometimes poisoned. The calthrop is a handy tool if you have to run for it, particularly if the guys after you are going to be on horseback. You scatter calthrops where horses have to follow narrow paths and you have yourself a guaranteed head start—or even grounds for a nasty ambush.

Aha! I spied the missing complimentary in-law.

Uncle Doj was dressed up in his best outfit, his holy fencing duds, like he maybe did not want us going to a whole lot of trouble when we laid him out. Hell. I would have to check with Thai Dei on Nyueng Bao funeral customs. A lot of Nyueng Bao had died around me but I never took part in what went on later.

I still resented being left out when they took care of To Tan and Sahra without me.

Uncle Doj strutted uphill till he was just fifty feet from the first line of Shadowlanders. He stopped and bellowed a challenge to Narayan Singh.

Guess who did not come out to fight? Nobody even answered.

Nobody even bothered to relay the message to the Deceiver camp.

Uncle Doj began issuing a series of formal insults, belittling the Deceivers and all their allies. Trouble was, they *were* formal insults from a stylized school of challenge and response. He did not know how to make his presentation in a manner accessible to people who did not speak Nyueng Bao.

Poor Uncle. Forty years of intense preparation brought him to the ultimate moment—and all those guys over there saw was a crazy old man.

Doj began to get it.

He began to get angry for real. He started yelling his challenges in Taglian. A few Shadowlanders understood him. His message soon reached the Deceivers. It was not well received.

I found the show as amusing as anything could be out there.

None of this was part of the Captain's plan.

Uncle kept hollering.

Over in the Deceiver camp the miniature messiah of the Stranglers told his cronies, "We will not respond. We will wait. Darkness is our time. And darkness always comes." After a pause he asked, "Who is that man?"

A wide, creepy-looking guy told him, "He was in Dejagore. One of the Nyueng Bao pilgrims." The man speaking was named Sindhu. He had come into Dejagore during the siege to spy for Lady and for the Deceivers. He was a real villain. I had been sure he was dead.

The Sahras die but the Sindhus and Narayan Singhs go on. Which is why I cannot be a religious man. Unless the Gunni are right and there is a wheel of life and eventually everybody gets what they deserve.

Sindhu continued, "He was a priest of some kind and their Speaker. A member of his family eventually wed the standardbearer of the Black Company."

"It becomes clear. The Goddess is scribbling one of her subtle death plays." He glanced at the Daughter of Night. The kid sat so still it was spooky. Spookier than usual. No four-year-old could do that.

Narayan Singh seemed vaguely troubled. His goddess enjoyed the occasional death joke at the expense of her most devout followers. He did not want to become one of her pranks.

"Darkness is our time," he said again. "Darkness always comes."

Darkness always comes. Sounded like Kina's motto. I took another look at Lady and Croaker's brat. She bothered me bad. She was spookier every time I looked. If it had not been so hard to care out there I could have cried for Lady and the Old Man.

Actually, I almost could. Maybe I was becoming capable of feeling while I worked.

I drifted away, found that Mogaba was taking stronger exception to Uncle's antics than was Singh. But he remembered Uncle Doj from the bad old days. "I want that man silenced," he said. "The soldiers are watching him instead of their enemies."

When he drew no response from the Deceivers, Uncle Doj began insulting the Shadowlanders and their masters. A javelin streaked his way. In a motion too swift to follow he drew Ash Wand and brushed the missile aside. "Cowards!" he called. "Renegades! Are any of you Nar men enough to come out?" He exposed his back contemptuously, headed for friendly lines before a missile storm could devour him. A masterful move, it did not look like a withdrawal at all.

24

ALL HELL BROKE LOOSE.

Horns shrieked. Drums grumbled. A stumbling, shambling, inept, mean-spirited and poorly armed rabble headed uphill wailing, sixty thousand hungry and hard-up camp followers attacking the servants of shadow. Our soldiers drove them at swordspoint.

I was stunned. I was awed. The Captain had his hard moments but I never figured him for hard enough to let camp followers accumulate and tag along so he could use them as a human avalanche. But on reflection, yes, for weeks he had been warning the soldiers not to let anyone they cared for join the march. Those who discussed it at all thought it meant that the Old Man did not expect to be successful.

Those people were going to get slaughtered. But they would hurt some Shadowlanders and grind the rest down, which would work to our advantage.

The soldiers were merciless. They whipped the camp followers into a terrified frenzy. When they hit Mogaba's center and right they actually penetrated the Shadowlander front rank.

Blade's division remained untouched.

While everyone was concentrating on our attack, Croaker's special forces left Lady's shadow and hastened into the wastes flanking the pass. Mogaba had sentries concealed in amongst those rocks, of course. Fighting broke out immediately.

Our elephants moved forward behind the troops pushing the camp followers. The Shadowlanders were too busy to bother them. The elephants used huge mallets to drive big iron spikes into the earth.

Came a shrill of brassy Shadowlander trumpets. For no reason I could discern Blade's division suddenly moved out, left oblique, downhill, at an angle that would take it around our right flank. I marvelled at how well his men maintained formation crossing that rough ground.

Now I got to witness one of Longshadow's epic rages. "You have gone too far this time!" he thundered at Mogaba, once he controlled himself enough to manage a coherent sentence. "What the hell do you think you're doing, making moves like that without consulting me? At least explain your thinking!" While he yelled he stamped around the rough platform, shaking, clawing at his mask till I thought he might show the world the face he kept hidden except when he was alone.

"I have no idea what he's doing." Mogaba ignored the Shadowmaster's rage. He leaned on the platform rail, stared at Blade's division and looked as confused as ever I had seen. "Be quiet."

Howler punctuated the racket with a series of shrieks.

Longshadow became incoherent again.

Taglian trumpets blared. Shadar cavalrymen galloped out of the gap between the Old Man's two divisions and rushed into that between Blade's division and the rest of the Shadowlander army. Their movement was a lot less impressive than Blade's. They did not even pretend to maintain formation once they were moving.

Blade ignored them. He continued his march.

Mogaba became as excited as ever I have seen him. He did not have a clue what Blade was up to.

Longshadow and Howler nearly came to blows.

What the hell was going on?

Sudden drums announced the advance of Croaker's lead division. It headed straight into the space vacated by Blade's force. The cavalry drifted onward, screening the division's outside flank. Then the reserve division faced right and began to follow Blade.

And I gawked.

Events were unfolding as though carefully choreographed yet nobody knew what was going on. Confusion was universal. In some more remote areas, like Lady's command post, people had no idea at all.

The Captain might have had some idea but he seemed to be running in three directions at once, trying to obtain control, keep control, keep in touch. He was unable to keep a grasp on the bigger picture.

I could give him no help. By the time I could return to flesh, get myself moving, find him at the front a mile from One-Eye's wagon, the whole situation would have changed radically.

On our left and in our center our soldiers continued to drive the camp followers ahead of them. That was turning into a horror show of proportions sure to be recalled for generations.

Croaker's lead division engaged the Shadowlanders directly, attempting to secure the position Blade had abandoned. Mogaba's reserves rushed in. They fought very well. They pushed Croaker back. Barely. I got the feeling the Old Man was not ready to make a total effort to gain the position.

One company of Shadar, towering over their enemies, did get within bowshot of the Strangler camp. For several minutes a handful of archers laid down a desultory barrage that did no apparent damage.

At the same time Howler managed to get through to Longshadow. "We do not have the luxury of spending time squabbling among ourselves! The woman could strike any moment. If you're not paying attention . . ."

Several strong sallies in the same vein led the Shadowmaster to understand that indulging in a fit left him vulnerable to sorcerous attack. And his sidekick could not protect him all the time. He was having a rash of his own screaming fits.

Still shaking, unable to articulate clearly, Longshadow concentrated his attention on Lady.

Lady was just standing there, waiting.

Mogaba tried to get Longshadow's attention. The Shadowmaster remained focused on Lady. Mogaba persisted. He got Longshadow to turn around only after it looked like the crisis had passed. The terror applied by our troops no longer was sufficient to keep the camp followers moving uphill. The Captain's division had withdrawn to its jump-off position. Blade's force had halted two miles west of the battlefield. It was surrounded by our cavalry and the reserve division. The Shadowlanders in the unit were as baffled as everyone else. But they were good soldiers. They carried out their orders.

Mogaba told Longshadow, "We have been deceived, not in any way we anticipated. With one clever stroke Croaker has decimated us. It is now unlikely that I can hold this ground if you won't modify your general orders."

Longshadow grunted an angry interrogative.

Mogaba told him, "Our best hope now is to attack while the Taglians are disorganized and scattered, before our own soldiers realize how suddenly desperate our situation has become."

Longshadow did not see it that way. "Once again you forget that your mission is to carry out my wishes, not to question them. Why must you be so negative?" He stared at Blade's force, only part of which was visible from where he stood. Clearly he was troubled by negative thoughts of his own. "You repelled their attack easily."

Mogaba restrained his anger with difficulty. I wished someone, anyone, had an idea of Longshadow's antecedents. Sometimes the man was as naïve as he was powerful.

Mogaba threw an arm up as though indicating Blade. "We were taken in. An entire legion has just been lost because you were so eager to enlist another ranking defector."

Dumb old me, I did not understand what he was saying. I had not made the intuitive leap.

Longshadow did not yet understand that there was a leap to be made. He saw only a triumph in the opening bout of the contest. "How many have we killed? See! The dead fell in windrows. They lie there in veritable hills. Count them in their thousands. These crows will feast for an age to come."

But the man inside was troubled. He continued to stare toward Blade's force.

Mogaba barked, "Maybe one out of a hundred of those dead was a soldier. Those were all camp followers, the thieves and whores and hungry mouths that become parasitic on any army that permits it. They were useless tagalong scum. Croaker used them to keep us occupied while he stole a quarter of our strength and all of our hope. His veterans now outnumber ours significantly. And most of them are fresh." He indicated the heights to his right, where Croaker's special forces continued to gain ground. "They'll soon take the high ground. They came prepared to take it."

"And you aren't prepared to defend it?"

"I anticipated Croaker's effort. Only a fool would ignore those heights. But I didn't anticipate the firebombs he's using."

Those were the finest product of One-Eye's weapons shops back in Taglios, transported here at great cost in treasure and labor, which now looked worthwhile. It was hard to hold your ground in the face of those bombs.

The Captain and his staff were headed for Blade's division. Something was up. I streaked that way.

Blade came outside the wall of his soldiers, faced the Captain across a hundred yards of rocky ground. Our men were posted outside bowshot, relaxed but alert, awaiting developments. They were only slightly less baffled than the traitor's soldiers, who were drawn up as if for review now, not for combat.

Blade and Croaker met midway between. They exchanged a few words. Silly me, I expected the Old Man to settle the feud he had been prosecuting so vigorously for so long. Instead, he threw his arms around Blade and started laughing.

It had been a long time for the Captain. His laughter had a definite mad edge.

They started jumping up and down, holding on to one another.

Then Blade spun away. He bellowed at his soldiers, "Stack your weapons and surrender. Or you'll be exterminated."

I was so dense that only now, as Blade's soldiers began obeying orders, as they had been taught, did I recognize the swindle.

Blade's defection had been staged. Croaker's years-long mad pursuit of him had been cosmetic—except where he had used Blade to rid himself of obnoxious religious fanatics.

Nothing like having your enemies do your dirty work for you.

More, Blade had worked hard to make the Shadowmaster unpopular with his subjects. Whole territories had surrendered without even token resistance.

And now Blade had delivered a quarter of the Shadowmaster's finest troops.

Nowhere in the Annals was there a con to match this con. And this one Croaker created for himself. He would laugh up his sleeve for a long time, knowing Mogaba could not have imagined him capable of such an unprecedented move. Mogaba did not think Croaker capable of taking a deep breath without consulting the Annals.

25

I LEFT SMOKE. NOBODY WAS ANYWHERE NEAR THE WAGON EXCEPT MOTHER Gota and Thai Dei. I joined them. They said nothing. I ate without speaking myself, drank a lot of water, climbed back into the wagon and took a long nap. I dreamed. The dreams were not pleasant. Soulcatcher was there and she seemed to be having a wonderful time. Messing with us, no doubt, because that is where she found her fun.

I woke up and ate again, barely aware that I was devouring some of Mother Gota's worst cuisine. I swilled water as though this was my first chance in weeks. I was vaguely aware that Thai Dei seemed troubled whenever he looked at me. I tried to figure that out but I could not concentrate.

It was late. The camp itself was quiet. The soldiers were still forward. Night sentries prowled watchfully, warned that there were Stranglers in the enemy camp. They gossiped softly as they paused to warm their hands by the fires. Farther back, some survivors from among the camp followers gathered their pitiful belongings and stole away before they got rounded up and herded forward again.

Vicious fighting continued on the heights. Mogaba intended to contest every foot of ground.

Not all the camp followers had been able to get away. Fires on Lady's flank once again began to mask our camp with smoke. Did the Captain have some new devilment in mind?

I asked him when he turned up a while later. "I hope they think so up there," he said. He could not stop grinning. "For the rest of his life I want Mogaba looking over his shoulder, jumping at shadows, thinking there's another trap about to open under his feet. Maybe there'll be one sometime." He laughed again.

All the senior officers began gathering at a fire laid like a Gunni festival bonfire. Politically neutral priests of all faiths performed rites of thanksgiving. Even Lady came in, accompanied by her officers and admirers. She looked like a demigoddess, more real than any Taglian deity but the dreaded Kina. In the modern era only Kina seemed interested in mundane affairs.

But she had a personal interest.

Hard to tell who among the crowd was most boggled. Blade settled beside the Old Man. He could not stop grinning. He could not stop babbling at his old buddy Swan. Pity Cordy Mather was back home with the Woman. He would have gotten a kick out of this, too.

I had not seen Blade for years. Back then he had been a taciturn cynic. Nothing like this. And One-Eye had not had time to get a still running yet.

Blade bellowed at Croaker. Croaker bellowed right back. Swan told me, "Don't mind them two. They haven't gotten over the hand-holding stage yet."

"I guess there must have been a lot of strain while the con was running."

The Old Man heard Swan but ignored him. "Tomorrow it's good old-fashioned hey diddle diddle, straight up the middle. The last thing Mogaba will expect from me. Prince, you get first go. Have your men show us how good they are."

I took a long drink of water, wishing One-Eye had managed to get *something* made for tonight. But that would not have gone over. None of the Taglian religions tolerated beer, nor did Lady or the Prince, who did not want drunken soldiers screwing things up. But what they did not see they could not condemn. So I might just suggest to One-Eye that he get a move on.

I asked, "You're actually going to tell us what's going on?"

A lax humor entered the Captain's eyes. "Nope." He leaned close, whispered, "Don't let this get out. I don't want anybody easing up. But they're not sending shadows out to spy." He pointed as a fireball headed up the pass. We had not seen much of Lady's big magic here yet.

"How come?"

"They're saving them." He grinned again. This grin took in everyone around us. He spoke to the assembly. "I think you all know what you're expected to do next. Get some rest."

How did everybody know what they were expected to do next? The little he had told anyone had been extremely vague.

Croaker looked at Lady. She seemed at the point of collapse. This was tiring work but her exhaustion went beyond what you would expect.

Some hard guy, my Captain. Sometimes his feelings were obvious. He hurt for the woman he loved. "Swan. Hang around. I want to talk to you."

I was politely invited to move my unwelcome ass along and get some rest of my own.

26

I WANTED TO SLEEP. I WAS TIRED DESPITE HAVING DONE SO LITTLE THAT WAS physical. But when I retired to One-Eye's wagon I lay there tossing and turning. Outside Mother Gota was engaged in an endless litany of complaint. Evidently I was only a minor character in her cast of troubles. Uncle Doj was a star. Hong Tray was a star. Sahra was a star for having gone along with Hong Tray. Or for having gotten Hong Tray on her side. Witches, both of them. Thai Dei did not say much more than usual. He might have wanted to enter a fact or two but his mother never gave him the chance.

Same old same old where Mother Gota was concerned. Most of the time I did not hear her anymore. I wondered if she could be insulted into silence.

She did get me thinking about the woman I loved.

I turned and tossed and wrestled with the pain. I thought it might be getting a little less potent. And, of course, I had to worry about that. Was it right? Was it a betrayal of Sarie?

I reminded me that I am a grown man used to a hard life and should not be getting caught up in this sort of obsessing, however great a treasure Sahra had been.

I did drift off into that state where you are not entirely asleep but you are not awake, either. Where you can rewrite your dreams as you go along.

Suddenly I was back in the past, whipped through time by a gust of laughter and a mocking voice that asked me where I had been. I was not expecting this after all this time but it did not take me off guard, either. I was experienced at this sort of thing now.

Not surprised, I was not lost or disoriented. I had walked with the ghost enough to have developed some resilience. I tried to take hold just as I would have had I been out with Smoke.

The aura of amusement surrounding me gave way to startlement. I did a sort of transdimensional fast spin—and right there caught a glimpse of the prime suspect, Soulcatcher, kneeling over some array of sorcerous objects near a fire somewhere in the gorsy approaches to Charandaprash. My turn to be amused. Even if I was not in control I now knew who was manipulating me.

Now, how could I put another move on her and find out why?

The laughter of crows enveloped me. Like it did not matter if I knew who was doing what.

That sounded like Soulcatcher, the way she was described in Croaker's Annals. A force for chaos, seldom giving one rat's ass *what* happened as long as *something* did.

I tried to recall where those Annals were right now. Another look at Soulcatcher might be worthwhile. Or maybe even a long heart-to-heart with the Old Man. He knew Soulcatcher better than anyone alive, her sister included. I do not believe Lady had a clue about her sister's thinking anymore. Maybe she did not care.

Maybe I was seeing things that were not there. What did I know about what Lady was thinking, really? I had not exchanged a hundred words with her in the past three years. Before that our exchanges were limited to information destined for the Annals.

The laughter of crows became the laughter of Soulcatcher. A voice said, "I do not think I want to play today after all."

A great invisible hand grabbed me and threw me into a windy darkness. I spun like a thrown walnut even though I was nothing but a dream.

I tried controlling it same as I would have had I been walking with the ghost. Once again I was able to take a measure of control. The sensation of spinning went away. As it faded a feeling of place and time returned, along with an ability to see.

It was not good seeing. It was fuzzing and short range, like Hagop talked about his vision getting as he got older. But I was in a jungle. Was it familiar? It was a jungle. I have seen a few and they are all pretty much the same if you cannot see more than twenty feet clearly. Bugs out the wazoo. Muted, the screeching of a thousand birds. A couple of those were inside my circle of vision. I noted that they seemed to see me just fine. I was the reason for all the excitement.

I rotated quickly. Jungle for sure. But not short on water. A nasty black pool lay only inches from where my heels would have rested had I had any heels.

Monkeys scampered along a branch overhead, rattled by the screeching of the birds but, apparently, unable to see me. At least not at that range. One came swinging past a foot from my point of view. She saw me. She was so startled she lost her grip, shrieked in surprise, fell into the black pool, where she started hollering in terror.

The crocodile almost got her. Almost. She got out of the water an instant before the jaws snapped. Nothing like some big teeth moving fast to motivate you.

The crocodile's effort, however, betrayed it to the crocodile hunters who materialized an instant later, casting barbed spears.

Life is cruel.

Those crocodile hunters were unusually nervous. They wondered why the birds were going crazy. They wondered why the monkeys had gone berserk, why one had fallen into the black pool. Understanding them was no problem. They spoke Nyueng Bao as though it was their native tongue. Which it was.

I was somewhere in the delta.

Faintly, faintly, behind the raucous birds I could sense the amusement of crows.

I had no sense of direction.

There was no Smoke to take me home.

I was not just dreaming. I had control but did not know what to do with it. . . . Up. Up was always good with Smoke. The higher you went the more the earth looked like an incredibly detailed map. Then you needed only find a landmark you knew. I went up.

I was in the nastiest, most untamed part of the delta. The whole world was black water, bugs and densely packed trees. That was very nearly my idea of hell.

I had to go way up above where the buzzards soar to see anything else. In the meantime psychic chills twisted the imaginary me; fear gnawed hard and deep. Rising with me was a momentary certainty that I would never find any landmark.

The sun was a landmark. If you had eyes to see it.

I could not see much very well. Not even the birds that shield away.

So I could not find a landmark the logical way. Well, there was a different green over that way.

The different green proved to be empty rice paddies. I zigged this way, zagged that, found a village, found the path that ran out of the village and followed it. I moved at wild speeds. Still, I knew, it was going to take me a long time to get back to where I started.

Damned Soulcatcher!

I heard the voices mocking crows.

I saw a village that looked familiar.

Some would say all Nyueng Bao hamlets look alike. They do, pretty much, from what I have seen. But their temples vary radically according to the wealth and status and age of the town. I had seen this temple before, weeks ago when I was searching for Goblin. I had, in fact, glimpsed a girl who looked so much like Sahra that I wanted to cry when I left Smoke's world.

I paused there, drifted around, watched the villagers about their early morning business. Everything seemed typical of a Nyueng Bao hamlet, from all I had heard. Even though it was the middle of winter there was work to do. People were getting set to do it.

It was a very prosperous town. Very old, too, probably. The temple was large and looked like it had been there for ages. A pair of mighty two-headed elephants formed pillars to either side of a door as tall as three Nyueng Bao men. The two-headed elephant represented the god of luck among the Gunni. I recall One-Eye saying luck took that form because it was powerful and two-faced.

Oh. That must be the girl I had seen before. The ringer for Sarie. She came out of the temple looking exhausted, sad. Could this be the same woman? The earlier one had looked like a slightly younger version of Sarie. This one looked like an older one, after having gained ten pounds and several years. She had that incredible face but both her hips and breasts were slightly heavier than Sahra's had been and she was ill-kempt, something Sarie never was, even in the worst of times. This woman was dirty, ragged, in despair.

But she did look so much like Sarie that I wanted to go to her and take her pain away, whatever it might be.

I drifted closer, almost enjoying my own self-pitying pain, wondering why the woman wore white when almost all Nyueng Bao except priests dressed in black. Except on special occasions.

I could ask Thai Dei when I got back. If I ever found the way.

I was so near the woman I could have taken her into my arms and kissed her had I been in flesh. I wanted to, she resembled Sarie so much in her face.

Had Sarie had cousins? I know she had uncles because at least one died during the siege of Dejagore. She might have had aunts who stayed behind, too. The party of pilgrims had included only a fraction of the delta population.

The woman in white looked square where my eyes would have been. Her eyes widened. Her skin went pale. She let out a shriek, then collapsed. Several old men in colored robes rushed out of the temple. They began trying to bring the woman around, gabbling at one another too fast for me to follow. She regained her composure as they helped her to her feet. "I thought I saw a ghost," she said in response to insistent questions. "It must be the fasting."

Fasting? It did not look like she had been missing many meals to me.

So she had sensed my presence, eh? Worth remembering. But I had a battle to get back to. I was no use to anyone down here, all but lost. I found the road out of town, followed it in a direction I believed would eventually bring me to Taglios. From Taglios it would be an easy course to chart south.

27

I DID NOT HAVE TO MAKE THE TRIP THE HARD WAY. NOT LONG AFTER I FOUND the river my whole universe began to rock. After its third unnatural shaking I began to feel pain. Twice more and I went into darkness, passed through, and came up to awareness inside One-Eye's wagon. The little shit was holding me up by the shirt and slapping me while he growled something about waking my ass up.

I was sitting up beside Smoke when I opened my eyes. I was soaked with sweat. I was shaking.

One-Eye demanded, "What the hell is the matter with you?"

"I'm not sure. Soulcatcher, I think. It was sort of like when I used to fall through time to Dejagore. Only I kind of squirted like a sugarmelon seed, right off to somewhere in the delta. I knew what was happening but I couldn't control it. In a way it was like walking with the ghost. But I couldn't see very far. . . ." I realized I was babbling, in Taglian yet. I managed to bite down on it.

"We'll talk about it later. I've got work to do."

I opened my mouth to protest.

"You want to talk, go see Croaker. Or do whatever else you want. But get out of the way. I'm not kidding about the work."

Angry, I clambered out of the wagon. It was daytime out there, just as it had been in the swamp. There was a lot of smoke. There was plenty of noise from the front, where the situation seemed to be static. There was not much chance the Old Man would take time out to hear about my misadventure. It did not affect what was happening right now.

I went over to the campfire. It had gone out. In fact, it had gone cold. Where were Thai Dei and his mother? Where was Uncle Doj? Not here.

I found water and drank, wondering how long it would be before the water supply became as critical as the food. I napped. Eventually One-Eye completed his business. He came out and sat beside me. "Now tell me about it."

I told him.

"You might have learned something important this time, Kid."

"Like what?"

"I'll let you know after I talk to Croaker."

28

I WAS AN AFRIT BUZZING BEHIND MOGABA'S SHOULDER. HE AND HIS CAP-tains were rattled.

Longshadow exhorted them to stop embarrassing his warrior empire.

"Somebody pour mud in that idiot's mouth," one of Mogaba's few loyal Nar growled. "What a cretin."

I agreed.

A cretin with a hearing impairment, apparently. He did not respond to the most direct provocation I had yet heard from any of those who served him.

Mogaba pretended to hear nothing himself. He watched the cliffs. Vicious, incessant fighting continued there. Our troops worked the attack in shifts. Mogaba's men were unable to do so themselves. He had almost no reserves. There was little hope in his eyes as he sent his commanders back to their units. But he was a soldier's soldier. He would fight until he fell.

Just like he had tried to do at Dejagore.

He had us by the short hairs if his troops went to eating each other in order to outlast us.

Our siege towers crept forward like tall, slow ships. Our elephants and surviving camp followers pulled them using cables passed through blocks attached to the steel spikes the elephants had planted earlier. When the towers finally stopped soldiers brought mantlets up to fill the gaps between. Protected by the mantlets engineers began erecting a wooden wall.

Missiles left the towers in swarms.

Mogaba had no engine powerful enough to penetrate the coverings on the towers. He had to do something.

The Shadowmaster forbid his doing the one thing that would have helped. Longshadow was worse than any spoiled child, stubborn as a rock. Things were going to be done his way and that was that. Mogaba was not going to take one step forward.

Mogaba was very near his limit but not yet ready to defy Longshadow. He was aware that Lady was over on our side just waiting for a chance to make his life miserable. That would happen seconds after the Shadowmaster took his toys and went home.

If he could not attack, Mogaba decided, he would pull back, leaving his forward works manned by minimal forces. They were to withdraw in such a way that we should not notice them moving out of harm's way.

But I was watching.

Mogaba told Howler, "You'd better keep your carpet ready. I'm doing this with both hands tied. I won't last long."

Longshadow turned. If looks could kill.

Howler's stance turned ugly, too. He did not want to be labeled a coward in front of witnesses.

A sudden uproar exploded on the far side of the pass. I darted over to the Deceiver camp. And there was Uncle Doj with Ash Wand, butchering Stranglers wholesale. Nasty old Mother Gota covered his back, moving about as slickly as he did.

Not bad for an old gal who practiced only when she could not duck out of it.

How had they gotten over there?

Then the real shit splashed down.

The Prahbrindrah Drah finally launched the attack the Old Man had dropped into his lap.

A dozen war elephants spearheaded the Prince's assault.

Shadowlander troops rushed to man their forward works. Arrows felt in sheets.

Mogaba showed us. He jelled his defense. He murdered our elephants. His men showed their superior discipline. They sent the Prince staggering back with losses as appalling as those I had anticipated before we saw any of the Captain's trickeries.

Mogaba launched a vicious counterattack he claimed was just a heavy pursuit. The wooden walls between our siege towers held until Longshadow recognized what Mogaba was doing and ordered him to pull back.

Immediately, as though he knew what was happening even without my reports, Croaker launched an attack on his flank. Only minutes later Lady attacked on the left.

Fighting on the heights grew even more savage. I lost track of my feisty in-laws. Narayan Singh and the Daughter of Night fled the Deceiver encampment and went into hiding beneath Mogaba's watch-tower.

There were no surprises from our side. Our divisions took turns attacking. Mogaba's men repelled them but had to come out into the missile storm to do it. Workmen edged the towers forward again, inch by inch. Long-shadow persisted in his irrational behavior. He began to look not only a lackwit but actively suicidal. He kept poor Mogaba operating with his hands tied and his ankles in chains, yet dumped buckets of blame on him because it looked like he was going to fail.

And the heights were aflame.

That facet of the fighting was almost over.

29

I TOLD CROAKER, "I FOUND OUT WHY LONGSHADOW REFUSES TO TURN Mogaba loose when even he's got to see that that's best. He's scared Mogaba might do a Blade of his own."

"The Shadowmaster is a blind fool," Blade said. "He doesn't know how to look at people."

I said, "What?"

"Mogaba has to destroy Croaker. He can't do anything else and live with the image of himself he's created for himself."

Croaker made a rude noise.

Blade continued, "Mogaba has his own troubles keeping in touch with reality anymore. This confrontation has become what his life is all about. There's no future if there's no victory."

Croaker was not flattered. "I feel pretty much the same way." He told me, "Longshadow is right about one thing. The whole world *is* out to get his ass. What's morale like over there?"

I winced. Was I supposed to tell him in front of people who knew nothing about Smoke?

"Lower than a snake's butt," One-Eye said.

I glowered at him.

"They likely to break?"

"Only if Mogaba runs. They may not like him a whole lot but they believe in him."

I stared at Lady. Her eyes were closed. She might be grabbing the chance to nap. Seldom on stage doing anything obvious, she was working harder than anybody else. She had to be completely alert every second.

I wondered if Longshadow and Howler had any notion how exhausted she must be, if they would try to turn things around by taking advantage of that. I shivered.

The Captain nodded to himself. "We go at three in the morning. Meantime, everybody rest." His general's mask faded whenever he looked at Lady. In those moments his feelings were pretty obvious.

I drifted off into a reverie, recalling the nightmares Lady had described in her book, all so obsessed with death and destruction, much like the ones I kept having. I was sure she was suffering those again. She was fighting sleep most of the time, trying to avoid them. I visualized Kina as Lady had described her, black and tall, naked, glistening, with four arms and eight teats, vampire fangs and nifty jewelry made from babies' skulls and severed penises. Not exactly a girl just like good old mom.

I wondered if Lady had been dreaming any of the times I had glimpsed something that might have been Kina.

I started. For an instant I thought I had caught a whiff of Kina's perfume, which was the stench of rotting corpses.

There would be plenty of that here soon enough. Only the cold kept it from being really bad already.

I squeaked. Thai Dei was shaking me. Where had he come from? He looked troubled. Croaker was staring at me, too. So were the others. I had drifted right off into a nightmare, never realizing I was gone. The Captain asked, "What's the matter?"

"Bad dream."

Lady was just leaving with Swan and Blade. She stopped, looked back at me. Her nostrils moved restlessly, as though she could smell that stench, too. She eyed me hard.

"Excuse me?" I had missed another question while Lady and I exchanged looks.

"Your in-laws, Murgen. Where are your in-laws?"

"I don't know. This morning they turned up over there in the Deceiver camp and went berserk." I spoke softly because I was not sure there was any language I could get past Lady and her tagalongs. "Uncle Doj sliced up about fifty Deceivers while Mother Gota covered his back.

It was a sight. You don't want to get that old woman mad." I shifted to Nyueng Bao. "Thai Dei. Where are Doj and your mother?"

He shrugged. That could mean he did not know or that he was not going to say.

"Thai Dei doesn't know, either." But where had Thai Dei been lately? He had not been underfoot for nearly a day.

Referring to what I had said about Uncle Doj and Mother Gota, Croaker said, "I've told you a million times not to exaggerate. Old people can't—"

"I'm not exaggerating. Blood and shit were everywhere. That old boy's sword moved so fast you could hardly see it. All those assholes wanted to do was get out of his way. Singh grabbed the girl and ran for it. He's hiding out under Mogaba's tower right now. Even the Daughter of Night was a little rattled by the way things were going."

"What about your in-laws?"

Stubborn bastard. "They've disappeared, all right? I haven't looked for them. Maybe the soldiers got them." I doubted that, though.

The old man nodded. He glanced at Thai Dei. "I'll get the angle on them yet. Get some sleep. Be long hours tomorrow."

Seemed to me like I ought to be plenty well rested.

Thai Dei looked like he really wished he understood a few more languages.

30

I WAS RIGHT. THE HEIGHTS WERE THE KEY TO THE PASS. BUT NO GENIUS WAS needed to figure that out, was it?

Renewed fighting began with a shower of firebombs. For the first time our entire front discharged bamboo poles uphill. Lady foamed at the mouth, cursing the waste.

Once again the Prahbrindrah Drah had been awarded the honor of the first charge.

It was hard to believe that Mogaba's soldiers had not been obliterated by the preparatory barrage but the Prince ran into fierce, stubborn resistance. The Shadowlanders fought ferociously now because they saw no other options. Their training took over, the way it is supposed to do in deadly situations. The Prince pushed hard but got nowhere.

Mogaba had managed to create a small reserve mostly out of imagination. He shuttled them here and there, applying mind, spirit and will to his own salvation. But he was accursed. And his curse was his lunatic employer.

Longshadow was nothing if not flexible when his own ass was in a sling. Till now the whole point of existence had been to hold the pass against the Black Company. The world would end if we crossed the Dandha Presh. But when the fireballs started zipping around his ears, sizzling black pockmarks out of the tower, he developed a new idea. He told Howler, "Get your carpet ready. General. Summon the Deceiver Singh, the child, and your five most valuable officers." Of a sudden he seemed entirely calm, totally rational, completely in control, apparently the sort of supreme ruler any man would prefer.

Howler stared at him half a minute before he nodded. The little wizard wore a mask of his own but that did not hide his contempt.

"Withdrawal at this point would be premature," Mogaba said. I was about ready to concede that the man was a saint. A devil saint, but a saint nonetheless. His patience seemed almost infinite. Longshadow was worse than a spoiled child. I wondered how he had become so powerful. "The situation can be retrieved if you'll just let me do it."

"You will do as I tell you, General."

"I suppose. Just as I have for four years. Which has brought us to this. The finest army of this age is being brought to despair by men who have only to design strategies that exploit the egotism, fears and fantasies of one wizard whose knowledge of things material does not extend to which end of a spear you grasp. I find that they are, by the by, astonishingly well informed about your character flaws."

Mogaba brushed Howler with a jaundiced glance. Paranoia and suspicion were not exclusive to our side. Neither were private agendas.

Longshadow sputtered in outrage.

Mogaba did not let up. "I will not summon my captains. I will not abandon my positions or desert my troops simply because your courage has deserted you. If you wish to go, go. Let us fight. We may die in fires sent up by the Senjak woman but at least no man of mine will be cut down from behind."

Longshadow sputtered. He was about to go berserk.

"Find some backbone, man. Find the guts to let the professionals do their jobs. Make your soldiers want to fight for you." Mogaba turned his back on the Shadowmaster. "Messenger." He sent word to the heights above that he was not pleased with the way things were going there.

A tall Shadar with an exceptional arm was lobbing firebombs fearfully close to Mogaba's tower. He had Narayan and the Daughter of Night very nervous down below.

For a while I thought Mogaba was going to carry his point and get away with his rebellion. He scattered messengers everywhere, steadying his troops. And Longshadow actually calmed down after a few minutes instead of flying into an inarticulate rage. He was reflective for quite some time. I feared that Mogaba had gotten through and convinced him of the truth that there was no better ground to meet us, no better men to fight us, no better commander to crush us. I feared his well honed instinct for self-preservation had kicked in.

Then some darkness gradually enveloped the Shadowmaster. I could have sworn that it did not come from within him.

Longshadow squealed like a wounded hog. He stomped and shrieked in a tongue no one understood and fell to his knees. He shuddered all over, having some sort of seizure. This was not like his usual fits of rage. He moaned and wept and talked in a way that made me wonder if even he understood what he was saying. Everyone on the tower gaped. Howler looked around like he expected incoming trouble of the cruelest kind. I took a swift look at Lady but found her doing nothing. She was just more alert than usual, sensing something but not knowing what it might be.

Whimpering, Longshadow climbed to his feet. He faced Mogaba. He began to stomp and shriek while he did something with his skinny, gloved fingers.

Mogaba suddenly dropped like he had gotten crowned by an axe handle.

Longshadow raged at the waiting messengers. He sent one to summon Singh and the child, others after his preferred officers. Those couriers went without any enthusiasm, which you would expect of guys who had just heard they were going to be allowed to stay behind and die so their nutcase boss could make his getaway.

Only the man sent for Narayan Singh actually did his job. The rest decided to get a head start hiking south. They saw no reason to accept betrayal.

Our guys on the heights managed to get a few firebombs into the structure of the observation tower. A sniper plinked away with a bamboo pole. His marksmanship left plenty to be desired. But those little balls of fire would not fly as predictably as an arrow.

Longshadow had Mogaba carried onto Howler's carpet. Howler said nothing though I thought it was obvious he agreed with Mogaba that the day was not yet lost.

Hell, it seemed to me they were a lot more afraid of Lady than they needed to be. I thought one big sorcerous shitstorm would take care of her. But maybe she had them fooled. Maybe Howler remembered the old days too well to go head-to-head with her now.

No matter. They were not willing to employ their strengths.

The carpet Howler had brought to Charandaprash was far larger than the one that he had had damaged earlier. It could haul a dozen people and all their gear.

Longshadow stopped raging. He seemed baffled by his own behavior, once actually whispering, "What have I done now?" He knew that he had screwed up but he was the kind of guy who, after he shoots his mouth off, cannot back down or admit any failing. The world is full of those people. All of us would be better off if their fathers would strangle them as soon as they showed signs of being that way. This particular fool was willing to sacrifice an army rather than admit his error.

A dozen men were on the platform when Singh and the child arrived. Mostly they were messengers not yet sent out. A few were officers. As Narayan and the Daughter of Night boarded the carpet even the dumbest soldiers realized that the big boys were running. After Longshadow stepped aboard and started to rave again, those about to be left decided not to stay. They joined the rush as Howler lifted the carpet. The carpet shuddered, sank to one side, banged off the edge of the platform, started sliding sideways toward the cliff.

Instantly firebombs came down. Soldiers dodged. The carpet wobbled worse. Men fell off. A firebomb scored. As the flames spread Howler gained better control. The carpet headed south, staggering like a drunken comet.

The men on the heights opened up with their bamboo gizmos. Howler dodged madly through the shitstorm. He did not dodge everything. Longshadow's desperate sorceries barely kept them from being eaten alive.

What was wrong with Lady? This was her chance. The villains were preoccupied with saving their own butts. If she brought them down now the thing would be done. And Narayan Singh and the kid would be ours for the collection.

Came a sound like ten thousand competing whispers, like a million, like a hundred million, swelling into the rush of a cyclone. It passed me, invisible, and chased up the pass. A horror-struck silence occupied its wake. It must have been a hundred times as terrifying outside the ghost-world. Soldiers from both sides put down their arms to watch.

Howler loosed a wail of despair heard above all the other racket. That woke up the gawkers on the cliffs who really had nothing better to do than blow fireballs at flying wizards. The fireworks show resumed, redoubled.

Howler headed for the ground. His companions' help was inadequate. He could not fly and fight at the same time. The carpet hit hard. Soldiers were thrown all over the slopes, Mogaba among them. Most just ran for it. Mogaba, when he recovered consciousness, began stumbling back toward his troops, oblivious to the shitstorm around him. He must have had divine dispensation because no harm found him.

Despite the flatness of the ghostworld I felt a surge of elation. We had them! This battle was won. This war was moments from being over! Lady's whispering witchery would gnaw away at Howler and the Shadowmaster while the guys on the cliffs inundated them with fireballs.

The expanse and depth of the Captain's ambush, crafted over years, all predicated upon the Shadowmaster's character, was only now emerging from the shadows. It overwhelmed me, not just because it had worked but because every contingency had been foreseen. Only he and his gods knew what else he had been ready for. There were tons of materiel down there still unused.

It was over. The road was open. I started back to One-Eye's wagon. We would have to move fast to make sure the Company stayed in a position to take advantage. First thing might be to get all our Company brothers together.

How long before I learn not to rack my eggs up as guaranteed fryers?

The Old Man was not trying to provoke the response he got. Neither was Lady, though she might have feared it. I do not believe Croaker had any idea anything of the sort was possible.

I was almost to the wagon when the ghost realm filled with a stench like somebody just kicked open all the tombs that ever were. I had not encountered much in the way of smells there before and all those had been nothing compared to this.

Fear hit me. Panic was a scant half step behind. I got out of there fast, before the fear made it impossible for me to recall how to escape.

Back up the canyon the Daughter of Night stood atop a boulder, oblivious to the fireballs streaking past, her little arms uplifted to greet oncoming darkness, summoning, her lips taut in an evil smile.

Something was coming. Something that I had glimpsed before.

31

I TUMBLED OUT OF THE WAGON, SORT OF HUNG ON TO THE SEAT WITH ONE hand, dangling like a monkey. It was far later than I had thought. Not only was it dark out, dawn seemed to be coming again.

No. This was no dawn. This light came from neither sun nor moon. It came from the pass. Had the firebombs ignited some Shadowlander supply dump?

I wished that was it. I knew better. That was no mundane fire.

I ran toward Lady's headquarters, stumbling more than making good time. My body was drained. Whatever was happening, Lady would be involved. And being near her might be the safest place.

I did not have far to run but the show was about over before I arrived. Surrounded by her intimates Lady was trying to get the Howler still but failed through no fault of her own.

A new player had come to the game.

Initially its shape and color were unclear. Then it collided with Lady's power. Power killed power in light. That light showed me something I did not want to see.

It was black. It was a hundred feet tall. It had four arms. It was the thing that haunted Lady's dreams and, sometimes, ghosted into mine. It was the darkness that had claimed Croaker's daughter.

Lady battled that colossus before a hundred thousand eyes and, by doing so, confused a lot of people.

The Deceivers had to be whooping it up. Things had gotten tough for them but here was concrete proof that the Year of the Skulls could be achieved. That it might be at hand. That their goddess had grown strong enough to reach into our world to protect her chosen daughter and the living saint, Narayan Singh.

That image of Kina was a lot like Longshadow's pets, though. It was not immune to fireballs from Lady's bamboo poles. The panic its appearance caused lured plenty of those into the air. Soon it resembled some mythological creature on a moth-eaten tapestry.

The thing ended before I could catch my breath. Kina guttered, vanished. It persisted only long enough for her child and her protectors to make their getaway. Still listing and smoldering, Howler's carpet passed from sight. The hundred million whispers began to fade.

Lady collapsed. They lifted her onto the stretcher. Swan and Blade manned its ends. Her most loyal soldiers surrounded them, men who had been with her for years. I told Swan, "You don't have to worry about them up there. They're headed for Overlook with their tails between their legs. Mogaba is unconscious and probably hurt. Nobody is in charge anymore."

Swan gave me an incredulous look. "What the hell you telling me for? Find your damned Captain and tell him."

"Good idea." I went.

32

THE PRAHBRINDRAH DRAH'S DIVISION SUFFERED HORRIBLY YET AGAIN. Mogaba's men refused to forget the first law of survival: never turn your back. It is hard to kill a soldier who clings to his training when every instinct and emotion tells him to throw down his arms and run away or to curl up in a ball to shut out the terror.

The whole point of drilling soldiers till they whine about the stupidity of it all is so those soldiers will do the right thing automatically when the terror comes. Combat is fear and management of fear far more than it is organized murder. Those who manage fear best will seize the day.

The Old Man observed for so long, without intervening in the Prince's situation, that his own staff started grumbling. I asked him why he was holding off.

"I want him to show Taglios what he's made of. I want to see that myself. I don't want there to be any doubts about him when he takes charge."

It had a nice ring but still sounded suspect. I was developing a very suspicious attitude where Croaker was concerned.

Later he had Lady's division, supported by Willow Swan's Guards, replace the Prince's division. Lady made rapid gains until Mogaba managed to reassert his control on the other side. She was so exhausted the witcheries she could manage amounted to little more than distractions.

I wondered why Croaker did not just back off until she recovered. I no longer spent much time trying to unravel his thoughts, though. Dark designs or otherwise, I did not know the man anymore.

He withdrew Lady's division shortly before noon. He moved archers up on the flanks, arrayed his own two divisions for the advance, in the follow-on mode where one force fights to exhaustion, then the next advances through its positions to attack the hopefully decimated enemy. But before the drums began their grim chant he took a white flag forward. I tagged along, carrying the standard. The damned thing needed to go on a diet. It seemed to be getting heavier.

I was put out. I was here only because Croaker insisted. I wanted to be out riding Smoke, finding out what Longshadow and Howler and Soulcatcher and whoever were up to. The Radisha needed checking, too. I had not looked in on her in far too long.

At least she would not be aware of events here for a while.

Mogaba surprised me by coming down to meet us. He limped. He sported an array of bandages. I imagine that if he had not been so dark he would have shown a fine crop of bruises. One of his eyes was swollen shut. His lips were compressed against the pain. But he betrayed no more emotion than an ebony statue. He said, "You managed to exploit our vulnerabilities very skillfully."

Warily and wearily, Croaker said, "The asshole hamstrung you. Do we have to waste any more lives?"

"This battle may be decided but the war goes on. Its outcome may yet be determined here."

That had the ring of truth. If we did not get moving forward real soon we were not going to be able to hold this army together.

Croaker's smile suited his Widowmaker armor, which he seemed unwilling to shed lately. "Time and again I've told you to study the Annals. Time and again I've reminded you that you'll regret it if you don't."

Mogaba also smiled, as though he knew something. "They aren't holy writ."

"What?"

"Your precious Annals. They aren't holy. They're just histories, made up of legends and outright lies in about equal parts." He glared at me. "It will cost you dear if you put your faith in the past, Standardbearer."

Now the Captain smiled gently. A battle fought with smiles?

Croaker had shown a lot of originality but Mogaba did not recognize that. He did not because he had not read the books. He would not confess it publicly but he had not read the books because he could not read. In Gea-Xle, whence he came, reading was not a warriorly skill.

Right now there was no doubt who held the initiative on the psychological front. Croaker said, "So I have to kill a bunch more of you before you'll face the truth?"

"Truth is mutable and subject to interpretation. In this case its final form remains undetermined. Perhaps you brought a good recipe for rock." Mogaba turned away, his piece said. He limped uphill. The set of his shoulders said his pride ached just having to show us his pain. He muttered to himself, something about the Shadowmaster no longer being there to hobble him.

I said, "Hey, chief, he don't got Longshadow on his back no more."

"He doesn't have him to stand in front of him anymore, either. Look out!"

Thai Dei jumped up and got a shield over my head just in time to keep me from drowning in a shower of arrows. "Wow! The weather really turned bad fast."

The boys uphill had a laugh at our expense. We made a spectacle backing away, three of us trying to stay under one undersized shield.

That crafty shit Mogaba had come down only to buy a few minutes for his troops. They attacked as soon as he reached them. Their nerve was no longer what it had been but their discipline remained firm.

Arrows from the the flanks and towers and fireballs from everywhere made their effort look ill-advised. Nonetheless, they pushed us back like they thought this attack was their last hope. The situation began to look desperate. But then Lady decided she had rested enough.

Charandaprash became quite colorful.

The fighting did not last long after that. But when the silence fell even our reserves were too exhausted to chase anybody. Croaker let the remaining camp followers have that honor, telling them they could keep any loot they took.

Those who tried mostly got themselves killed.

Mogaba's plans were the hot topic around the big bonfire. It seemed like everyone over the rank of lieutenant was there and every man had a theory. Or two. And not a one of those was sound.

I had gone ghostwalking and had not been able to find Mogaba, even by backtracking through time. But just a hint of a specter of a death stink had sent me running before I could get a real good look around.

Was she going to be out there every time I went?

Croaker kicked nothing into the speculative stew. He just sat around looking smug and more relaxed than I had seen in years.

Lady sat beside him and she looked pretty good, too. Like she had gotten some real sleep for once. I told her, "I want to talk to you when you get a few minutes. I don't have hardly anything about you to put down."

She sighed, said, "I don't think I could tell you anything interesting."

I could use Smoke to study her backtrail. But that would not tell me what she was thinking.

She asked Croaker, "Why do you look like the cat who stole the cream?"

"Because Longshadow and Howler didn't come back." He looked at me. He wanted to know why. But not right now. It could wait. "And because you have." After her rest she seemed none the worse for wear despite her head-to-head with Kina. Or whatever that was. "Because now they're just going to hide out in Overlook while Longshadow tries to cobble together something from garrisons and militias made up of men who'd rather not get involved at all."

He was still the Shadowmaster. He had not played his trumps to their limit. And the walls of Overlook were a hundred feet high. I hoped Croaker did not think all we had to do now was coast.

"You notice he hasn't really said shit," Swan grumbled to Blade. He had not had any trouble accepting his buddy back. Some of the men could not believe the whole defection had been a swindle. Especially those who had had relatives among the temple troops Blade had exterminated. "The son of a bitch flat ain't going to tell nobody what he's up to. Not even you and me. He's got tricks up his sleeve and we've got to find out about them same as any poor dork that they're going to happen to."

He stared at Lady sadly for a moment, unable to see what she saw in the Old Man. I had wondered that a few times myself before Sarie and I fell in love.

It does not have to make sense. Just pray for the freedom to indulge it.

Speaking of limits to freedom, my in-laws were still missing. Except for Thai Dei, of course. He was there even when my shadow was gone.

Blade laughed at Swan's sourness. He was a changed man after his adventure. He had found his niche. "You really want to know, you'd better borrow those books from Murgen. They say it's all in there if you know where to look."

Murgen lied, "Good plan. But Murgen didn't bring the books along. Except for the one he hasn't been working on enough lately."

Swan's comment was brief and obscene. Like Mogaba, he did not know how to read.

Blade suggested, "Get Murgen Big Ears to tell it to you. He can quote chapter and verse almost as good as Croaker. He's Croaker's handpicked boy."

The old Blade did not have a sense of humor. I was not sure I liked this one better. He was not interested in being funny.

"I'll do it if the pay is right," I told them. "Us mercenary types don't do diddly unless we get paid."

I did have to put some thought into staying away from Smoke long enough to get some solid notes made. Charandaprash was a critical juncture in Company history. I was not doing it justice.

And when I did go walking with the ghost I would have to concentrate on things I really needed to observe.

I could not go just to get away from the pain.

The pain was not so all-devouring anymore. Maybe a couple of brushes with Kina were the cure for romantic excess.

"Thai Dei," I said, softly and in Nyueng Bao to show this was merely a personal matter, not business. "What does it mean when a Nyueng Bao woman wears white?"

"Ai?" He seemed surprised. "I don't understand, brother."

"I just remembered a dream I had a couple nights ago. Somebody who looked like Sahra was in it. She was wearing white. Nyueng Bao always wear black except sometimes when you're out here in the world. Or if you're a priest. Isn't that so?"

"You dreamed of Sahra?"

"I do all the time. Don't you dream about My?"

"No. We are taught to let their spirits go."

"Oh." I did not believe that. If that was completely true there would be no call to seek revenge. "So what does it mean, wearing white? Or does it mean anything?"

"It means she is recently widowed. A man who lost his wife would wear white as well. She may do so for as long as a year. While she is in white no one may advance a marriage offer—though of course the men of her family will be looking around unofficially. In the case of a man his father and brothers may examine the possibilities but not be allowed to speak on his behalf until he puts off the white."

This was news to me. "The whole time we were in Dejagore I never saw one Nyueng Bao in white. And Sarie sure didn't wait any year after Danh died to get interested in me."

Thai Dei showed me one of his rare smiles. "Sarie was interested in you before Danh died. Sarie was smitten the first time you came to see Grandfather. You have no idea the quarreling that went on. Particularly after Grandmother announced that it was fated that Sarie take a foreign lover."

So the smile was not one of good humor.

I could imagine Mother Gota's take.

"But Sarie never wore white. Nor did anybody else."

"Nor was there a square inch of white cloth in that city that was not worn by a Taglian soldier. Grandfather did not think it politic to take their tunics." Thai Dei smiled again. That only made his face more skull-like. He added, "We were a small party. After all that time on pilgrimage we knew one another. We knew who had lost a mate. And we knew nothing could be done till we got back to our villages and priests anyway."

So the woman I saw while I was lost in the delta was a widow. I guess that explained why she was haggard and unhappy.

"You should tell me more about Nyueng Bao. I'd feel less stupid when something like this comes up."

Thai Dei's smile died. "There is no longer any need for you to know our customs, is there?"

I was not one of them, even by marriage. He was here because he had assumed an obligation, not because I was family.

I needed to think about that.

33

CROAKER LET EVERYBODY REST THOROUGHLY BEFORE HE LAUNCHED WHAT he hoped would be the final assault on the Shadowlander defenses. I had an ague or maybe something I picked up from the proximity of Kina for a while, hot sweats alternating with cold shakes. Consequently I did not get out to scout our enemies.

No matter. The Old Man was able to gossip with his crows.

There were no living Shadowlanders anywhere in the defensive works that Longshadow had deemed so critical. While we were being soft, sitting around on our behinds resting, Mogaba and his captains had gotten their soldiers moving. They had even tried to destroy the stores they could not drag with them but were forestalled in that by the efforts of an alert Shadar cavalry detachment.

Death is eternity. Eternity is stone. Stone is silence. Stone is broken.

In the night, when the wind no longer moans and the small shadows go into hiding, stone sometimes whispers. Stone sometimes speaks. Stone sometimes sends its children plunging into the abyss. Sometimes a tendril of colorful mist rises to caress the figure pinned to the tilting throne.

Shadows scamper playfully about the plain glittering in the moonlight, devouring one another and growing stronger. Their memories are as old as stone. They remember freedom.

Sometimes the leaning throne slips a millionth of an inch, tilting farther. This happens more and more frequently now.

Stone shudders. Eternity sneers as it devours its own tail. This cold feast is almost finished.

Even death is restless.

34

I COULD HEAR ONE-EYE CURSING FATE IN GENERAL AND SEVERAL VEHDNA Taglians in particular. One wheel of the wagon had become pinched between boulders and the soldiers were not getting it pried out fast enough to suit the little wizard. He had been in a foul temper all morning. I do believe he thought we would not continue on south after we won at Charandaprash. I do believe he thought the Old Man would be content to occupy the pass, then withdraw to warmer climes and wait for summer.

Where was Longshadow going to go? Home. And because of the earthquake home was a house that would not be completed any time soon. So where was the big hurry? What kind of tunnel-vision fanatic did not even take time out for one good drunk after winning a battle so huge and obviously unwinnable going in?

One-Eye had been saying all this and a lot more from the minute Croaker had told him to move out. One-Eye was not a happy trooper.

He was even more unhappy because I got to ride. My fever and chills thing kept coming and going. The Captain saw that as a good excuse to keep me near Smoke—against whom he continued to caution me regularly. I did not tell him that walking with the ghost was becoming as unattractive as attractive, that it was getting scary out there. I had not talked it over with One-Eye yet, either. I knew I should. I would not like myself much anymore if something happened because I failed to warn them.

But I did not want to cry wolf, either. One-Eye had not mentioned running into anything unusual during his occasional trips out. Maybe I was letting my imagination get the best of me.

I was in pretty good shape for the moment. A little shaken by the ride but neither feverish nor fighting a chill. Might be an opportune time to take a look around.

Outside, One-Eye snarled something at Thai Dei. "Not a good idea, One-Eye," I snapped in Jewel Cities dialect. "He'd as soon kick your ass as look at you."

"Ha! That ought to be interesting. See what JoJo does. Might even wake him up."

Like most Company members One-Eye had a Nyueng Bao bodyguard. His was Cho Dai Cho, as unobtrusive and unambitious a bodyguard as ever lived. He was around only because the tribal elders had decreed it. He did not seem to have much interest in saving One-Eye from himself or anyone else. I had not seen Cho four times in the last month.

I could not find Soulcatcher. I knew she was there and Smoke was not fighting me but the woman was operating under a spell that hid her from even this sort of seeing. I could guess where she was roughly, though, because of the comings and goings of crows in the mountains west of us.

I looked around for One-Eye's shapeshifter friend Lisa Bowalk but there was no trace of her, either. Nor could I pinpoint Mogaba and the couple of Nar who had chosen to stand by him when he deserted the Company for service to the Shadowmaster.

This was something to think about. If people had begun to suspect we were watching . . . But there was Longshadow in his crystal dome atop Overlook's tallest tower, seated at a stone desk, calmly giving orders to messengers, arranging for the defense of his dwindling empire rationally and with vigor and making no effort to hide himself from me.

And down below, in a private apartment, here was an uncomfortable and weakened Narayan Singh cringing in a corner while the Daughter of Night, like a dwarf rather than a child, apparently carried on half of a conversation with her spiritual mother. There was a smell of Kina in the room but not that terrifying sense of presence I had encountered before.

I observed for a while. I ran back the hours. There was no doubt. Narayan Singh was not running anything anymore. He was an adjunct to the Daughter of Night, useful principally as a voice through which she could communicate with the Shadowmaster and the Deceivers. But Singh was beginning to suspect that his usefulness was running its course, that it would not be very much longer at all before the child would be ready to dispose of him.

When the time came she would do it with no more thought or emotion than she would discarding a well-gnawed pork rib.

Her communions with her divine parent were reshaping her fast.

Kina seemed to be in a hurry, perhaps pressed for time, so that she did not have time to wait for the child to mature into her role.

I was very uncomfortable around the kid even though she was a hundred miles away. I got out of there.

I tried tracking Howler down but caught only glimpses as he buzzed here and there on his raggedy-ass, oft-patched smaller carpet. He seemed to have upped his level of precaution dramatically, too. I could spot him only when he was in a really big hurry and, apparently, outrunning his invisibility shield. Who would he be hiding from? If he did not know about me?

There was still the Radisha, whom I had not spied on for way too long.

In present time she was in the midst of a large audition with the chief priests of the major temples of the city. The subject was, not surprisingly, the war. In particular, the sacrilegious, atheistic, anticlerical stance of the men directing the Taglian effort. The new generation of priests were much less contentious amongst sects than had been their predecessors, who had paid for their stubbornly parochial attitudes with their lives.

"There's no doubt," the Radisha admitted to a priest of Rhavi-Lemna, a goddess of brotherly love, "that the Liberator has been sending troops raised among the devout to pursue his feud with Blade." News from the war zone was still far away. "He's blatant about it, it's true, but you people keep going along with it."

A priest in vermilion grumbled, "Because Blade has been promised the protectorship here when the Shadowmaster triumphs. He'll exterminate us all. If he's still alive."

"Which brings us to the crux again, doesn't it? Even though my brother has become a competent commander and a corps of experienced officers has developed, neither the soldiers themselves nor the people believe we can defeat the Shadowmaster without the guidance of the Black Company. We're still in a position where we're compelled to let darkness wrestle darkness, hoping our hand of darkness triumphs and we can control it after it does so."

Rhavi-Lemna was a reasonable goddess. It would not be natural for her priests to be firebrands. But the Gunni have a hundred gods and goddesses, great and small, and some of them are a lot less tolerant. Someone shouted, "We should kill them now! They're a greater danger to our way of life than any masked sorcerer eight hundred miles away."

There were still many Taglians who had not served in the armies nor traveled south to see what legacy the Shadowmasters had left in the lands retaken from their rule. Men who did not believe simply because they preferred something else to be true.

This was an unending squabble that might not be settled in my lifetime. There was a war on and as long as we did not yet have it won the "Kill them now!" school of thinking would remain a distinct minority. But the "Kill them later!" school had plenty of members.

"There aren't more than fifty or sixty of them," the Radisha countered. "How hard can it be to dispose of them once they've outlived their usefulness?"

"Pretty damned hard, I imagine. The Shadowmasters haven't managed. Neither have the Deceivers."

"Steps are being taken."

Interesting. I had not seen any sign of that.

Time to cruise days gone by, then.

Away I went. Skipping like a seven-year-old girl, toes coming down every hour or so as I headed toward the last time I checked on the Woman. There was not much there. A lot of the same stuff. One idea after another bounced off Cordy Mather in the deeps of night, every one rejected by Mather, and the more vigorously so the better the Woman seemed to like them.

Of more interest was the fact that she had started looking for Smoke. In fact, she was getting suspicious, though not yet in any major way. Mather kept telling her we were all right and must have made some arrangement to look out for Smoke. We would not just let the old boy starve.

"They hate him, dear. He did everything he could to undercut the Black Company."

"They would find a crueler way to get even. After they woke him up. So he could appreciate the pain."

Cordy echoed my thoughts perfectly. Starvation would do fine but I wanted him conscious while he went.

Waking up to find himself in our hands might just be enough. He would have a shit hemorrhage.

All the way back to my last visit I found nothing particularly exciting. The Woman never said anything interesting except when she was finished using Mather and then she said nothing original. Yet I could not help thinking that something was going on.

She was the Radisha Drah. Her whole life had been spent aware that everything she said or did might be observed by someone who did not wish her well.

I skipped back to today but did not find anything to hurry back to the Old Man.

There would be some excitement when the news from Charandaprash arrived. People would stop thinking as clearly and carefully. I would be back.

I took a dive into Smoke's old hiding place before I left. The old Annals were right where I had hidden them.

Interesting to note, though, as I departed, that there were crows all over the Palace district.

One-Eye was still cursing when I came out. Cursing again, I learned, as I let myself down from the rear of the wagon. A different wheel was stuck. We had moved several miles. I was bone dry. I lifted the lid on One-Eye's waterbarrel. There was not much there. The little that remained was pretty nasty. I drank it anyway.

I walked around to where One-Eye was abusing a fresh crew of victims. "You little shit. Quit barking at the help. They'll stuff that damned hat down your throat and I'll end up having to walk. Where's the Old Man?"

35

"CROWS ALL OVER, EH?" CROAKER MUSED. "INTERESTING. GUESS IT DOESN'T surprise me."

"Hers?" There were crows around us right now. Naturally. He would not let Lady run them off.

"Probably."

"Are they all nowadays?"

"Take it for granted. You won't be unpleasantly surprised. Tell me about Longshadow." The last sentence was not verbal at all but in the finger speech we had learned way back when Darling, the White Rose, was with the Company. We employed it sparingly anymore and I had not thought of using it to get around the crows. It was so obvious when you considered it. There would be no way for the critters to relay the signs.

Nobody believed that the birds understood what they relayed now. They just carried the words.

My fingers were no longer as nimble as once they had been. I had a hard time telling him that Longshadow had done a turnaround and was all business now, calm and sane and decisive.

"Interesting," he said. He looked up the pass. The Prince's troops, in the vanguard, had sprung a Shadowlander ambush. The fighting was getting heavy. The column was crushing up behind it. This could get bad.

I looked at the slopes rising to either hand. If Mogaba had a lot of men up there he could embarrass us easily.

"He doesn't," Croaker said, as though I had spoken my thoughts.

"You're getting spooky." He wore most of the fancy Widowmaker armor most of the time now. There was hardly ever a time when he did not have a crow on his shoulder. He seemed to know his favorites because he always had tidbits for them.

"When I have to play a role I try to live it." He began talking with his fingers again. "I want you to find Goblin. It is critical."

"Huh?"

He signed, "I would do it myself but there is no time." Aloud, he added, "These delaying tactics are working very well for Mogaba. This pass is just too damned tight." He turned away, strode up the stalled column. The Prahbrindrah Drah was about to get talked to like a new recruit.

Suddenly, over his shoulder, he shot, "Where're your in-laws, Murgen?"

"What?"

"Where are they? What're they up to?" He used colloquial Taglian, which meant he did not care what Thai Dei heard. Or specifically wanted him to know about the query.

"I haven't seen them." I glanced at Thai Dei. He shook his head. "Maybe they went home."

"I don't think so. If that was the case the rest of these clowns would be gone with them. Wouldn't they?"

I did not think so but there was no need arguing the point. Croaker would never be comfortable with the Nyueng Bao. I told him I would keep an eye out and would let him know if I learned anything, then moved along.

I ran into Sleepy on the way back to One-Eye's wagon. "Hey, kid. How you doing?" I had not seen him since I gave him his assignment that night in Taglios. He had been working with Big Bucket, helping oversee the special forces teams. He looked tired but still not old enough to be a soldier.

"I'm tired and hungry and beginning to wonder if being buttfucked by my uncles really was worse than this."

Anybody who could sustain a sense of humor after what Sleepy had suffered was all right by me.

I wondered if he would ever go back and kill them. I doubted it. That sort of thing was acceptable in this bizarre southern culture.

Sleepy asked, "You talk to the Captain yet?"

"I talk to him all the time. I'm the Annalist."

"I mean about the standardbearer job. You said you might . . ."

"Oh. Yeah." His excitement was obvious. But becoming standardbearer meant those above you thought you were destined for big things in the Company. The standardbearer often became Annalist. Frequently he became Lieutenant because he was always near the center of things and knew everything that was going on. The Lieutenant almost always becomes Captain when the job comes open.

Croaker was an anomaly of epic proportion, elected at a time when there were only seven of us, none more qualified, and nobody else would take the job.

"I bounced it off him. He didn't say no. He'll probably leave it up to me. And that means it's a someday sort of thing because right now everybody in this army is working twenty hours a day. There's no time to teach you anything."

"We're not doing anything. I could just hang around you and—"

Big Bucket's voice rose above all the other tumult of an army on the move, telling Sleepy to get his dead ass back up here, they've decided nobody else can crack this nut but us.

"Good luck. And don't get in a hurry, kid," I told him. "Hell. Do like I'm doing with the Annals. Wait till the siege of Overlook. We'll have plenty of time then. Including learning to read and write."

"I've been learning. Believe it or not. I know fifty-three common characters already. I can puzzle out almost anything."

Written Taglian is fairly complicated because there are more than a hundred characters in the common alphabet and another forty-two in the High Taglian used only by Gunni priests. A lot of the characters duplicate what they mean but distinguish caste. Caste is very important among the Gunni.

"Keep at it," I told Sleepy. "You'll make it on determination."

"Thanks, Murgen." The kid began scooting uphill, sliding through the press like he was greased.

"Don't thank me," I mumbled. Most standardbearers are not as lucky as I have been. It is not a job with an extended life expectancy.

I spotted Lady across the pass, as always surrounded by her admirers and most of the Nar who had not deserted the Company. I headed that way.

36

MEN MOVED TO LET ME THROUGH. THINGS LIKE THAT HAPPEN WHEN YOU can leave someone as a good taste or foul odor in history's mouth. Croaker really made the importance of the Annals an article of faith with everyone in the Company.

Lady looked around. Her ordinarily impassive expression betrayed an instant of irritation. I said, "Looks like we're going to be stalled here till Bucket's crew convince Mogaba's people they'd really rather go home and get in out of this weather."

That was looking kind of bleak. A wind was building. It was colder than the wind had been for days. Heavy clouds were piling up overhead. Looked as if we were going to get some snow.

"Yeah. Let's hope," Swan said. "We need to get down out of these rocks." He was not talking to me, really. "I hate mountains."

"I'm not too fond of cold and snow, either," I said. Of Lady I asked, "You really need to keep avoiding me?"

"What do you want to know?"

"How can you be getting your powers back? I thought that business in the Barrowland stripped you forever."

"I'm a thief. Otherwise, none of your business."

Her entourage sneered at me, mostly because they thought that would make points with her.

"Have you been dreaming again?"

She thought about that one before admitting, "Yes."

"I thought so. You've been looking a little ragged."

"You want to play you have to pay the price. What about you, Annalist?"

I found I was reluctant to reveal anything. Especially in front of those guys. I forced myself. "Yeah. Something that might have been Kina turned up in my dreams a couple times. Almost like an intrusion from outside. I wondered if that might have been the same time she was bothering you."

That interested her. You could see the thoughts begin moving behind her eyes, the consideration, the calculation. She told me, "If it happens again, note the time. If you can."

"I'll try. How did you manage to go head-to-head with Kina the other night and come out in one piece?"

Without missing a beat Lady shifted to Groghor, a language on its last death rattle. "That was not Kina." I learned it from my grandmother, whose people had all been wiped out in the consolidation wars that had built the Lady's empire. Granny was dead and so was my mother and I had not used the tongue except to cuss people out since I signed on with the Company.

"How do you . . . ?" I sputtered. "How could you know that I . . . ?"

"The Captain has been kind enough to have your work copied and forwarded to me. You mentioned Groghor somewhere. I am a little rusty. I have not spoken this language in more than a century. Pardon my lapses."

"You're doing fine. But why bother?"

"My sister never learned the language. Nor did this bunch, half of whom are probably spies for someone."

"What's the deal? You said that wasn't Kina. Sure fooled me if it wasn't. Sure fit the description."

"That was my beloved sister. Pretending to be Kina. I expect she surprised Kina's worshippers as much as she surprised the rest of us."

"But . . ." The Daughter of Night had seemed happy enough.

"I can touch the real Kina, Murgen. Believe me. It's why I don't sleep well. The real Kina is still in her trance. She can only touch the world in dreams. And I have to stay a part of those dreams."

"So Kina is definitely real, then?"

"There is something that fits the bill of particulars, Murgen. I'm not sure that when it's awake it thinks of itself as Kina or as a goddess. It does want to bring on the Year of the Skulls. It does want to get free of its chains. But these are just emotions I have gained from it over the years. It is far too alien for me to know it well."

"Like Old Father Tree?"

She had to think to remember the tree-god thing that had ruled the Plain of Fear and defied her when she was still the Lady.

"I never touched that mind."

"Why would your sister pretend to be Kina?"

"I have never known why my sister does any of the things she does. She has never been rational. Two does not follow One in her scheme, nor does Three come before Four. She is capable of spending incredible energies and vast fortunes on the execution of a prank. She is capable of destroying cities without ever being able to explain why. You can know what she is doing but not why or you can know why she is doing something but not what. She was that way when she was three years old, before anyone knew she was cursed with the power, too."

"You believe you're cursed?"

She actually smiled. When she did her beauty shone through. "By an insane sister, for sure. I wish I had even the foggiest notion why she's just out there, doing nothing but watching and constantly reminding us that she's there."

"Reminding us?"

"Don't you get a little tired of those damned crows?"

"Yes, I do. I thought revenge was her thing."

"If that was all she wanted she would have squashed me a long time ago."

There was a stir behind me. Scores of eyes were staring at us as everyone in earshot tried to figure out what was going on. It had to be some secret if we were going to talk it over in a language nobody knew.

Willow Swan looked like his feelings were hurt.

"Excuse me, sir," said a voice from behind me. "The Liberator's compliments and would you be so good as to get your ass on about the job he gave you? He said to suggest that he wants the answer before sundown."

That was not in a language no one else understood. It cheered Swan right up. Even Lady chuckled.

I do believe I blushed. "I'll want to pursue this further," I told Lady, who did not seem thrilled by the prospect. To the messenger, who happened to be the nephew of a prominent Taglian general, I said, "Just for that I think I'll go do what the Old Man wants."

37

IT TOOK ME A LONG TIME TO FIND GOBLIN BUT THERE WAS NO HURRY. THE Shadowlanders up the pass were being particularly stubborn. Big Bucket was having to use a lot of firebombs to root them out.

I found it hard to believe. Goblin was on the other side of the Dandha

Presh. His Shaded Road was an expedition that had pushed a commando force across the Shindai Kus. Croaker had talked about the possibility once, ages ago, before we ever even went after Dejagore, but I always thought it was completely impractical. So much so that the possibility had not occurred to me even when I had found Goblin on the shore of the Shindai Kus.

Goblin was still Goblin. The desert only baked it in. "I'm one step and ten seconds short of exhaustion," he complained to the man nearest him, a Company brother named Bubba-do who was not too bright and who, I noted, kept Goblin on his left side, which was where he had the bad ear. "But I'm here. I'm in place. I'm on time. And nobody knows we're here."

Lights flared in the mountains above. Tiny balls of fire rose over the high Dandha Presh. Bubba-do said, "Looks like da Captain won his bet."

"I'm worried. This damned thing's been going too good. I've been fighting these people for years. I know how they think. I know Mogaba." So did Bubba-do but that did not matter in Goblin's view. "He ain't going to let himself get whipped by Croaker. Whole point of him going over to the Shadowmaster was he wanted to prove he was a better soldier and general."

Goblin went on and on. His men ignored him most of the time. After he had heard scouting reports about the surrounding terrain he allowed his men to build several small, carefully hidden fires. That side of the Dandha Presh was colder than the northern slope. It was impossible to manage without heat if you were not moving.

"I should've found a farm. Maybe a small town. Someplace where we could get inside."

"That would mean killing a bunch of people so they couldn't rat on us and that probably wouldn't do any good anyway because somebody probably would've got away."

It was almost dark. The excitement in the mountains was getting colorful. I began to wonder if Mogaba himself was not up there directing the resistance.

"You got company," somebody said. Instantly everybody at Goblin's fire found a chore that had to be handled right away somewhere else. Everyone but Goblin's Nyueng Bao bodyguard, who was a man so unobtrusive I had yet to learn his full name. It was Thane, Trine, something like that. This man merely moved to a place more comfortable on a taller rock and laid his sword across his lap, ready for business.

The reason the others wanted to be elsewhere was evident a moment later.

I had found one of my missing targets.

A huge, cruel-looking black panther stalked out of the darkness, set-tled near the fire. Goblin reached out and scratched her behind the ears.

What the hell? This particular panther had no love for him. Though her squabble with One-Eye was an order of magnitude bigger.

"So you decided to help out after all, eh?" Goblin said. "It never was that hard to get along." Off he went on an odyssey of the imagination, describing in fantastic detail why she was a natural ally of the rest of us despite One-Eye's having had to do in Shapeshifter. Shifter really had given him no choice, now, had he? Anyway, it was only a matter of time before they completed their research into the character of release spells. Last time he saw One-Eye they were just three terms and a postulate short of putting a wrap on it.

The wind had a real bite as I went looking for Croaker. There were bits of snow zinging around. Nobody had moved since this afternoon. Fireballs flickered across the sky up ahead. There were almost no fires. There was nothing to burn. Men huddled with one another for warmth. Hardly any-one lifted their eyes as I passed. I could have been the Shadowmaster himself and nobody would have cared. Had I been carrying hot food I would have been hailed as a messiah.

Croaker did not have a fire, either. But he had a girlfriend to keep him warm. Something nobody else had. The rat bastard.

"You want to go for a walk?"

Hell, no, he did not. Neither would you if you were bundled up in some blankets with a beautiful woman on a freezing night. "Use your imagination here, Murgen. Do I look like somebody who wants to be interrupted?"

"All right. Be that way. I've finally located the man you asked about. He seems to be where he's supposed to be. But—"

"Then go keep an eye on him."

"There's a complication."

"Keep an eye on him. He's not likely to get into much before I can come check on him. Later."

With him and Lady both scowling at me I decided I would take the hint and go away. Shaking my head. There are things you can accept intellectually but still not imagine. Those two in the throes of passion fell into the latter category.

If he was in no hurry I was not, either. I had a snack and a nap and a dream about Sarie before I got back to work. It was not a dream I wanted. It was Sarie looking aged and haggard and wearing white. But that was a better dream than the visit to ice hell that followed.

That one did not change much with time, nor did any more details develop. But I never got comfortable with it.

Goblin had all his illusions in place but he did not bother the first fugitives to hurry out of the Dandha Presh. Those would be the men least likely to be trouble in later times. He did have a few individuals captured so he could get a better idea of what had happened to the north. He told the panther, "A shithead like Longshadow don't deserve followers like Mogaba."

The panther rumbled deep in her throat.

"You got to wonder about Mogaba. Why the hell don't he just walk?"

Mogaba had everything under control. His fighting withdrawal was going well for him.

The hundred men with Goblin were all young Taglians interested in becoming part of the Black Company, I gathered. Clever Goblin had sold them the notion that this operation was an entrance exam. The nasty little shit.

He had to feel lonely out there. His bodyguard, Thien Duc, knew only a few words of Taglian and had no more inclination to gossip than Thai Dei did. The panther's conversational skills were limited. The commandos were all under twenty-five. Goblin spoke Taglian well enough but did not speak the language of the young.

In the dialect of the Jewel Cities he muttered, "I miss One-Eye. He may not be worth two dead flies but . . . Nobody heard that, did they? Us old farts got to stick together. We're the only ones who know what it's all about.

"Or do we?"

"Yeah. I think we do."

"Were you saying something, sir?" one of the young sergeants asked, rushing up.

"Talking to myself, lad. Guaranteed intelligent conversation. I was thinking out loud about Mogaba. How everybody on the other side's got their own thing going. Ten minutes after they whip us everybody over there is going to be measuring everybody else for a dagger in the back."

"Sir?" The young Shader seemed scandalized by the suggestion that our side might yet lose this war.

"If they blow it, with everything they've got going for them, and we come out on top, the same shit is gonna happen on our side."

Goblin began using his illusions and commandos to begin picking off Shadowlander fugitives, to teach job-appropriate skills while the work was still easy, and to keep the boys from getting bored.

Larger Shadowlander forces began to come down, hurrying, in disarray, walking into Goblin's setup like they had rehearsed it. Snipers picked off obvious officers. Missile fire drenched the troopers. When they organized for a counterattack they found themselves fighting illusions and shadows.

From my vantage I began to wonder what Goblin was expected to accomplish. He was causing trouble out of all proportion to his numbers but what he was doing was unlikely to have any permanent impact. Unless, of course, him being here meant he was not somewhere else. Which was just the sort of thing that might occur to Croaker. Cook up some cockamamie mission for Goblin so he would not be around getting drunk and feuding with One-Eye and generally obstructing progress.

Still . . . The Shadowlanders could not find him. He kept giving them ghosts. Word rolled back up into the mountains. Panic rode its back. That effect was all out of proportion to Goblin's numbers, too.

There was one major theme to Goblin's ambushes. He was directing his strongest efforts toward eliminating officers. He seemed to have a way to identify those in plenty of time to slide his commandos into position.

The forvalaka. The woman in cat form. She was scouting for him. But how was she communicating?

I spend a lot of time being puzzled by things going on around me.

"I feel like I'm a mushroom on a mushroom farm," I told Croaker. "Kept in the dark and fed a diet of horseshit."

Croaker shrugged, said the famous words. "Need to know."

"He didn't get Mogaba, if that was the plan. That son of a bitch must take a bath in grease every morning, he's so slick. He did get that Nar Khucho."

Croaker grunted.

"Not much of a triumph," I agreed. "He was already on a stretcher with one leg amputated. But I had to let you know and I'm going to have to put it into the Annals because he did belong to the Company once."

Croaker shrugged, grunted. That was how we did it.

"He's got nobody left, then," I said. "He's over there all alone, without one friend."

"Don't cry for him, Murgen. He's there because he chose to go there."

"I'm not crying for him. I had to go through the siege of Dejagore with that guy in charge. Far as I'm concerned anything that happens to him won't be pain enough."

"You thought any more about turning the standard over to somebody else?"

"Sleepy's been bugging me. I told him we'd look at it once we get set up around Overlook."

"You think he's the right one, go ahead and start breaking him in. See about his literacy level, too. But I want you staying with the standard for the time being."

"He's learning his Taglian. He says."

"Good. I've got work."

Son of a bitch was not going to let me in on anything.

Goblin's efforts were the straw that broke the Shadowlander force. They cracked. The survivors scattered. Goblin and his crew faded into the wilds, headed south.

Fear spread before them, far exceeding their capacity for creating despair.

I liked how things were going over there now. The little wizard and his boys were running free in a land not yet prepared to resist. A land not sufficiently recovered from its earthquake horrors to be able to resist.

Still, I felt like we were rushing toward some great doom.

We had done that before. Everything had fallen into our laps—till we found ourselves decimated and besieged in Dejagore.

38

CROAKER TOOK THE CAVALRY AND ME AND RACED AHEAD OF THE ARMY. Fleeing Shadowlanders fell to our lances. Opposition was spotty. Our foragers spread out. The idea was to scavenge whatever supplies were available quickly so we could keep the main force concentrated once it came out of the mountains.

I kept thinking how we had done this same thing after our unexpected victory at Ghoja Ford years ago. But when I mentioned that to Croaker he just shrugged and said, "This is different. There aren't any armies they can bring up. There aren't any new sorcerers they can bring out of the woodwork. Are there?"

"They don't need to. Between them Longshadow and the Howler can eat us alive. If they decide to do it."

We entered a moderate-sized town that was absolutely empty of people. Nor had there been many there before our appearance in the region. The earthquake had not been kind.

We did find enough shelter to get in out of the cold. We got fires going, which was maybe not a brilliant idea tactically. Nobody warm wanted to go outside again.

This was a problem that would be universal among our troops. Hunger would be the only force capable of keeping the men moving.

It had been a week since I parted with Smoke. I missed him more than I had thought possible a week ago. I had convinced myself that I no longer needed him to deal with my pain. But that had been while he was always there and I was always out roaming the ghostworld.

When you are riding around the east end of hell, trying to keep your mind off the fact that you are freezing your ass off while starving to death, you tend to think about your other troubles.

My big one came back with a vengeance.

The only good of the venture, so far, was the humor to be found in watching Thai Dei try to keep up on that ridiculous swaybacked grey. The man was one stubborn little shit.

At least once every four hours Croaker asked me about my in-laws. I did not know anything. Thai Dei claimed he knew nothing. I reserved judgment on his veracity. Croaker took a jaundiced view toward mine.

Word came in that a Shadowlander deserter had been picked up who knew the location of an ice cave stuffed with edibles.

"You buy it?" I asked.

"Sounds like somebody thought he was going to get his throat cut and made up a story. But we'll check it out."

"Just when I was getting used to being warm."

"You used to being hungry, too?"

Out we rode, and onward and onward we rode, day after day, through fields and forests and hills marred by quake effects and abandoned by the population. The Captain and I rode those giant black stallions, him outfitted in his cold Widowmaker armor and me lugging the bloody standard while Thai Dei tagged along behind like he was trying to become some sort of clown sidekick. We found the prisoner's ice cave. Near as we could tell, it was a real treasure trove. The earthquake had dropped an avalanche down its throat. The good people of the province had been trying to open it back up. We relieved them of all that hard work and left a troop to await the coming of reinforcements hungry enough to dig for their supper. We continued on toward Kiaulune and Overlook, managing to sustain ourselves and avoid trouble until we were just forty miles north of the stricken city.

The countryside there was unmarred by disaster, quiet, orderly, almost pretty—but a little too wintry for my taste. Suddenly, without warning, despite the Old Man's crows, we ran into Shadowlander cavalry and not a man among them was in a good mood. Their charge broke us into half a dozen clumps. Whereupon a horde of infantry types tried to horn in. Lucky for us they were regional militia, poorly armed, completely inexperienced peasants. Unfortunately, it is true that some totally untrained and inexperienced dickhead can get lucky and kill you just as dead as a martial arts priest like Uncle Doj can.

I managed to get the standard set atop a knoll, the Old Man there with me inside a circle of friendly folks. "The one day you don't wear the damned costume," I yelled. "They wouldn't have had the balls for this shit if you'd dressed up." Who knows? It might have been true.

"It was getting heavy. And it's cold and it stinks." He shrugged into the hideous, grotesque armor. As he lowered the nasty winged helmet onto his head a pair of monster crows dropped onto his shoulders. Traceries of scarlet fire began crawling all over him. A few thousand more crows began zooming around overhead, every one bitching his little heart out.

After a chance to take in the crows, Widowmaker and the Company standard most of our attackers decided to take the rest of the day off.

The stories had to be really bad down here.

The cavalrymen were made of sterner stuff. They continued fighting. They were veterans. And Longshadow probably had them convinced we were going to roast their wives and rape their babies, then turn the rest of them into dog food and shoe leather.

But we scattered them. Before the soldiers could get carried away chasing them, the Old Man headed south again, declaring, "We have bridges to capture and chokepoints to clear."

A few men did not heed the recall. I asked, "What about them?"

"They have a chance to serve as a valuable object lesson. Those that survive can catch up." He was feeling hard.

He did not think about arranging care and protection for the wounded. That was not something he had overlooked ever before.

It might be that there were no Company brothers among the wounded even though we had nearly a dozen with us.

That consideration often seemed to lie at the root of his decisions, yet never so blatantly that outsiders were conscious of it. I hoped he would keep it low-key. We had troubles enough.

I had seen Shadowcatch a hundred times in Smoke's dreams. I had spent cumulative days prowling Overlook. I thought I knew the city and the fortress about as well as anyone who lived there. But I was not prepared for a reality unfiltered by Smoke's thoughtless mind.

The remains of Kiaulune were plain hell. Famine and disease had claimed almost everyone who had not been killed by the earthquake. Longshadow, taking unwanted advice, had tried to help. Too late. But he had allowed refugees to establish themselves in the shadow of Overlook and had been making provision to care for them. In turn, those people were replacing the lost workers who had been building Overlook before the earthquake.

Very little work had gotten done since the disaster. Even Longshadow had been forced to stipulate that survival demands superseded his desire to complete his invulnerable fastness.

There were no children. Some arrangement had been made to care for them elsewhere. A clever step, uncharacteristic of the Shadowmaster. That idea had to have originated with someone else. In fact, I could think of no one in Longshadow's coterie to whom such a thing would occur.

It looked as though the little construction effort put out lately had been directed principally at providing housing.

This would not keep up once the pressure was off. To Longshadow all the people of the Shadowlands were his to use and dispose of as he saw fit. He just wanted to keep them alive long enough to be used.

"Hell really is leaking into the world," Croaker observed. He stared at the bleak, stinking, unwalled remains of Kiaulune. He paid no attention to the gleaming magnificence beyond the city.

I did. "We're too damned close here, boss. We don't have Lady to cover us."

That did not seem to trouble him. The only time he paid Overlook any attention was when he paused once to glare and say, "You didn't get it done in time, did you, you son of a bitch?"

From the limited point of view of someone seeing the fortress with mundane eyes the place seemed immeasurably huge. Mostly the towering walls had been constructed of a grey-white stone but in places blocks of different colors had been worked in, along with silver, copper and gold, to scrawl the whole with cabalistic patterns.

What forces had Longshadow gathered to defend those ramparts since last I walked with the ghost? Did it matter? Could any army scale those incredible walls if the construction scaffolding was cast down?

Most of that was still in place.

Croaker mused, "You may be right. I shouldn't rub their noses in the fact that I'm out here personally." He turned a little more and looked past Overlook, at the escarpment in the distance. "Have you ever gotten up there?"

I looked around. No one was there to hear. Not even a crow. "No. I can get about halfway across the space between Overlook and a place on the road where there's a landslide that seems to be what they call the Shadowgate around here. Not much to look at. But that's all the farther Smoke will go."

"I've never done better. Let's get out of here."

We withdrew and pitched camp north of Kiaulune. The soldiers were not comfortable there. None of them wanted to set up housekeeping so close to the last and craziest Shadowmaster.

I tended to agree.

Croaker said, "You could be right. I'd feel better myself if Smoke was down here and you could do some scouting." Then he grinned. "But I do believe that we have a guardian angel better than Lady looking out for us."

"What? Who?"

"Catcher. She's as goofy as a squirrel with three nuts but she's predictable. You been able to get close to her?" Like he was sure I would try.

"Not really. Smoke won't go."

"You have to remember how determined she is to use me to get even with Lady for having kept her from getting even before. That means she has to take care of me."

"Oh." Dumb me. I had not thought about how he could be using Catcher. "You're willing to bet your life on Catcher?"

"Hell no. She's still Soulcatcher. She could get interested in something else and just walk out on everything here."

"But she does have a score to settle with Longshadow, too."

"That she does." He grinned. He was pleased about the way things were going.

I was worried about Soulcatcher. She seldom did anything overt but in her own mind she would be one of the major players. Eventually she would do something dramatic.

Was there anything Croaker had not foreseen and made part of his plan? He did not think so, I am sure.

I did not agree. Because I had rock-hard evidence that he was not ready for everything. There is no way he could have anticipated me starting to have the same sort of nightmares as Lady—though I am just as certain that he did expect hers to continue.

Here near Kiaulune my nightmares were powerful and frequent. I could not take a nap without a visit to the cavern of the old men. Frequently I went to the plain of bones and corpses. On occasion I slipped off to the land of myth. Or so I interpreted it. It was a vast grey place where gods and devils met in divine battle and the most ferocious thing on the field was a gleaming black monster whose footfalls shook the earth, whose claws rent and tore, whose fangs . . .

The hideous cold place with the slimy old men was there every time, though. Every time. It was repellent in the extreme, yet attractive. Each time, as I walked the cold shadows, I found another familiar face among the old men.

I thought I had it handled. I really did. But that was because I did not think Kina would bother being subtle with a dim candle like me. I ignored the fact that she was the goddess of Deceivers. And forgot that Lady had told me that all that appeared to be Kina did not have to be Kina.

The dead place came to smell sweeter. It became more relaxing, safer, more comfortable, just as walking with the ghost had become comforting. I had a suspicion my enjoyment of that comfort was one reason the Old Man brought me down here ahead of everyone. He wanted me to go cold turkey.

I wanted to tell him I had it handled because I believed I did. But as we lay there in the hills waiting for the rest of the army to trudge up the road I spent a lot of cold days and colder nights huddled by a fire, spooking out Thai Dei, fiddling with my notes and napping. A lot. Because when I slept I could go away from the center, where the pain remained in a hard little core that would not die. Sometimes I even seemed to fly the way I had with Smoke, though not far, nor to anywhere interesting. I was the opposite of Lady, who fought her dreams all the way.

It was a gentle seduction. Kina gradually replaced Smoke.

I noticed that the Captain watched me sidelong in the mornings, warily, when I arose reluctantly. Thai Dei did not say anything but he seemed worried.

39

THE MEN WERE SINGING AROUND THE CAMPFIRES EVEN THOUGH IT HAD snowed. Morale was up. We were finding enough to eat. We had halfway decent shelter. The enemy was making no attempt to discomfit us. Lead elements of the main force were in the province and scattering in a wide arc around Kiaulune, settling in to await the final phase of the campaign. But even when the mob is sitting around, playing tonk, somebody has to do something to keep things moving. The Old Man reached into his trick bag and pulled the straw with my name on it.

I think he rigged the draw.

I got the job of taking a patrol north to meet a quartermaster crew inbound to begin surveys for camp layouts once we got serious about besieging Overlook. They were bringing in some prisoners Lady thought the Captain would find interesting.

Three times outbound we had brushes with partisans. We had another coming back. The tension was draining. I was exhausted. Still not a hundred percent despite his protests to the contrary, Thai Dei was used up, too. "Message from your honey," I told the Old Man, tossing him a leather packet that was heavy enough to have a couple bricks inside. "Clete and his brothers are with this bunch. They're already talking about building a ramp to get over Overlook's wall."

"Fat chance. You all right?"

"Dead tired. We ran into partisans again. Mogaba's changing his style."

He gave me a hard look but told me, "Get some rest. The guys have found a house I want you to look over tomorrow. You might grab Clete and them and have them tell you how much work the place needs."

I grunted. I had a nice place now, dug out of the side of a hill, a real blanket hanging in front to keep out the wind and contain the warmth of my fire. Our fire. My brother-in-law holed up there with me. We were turning the place into a manor house in our spare time. Compared to anything we had had since leaving Dejagore.

Between us we had just about enough energy left to grunt at one another over some hard bread while we got the fire built up, then collapsed into piles of rags we had harvested from the ruins of Kiaulune.

I fell asleep wondering how bad the guerrilla problem could get. This time of year we could starve them into submission simply by keeping a lot of foragers out. But if they survived the winter we would have big trouble with them in the spring, when we would have to plant our own crops, then would have to work and protect them through the harvest.

I did not worry about it long. Sleep jumped up and grabbed me. And the dreams were waiting for me.

This time it started with the dead waste, the expanse of corpses and bones, but it was not quite the night land it had been before. The stench was absent. The corpses looked like corpses in paintings, pale, with little blood showing. There was none of the corruption that finds us after we have lain in the sun for a few days. There were no flies, no maggots, no ants, no scavengers tearing at the bodies.

This time some of the corpses opened their eyes as I passed. A few looked vaguely like people I knew long ago. My grandmother. An uncle I had liked. Childhood friends and a couple friends from early days in the Company, now long dead. Most of those seemed to smile at me.

Then I encountered the face that I should have expected, the one the whole series of dreams must have been choreographed to throw at me. Yes, I should have expected it but it did take me completely by surprise. "Sahra?"

"Murgen." Her response was no more than the stir of a faint breeze. A ghost's whisper. As you would expect. As I would expect, anyway, being naive about such things.

I saw the trap instantly. Kina was going to offer me back my dead. What she had taken away she would ransom. At that moment I did not care. Of course.

I could get my Sarie back.

I had my Sarie for as long as it took for my emotions to become totally engaged. Then I was in a dark, cold, terrible place I was meant to believe was where Sarie went when I was not there to pull her into the light.

Not real subtle.

I guess Kina never needed subtlety.

The gimmick tore me right up. But . . .

The outside influence quickened my reason as well as my emotions. I realized Kina was playing to a native audience, as though I was Taglian or from one of Taglios's cousin states, where the religions are closely related. She could not encompass the fact that I had not been raised up steeped in southern mythologies. Even this touching of me in my dreams did not convince me that she was divine. Her scheme was something Lady could have pulled off at the peak of her powers, something her dead husband could have managed from his grave.

I did not let her set the hook, sweetly baited as it was.

So she grabbed the pain of my soul and dragged it naked and screaming through the briars.

I wakened with Thai Dei shaking me violently. I yelled, "Take it easy, man! What's wrong?"

"You were screaming in your sleep. You were talking to the Mother of Night."

I remembered. "What did I say?"

Thai Dei shook his head. Lying. He had understood. And what he had heard had upset him.

I put my mind and face in order, dragged my dead ass over to the Captain's place.

Something was wrong with that man. I mean, I have pretty spartan tastes myself but I can think of a few luxuries I would demand if I were dictator to a vast empire, a powerful warlord, Captain of the Black Company, and there were people around who would be just thrilled to make me more comfortable. But he was living in a half tent, half lean-to thing, partly a sod hut, just like the meanest groom. It kept him out of the wind. His only claim to status was that he did not share.

He did not have sentries hulking around him despite our presence deep in enemy territory, despite our suspicion that a few dedicated Stranglers still lurked within our ranks.

Maybe he did not believe he needed guards because an old dead tree loomed above his shelter. That almost always boasted a crew of bickering crows.

I let myself in. "You're counting on Catcher's obsession way too much, boss." Though I had had the feeling that I was being examined closely as I approached. Maybe Croaker had cause to feel confident.

He was asleep. He had left a lamp burning. I turned it up a bit, went to work trying to wake him. He came around but he was not pleased. Seldom did he get a chance to sleep as much as he wanted. "This better be good, Murgen."

"I don't know if it is or not but I do have a point," I assured him. "I'll try to get through it fast." I told him about the dream. And about the dreams that had gone before it.

"Lady told me you might be vulnerable. Not knowing about Smoke, though, she didn't see how you could be."

"I'm sure there's a reason," I said. "I think I know what she's trying to do. What I can't figure is why."

"That tells me you really haven't thought it through."

"What?"

"You know exactly why but you're too lazy to figure it out for yourself."

"Bullshit." But I capped my temper. I sensed that I was about to enjoy one of his lectures.

"You're of interest because you're the standardbearer, Murgen. You've spent the last several years backfilling new material into my Annals and Lady's so you know them pretty well. By now you ought to suspect that there's something special about the standard."

"The Lance of Passion?"

"According to the Shadowmasters. We don't know what that means. Maybe the answer is in those old Annals you squirreled away at the Palace. Whatever, it's clear that some people would like to lay hands on the standard."

"Including Kina. That what you're saying?"

"Evidently. You studied the Kina myth while you were trapped in Dejagore. Weren't the standards of the Free Companies of Khatovar supposed to be the pizzles of demons or something?"

That led to an exchange of crude speculations about why Kina wanted the standard, a couple of chuckles, then the Captain said, "You did the right thing, letting me know. We've all got these things going on inside us. We're keeping them locked up and secret and we're getting used. I think. Look, hang in there. Stay aware. One-Eye will be here tomorrow or the next day. You talk to him—then you do exactly what he tells you. Understand?"

"I got it. But what do I do about it?"

"Gut it out."

"Gut it out. Right."

"On your way back to your den take a look at Kiaulune and ask yourself if you're the first guy in this world who ever lost somebody he loved."

Oh-oh. He was getting impatient with my refusal to heal.

"Right. Good night." I wished. It was more like hell night for a while. Every time I slipped off I fell right into the plain of death. Not once did I get to the cavern of the old men. As soon as it got bad I awakened, usually on my own but twice with help from Thai Dei. Poor guy. No telling what he really thought about me after four years of watching me go through these bizarre behaviors.

Finally, apparently baffled by my lack of receptivity, Kina abandoned me—trailing more than a hint of exasperated threat behind her.

And when it was over I was not quite sure the whole thing had not been some monster entirely of my own imagining.

I slept. I awakened. I crawled out of my shelter. As another privileged character I could have gotten by without sharing, too, if I had wanted. In fact, as Annalist, I rated a tent of the sort used for small conferences, a veritable canvas palace where I could spread out and work.

I rated it but I would never see it.

The standard stood outside. It did not look like something that ought to excite the envy of a blacksmith, let alone great powers. It was nothing but one rusty old spearhead atop a long wooden shaft. Five feet down from the head there was a crosspiece four feet long tied to the shaft. From that hung the black banner bearing the device we had adopted in the north, the silver skull exhaling golden flames that originated as Soulcatcher's personal seal. The skull was not human because it had exaggerated canine teeth. No lower jaw was present. One eyesocket was scarlet. In some representations that was the right eye, in some the left. I have been assured there is significance to that but nobody ever told me what. It may have had something to do with Soulcatcher's changeable nature.

Every Company man wore a silver badge bearing a similar design. We have them made where we can. Some we take off our own dead. Some men are carrying three or four as part of Croaker's thing about returning to Khatovar. In fact, I think Otto and Hagop have several dozen of them they brought down from the north.

The skull device is not that intimidating in itself. It is scary because of what it represents.

Everyone in this end of the world at least pretends to be spooked by how nasty the Company was the last time it passed through. Hard to believe that anybody could have been so cruel that the fear would persist for four centuries. There is nothing so terrible that it does not get forgotten in a few generations.

Kina had to be responsible somehow. She had been manipulating these people for an age, sending out her dreams. Four centuries was plenty of time to create an enduring hysteria. In fact, if you assumed the great black goddess was behind that you could explain a lot that never made sense before. It even explained why there were so many crazed people involved, great and small.

Might it be that Kina's departure from the play would cause an outbreak of sanity at all levels?

But how do you get rid of a god? Is there any religion where they teach you that? How to get your god off your back if he gets too damned obnoxious? No. All you ever get is advice on how to bribe them to leave you alone for a few minutes.

40

ONCE AGAIN ONE-EYE THREATENED TO PROVE USELESS. "YOU GOT ME BY the balls," was his response when I asked him how I could deal with my dreams.

"Goddamn it! Croaker said you'd have the answer. But if you're going to be that way, screw you. Stick it in your ear."

"Hey, Kid. Take it easy. What way?"

"Purposely stupid."

"You're too young to be so cynical, Kid. Where'd you get the idea I couldn't straighten out something as simple as a dream raider?"

"I got it from something this lazy-ass little old man told me about twenty seconds ago."

"Did not." He stomped around. "Shit. You're sure the Old Man told you come to me about this?"

"I'm sure."

"And you told me everything? Didn't leave some little detail out, you're too proud to mention, that's going to get me bit on the ass if I do something?"

"I told you everything." It had been hard but I had.

"I got to get out of this. I'm losing it." He showed me his best glower. "You're sure the Old Man sent you to me? You weren't just hearing voices?"

"I'm sure." I stared at that stupid hat of his, wondering if I could get it to hold still long enough for me to put it out of its misery.

"Nobody likes a smartass, Kid."

"Even you have friends, One-Eye."

He pranced around some. "I don't want to do this. I don't think Croaker knows what he's doing. Why should I?"

I did not realize that he was talking to himself, not me. "On account of I'm a brother and I need help."

"All right. Don't tell me you didn't ask for this. Come on up to the wagon."

A shiver of anticipation overcame me. It was so strong both One-Eye and Thai Dei noticed. One-Eye muttered to himself. As he started to turn he told Thai Dei, "You come along, too."

The why of that proved to be Mother Gota. "She turned up, eh?" I observed. I probably did not sound thrilled. The fact was, I was not thrilled. Having Mother Gota around generally made me wish I had boils on my butt instead.

"Found her sitting beside the road looking downright forlorn as we started down the south slope of the pass."

I knew it was a waste of time but I asked anyway. "Where have you been? Where is Uncle Doj?"

Did I say something out loud? Apparently not. She did not respond. She began carping at Thai Dei about how he was keeping himself. Maybe his hair was too long or his beard not plucked. What was insignificant. There was always something to complain about and something to criticize.

One-Eye said, "While they're getting caught up I want you to climb in the wagon and go for a stroll with the ghost. Whoa, boy! Let's not get so eager. If the Old Man wants you to see me about your dreams there's only one possible reason." He looked over his shoulder. He laid a really hard look on mother and son. "Something he told me to spend some time on before you all took off for your adventures over here."

"Think you can get to the point?" I had both hands on the wagon's tailgate.

"All right, smartass. You get in there, you take Smoke back to the night your wife died. You watch it happen."

"Goddamn it!"

"Shut up, Kid. I've had all your self-pity I can handle. So's the Old Man, I guess. You want to be able to deal with these dreams, you go back there and take a damned good look at what made you the way you are right now. You watch every second of it. Three times, if that's what it takes. Then you come back and we'll talk."

I started to argue.

"You shut your mouth and do it. Or you just stay away and spend the rest of your life living in your own fantasies."

He pissed me off so bad I wanted to jump his ass. Which would not be wise on several counts. I let the anger give me a boost as I hoisted myself into the wagon.

I guess you do not quite know yourself, ever. I really did believe I had it handled until the encounter with Kina, the temptation of the impossible promise to give me back my dead. After that the pain had grown back up again.

It was amazing how much I did not want to go watch Sarie die. The force that moved me on, that convinced me I had to do it, was a whiff of carrion I caught as something that might have been Kina passed me in the ghost world. Looking for me?

I found the Palace. I stalled by looking in on the Radisha Drah. Not much had changed except that word had arrived about the triumph at Charandapresh. Debate was more lively now, with the Radisha forced to take the unpopular viewpoint and remind her fellow conspirators that this unexpected victory did not mean that Longshadow had been conquered. In the end she closed debate by ordering Cordy Mather to take a party of fact finders south to gather reliable information. A bureaucratic solution that just pushed back the day of treachery.

With a reluctance I did not entirely fathom, so powerful was it, I rode Smoke to my old quarters. They were unoccupied still. Everything lay where I had left it, gathering dust.

I had Smoke move backward, very gingerly as we approached the time when the evil had occurred. For some reason I felt it was very important that I not encounter my previous self. That if I did so I would get caught back there living the whole thing over again just as I had a number of times with my plunges into the darkness of Dejagore.

Maybe I could warn Sarie. That woman in the swamp had been aware of me for an instant. Maybe someone who knew me as well as Sahra did, and me wanting to change things as much as I did, could force a warning across the barrier of time.

It seemed my trips back to Dejagore may have changed a few things, though there was no way to be sure.

There. Guards and whatnot rushed all over the place. Some chased Stranglers, some headed for my apartment. This would be after I had arrived myself. So I needed to jump maybe another half hour.

I did so, going down to the entrance the Deceivers had used to penetrate the Palace. I had seen these murders before because I had been curious how men so alert could be taken by surprise. The first couple of Deceivers came disguised as temple prostitutes fulfilling their obligations to their goddess. It had not occurred to the guards to turn the ladies down. That would have been sacrilegious.

This was before I became involved. I jumped upstairs, to the apartment, where my mother-in-law and Sarie were doing housework, concluding the day. Uncle Doj and To Tan were asleep already. Thai Dei was not, probably because he was waiting for me to return from a job where he had not been welcome. He had his eyes closed and seemed to be trying to shut out his mother's carping two rooms away.

How Sarie managed I do not know. Particularly when I was the object of this diatribe.

Mother Gota was more fierce than usual. She wanted to know when Sahra was going to abandon this headstrong idiocy—a thousand curses upon the head of Hong Tray—and get herself back to the swamps where she belonged. There was still a chance she could marry, though certainly not well, seeing as she was past her best years and she had allowed herself to be defiled by a foreigner.

Sarie took it with such calm I knew she was accustomed to it and did not let her emotions be touched. She went about her business as though her mother was not speaking at all. Soon they finished what they were about. Sahra went to our room without so much as a "Good night," which only irritated her mother more.

I always knew Mother Gota did not approve of me and suspected she talked behind my back but I never guessed it had gotten that virulent. The sound of it told me the only reason Mother Gota had come to Taglios was to get her daughter back home.

I was aware that she had broken some tribal taboos in coming to me but I had misjudged the true depth of feeling of the Nyueng Bao toward outsiders.

The apartment became very quiet. To Tan and Uncle Doj were snoring. Sarie fell asleep almost instantly. Mother Gota was too busy complaining to turn in immediately.

She did not need an audience, apparently.

I was there hovering when the apartment door opened and the first Strangler slipped inside. He was a black rumel man, an assassin who had killed many times. One after another, a whole troop followed him in. They believed they were going to attack Croaker, the Liberator. The last reliable intelligence they had from inside the Palace had Croaker living in this apartment. He had turned it over to me little more than a week before.

The results were unfortunate for everyone but the Old Man.

Moments after they entered they were aware that there were several people in the apartment. They whispered too softly to be heard. Fingers pointed. They split into four teams, three of three men each while another half dozen stayed in the main room, just inside the hall door.

To Tan, Thai Dei and Uncle Doj were nearest that room. To Tan was nearest of all. Then Uncle Doj. Then Thai Dei.

To Tan never had a chance. He never woke up. But Thai Dei was not asleep yet and Uncle Doj must have had a guardian angel. He popped up as the Strangler team hit him. The arm-holders, whose task it was to keep the victim from defending himself while the senior Strangler got his rumel around his neck and finished him, were not strong enough for their task. He threw them off, then dropped the master Strangler with a violent smash from an elbow. Before the other two could get back at him he reached Ash Wand.

Thai Dei came to his feet as the door to his room swung inward. The arm-holders hit him as he headed for his swords, flinging him violently across the room—but not before he got hold of his shortsword.

Thai Dei shouted warnings as he lashed out.

The Stranglers waiting in the main room stormed back to help their brothers. By the time they arrived Mother Gota was up and flailing around with a sword and Sahra, who had no weapon whatsoever and no way out of our room except through the melee, was trying to find some way to block the entrance.

I studied the next two minutes over and over. During them a dozen people died. *All* of them Deceivers. Thai Dei managed to get his arm broken. Uncle Doj chased survivors into the hall.

It did not happen the way I had been told but it was close enough—to that point. But afterward no bad guys got in behind Doj and murdered Sahra. Sahra was in bad shape but she was alive. When Doj returned from the chase Mother Gota suggested she be given something to calm her down. Uncle Doj agreed. In minutes Sahra was out, in the bed where I would see her shortly.

I had to go away for a while. I would be arriving any minute. I came back when I knew I would be out cold, having drunk something offered me by Uncle Doj while I lay down with my beloved.

I watched them take Sarie and To Tan away. Uncle Doj, Thai Dei and various relatives, as Mother Gota would tell me after I awakened, carrying their bodies off for proper funerals at home.

I managed a fair amount of anger out there despite the emotion-deadening environment.

I followed the party off to Nyueng Bao land. There were other bodies, too. The Strangler raid had taken the lives of several Nyueng Bao bodyguards.

Surprise, surprise. Sarie came back to life before the party ever cleared the city. She acted just about the same as I had on wakening and finding her gone. "What's happening?" she demanded. "Why are we here?" She directed her questions to Uncle Doj but Doj did not respond except to make a gesture toward Thai Dei, who was distracted by the pain of his broken arm.

Thai Dei mumbled, "We are taking you home, Sarie. There is no longer any reason for you to remain in this evil city."

"What? You can't do this. Take me back to Murgen."

Thai Dei stared down at the cobblestones. "Murgen is dead, Sarie. The *tooga* killed him."

"No!"

"I'm sorry, Sahra," Uncle Doj said. "Many *tooga* paid with their lives but it was a price they were willing to pay. Many of our people died, too, and where they failed or they were not present many of the others perished as well." The word he used as "others" was Nyueng Bao for anyone who was not Nyueng Bao.

"He can't be dead," Sarie cried. She for sure had the wail of grief down pat. "He can't die without seeing his child!"

Uncle Doj stopped dead in his tracks, as numb as a poleaxed steer. Thai Dei stared at his sister and began making a whimpering sound. Since I was getting used to Nyueng Bao ways I assumed he was distraught because it would be impossible for him to marry off a sister who carried the child of an outsider.

Uncle Doj muttered, "I am beginning to believe your mother is wiser than we thought, Thai Dei. She blamed all this on Hong Tray. Now it begins to look like your grandmother was entirely too clever. Or we just misunderstood. Her prophecy may have included Murgen only indirectly. It might be about the child Sahra is carrying."

I understood that the woman in the swamp, twice seen already, must be Sarie herself.

"There will be no place for Sahra, then," Thai Dei said, pain obvious. "If she bears an outsider's bastard . . ."

"Take me back," Sahra said. "If you won't let me be I will be Nyueng Bao no longer. I will go to my husband's people. There will be a place for me with the Black Company."

This was social heresy of an order so high that both Thai Dei and Uncle Doj were stricken speechless.

I do not believe I would have been speechless had I been able to get at those two right then. I lifted away. I had heard enough to know where I stood, where Sarie stood and where my faithful companion Thai Dei stood. The Old Man might not be right about the Nyueng Bao but he was for sure not wrong.

I skipped forward in time rapidly, tracking Sarie. Thai Dei and Uncle Doj took her to that temple where I had spotted her before. They left her in the hands of a great-uncle who was a priest. Sahra was, in essence now, an orphan, though she was a grown woman twice married. The temple was where Nyueng Bao without family went. The temple became home. The priests and nuns became family. In return, the orphan was expected to dedicate his or her life to good works and whatever deities the Nyueng Bao worshipped.

Nobody ever set me straight on that, though the temple where they stashed Sahra boasted several idols that looked a lot like various Gunni gods.

Shadar have only one god of sufficient magnitude to warrant an idol and Vehdna doctrine proscribes any graven images at all.

I focused in on Sarie as she was today. I followed her about her duties for an hour. She was helping keep the temple clean, carrying water, helping with cooking, pretty much exactly what she would have done had she been living in one of the hamlets with a Nyueng Bao husband. But the people of the temple shunned her.

No one spoke to her except a priest to whom she was related. Nothing needed to be said. She had defiled herself. Her only visitor was an elderly gentleman named Banh Do Trang, a commercial factor whose friendship Sahra had won during the siege of Dejagore. Banh had been the interlocutor between us the last time Sahra's family had tried to keep us apart. He had made it possible for Sahra to slip away and reach me before she could be stopped.

Banh understood. Banh had loved a Gunni woman when he was young. He spent most of his time trading in the outside world. He did not think everything "other" was purely evil.

Banh was good people.

I searched hard and picked my moment carefully, when Sarie was at her afternoon prayer. I brought my point of view down in front of her, right at eye level. I exercised all my will. "Sarie. I am here. I love you. They lied to you. I am not dead."

Sarie made a little sound like a puppy whimpering. For an instant she seemed to stare right into my eyes. She seemed to see me. Then she bounced up and fled the room, terrified.

41

ONE-EYE JUST KEPT SLAPPING ME TILL I CAME OUT OF IT.

"Goddamn, you little shit, quit it!" My face was sore. How long had he been pounding me? "I'm here! What the fuck's your problem?"

"You're doing a lot of yelling, Kid. And if you was talking any language your in-laws could understand you'd be up shit creek. Come on. Get it under control."

I got it under control. You have to learn to manage emotion if you are going to survive in our racket. But my heart continued to pound and my mind to race. I shook like I had a bad ague. One-Eye offered me a large cup of water. I drained it.

He said, "It's partly my fault. I wandered off. I didn't think you'd stay out that long. Thought you'd figure it out and get your ass back to see what we plan to do about it."

I croaked, "What you plan to do about it?"

"Don't got no plans. I think the Old Man was just gonna let it slide and keep his eyes open till he decided you needed to know."

"He wasn't going to tell me?"

One-Eye shrugged. Which meant probably not.

Croaker was no more enthralled by my marriage than were Sahra's people.

The bastard.

"I need to see him."

"He'll want to see you. When you've got yourself under control."

I grunted.

"You let me know when you can get by without a lot of screaming and carrying on."

"I can do that right now, you little shit! What did you guys mean, not letting me—?"

"You let me know when you can get by without a lot of screaming and carrying on."

"You little shit." I was running out of venom. I had been out there a long time. I needed to eat. I had a feeling I would not be allowed a snack till after my interview with Croaker.

"You ready to talk?" Croaker asked. "Done with screaming and carrying on?"

"You guys spend the whole time I was ghostwalking rehearsing your act?"

"So what are your in-laws up to, Murgen?"

"I don't have the faintest fucking idea. But I'm thinking maybe I want to put Uncle Doj's feet in the fire and ask."

Croaker was drinking tea. Taglians are big tea drinkers. The Shadowlanders of these parts were bigger tea people. He took a sip. "You want some?"

"Yeah." I needed liquids.

"Think about this. We put him to the question on account of you suddenly know they fucked you over. You think anybody, Nyueng Bao or otherwise, might wonder how you suddenly knew when you're only like eight hundred miles from the evidence?"

"I don't care—"

"Exactly. You're not thinking about anything but you. But anything you do is going to touch every member of the Company. It might touch every man who came over those mountains with us. It might change the course of this war."

I wanted to belittle his claims because I was hurting bad and very much wanted to do some hurting of my own. I could not. Time enough had passed for reason to begin rearing its reasonable head. I bit down on the words that rose in my throat. I drank my tea. I thought. I said, "You're right. So what do we do?"

Croaker poured me some more tea. "I don't think we do anything. I think we go right on the way we have been. I think we do the trap-door spider thing. I think only three guys know what an incredible tool we've got and nobody else needs to know."

I grunted. I drank some tea. I said, "She thinks I'm dead. She's living her whole life based on that lie."

Croaker fiddled with his fire. He looked into his bag of liberated tea. One-Eye finally caught on. "Oh. Yeah. I figured you was familiar with that book of the Annals that was written by the Captain's woman." He showed me a sneer with a couple of teeth missing.

"Right. You just keep on being reasonable. See if I care. Shithead."

"I got a great idea, Kid. Come on back to the wagon with me. Something I found the other day you might be interested in."

Croaker said, "You guys don't wander too far. We're getting enough people in here now, it's time to start harassing Longshadow."

"Of course," One-Eye said. He ducked out the doorflap grumbling, "Just can't leave shit alone." I ducked out behind him. He did not stop. "We could sit out here for the next hundred years and not hurt nobody. Set up our own damned kingdom. Starve the son of a bitch out. But no!

We got to do some kind of . . ." One-Eye glanced back. We were out of earshot of the Old Man. "Enough of that shit. You dickhead. You never told me about Goblin."

"What's to tell?"

"You knew where he was all along, didn't you? He wasn't dead or nothing. You got around the commands Croaker laid on Smoke and found the worthless little shit."

I did not say anything. Goblin was still out there on his own somewhere, presumably continuing his mission. Presumably still needing secrecy.

"Ha! I was right. You never could lie for shit. Where is he, Kid? I got a right to know."

I started to back away. It might be time to take my act elsewhere. "You're wrong. I don't know where he is. I don't know if he's even still alive." Which was true.

"What you mean, you don't know?"

"I got a speech impediment? You've had Smoke all month, remember? You. The short shit who was loafing around up there in those hills while I was down here dodging shadows and Shadowlander ambushes."

"Now I know you're shitting me. There ain't been one shadow seen since the night we broke them at . . . Bullshit! You're feeding me bullshit."

"Yeah. I guess I forgot the first rule."

"Huh? What's that?"

"Never confuse you with facts."

"You smartass. I hung on in this world two hundred years so I could put up with this shit." He jumped up on the tongue of his wagon and leaned inside. I began to put a little more distance between us. He dug around in some rags behind his driver's seat. He glanced over his shoulder, saw me moving. "You just hang on right there, you peckerhead."

He jumped down, started waving his arms around while he went to squeaking and squealing in one of those languages wizards use so the rest of us will think there is something terribly strange and mystical about what they do, kind of like lawyers. One-Eye sometimes flew off into unprovoked fits of lawyerism, too.

Blue sparks began to crackle between the tips of his fingers. His lips stretched into an evil grin. I would not give him Goblin so I would have to take Goblin's place.

Damn, I wished Goblin would come back.

"What's this?"

I whirled. The Captain had followed us. One-Eye gulped air. I scooted a few fast steps, which brought the Old Man into the field of fire, too.

One-Eye shoved his hands into his pockets to hide them.

"Ouch!" he said with sudden, quiet fervor. The sparks had not stopped.

Croaker asked me, "He been drinking again?"

"I don't know when. Unless it was before he got me up. But he's acting like it."

"Who? Me?" One-Eye squeaked. "Not me. No way. I don't touch the stuff anymore."

I observed, "He hasn't had time to get set up."

"That means jack shit. There's any to be stolen, he'll find that. You know anyone else who'd suddenly start a fight for no good reason?"

"Ain't nobody in this outfit like that," One-Eye insisted. "Unless you count Goblin. Sometimes he . . . He in this outfit anymore, Captain?"

Croaker ignored him. He asked me, "You planning to take Smoke back out now?"

"No." That had not occurred to me. Food had.

Croaker grunted. "I need to talk to my staff wizard, here. One-Eye?"

I moved out. What now?

That food.

I ate till the cooks began to grumble about some folks thinking they were special.

After I finished I strolled across the snowy slopes trying to calm the storm inside me. The sky promised more snow. We had been lucky so far, I suspected. None of the snows had been heavy and none had stuck long. I spied Thai Dei and his mother, the latter offering a piece of her mind. Still.

It kept them at a distance.

I glimpsed Swan and Blade, far off, trotting somewhere in a big hurry. That meant Lady had come in, or at least would arrive soon. Her advance force had a camp under construction.

South, beyond Kiaulune, a spear of sunlight broke through the overcast, struck Overlook. The whole vast fortress gleamed like some religions' notion of heaven. I needed to take Smoke over there and get caught up. But not right away. One-Eye and the Old Man still had their heads together. Maybe talking about me.

I strolled downhill toward where Lady's soldiers were building their camp.

I wondered how Lady and Blade were getting along. He had been her main helper before his defection. He had not let her know what was happening when he did that. I could not see her forgiving him the deceit, however successful its end result.

Crows fluttered over the camp. Maybe Lady was there.

Croaker was right. We had to be paranoid. All the time. If it was not the Shadowmaster spying it would be Soulcatcher or the Deceivers or the Howler. Or Kina herself. Or the Nyueng Bao. Or the Radisha's agents. Or spies for the priests, or . . .

42

LADY HAD COME IN WITHOUT ME BEING TOLD. I HAD NO TROUBLE GETTING IN to see her. That made me wonder if it was going to be easy to get out.

She had questions of her own. "What are we doing now, Murgen? What's his game this time?"

I halted one step into the presence, mouth open. There had been changes since last I saw her. This was not the Lady with whom I had ridden south. This was not the woman who had seemed so haunted in front of the Dandha Presh. This creature was the Lady of olden times resurrected, a being of such terrible power it had trouble constraining itself in a presentable form.

"What the hell happened?"

"Murgen."

"What?" I squeaked. I reminded myself that I was the Annalist. The Annalist is fearless. He stands aside from squabbles within the Company. He is not intimidated by his brothers. He records the truth.

She scared me anyway.

"I want to know—"

"Anything you want to know, you'd better ask the Old Man. I couldn't tell you even if I was as goofy as Willow Swan. He don't tell me anything, either. He's still keeping it all inside his head. You seen that place over there? Worse than the Tower at Charm. He hasn't paid any attention to it since we got here. I haven't seen him do much of anything. Longshadow and Howler haven't done much, either, though."

"It's frustrating."

"Yeah. And maybe not even very smart considering what shape we'd be in if the Stranglers got him."

"Less likely than you think."

"Because of Soulcatcher?"

"Yes."

"She can't be everywhere any more than you can. And they call them the Deceivers for a reason." I hoped my voice was not squeaking. I was trying to play the fearless man.

"None of that is why you wanted to see me."

"No. I've got a problem. My dreams are getting worse. They're really bad now. I want to know how to shut them out."

"I haven't found a way. You have to learn to remember what they are. Has Kina been calling you?"

"I don't think so. It's more like she's passing through my dreams and doesn't notice me if I lie real still. Or maybe I'm eavesdropping on someone else's nightmares."

"Tell me about them."

I told her.

"Those are pretty much the dreams I've always had. Mostly I'm on the plain anymore."

"Are there crows there?"

"Crows? No. There isn't anything alive there."

I considered. "Actually, what I said before isn't quite true. She does seem to be aware of me specifically. The other night I got led through a version of the plain dream where I saw my wife. I talked to Sarie. The implication was there that I could get her back."

"That's new. For me the horrors just get worse. I think they're supposed to overwhelm me eventually."

I had a feeling she was not telling the whole truth, either. I said, "I find it hard to believe that she could feed me anything worse than what I've seen in real life. Knowing what she's trying to do—"

"She managed to use *me,* Murgen. Because I thought I knew what she was doing. But I didn't. She is the Queen of Deceivers. I wasn't her Daughter of Night at all. I was just a brood mare who was going to carry a Deceiver messiah for her. Don't make the mistake I made. If she really has noticed you, you be very, very careful. And keep me posted."

I grunted.

"Did you keep track of times when you thought you sensed Kina?"

"Uh . . ." I had. But most of the time she came near me I was out with Smoke. "Not very well." I gave her a couple of times that seemed harmless.

"That isn't much help. Control your emotions. Your wife would be an obvious way to manipulate you. You have any idea why?"

"I'd guess the standard."

"Of course. Hints pile up but we never get the story. The Lance of Passion. Only the thing's never shown any special properties."

It had, but in a time and manner I could not explain without exposing Smoke. Croaker stuck Howler with it once, just a flesh wound, but the little wizard almost died. "Maybe we don't really have the Lance. People might just think we do."

She murmured, "Is this another complicated deceit?"

I asked, "How do I stop the dreaming?"

"Weren't you listening? You don't."

"I don't think I'm strong enough just to live with them."

"You learn. Mine went away after the baby was born. But not for long. I think Kina forgot to sever the connection."

"Maybe Narayan was supposed to do that when he took your daughter."

"Of course he was."

"I didn't mean to remind you of—"

"I don't need reminding. I remember just fine. Every minute of every hour. And someday soon I plan to discuss it with Narayan, up close and personal." When she said that she seemed as nasty as Kina herself, though maybe you had to be there and had to know her history to enjoy the full impact. "He's going to get his Year of the Skulls now. He's run out of places to hide."

"You've seen Overlook. You think he needs to hide?"

Before she answered Blade shoved his head into the ragged tent. "A Strangler just took a crack at Willow. Willow's having a little trouble breathing but he'll be all right."

"You take the assassin alive?" Lady asked.

I eased toward the exit. Her mood was getting blacker. I did not want her pressing me hard.

Blade grinned. "He's in perfect health. Though he'd have a heart attack if he could."

I began easing around Blade. Lady gave me an eyeball-the-bug look that said she thought we ought to talk more later. I might consider staying out of her way. Maybe I had been too open with her already.

I stayed at a distance but watched. Lady's interrogation methods were deft, vicious and effective. The lesson was not lost on any witnesses.

Within minutes the Strangler admitted that he had infiltrated the camp-follower crowd after our victory at Charandaprash. The order had come from Narayan Singh himself. Willow Swan had been his primary target. Other red rumel men had been assigned other targets. They, too, had concealed themselves among the camp followers. They had been directed by the Daughter of Night herself to be very careful executing their missions. The Children of Kina had become so few that part of their obligation to their goddess now was to preserve themselves for her sake.

Lady knew just how to charm a man into talking. One of those things you learn when you are around forever, I suppose. One of those things people like Longshadow would like to mine out of your head.

She was so effective the Strangler abandoned hope of his eternal reward to tell her names.

I took a walk as Blade began organizing a throat-cutting expedition.

Just to underscore her disaffection with them Lady strangled one of the Deceivers herself. She used her own black scarf, taken from a black rumel man years ago. Every Deceiver knew the tale.

She sent her messages thus.

Crows took off in multitudes.

By way of conversation with Narayan Singh, Lady had the heads of the Deceivers put on lances and carried across to Overlook.

Croaker joined me. "That's my sweetie," he said, shaking his head. Like he would have been kinder had he gotten to those men first.

He knew what I was thinking. "A lady doesn't murder people in polite company." He grinned.

"What polite company? The Company ain't polite. And I think it was a very Lady-like thing she did."

"Yeah." He seemed almost cheerful about it all.

43

I SPENT A GOOD MANY HOURS AT IT BUT I FINALLY LOCATED SLEEPY WITH some base-camp elements from Big Bucket's special forces battalion. Bucket's gang was doing the biggest part of the work of hunting Mogaba's partisans. I told the kid, "Let's go for a walk. I need to talk to you." I collected a handful of flat stones to throw at crows if those squawking nightmares got too curious.

"This about what I hope it is?" The boy was excited. I could not remember having been excited about becoming the standardbearer. But I had gotten the job by default. There had been no one else able to do it. It had had to be handled.

"Partly. I got the final word from the Old Man. He says you're all right with him. He's leaving the choice up to me. So you're in, far as I'm concerned. But he wants me to handle the standard myself till after we know one way or the other how it's going to go with Longshadow. We can start teaching you some stuff right away. And see that you get out of some of the more unpleasant duties so you'll have time. Especially for working on your reading and writing."

The boy beamed. I felt a little shitty. "But there's one special job I need you to do first." I saw Big Bucket headed our way, probably to hand the kid one of the very jobs I had just mentioned.

"What? I can handle it."

Absolutely. Which was why Bucket would pick him out of the crowd.

"I've got a secret message that needs to get to Taglios. It's critical. You can take a few guys with you, just in case. Use guys who can ride hard. I'll give you authorization to use courier remounts." I raised a hand to forestall anything Bucket had to say. "This has to go through as fast as it can."

Bucket had heard some of it. "You taking away my best man to carry a letter?"

"Yes. Because it has to get through."

"This really serious?" Bucket asked.

"That's why I have him out here where nobody can hear us."

"Then I'd better go away." For a fugitive thief Bucket made a very good soldier.

"Probably."

"Hate to lose you, kid." Bucket shuffled off to dump whatever it was on somebody else.

Sleepy said, "If you loan me your horse I won't have to take anybody with me. And I'll get there and back a lot faster."

He had a point. He had a marvelous point—and it had not occurred to me. "Let me think about this."

There was an iffy side. The Old Man might want me to do something before Sleepy got back. If I did not have my horse he would ask questions.

I was not planning to share my plan with the Captain. If I did he would forbid it.

"I'll be back in less than a month."

With my horse he could manage that—if he had a butt of iron. He was young and hardy but I did not think anybody was that tough. Still . . . Nothing was likely to happen around here for at least that long. It would take more than a month for all the stragglers to come in, for our leaders to hash out some kind of plan. It was not possible that Croaker had a plan worked out for Overlook the way he had had for Charandaprash. I was not likely to get caught.

And once the kid had a week's head start even Soulcatcher would not be able to intercept him.

"All right. We'll do it your way. One thing, though. The message has to be put into the hands of a specific person. He might not be available right away. You might have to wait for him."

"I'll do whatever the job calls for, Murgen."

"All right. Come down to my . . ." I could not do that. Thai Dei was sure to overhear something. "No. First, I have to tell you who to find." I glanced around. Sleepy was one of the few veterans of Dejagore who had not acquired a Nyueng Bao bodyguard, but the Nyueng Bao as a group did keep an eye on him.

"I'm listening." The kid was eager to prove himself.

"His name is Banh Do Trang. He was a friend of my wife's. He's a trading factor who goes back and forth between Taglios and the delta. He sells everything from rice to crocodile skins. He's old and slow but he's the only way to get a message into the swamp."

"You have a whole family—"

"You might've noticed how little the Captain trusts those people."

"Yes."

"There's good reason not to trust them. Any of them who're here with us. In this case, any of them but Banh Do Trang himself."

"I understand. Where do I find this man?"

I gave him directions. "You can tell him who the message is from but only if he asks. He should deliver it to Ky Sahra at the Vinh Gao Ghang temple of Ghanghesha."

"You want me to wait for an answer?"

"That won't be necessary." If the message got through I would get my answer directly from Sarie. "I'm going to go write several copies of the message. You do what you think is best to make sure one of them survives the whole journey."

"I understand."

Though he had not reacted to Sahra's formal name I suspected that he understood more than I was telling.

Later, I introduced Sleepy to my horse and made the stallion understand that it was time to earn his oats. The animal was smart enough to be as disgruntled as any soldier asked to get up and bust his butt.

The kid slipped away without anybody but Bucket knowing that he was going.

44

THE SHADOWMASTER WAS IN HIS CRYSTAL TOWER, IMMERSED IN SOME arcane experiment. He was seeing no one. The stinking ragbag that contained the Howler was perched atop some of the highest scaffolding surrounding Overlook. Work had resumed, though at a snail's pace. Longshadow would not quit just because an army was nearby.

The sky was heavily overcast. A chill breeze whined through the scaffolding. Unpleasant weather was headed our way.

"You sent for me?" Singh sounded offended. He was cold for certain.

"It was not a summons, friend Narayan," Howler replied. The Deceiver's approach had been impressively discreet. Easy to see how he had become a master Strangler. "An invitation only. Perhaps my messenger failed to relay my exact words."

A crow whipped past. Another settled nearby. It pecked at crumbs left scattered where workmen had paused to eat. Singh ignored them. There had been crows everywhere since the earthquake. Times were good for the black birds. Howler said, "It occurred to me that you might be interested in what's been happening outside. I believe Lady has sent you a personal message."

Singh stared down at the array of severed heads indicated by Howler. Undaunted by the presence of workmen, Taglian cavalrymen had set up their trophies close enough for their faces to be recognized.

Narayan counted heads. His skinny shoulders slumped. Howler's stance became subtly mocking. "I was right? It is a message?"

"A prophecy. She's trying to foretell my future. She does these things."

"I worked for her. And her husband before her. This is nothing." Howler tried and failed to stifle a shriek. "Seems to me Kina hasn't taken good care of her children lately."

Singh did not argue.

"How will you bring on the Year of the Skulls now? How many of your freak brothers are left?"

"You risk more than you know when you mock the Goddess."

"I doubt it." Howler controlled another rising scream. Like a man choking down a persistent cough, he could manage for short times. "In any case, I don't think I'm going to stay around to find out. Longshadow is too damned crazy to do what he has to do. I refuse to be dragged down with him." He eyed Singh sidelong, watching for a reaction.

Narayan smiled as though privy to a huge and ugly secret. "You fear Lady. You cannot control your functions when you think of her."

Me, Murgen, ectoplasmic spy, sat on the runt's shoulder and wondered if these two would be kind enough to take it a little further and give me something I could use. Howler had something on his mind.

Singh started to leave. It was obvious that those heads out there did little to sustain his faith. Unlike his spooky ward he did not enjoy visitations from his goddess. Neither she nor the Daughter of Night had bothered providing explanations for the countless disasters befalling his brethren.

Howler read his mood perfectly. "Makes you wonder about the divine order, doesn't it?" He screamed before Singh could respond.

He had lost control because he was startled.

I was startled, too.

Swarms of those colored balls from the bamboo poles hurtled toward Overlook. They ripped into workmen and scaffolding and splashed against the wall. They gnawed at men and material and even stained the ramparts wherever Longshadow's spells were not yet sufficiently dense. Workmen shrieked and fled. Some scaffolding collapsed.

A band of Taglian horsemen appeared out of a ravine, chased the workmen toward their makeshift housing. I raised my point of view as the horsemen withdrew across the rocky ground. I spied Taglian infantrymen crawling forward everywhere. Large numbers were stealing into the laborers' housing complex from its blind side. Many wore clothing similar to that worn by the locals.

What the hell?

These were Lady's troops, I was sure. What was she up to? And why did the Old Man keep it from me?

Or was he unaware, too?

The workmen turned back, chased by the soldiers they found in the housing complex, their families fleeing with them, in a wild tangle of panic and confusion.

I got a glimmering then.

They clambered up the surviving scaffolding and took shelter inside Overlook. And a whole bunch of Lady's men climbed right with them.

Fireballs continued to splash away against the walls and towers. Whole batteries seemed particularly interested in the tower surmounted by Longshadow's crystal chamber. In some places bits of wall wisped or melted away. In most areas—and especially so everywhere Longshadow had the habit of going—the protective spells were already too well established for the fireballs even to cause discolorations.

Howler did not understand exactly what was happening. From his angle of view he could not see the nature of the attack. He just saw his associate's subjects running for their lives. "Forbidden," he muttered. "Forbidden forbidden forbidden. Longshadow is going to shit rocks. I hope he doesn't get any ideas about having me punishing these people."

"You're so mighty a sorcerer," Narayan Singh said. "Why don't you hit back?"

"That's the point," Howler said, seeing the possibility Lady wanted him to see. "It's a trap. Somewhere down there are whole battalions with those devices that throw fireballs. They're waiting for me—or Longshadow—to counterattack."

I took a quick swoop across the countryside. Howler was right. There was a guy behind every bush and rock with a bundle of bamboo poles. Few were contributing to the continuous barrage. Yet.

And what was Lady doing?

When I returned Howler had gotten down out of sight. Narayan crouched. Neither seemed anxious to move. Howler said, "I'm not staying much longer, Singh. If I was you, right now I'd be doing some serious thinking about how I could wake up an ally who's completely lost his grip on reality. That or I'd think about finding friends who could do me more good."

I pricked up my ghostly ears. At the same time I turned slowly, using my ghostly eyes. We had several hundred of our men inside Overlook now and neither Howler nor Longshadow realized it.

I wondered if the Old Man knew. I think he would have hinted something so I could watch for a particular reaction.

Narayan asked, "You have a suggestion?"

Howler fought through one of his shrieks. "Perhaps."

Pretty lights filled the air around me. I almost let myself be distracted. But I managed to hang in there, listening.

Singh asked, "What do you mean?"

"Longshadow is clever but he's no major intellect. Back when the Shadowmasters took control of the shadows they used to conquer their empire, before they understood the darkness they were tapping, they messed up royally. They broke some seals permanently instead of cracking them temporarily. You get in a hurry, you screw up. To keep things from going completely rotten they had to have somebody watching the Shadowgate all the time. Longshadow volunteered for the job. The others thought that would keep Longshadow out of trouble because he wouldn't be able to travel. They already knew he was a lunatic. But he was more cunning than they thought. He wove a skein of spells that keeps the Shadowgate closed to everybody but him. His true name is part of the spell complex. That's probably the biggest risk he's ever taken and one he's regretted from the instant he cemented it in place and discovered the price he'd paid for power. The shadows know his name. Every one he lets wriggle through that gate so he can use it wants to devour him. The price he pays is eternal vigilance. If he slips, he dies." Howler let loose a shriek pregnant with passion as well as pain.

Narayan Singh sensed the difference. "What is it?" he asked.

"It was a stupid thing he did. For power. If he dies and his name fades, the clamping spells unravel and the Shadowgate opens. And that means the end of the world."

"Do they know that out there?" Singh asked, indicating the besieging army—some of whom continued to sneak up the scaffolding unnoticed because that was considered impossible.

"Probably not. Though Lady might reason it out."

Sneer. We knew it now.

Narayan pondered for a moment, then said, "If all that is true, then I think you cannot leave Overlook. Without your aid, I fear, the Black Company will triumph. Whatever he believes. In which case doom will find you wherever you run."

Howler shrieked, angry, despairing, seeing the logic of Singh's observation. "He is not competent to lead yet we cannot wrest command from him."

"That would do no good, would it? We are slaves of his strategy now. And that requires completion of the fortress."

Which no longer seemed likely. If many more of Lady's soldiers got inside, Longshadow's skeleton garrison would not be able to overcome them.

Narayan continued, "Maybe the general will have an idea."

Both sides knew Mogaba was alive and directing the partisans. I had had no luck finding him. I had had an equal lack of success tracing Goblin. Smoke was a handy tool but you had to have some reference points when you started. That or an age to go back and forth in tiny jumps so people working hard not to be found could be caught in each of their tricks.

"We'd have to find him."

Good luck, guys.

"There are ways," Narayan said. "The Daughter of Night has eyes that can see from afar. And you are correct when you say that something has to be done."

Howler agreed.

I agreed with everybody.

Taglian soldiers continued to reach the top of the wall. Most were surprised to have made it. Few had any definite objective once they reached the top.

Again I wondered if the Old Man knew what was going on.

I started to drift away, thinking maybe it was time to see Croaker. The Daughter of Night came to the top of the wall, galloped toward Howler and Singh as fast as her short legs would carry her. Fireballs scarred Overlook's wall. There appeared to be a purpose to the way they fell but I could not discern it.

More and more soldiers climbed the scaffolding.

The child shrieked at Singh and Howler. Then Howler shrieked.

The news was out.

45

I TUMBLED OUT OF THE WAGON. AFTER A COUPLE OF STEPS I FELL TO MY knees.

"Whoa, there!" One-Eye said. "What's up?"

"Spent too long out, maybe. Weak." Hungry and thirsty. I took water from him. It had been sweetened but included nasty additives as well. He must be making something that would turn alcoholic. "Where's the Old Man?"

"I don't know. I see Thai Dei, though." By way of suggesting caution.

I shifted languages. "Lady isn't playing with them over there. She had troops climb the scaffolding. They made it to the top. There's a mob of them inside. They've just found out on the inside. And some of the Prince's men are in the ruins of Kiaulune. They were sneaking up to help Lady but they got bogged down. There're actually people hiding out there now. Some of Mogaba's bunch. They're putting up a fight."

I had passed over the ruins coming back and had been surprised to see the fighting. The presence of fighters there needed examination. It had not been long since the ruins were occupied by only a handful of survivors incapable of helping Longshadow with his construction project.

Mogaba had to be sneaking men in a few at a time.

"I think Croaker went off with one of the patrols looking for Mogaba. What do you need him for?"

"I don't think he knows what's happening. I think Lady did this on her own." Which had been fine when she was in charge of the frontier but not now, when she commanded only a quarter of the army. "I have no idea what his plans are but I'll bet he don't want them taken away from him like this."

One-Eye grunted. He considered Thai Dei and Mother Gota, who was a dozen yards farther away, closing in, bent under a huge load of firewood. Give her credit. She carried her share of the work. One-Eye's own bodyguard, JoJo, was nowhere to be seen, which was the usual state of affairs. They were two of a kind.

One-Eye said, "I'll jump in the wagon and find out. You get your strength back." He went up with a frown, tossing one concerned glance back before he disappeared.

I helped Mother Gota with the firewood. So did Thai Dei. We got it sorted and broken and in out of the wet in minutes. Mother Gota actually thanked me for helping.

She had moments when she could manage courtesy toward an outsider who had not been able to help his bad choice of parents. Those were rare. They seemed to come only when she was feeling particularly good.

I remained courteous myself. In fact, now that I knew what they had done to me and Sarie, I found myself becoming more formal and courteous. I hoped my manners did not make them suspicious. I smirked when I thought about Sleepy. Then I worried about the kid. I had no business burdening him with a personal mission like that.

I started pacing, wondering if I ought to confess to One-Eye or the Old Man.

One-Eye descended from his wagon. He looked like he had seen a ghost. Or something equally unexpected and unpleasant.

I headed his way. "What's up?"

"I don't know. I don't have time to find out." He sort of sighed his words.

"Tell me."

"I found Croaker."

"All right. So where is he? So what's the problem?"

"He's out there talking to the keeper of the crows."

"Catcher? He went out to meet Soulcatcher?"

"I didn't track him back. I don't know if that was his plan. But that's where he's at. That's what he's doing."

"Did he look like he was a prisoner again?" I did not wait for an answer. I piled into the wagon.

Silly me, I did not ask One-Eye where Croaker was so I ended up having to track him from his quarters to his meeting with the madwoman.

He did go specifically to meet her. That I determined by taking Smoke in so close that I could hear Croaker's twin crows squawk instructions. The trouble I did have was after I trailed him through the wilds to his rendezvous inside a snowbound, rocky ravine that was almost invisible beneath overhanging pines.

I did not get close enough to hear what was said. It was a miracle that I got Smoke as close as I did, to assure myself that the Old Man did indeed have a date with Soulcatcher.

The crows were thick there and they sensed me hovering. They became so agitated that Catcher came out to find out what was going on.

I got out of there.

I wondered if Croaker would suspect anything.

I came back out. Thoughtful One-Eye had a bucket of warm tea ready along with some fresh bread from a nearby regimental bakery that was just getting started. I asked, "You get close enough to hear anything?"

"Can't push that little shit anywhere near her. He's three-quarters dead but he's still five-fourths chickenshit."

"I don't feel like going after him. It'll have to wait. In the meantime . . ."

In the meantime things were happening in Overlook. Flickering lights illuminated the whole region. A dark cloud ribbed with fire boiled up and fell apart in the teeth of the wind. Horns and drums bickered. Fireballs by the thousand pelted the fortress wall.

"In the meantime you might want to take a look at that so you can tell the Old Man whatever he needs to know when he gets here. Which he's going to be when he realizes that something is happening."

Not unsound advice. If Croaker was going to make decisions he was going to need all the information he could get. "Keep my loving family away, eh?" I could not keep bitterness from creeping into my voice. One-Eye caught it but he did not ask.

I swallowed one last mouthful of warm bread, settled, grasped Smoke and took him out. The process had become so easy I could practically do it in my sleep. I hardly had to think about where I wanted to go. As long as that was not one of the places Smoke did not like to visit.

Overlook was the proverbial overturned ant's nest. People were running everywhere. It did not look like anyone knew where they were going. Almost everybody was interested only in not being where they had started. Occasionally Taglians came face to face with the Shadowmaster's men and fear took its inevitable course.

Some of the invaders had sense enough to stay up on the wall and use their bamboo poles to make life miserable for folks inside Overlook. One lieutenant screamed his head off at the men outside and below, telling them he wanted more poles up here *now!* His snipers were having great fun tearing the place up. Overlook's defenders did not dare show themselves.

Some of our men had Narayan Singh and the Daughter of Night cornered in a tower. They pasted it with a blizzard of fireballs. The tower held up only because it was layered with scores of protective spells. It was one of Longshadow's favorite hideouts.

The Howler was on the run. Taglians whooped after him, spraying fireballs around so liberally that the little wizard had no time to counterattack. He screamed as he ran.

More and more men, all lugging bundles of bamboo, got into the fortress.

It could not possibly be this easy. Could it?

Where was Longshadow? He was not taking part.

The Shadowmaster remained in his own high tower, staring south toward the grey plateau, apparently unaware that hell had come calling. How could the man be that preoccupied?

No. He was not that preoccupied. He did know.

Scaffolding all the way around Overlook burst into flames. It was a ferocious fire spell. Flames devoured everything consumable in seconds. Scores fell to their deaths.

Before that ever happened Lady's men had begun lowering rope and slat ladders obviously created specifically for scaling Overlook's walls. They were long enough for the climb and each dozen feet they boasted a frame box meant to hold them away from the wall so the climb would be easier for the soldiers.

Longshadow could not see those from his vantage. It would be a while before he understood that his stroke had gained him very little.

Now he was shut up inside without hope of completing his fortress because he could acquire materials for scaffolding only on the outside.

Whatever else, Lady had accomplished that much. She had taken away the one weapon that might have given him an incontestable victory. He could not unleash a flood of shadows to cleanse the earth of his enemies because he could not protect himself from the darkness.

Lady's soldiers continued entering Overlook, slowly, under the impression they were headed toward victory because the only resistance they encountered initially was that of gravity. Their comrades already held the top of the fortress's north wall for the two hundred yards between two crystal-topped towers. Both towers were slagged and blackened, the crystal dead from fireball bombardment.

To my puzzlement Lady had teams outside the wall still hammering away with their bamboo poles.

I had no hope of figuring anything out. Lady had brought this mess on with less warning than the Old Man did his surprises.

Would we have two of them playing this game now?

Actually, I suppose, Lady had been playing all along. I just did not pay attention because she was never in the primary role.

The Prince's men remained bogged down with the unexpected mob of partisans in Kiaulune. But now he was routing his men around the skirmishing. It looked like there would be plenty more soldiers to follow Lady's mob up the rope ladders.

The fighting inside Overlook was crueler than I thought it could be. The garrison were all veterans who had been with Longshadow a long time. They might not love him but they were dedicated and determined and convinced that the Black Company would show them no mercy whatsoever. They fought like it. In territory they knew well and their enemies knew not at all. With the help of several clutches of those little old brown men called skrinsa shadowweavers.

Shadows did lurk in the fortress. The shadowweavers knew where they were hidden and how to send them slithering after invaders.

The bamboo poles helped. But not enough to save everybody. The inside of the fortress was all winding hallways and dark rooms and there was no way to know that a shadow was around till it attacked.

I could locate the little old men but I could not tell anyone where they were so they could be erased from the equation.

The deeper the soldiers pushed the worse it got.

Longshadow was not doing much. He had taken that one shot, then nothing. And the Howler . . . What had become of him?

Howler had eluded the soldiers trying to kill him. He was sneaking around, trying to join forces with the Shadowmaster. Longshadow went on to suffer one of his fits.

It was a big one, so bad he collapsed, thrashed around, tore his clothing, lost his mask, nearly swallowed his tongue. Floor and face alike became soaked with spittle. How had this guy survived to become one of the most powerful sorcerers in the world if he had seizures whenever he was under stress?

Again, though, I could tell no one that he was down and it was a perfect time to kick him in the head.

The protective spells shielding the tower where Singh and the Daughter of Night had gone to ground were particularly strong. The Taglians trying to reach them knew who they were, though. And they were dedicated to their commander. And to the huge reward she had offered for Narayan.

Lady said Singh was worth his weight in rubies if he was delivered alive.

She never offered anything for her daughter.

The sky darkened suddenly. Never have I seen so many crows. It seemed the sun would go out.

46

I RACED TO FIND CROAKER AND SOULCATCHER. SMOKE WAS SO FAR OFF BALance I actually got close to Lady's mad sister. She was dancing around in a rage, talking to herself in different voices, cursing Lady for having too much initiative, cursing her crows for not getting to the battle and back with information fast enough to suit her. "It's not time!" she raged. "There's no conjunction yet! This can't happen now!"

I hustled off to find Croaker when Smoke began to strain away from the woman. We soared upward, terrifying the crows, leaving a discernible wake through their swarm. I hoped Soulcatcher was not alert enough to catch it.

There had been times when she had seemed aware of my presence. Though that had been on occasions when I was loose from my own place in time, mostly.

Croaker was easy to spot. He was headed for camp at a gallop, trailing a comet tail of crows. His giant black stallion seemed almost to fly.

I rose higher still, to see if there were developments elsewhere in need of noting.

Smoke seemed to enjoy rising up where the eagles soar. We went higher than ever before, until the surface of the earth was so far below that I could not make out such trivial details as men and animals, till only the most vast works of man stood out from the snowy background. The Dandha Presh gleamed like a row of teeth in the north. In the west a pile of dark clouds promised more hard weather for later. In the south the plain of grey stone sparkled as though strewn with newly minted coins. The plain as a whole faded away into grey nothingness, yet at the extremity of vision something loomed within the grey.

All Overlook's north face seemed to be on fire.

I swooped down there to discover that Howler and Longshadow had gotten together and launched a counterattack against the troops holding the top of the wall. Then Lady had come to the aid of her people. Every man who could work a bamboo pole was doing so, often apparently not aiming at anything.

Amidst all the other lights the air shimmered with fragments of something that recalled the northern lights we had seen ages ago when the Company was way up at the Barrowland. None of these shards was bigger than a platter. They flew around like a swarm of gnats. The air was filled with a sound like sharp steel in rapid motion. The shimmers slashed everything but Longshadow's most densely spell-protected stone.

Lady was up near the edge of the emergency housing that had been erected for Shadowlander refugees. Her usual gang of worshippers surrounded her, ready to repel any physical attack. She was doing whatever it was that was throwing those blades of light around up there, keeping the defenders under cover and Howler and Longshadow too busy to trouble her or any of her soldiers.

The blades of light did not appear to be under Lady's direct command but orbited a point she did control—most of the time.

A tower collapsed into the interior of the fortress. A pillar of dust, reflecting colorfully, rose to be carried away by the wind bringing the storm from the west.

The outside of the fortress, once so ivory, was a mess of stains. I figured the housekeeping staff would be real put out.

The flying black speck that was the Old Man was almost back to his headquarters. I knew he would want to see me first. Reluctantly I left the great show for flesh.

"What the hell is going on?" One-Eye demanded as I let myself down from the wagon. The show must have impressed him because he was all business. He had food and drink waiting.

"Croaker's almost here. I'll tell you both."

Right on cue the Old Man popped over the nearest rise and hurtled toward us. His mount was still in motion when he left his saddle. He grunted as his boots hit the ground. "Tell me." He understood that we were waiting.

I told him everything I knew. Including the fact that he was sneaking around with his wife's sister when the shitstorm hit. He stared over my shoulder toward Overlook the whole time. His expression was cold, stony. I offered the observation that Lady had in no way exceeded her authority within the general orders of the organization. That cold look turned my way.

I had no trouble meeting it. A couple of brushes with Kina can do wonders for the trivial fears of the world.

"You got something on your mind, Murgen?"

"You don't tell anybody what's going on, you got to accept it when they go ahead and get on with the job."

I thought smoke was going to roll out of his ears.

A skinny, mangy mongrel raced past and on the dead run clamped jaws on a startled crow. He got a wing.

All the crows in the world descended on him before he could enjoy his dinner.

"A parable," One-Eye said. "Observe! Black crows. Black dog. The eternal struggle."

"Black philosopher," Croaker grumbled.

"Black Company."

Croaker said, "Let's go have a chat with my esteemed paramour. Where is she, Murgen?"

I told him.

"Let's go." But he had to stop and pick up his Widowmaker costume. Which allowed me time to borrow Thai Dei's grey mare and get a head start. Croaker frowned but did not ask when he caught up. Thai Dei insisted on coming along even though he had to jog now.

He did not keep up.

Neither did I, of course.

If Lady and the Old Man indulged in a head-butting contest it was over before I got there. Maybe I could take Smoke back to look their meeting over. When I got there they were looking up at the tall white wall and deciding how best to exploit the situation.

Lady was saying, "I fear our supply of bamboo poles is growing too small. It's certain that Longshadow will send shadows against us at least once." She spoke Taglian. She did not care who heard what she said. And plenty of ears were nearby, including Blade, Willow Swan and the Nar generals Ochiba and Sindawe, none of whom enjoyed my complete trust. Crows were, as always, plentiful, too.

They were turning the ruins of Kiaulune into a major rookery. Good eating there, I suppose, with the cold weather preserving the corpses of the Shadowmaster's subjects.

Almost everyone threw rocks at the birds. They had become adept at dodging. I suspected resignation would set in eventually and the only time we would enjoy any privacy would be when Lady used one of the spells she had developed for frightening the birds away.

A ripple of astonished disturbance passed through the circling birds. No one else noticed. But I was alert for it because I had been wondering if One-Eye was going to watch.

If anyone else figured this out . . . You can do nothing in this world without leaving some mark, somehow. If someone else knows what sort of trace you will leave . . .

One of the crystal tower tops received so many fireballs that it began to ring. The sound started as a soft hum and rapidly swelled to a raging shriek. The tower top exploded in a cloud of smoke and dust and spinning shards that melted holes in the snow and earth wherever they fell. The event so startled everyone that it distracted even Lady for a moment.

In that brief moment Longshadow counterattacked.

The boots of an invisible giant a thousand feet tall began stomping and kicking the men atop Overlook's wall and those trying to join them. In the moments it took Lady to overcome her surprise and respond, every ladder got stripped away and the bands holding the secured section of wall got scattered. Many fell to their deaths.

Lady stopped the stomping but all efforts to reestablish a ladder link to the men up top failed. Longshadow was fully into the game.

Croaker stayed and watched for the rest of the day. I stayed with him. Nothing much happened.

We walked back. Croaker said, "Overall, that may have been a net gain."

"We still have people inside. If we can preserve them."

"We shall make every effort."

His mind was racing. Something had happened outside whatever playscript he had written and he was trying to incorporate it as a positive. He had no attention left over for little questions like why I was using Thai Dei's horse while my brother-in-law was hoofing it.

Which reminded me that I needed to check up on Sleepy. The weather and the war had not gone the way I had expected here so his life might not have been comfortable lately, either.

The wind rose dramatically during our walk. Pellets of ice came as precursors of the storm. "I've got a feeling this is going to be a bad one."

Croaker grunted. "Pity she didn't pull it off this morning. We could be inside and warm."

"At least it ought to be about the last big one of the winter."

"That reminds me. How are we doing finding seed grain?"

47

THE STORM LINGERED A LONG TIME. A COUPLE TIMES I ALMOST BECAME lost just getting from my shelter to One-Eye's wagon or Croaker's shelter. The blizzard brought air so cold we had to move Smoke into Croaker's place to keep him from freezing. The soldiers suffered badly, though mostly through their own failure to provide themselves with adequate shelter. Captives had warned them that winter here would be much harsher than any they had ever known.

Once again I got to know the joys of sharing quarters with Mother Gota.

Thai Dei insisted she had to get in out of the weather and I have been developing a soft streak as I get older. I allowed it.

She behaved uncharacteristically for Ky Gota. She kept her own counsel most of the time. She stayed out of the way. She helped Thai Dei dig out cold earth and carry it away so we would have more room. She did not say a disparaging word about all the time I spent writing. She worked hard, though I never had been able to criticize her on that account, ever.

She made me nervous. She was almost human. Though she made very little effort to be pleasant or friendly.

The Captain, though, was sharing space with One-Eye and Smoke for the duration. He was much less happy than I was. And I was not happy because I was getting almost no chance to travel with Smoke. When I did stumble over there they would not let me go ghostwalking long enough to do more than check something specific, which was always something on a list they had prepared but claimed not to have had time to check for themselves.

Croaker did not ghostwalk much but he did not let the blizzard and its aftermath keep him from working on other stuff.

Over there in Overlook, Longshadow and Howler were putting in hours as long as ours. And when he was not with his ally Howler, the Shadowmaster had his head together with Narayan.

Singh seemed to have perked up now that he had an almost friend. The Daughter of Night seemed content to ignore everybody and live entirely within herself.

Fighting continued inside the fortress. I almost had to envy our guys who were trapped in there. They were scared all the time but they were warm and most of the time they had enough to eat.

Fresh snow fell every three days. Harsh winds never stopped blowing. I began to worry about the wood we needed to keep going. The snow was so deep it was almost impossible to get around. Nobody knew how to make snowshoes. Probably only three or four Old Crew guys besides me knew what snowshoes were.

I thought it was a great time for Longshadow to send out some of his pet shadows but he failed to grab the advantage. He was not confident that Howler could withstand Lady by himself, nor, I suspect, did he want to turn his back on his partner for long.

The dreams intensified. They diversified as well. I went to the plain of death and the caves of ice—and I went to the Nyueng Bao delta swamps to see Sahra and into the hills and mountains behind us where I caught glimpses of Goblin and Mogaba in huddled hiding places trying to wait out the weather.

Those dreams all seemed very real.

Even more real seemed my dreams of Soulcatcher, whose lonesome misery was epic. The place she had chosen to hole up seemed to pull snow and wind both, till the former was deeper than she was tall.

The first two times I suffered these dreams I took them passively. The third night my own presence there seemed so real that I tried tinkering with reality.

The dream did not change but my place within it did.

I experimented much more next night.

The morning afterward, after a not entirely inedible breakfast prepared by Mother Gota, I slogged through the snow to visit the Captain.

"Had to get away?" he asked.

"They're not being bad. The old woman's even fixing food that's palatable. If you're not real picky."

"What's up? Where's your shadow?"

"I guess he didn't want to deal with the snow." The snow was the first thing I had seen that made Thai Dei want to back down. This winter was his first extensive experience with the white stuff.

"None of us do. Anything from the old guy?"

"In this weather? You're kidding." He was still sure that Uncle Doj was up to something. Maybe I ought to dream about him. "What I wanted you to know is, my dreams are getting really strange." I explained.

"Is it your imagination or are you really going out?"

"It feels like being out there with Smoke. Almost. I don't have any feeling of control. So far."

Croaker grunted. He looked thoughtful, seeing some possibilities. I saw a few myself.

"What I thought was, I could make a quick circuit with Smoke to see how closely reality conforms to what I dreamed." I had little trouble accepting the possibility because I had been experiencing such unusual dreams for so long.

"Do it. Without wasting any time."

"What's your hurry? This snow isn't going anywhere for a while."

Croaker grunted again.

He was turning into a genuine old fart.

The flight with Smoke showed me nothing I had not seen in my dreams. It did not show me Soulcatcher. Smoke still refused to get close. But I passed high overhead and saw that she was indeed caught in a side canyon where the snow was extremely deep.

48

THE WEATHER CHANGED EVENTUALLY. THE SNOW MELTED. WE CAME OUT OF our shelters like a bunch of groundhogs. So did the rest of the world. But most everyone was interested in recovering, not in getting into fights.

Fighting did continue inside Overlook, though mostly Longshadow's soldiers were satisfied to keep Lady's troops bottled up. Those men were in no hurry to get themselves killed now they were cut off from the outside. They had control of stores enough for a long time and complete confidence that Lady would make every effort to relieve them.

She would. I used Smoke to look in on some of her planning. She had expected any men who got inside to be cut off for a while. She had chosen shock units and commanders she believed would be able to handle the hardship.

The Prince's division was fighting in the ruins of Kiaulune and in the hills north of us, where Mogaba persisted in harassing the shit out of us. Lady's division held the ground between the city and Overlook. One of the Captain's divisions was around the other side, astride the road to the Shadowgate. The other remained in reserve.

Spring was a real threat on the horizon.

I asked Croaker, "You think the Prahbrindrah Drah is maybe going to get tired of getting the honors in all these fights?"

He gave me a startled look. "Am I that obvious?"

"About what?" I looked around. Only Thai Dei was close enough to hear anything.

"You just . . . It could be his division is the most incompetent."

"And least reliable?"

"This army will suffer a lot of casualties before we get to Khatovar, Murgen. Correct me if I'm wrong. It seems to me it would be in the Company's interest if most of those happened outside our own ranks."

"Uhm?"

"I trust my Old Division. A lot of those men want to join the Company. Most of them would fight the Prince if I gave the order."

Lately a lot of Taglians wanted to join the Company. I think most of the applications were genuine. Guys who take the oath always stick. They never take the oath lightly.

The oath is always administered in secret. Recent recruits have been asked to keep their new allegiances to themselves. No one outside the Company had any idea how strong we really were. Some people inside were getting the mushroom treatment, too, if their name was something like Lady.

The Old Man was turning paranoia into a fine art.

"I understand that. What I'm wondering is, how come Lady is getting the hurt, too?" If something did not end up on the Prince's back usually it went to her.

Croaker's shrug told me he was not quite sure himself. "I guess I don't want her in any position where she has to deal with too much temptation."

"And the New Division?"

"I wouldn't ask them to face off with the Prince. They probably won't ever be ready to take our side in a civil scrimmage." He looked me in the eye. This campaign had elevated him to a new level of hardness. This was like trading looks with Kina.

I did not look away.

Croaker explained, "I'll deliver on *my* promises."

He meant that our employers would not deliver. The Radisha, especially, was determined to screw us. The Prince had been out here long enough to become one of the gang.

We never did get a chance to work our magic on his sister.

I said, "I spend a lot of time wishing I'd stayed a farm boy."

"You still having trouble with the nightmares?"

"Every night. But it's not like it's a direct attack. I always work my way through and use the opportunity to scout around. Sure as hell ain't pleasant, though, I'll tell you that." Kina, or somebody or something who wanted me to think she was Kina, was in my dreams all the time. My own conviction was that it *was* Kina, not Catcher. She was still trying to promise me Sahra back.

I wished she would do something about the odor.

"She trying to work Lady, too?"

"Probably." Almost certainly. "Or maybe Lady is working her."

"Uhm." He was not listening. He was concentrating on Overlook now. Fireballs had begun zipping around over there.

Several fireballs flashed in the ruins of Kiaulune, too. The people Mogaba had in there were stubborn. The man really could find good soldiers and could motivate them. The Prahbrindrah Drah had begun razing parts of the ruined city, building by building, salvaging burnables where he could.

It was still cold. At the moment there were eight inches of snow on the ground, atop a couple of inches of hard-packed sleet. This was spring? How many more storms would we have to endure before the weather gave up delivering unpleasant surprises? Longshadow's surviving crystal turrets sure looked comfy. I wondered why he had not bothered us much lately.

I checked the smoke rising from Kiaulune. I hoped the Prince would save a few nice places where us special folks could hole up in comfort after he rooted out the last partisans.

I was tired of living like a badger.

"What's going on in there?" Croaker asked, indicating Overlook.

"Nothing's changed. I don't understand Longshadow. Not even a little. It's like he's determined to destroy himself. He's in some kind of emotional slough where he just can't exercise any initiative. You've been there, I expect. I have, I know. You know what needs doing but you just can't move. It doesn't seem like it's worth the effort. It's the same sort of paralysis that came over Smoke those last few weeks before he got knocked into his coma."

Croaker looked thoughtful. "How about you? You feeling like you're getting enough rest? With these dreams?"

"It isn't bothering me yet." I lied. Though I did not need sleep. I needed an emotional respite. I needed a few weeks alone somewhere with my wife.

"Where are your in-laws?" The eternal question. Uncle Doj was still missing.

"Good question. And before you ask, I still don't have a clue what they're up to. If they're up to anything."

"I worry about so many Nyueng Bao being so close to us."

"Bad can't happen, Captain. Not ever. They're with us as a debt of honor."

"As you always tell me, you had to be there."

"That'd sure help you understand."

He glared at the great white fortress. "You think we could let refugees get through?"

"Huh?"

"Put another burden on Longshadow. More mouths to feed."

"He wouldn't let them in." I was still amazed that Longshadow had provided himself with such a small garrison. There were never more than a thousand people inside Overlook, including servants and families and those refugees who had gotten in before the destruction of the scaffolding. There was no mundane way the fortress could have been defended against multiple attacks.

But Longshadow had not planned to deal with the mundane. He had expected to be safe behind countless adamantine spells for as long as he liked.

"I don't think it'll be much longer, Murgen. Not much longer at all."

Fireballs flew around over there. A rising breeze lifted some of those box kites the quartermasters had dragged all the way from Taglios. In this sort of wind they could lift twenty-five pounds to the top of the wall.

That was not what Croaker had brought them along for, he said. But he did not expound.

"I admire your confidence, boss. Yeah. Next year in Khatovar."

"Next year in Khatovar" had become the sarcastic slogan of the Old Crew these past few years. Most would just as soon have faded away and gone back north. The constant stress of being in service to Taglios suited nobody but Lady. Despite her bouts with exhaustion she seemed to thrive emotionally where raging paranoia was the only sane way of facing reality.

Croaker was not amused. His goals for the Company were not acceptable butts for humor.

His sense of humor had been assassinated by this campaign. Or, at least, it had gone as comatose as Smoke.

"Thai Dei. How about we go for a walk?" When the Old Man got in a mood it never hurt to be somewhere else.

49

ONE-EYE IS SUPPOSED TO BE MY BACKUP AS ANNALIST, AT LEAST TILL Sleepy gets back and learns the ropes. Those few times I have handed him the job, or Croaker did when he was doing the Annals, he proved conclusively that we need Sleepy desperately. The old fart cannot live beyond the moment most of the time. Not that I blame him at his age.

So I was surprised when he bothered to tell me, well after the fact, that he had witnessed something interesting while he was out scouting with Smoke. No, he never wrote anything down and he could not recall all the details now but better late than never, right?

Maybe. Old Smoke was not anchored in time.

He and I drifted back to a moment not many hours after Narayan had visited Howler on the wall and their little chat got interrupted by Lady's gang of insensitive brutes.

Singh and the Daughter of Night had reached safety in her quarters. The child did not talk much. Narayan was obviously extremely uncomfortable in her presence now, though she was a tiny thing even for her age. She ignored him, settled at a small worktable and turned up the wick on a small oil lantern. The stunner, for me, was seeing her set about the same sort of work that I did almost every day.

Astounded, I watched as her little hand slowly, laboriously recorded words in a language I did not recognize and which, I discovered, she did not read. For as soon as I saw what she was doing I darted around through time looking for an explanation.

The writing got started a week ago.

It was the middle of the night. Narayan had stayed up late, praying, calming his soul, trying to reach the state the Daughter of Night achieved when she touched the goddess. He had tried a hundred times. He failed this time as well.

Failure no longer ached inside him. He was resigned. He just wished he could be allowed to understand.

Hardly had he fallen into his dark dreams before the Daughter of Night was tugging at his shoulder. "Wake up, Narayan. Wake up."

He cracked an eyelid. The child was more animated than he had seen since before she learned that she was to be the instrument of Kina, the hands of the goddess in this world.

He groaned. He wanted to swat her, wanted to tell her to go back to her pallet, but he remained wholly dedicated to his goddess, prepared to execute her will. The will of the Daughter had to be considered an extension of the will of the Mother, however difficult that might make life.

"Yes? What is it?" He rubbed his face and groaned.

"I need writing materials. Pens. Ink. Brushes. Inkstones. Penknives. Whatever is involved. And a big bound book of blank pages. Quickly."

"But you can't read or write. You're too little."

"My mother will guide my hand. But I must begin my task quickly. She fears we may not have much time left here, in safety."

"What are you going to do?" Narayan asked, wide awake now and completely baffled.

"She wants me to make copies of the Books of the Dead."

"Make copies? They've been lost for thousands of years. Even the priests of Kina doubt that they exist anymore. If they ever did."

"They exist. In another place. I have seen them. They will exist again. She will tell me what to write down."

Narayan considered the notion for a while. "Why?"

"The Books must be brought back into this world to help us bring on the Year of the Skulls. The first Book is the most important. I don't know its title. But by the time I finish writing it down I will be able to read it and to use it to bring forth the other Books. I will be able to use those to open the way for my mother."

Narayan gulped air. He was illiterate. Most Taglians were. Like many who were illiterate, he was possessed of a vast awe of those who did read and write. He had seen great sorceries since associating himself with Longshadow, yet considered literacy the greatest witchery of all. "She is the Mother of All Night," he murmured. "There is None Greater."

"I want those materials, Narayan." That was no four-year-old talking.

"I will find them."

Back in the hours after their escape from Lady's soldiers, while fighting persisted only a short distance away, the child wrote slowly and Narayan paced and shivered. Finally, she looked up, considered him with those disturbing eyes. "What has happened, Narayan?" She seemed to see right through him.

"Events have surpassed my understanding. The small, smelly one called me to the wall to show me the heads of my brothers displayed on spears. A gift from your birth mother." He picked at himself, reluctant to go on. I thought maybe the worst torture we could visit on him when we caught him would be a bath. "I cannot fathom what purpose moved the Goddess when she allowed all those faithful sons to fall into the woman's hands. Almost none of our people remain alive."

The child snapped her fingers. Singh shut up instantly.

"*She* killed them? The woman who gave this flesh life?"

"Apparently. I made a bad mistake in not making sure of her when I brought you away to your true mother."

Not once did the child ever call Lady her mother. She never mentioned her father at all.

"I am sure my mother had an overpowering reason for allowing that to happen, Narayan. Have the slaves clear out. I will consult her." Several Shadowlander women attended the child most of the time. She treated them like furniture. They were not in fact slaves.

Singh shooed the women while keeping one eye on the girl. She really did seem disconcerted by his complaints.

Singh shut the door behind the last servant. The woman had made no effort to conceal her relief at being away from the little monster. The people of Overlook did not like the Daughter of Night. Narayan settled into a squat. The child was in a trance already.

Whatever other place she went off to she did not stay long. She grew pale while she was there, though, and when she returned she was more troubled than when she had gone.

The odor of death filled the ghostworld while she was away. I gutted it out. Kina did not come.

The girl told Singh, "I don't understand this, Narayan. She says none of it was her doing. She neither caused their deaths nor allowed them to happen." The child sounded like she was quoting, though when she did speak she always sounded older than her years. "She was unaware that it had happened."

Now they both faced a crisis of faith.

"What?" Narayan was startled, frightened. Fear was a constant of life these days.

"I asked her, Narayan. And she didn't know. The deaths were news to her."

"How could that be?" You could see the fear shove its cold claws deeper into the Deceiver's guts. Now the enemies of the Deceivers could murder them wholesale without their goddess even knowing? Then what protection did the Children of Kina possess?

"What fell powers do these killers from the north command?" the child asked. "Are Widowmaker and Lifetaker more than created images? Can they be true demigods walking the earth in the guise of mortals, powerful enough to spin cobwebs of illusion before my mother's eyes?"

You could see the doubts gnawing at both of them. If those red and yellow rumel men out there could be taken so easily and killed without alerting their protectress, what could save a living saint or even a Deceiver messiah?

"If that is the case," Singh said, "we had better hope this place is as impregnable as that madman Longshadow wants to believe. We had better hope that he can exterminate all the Taglians already inside."

"I do not think he's finished, Narayan. Not yet." But she did not explain what she meant.

50

YOU WHO COME AFTER ME, AND WHO READ THESE ANNALS ONCE I AM GONE, will have difficulty believing this but there are times when I do dumb things. Like the day I decided to stroll over to Lady's forward command post to see the fighting with my own eyes instead of watching it from the comfort and safety of the ghostworld or my dreams.

I suspected I had pulled a stupid before I ever got there. I kept stumbling over corpses, most of them just lumps in the snow, slowly emerging. There would be another feast for crows, another celebration of corruption, after the weather turned.

And it was turning.

It was raining, steadily though not heavily. The rain was melting the snow. In places a mist almost as thick as fog hung in the air. I could not see a hundred feet. This was a new experience for me, walking in the rain on thick snow, through a fog.

Actually, it was a journey through silent beauty.

I could not appreciate that because I was so miserable.

Thai Dei was more miserable. The delta was warm even during the winter.

Sleepy was up there enjoying the earlier spring overwhelming Taglios and its environs. I hated and envied the kid now. I should have gone myself.

He had delivered my message to Banh Do Trang. I was a fly on the wall when it happened. The old man took the letter calmly, without reaction or comment—except that he did ask Sleepy to wait in case there was a reply. My message began its journey to the temple of Ghanghesha. Banh Do Trang carried the message himself.

Meantime, I was so far away I was in another world. Freezing my ass off.

"Why are we here?" I asked suddenly. I am not sure why. It seemed like a good question at the time.

Thai Dei took it literally. The man could not help himself. He had no imagination. He shrugged. And he kept on being as alert as was humanly possible while trying to keep cold water from running down the back of his neck.

I have never seen anyone as capable of carving his life into exclusive slices. And of giving each slice all the attention it deserved.

He was alert because dumb boy me had decided to take a shortcut through the ruins of Kiaulune. The Prahbrindrah Drah had rooted out all the enemy, had he not?

Maybe. But if that was true who were the snipers we had encountered twice already, slingers who operated from the remains of what had been tenements before the earthquake? My right thigh hurt where a lucky ricochet had gotten me. I was not hot for revenge, just for getting out of there.

I said, "I don't mean why are we here freezing our butts off. I mean why are we here in this end of the world freezing our nuts off while lunatics without sense enough to surrender sling rocks at us and Croaker and Lady figure it's a cinch to impregnate an impregnable fortress."

Thai Dei indulged himself. "Sometimes you don't have any idea what you're going on about, do you?" He regained his self-control and returned to character. "You follow the path of honor, Murgen. You strive to pay the debt of Sahra. As do we all. My mother and I follow you because your debt is our debt."

You lying dicklicker. "Sure. Thanks. And we'll collect, won't we? But this weather just drains the fire out of me. How about you?" Like most young men dream of spending their summers in Kiaulune.

"The fog is disheartening," he admitted.

An arrow wobbled between us, sped by someone who did not know what he was doing at targets he could not see well. "These are some pretty stubborn little bastards," I said. "Mogaba must have them convinced that we're going to eat them alive."

"Perhaps they have seen no evidence otherwise."

I gleaned the arrow. "You all of a sudden gonna turn talkative and philosophical on me?"

Thai Dei shrugged. He had become more loquacious lately. It was as though he did not want me to forget that he was closer than my shadow.

We entered an area that had been a square before the earthquake. The fog made it impossible to discern any landmarks. "Shit!" was my philosophical take on the situation.

"There." Thai Dei indicated a glow to our left.

I made out noises that sounded like muted curses in Taglian. Like soldiers grumbling over a game of tonk, a pastime the southerners had adopted enthusiastically.

I headed that way, slush splashing. The stuff was ankle deep now, except where it was deeper, like the place where I put my foot down and it just kept going till I was in up to my knee.

The stumble was a piece of good luck. It started me cursing in Taglian. Some nearby soldiers came to help. They had been about to ambush us, having heard us stumbling around earlier. They recognized me. I did not know them.

Turned out they belonged to the bunch playing cards. They had lost their officer and their sergeant had been slain and they had no idea what to do with themselves so they were just trying to stay out of the way and keep warm. One of our failures as military educators. We have not encouraged innovative thinking at the squad level. Or at any other, for that matter.

"I can't tell you guys what to do because I don't know your situation. Try to go up the chain of command, I guess. Find your company commander."

They explained that their whole company had been sent in to clear the area of snipers. In the fog those snipers had no trouble telling who *their* enemies were. Everybody who was not them, a luxury the Taglians did not enjoy. The rest of the company was out there in the fog somewhere.

"The fire get started on purpose?"

"No, sir. Some guys got excited and used their bamboo. Then we just kind of kept it going."

"Why didn't you burn the buildings and roast the snipers out?"

"Orders. These here buildings are all in good shape. The Prince wanted to set up a headquarters here."

"I see." Maybe more than the Taglian realized.

The Prahbrindrah Drah already had a headquarters. It was in a better neighborhood boasting much better living conditions.

"Nobody told me," I said. "I'll tell you this. Don't get yourselves killed trying to save a pile of rocks and timber. If the little shits snipe at you, burn them out." Anywhere in the Annals that city fighting is mentioned one lesson stands out. That one lesson was bitterly reinforced by my own experience in Dejagore. If you worry even a little about preserving property, the guys on the other side will eat you up. When you are in a fight you do not worry about anything but getting your enemy before he gets you.

Missiles kept coming out of the fog. They did no damage but did advise us that the snipers had a good idea where we were.

Given my encouragement the Prince's troops went off to commit wholesale arson. I chuckled. "I'm proud of me, I am, I am."

"What must be done must be done," Thai Dei said, misunderstanding.

There was no need to tell him that I had just scuttled some plan of the Prahbrindrah Drah's. "You'll whistle a different tune if we end up freezing our butts off because these assholes waste the whole damned city." The remains of Kiaulune were a rich source of firewood, not to mention stone for reinforcing earthworks. Fires began to spread. I felt giddy. Is this what power does to you?

I stayed around, directing those men and other leaderless types who accumulated. The snipers were stubborn about not getting caught. Fires became more numerous.

The weather turned colder as evening arrived. Rain came. It turned to sleet and freezing rain that coated everything with crystal. The fog thinned. As visibility improved I discovered that the fires were more widespread than I had thought. Out of control and spreading, they soon yielded enough heat to turn the sleet back to rain.

Smoke began to replace the fog. I told Thai Dei, "We're going to have to start hauling firewood all the way from the mountains." I sent word out not to start any more fires. It did not do much good.

The soldiers were so jumpy they kept plinking at each other with the bamboo poles.

Mogaba would get a good laugh out of this one.

Full night arrived. I had been having too much fun. I did not want to be down in Kiaulune after nightfall. The dancing firelight only made me more nervous. What a time for the Shadowmaster to loose his pets.

"Did you see that?" I demanded.

"What?" Thai Dei sounded righteously baffled.

"Can't swear to it. My eyes aren't what they used to be. But. . . ." But I did not need to tell Thai Dei I thought I had seen Uncle Doj flickering through the tricky light as though he was a shadow himself. A troll-like figure had been right behind him. Mother Gota.

Interesting. Very interesting.

"Let's go for a walk." I headed the direction my in-laws were going. Thai Dei followed. Of course. "Thai Dei. What do you really know about Uncle Doj? What moves him? Where is he going?"

Thai Dei responded with one of his all-purpose, neutral grunts.

"Talk to me, dammit! I'm family."

"You are Black Company."

"Damned straight. So what?"

Another grunt.

"I admit I ain't brown enough, short enough, skinny enough, ugly enough or dumb enough to be a genuine swamp-loving master race Nyueng Bao De Duang, but I did just fine as Sarie's husband." I overcame the impulse to throw him up against a handy ruin and slap the pigshit out of him till he explained what they thought they were doing, stealing my wife and pretending she was dead.

In recent days I had found I could not help rubbing Thai Dei's nose in Nyueng Bao racism.

"He is a priest," Thai Dei confessed, after considerable reflection.

"Oh! You surprised me there, brother. Pretend that I'm not stupid. Not *jengal.*" Which is a Nyueng Bao word meaning something like "congenitally deformed, brain-defective foreigner."

"He is a repository of old things, brother. Of old thoughts and old ways. We were a different people from a different land, once upon a time. Today we live where and how we must but among us are those who preserve ancient skills and customs and knowledge. As Annalist of the Black Company you should be able to understand that mission."

Maybe.

Accumulated precipitation had filled the streets with slush. It was only inches deep but it recalled the water-filled streets of another city in another time. This is a nightmare, I told myself. This is a torment from Kina, maybe. The smell is here but this is not Dejagore. Here we will not eat rats and pigeons and crows. Here no one will indulge in dark rituals requiring human sacrifice.

I studied Thai Dei. He, too, seemed to be remembering when. I said, "At least it was warmer than this."

"I remember that, brother. I remember everything." Meaning he recalled why so many men of such a proud race had attached themselves to the Black Company in almost subservient positions.

"I want you to remember those days always, Thai Dei. We were trapped in hell but we survived it. I learned there. Hell no longer has any surprises for me, nor any secrets from me." A bit of veiled criticism and an exposure of the bedrock philosophy that continues to get me through.

I have been to hell. I have done my time. This dark goddess Kina could not throw anything at me worse than the things I had seen already with my own eyes.

I scurried around but never caught another glimpse of Uncle Doj. If that was him that I saw. Thai Dei and I stayed in the streets, spreading encouragement while trying to forget our holiday in hell.

The little shit would not give up another word about Uncle Doj.

51

CROAKER WAS NOT PLEASED. "I DON'T WANT YOU PULLING A STUNT LIKE that again, Murgen. There was no reason for you to put yourself at risk like that."

"I found out the Prince is up to something."

"Great big old hairy-assed deal. We knew that. Had to be."

"I saw Uncle Doj sneaking around down there, too."

"So?"

"You're always worried about my in-laws."

"Not as much anymore."

His tone alerted me that, once again, he knew something he was not going to share. Or he had an angle he meant to keep completely secret. "What happened?"

"We reached a milestone. And no one noticed. Which puts us at a hell of an advantage."

"And you're not going to tell me?"

"Not a word. A little birdie might hear."

"Why were you visiting the bird lady?" I made a habit of asking— like he used to ask me about Uncle Doj. He was not pleased.

He offered no answer. "You have a job to do. Two jobs, in fact. Stick to those. If I lose you I've got nothing left but One-Eye." He eyed me hard.

"Wouldn't that be awful."

He caught my sarcasm. "When will Sleepy be ready? I haven't seen him around."

"Neither have I." I did not lie, did I? "I've been mapping the inside of Overlook." Which I had, whenever there were no other demands on my time. I had not put much effort into following up on the people I was supposed to watch. "You know how deep into the earth its basements go?"

"No. And neither do the crows."

He was probably wrong about that. Soulcatcher had been a prisoner in Overlook's deeps, once upon a time. But the point got through. Our days of paranoia were far from over.

"Gotcha. Think I'll go for a walk."

I found One-Eye seated across the fire from Mother Gota. They were not talking but them just tolerating each other was an epic amazement.

Was the little wizard trying to sell her on Goblin? He did have that sneaky look, like he was up to something really villainous.

I went on to One-Eye's dugout. My tagalong sat down beside his mom. She dished him up some nasty imitation Nyueng Bao chow. He ate in silence.

I slipped through the ragged blankets into One-Eye's den. It stank in there. I do not know who he thought he was fooling. There was no mistaking the smell of the mash. The results would taste as bad as that mess smelled. He put in anything he thought would ferment.

Smoke lay sprawled on a cot. One-Eye had gotten Loftus and his brothers to make it. The comatose wizard had the best bed in the province. I settled into the chair beside it, wondering if it would be possible to manage without him entirely.

I would experiment later, I decided. At the moment reliability was important.

I had to get him out of that hole, though. As soon as I could sneak him over to Croaker's. Who would shit a brick.

I went after Sleepy first. I found him still waiting at Banh Do Trang's city place. I followed Trang into the swamp. The old man appeared troubled. I could not tell why. In present time he was still far from the temple where Sahra was getting bigger by the minute.

It was scarcely a week since I had seen her yet she seemed to have swollen dramatically. I recalled the jokes the grown-ups had cracked about pregnant women when I was a kid. They did not seem that funny now.

I wanted to be there even though I knew my presence would be valueless. Babies get born every day with no help from their fathers and, everywhere I have ever been, no help wanted. At birthing time women stood united and wanted no men around.

Once again I found a time when Sahra would be alone, then tried to materialize in front of her. My luck held. It was bad again. I managed only to frighten her thoroughly.

"You'll know soon," I tried to say, but managed only to scare the swallows in the thatch overhead.

I could be patient. This game was all in my hands now. Uncle Doj and Mother Gota did not have a clue that I knew.

I went to check up on the Radisha Drah.

At a glance I had to say she regretted sending Cordy Mather off to check up on us bad boys. She was a cranky old witch without her playtoy.

People noticed, too. Not a good thing, with priests always looking for an angle.

More work for me, keeping an eye on them. Have to talk it over with Croaker, see if he wanted to make a project of it.

I saw nothing else of interest in Taglios. The victory at Charandaprash was general knowledge now. People of all castes and religions, rich and poor, supporters of the Black Company or its enemies, apparently took it for granted that Overlook would come next, easily. I found no fear of the Shadowmaster anywhere I looked.

Looked like Taglios was headed for peacetime and its good old backstabbing ways—perhaps prematurely.

I moved back south, tracing Cordy Mather.

Mather must have been disgruntled. He had not taken his assignment to heart. He and his companions had not yet reached Charandaprash. I did not take time to explore but they seemed to be waiting for good weather. And nobody was any more eager than Mather to get to the fighting.

They thought the war was won, too. Why go over there where people were still killing each other? A guy could get hurt! Not to mention the cold, the primitive living conditions, the lack of entertainment and gourmet cuisine . . .

I came back over to the cold and bloody side of the Dandha Presh, zoomed around looking for signs of Mogaba, Goblin, the forvalaka, Soulcatcher. Smoke could not, or would not, find any of them, though Catcher's general location could be determined by the density of crows.

She had not moved from where I had spied her meeting with the Old Man.

Smoke would approach the Shadowgate no more closely than ever before.

Damn! Almost the entire strength of what Croaker called his Old Division was established now in the gullies and rocky slopes of the ground between Overlook and the Shadowgate, astride the road south to Khatovar. Some of those fools, posted up close to the Shadowgate, kept sniping at what they thought they saw on the other side. A few fireballs always drifted through the chill air.

I wondered if the Old Man knew they were doing that. I wondered if it was a bright idea. It might take only one badly aimed fireball to cause the collapse of the gate.

I went back into Overlook. It was always an adventure ambling through that fortress's dark corridors. As frightened as Longshadow was of shadows you would think that he would keep the whole inside brightly lit. I suppose he realized that was impossible and was satisfied to live in his crystal chamber and surround himself with intense light only when he *had* to move around. He chose not to go out very often.

The Howler, Narayan and the Daughter of Night had free run of the place. They were not afraid of its dark corners. They never ran into anything scary. The child had grown contemptuous of Longshadow's fears.

Neither she nor Narayan had witnessed all that could be done by the Shadowmaster's pets.

Neither had we, I feared.

Lady had established a factory for replenishing spent bamboo poles. She had been confident that we would need them.

I was afraid she was right.

Stone shudders. Eternity sneers while it devours its own tail. This cold feast is almost finished.

Even death is restless.

The walls are bleeding.

In the darkness of the grey fortress it is hard to distinguish but dribbles of cardinal venous blood have begun to leak from the cracks between stones. It glistens in the light rising from the abyss. Small shadows squabble around it hungrily.

One crow watches.

The mist from the abyss has begun to fill the fortress. Half the tilting throne is covered. The throne is tilting precariously now. It looks like the figure there would slide away into the mist if it were not pinned in place.

The throne slips another millionth of an inch. A groan rises from the tortured figure. Its blind eyes flutter.

One crow cackles.

There is no silence. Stone is broken.

Where there is even a crack life will take root.

Light will find a way in.

52

I TOLD THE OLD MAN ABOUT THE TROOPS SHOOTING OVER THE SHADOW-gate. He scowled blackly. "I don't think that's a good idea." He bellowed for a courier. He sent out a strong suggestion to our brothers with the division to the south.

"No crows around here," I noted.

"One-Eye custom-built me a spell I can use to make them get hungry and go away for a while. But not forever."

I got the hint. "I don't think we're doing enough to support Lady's men inside Overlook."

Croaker shrugged. "I'm not concerned about Overlook anymore. Much."

"What? Not worried about Longshadow? Howler? Narayan Singh and your . . . the Daughter of Night?"

"Don't get me wrong. I'm not indifferent. They just don't matter as much as they did."

"I must've missed something. What're you saying?"

"I'm just suggesting it, Murgen. But we could go on south now. If we wanted. If I'm right about the standard."

"Uh . . ." I said. No flies on me.

"The standard has to be the key to the Shadowgate. I think we could walk right through and keep on going, without any danger, as long as we carry the standard."

"Uh . . ." I said again, but this time I had a few more thoughts. "You mean we could just get everybody together, say screw you to the rest of this mob, and trot off singing merry marching songs?"

"Exactly. Maybe."

So he was not completely sure.

"Wouldn't that leave a lot unsettled? Not to mention risk opening the Shadowgate the wrong way?"

"Longshadow is the master of the Shadowgate. He can keep it sealed."

"What if he can't?"

Croaker shrugged. "We don't owe anybody. . . . You just got finished telling me the Radisha is still fixing to screw us. The Prahbrindrah Drah was up to something down here. Howler is no friend of ours and Catcher has been helping me only because she thinks that'll help her get an angle on Lady."

"I've got a wife out there, Boss. And she's got a bun in the oven. Not to mention Goblin and his crew. Whom I can't find, but I'm sure they're out there somewhere, on some mystery mission from you."

"Hmm? Didn't think about that. There's no mystery. Goblin's job is to be forgotten. Then he's supposed to be in the right place if the Prince runs out on us. Or decides to pull some other stunt where we could use some help that comes from the blind side."

I grunted. It might be true. Or it might only be what he wanted me to think. I set it aside. I could answer the question using Smoke if I was determined and clever and felt any real need. I asked, "What about Singh? You just going to walk away from him?"

I did not believe Lady would accept that. It was hard to tell what was going on inside her head but I did think that no one and nothing would make her walk away while Narayan Singh remained in good health.

"I've been letting things work themselves out. I'll go on doing that for a while. But when the moment comes I won't hesitate to take the Company on down the road to Khatovar." His voice turned cold and hard and confidently formal.

I was getting angry. That was not good. I told him, "I think I'd better excuse myself now."

"Just in time, too." He flashed a wan smile.

One of his huge crows had shoved its beak into the room. If it was possible for a bird to look puzzled this one did.

It also smelled. It had lunched in the ruins.

I asked One-Eye, "How much weight should we put on our contract with the Taglians?"

"Uhn?" He gave me nothing but the puzzled grunt. He wanted me to go away so he could play with his still.

"I mean are we obligated to keep our part of the bargain until they actually try to screw us?"

"What's your problem?" He gestured. There were no snoopy beaks over here.

"The Old Man's talking about walking on past Overlook. Forgetting Longshadow and everything else. Leaving them to enjoy each other while we head on south."

That idea startled the little wizard. He stopped trying to get rid of me. "He figured out how we could do that?"

"He thinks maybe. I don't think he knows for sure. But I do believe he's willing to test it the hard way."

"That's not good. That could bring on a shitstorm the likes of which . . . Like nothing we can imagine, probably. Like something out of the myths."

"I thought so, too. He could be just shooting his mouth off. But it might be a good idea to remind him that we still haven't read those three missing volumes of the Annals. I've got a feeling we shouldn't overlook that."

One-Eye does not have a quarter of my faith in the Annals, nor a tenth of Croaker's, but he grimaced. "A good point. I'll remind him."

"Subtly? You hit him with a hammer, he tends to get stubborn."

"Subtly? You know me, Kid. I'm slicker than greased owl shit."

"I do know you. That's what scares me."

"I don't know what's got into your generation. You got no trust. You got no respect."

"And not much patience with bullshitters, either," I admitted. "I've got journals to write. Not to mention worries to worry." And food to eat. I was hungry again. Much as I ate when I was walking the ghost I should have gotten too fat to waddle.

I joined my in-laws beside their fire. Mother Gota dished me up a bowl of whatever it was she kept simmering in her pot. Nobody said anything. I had not talked to them much lately. They had begun to suspect that I was not real social anymore.

I wondered why the old woman would not do her cooking inside. Thai Dei and I had set her up a whole private suite in our ever-expanding dugout but she would go inside only when the weather turned foul or it was time to sleep.

Thai Dei did most of the work on our shelter. There was not much else for him to do. He was not involved in the schemes of his mother and Uncle Doj.

"Thank you," I told Mother Gota as I finished. "I needed that." I could not compliment her on her cooking. If ever she did screw up and make something palatable she would not buy the real thing. She never did claim any culinary skills.

"You," she said, initiating conversation, which she did rarely, "Bone Warrior, you are wary of crows? They are significant?" Her Taglian was abominable. I spoke Nyueng Bao much better but she would not do me the courtesy. I suppose that would, somehow, lend legitimacy to my relationship with Sahra.

I stopped trying to make sense of Mother Gota's thinking years ago.

I responded in Nyueng Bao. "They carry messages sometimes. They spy. We know this. Mice and bats do the same. Those who use the animals aren't our friends."

I exceeded myself telling her that much. Croaker would not be pleased. But I was fishing. It would be nice to find out what she knew or suspected. Sometimes she just could not help showing off.

"I have seen owls in the night, too, Stone Soldier. They do not behave the way owls should."

I grunted. That was news. And it told me that if owls were being used and no one else had noticed, then the old woman was a lot sharper than I had suspected.

"Last night many crows came and went from the shining fortress."

I looked at her more closely. Last night. While Thai Dei and I were in town with the lost boys. While she was traipsing through the night with Uncle Doj. She had seen something that I missed. Maybe.

Crows had been scarce near Overlook lately. Longshadow had taken a dislike to the dark harbingers. His crystal turrets were surrounded with nasty little spells that worked like trapdoor spiders, striking when birds came too close.

"That's interesting," I said. "That might be something new."

"There have been crows before. But never so many."

"Uhm." What went on in there last night that Soulcatcher found so interesting? I had seen nothing abnormal today. It might be worth checking.

Maybe I was being worked. Maybe Uncle Doj and Mother Gota were bound to start checking out the oddities they had noticed about my behavior in recent months. Maybe they were getting ready to do whatever Croaker suspected they were going to do. If he did anything more than just suspect.

He suspected everybody of something.

"The one who flies went out last night, Soldier of Darkness."

"Ah." She *was* trying to manipulate me. She knew I hated those enigmatic titles first employed by her father, Ky Dam. The old Speaker never explained them and Mother Gota would not waddle where her dad had refused to tread. "That *is* interesting." There had been no aerial sightings of the Howler for a while. He liked to use spells of concealment when he was aloft, though.

She wanted me to ask questions so she could toy with me and frustrate me. The information she had given was all I was going to get. Right now.

I refused to play her game. I turned to Thai Dei. "Did I just get promoted to honorary member of the tribe?"

He shrugged. He seemed mildly surprised that his mother had told me anything at all.

I did not rush right over to visit Smoke. If that was what the old woman wanted I meant to disappoint her in a big way. I tended to chores, helped Thai Dei work on our dugout, ate again, drank plenty, worked on the Annals for a while. I could change nothing that had happened during the night. And whatever that was, it had not been so earthshaking that it was an immediate threat.

One-Eye actually made it easy. Shortly after sundown he came over with a clay pot. "Soup's ready," he said. He sloshed the pot's contents. The stink of a really bad beverage quickly filled my dugout.

"All right!" I got up and followed him into the darkness.

53

"THAT WAS A STROKE OF LUCK, YOU SHOWING UP JUST THEN," I TOLD ONE-Eye. "I needed to get away." I relayed what Mother Gota had told me.

"How would she know that?"

I told him about spotting her and Uncle Doj during the night. "Maybe they spotted me, too."

"Thai Dei could've told them."

"I guess."

"You think it's important?"

"They make a special point of making sure I know, I'd better check it out. I didn't notice anything when I did my routine snooping."

One-Eye grunted. He looked thoughtful. "Goes to show you. No matter how well set up we are we're going to miss stuff because we don't know what to watch for."

Which was true. Things could be right there in the open and even with the advantage Smoke gave me I could miss them if I did not know to look.

There just was not enough time to look everywhere all the time.

I suggested, "Why don't you take some of your magic potion over to my in-laws? Screw up their thinking for a while."

"Thought they didn't touch the stuff."

"They're not supposed to. But I've seen Thai Dei take a tummy-warmer a time or three, to be sociable, and his mother would've developed a taste for it if Uncle Doj hadn't been there most of the time we were in Taglios. She'd sneak a few pints whenever he was away. She hasn't had a chance since we've been on the road."

"Very interesting." The little black man started rustling around. "Tell you what. I'll just go over there and keep them company while you're out. I'll tell them you're working."

He left before I finished my preparations. He lugged a slimy old wooden bucket with him. I muttered, "I got to get him to talk to Swan." Willow Swan made bad beer, too, but he did know a little about the brewer's art. Compared to One-Eye's product Willow's was ambrosia.

There was very nearly a warmth to Smoke when I took hold of him, as though some part of him sensed that he was no longer alone and was pleased. I took him directly to Overlook, sliding backward in time as we went, avoiding the ruins where the fires burned so I would not see myself. I had to shuffle forward and backward to find Mother Gota's crows. They were visible only briefly and were never obvious. They streaked in from the north, high above the fortress, then plummeted into Overlook like falling stones. There were no more than a dozen so any message they carried, either direction, would be severely limited. I expected greater numbers from what my mother-in-law had said.

I followed the last one down. The flock did not go near Longshadow's glowing towertop, where the Shadowmaster labored late over some esoteric text. They plunged into the darkness of a courtyard and entered the fortress through a door standing just a crack ajar. They muttered among themselves, uncomfortable with where they were. A sharp cry, broken off, nearly spooked them.

A voice whispered. I could see nothing but the vaguest shape in the darkness but recognized the Howler's aborted cry. I did not understand a word he said. I did not understand the crows, who took turns making noises that might have constituted a message. For me the critical piece of information was not included in the body of the message but in the existence of the message.

Soulcatcher and Howler were communicating.

I ran back in time another hour. Howler did nothing but sit there and wait. I jumped forward, planning to bracket him till I found something else interesting.

I had to advance only a few minutes beyond the arrival of the crows.

They stayed only briefly. Then Howler rustled back into the darkness. I drifted along behind him, tracking him by ear and by smell. Even in the ghostworld Howler had an air about him.

He stayed in darkness, away from routes Longshadow might use, till he reached a particular door. He knocked, which surprised me. Howler was the kind of guy who just invited himself in.

Narayan Singh opened the door a crack. Howler fought down a shriek. He was developing a talent for silence. Singh stepped back and allowed him to enter. Howler slipped in like a diminutive Deceiver on a deadly skulk. "It's time," he whispered.

Time for what?

Singh knew. He went to the Daughter of Night immediately. The kid was hunched up in front of a small fire, fanatically transcribing that first Book of the Dead. Looked to me like she was almost done. But who knew how long a book it was?

Singh seemed unsure how to approach the girl. He seemed unsure about a lot lately. He was close to superfluous and knew it.

Lady always would have a use for him, though.

He got the girl's attention. Gods, she was getting spooky! There was an aura about her, something you might call a glow of darkness. In that light her eyes seemed to shimmer like those of a big cat stealing toward your dying campfire. You were drowsing and she was hungry.

"It's time," Narayan told her, his whisper barely strong enough to stir the air.

The child nodded curtly. She made a tiny gesture. Narayan bowed, backed away.

There was no doubt who was in charge here, who ruled and who obeyed. Nor any doubt that she was herself controlled by a determined power. She extended her writing hand to Narayan for help rising. It was a claw she could not relax. Her legs were too stiff to unfold on their own. For a moment I pitied her, forgetting she was no true child.

Howler returned to the corridor. He drifted along ahead of Singh and the girl, scouting. Those two insisted on a lamp, which troubled Howler deeply. He muttered and fussed the whole time they were doing their sneak.

By a tortuous route that avoided Longshadow, the garrison and the enclave still held by Lady's soldiers, Howler led them to an unguarded piece of wall overlooking Kiaulune. Fires were burning down there. I was down there with Thai Dei, cold and disappointed with myself for having been dumb enough to insist on the eyewitness view.

I did not tag along in real time. I skipped forward, compressing events. Howler's destination was a small carpet concealed atop a domeless tower otherwise not in use. It was a new carpet, smaller than those we had seen before, black as the night around us. More evidence that you cannot know everything that is happening unless you want to spend every minute watching. I had not seen Howler working on this carpet.

With no words exchanged the three lifted it, walked to the edge of the parapet, lockstepped right off into space. They clambered aboard as they fell. Narayan moaned softly, eyes closed. The Daughter of Night was not impressed.

Howler took control in time not to smear them all over the rocks and wreckage below. He began sliding gently along just a few feet above the ground, trying to keep solid objects between himself and Overlook.

I took a quick look at Longshadow.

The Shadowmaster was restless. He had left his studies to stare vaguely toward Kiaulune. He sensed that something was happening but could not determine what.

Howler was playing around behind his ally's back.

I almost lost the little shit. I had to go back to the moment I left him to pick him up again. Soon afterward he drifted past a band of Mogaba's guerrillas in the ruins. The guerrillas did not see him but sensed him and panicked, thinking one of the Shadowmaster's pets was on the prowl. The racket they made drew the attention of nearby Taglians. The soldiers saw something shadowy drifting through the darkness. They wasted no time getting off a volley of fireballs.

Howler changed tactics.

He put on a burst of speed and employed a spell of concealment—neither of which he wanted to do that near Overlook. I would have lost him then had not chance favored me.

A wild fireball clipped the corner of the invisible carpet, which began to smolder. The spell of concealment did not include the glow as long as I stayed close.

Howler hauled ass. But he did stay so low that brush scraped the underside of his carpet. At one point he ploughed through some tents and clotheslines in one of the Prahbrindrah Drah's division camps. He was less concerned about being noticed by our side than by his own.

The race brought on a mild sense of exhilaration. I did not notice it immediately. Then it hit me that I was feeling more emotion than usual. Eventually I realized what I was feeling was some feeble spillover from Smoke.

Sometime during the flight we passed close enough to Uncle Doj and Mother Gota to be noticed but I saw no sign of them. We also swept over my own headquarters close enough to startle the sentries and horses.

I was not entirely surprised when Howler headed for a certain snow-choked canyon. Smoke did not notice until we were close enough to watch Howler land in front of a waiting Soulcatcher amidst an explosion of terrified crows.

In my amusement at the birds I relaxed just a little bit. And Smoke rebelled. *She is the darkness.*

What?

That was not me. But it did not happen again.

I backed out and up and away, content to go back to my flesh with the knowledge that Howler and Soulcatcher were up to some treachery that included Narayan Singh and the Daughter of Night.

The mood Smoke exuded now, if so feeble a thing could be called a mood, was terror.

And terror was out there roving the night, though it was not the terror that haunted my spirit steed.

I caught a whiff of corruption as I moved toward my flesh. I saw nothing. I stopped, experimented, moved in a direction away from the invisible source.

Maybe it caught a whiff of me. The stench grew stronger suddenly. I felt a sensation as of something onrushing. Light flickered in the ghost-world. I saw Kina's hideous face for an instant, looking directly toward me. But her eyes were blind. Her nostrils flared as though she was trying to catch my wind.

Smoke's terror might have been what she smelled. He fled in total panic. *She is the darkness.*

It was more feeble this time but it was there. It was not my imagination.

54

THE OLD MAN DID NOT SEEM SURPRISED TO HEAR THAT SOULCATCHER might be up to something with Howler. "I wasn't counting on it but it seemed like a possibility," he said. "They've worked together for ages. We may have Longshadow by the nuts."

"Somebody better have him by something if he controls the Shadowgate. The other thing is . . ." How could I put it?

"Other thing?"

"Smoke is showing signs of personality. I think." I told him what had happened.

"Damn! We don't want him waking up now." He thought for a while. "I don't see how we can stop it if it's happening."

"Better see One-Eye about that."

"Send him over. Wait! Don't leave. Tell me about the part of the fortress where Singh and the girl hide out."

It turned out this was more than a passing interest. He wanted maps.

I had that part of the place charted already. All I had to do was get the drawings from One-Eye's dugout. I brought the little wizard along. He kept grumbling about being wakened in the middle of the night. Once the Old Man had what he needed I shut the curtain to Smoke's alcove and went off to bed, leaving them to their schemes.

I did not escape Kina just by getting back to my flesh. She was waiting in my dreams. No sooner did I lie down than I found myself in the place of bones. Sahra was waiting.

I had no trouble recalling that she was an illusion. She looked nothing like the Sahra who lived so miserably at the Vinh Gao Ghang temple. This one was too young, too unworn, despite her pallor and the neck crook characteristic of a Deceiver victim.

I had begun to suspect that Kina was slow and unimaginative, although extremely powerful. How had she gotten the angle on Lady?

It was true Lady had not known what she was up against. And ignorance is a chink in the armor a knowledgeable enemy can exploit at will. And, of course, Kina was Queen of the Deceivers.

It no longer mattered how Kina had fooled Lady. What mattered now was that she did not fool me.

That thought left me unable to pretend that I was being deceived. I was not kind to the false Sahra.

Her flesh corrupted and melted right before me. The perfume of Kina, which was the stink of dead bodies, assailed me. A shadow in the grey distance coagulated into a four-armed black dancer a hundred feet tall whose pounding feet threw up clouds of bone dust as she stamped and whirled. Her fangs dripped venom. Her eyes burned like dark coals. Her jewelry of bones clattered and rattled. Her breath was the breath of disease.

The Daughter of Night rode upon her shoulder like a small second head. She was excited as a child making her first trip to the county fair.

Kina was not pleased with Murgen.

Armbones lifted out of the litter, grasping with fleshless fingers. Sahra's skeleton stumbled toward me. I willed myself away and, behold!, I drifted up and backward a few feet. I willed myself again and moved again, not far, amazed that I had control and bewildered because I had not tried to exercise it before.

Kina stopped dancing and stomped toward me. Her fangs grew longer. Her six breasts dripped poison. She put on another pair of arms. The Daughter of Night bounced excitedly on her shoulder, immune to the lure of gravity.

I willed myself away.

I had control but that was not my world. I could not run away faster than the world's creator. A great gleaming, taloned black hand swooped down. I dodged. A claw brushed me. I spun ass over appetite into darkness.

And I was in the cavern filled with old men caught in spiderwebs of ice. I drifted along past faces I not only knew I knew, I remembered the names that went with them.

I felt a panic like what you would feel if you were closed up in a small place in the dark. A buried-alive panic. I did not let it manage me. I tried, again, to manage myself and found I could move along the cavern if I willed it, like I did when I was walking with Smoke. I moved a whole lot slower here, though.

I tried moving out through the walls. Like the real world, and unlike riding Smoke, I was constrained pretty much by physical rules. My only way out of the cavern would be forward or back. Which did not make much sense if I was dreaming and had gotten in there without following any complicated route.

Was it possible physical laws operated only when I was in control? Could it be that I was unable to walk through walls because I never learned the knack in daily life?

I decided to go forward, up the slope of the cavern floor, because that is what I always did in the fragments of dream I remembered. As I did so I became aware of an inchoate anger growing behind me, as of something hunting that was frustrated. I did my best to speed up.

There was more in those ice caves than old men. There were more old men, none of them known to me. There were treasures. There was junk, like everything that ever fell down a crack ended up there. There were books.

Three huge tomes bound in worn, cracked dark leather rested on a large, long stone lectern, as though waiting for three speakers to step up and read at the same time. The first book was open to a page three-quarters of the way through. I caught only a glimpse of the page before some compelling force pushed me away. It was identical to the page the Daughter of Night had been transcribing when Narayan Singh interrupted her so they could go visit Soulcatcher. The calligraphy was superior, more colorful and ornate, but the child had missed nothing important, I was sure.

The anger behind me grew stronger. It seemed to be looking for a focus. I learned early never to volunteer. I moved on as fast as my will would carry me, wondering what sort of nightmare this was. Its most bizarre and fantastic elements were most real. Maybe it was a mirror of the waking world.

The anger kept gaining although I saw nothing when I looked back. It did not catch me. I do not think. But without actually passing through anything suddenly I was in another place. There was a full bowl of stars overhead but not even a sliver of moon. I was high in the air. I could distinguish no features on the ground below.

It was like ghostwalking without the ghost. Only I could not just tell Smoke where to go and get there almost instantly. I could move, it seemed, though it was hard to tell. . . . I had to have landmarks, I realized. I pushed back my panic.

I thought. I did have information. I knew up and down. I had a full field of stars overhead, so numerous they almost overwhelmed the out-standing constellations normally used for navigation. Trouble was, I had not studied the southern skies closely. Any astronomical navigation I did would be only slightly better than a guess.

I caught a faint whiff of corrupt flesh. That whipstroke got me moving toward a cluster of stars I vaguely recalled hanging close to the northern horizon during the spring. There were three of them in a flat triangle, all bright. The star at the peak of the triangle waxed and waned. Many legends attended it, most of them unpleasant. I was not intimate with them.

From that altitude I could see a fourth star in the constellation, equally bright, below the other three. I recalled seeing that formation when the Company was still far north of Taglios.

How high was I? Or was I somewhere far north of Kiaulune?

I stopped moving forward and slanted down toward the earth. I found myself over a region where agriculture was extremely orderly, commu-nal, making the most efficient use of man, animal and equipment, various operations having been laid out in a circle around a central manor with hamlets and single dwellings strung out along the spokes of wheels. Preparations for spring planting had begun although there were no work-ers in the fields at night.

I passed over circle after circle. The ground between had been left wild. I suppose it supported game and provided timber and charcoal and firewood.

I had heard of the region. It was in the Shadowlands west of Kiaulune. Longshadow had been experimenting with agricultural effi-ciencies in an effort to produce more with fewer workers so he could free up manpower to work construction on Overlook and serve in his armies.

I was not all that far from my own gang.

I worked my way eastward. After what seemed like hours I spied the glow from fires burning in the ruins of Kiaulune. I found my own part of our encampment, then my own shelter. I was comfortable enough with my condition to do a little experimenting now.

It took only moments to learn that while I could not will myself through a wall, or even the blankets One-Eye had hung for a doorway, or the side of a tent, I could slide my point of view through a crack or hole too small for a mouse or snake.

I could not go back or forth in time. I was confined to the now of my sleeping flesh.

I had control of the dream. It seemed real. What I saw of the camp was exactly what the camp should have been like while I was sleeping. My imagination was not good enough to make up a whole dream world that mimicked the real world exactly. A big question occurred.

Would I be able to do this again? Would getting here always be out-side my control, the way it had been when I kept tumbling off the wall of today into the horrors of Dejagore?

If this was going to be one-time I had better use it for all it was worth.

I snaked back out into a cold I did not feel. For a second I thought about heading for the plain but just the thought stirred up an instant, pow-erful revulsion. Maybe later.

I went toward the mountains instead.

Spying on Soulcatcher would do. Up close. Without disturbing the crows, I discovered. They remained asleep. So did their mistress.

Her company had left. I was not going to find out a damned thing.

I could go over to Overlook and see what everybody was doing. . . . I saw the faintest hint of light in the east. Dawn was on its way. And I began to feel a compulsion to head for the safety of my flesh. That drive grew stronger as the light did the same.

I headed for my body wondering if I was a dreaming vampire now.

Mother Gota was awake already. Though Soulcatcher had not been able, Ky Gota seemed to sense me somehow. She turned when I weaseled inside, looked almost directly at me, frowned when she saw nothing, then shuddered the way you do when a chill runs down your spine.

She went back to her cooking. I noted that she was preparing more food than she, Thai Dei and I could possibly eat all day. I supposed she planned to take some out to Uncle Doj.

55

"YOU LOOK LIKE SHIT," ONE-EYE TOLD ME OVER BREAKFAST.

"Thanks for the boost."

"What's up?"

"Bad dreams last night." He did not know what I had been going through. I chose not to share everything now but I did practice my Fors-berger long enough to tell him, "It looks like our friend the crow woman is up to something with her old pal Howler, our favorite Deceiver and the kid."

Both Thai Dei and Mother Gota glanced at me sharply. I had used the Taglian for "Deceiver," *tooga.* It was the same in Nyueng Bao.

"And old Longshadow thinks he's got nothing to worry about."

"Yeah. The Old Man always says even paranoids sometimes got somebody trying to stab them in the back." Usually when I let him know I thought he was overdoing the paranoia himself.

"That kind of thing is nice to know but how can we use it?"

"Not my problem. I just work here. The Captain gets to make the decisions. That's why he's the Captain." Just for the fun of it I slipped in the Taglian for "captain," *jamadar*. Thai Dei and Mother Gota looked me over again. In the context of the Deceivers *jamadar* means more than just "captain." It indicates a leader of a band, which is like a small nation of Deceivers. The only Deceiver *jamadar* now known to be alive was Narayan Singh, who had become *jamadar* of *jamadars* before the destruction of his cult.

They would think we were talking about the living legend, the saint who still walked the earth on his goddess's behalf.

I tucked the last of my breakfast away, thanked Mother Gota, got up and left the dugout. Thai Dei followed me. I told him, "I'm just going to see the Captain. If you want to you can stay and work on the house." We called our hole in the ground the house now.

Thai Dei shook his head. He had gotten lax about bodyguarding me lately. I did not feel neglected.

Time has a way of blunting the sharpest edge of determination.

I waited a moment for One-Eye to join us but he did not come out. More and more the little shit seemed perfectly willing to invite himself to my family meals rather than go to any trouble on his own.

I should be surprised after all these years?

Croaker looked about as happy as I felt. His night had been no bed of roses, either. He grumbled, "What is it this time?"

"Did a little dreaming last night. Went to hell and came back and then went out roaming without using Smoke at all." I gave him the unhappy details.

"Could you do that again?"

"I been falling through rabbit holes in space and cracks in time for over a year. Maybe I'm getting the hang of it."

"We wouldn't need Smoke."

"Especially since he's threatening to wake up." I must have had a nasty look on my face because he raised an eyebrow. I said, "It'd be fun to watch him try to get used to the new world he'd wake up in."

Croaker smirked. "You'd want to stand upwind. He'd shit his guts out when he saw how far we've come. By the by, as long as you're here, it'd be handy if you'd go see Lady. I sent her your maps. She's going to pick off Narayan and catch the girl. If *anybody* asks you about the maps all you know is that we captured a couple of Mogaba's officers who used to belong to Overlook's garrison."

I grunted, not entirely thrilled. I would not be able to lie to Lady convincingly.

"Experiment with this. I have to know if we can get along without Smoke."

"I already know about one severe handicap."

"Uhm?"

"I can't travel back in time when I'm on my own."

He sucked a bunch of air in, blew it out. "Wouldn't you know? There had to be a catch. Smoke's got job security."

"You said you'd take to One-Eye about keeping him from waking up."

"He wasn't much help."

"Is he ever?"

"If you see him, send him over."

"Right." I got out of there, paused outside to stare across at the encampment below Overlook's wall. I said, "The boss wants me to go over there and show Lady how to manage her business."

It was a bright, sunshiny day. There was enough breeze to carry the smoke and stench away. Thai Dei observed, "Maybe some of the ground will dry up."

Most of the snow had melted. It was springtime. Around Kiaulune that meant mud season. Mud would mean bugs eventually.

I wondered if melting snows would cause floods that would chase Soulcatcher out of her hideout.

It was time spring came to Kiaulune. It had arrived already everywhere else.

56

"I FIGURED YOU'D CRAWL OUT OF THE WOODWORK PRETTY SOON," WILLOW Swan grumbled when I joined the crowd around Lady. Her staff were munching rolls one-handed while she told them what she wanted done so she could catch Narayan. "You turn up every time things get nasty."

Blade showed me a smile. "The man needs a girlfriend."

"Thought he had one, only she already has a boyfriend."

"That's where she was last night, eh?"

"Maybe." It might explain why Croaker was so damned groggy this morning.

That man just had one adventure after another.

Lady was saying, "There were shadows in there before but Jarwaral says they haven't been a problem lately. These charts supposedly show us where we can find the shadowweavers—if we want. I want. We'll take them out before we go after the Deceiver. Ah! Murgen."

"She had to spot me," I muttered to Blade. I looked for the inevitable crows. They were notable for their scarcity. The couple I did see acted like they were blind drunk.

Lady had employed some spell to diminish the flow of information to her sister.

"You stand out in a crowd," Swan told me. "The women always notice you."

Lady continued, "Come here. The Captain sent these charts. What do you know about them?"

"They're supposed to be reliable." A hundred percent—unless there had been some heavy renovations in the last few hours.

"They aren't very extensive."

Bitch and gripe, bitch and gripe. Nobody is ever satisfied. "Want I should go dig the guy up and let you do some kind of necromantic thing on him?"

She gave me such an ugly look that for a moment I was afraid she would call my bluff. But she did not doubt me, she just was not getting the kind of fear and respect she expected. She relaxed, told me, "Except for the locations of the shadowweaver hideouts and where Singh is holing up there isn't much here we didn't know already."

Which stuff was what the exercise was all about, woman. "There's a little more. Longshadow is almost always locked up in this tower here, doing whatever he does instead of giving us grief. Howler has an apartment somewhere around here. He keeps two carpets on a flat place over here and a little-bitty, brand-new one rolled up right beside his bed."

Lady gave me a piercing look. How could I know that?

I told her, "The day he got here Howler started covering his ass in case his partner turned on him someday."

"Uhm?" she grunted. "Howler would. Particularly in view of what Longshadow tried to do to his previous associates." She turned her attention to the charts. But I knew she was not satisfied. She could not be satisfied when somebody else knew anything that she did not.

She beckoned Isi, Ochiba and Sindawe closer. The Nar generals worked well with her. They did not do so with the Old Man. Croaker could not trust them even though they stuck with the Company against Mogaba. "Should we do this in the daytime or at night?"

Ochiba, a man I had heard speak maybe five times in that many years, said, "It won't matter in there."

"True. But I prefer by daylight. For the impact on morale."

"It's daytime now," Swan observed.

I told Blade, "You can't get anything past this guy."

Lady glanced at Willow. "You want to see how well your Guards can perform in there?"

"I'd love to. But that isn't their job."

Their job was to look out for the Prince and Princess, neither of whom he or they had been near in recent times.

Everybody there had that thought at the same time I did. Everybody gave Swan a long look. He reddened.

"Sindawe, you're my second choice." Lady stepped aside so the tall Nar could move closer to the charts. I had kept wriggling forward. Now I could see that there was more than one set. Only one was the one I had prepared. The other, structured differently, may have been put together by Lady's people based on what her soldiers had found inside Overlook.

The Nar officer stared for a while. "We ought to rotate fresh troops in before we do anything else."

Isi agreed. "The men inside have been there a long time, under a lot of pressure."

Lady said, "I'll approve that."

Sindawe said, "We should add numbers for this. Once we start moving there won't be any point to pretense. Will there?"

"Probably not. Succeed or fail, going ahead will attract some close scrutiny. And the Captain hasn't given us the option of not going ahead. Has he, Murgen?"

I shrugged. "He'll always defer to the commander on the scene. You know that. As long as you can make a good argument."

"We don't have an option, then. We've been stalling in hopes somebody else would come up with a workable solution to the Longshadow dilemma."

"What's that?" I asked.

"The fact that we can't kill him. You know that, don't you?"

I knew that. What I did not know was how they planned to send fresh troops into Overlook.

Sindawe said, "We ought to pursue every phase of the effort at once. Here, here, toward these shadowweaver hideouts. Here, toward the Deceiver's holeup. And a general raid against the garrison and servant population, too. So they don't interfere in our other efforts."

"Go for Longshadow, too," Lady suggested. "You might get lucky."

I was missing something. There was a hundred-foot wall over there, not nearly as shiny as it used to be, and absent some of its pretty towers, but not one foot shorter than it ever was. Why were these people not impressed? "You all walk through walls or something?"

"If that's convenient," Lady replied.

"We'll crawl," Sindawe told me.

Soon enough I discovered something else that I had missed while doing my all-seeing thing in the ghostworld—because I had not been looking.

57

THEY HAD A TUNNEL UNDER THE WALL. THROUGH THE FOUNDATION, REALLY. But just a wormhole of a thing. A guy my size had to slither on his belly like a snake. I know because I did it.

Fool.

Why did I have to do it in the flesh? I could have gone back and ridden Smoke. I could have seen everything with no claustrophobia, no bruised elbows or knees, no pops in the snot box from the heels of the clown in front of me. No weaseling through the farts and fear smells of the hundred little vegetarians snaking along ahead of me, raising the dead with all the clatter of their weaponry.

Where were the Shadowmaster's boys? All this racket, they had to be chuckling while they sharpened their swords. They were going to have Tals for their afternoon snack.

The tunnel had been created in part by a liberal application of Lady's fireball tools. In places its walls were still hot. It was completely new. All I saw when I got to its nether end was a gang of raggedy-ass Taglians who had been on the inside way too long. They looked like they had had a glimpse of heaven but a bunch of assholes like me were blocking the way.

I was the last guy in my string. Number one hundred one. When I crawled out of his way number one of the guys being relieved dove into the hole and slithered away.

Only twenty got to leave for each hundred who came in. The twenty were very enthusiastic. But nobody heard the clatter upstairs.

Ochiba, Isi and Sindawe began choosing up teams to go thump on Longshadow's guys. Sindawe always was decent to me, even when he worked for Mogaba. He was willing to change his ways, though. "Would you like to lead an attack group, Standardbearer?"

"Obviously you have me confused with somebody who thinks he's a hero."

"You could make big points by catching Narayan Singh."

"I don't need big points. Talk to Blade or Swan."

Sindawe chuckled. "You won't see them in here."

"Why not?"

"They aren't Company. Lady wouldn't trust them in a tight place."

Interesting. She *would* trust these Nar.

Croaker did not. Not one hundred percent. Never.

Sindawe read me plain. He smiled. "This place is tight enough."

"Yeah. I still ain't going to be a hero. I'll just come along behind and watch so I can write it down right."

"Sin," Isi called. "Got to move. The garrison knows something's going on."

The Shadowlanders were slower than I expected. Sindawe and his pals were faster. About as quickly as it took to think it they led three groups off to the attack, going like they were right at home although none of them had been inside Overlook before.

Overlook inside was no shiny white marvel. Wherever we were, it was way down deep in the ground where it was dirty and damp and unpleasant creatures with two, four or six more legs than me lurked in every shadow. Thai Dei did not like it at all.

He had needed several hundred-man shifts just to find nerve enough to come inside.

"Move back," I growled at the troops waiting to go out. "For now this tunnel only runs one way. Thai Dei, slap that moron up side the head. Then thump that fool sitting in the mouth of the tunnel gawking. Let's go, people. There's a war going on in here. We don't have time for lolligagging." I was turning into a real top kick. Now if I could get the vocabulary working.

"Lolligagging" does not exist in Taglian. The word got me a lot of dazed looks. The pithier nouns, verbs and adjectives do exist, mostly, with much of the usual impact. Religious insults work real good, too.

"You," I said to a head being birthed by the tunnel, "pass the word back that we're engaged. We need people in here as fast as we can get them."

Sindawe reappeared. He was the commanding officer for this death-dance. He was amused by my barking. But he was politic. He was a big general only where the Taglian troops were concerned. The day might come when I was his boss inside the Company. He told me, "There's still the attack on Longshadow to launch. You could spearhead that one."

I recalled the black spear One-Eye made specially for sticking Shadowmasters. Be a handy tool if I was to do something dumb like go after Longshadow. "I'll let somebody else have that honor. I don't want to hog everything."

Tell the truth, the place had me spooked. The smell of damp stone, vermin and old fear, combined with the cold and bad light, recalled too strongly all my nightmares about old men trapped forever in caverns where never-seen spiders spun webs and cocoons of ice.

Coming inside Overlook had been a dumb idea. I suspected that when I made the decision to visit, but I did not listen to the little voice of fear because all those guys like Blade and Swan were hanging around grumbling about how the boys from headquarters never risk their cute and precious butts when the blood and shit start flying.

It was the usual stuff. I started the same sort of crying about an hour after I took the oath. I just did not want to be the guy the troops thought had spent his last thirty years with his head up his butt.

My message reached the other end of the tunnel. People started arriving at double speed.

I had no idea if Longshadow and Howler realized we had a way into Overlook. They did not act like they were desperate to plug an unexpected breach in the wall. Their response was angry and vigorous but only with the power you would expect if they thought the bunch already inside were getting frisky.

Our people did not reach Longshadow. Which was no surprise. The surprise of the century would have been if the crazy son of a bitch *had* come floating belly up.

Likewise Soulcatcher's little screaming buddy the Howler. Except that Isi, who was running that try, was clever enough to know he just might not be one hundred percent successful at squashing the little shit. So while he kept Howler dancing saving his ass from fifty guys with bamboo poles, five other guys burned his flying carpets. All but the little one that he kept right beside him. And Isi would have gotten that one, too, if Howler had had the balls to chase Isi's men the way Isi wanted. What Isi failed to appreciate was that very few men were hung as heavy as him.

However she managed it Lady had a good grasp of events inside the fortress. She recognized the failures where Longshadow and her former employee were concerned. She also knew, somehow, that Narayan Singh and the Daughter of Night, by coincidence or the grace of their deity, happened to be away from their quarters when our gang turned up to collect them.

Their servants were not so lucky.

Most of those who had chosen to come into Overlook, either to serve the Shadowmaster or just to be safe from pestilence, hunger, or other terrors of the world, were not as lucky as their master. Ochiba took the garrison completely off guard. He and his men must have had trouble hearing their parents when they were growing up. They never got a grasp on the concepts of mercy or noncombatants.

Which I really did not get a good look at till much later. After I got out of that slaughterhouse. After the casualties started coming in to the tunnel head, for evacuation if the chance came. After Lady stopped sending men in because she thought that would be a waste. After I got me back out of there, in one uncarved piece, dragging one end of a wounded Taglian while Thai Dei pushed the other, with the Taglian complaining all the way and the tunnel about a mile longer going out than it had been coming in. After coming up into free air only to find Willow Swan and Blade there wondering aloud why I was not back inside collecting Longshadow's ears.

"Didn't want to steal your chance to count coup. Sindawe's got you all set up. All you guys got to do is pick up a couple of sharp knives and slide on in there. You can collect Howler's scalp while you're at it. You'll find them waiting for you together, I think. Up by the Shadowmaster's tower."

"You ready?" Blade asked Swan. "I got my knife." Blade had a grin on. He was perfectly willing to give Swan just as much crap as he gave me.

Lady came striding toward us. She was decked out in the complete Lifetaker armor. Threads of red fire slithered over its black, hideous surface faster than the eye could follow. Taglians thought the Lifetaker image matched one of Kina's Destroyer avatars. Despite what had been done to her and her daughter, plenty of people still thought she was a creature of the dark goddess. Sometimes those people included me.

There was a connection for sure. She would not discuss it.

But I did not tell her about me and Smoke. So we were even.

"Any success to report?" Her voice was a bass boom rolling down a long, cold tunnel. "Anything at all?"

"Lots of dead people. Both sides. A lot of them aren't people we especially wanted dead. But I'd say they've only got one way left to hang on to the place."

"Which is?"

"Loose the shadows." I sort of croaked it out. I did not want to be a fortune-teller but that was a future that did not require a lot of divination. "Unless these two get to Longshadow first." I indicated Swan and Blade.

Lady was not in a mood for banter.

She never was. The woman had about as much humor in her as my mother-in-law.

She did enjoy a good impaling, though.

She did the thing that created the cyclone of light blades and turned it loose among the taller towers. It drifted around on its own, doing plenty of damage and keeping Longshadow and Howler too busy to finish off her troops.

58

"THAT'S THE SECOND TIME," THE OLD MAN GROWLED. "I THOUGHT I GOT through to you after the adventure in Kiaulune." He was pissed off because I had gone inside Overlook. "You take Smoke down there and find out what the Shadowmaster and Howler are doing."

When Thai Dei and I had gotten back we had found Croaker already barking and snarling at a gang of couriers. Obviously he thought Lady had started something the rest of us were going to regret.

I got the feeling Soulcatcher clued in late and was about as thrilled as the Captain. Crows appeared everywhere. They were unpleasant, even for Catcher's agents. They swooped around shooting crow shit everywhere.

"When you're done checking on Longshadow and Howler I want you to start identifying the whereabouts of every man of ours."

"Ours?"

"The Company. Old Crew. Nar. I want to get everybody together. Real soon now."

"You got it."

"Of course. But add in a dab of common sense, Murgen. To get to Khatovar the Company needs a standardbearer. Probably more than it'll ever need a Captain or Lieutenant."

"I've said it before and I'll say it again. If anybody had a clue what you were up to it's just possible they could do the things you want done when you want them done." I walked away before we squabbled in front of the troops.

Longshadow was taking it out on Howler. And Howler was getting him even more pissed off by not paying a lot of attention. He was witching up some colorful little construct out of thin air. I had to study it a while before I recognized it as a representation of the areas of Overlook that were in our side's hands. It was a complicated little cyan and magenta mess—with a tail that dipped through the foundations of the wall to Lady's positions outside.

He did nothing to restrain his screams. Several came in quick succession, howls that seemed to have a little extra emotion behind them.

The third howl triggered something inside Longshadow's head. He shut up. He adjusted his mask, leaned forward to stare at Howler's construct. He reached out with fingers as skinny as spider legs despite being inside a glove, poked at the tail leading to the outside. "How did she manage that? That should not have been possible." His lunacy, his rant, vanished like mist in the morning sun. It was almost as if his reason had cleared. "The stone cannot be worked."

"That's Senjak out there, if you'll recall. She'll work the stone the same way you did."

Longshadow made a noise like a cat's growl. I thought his moment of lucidity had passed. I thought he was about to have an all-time fit. He fooled me. "Find the Deceiver and his brat. They need to be here, inside this tower, before midnight. If they want to survive."

Howler replied with an interrogative grunt.

"I have no use for them anymore. I owe them nothing. They have done nothing for me. But I will give them this opportunity to survive."

I did not wait around to learn what happened next.

"What're you doing back already?" Croaker demanded when I sat up. "You haven't been out long enough—"

"Excuse me, boss. I've already got a mother-in-law. Yes, I *was* out there long enough to hear Longshadow say he's going to turn the shadows loose tonight."

Croaker shut his mouth. I hurried through the information. He said, "You're right. He didn't say shadows in that many words but it can't be anything else. Get back to it. I'll round up One-Eye and get the word out."

"How long do we have?"

"I don't know. I'm not sure what time it is now. Just get going."

"I'll need water and food brought in. The water should be sweet."

"Go."

I went.

59

I CAME BACK TO FLESH EVERY FEW MINUTES TO REPORT THE WHEREABOUTS of those Company brothers I could locate. The Old Man sent warnings to those he could, telling them to get over to the division at the Shadowgate.

Wagons were on the move soon, leaving Lady's crude factories with stocks of bamboo her workers had been able to reload. The supply seemed woeful to me.

I darted everywhere. When I thought it would not hurt I fluttered northward. Swarms of crows came and went from the ravine where Soulcatcher holed up. I skipped backward in time, watched the Old Man and, sure enough, I found a time when he whispered to those two huge crows of his and they promptly flapped off to gossip with the crazy sister. I could not get Smoke anywhere near her, of course, and anytime I pushed even a little I got that tickling *she is the darkness* sensation.

I got a ghost of the same thing when I swarmed off to see what the Daughter of Night was doing, though Smoke showed no reluctance to move a little closer. The child was writing furiously, her little face contorted in pain. She was working on a different volume. This one she had only just begun.

"Oh, shit!" She finished the first one already? Croaker needed to know that. We might be in deeper shit than I had thought.

Where *was* the Book? I did not see it anywhere. I had better find out.

I took a dive into the past.

I found the Daughter of Night crying. I found Narayan Singh stunned by that. He had not seen that before and did not know how to comfort her, though he had had children of his own in another time, another world, before the Black Company came to Taglios.

I pushed back farther, to discover the cause of this bizarre circumstance. I could think of a hundred unlikely candidates I expected to see cry before that grim midget broke down.

It started when she and Singh returned to their apartment after having escaped it only a step ahead of Lady's raiders. Though forewarned the child had been too busy writing to pay close attention and had waited almost too long.

Their exit had been so hasty they had had to leave the Book behind.

So, I thought, some lad from Lady's gang realized it was important and decided to take it back to the boss. I would have suspected Swan or Blade had they been inside Overlook.

I was surprised again when I did identify the culprit.

Howler. The little snake managed to slither into those quarters while supposedly driving our men back, while Narayan and the girl were suffering the effects of a mild disorientation spell not fifty feet away. He made the Book vanish.

The screaming wizard must have feared that he could be seen from afar because he pulled a bunch of stunts and used a handful of spells, over the next several hours, to make sure the Book got lost to everybody but himself.

He left a blank book behind. It was a twin of the one he took.

Curious. How did Howler know about the Book? I checked my memories against whatever Smoke could find fast. Yep. Neither the kid nor Singh mentioned it to anybody. Longshadow's people did tell him that they had asked for writing stuff but the Shadowmaster had not passed that on to Howler.

I knew about the Book. I had told Croaker about it. Howler had visited Soulcatcher. The Old Man communicated with Catcher.

Could it be?

If I got a chance to dream my way around there again I might try to find out. . . . Shit! I could see only what was happening right now.

I ripped out of there, went back to my flesh. I was starving and thirsty when I came out.

"About time," One-Eye told me.

I guzzled water. "Where's Croaker?"

"Out making sure everybody knows they need to keep their shelters buttoned up tight tonight. Trying to get those shadow-repellent candles out where we're thin on bamboo poles."

"Oh." I ate for a few minutes. My manners were not upper-class. Then I asked, "You got any idea what's going on between the Captain and Soulcatcher?"

"I didn't know anything was."

I groaned, drank some more water. "You blind?"

He shrugged. "What did I miss?"

"Those two have been swapping information all along. That don't sound that smart to me."

"You figure the Old Man ain't smart enough to deal with her?"

That was exactly what I figured. Soulcatcher was a slippery old fish when Croaker's grandfather was wetting his diapers. "Me? Doubt the Captain in any way? How could I do such a thing?"

"Not you. You're a veritable worshipper of the cow flops he walks on. You got a reason to be in a panic? Soon as we get straightened out here I want to get back to my hole. I've got some suckers coming over for a game of tonk."

That was One-Eye. The world was coming to an end and his main interest was cheating somebody at cards. "Tell the boss Howler snatched the copy of the book his kid was writing. He left her a blank so she could start over." I took a deep drink while One-Eye stared at me dumbly, waiting for me to explain what I meant. I told him, "He'll understand."

"Everybody's got to keep secrets from everybody else. So the only people who know what's going on are their enemies."

I grunted as I turned back to Smoke. One-Eye had a point.

As we neared Lady I sensed Smoke's *she is the darkness* emotion, not very strongly. He must have a thing about females in general since he seemed to respond the same to all of them.

Lady had received word but she did not seem troubled. Longshadow loosing his pets had been a concern of hers for years. Her men were trained. What needed preparing was kept at a state of near readiness all the time. Her division might succumb but not through their own failings.

That had been Lady's way from the dawn of time.

I yielded to temptation and sped off to the north. I told myself I wanted to see if I could find Goblin and Mogaba. It would be good to know how exposed they might be in the coming mess. But I wanted to go on, past there, a long way. All the way to the wellsprings of my heart.

I might not get to see her again, ever. This might be the last night of my life.

60

GOBLIN WAS ALMOST IMPOSSIBLE TO FIND DESPITE THERE BEING CROWS wobbling all over above the south face of the Dandha Presh. His handiwork was obvious, though. Anywhere that the locals were insane enough to cooperate with Mogaba, Goblin's band had pillaged and burned and made examples. Mogaba's troops had done the same to everyone dim enough to cooperate with Goblin or any of our allies. From a strictly practical, aftermath sort of viewpoint it was impossible to tell who had provided which instructional display.

The locals did not seem to care who was fighting whom, or why. They knew they did not see any good guys or bad guys anywhere. During the few minutes I took to dip around in time I saw several villages and manors attacked. The nearer the present the violence occurred the more likely its victims were to resist—whoever came calling.

The forvalaka participated in some of Goblin's night raids. Crows came and went when she did, but a few always did so even if the big cat was elsewhere.

They visited Mogaba, too. Apparently. Longshadow had provided Mogaba with an arsenal of mystical objects capable of distracting a seeker like myself, of averting any other watching eye.

But this was not getting me to what I wanted to see.

I did take a moment to check in on Cordy Mather's party. Old Cordwood was on the south side of the Dandha Presh now, moving slowly and moving at all only because the mountains remained incredibly inhospitable.

Cordy did not have crow trouble. That I could see.

I was startled, though, to discover that a flock of the little monsters had nested amongst the crags and crumbles of the exterior of the Palace at Trogo Taglios. Though that should not have amazed me so, on reflection. Events in the Palace would be of particular interest to Soulcatcher, who liked to push her nose deep into everybody's business.

I was too eager to visit the swamp to waste time rooting around in the Radisha's secrets. *She is the darkness.* She was still holding a lot of meetings with priests and leading men. Our books remained hidden where we had left them.

I was surprised that the Radisha was making no great effort to find Smoke anymore. I did not believe that she had forgotten him.

But I wanted to travel on. Banh Do Trang should have had time to reach Sahra.

Oh, he had. He had! For the sheer power of the self-tantalization I joined him late in his journey and followed him as he approached the Temple of Ghanghesha. Shortly before he reached the place he stepped off the trail, which was just a raised path meandering through swamp converted to rice paddy, and took time to adopt a disguise using materials he had brought along. A little more dirt, a change in the hang of his hair, the quick adoption of a raggedy orange robe, and he became a wandering mendicant of one of the Gunni cults. Their vows-of-poverty missionaries went everywhere. Even the Nyueng Bao tolerated them. Their holiness was beyond question, however mad they might be as individuals.

I have always found the religious tolerance of the southerners amazing and disconcerting, though it was really only an ancient habit predicated on the fact that no religious community was strong enough to show the rest the errors in their thinking at swordspoint.

Trang continued on his way. He did the mendicant part very well. I think he may have played it before, maybe while first visiting Taglios. Nyueng Bao were not welcomed warmly there. They were too arrogant a minority.

No matter. Trang was admitted to the temple. The older priests seemed to know the character he pretended to be.

Trang did not approach Sahra immediately. In fact, he waited till evening before contriving to stumble into her. They had encountered one another several times during the day. Sahra had not recognized him.

He made his apologies in softly whispered Taglian while Sahra was still too rattled by the collision to give herself away by jumping.

I did not hear what Trang said. I did see Sahra's eyes focus and fill with surprised life. She accepted his profuse apologies and went her way.

That night she left the door to her cubicle unlatched. She indulged in the extravagance of leaving her candle burning.

Trang arrived very late, when the only priests still awake were the three making the regular midnight offering to Ghanghesha in hopes of inspiring the god to grant the world another complete daily cycle free from calamity and despair.

Trang scratched at the door to Sahra's cell. It was a crude wicker thing that would not have thwarted a determined woodchuck. More a symbol of the thing than the thing itself, really. A rag curtain hung behind it, containing the light. Sahra let Trang inside, gestured him to a seat upon her mat. The old man sat, taking his due. He looked up at Sahra with liquid eyes. I knew he understood the substance of the message he carried even though he was far too honorable a man to have read it.

In that instant I nearly panicked. I had tried some to teach Sarie to read but she had not picked up much. How would she be able to . . . ? She would ask Trang, of course. And then I would find out just how good a friend the old man was. If his secret self sided with Uncle Doj . . .

Sahra's manners were perfection, which maddened me. Even though she could not serve tea or indulge in any of the other ceremonial delays Nyueng Bao use to avoid getting to the point, she managed to delay the crisis of the visit for fifteen minutes.

"I have a message," Trang said at last, in a whisper that could not have been heard by someone listening outside the door, even had that eavesdropper spoken Taglian. "It was delivered into my hand by a Stone Soldier who carried it north all the way from the last stronghold of the Shadowmasters. He insisted that it be delivered to you. Here."

Sahra lowered herself to her knees before him. It was difficult for her. She was getting big. She met his eye, frowning slightly. She did not speak. I do not think she trusted herself to open her mouth.

"The Soldier of Darkness knew where you were. He knew what name you were using. This when I myself did not suspect that you had survived the *tooga*. Your family are cunning in their cruelty."

Sahra nodded. Still she did not trust herself to speak.

Gods, she was beautiful!

"They knew from half a world away, child. This frightens me. These are terrible times and terrible people walk among us. Some of them we cannot recognize. The Bone Warriors appear no more frightful than any others, yet—"

"A message, Uncle?" She used that word as an honorific. Trang was not related in any way.

"Yes. I'm sorry. I grow so frightened whenever I spend too much time thinking."

Sahra took my letter, stared at it a moment, reluctant to find out what was inside. But she was happy, too, I could see. Her husband's brother-hood knew and cared. "Who brought this?"

"He did not give a name. He is very young. He is Jaicuri. Vehdna. Low caste."

"He has a scar that makes his left eyelid droop so when you see him from that side it looks like he's having trouble staying awake?"

"Indeed. You know him?"

"I remember him." She turned my letter over again.

"Do it, child."

"I'm scared."

"Fear is the mind-killer."

Damn! All of a sudden he sounded like Uncle Doj back when he was giving me fencing and fighting lessons. Was old Trang another one of these secret priests?

Sahra opened the message. She stared down at what I had written, in big, careful, clear characters. Finally, she said, "Read it for me, please, Uncle."

Trang stuck a little finger into his left ear and dug around amongst the tufts. That old man had more hair there than on top of his head. He scanned my message, which he held in his other hand. He took a while to digest and think. Then he looked up at Sahra. He opened his mouth to speak, suffered a thought, looked around as though startled.

It had occurred to him that it was, apparently, somehow, possible for us to see what was happening inside the temple of Ghanghesha. It had occurred to him that this was a moment that would interest us very much. Particularly a Soldier of Darkness name of Murgen.

"It purports to be a letter from your husband." He hesitated just a fraction of a heartbeat as he decided to leave out the adjective "foreign."

"It is. I know his hand. What does it say?"

"It says he isn't dead. That they told him you were dead. That he knows where you are and what your circumstances are because a great magic has been made available to him. That he will come to you as soon as the Shadowmaster is crushed."

That was actually pretty close to what I had written.

Sahra started to cry.

Sahra? I wanted to hold her. She was always the strong one. The disasters that overtook her could not break her. Always she soldiered on. No tears for Sahra, ever.

I did not like seeing her emotionally distressed.

I drifted nearer Trang. He shuddered, looked around. "That's not all he said. He said he loves you and he hopes you'll forgive him for the failure that let this happen."

Sahra stifled her tears. She nodded. "I know he loves me. The question is, why do the *gods* hate me? I've done nothing to harm them."

"The gods don't think the way we do. They scheme schemes in which a life is only a flicker, just a second in a century. They do not ask us if we want to participate, perhaps as an alternative to happiness. They use us as we use the beasts of forest, swamp and field. We're the clay they sculpt."

"Uncle Trang, I don't need a homily. I need my husband. And I need to be free of the machinations of old men. . . ." Sahra started. She gestured, indicating that someone was outside, that Trang should be quiet.

I drifted out of Sahra's cell.

A priest stood a step away from her door, poised in uncertainty. He must have heard something as he was passing. He glanced both ways along the unlighted hall, down at his own small lamp, then moved to Sahra's door and cocked an ear.

I swooped in close, poured all my anger into my will and tried to butt heads with him.

He spun around. He started to shake. He hurried away. I could scare more than birds if I got mad enough.

I went back inside. Sahra wanted Trang to send a reply. Her speaking the words were all the reply I needed although I would look forward to the note as a physical confirmation of our eternal connection, an icon to carry with me till we saw one another again. Trang agreed but he chose his words carefully. He kept looking around like he thought the place was haunted.

He asked, "How is your pregnancy going?"

"That is one thing I do very well, without great effort or trouble, Uncle. I have babies."

"This one will be bigger than your first two. Your husband is a big man."

"Do you expect the child to be a devil, too?"

Trang smiled thinly. "Not in the sense others might mean. But in the sense of Hong Tray's prophecy, probably. Your grandmother was a wise woman. Her prophecies all come to pass—though not always in the manner we imagined when she offered them."

"She said nothing about any monster."

"What she said and what your mother and Doj heard were not necessarily the same. There are things people just don't want to hear."

He had my interest on several fronts. I might learn something more about Uncle Doj. I might learn something about this prophecy of Hong Tray's, which, so far, was almost as mysterious as the concerted determination of all Taglians that the Black Company had to be some sort of catastrophe in the making, worse than any flood or earthquake. Trang disappointed me. He said nothing more. In fact, he struck a listening attitude.

I popped into the hallway.

The man I had frightened before was returning. And he was bringing friends.

I swooped at him again, angrier than before. He was no hero. He squealed and took off. His companions yammered among themselves. They decided their friend must have mental problems. They went after him instead of going on to Sahra's cell. I followed to make sure.

Trang was gone when I got back. A flick through time provided me no useful information.

61

SAHRA HAD MOVED TO HER PALLET. SHE WAS ON HER KNEES THERE, PALMS atop her thighs, staring straight forward. Waiting.

I drifted into position in front of her.

"You're here, aren't you, Mur? I can feel it. You're what I've felt before, aren't you?"

I tried to answer her. I got *she is the darkness!* from Smoke and a reeling back. Why now? Sahra had not bothered him before. Had she?

He did not like any female these days. He even tensed up around the Radisha when we were there.

I pushed inward. Smoke pushed back. Sahra sensed something. She said, "I'm too heavy to travel now. I'll come as soon as our son can travel."

A son? Me?

I became a different man in that moment. But it lasted only a few seconds. Only until I wondered, how could she know that?

Some people called her a witch. Well, spooky. I never saw it myself. But maybe she *could* know.

My world began to shudder and shake. I had enough experience ghostwalking to know that meant somebody back at the shop wanted me to wake up. Reluctantly, I responded. I wished there was some way, any way, to let Sahra know I had gotten her message. "I love you, Sarie," I thought.

"I love you, Murgen," Sahra said, as though she had heard me.

The shaking grew more insistent. I turned loose of the temple of Ghanghesha but refused to be managed completely. I tried to drop in on the Radisha for a closer look at her scheming but Smoke shied away with an aversion almost as strong as that he showed for Soulcatcher. *She is the darkness.*

The earth blurred beneath my point of view. I was low and moving fast. Maybe that helped defeat some of the spells making Goblin and Mogaba so hard to find. I got a clear, if brief, look at both as I whipped past.

They were on the move. Mogaba seemed to be gathering strength. The forvalaka was with Goblin. Both groups moved inside an envelope of crows.

Soulcatcher probably had a better idea of the big picture than I did.

"Don't you ever learn?" Croaker snarled.

I barely had strength enough to sit up and reach for something to drink. I had spent a lot more time out than I realized while it was happening. Sarie always did make me lose track of time.

"Shit," I murmured. "That took it out of me. I could eat a cow."

"You weren't supposed to be dealing with family things. You keep it up, it's going to be crow, not cow."

You could not find an edible cow in this end of the world, anyway.

I grunted. I had a pitcher of something sweet in one hand and a warm loaf of bread in the other. At that moment it did not occur to me to ask why he would accuse me of getting involved in family things.

"It's dark already. Our people are all climbing into their holes and pulling them in after them. I need you rested and ready because I want you over there watching the Shadowgate. And not sightseeing, either. We need to get a signal up the instant Longshadow cracks the gate."

I lifted a hand. As soon as I cleared my mouth I asked, "Why don't I watch Longshadow? Smoke don't want to get close out there. I might not see the shadows moving till it's too late. Longshadow I can see while he's making his summons." I dumped some sugar water in behind the last bite of bread.

Smoke groaned.

"Shit." Suddenly, the Old Man looked like he wanted to cry.

"Where's One-Eye?" I asked. "Better get him in here."

Smoke had not made a sound in years.

"You find him. I'm the physician here." He headed for Smoke's cot.

"Good idea." I got myself up and stumbled toward the doorway on still feeble legs.

62

IT WAS A GREAT NIGHT FOR ALL HELL TO BREAK LOOSE. I HAD NOT REALLY noticed the gathering darkness while walking the ghost, so lost in thought had I been. But clouds were moving in to deepen the darkness. "One-Eye!" I bellowed. "Get your dead ass over here now!"

I considered the clouds. My suggestion looked real good now.

Where the hell was that little shit? I climbed on up out of Croaker's dugout. "One-Eye!" I headed for his hole. Surely he did not intend to spend the night there? He had not done nearly enough work on it to make it a good place to wait out a night when shadows were slithering about, wizard or not.

I was almost there when the little wizard came scuttling from the direction of my shelter. "What do you want, Kid?"

"Where the hell you been? Never mind. We got trouble with the ghost."

"Uhm?"

"He's making noise," I whispered. Then I glanced around. I had forgotten to guard my tongue.

It was my lucky night. There were no crows anywhere around.

One-Eye glanced over his shoulder. "Making noise?" He did not believe me.

"Did I stutter? Get your ass in there. Croaker's already checking him for physical problems." I continued to look for listeners. Mice and bats and shadows have little ears, too.

A boreal light rippled between Overlook and the jagged ruins of Kiaulune, reflecting brilliantly off the metal in the fortress wall. It was just a sputter, though, as Lady got tuned up. A moment later the only light visible anywhere came from the surviving chambers of crystal atop Overlook's towers. Longshadow's favorite was particularly bright.

"You gonna stand around and gawk or are you gonna get on with business?"

That was One-Eye. Turn everything around so any delays would be my fault.

I took one last look around before I went inside. Still nothing. I dropped the rags covering the doorway, moved a shadow-repellent candle on a stand into place between the doorway and the rest of us. I lighted it from the nearest lamp. We ought not to count on Longshadow to keep our timetable. "I wonder if the Shadowmaster isn't curious about why we aren't showing any lights and making any noise."

"Hush," One-Eye told me. He whispered, "Thought you said Croaker was giving him a physical."

Croaker was sitting in my chair, slumped. "He was when I left." I grabbed a pitcher and sucked down a bellyful of sweet water.

"He don't look real frisky to me," One-Eye said. He poked Smoke.

"I didn't say he got up and danced a hornpipe. He groaned. In all the time I've been around him the only noises he ever made was when we thought he was coming down with pneumonia. A groan looked like a big thing. Croaker agreed."

The Old Man made a noise. He returned to flesh. As soon as his head cleared he told us, "It's going to be interesting. Longshadow just sent for Howler, Singh and the girl. He's ready to get started."

One-Eye grumbled, "A thrill a minute around here. Shadows again. I knew I should've picked up that farmland and got out. Swizzledick here says the runt's been getting uppity. Talking back and everything."

"He made a sound," Croaker snapped. "Call it a groan. And when I tried to take a look at the girl he shied away and gave off a sort of feeling to do with shadows."

" 'She is the darkness,' " I quoted. "Lately he's done it any time I take him close to anybody female. It's strongest near Soulcatcher. Sarie and the Radisha tie for number two."

"Ah," One-Eye said. "I'd almost forgotten that old witch. How's she doing, Murgen?"

"You care?"

"I hear Cordy's on his way. He might want to know."

"You're going to tell him we can spy on his bounce baby?"

"Grr. I guess not. But I owe him a couple, three big tweaks."

Personally, I doubt that anybody has ever gotten ahead of One-Eye anywhere. Except maybe Goblin. One-Eye is the kind of guy who gets even with you first.

One-Eye is also the kind of guy who can still hand out the occasional surprise after two hundred years. "I don't make it through the night tonight, there's a will in my bedroll. Most everything goes to Goblin. Couple things, though, I want Gota to have." He was peeling back Smoke's eyelids at the time so did not notice when Croaker and I exchanged startled looks.

Croaker said, "You don't make it, there's not much chance we'll still be here, either."

"The Kid will be. His mother-in-law claims he's destined. What for, who knows? The only one who ever did is dead."

Before the Old Man could ask, I said, "He's talking about something Hong Tray came up with way back in Dejagore. I'm not sure what it was. Sarie and I talked about it but they never made it clear to her, either. Something about the future of the Nyueng Bao. I know it bugged the shit out of Uncle Doj and Mother Gota. Thai Dei's more neutral but he's not keen on it, either. I think he's glad he doesn't really know what's going on."

"I think you've pretty well shaped the future of those people already," Croaker told me. "We've still got half the tribe traipsing around behind us. Where's your pet, One-Eye? I haven't seen him in a week."

"JoJo? Damned if I know. Long as he stays out from underfoot. . . . Look, I don't see anything different about this guy. Not from here. Let me take him out, see if there's any change in him where he's at."

I said, "I already told you—"

"Yeah, yeah. Shut up. I got to concentrate here." But not much. Smoke was so used to being used this way that taking him out required no effort at all.

Croaker said, "He did feel a little different. But it's been a long time for me."

"It just occurred to me that I haven't run into Kina out there lately."

"How about in your dreams?"

I could not remember. "That's odd. I don't remember. But it has to be. I have the same dreams all the time. I'm almost comfortable with them now."

"Maybe that's the point. Be careful."

"Like One-Eye says, careful is my middle name."

"Stupid is One-Eye's middle name."

"I heard that. I'll turn you into a toad." The little wizard was back already.

"I've said it before and I'll say it again. You're not even good at turning food into shit. What's the word?" I asked.

"We may have to wait for a day when we have more time but you and me are going to have to sit down and see what we can figure out about what you've been doing."

"What?"

"It feels to me like a couple of the walls he's hiding behind have started to fall down."

Croaker asked, "Is he going to wake up on us tonight, right in the middle of things?"

"I doubt it. He's still buried way down deep." He watched me suck down some more water, then follow that with a leg from a roasted chicken. You do not eat badly if you are the Liberator. "You going to suck down everything in sight, Kid?"

"It's going to be a long night."

"You stay here and stick to business," Croaker told me. "Short trips out only. Let me know what's happening when it happens."

"Right. Will do, boss."

"One-Eye. We need more spells around this place. Something that will keep the shadows away but that will let us come and go if we want to."

One-Eye put on a big, gap-toothed grin and cocked that ugly hat of his at an uglier angle. "I done come up with the perfect amulet, chief. Figuring we were going to need to have messengers moving around during hard times."

"How many do you have?"

"Right now, an even baker's dozen."

"That's all?"

"Hey. They're hard to make."

And, no doubt, fooling with them took time away from his still and black market projects.

We had been in one place long enough for him to have gotten involved in some sort of black marketing, however feeble its prospects were. Which would take time away from less interesting avocations. Like making amulets that might save lives.

I was willing to bet that he had more than the thirteen he was willing to turn over to the Old Man. He would have at least one for each of his own wrists and ankles plus a few socked back to retail to the highest bidders once we saw how well they worked and how badly they were needed.

That little shit really is a villain.

But he was on our side, our villain, the best we had. Unless you counted Lady, which I did not even though she was the Lieutenant. I never have been able to count her part of the Company. She came with too much baggage.

"It's getting late," Croaker remarked. "You might take a quick run at Overlook, see what they're doing now. One-Eye. I want to stash my couriers in your dugout."

"What? No way, chief. I just got the place cleaned up."

I took another drink, then sat down beside Smoke.

63

THE LIGHT IN LONGSHADOW'S CRYSTAL CHAMBER SEEMED BRILLIANT enough to hurt fleshly eyes. Magically created, it came from everywhere at once and left no place at all where a wild shadow might lurk. The few furnishings up there were smooth and rounded and left no little pockets or crevasses or corners where even a pinhead of untamed darkness might come to life.

No feral shadow was going to sneak up on him.

Longshadow seemed to have changed clothing and even bathed in preparation for the night's events. Certainly he wore a new mask, black and silver with inlays of cyan, cardinal, and a particularly intense dark green. The patterns on the mask altered every time I looked. I told myself when I got a minute I ought to go back and have a look at Longshadow making himself over. He had not done anything like this ever before.

Narayan Singh and the girl arrived only moments before I did. I determined that by a quick dip into the past. Longshadow asked, "Where is Howler?"

Singh shrugged. The girl reacted as though Longshadow had not spoken at all. Singh said, "We have not seen him in days." Which was an outright lie.

"He should be here. I warned him to be here. For his own safety."

The girl sat down on the floor, cross-legged. She paid the Shadowmaster no mind whatsoever. Singh probably had had to badger her to get her to leave her writing.

Curious, I did a dash back in time. And got surprised. I found the child hurrying Singh. "We must be there in time."

I went back some more. I found the child in that trancelike state where she claimed to be in touch with Kina. Certainly the odor of Kina was strong. I got out of there before I attracted her attention. She had not paid me much mind lately and I liked that just fine.

I took a couple of quick dips into times nearby and concluded that Narayan and his ward had responded to Longshadow's summons because Kina had told them to respond.

Interesting. But what did it mean?

When I got back to present time I found the Howler puffing his way up the last spiral of stairs to Longshadow's chamber. The Shadowmaster had sensed his approach and had faced the entrance. The smelly little wizard appeared, let out a shriek before the Shadowmaster could start giving him a hard time. It sounded almost amused.

Longshadow turned away although he had been suffering a bad case of the nags lately. He seemed to be in such a good mood that he was willing to overlook petty transgressions. He said, "Good. We're all here. Now we go ahead with the game the way I should have played it from the beginning." He sounded slightly puzzled, as though, suddenly—like every man and woman in the army besieging him—he wondered why he had done so little for so long. He acted as if a powerful psychic wind had torn away a dense fog that had gripped his mind for ages.

I suspected that was close to the truth. I could not identify the villain but I was sure that one of our nastier female players, most likely Kina, had reached him somehow long ago and had been blunting his sword ever since. If I was right I had to admire the subtlety of it. Longshadow had not worked it out. That might be because the manipulation had been limited to dumbing him down and exaggerating his natural prejudices and bullheadedness.

I recalled that he had had a few sharp spells. Things had not gone well for us during those interludes.

"Close the door, Deceiver." The Shadowmaster's voice was strong. "There must be no interruptions."

Howler seated himself on a tall stool. I gathered that it had been brought in for him specifically, back when he first attached himself to the Shadowmaster. He did not use it often but no one else used it ever. He and Longshadow were not the sort of colleagues who watched over one another's shoulders, sharing suggestions and expertise.

The Shadowmaster had done some housekeeping. Usually his chamber contained an arsenal of magical gewgaws, all laid out strategically. Most of those were absent tonight. Maybe Longshadow did not want to test the honesty of his guests.

After some nervous shuffling Narayan Singh assumed a protective stance beside the Daughter of Night. I noted a triangle of black silk peeping from the top of his loincloth. He had dressed formally tonight, then. That would be his strangling cloth, his rumel.

"In more normal times," Longshadow said, "I would go out to the Shadowgate personally and employ the traps there to collect the shadows I want to use. To obtain the best effect they have to be trained. Once they are properly trained they will leave their friends alone. The skrinsa can employ them without troubling me. But these are not normal times."

No. They were not. And when he mentioned the shadowweavers I began to wonder if he knew just how bad off he was when it came to followers. At no time had he ever had much contact with those who managed the daily business of his fortress. He gave orders. They got executed. Only a handful of his people had survived Lady's last attack. They continued to care for him. Howler had seen to that.

He no longer had any shadowweavers to manage any trained shadows he might have.

On the other hand . . .

At one time there had been a crystal chamber atop a tower every seventy feet along Overlook's southern wall. Inside each was a mirror that could be used to cast the light there in a beam onto the ground surrounding the road down from the Shadowgate. It had taken a couple of men to aim each mirror.

Longshadow did something by moving small figurines in a collection on a table, as though making multiple moves in a board game. He said a single word.

The lights in the surviving tower tops waxed brilliant. Light beams reached out across the night. Like accusing fingers they swung to point in the general area of Croaker's Old Division. They did not light up the slope nearly as well as they had in former times but I was impressed. They did their jobs without the aid of one human hand.

The others there were impressed, too. Narayan seemed a little troubled, the Howler suddenly restless. Longshadow did not notice. He moved on to his next step. He said, "The lights are unnecessary to coming events. I just thought it would be amusing if our enemies watched one another scream their lives out."

He giggled.

Howler sat up straight as a spear, suddenly alert. He did not like the way things were going.

Maybe Longshadow was not as big a fool as everyone thought.

I spent a moment too long watching the girl for a reaction. Smoke did his *she is the darkness* reaction and started to back off. I held him. We were about to witness some excitement.

Longshadow stepped up to the big crystal sphere standing on a pedestal at the center of the chamber. His audience watched carefully, nervously. This was not something he had done in front of witnesses before. I doubted they knew what the sphere was.

The globe was four feet in diameter. What looked like little tunnels followed wormtracks in to a hollow place at its center. As Longshadow stepped closer shimmering light rippled over its surface, like oil on water but much more intense. Snakes of cold fire wriggled through the channels inside. It was a hell of a show.

Longshadow raised his spidery hands. Carefully, he removed his gloves and pushed up his sleeves. The skin he revealed seemed both translucent and pus-colored, with speckles of blue beneath, like cheese. He had a fine crop of liver spots. There was almost no flesh on him at all.

The Shadowmaster rested his hands on the surface of the sphere. The lights inside became excited. The surface shimmer climbed his fingers, covered his hands. His fingers sank into the globe like hot rods slowly melting their way into ice. He grabbed the worms of light and began twisting.

He began to talk in a conversational sort of voice, of course using a language that nobody recognized—though the Daughter of Night frowned and leaned forward as though she was able to puzzle out a word here and there.

The Shadowmaster summoned a shadow. I could not see it. It was inside the pedestal supporting the globe. But I felt it. There was not much to it but it was very, very cold.

The Howler dropped to the floor and leaned closer to watch. Narayan and the Daughter of Night stared, bemused. The kid took a few steps forward. Singh moved closer to the door, for a better angle of view.

Longshadow spoke for several minutes, his eyes closed tightly. As he finished the brightness inside the globe began to fade. He opened his eyes and stared out southward as he had done ten thousand times before, watching the area illuminated by the mirrors.

She is the darkness!

I was not looking at the brat. . . .

Not that darkness.

A very special darkness. A surprise darkness that should not have caught me that far off guard, considering.

Soulcatcher.

She stepped in through a door opened by Narayan Singh as though she had been about to knock.

Longshadow was not ready for this. Not at all. He was surrounded, totally betrayed, before he realized Catcher had arrived.

I clung there with all the power I had to resist Smoke's terror. The little shit whined and repeated *she is the darkness!* like that was some mantra against the fangs of the night.

"The game ends," Soulcatcher said in the booming, basso voice of a crier in an amphitheater. Then she giggled like a teenaged girl. "It's been hard work but worth it. I really like my new house." Both those sentences arrived in the voice of a little old man who keeps account books.

Longshadow was caught, trapped, pinned like a butterfly on a collector's display board. He was surrounded, outnumbered, and did not have a chance even if he was the greatest wizard who ever lived. Which he was not. Even so, he did not surrender.

He knew his value. His mind was not clouded. She dared not kill him because the Shadowgate would collapse.

I had to give in to Smoke. I had to get this news back fast.

I really needed to get it to Lady fastest but there was no way.

Longshadow moved slowly to pick up his gloves. As he began to pull one on, Soulcatcher said, "I think not." Her voice was the velvet tenor of a tombstone salesman. "In fact, it's time . . ."

Longshadow's right pinky was crooked, as though it had been broken and badly set a long time ago. The nail looked like a bit of rotten, dried out, blackened spinach leaf.

The Shadowmaster flicked that little finger.

The nail flew off just as Catcher said, ". . . time. . . ."

I shook my ghostly head. You never see everything.

In one eyeblink that nail became a shadow filled with hatred for the light.

Smoke's wriggling became irresistible.

64

I REACHED FOR A MUG OF WATER EVEN AS I SAT UP. GROGGILY, IT DAWNED ON me that I had been shoved into the cramped little alcove where the Old Man had been keeping Smoke since we sneaked him over from One-Eye's pesthole. There were voices beyond the ragged hangings concealing me.

I took a long drink, stirred Smoke's blankets around so he would be hidden, ran my fingers through my hair, stepped out of hiding.

The voices stopped instantly. Croaker looked about as angry as he could get. I told him, "It's that important." Which left a baffled look on the faces of Swan and Blade. "Good thing they're handy. You guys go outside for a minute? Take the candle."

"What the fuck are you doing?" Croaker demanded. He had to make a major effort to keep his voice down.

"Soulcatcher just took over Overlook."

"Huh?"

"She walked in while Longshadow was cutting the shadows loose. Which he did, by the way. And she and Singh and the kid and Howler all jumped him. You needed to know right now. This changes everything. Lady should hear as soon as possible, too."

"Uhn!" Croaker was still angry but I could see the changes taking place behind his eyes, see the focus of his anger shifting like a ship changing course. "The bitch. The deceitful, conniving, treacherous bitch."

"Way she talked, she's planning on moving into Overlook and making it home."

"The bitch!"

"I wish I could tell you more. Smoke refused to stay around where she was at. Think you better tell Lady?"

"Of course I'd better tell her. Shut up. Let me think."

"Hey in there!" Swan yelled from the other side of the hangings keeping the wind out. "You guys better come and see this."

"Now what?" Croaker snarled.

"I'll check it out. Write them a message they can take to Lady."

"Damn it. It may be too late. She was going to try to sneak up on Longshadow herself."

Shit. We were in the brown stuff deep. Maybe.

I made a wobble-legged dash for the open air. I slipped on the steps going up to ground level. The earth was still soggy, even up here on the hillside.

I did not have to ask Willow what troubled him.

The biggest fireworks show of all time was going on over by the Shadowgate. Maybe the dustup at Lake Tanji was a match but I got to see that one only from the inside. "Gods damn!" I swore. There were so many fireballs flying around that no expletive could do the event justice.

I flung myself back down the muddy steps.

Croaker was wriggling into his Widowmaker costume. I told him, "It's started at the Shadowgate. You have to see it to believe it. I hope those guys have enough bamboo."

"Lady gave them everything she could. It'll be a matter of numbers. Which we've known from the beginning. If we have more fireballs than they throw shadows, we win. If we don't, we end up sorry. But not for long."

"Longshadow didn't seem to do much. If that tells you anything positive."

"It doesn't. I don't have any idea what he would or wouldn't have to do to unleash some or all of the shadows. And there's no way I can guess how he'd think about it. Except that he wouldn't want to let go so many that they'd come after him, too. He'd want to be able to control the survivors after he got rid of us."

"He doesn't know that he doesn't have any more shadowweavers. Singh and Howler have been feeding him very selective information lately. The true extent of what Lady accomplished the other day is a complete mystery to him."

"More treachery from our friend Soulcatcher, no doubt."

"I'd bet on it."

"You need to get back out there. She wouldn't do just that one thing. It would leave her too vulnerable."

"Huh?" My turn to make funny noises.

"She's got to know we can get in and out of there whenever we want. She has to cover her sweet little ass. Go see what she's up to before she really gets going."

"On my way, boss."

I drank some sugar water and went out.

Smoke did not want to go back to Overlook. I got my way. I tricked him, sort of, by ducking back to before Catcher pushed her way into his awareness. Then I zipped forward and watched the shadow explode off Longshadow's pinky.

It went for Howler. It hit Howler. Howler howled. And fought it off somehow. It darted at Narayan Singh, who shrieked as it struck him. Howler and Catcher together forced the animate darkness away from the Deceiver. Singh lapsed into unconsciousness immediately.

The shadow was not whipped yet. It struck at the Daughter of Night.

The instant she screamed the ghostworld began to fill with the stench of Kina. A cyclone of rage roared toward Overlook. Smoke squeaked *she is the darkness* and away we went, streaking out of there like a shaft from a ballista. We went high and we went north and we went fast. The fireworks at the Shadowgate vanished behind the Dandha Presh. We were north of Dejagore before I could exert any control.

The ghostworld had become one protracted whimper from my steed. He was fleeing somewhere where he expected to be safe. Somewhere that the deepest part of him recalled from days when he was still an ordinary mortal.

He had only just begun to respond to directions when we drifted into the Palace.

The place was a beehive. Priests and Guards and functionaries rushed everywhere. There was excitement out on the city streets, too. Shadar watchmen roamed in packs, making arrests by the score.

This bore closer examination.

I checked the prisoners. A few seemed vaguely familiar. I dipped around in time and discovered that they were being collected in the empty Black Company barracks. I found some definitely familiar faces in the crowd there.

They were all people who had been friendly to the Company.

I zipped around for a look at the Radisha, ran back in time to the beginning. . . . Near as I could tell her adventure had been going on for only a short while, though she had spent hours earlier getting her assets positioned. Actual arrests commenced just about the time Soulcatcher strolled into Longshadow's chamber at Overlook.

Sleepy!

Shit! I sped to Banh Do Trang's warehouse.

Sleepy had not been arrested. Not yet. Several Shadar were in the neighborhood. They were looking for Sleepy. Their curses left me no doubt that they were after him specifically. But they could not find his hiding place.

I went after the kid. I gave it everything I could. If it worked in the swamp it ought to work in the city. I got right down there in his face and screamed. I tried to mess his hair and pull his ears.

He spooked.

So he did happen to be out of the way when the watchmen arrived, though he was still close enough to overhear and understand.

I did not wait around. He had sense enough to saddle up and get out of town and never mind waiting for an answer from Sarie.

I grabbed Smoke by the ectoplasmic short hairs and headed south. He was not even a little bit eager to go.

I returned to my flesh. The Old Man was waiting for me. "What's the word?"

"Kina was coming. Smoke spooked. He headed north. I just got back. The shit's flying up there, too."

"Oh? How so?"

"The Radisha is rounding up anybody who ever smiled at one of us. She started at almost exactly the same minute that Soulcatcher jumped on Longshadow."

He did not ponder that. "We've got a problem, then. Get back out there. I want to know if anything else is going wrong."

I sucked some sugar water and went.

What else was going wrong? Right here in Kiaulune the Prahbrindrah Drah was trying to disarm Lady's troops. She was inside Overlook. She did not know yet. I did not know how to get word to her quickly. I decided to try the same tack I had with Sleepy. Maybe I could startle her into doing something.

I found her already in the stairwell leading up to Longshadow's crystal chamber. Several of our best Company brothers were with her.

I dropped down in front of her and screeched, "Booga! Booga! Booga! Get your ass back outside!"

She jumped. She squinted into the darkness right about where the eyes of my viewpoint floated. "Murgen?"

"Get your butt out of here, woman. It's a trap. And the Prince's troops are trying to disarm your men."

She turned and barked orders.

Damn! She was a whole lot more sensitive than the others.

I whipped out of there. The stink of Kina had begun to fill the stairwell.

A dark nimbus clutched itself to Longshadow's crystal tower. Kina had little strength she could project into this world but it was all focused now. I made Smoke move higher so I could look down into the chamber.

The Daughter of Night had recovered from the attack of the shadow. She used the strength lent her by her goddess to drive the thing back at the Shadowmaster.

Longshadow, of course, had been completely mad from the beginning, as paranoid as they come. He never trusted Howler. About all he and the little stinker had in common was their hatred of the Company. Mutual hatred for somebody else never has been sound grounds for a marriage.

The Shadowmaster had planned for a moment like this—though he had not anticipated Soulcatcher being there to help the turncoat, nor had he expected the Strangler and his brat to contribute distractions of their own. Nevertheless, he had been thorough. He had overengineered by a large factor. It might be enough. If they had underestimated him.

The towertop chamber became a bizarre pot filled with growls and shrieks, bits of smoke that came and went too fast for the eye to track, changing colors, knives of pure energy that slashed stone and crystal and ricocheted off stubborn protective spells and never considered the loyalty of anyone who got in the way.

Soulcatcher cried out like a child suddenly injured. She dropped to one knee, whimpering, but did not abandon the fight. Howler howled. The Daughter of Night babbled passages from the first Book of the Dead. The stench of Kina was awful in the ghostworld but the child had not finished copying the book before Howler stole it. She could not bring Kina all the way home without all of it.

Longshadow edged toward the doorway. It looked like he might actually get out. Presumably once he did the chamber would implode or in some other fashion destroy everybody still inside. That was the sort of trap I would have set.

They called Singh a living saint. He was, supposedly, the best of his kind of his generation. A dubious distinction in most of our eyes, but every man should be lucky enough to discover the one thing he can do better than anyone else alive.

The Shadowmaster thought no more of Narayan than he did of a mouse. The Deceiver was just there.

He was *there* one moment and *here* the next. His strangling cloth encircled the Shadowmaster's throat like black lightning.

A black rumel man becomes a master Strangler in part by mastering his own fear and excitement in times of stress. Narayan Singh had that knack though he had had little opportunity to exercise it recently. He had done so now. He remained calm enough not to break the Shadowmaster's neck. He understood the cost.

Strangulation is a slow process. Its victim seldom cooperates. Singh shouted, "I need armholders!" At first he said that in Deceiver cant. Only the child understood. She did not have the strength to restrain the Shadowmaster.

She told Soulcatcher, "You! Take his right arm and pull. You. The smelly one. Take hold of his left arm. Now. In the name of my mother."

Catcher snapped, "In the name of your real mother, who happens to be my pain-in-the-ass sister, you're going to get a paddling as soon as we finish with this piece of shit." The voice she used was a dead ringer for that of somebody I used to know who had been a devout believer in not sparing the rod.

Longshadow was one stubborn fish. He thrashed a lot longer than I thought any human could without air. The kid told the others, "Make sure you don't kill him."

"Go teach your grandma to suck eggs, brat." This time Catcher's voice was identical to Goblin's. I felt a sudden fear for the little wizard.

Longshadow collapsed. "Tie him and gag him and put him in that chair of his," Catcher told Howler. "Fix him good. Then look around for any more surprises he may have here." The shadow had vanished, either out the cracked door, into hiding or destroyed.

Howler, panting, asked, "And what'll you be doing, O mighty one?"

"Setting the pecking order straight." She grabbed the Daughter of Night, dropped to one knee, bent the struggling child over the other, mouthed a spell that flung Narayan Singh across the room hard enough to knock him cold, then yanked the kid's pants down and proceeded to apply a well-deserved tanning.

The child never cried but tears filled her eyes once Catcher finished. She felt both humiliated and deserted. Again she faced a crisis of faith. The stench of Kina had faded as soon as the kid got too busy to mess with her incomplete summoning.

Catcher said, "You give me any more crap, sweetheart, and next time you get intimately acquainted with a willow switch. You got him tied up good?"

"I'm working on it. You've waited this long you don't need to get in any big damned hurry now."

"I want to get control of his shadows. They're not going to sit still—"

"I know the plan. I helped write it." Howler screeched. There was a world of irritation in his cry.

I had to see the Old Man.

65

"THEY'RE SQUABBLING AMONG THEMSELVES ALREADY," I TOLD CROAKER after he shooed everybody outside. "But they definitely have Longshadow on the hook. Catcher intends to make him do whatever she wants."

"She going to do a Taking?"

I had not thought of that. That kind of stuff had happened only way, way back. "Would she know how?"

"She might. But she might not have enough to work with where Longshadow is concerned. She might need to know his true name. We know he's got that hidden in the Shadowgate spell."

"What's going on here?"

"I've ordered the New Division to move over to the Shadowgate and relieve the Old Division. If I get them entangled with the shadows before they understand what the Prahbrindrah Drah is doing, they won't be able to participate. All they'll have time for is fighting shadows."

"What excuse did you give them?"

"The Old Division doesn't have enough bamboo."

On a night like tonight no general was going to let his men surrender their bamboo to another outfit.

"Also, that I want the Old Division to attack Overlook from the south. Those are the orders I actually sent to get them started. They won't get their real orders till after they separate."

We had rehearsed a move from the Shadowgate to the south wall several times. Maybe the Old Man was still thinking way ahead of everybody else.

"I think I was able to warn Lady." I told him what I had done. "It seemed like the right call in the circumstances. I know she'll ask questions later."

"Oh, she will. And she'll crap bricks when she gets her answers."

"You don't seem particularly terrified."

"I was her prisoner in the Tower at Charm before she learned to love me. I used up my scared then."

I would not count on her love if I was him. They had not been much of a loving couple lately. Guys like me never stop loving their Saries but other people do fall out of love when there is a lot of stress for a long time. I said, "I have to check on Goblin. I had a really ugly thought while I was watching them fight over there. If Catcher was as thorough as I think she'd be, old One-Eye might be an orphan."

"Shit," Croaker said softly. "I overlooked that angle completely. Look, while you're searching for that little shit tell Smoke 'white wedding' and 'white knight' every little bit. Alternate them. That'll make Goblin easier to spot."

"I figured there was something—"

"And any time you see crows, anywhere, panic them. We need to blind Catcher as much as we can."

"She fooled you, eh?"

"Say I underestimated her ambitions. Obviously, now, she's up to more than just getting even with Lady. Go on."

The "white wedding, white knight" mantra worked wonders. Smoke and I found Goblin almost immediately. And he was in deep shit, just as I feared, only it was not nearly as deep as some probably hoped. When Smoke and I got there we found him and his boys lying very quietly amongst some rough rocks feeling very nasty. In a very few minutes somebody was going to get hurt. Bad.

I had to dive into the pool of time to find out why.

Goblin is just a minor wizard but he *is* one. He comes equipped with a normal Company complement of distrust, too. He could not control shadows or crows, bats or mice, or any other creature well enough to use it to collect information but he could manipulate some creatures some ways. His choice was a miniature owl common on the south side of the Dandha Presh. It did not grow much bigger than your fist.

He kept the critters posted in the bushes around his camp wherever he went to ground. And they always fluttered ahead when he was on the march. He moved only by night except when he chose to attack some of Longshadow's loyalists.

Goblin suffered no surprises.

He was not surprised when the forvalaka came padding through the darkness and leapt at him with a thunderous growl. Owls using a call unique to that particular danger had cried out as the beastwoman passed.

There were no official plans for her to be anywhere nearby tonight.

There had been a lot of unnecessary, unexplained crow activity in the neighborhood lately, too.

Goblin had become suspicious. He had prepared. Just in case. After a while even a Company man as lazy as One-Eye will react to signs and portents.

The forvalaka attacked—but what she sank claws and fangs into was not Goblin. It was only vaguely human in shape, sacking stuffed with leaves and straw. A spell had been put on that so the forvalaka could not let go once it grabbed hold.

That happened at virtually the identical moment that Soulcatcher stepped into Longshadow's workplace, when all hell broke loose everywhere else.

A little something that did not look like Goblin at all and probably smelled even less like him bounced out of the darkness. It awarded the panther an enthusiastic kick in the ribs. "I knew you were too good to be true. And after I went to all that trouble to try to fix things for you." Boom! He kicked her again. She roared and thrashed.

A voice from the darkness said, "You make her any madder, she's going to bust loose and tear you a new asshole."

"If I didn't make that spell strong enough to hold four more just like her then I deserve to get my shit chute rerouted." The forvalaka roared again. "But I do need to do something about all this racket." It could be heard for miles.

Owls hooted. This time they conveyed no sense of alarm. Nevertheless, only the forvalaka was out in the open when a lone Taglian stepped into the clearing where the beast still struggled to let go of its prey. The newcomer told the darkness, "White wedding, white knight." I would have laughed had Smoke permitted me that option.

Goblin materialized. "What's the word, Mowfat?"

"Somebody's coming. Sneaking. And they know where they're going."

"Surprise, surprise." Goblin gave Lisa Bowalk another kick that would have broken normal ribs. "When they sell you out they sell you all the way. I ever tell you what this bitch was doing first time we met her? She was barely old enough to bleed at the crotch but she was killing people to sell their bodies."

"We've heard it all before, boss," a voice called from the darkness. "If we've got company coming let's get ready to have a party."

"I hate this shit," Goblin told Mowfat. "I hate this country, I hate these people, I hate—"

"I hate to tell you this but they're less than a mile away."

"Mogaba with them?"

"I don't know. I didn't wait around till they got that close."

Goblin went to work being a wizard. He cooked up some of his favorite wizard dishes. Those, it was obvious immediately, would include illusions.

One-Eye and Goblin love to make people see things that are not there.

I stole away to take a look at the people approaching.

These events were taking place in rocky, wooded, brushy mountain country in the dark. The seeing was bad even for me. I could not find Mogaba though I did confirm that the folks hunting Goblin were Mogaba's partisans. They were hard little snots, too, after having spent a winter in the business. They were wary and they were quiet.

I backtracked them. I had to go all the way back to before sunset to get a glimpse of Mogaba. I caught him sitting around with his boys not five miles from Goblin's camp. He was sharing his venison roast with a big black kitty.

That led me backward again instead of just humping off to see where everybody went. The mantra that cleared the mists around Goblin also helped disperse those around Mogaba. But only for a few seconds at a time.

I found out what I wanted to know, then rejoined Goblin's bunch in time to watch them ambush the bad boys who were supposed to clean up after sweet Lisa Bowalk.

What looked like a shimmering ghost materialized on the slope opposite the one where Goblin and most of his gang waited. Although the specter grabbed the attention of the Shadowlanders that was not its function. It was a signal meant to warn Goblin's gang to protect their night vision. Four, three, two, one. Flash!

I had no eyes to close. For an instant I was as blind as Mogaba's raiders. Then I asked myself why I should be blind and decided I was blind only because I expected to be blind. I could see again as soon as I decided I should. Which was more proof that lots of things really are a matter of viewpoint and expectation.

The flash not only blinded the Shadowlanders for a while, it splashed them with something that left them glowing in the dark. They made good targets.

Goblin's men were outnumbered. They took the opportunity to rectify that. Life became very unpleasant for the southerners. Short for some of them, too.

Goblin made their situation more unpleasant by conjuring numerous simulacra of brothers present and past. It was an old device and one of his favorites. He did not use it so often anyone figured out how to deal with it. The southerners struggled with spooks and shadows while Goblin's rangers picked them off. They did not jump on the option of using anti-ambush tactics because they took too long to comprehend the full scope of what had befallen them.

Mogaba never appeared. I could not find him no matter how hard I looked. Eventually it dawned on his lieutenants that they had taken a bite that was beyond their ability to chew.

They began to withdraw. They flailed at themselves and one another, trying to shed the luminescence that made them easy targets. Some tried to strip, though that meant staying in one place for a length of time definitely not conducive to continued good health.

The spooks and Goblin's men kept after them. Organized withdrawal collapsed into panic. Goblin kept close contact. He had spun Fortune on her ear and tripped his enemies good. Now he wanted to ride his good luck for all it was worth. He wanted to catch Mogaba while the Nar remained unaware of the scope of the disaster.

I wished him luck.

My fears for Goblin having proven unjustified I headed back to report what looked like the only good thing that had happened all night.

66

"IT'S NOT AS BAD AS IT SOUNDS," CROAKER TOLD ME. "YET." HE WATCHED ME suck down a quart of sugar water. "It looks like the Old and New Divisions are swapping places without any problems. And we haven't seen any evidence that many shadows are getting through. And I think Lady can get her situation under control. So whatever kind of stunt Soulcatcher is pulling it isn't gonna go all her way."

There were some unspoken yets in there that were pretty damned big.

Croaker asked, "How are you holding up? Should I have One-Eye come take over?"

"He's probably more use wherever he is now."

"I don't know. He's being One-Eye. A few minutes ago he was running around waving a fancy black spear and mumbling incoherently. I do believe he was a bit tipsy."

"Shit." One-Eye drunk and in a mood to show off his talents seldom bodes well for anyone. "That's the spear he made while we were trapped in Dejagore. He was drunk the last time he tried to use it."

"The one he made to kill Shadowspinner?"

"To kill Shadowmasters in general, but yes."

"We don't want him killing *this* Shadowmaster. Not yet."

"He's probably worried about the shapeshifter. You can tell him she's no threat. Goblin's got her under control."

"You're sure you don't need a break?"

"I'm fine." I got back into the alcove with Smoke.

Croaker called, "Your in-laws understand about the shadows?"

"Thai Dei saw them at Lake Tanji. They'll keep their heads down."

Smoke and I went straight up half a mile so I could get an idea of who was doing what to whom, where and when.

Everybody was doing something to somebody. The night was alive with trails of fire down around the Shadowgate. It looked as though some of the Old Division were still there giving their replacements a hand.

There were a few fireballs flying around in Kiaulune and the wastes between the ruins and Overlook, though not so many as I had expected. Maybe I had gotten the warning to Lady too late.

I headed downward. Below me the ruins and surrounding area began to develop a case of measles as ruby dots took life. In moments those gave birth to red threads that slithered through the night in search of other measles.

Whatever it was, Lady was behind it. It encouraged a lot of yelling and running. The people getting excited all proved to belong to the Prince's division.

Lady's men were rounding them up and disarming them. Those who chose to remain loyal to her, of course.

The worm had turned real fast.

The Prince himself exercised the better part of valor, accompanied by his staff, his bodyguards and anyone else who could run fast enough to keep up. Lady had impressed them quickly and thoroughly and the survivors fully understood that their futures might be much more pleasant if welcomed somewhere else.

There were a lot of dead people around. Most appeared to be stubborn Taglian loyalists.

The rubies grew larger and brighter. The threads connected, then contracted into straight, rigid lines. Seen up close those hummed and crackled and popped ferociously when some fool touched them. Said fool always fell down stone dead. The red light smelled bad. It took me a moment to recognize the odor because I was not expecting it.

The ruby light exuded the smell of Kina. Lady was drawing upon the goddess to create her sorcery.

The lines of power she laid down carved the area into triangles of isolation that could be escaped but only by using great caution. The lines kept the Prince's faithful from supporting one another. Consequently, Lady was emerging triumphant although she was outnumbered dramatically.

She was a nasty old bitch.

I closed in on her. She had reached a state where she was happy with the way things were going. I presumed. It was hard to read her emotional state when she was buttoned up inside the Lifetaker costume. She told Isi and Ochiba, "That should take care of that. For a while."

Isi said, "I guess this means no more warm barracks and no more combat pay." There had been no pay for anybody since the battle at Charandaprash. Not that there was anything to spend pay on. Unless One-Eye's brewing scheme was more successful than I believed.

"I suspect our contract has been terminated, yes. And the Captain is likely to be put out because all its terms have not yet been met."

That was true, though the Prince and his sister had been cautioned repeatedly against failing to fulfill their end of the bargain. And right now those warnings had to be weighing heavily on the Prince's mind. He had cast his fortune with Soulcatcher, for whatever reason, and the snake had turned in his hand. How many times had he heard Croaker tell what had happened to past employers who had turned on the Company?

Plenty. Catcher must have done some strong selling to make him turn on us. She must have been convinced that she could handle Lady.

Might be worth a few minutes trying to find out what kind of a deal they made.

Lady's bunch had a gang of prisoners seated in neat lines, cross-legged. None seemed inclined to protest their situation. Willow Swan and Blade were among the captives. They seemed depressed.

I guess Sindawe was right when he said she did not trust them.

I almost wished I was there in person.

"I hear Cordy's supposed to get here tomorrow," Swan muttered to Blade. "Nothing like timing."

Blade grunted.

"Why the hell did the fool go and do something like this?"

It took me a moment to realize that Swan meant the Prahbrindrah Drah, not Cordy Mather.

Blade grunted again. Swan seemed to understand.

"Why the hell didn't he tell me? I'm supposed to be the goddamned commander of his goddamned bodyguard."

"Because you're always over here watching her body instead?"

"So I'm sorry. He don't appeal to me. You suppose this crap is happening all over? Or did just the Prince go bugfuck?"

"No talking over there," Lady said, not unkindly. She asked, "Anyone have any thoughts concerning what we can do about our friends in there?"

"Stay out of their way?" Isi asked. He was turning into a real comedian.

"I think we need instructions from the Captain." Lady turned around slowly, studying the air almost as if she sensed an extra presence.

It was, I suspected, a direct experiment meant to illuminate her suspicions.

Nevertheless, Croaker did need to know her situation.

67

"YOU SMELLED THE KINA SMELL? YOU'RE SURE?" The Old Man did not seem interested in details of how Lady had visited disaster upon the Prahbrindrah Drah. The fact of her success was enough.

"Yes. But the goddess wasn't there. I've felt her close up often enough to know when she's been around. Especially tonight."

"She wants instructions?"

"She may. But she was fishing for a reaction, really. She suspects."

"She probably knows. Have you been back to the Shadowgate? Are we holding?"

"No, I haven't. I assume we're doing all right. There aren't so many fireballs flying around as there were a while ago. That seems to be because there's a lack of targets, not a lack of bamboo. Once in a while there's still a big barrage, though."

"You need One-Eye to spell you?"

"I'm all right for now."

"Be careful. And watch out coming back. I'm sending for Lady. She might be here."

I tried to take Smoke south. He would not go. I tried to get back into Overlook to spy on Catcher and Howler and Longshadow but Smoke refused to get anywhere near them, either. *She is the darkness!* He would not be fooled and he would not be bullied. He was gaining substance again. And that substance was in keeping with what I knew about his chickenshit character. Which suggested that we might not be getting a lot of use out of the old boy in days to come.

He *would* go upward. So I took the opportunity to survey the situation from above once more.

The distribution of fireworks suggested our situation was not bad now. The Shadowgate had held. The Prahbrindrah Drah was headed north. He showed good hustle and a fair amount of thought as well. He left messages for his scattered troops, confident that we would be much too busy to chase them hard. He had no actual plan yet, though, other than to get clear and reassemble his division. He was not pleased by the way the tables had turned so suddenly. He had been promised that Lady would be handled. He had taken a major princely step when he had set aside his emotional disinclination to buy that.

If he had thought he had some chance with Lady he might not have pursued his treachery.

Not that his action came as any great surprise, except in its timing.

Longshadow's pinky-nail pet had ruined the whole conspiracy's timing.

Smoke did not seem keen on getting close to Lady, now, either, though he did let himself be bullied.

We needed to find a way to encourage Smoke to be more cooperative. Maybe red-hot branding irons.

Shadows definitely were leaking through. I arrived about the same time as the first reached the vicinity of Lady's force. This was no onslaught like the one at Lake Tanji, though. The only evidence was an occasional scream.

Lady's mood had blackened since my last visit. She stamped around angrily. Pink fires jumped off her Lifetaker armor. They flew around like sparks in a forge. She had become unhappy in a big way but I could not make out why. She looked like she wanted to take it out on Willow Swan and Blade. They received a few choice words each time she passed. But their behavior remained impeccable. They offered her no excuse to strike.

I failed to see why Blade was a prisoner, anyway.

The smell of Kina was strong around Lady but I got no sense that the goddess herself was anywhere close by. I had expected great horrors splattered all over the region after her wild response to Longshadow's assault on the Daughter of Night.

Lady paused in her pacing. She listened. She cursed.

Horrors were coming but these nightmares were not spewing forth from Kina's forehead.

The cries of men attacked by shadows became increasingly frequent.

"Idiots!" Lady growled. "They won't listen and they won't protect themselves."

Then the smell of Kina began to grow stronger, too.

I tried to grab Smoke in a spectral hammerlock, to force him back to Longshadow's crystal chamber.

From the first moment I saw it with ghostly eyes, that chamber had blazed with the intense cold light of a brilliant star. It made a landmark more easily seen than any beacon or lighthouse. But tonight, now, the light was flickering.

Smoke whimpered *she is the darkness sheisthedarkness sheisthedarkness!* like some protective mantra and fought me tough, but this time I enforced my will upon him. Apparently I could if I worked up a strong enough case of emotion. And sustained it. Smoke never stopped resisting.

He did not seem to need tons of energy, the way I did. Maybe he fed off me like some vampirish spirit.

The crystal chamber was a shambles. In one corner, still tied to his chair, the Shadowmaster lay trapped inside a cocoon of glimmering force, unconscious and in terrible shape. I guessed he had several broken bones. His clothing was torn all to hell. Clotted blood had splashed the inner face of his defensive shell. Must have been some major excitement in my absence. He must have tried another trick or two. And had paid the price for trying. Maybe he was close to death. Maybe that was why there was so much more screaming going on outside Overlook.

I thought the Daughter of Night was gone altogether but then I spotted her hiding inside her own egg of protection. Hers was eggplant black and just barely translucent. She had curled into a fetal ball but she did not appear to be injured.

Howler looked like he had tried to rape a tiger. He was making noise continuously but not of the usual sort. This was more like a continuous whine punctuated by the occasional rattle of air in a punctured lung. Soulcatcher was trying to doctor him but she was in bad shape herself. She looked like she had wrestled the same tiger, with only marginally more positive results. Right now she had no time for anything going on outside the chamber.

The smell of Kina remained strong there.

I dislocated Smoke's ghostly knuckles and applied pressure till he moved back toward the moment when he had dragged me away. We never got there. Kina arrived first, making a second, surprise visit that caught everyone off guard.

When I got close enough to feel Kina's presence, to catch glimpses, I became unfocused. Smoke made a run for it. I regained control, dove right back in there.

We bounced in and away, in and away. I caught several more glimpses of an animate darkness that, seen from the corner of my invisible eye, looked like a miniature version of the many-armed goddess. Kina concentrated on enveloping the brat in the dark shell that surrounded her now. Howler and Soulcatcher took their lumps in a minute of vain resistance in which they caught the goddess's attention about like an annoying yellow jacket buzzing around an outdoor lunch catches the attentions of picnickers.

Longshadow grabbed the chance to employ a ready protective catechism to create the egg enveloping him now. Most of the damage he suffered was accidental and collateral and happened during the scrimmage between Kina and the others.

Narayan Singh appeared to be splashed all over the floor. I could not tell if he was alive.

I let Smoke pull away, drove him toward Lady. She ought to resemble a bouquet of posies on his fear scale now.

I positioned myself right in front of her, at eye level, as I had done before. That took some doing. She would not stand still. She continued to mutter curses about the screaming, which had become more common.

Longshadow had to be teetering on the brink of eternity.

I shrieked.

Lady froze.

I glared into the eyeholes of her ugly black helmet. Those glowed with an unnatural intensity. If something so unnatural initially could become more unnatural. She whispered, "You're there again."

I tried to bellow. "Your pal Kina whipped their asses upstairs. They're all down right now. There'll never be a better time to get them."

Lady turned slightly. She stared up at Longshadow's personal tower. The light in the crystal chamber was feeble, guttering like a spent lamp.

The fate Longshadow feared so much might catch up with him yet.

Lady shouted at Isi and Sindawe.

She did not get my message exactly but she did hit on the notion that right now might be a good time to take one last whack at the Shadowmaster.

68

THIS TIME WHEN I RETURNED TO FLESH I WAS WIPED OUT COMPLETELY. I HAD just enough strength to grab some sugar water. I consumed my resources a lot faster, apparently, when I had to fight Smoke all the time.

Croaker was talking to somebody on the other side of the curtain. I did not recognize the voice so I did not include myself in the discussion.

The subject seemed to be a rapid deterioration in our fortunes due to a sudden increase in the number of shadows getting past the troops below the Shadowgate. Shadows were turning up everywhere now, though not yet in disastrous numbers.

The man reporting to Croaker was a courier who had come all the way around Overlook from the Old Division. Mission completed now, he did not want to go back out into the night even when Croaker offered him one of One-Eye's amulets.

"You're perfectly safe now," Croaker told him. "The shadows won't know you're around."

"I don't trust—"

"Don't test my temper, soldier. I'll call the guards."

Smoke groaned. It was a for-real, out-loud, full-throated kind of groan.

Croaker started to snarl at the messenger again.

The ground shook as though somebody had dropped a seven-ton boulder next door. Dirt rained down. Some got into my food. Some went down the back of my neck. I was too tired to care much, or even to wonder what was happening.

Croaker pulled the hangings aside. "What was that?"

"The old fart made a noise."

"He didn't make the earth shake, did he?"

I shrugged. "I don't know about that. I do know Lady wants to take one more crack at Overlook." I explained the situation there. "Wouldn't it be something if we could just round them all up? If we ended up getting the best of everybody because they couldn't stop feuding among themselves?"

"We've been doing that for the last five years. More or less. I don't like the idea of her going in there again. She ought to hunker down till morning. A place like Overlook could turn into a death trap if the shadows infest it."

I said, "We'd really better worry about Longshadow's health. If the well-being of the Shadowgate depends on his well-being."

"Uhm?"

"A lot of the insane stuff he did the last several years he did because Soulcatcher and Kina were manipulating him. But he was paranoid about the shadows twenty years before any of us showed up in these parts. He's convinced they're out to get him. What if he's right? What if they do get him? I don't know what happens to a man when the shadows come, except that he dies horribly. If one of *them* kills Longshadow, will that break open the Shadowgate? Would that be why they want to get him so bad?"

"I don't know. I'd have to ask One-Eye."

"Where is that little shit? He should have been hanging around here instead of playing tonk."

"Tonk?"

"A while ago he was bitching because he wanted to get back to his burrow. He'd suckered somebody into coming over to play."

"He was bullshitting you, then, Murgen. There's nobody in this army stupid enough to play cards with him anymore. Maybe he was going to get drunk. Why don't you run over there and—"

"I'm wiped. That's one reason I wanted to see One-Eye. I don't have anything left to give."

Croaker sighed. He started to settle his winged Widowmaker helmet onto his head. "What should he look for?"

"He'll want to keep track of Lady and what's happening in Longshadow's chamber. He'll have to fight Smoke every step to do it, though. The little shit is really turning into his old chickenshit self. He don't want to get near this or that or . . . Never mind. Tell him if he sees something Lady ought to know about, he can sort of warn her by getting his point of view down right in front of her and screaming. She won't pick up anything word for word but she'll understand that there's something she needs to know. Then she'll pick up the gist of it."

Croaker frowned. He was really worried about Lady going back into Overlook. He asked, "Can you make it back to your place?"

The sugar water had given me strength enough to attack some hard rolls and fragments of a scrawny chicken that had not been able to outrun the headquarters cooks. "Yeah. Now. I wish we'd brought more cattle. I'd cut somebody's throat for a good hunk of rare beef."

"One-Eye is supposed to have woven a network of spells around here to make the area proof against shadows. But I want you to take this amulet, too. Just in case."

It is never wise to count on One-Eye one hundred percent. Sometimes he gets sloppy. Sometimes he forgets. Sometimes he is too lazy.

Croaker said, "Bring the standard when you come back. Then I can give that amulet to somebody else."

"Still want me to go past One-Eye's hole? I'm better now."

"I'll handle it. Get some rest. If you've turned into the religious sort while I wasn't looking, beg your gods to get us through the rest of the night." Fortunately, there was not a lot of night left. The shadows would have to go into hiding before long. The tables would turn. Soldiers would spend the daylight hours hunting them.

During our conversation we had heard several remote screams. "Yeah." As I was about to leave I observed, "Shouldn't most of the stupid

ones, the ones who didn't want to do the work or to inconvenience themselves, be dead by now?"

"I expect so. I imagine the shadows are learning from their successes,
though. And their failures."

Shaking, I went out into the night.

Clouds masked the stars. I could see nothing but the occasional flight
of a fireball and the glow atop Overlook's remaining lighted towers.

I listened for crows and owls and bats, for rats and mice. I heard none
of those. There was no noise anywhere that was not of human origin.
Shadows found nonhuman life nearly as tasty as human. And a whole lot
less difficult about being hunted.

A breeze had begun to blow. I sniffed the air, considered the overcast.
Looked like we were going to get some rain.

I descended into my own dugout. Inside I found Thai Dei huddled
beside the fire, pallid for a Nyueng Bao, obviously frightened. Weird. I
had trouble picturing him being scared of anything.

I told him, "We'll be fine here. This candle will keep out any shadows
that get through the spells One-Eye spread around outside." I did not
mention the standard. He did not need to know. I tossed him the amulet
Croaker had given me. "For insurance. You wear that, you can go anywhere safely."

"I'll go nowhere till the sun is high in the sky."

"I like your attitude. Shows good sense. I'm exhausted. I need to get
some rest before I collapse." I looked around. "Where's your mother?"

Thai Dei shook his head. "I don't know. I wouldn't know where to
start looking—if I could summon the courage to rid myself of the cold
water that has replaced my bones."

"She isn't out there with Uncle Doj, is she?" Concerned, tired, I
spoke without thinking.

Thai Dei was not so frightened and worried that he missed my slip.
"Uncle Doj?"

Why pretend? "Oh, I know he's prowling around out there. I saw him
the other night. Him and Mother Gota were prancing through the ruins of
Kiaulune. Doing who knows what the hell why. Or maybe hell knows
what the who. What's he up to? I'm sure he wasn't looking for plunder
Mogaba's and the Prince's men missed."

Thai Dei just looked at me. Maybe a hint of a smile tried to break
through. It did not last. "Will that candle last all night?" Evidently he
could become mildly talkative if he was scared and worried.

"It'll last a lot of nights. I'm going to crap out. If it makes you more
comfortable, put on the amulet and sit next to the candle. Just don't move
it. It has to block the doorway."

Thai Dei grunted. He had the amulet on his wrist already and was back at full worry.

I said, "We'll look for your mother first thing." Now that there was a chance she was dead I was concerned. Result of a whole lot of boyhood teaching that insisted that even the most hated member of your family was immeasurably precious. And there was some truth to that. Who will watch your back if not family?

It is the same here in the Company. The most loathsome, most despicable of my brothers has to be of more value to me than any outsider. On one level we are a big, ugly family.

There are, of course, rare exceptions, bullies and assholes so bad they have just got to be fragged. That has not happened in a long time.

I would look for my mother-in-law even though I had wished her away at least a hundred thousand times.

I was not yet all the way horizontal when sleep overcame me.

69

I DREAMT. OF COURSE. AWAKE OR ASLEEP I SPENT MOST OF MY LIFE IN dreamlands.

I was in the place of bones. Some great force troubled the plain. The bones themselves drifted on tides and currents. Scattered skeletons pulled themselves together, rose up and wandered aimlessly for seconds or minutes before falling apart again. Skulls turned to stare wherever I floated. Crows cawed drunkenly from perches in the few enwintered trees, afraid to fly because their equilibrium was all off and every straight flight nevertheless warped groundward where the stricken bird flopped and struggled amongst the bones like a moth caught in a spider's web. Dark clouds scurried across what had always been iron-grey skies. The wind was icy. Gusts made the bones rattle.

The smell of Kina was strong but I did not see her.

There was something behind me, though. I just could not turn fast enough to find out what.

Turning did inform me that I had some control, which I exercised immediately by wishing myself out of that place. Naturally, the move failed to be an improvement.

I went to the caverns of ice and old men. Those ancients made no sound but they were bickering. Something was in the wind. The smell of Kina was strong there, too, but she was nowhere to be seen.

Some of those old boys had their eyes open. They watched me as I passed.

Again I had the feeling that there was something behind me but saw nothing when I looked back.

I did have control. I followed the tunnel, eventually reached the place where the Books of the Dead rested upon their lecterns. The first, which the Daughter of Night had been transcribing, was now open to a page near the beginning.

The stink of Kina was particularly strong there.

I had no business in that place. There was nothing I wanted there.

Except out.

I tried to recall how I had gotten away last time. By just wanting to do it badly enough, I guess.

Darkness came.

It reminded me of something Narayan Singh said one time: "Darkness always comes."

It seemed I was in the darkness a long time. Fear began to build. I reflected on just how right Narayan had to be.

Though it might wear a thousand different names in a thousand different times, and might come from a thousand different directions, darkness always comes.

When the light came back I found myself way up high above everything again. So high up, I was above the clouds that had been moving in as I headed for bed, leaving me at the mercy of those unfamiliar stars.

I picked out the ghoulish dagger constellation in the north, took a guess at the direction I had followed before, put on all the speed I could and dived into the clouds. In moments I was down where treetops whisked right under where my love handles would have hung had I had any belly at all. I thought I could learn to enjoy this—if I could just get rid of the feeling that something was close behind me and gaining.

There were no lights down there this time. The whole world smelled of fear, as though every rock and animal and tree sensed something dire about to happen. I located a village. The entire population was wide awake, despite the hour. They huddled in frightened clumps, babies clutched tightly, livestock gathered into their homes with them. They did not talk much. The children whimpered.

How could they know what was happening at Overlook? Was there some prophecy or something that said tonight was the night the Shadowgate would go down? Had there been signs and portents unseen by me?

Did they know anything at all? Maybe their terror had nothing to do with Shadowmasters or the Black Company.

I streaked onward. Far, far ahead the occasional spark flipped into the sky. Those had to be the home fires burning.

The quarrel with the shadows was not over.

It was a long night.

The Shadowgate had not collapsed. Not yet. Longshadow was still alive.

I recalled having no problems getting close to any *she is the darkness* when I did not have Smoke along. I headed for the flickering remnant of Longshadow's crystal chamber.

Soulcatcher was on her feet and in nasty form, carping at Howler. The screaming wizard hardly knew where he was. "Come on, you worthless ball of rags!" Catcher raged in a fishwife's voice. "We've got to get out of here before my beloved sister realizes the lovely chance she's missing!"

Her darling sister was on her way already, thanks to me. I was surprised she was taking so long. She seemed to have grown cautious in the last hour. Of course, she did have to slither through a long tunnel, then wander around a dark fortress, then make a long climb, all the while making sure no little shadows jumped on her back.

Howler let out a groggy, interrogative sort of cry. He was not yet clear on where he was or how he had gotten there. He concentrated on getting his feet back under him.

Catcher had to keep her back clean, too. She cast some little spell that sent a worm of light slithering into all the dark places in that tossed salad of a chamber. It rooted out several tiny shadows. They evaded the light easily. Soulcatcher cursed. "Damned thing isn't fast enough!" The shadows darted at Longshadow, who was in far worse shape than Howler. He was, however, more in touch with what was happening around him. He whispered a cantrip before the darknesses reached his shell. The little shadows spun and went after the invaders.

This battle would not end while he was alive, apparently. He was a stubborn shit.

Soulcatcher cuffed Howler around the ears. The fishwife's shrill insisted, "Come on! This place is going to be your death if we don't get—" She sensed imminent danger. Lady was not far away now. "It's her." New voice. Baffled, frightened, childlike. "How does she dare? She *can't* have any real powers anymore. It doesn't *work* that way."

Lady was in the stairwell now. She did not seem afraid of a confrontation with her little sister at all.

She carried a bundle of short bamboo poles.

So did the dozen men behind her. They would be able to launch a small blizzard of fireballs. Those at the rear of the party backed up the steps. They kept poles ready to discharge at anything coming up behind them. The smell of fear grew stronger than the lingering perfume of Kina.

Soulcatcher thumped Howler a few more times, trying to get him to come alert. He remained too groggy to be much use.

She turned to the doorway. With some small but well-chosen spell she sealed it, then resumed trying to get Howler into shape for a flying escape.

The small shadows had gone into hiding again.

The door began to glow. Its surface rippled colorfully, according to the hue of the fireballs hitting its far side.

Soulcatcher produced a knife and slit Howler's clothing. I did not understand till she found what she was looking for. That proved to be a piece of silk, four feet by six when she spread it, and a little bundle of sticks. The silk rectangle became almost rigid when she spoke a certain word. It floated up off the floor like it was floating on the surface of a gently rippling pool. Soulcatcher broke the bundle of sticks and assembled them into a framework on which she stretched the silk. She muttered as she worked. The whole thing seemed much too fragile but in a minute she grabbed the Daughter of Night and clambered aboard. The carpet sagged but held their weight.

Sputtering, jerking like he was having a seizure, Howler staggered toward his stolen emergency conveyance. I wondered if this was his final secret or if he still had more flying tricks up his sleeves. I bet it was something like that piece of silk that got him out of dying, back when they thought he had crashed at high speed into the side of the Tower at Charm.

Soulcatcher did something incredibly violent. Most of the tower top vanished inside a globe of white light. The flare was so brilliant it betrayed every shadow slithering through the night but temporarily blinded half the men trying to exterminate them.

When the light faded a third of the tower's crystal roof no longer existed. Soulcatcher snagged Howler by the hair, dragged him onto the carpet, said some word that started the tiny thing moving.

It began to sink almost immediately. It barely cleared the turret. Then it went down, down, toward the unfriendly folks and unfriendlier shadows hunting one another amongst the rocks below. Catcher did not want to go down there but the carpet was overloaded. It was designed to help the runt get out of a tight spot, not him and all his friends and neighbors.

The smell of Kina grew stronger again. The whirlwind of rage was coming back for one more try.

The goddess did not want her daughter carried off.

The brat's eyes were closed inside her egg. That had proven to be flexible and slick when Soulcatcher was slinging it around. The kid's face bore that serene expression she got when she was communing with Kina.

Lady and her cohorts burst into the chamber where Longshadow and Narayan Singh still groaned and twitched. Fireballs routed the small shadows instantly. Seconds later a stream of fireballs reached down for Catcher and her companions. None hit home but they did alert our troops that something was on the fly. Anything that flew would not be friendly.

Kina's interest and anger heightened fast. A hurricane screamed in the ghostworld. Her stench leaked over into the real world. Men heaved up their last meals. The sky darkened more than the night and clouds insisted.

The earth shook.

The throne shudders and slips a thousandth of an inch. The tortured figure groans. Its blind eyes flutter.

One crow cackles.

The bird fails to recall that it dares not rest. Its claws touch down atop the sleeper's head. Before its wings finish folding it begins to scream. Small shadows have found it. They squabble over its life force joyfully.

The earth shivers. There is no silence anymore. Stone is broken. It continues to break. The light in the abyss is brighter. Pastel, gossamer mists rise like the questing tentacles of a sea anemone.

There is color. There is life, of a sort. There is light.

There is death. The crow shrieks out its pained outrage. And dies.

Death will find a way. Darkness will find a way inside.

Darkness always comes.

70

IT TOOK ME A WHILE TO REALIZE THAT THE SHAKING WAS NEITHER IMAGINARY nor metaphorical. The earth *was* shaking. This was a genuine badass earthquake as nasty as the one that had destroyed Kiaulune and much of the Shadowlands back before we headed south. Panic filled the air of the ghost world, apparently a divine panic on Kina's part. Her stink took on a whole new air.

Who ever heard of a god being scared?

Fireballs continued to scar the night.

I watched Lady and her people stagger around as they collected

Singh and Longshadow. They were extremely careful with both. Lady knew just how dangerous each could be. She had been both in her time.

She wanted to hurl some special farewell after her sister but before she could get a spell woven an aftershock rattled the fortress. Pieces began to fall off the battered tower. Lady decided it might be an opportune time to head downstairs and get out to ground where things were less likely to fall on her.

I decided it would be a good time to get back out and talk to Croaker. Then I recalled that I was not riding Smoke now so I did not have that kind of control. I could not force myself awake.

I decided to stick with Soulcatcher and her companions. It would be useful to know where she settled down to regain control enough to surround herself in mists and repulsions again.

For a second, as I went over the lip of the tower into the abyss of night, I thought I felt Smoke whiningly trying to shy away from the tower. Maybe I was getting too accustomed to being close to that little chickenshit.

The smell of Kina grew stronger, faded, grew stronger, as though the goddess was hunting blindly. Her anger never abated.

Soulcatcher managed to nag Howler awake enough to lend a hand keeping the carpet aloft. As soon as he had half his wits collected they began bickering. They must have gotten loud because the fireballs began streaking much closer.

Those things had a power that extended beyond the mortal plane, that was sure. I found out the hard way, by giving in to a childish temptation. I allowed one to go zipping through what, roughly, was my body space.

The pain was terrible. I felt what the shadows must feel when hit. But the fireball did not attach itself to me the way it did the shadows—though its momentum did drop dramatically enough for me to notice even in my agony.

I was not going to pull that damnfool trick again.

Catcher and Howler almost evaded me after I began to watch the fireballs too closely. But those that darted up after Howler's racket kept her trail warm.

She was heading for that same canyon where she had holed up all winter. It was unlikely that she would stay there long, though. We knew where it was.

I caught up. I could make some time out there when I concentrated.

Maybe I got too close. Soulcatcher seemed, suddenly, to realize that she was being watched. She stopped the carpet and spun it around. Even in the darkness I could feel the intensity of her glare. "Howler!" she snapped. "Do you feel something strange?"

Bad move, that. It encouraged the stinky little wizard to open his mouth. A grand howl ripped out when he did. Catcher had stopped right above some of the Prahbrindrah Drah's fugitives. They were very nervous men.

The first fireballs up illuminated the carpet well enough for other snipers to take better aim. Hardly had Howler gotten his mouth under control than a fireball winged him. He shrieked again. And lost his concentration.

The carpet began to slide toward the ground. Soulcatcher cursed in a cranky old man's voice, fought it. A fireball nearly parted her raven hair. Enraged, she opened her mouth to pronounce some deadly retribution.

The carpet began to fall.

Catcher shrieked in frustration, threw out a booted foot and pushed Howler off the edge of the carpet. He yelled angrily. Catcher grumbled an unfriendly goodbye. The carpet stopped falling. Muttering control spells, Catcher got it moving again. The boys on the ground never stopped sniping.

A fireball passed through the carpet between Soulcatcher and the Daughter of Night.

Kina, while unable to catch up and hammer Catcher, seemed to be aware of events. A whirlwind of rage filled the shadow world. A glimmer of the multiarmed idol began to show through on our side. It never coalesced completely but did materialize enough to send the Taglian loyalists running whatever direction they happened to be facing.

Howler howled. He plummeted toward the earth. He always was a lucky little shit and his luck held now. First he plunged through the branches of some heavy evergreens. They whipped the pudding out of him but slowed his fall. Then he smashed into a hillside still covered with unmelted snow. That was deep enough that he vanished into it.

I had not one doubt that he would be up and dancing like a dervish before lunchtime. And likely in a mood to show Soulcatcher just how much he loved her.

I sniffed around for a few minutes, marking the spot. Howler did nothing. I figured I had better go try to wake up. This looked like a once-in-a-lifetime chance either to recruit a first-line wizard or to put him out of our misery forever.

I suspected Croaker would prefer the latter option. We had had too many unfriendly encounters with the Howler over the years.

Did I mention Howler's luck? I could not wake up. Evidently my spirit had no power over my body when that wanted to sleep. It looked like I had to keep wandering, want to or not.

I recalled last year when I had gone off without even being asleep. When Soulcatcher somehow pried me loose by means unknown and for a purpose I never divined. Which she might do to me again. Particularly if anything I had done lately had caught her attention.

There was a good chance the whole thing had been just a game to her, something to while away some time while fragments of her scheme fell into place. Or maybe she had been experimenting. Or both things, and maybe more. What we know for sure about Catcher is that she walks in chaos and her motives are changeable.

I must be driven. I figured that as long as I had to stay out there I ought to keep scouting around. Working in my sleep. Ought to have the Old Man double my pay. How much is two times a stab in the back?

The Prince was making good time. He was headed straight up the road north, which was the only reason I found him. A whole mob of his guys were running with him. And they did keep moving briskly.

Shadows larked around them like wolves on the hunt for dangerous game. It was a running fight. The Prince's men did not have many bamboo poles but whenever one of the crowd began shrieking he died of fireballitis before the attacking shadows could finish their cruel work.

I wasted no time looking for Mogaba or Goblin. Too much work to find them. Maybe after it got light. Which it ought to be starting by now, only the clouds were so heavy.

I headed back toward Overlook.

Everywhere I went I saw evidence of the latest earthquake: landslides, toppled trees, a collapsed bridge the southerners had rebuilt after the last quake, then had cast down so we could not use it so Cletus and his brothers had had to put it up again. And lots of shelters knocked over or fallen in. And cracks in the ground. And even some damage to Overlook, up where Longshadow had bickered with his pals and then everybody had quarreled with Kina.

As I closed in a large block of white stone slipped out of Longshadow's tower and plunged toward the foot of the wall. Several more followed quickly. The tower seemed to wobble slightly, as if made of gelatin instead of stone. Then I realized I was seeing an aftershock in progress. Or maybe a temblor even bigger than the last.

Shit! Was the whole damned fortress going to come tumbling down? Lady and her crew were still inside. No. Not possible. No earthquake was going to lay Overlook low. It was just too massive. Practically speaking, there was hardly anywhere for it to fall since it was more stone than empty volume.

Longshadow's workbenches and mystery engines began to shift.

71

A JET OF WHITE FIRE SPURTED SKYWARD, RIPPED OPEN THE BELLIES OF THE low-hanging clouds. Even in the ghostworld I could hear the roar of energy being released. Crystal near the jet vanished in blue puffs. Farther away it melted and ran like candle wax. It dripped. I saw a glob plummet into a pail of water, sizzle. Right then I decided that if I survived I would climb that tower—if it survived—and claim that marble as a souvenir.

The jet faded from white to yellow to red, then went dark, but the heat was still there, squirting away less violently, for a while. The Shadowmaster had had a lot of power stashed atop that tower.

Everything burnable in the remains of the chamber was now on fire. Several small shadows scuttled hither and yon. They seemed unwilling to leave despite the disaster. Maybe they were domesticated.

The first raindrops fell. Those passing through the invisible energy jet sizzled into steam.

I was thinking about going down inside the fortress to check on Lady, and having no luck convincing myself, when one of the shadows decided it might be happier hitting the trail. The trail it chose was the one Lady had to have taken with her prisoners.

An entire section of my mind devoted itself to speculating about the futures of Longshadow and Narayan Singh. Narayan's prospects, I feared, were particularly bleak.

I followed the shadow.

I did not want to do that. But I felt compelled. It might sneak up on Lady and the guys. It might be devoted to its master. It might want to help him get away.

I sort of chuckled at the image of Longshadow trying to run, busted up the way he was.

I had no sympathy for the guy.

I tried sensing Lady's presence ahead, could not. And I could not go anywhere in a straight line, of course. I still could not walk through walls. Which meant I suffered the same constraints as shadows. Did that mean I could go anywhere shadows could? Did it mean shadows could go anywhere I could?

That was troubling.

There was no light inside Overlook, nor any sound or landmarks. I changed my mind about finding Lady quickly.

I can have nightmares about darkness and tight places even when I am awake.

I turned back. Insofar as I was aware there had been no branchings to make me lose my way.

I ran into a shadow head-on.

There was no source of light but the forge where the torturer heated his instruments. That flickered, illuminating the creased, weathered bronze face of the frightened little man who had not become a soldier because he wanted to but because he believed he owed his gods a service when they demanded it. Like all his own people (and as their enemies did also), he hoped his own gods were strongest and would prevail.

It was one slice of nightmare two seconds long, filled with information so alien most would never make sense to me. I was not sure I should assume that the shadow I had encountered actually connected with a man who had been tortured to death after having been captured in some religious war. No religion in these parts worked that way. Not even the Deceivers did—though they had tortured some victims, in ages past, in the Grove of Doom, during their Festival of Lights.

My encounter with the shadow had not been that bad, really. I did not think collisions would be troublesome as long as I was ghostwalking. But it probably would have been a fatal meeting had it come while I was in my own body.

The incident did leave me goofy and disoriented. I floated back up to the remnants of the crystal chamber. The place had cooled down. The light had gone dead. But there was another light in the world now, despite the overcast. Daylight was coming at last.

Just as I realized that night's siege was ending a final small volley of fireballs erupted near the Shadowgate. Then the world went still. And for a few minutes nobody and nothing was killing anybody or anything anywhere within sight.

I looked south and reflected that there was no Smoke to keep me from going over there and taking a peek. And shadows did not bother me in this state. And if they did try, why, they behaved like rodents. No matter how big and ferocious, they stayed close to the surface. They wanted to be able to get into hiding quickly. And I could fly.

I started southward. I really did. But something happened.

The earth shook again.

Lightning struck Overlook only a dozen feet away.

Thai Dei woke me up.

The effect was, I headed south but something grabbed me by the scruff of the neck and I spun northward like a leaf snatched up by a dust devil.

*   *   *

"I don't want to get up," I told the hand abusing my repose. "I'm tired. I worked all night." I *was* tired. I *had* worked all night. Hard. I did want to roll over and snooze for another eight hours.

Thai Dei poked me again. And then there was the other problem. Maybe a bigger problem.

My feet were wet.

I pushed myself up onto one elbow as Thai Dei told me, "You must get up!"

"I hate to admit it. You're right. I gotta get up." I had to get up because rainwater was running in in a stream, turning the floor to mud.

I banged my head against a log. "What the hell?" The overhead had fallen halfway in. The far wall had collapsed. The only reason I could see anything was that Thai Dei had brought a candle—the shadow repeller— when he came to visit. "What happened?"

"Earthquake."

Oh. Yeah. It had not occurred to me that I could become a disaster victim, too.

By the time I got my knees under me I saw that Thai Dei must have done a lot of work just to get to me. I was in a pocket. Most of our dugout must have fallen in. "Mother Gota?" I asked. I had shifted to Nyueng Bao without thinking.

"I don't know." He responded in the same language. "She never came home." His voice had an uncharacteristic edge. The strain was getting to him. Every few years he cracked and stopped being the ice man for minutes at a time.

"How'd you get in?"

"Where the roof fell in."

I had to duckwalk to look at the hole. Yeah. I could see where he had squeezed his way in. There was some ugly grey sky out there. It was drizzling still. Thai Dei was about half my size, though. "I'm going to have to stay down here for a couple months before I can get through that. I shouldn't have put on all that weight after we got out of Dejagore." We had looked bad back then. Like walking skeletons, most of us.

I wondered if that had anything to do with my dreams.

"Take the candle. I'll go up and make the hole bigger."

My bodyguard. This was about the first time he ever had a real chance to save my ass and it was from being smothered by a vicious sod roof.

He pushed himself up into the opening. He wiggled. He squirmed. He dropped back down. "You need to push me."

"Too many snacks while we were sitting around here bullshitting. Go." I set the candle aside very carefully. It had become very important to me. I did not want to be down there in that tight, cold, wet place without a light.

I grabbed his legs and pushed. There must have been enough water in the hole to lubricate it. He popped through. I chuckled at a mental image of the earth giving birth to that ugly little man, like some clay devil in the Gunni myths.

I heard voices. Something blocked the dirty light. Croaker called, "Hey, deadbeat, you still breathing down there?"

"I'm fine. I was thinking about taking a nap."

"You might as well. We're going to be a while getting you out."

"All right. I'll be fine." As long as the candle lasted.

I looked at it. It had a lot of life left. Those things were designed to last.

I began to think about what Thai Dei had had to do to come down into a place where shadows might be hiding just to see how I was doing. And that made me wonder that much more about the landscape of his interior world. Maybe I was a sloppy thinker. Or maybe just not yet experienced enough at being Nyueng Bao. I could not even work out how to treat Thai Dei like he was several different, distinct characters.

He and the Nyueng Bao believed he owed me a debt so great he had devoted his life to protecting me. He would lay that, and maybe even his soul, down for me. But at the same time he would willingly lie to and deceive the foreigner who was a cause for shame on his family. And, certainly, he would tell a Soldier of Darkness nothing that might cast *any* light upon Nyueng Bao attitudes toward the Black Company.

Come to think of it, not even my darling, beloved Sarie had gone that far. She could always change the subject without appearing to have done so.

I said something into the hole but nobody answered. Well, screw them. I was tired.

I sat down in the deepening mud and did go back to sleep.

I did not go anywhere. I did not do anything but sleep.

72

I WAS A TERRIBLE MESS WHEN PRISONERS FROM THE PRINCE'S DIVISION hauled me out of the ground. Otto and Hagop, who belonged with the Old Division and whom I had not seen since Charandaprash, came to stare down at me. "Looks like one a them mole-rat things they got down here," Otto said.

"Only filthier. It wasn't raining, Ott, I'd say get a bucket a water and throw it on him."

"Comics," I muttered. "You just gave away why you signed on. Your only way to get out of town ahead of an audience turned ugly."

"His disposition's improved since the last time we saw him," Hagop observed. "He don't let these little setbacks bother him anymore."

"How you guys been keeping? We don't get a lot of personal news over here."

Hagop frowned. Otto said, "A nick here, a ding there. Nothing serious." Practically ever since I met them one or both had been recovering from some kind of wound. It was what they were known for. They were icons, practically. Otto and Hagop could not be killed, only injured, and as long as they stayed alive the Black Company would survive.

Hagop said, "We was sent over with a bunch of stuff for the Old Man and some stuff for you to put in the Annals. Names."

"Oh." Croaker and I always tried to record the names of our fallen brethren the best we could. A lot of guys counted on it. Once they were gone it would be the only evidence that they had ever lived. It was immortality of a sort.

"Lot a names," Hagop persisted. "Hundreds. Last night was not a good night for the Old Division."

"You going to be able?" Otto asked. "Is everything buried down there in the mud?"

"It is. But I was more careful with the Annals and that stuff than I was with me. I kept them in a room with logs for the walls and floor and ceiling, with drainage and everything. Just in case. I figured the Shadowmaster would be the problem, though. Hundreds of names? Really? Any I know?"

"They're just all on a list."

"I'll have to add them on at the back of the volume I'm doing now." If there were hundreds they would be recent enlistees, their names likely unknown to me. They would be recorded on a payroll somewhere but that had nothing to do with me.

Thai Dei materialized. I had not noted his absence till he did. He said, "My mother was all right." He did not sound real sure about that, though.

"Uhm?"

"They found her in the wizard's hole when they dug him out. Which was why they were so long getting to you. Your Captain knew you were all right. He did not know if the wizard was dead or alive."

He meant One-Eye, I realized. Well, of course, if the quake had been bad enough to overcome the fine craftsmanship Thai Dei and I put into our place, then One-Eye's place could not be anything but a rainwater pool by now.

"She was in One-Eye's dugout?"

Embarrassed, whispering because there were other Nyueng Bao around, Thai Dei admitted, "They were both dead drunk. Passed out in their own vomit. Didn't even know the roof had fallen in till the rescuers pulled them out."

"I'm sorry," I told him. "But I'm just going to have to laugh." It came on me hard. It was more than just picturing those two getting plotzed together. It was the release of all the stress from last night.

Otto and Hagop stared at the slopes to the south, restraining their own amusement.

I suffered another laugh seizure. I realized that, before lunch, word would be all over what was left of the army. Undoubtedly it would suffer severe exaggaration and would evolve into some prurient epic before it reached our most remote outpost.

The slope that had been the home of the headquarters group had turned into thirty acres of pockmarks. Hardly a dugout had survived. Prisoners were digging in a dozen different places.

I spotted one familiar face, then another, directing rescue teams. "So. She didn't stay mad at them."

"What?" Thai Dei asked.

"Nothing. Just thinking out loud." Speak of the devil. There she came out of the Old Man's bunker. Which had survived unscathed. Croaker was right behind her. Neither looked rested. But they sure looked pleased with themselves.

I grumbled inarticulately, deep in my throat. *My* wife was half a world away.

Croaker ambled over. "Time for your annual bath, Murgen."

"If I just stand here in the rain long enough . . ."

Lady stared a hole through me. She wanted to interrogate me. But not now, not here, not in front of so many people who did not need to hear my answers because half of them did not themselves know where their loyalties lay.

I asked, "How bad did we get hurt last night?"

Croaker shuddered. Maybe some cold rainwater got inside his collar. "I don't know yet. Lady has almost two thousand people she still can't account for."

"They keep turning up, though," she said, joining us. "I imagine we'll find most of them eventually." Probably dead.

I said, "Otto and Hagop say we lost a big chunk of the Old Division."

Croaker nodded. "They brought a list. It's way longer than I hoped. We still don't have anything useful from the other divisions. The New Division is still disorganized and the Prince's fell apart completely. Did you have something you wanted to say in private? You have that look."

"Yes." Smoke rose from the crude chimney of Croaker's shelter. Warm sounded good. I would make up something to tell him if I had to.

I joined him in the warmth with no remorse and little sympathy for the guys I had left out in the rain.

Lady followed us inside. She wore a smug but hungry look.

Lady had one of Croaker's rough maps spread before the fire. "Can you pinpoint where he went down?" She meant the Howler. "Maybe we can still catch him if he was hurt bad."

"What's that?" the Old Man asked when I mumbled.

"Uh . . . I said, 'you never stop tempting trouble, do you?'"

Lady did not turn me into a toad. Nor even one of Otto's ugly little mole-rats. She was in a good mood this morning, as opposed to last night.

Smoke groaned. He startled me, though it was his second groan since I had come into Croaker's shelter. I glanced that way. The curtain was open. Longshadow and Narayan Singh had been stacked in the alcove with the stricken wizard. I could not imagine Lady and the Old Man fooling around with that crew piled up only a few feet away, but it was obvious that they had taken complete advantage of their opportunity.

I was mildly surprised Lady would turn her prisoners over—even to her old man. Longshadow represented a great opportunity to gain power. And Singh . . . Lady owed Singh a lot. But so did the Captain.

Maybe they would make a family project out of Narayan.

She asked fewer questions than I expected, mainly about Smoke's limitations. I did not mention that I was developing an ability to travel without the comatose wizard. She did not ask. Croaker, though, noted that I knew about Howler even though I had been in my own bunker during the Taker's run of bad luck.

"I'll send Blade," she decided. "He's levelheaded. He can get a job done without getting himself or Howler killed."

I wanted to ask how Blade and Swan had slithered back into her favor but management decisions were none of my business. I had had Lady explain that to me already, emphatically, regarding another matter.

She left to offer Blade his opportunity.

While she was away Croaker asked, "Where's the standard?"

"Buried in my dugout."

"Uhm. How about the Annals and stuff?"

"They're in there, too. But they should be all right for now. If we have another quake, or a lot more rain, though . . . I don't know."

"We'll go after that as soon as we've got our people dug out."

"How come she brought Singh and the Shadowmaster here?"

He understood. "Because I'm the physician. And they're both about half a heartbeat short of dying. Maybe if she'd had somebody of her own handy, whom she trusted . . ." He let it trail off. He would never trust his woman completely, where ambition might enter the equation.

"She's probably less risk than you think. I think I figured it out last night."

"What?"

"Her relationship to Kina. How it works and why it exists. I think I got it."

"You have time to think when you're out playing spook?"

"Some."

"So tell me about my sweetie and Kina."

"Begin with the premise that she's pretty damned bright."

"Oh. Yeah." He smiled at some private thought.

"Not to mention pretty strong-willed."

"You going to waste my time with understatements? Or are you going to get on with it?"

"Onward. I think that, a long time ago, before we ever got to Gea-Xle, when she first showed unexpected signs of regaining some power, she understood that some force down here meant to use her. And she let it happen. And that lulled that force into thinking that it had claimed a slave when in fact what it really got was a parasite."

Several possible responses stirred behind Croaker's eyes. But he said only, "Go on."

"That's pretty much it. While the goddess was using her, Lady was limpeting herself to Kina so she could suck off power she could use herself. I think she's burrowed in so deep Kina can't get rid of her without crippling herself. I think Lady may even have some control over what the goddess does. Kina got real upset last night. The Daughter of Night was being threatened directly. But when she tried to help the kid, even though she managed to get really destructive, her efforts never quite hit their mark."

"And you think Lady . . . ?"

"Yes. He's right." Lady stepped into the weak light. No telling how long she had been behind us, listening. She was the darkness when it came to moving quietly. "That doesn't leave this place. So long as they think I'm the real thing the end results will be the same as if I were."

I discovered some interesting mold formations developing on the wall in front of me. I gave them my devoted attention.

Croaker said, "If you're like some kind of leech or something, how come Kina hasn't tried to get rid of you?"

"Most of Kina is asleep. The part that isn't is interested only in bringing on the Year of the Skulls. And she's pretty stupid besides. She didn't understand what I'd done till recently. She may ponder it for years before she decides to do something about it."

I said, "She does seem to look at time in a different way."

Lady continued, "I'm concerned that my beloved sister may have solved the puzzle, too. Or will now that she has the girl. The girl knows."

I said, "Catcher's hiding out in the same place she has ever since she got here." The Old Man knew where that was.

Croaker said, "I'd love to take a crack. But we've only got ten hours to get ready for another night."

I understood. But boy would it have been nice to get Catcher tucked safely into the past.

Twenty minutes of speculation did nothing to unravel Catcher's ultimate motives. Not even Lady could guess what Catcher really wanted or what she might do next.

"She was that way when she was four years old," Lady said. "Hell. She was born unpredictable."

I must have looked too interested. The story stopped there.

I did not overlook the fact that neither Croaker nor Lady ever referred to their child in any way that might suggest that she was anything but an unnatural monster entirely unconnected to them.

73

I WATCHED WHEEZER DIRECT THE WINKLING OUT OF A SMALL SHADOW THAT had worked its way up close to the perimeter of One-Eye's safe zone before going into hiding from the light. Lady had modified One-Eye's amulets so that they could be used to detect shadows. Our guys were rooting them out with great enthusiasm—particularly considering that most of those guys were exhausted. I said, "I can't believe that old boy isn't dead yet."

On cue Wheezer tried to hawk up a lung. He was ancient when he joined the Company years ago and was dying of consumption even then. The only thing good that could be said about his situation was that he somehow managed to stay alive.

Thai Dei grunted. He did not care about Wheezer. Although he was supposedly helping excavate our bunker he spent more attention on his mother, who snored ferociously in the shelter of a tent that had belonged to somebody who had not survived the night. His face was stone. His eyes were ice. If another Nyueng Bao came anywhere near him his hackles rose. He was just waiting for somebody to say something, anything, that he could interpret as an insult so he could spend his embarrassment in a good fight.

When they dug Gota and One-Eye out not only were they passed out drunk, they were on the same pallet wearing less than their usual apparel.

So that was his tonk game, eh?

I worked hard not to crack a smile. Thai Dei might decide I was truly family after all and take it out on me.

I hoped he would not confront One-Eye. One-Eye would have a murderous hangover when he woke up. One-Eye with a hangover is not somebody to annoy.

Croaker was sorely exercised, I knew. The little wizard had rendered himself useless at a time when his talents were needed desperately.

Everywhere you looked people were scurrying to rebuild and to get ready for another night with a leaky Shadowgate. Lady and the Old Man hoped Longshadow would help improve that situation but no good news had been reported yet. They were having trouble getting him out of his shell.

They had no time to concentrate. Messengers came and went continuously, interrupting constantly.

"Another dozen shovels full and I think we can get it open," I told Thai Dei. I had conscripted a door somebody else had stolen from the ruins. I had used it to close off the little workroom I had managed to complete just in time for the earthquake.

One of Croaker's guards appeared. "The Captain wishes to see you, Standardbearer."

"Wonderful. I'll be right back, Thai Dei." I clambered up out of the muddy hole and headed for Croaker's dugout. I ducked inside. The crowd had thinned out. Amazing. "What you need, boss?" He and Lady had Longshadow stretched out on a table made out of another stolen door. The Shadowmaster was too long for it. His feet hung off.

Lady had managed to eliminate the sorcerer's protective shell.

"Fellow just came in from Blade's bunch, Murgen. They've found Howler. He's still buried in the snow. They don't know if he's unconscious or dead."

"He's been there long enough he should've froze to death." But he was one of the Taken. They did not die easily. Especially not Howler. I glanced at Lady.

She told me, "I can't tell from here."

Croaker said, "They also caught Cordy Mather and his gang. They asked what to do about them." He was poking and squeezing Long-shadow's limbs, looking for broken bones, I guess. He told Lady, "This man hasn't eaten right for a long time."

"Maybe he was worried about poison." She stared down at the Shadowmaster's mask. She started to reach.

"You sure you've cancelled all of his spells?" the Old Man asked.

"You can't ever be sure with somebody you don't know. Murgen. Did you ever see him with this off?"

The messenger from Blade pricked up his ears. He was collecting stories to share with the guys.

"No. How would I manage that? I never saw him before right now."

She took the hint.

Croaker said, "What I want, Murgen, is for you to round up some men, including One-Eye—even if you have to carry him—and go help Blade." And maybe keep an eye on him, eh, chief? Him and Mather being such good buddies? "Be careful with Howler but bring him in if you can."

I grunted unhappily. Lady took hold of Longshadow's mask.

The Old Man asked me, "You found out anything more about the planting season around here?"

I gave him a baffled look. That was an odd shift of subject. But he did that. His mind sometimes ran a dozen directions at once.

He continued, "We've got to get crops planted if we mean to stay here. That or pull a Mogaba and start eating each other."

Lady pulled the Shadowmaster's mask away.

Longshadow arced as though stabbed. His eyes opened. But he could do nothing else. He had been constrained and silenced by a master.

I asked, "Why don't we move into his place? There're supplies in there. Some. And Overlook is sure a whole hell of a lot drier inside than here. I don't recognize him." The Shadowmaster's face was gaunt and oriental but pale as lard. There were just a few teeth in his open mouth, supporting Croaker's assessment of his diet. He looked like a guy who had suffered repeated bouts with rickets or scurvy or something like that.

"Neither do I," Lady said. She sounded badly disappointed. I do believe she really expected him to be one of the Taken, or at least some-one she had encountered in the past.

I asked, "Is this a problem?"

"I was hoping for a break. Something to make life easier."

"You picked the wrong husband. Boss, can I get out there and back before dark?"

The messenger nodded. "Easy. It's only four miles. There's road most of the way and it's still in good shape."

Smoke groaned again. There was a taint of fear there this time. Lady frowned his way. He was a problem she wished she had time to explore.

"Get a move on," Croaker told me. "It'll get dark eventually."

Darkness always comes. "I love walking in the rain." I beckoned the messenger, went back outside. A walk in the rain would not be that awful. I could not get any more wet.

I told Thai Dei, "The Captain wants us to go collect some prisoners."

74

THERE ARE DISADVANTAGES TO TRAVELING WET. YOU GET A LOT OF CHAFING, for example. By the time I caught up with Blade I had blisters on my feet and a raw spot inside my right thigh that burned awfully. And I still had to go back the other way.

Thai Dei was no happier than I was. None of the guys tagging along were cheerful. They had to take turns carrying One-Eye. The runt's most ambitious effort yet had been to roll onto his side to puke over the edge of his litter.

I had had a notion about sneaking on up to peek into Soulcatcher's ravine. It was a notion that died stillborn about the time we left the road for the forest. A few hundred yards of slip-sliding around in the mud and pine needles and, in the shady places, snow, on steepening hillsides, quickly convinced me that this was no day to demonstrate individual initiative.

One thing I could be sure of. Soulcatcher would be around later.

I flopped down beside Blade. "Have a good trip down?" I asked Mather. "Sorry we couldn't reserve better weather for you."

Blade chuckled. So did Willow Swan, who observed, "This is about as good as it gets, Cordy. We did save the best for you."

"I knew you were my pals."

I asked, "Where's our boy Howler?" None of this country looked the same as it had during the night, from the air.

Swan pointed uphill, southward, toward where some tall evergreens held on to a thick clot of shadow. "Buried in some snow up there."

The guys with me dropped One-Eye's litter. The little wizard moaned but did not yet have enough ambition to curse or threaten anyone.

I asked, "What did you guys do to convince Lady she could let you run around loose?"

Blade chuckled. "She convinced *him.* By pointing out that anybody who doesn't stay close and friendly won't have any protection from the shadows."

I grunted. "It's a realization that's going around as people begin to examine their consciences." It was the kind of question that has led many men to select options for which they may be excoriated later, by people with full bellies sitting in front of cozy fires. "Anybody got any grease? Even anything that will pass for grease?"

My old pal Thai Dei was lugging a glob of lard. In case we had to do some cooking. Nyueng Bao never ceased to amaze. Though their religion had to be an offshoot of the Gunni, somehow they did eat meat and, unlike the Vehdna, that did include pork. The swamp did not allow them to become too picky. Thai Dei must have lugged that lard for years, using it over and over. . . . No matter. Lard was exactly what I needed.

I dropped my trousers, treated the insides of my thighs to a generous spread. "This'll keep me going for a while."

One-Eye began thrashing on his litter, fighting his blanket and complaining about being wet. His problem was trivial. It was not raining anymore.

He threw up over the side again, hacking and gagging, then settled down to sleep.

"That looks pretty raw already," Swan told me.

"Kiss it better," Mather suggested.

"Some reunion. Our old pal Cordy got above himself since he's been hobnobbing with the Woman—"

I said, "Let's go do our wizard mining."

Blade said, "I really don't want to do this."

"No shit. Me neither. Tell you what. Why don't we let Swan and Mather get him? We'll stay right here so somebody can get word back to camp in case anything goes wrong."

Mather said, "This guy is definitely starting to sound like an officer. You get a couple field promotions during the campaign?"

"I'm a god." I let Thai Dei help me up. He had not sprawled on the ground. His muscles were still loose. He started heading the direction Swan had indicated earlier.

Blade asked, "What about your pet?" He chucked a pinecone at One-Eye. One-Eye barely twitched.

"He's got liabilities enough." Let sleeping sorcerers lie.

One-Eye sat up. He slurred, "I heard that, Kid." Then he collapsed again.

I said, "I think I'll leave him here and take the other one back on the stretcher." An idea which proved popular immediately. Not even One-Eye came out against it. He was busy snoring again.

There was no evidence that Howler had moved an inch since his fall. There was just the hole where he had gone into the snow and at its bottom, about eight feet deep, a bundle of dark rags. A light dust of loose snow had blown in on top of him.

"Hey! Lookit here!" a soldier called from maybe thirty feet away, up the slope past Howler.

"What you got?" I asked. I was not walking ten feet if I did not have to.

"Looks like a dead wolf."

I worked my way up there. "Sumbitch, guys! He found a dead wolf." I knelt. "Looks like it got caught by a shadow." Evidence on the slope suggested that it had been sneaking toward Howler when bad luck got in its way. Then it had tried to run. It had not been alone, of course, but the tracks indicated a very small pack.

"I didn't know they had wolves down here," somebody said.

"Now you do." The death of the wolf did not seem critical. Except to tell us that a shadow had been around here last night and might still be hiding somewhere nearby. "Be careful if you're anywhere that's dark."

I went back down to check Howler. He had not moved. Of course.

"He alive?" Swan asked.

Blade suggested, "Get a long stick and poke him."

I said, "Let's dig him out."

"That smart?"

"He won't do anything till we get him out of the hole." I would not have in his position. Always let some other fool do the work if he insists.

The snow was old snow. Its surface had melted and refrozen numerous times. It was hard and heavy. Luckily, Howler was not really eight feet under. He had passed through eight feet of snow but that snow lay on a steep hillside and was only about four feet thick going in at the most direct angle.

I had a notion. "Don't scatter that stuff too far. We might want to use some."

"There ain't exactly a shortage," Swan grumbled.

Thai Dei, I noted, never offered to help. He stood back with his hand on his sword, alert, one eye cocked toward One-Eye. Perhaps his impulses were evil.

His vigilance proved unnecessary. As the more daring men brushed snow off Howler one of them announced, "He's froze solid."

A huge sigh of relief ripped through the crowd.

"Excellent!" I observed. "Here's what we'll do, then."

An hour later we had the little wizard tied to a carrying pole, packed inside a layer of snow six inches thick. "Just to keep him from spoiling on the way," I told the guys, some of whom had had to give up ragged bits of clothing to help keep the snow around Howler. They all whined and groaned and groused and wanted to know why we could not just pack him in with the other one.

They were going to break One-Eye's heart. They did not love him anymore.

75

"USE THIS SALVE," CROAKER TOLD ME. "AND TRY TO KEEP IT AS CLEAN AND dry as you can."

"I was walking bowlegged before we got back." I scowled at One-Eye, who was seated on the floor near Croaker's fire, not saying a word. He looked like he wished we would let him fall asleep for a year, so the pain would go away. He was still in such bad shape that he did not have energy enough to complain.

Mother Gota was more resilient. Her youth, I suppose. She and Uncle Doj had been working on the family dugout when Thai Dei and I returned from our adventure. Nobody, including Uncle Doj, had anything to say. I ignored his long absence. I had no time for Nyueng Bao mystery games. I left them stirring the mud in an effort to get a shelter up before night fell again.

Lady had Howler on the door table, examining him. She concluded, "He should recover."

I asked, "You get issued nine lives when you get Taken? That little shit is starting to look stubborner than the Limper was." We killed that asshole half a dozen times. We thought. And he just kept coming back.

Lady said, "No. But anybody who has the drive to become a wizard of his level is the sort who wastes no opportunity to further prepare for any imaginable possibility."

I asked the Old Man, "What's it look like out there?" There had been dramatic changes in the few hours I was away. Besides the passage of the rain. Most of the survivors had been collected either in the vicinity of the headquarters group or directly below the Shadowgate. A lot of manhours had gone into locating every surviving piece of workable bamboo. Lady's reloading factory was hard at work, too, but the effort there was little more than symbolic of the leadership's commitment to continue the struggle.

"Looks better than I thought it would. Lady got Longshadow stabilized. That should mean we're back to the slow leakage we had before he got hurt. If he mends all right we'll have him shut it down in a couple of days."

"We going to be able to control him?"

"Oh yeah. You've seen statues of dead generals that had more freedom of action than she's left him."

Lady looked up from her work. She wore the tiniest of smiles but it betrayed the confident amusement of an old, old evil. *She is the darkness.* Smoke was for sure right about that.

I said, "Wouldn't we be better off if we moved into Overlook?"

"Maybe. And we might do that. Once we get straightened out and know where everybody is. And figure out where, for right now, their loyalties lie."

"Speaking of which. Uncle Doj is back. He's out there helping my mother-in-law and acting like he was never gone."

"I heard."

"I'm wondering how he managed to survive. Especially last night."

Lady looked at me like I had sparked a surprise thought. She said, "Watch Howler. Call me if he moves. I'll be right outside." She hurried out the doorway.

I looked at Croaker. He shrugged. "I don't ask anymore."

"She looks pretty ragged."

"Don't we all? But maybe we'll get to rest up now. If we get the Shadowgate under control there won't be anybody to aggravate us for a long time. If ever."

Mogaba was out there. But he had no patron anymore. That meant that nobody could cover his ass magically. He would have to back off. And the Prahbrindrah Drah might not live long enough to become a problem. He had to evade both shadows and Goblin to reach friendly territory. And even so-called friendly territory would not be very friendly if he could not pull together a band big enough to look out for itself. Peasants are notoriously cruel to fleeing soldiers when they catch them at a disadvantage. Possibly that is because soldiers are so cruel to peasants when the advantage lies in their hands, though many from the hyperrefined warrior classes have insisted it springs from the beastly nature of the peasantry.

"Can you get over to the Shadowgate?"

"Me? Now?"

"You. Now. Before dark. Carrying the standard. To test my theory about what it is. And to help cover the troops there if I'm right."

"I can try. But I'm in pretty lousy shape."

"You could ride."

That was asking for another set of galled spots entirely but he was right.

With a slightly nasty smile he observed, "You could have your understudy do it for you—if you had one."

So he knew Sleepy was missing. I needed to check on the kid first chance I got.

Lady pushed back inside. She was not a big woman but she had a big presence. I was always surprised when I saw her after a separation because I always remembered her about a foot taller. She told me, "Your friend Doj isn't just a priest from some obscure cult. He's a sorcerer. Very minor. Less than One-Eye in ability. But he's carrying something—an amulet, an artifact, what exactly I couldn't determine—that protects him from shadows."

Croaker looked at me like I ought to have known all about that years ago. "I don't know, boss. This's the first I've heard about it." Though I had always suspected that Uncle Doj might be able to do something besides crochet with a sword. In fact, his skills with a blade always did seem almost magically augmented. How could a guy pull off something like that attack on the Deceivers at Charandaprash without getting swamped by sheer weight of numbers?

I do not know why but I told Lady, "My wife isn't dead. The Deceivers never touched her when they raided our apartment. Thai Dei and Doj and some cousins took her away, then told me she was dead. They also convinced her that I was dead while they were taking her back to the swamp. They've got her stashed in a temple there now, where she won't embarrass them by being pregnant. Doj and Gota don't want us two together. They only ever put up with it at all because Gota's parents insisted." Sarie, her family and the Nyueng Bao were not something I had discussed with Lady before. I never talked with her much about anything except stuff that needed to go into the Annals or the stuff that she had written there that needed clarification.

She checked Howler again while she listened to my chatter. She suggested, "Tell me all about this. I've always had a feeling that there was something going on."

Yeah? Right. Her and everybody else smart enough not to eat dirt.

Croaker went to the doorway and stuck his head out. He popped back inside. "Hey. Why didn't you say it'd stopped raining? Maybe I can get these assholes to move a little faster now." Out he went. I felt for him. He looked even more worn out than I felt.

I said, "I did tell him."

"He doesn't always listen. Talk to me about the Nyueng Bao."

I talked. Lady listened. She asked sharp questions. I returned the favor at times, when we touched on anything I thought I wanted to know.

She said, "I want to know about your dreams, too."

"They're different than yours. I think."

"I know. How they're different might mean a lot."

We talked a long time. But not long enough for me to get out of trekking over to the Shadowgate with the goddamn standard.

76

HORSES WERE IN SHORT SUPPLY. MOST THAT HAD NOT GOTTEN EATEN HAD been killed by shadows the previous night. And were getting eaten now. I ended up borrowing Lady's mount. Croaker never said a word. He did not have to. Down the road somewhere I was going to pay.

Thai Dei got up behind me. Lady's stallion, which was used to lugging only her hundred and a few pounds, plus armor occasionally, glared over his shoulder. I told the beast, "It's only for a little ways. I promise."

The Old Division and some of Lady's troops had moved into camp below the Shadowgate. Tensions were obvious as we rode in. A lot of faces were less than friendly. These were men who had stayed with the Company mainly because their chances of survival were better with us than away from us. Twilight was not far off, though, so no one was inclined to belligerence.

I decided not to tell anybody why I had brought the standard.

Word spread fast. Company brothers came out to see if there was anything special in the wind. I ran into people I had not seen for months. Some, even, whom I had not seen since we had left Taglios.

Sindawe and Isi appeared. They thought something big had to be up since I had come out of my hole. I could see how they might have gotten that odd notion. My job had kept me close to Smoke for a long time.

Ochiba materialized. He and the other two Nar were the senior officers outside the Shadowgate. All the most senior Taglians had deserted. They had respected their obligations to their prince.

I suspected they would regret choosing to maintain their honor. If they had not done so already, last night.

Sindawe caught the stallion's reins. Thai Dei and I dismounted. Everybody waited for me to say something. I just shrugged. I pulled my pants away from my burning thigh. Riding had been no improvement.

Just as I had predicted. "Don't ask me why I'm here. The Old Man said to come. So I came. What he's up to is his secret."

"So what else is new?" Big Bucket asked. "He ever does say what's what, nobody will believe him."

I glanced around. The ground there was harder than it was back across the way. It was also dryer. Most of the shelters, therefore, were aboveground. The camp gave poverty and squalor a bad name. I saw the ensigns and pennons of battalions that had, a year ago, been renown for their spit and polish. I asked, "Is morale really this bad?"

"It is over here."

"From what I hear the New Division suffered fewer casualties than anybody last night."

Sindawe observed, "You've been in this business most of your life, Standardbearer. You know morale can have little to do with the facts of a situation. Perceptions are more critical."

Absolutely. People want to believe what they want to believe, good, bad, or indifferent, and do not confuse them with facts.

I said, "We maybe shouldn't mention it to these guys but I think he expects to head on up there soon."

Bucket glared up the unwelcoming slope. "You're shitting me."

"You didn't believe him when he said that's where we're going? He's never made a secret of the fact that we're headed for Khatovar. It's what we've been doing since we left the Barrowland." Half a lifetime ago, it seemed. Before he ever joined up.

Grimly, Isi observed, "I don't think you'll find anyone here who actually believed we'd get this far." And he had not been with the Company as long as Bucket had.

Isi was not exaggerating. I do not think anyone but the Old Man ever really believed in Khatovar. The rest of us went along because we had nowhere else to go and nothing else to do but follow the standard. Every day was a gift, of sorts, and it did not much matter where the long night caught up. I said, "The last human obstacle went down last night. Lady has Longshadow wrapped up like a birthday present."

I glanced around again. Everywhere I looked men were hard at work. It was not something special suddenly put on for me but I did garner plenty of resentful stares just for being a guy from headquarters. Me turning up could only mean more demands, more work, more hardship.

The light was getting strange. There was not a lot of daylight left. "What are they doing over there?" I asked, indicating a work gang apparently digging a defensive trench. Against shadows that would be as useful as teats on a bull.

"Burying last night's dead," Bucket told me.

"Oh. Look. You stick with me. Unless you've got something critical going. The rest of you go ahead with whatever you were doing."

Sindawe told me, "Isi or I would be better guides, Standardbearer. We're in charge so we don't do much." He said that with such a straight face I almost thought he meant it.

I walked over to the mass grave.

They were digging a trench because that was the most efficient way to get bodies under the hard ground. I knelt, ran my fingers through what they had broken loose. Despite the rain earlier the hardpan was dry just inches beneath the surface. "It didn't rain much over here?" I asked.

"Mostly it just gets cold," Isi said.

I stared up the slope, past the Shadowgate. The ground grew more barren by the yard. There was some plant life up there but it was stunted, desertlike growth.

The corpses the soldiers were planting bore the stamp of shadow death. They were all shriveled up, with skin darkened several shades. Each dead man's mouth was open in a screaming rictus. The bodies were curled. They could not be straightened.

Crows circled but the soldiers kept them back.

I felt the hard soil again, eyed the slope. The rock itself looked like hardened mud, lying in hundreds of thin layers being gnawed away slowly by time. "I guess it wouldn't rain a lot up there, either, then. Or there would be more gullies and obvious washes." I wondered if erosion would create ways for shadows to escape from beyond the Shadowgate. Evidently not. Otherwise the world would have been overrun a long time ago.

I had never found any record of a time when the Shadowgate had not been there. It was ancient beyond reckoning but even so had not found its way into native religion in any form I recognized. Except, possibly, in the infrequently used idiom common to many southern languages, "Glittering stone," which seemed to mean an inexplicable possession of dark madness, a sort of demonically savage insanity complicated by congenital stupidity. One of those things Taglians will not discuss with outsiders, however pressed.

Until the rise of the Shadowmasters there had been very little historical mention of the land beyond Kiaulune, except that it tied in somehow with the rise of the Free Companies of Khatovar over four hundred years ago.

Though not religious myself I bowed and offered a short Gunni prayer for the dead before I ventured uphill for a closer look at the source of our trouble. Thai Dei beamed at me. I must have done right.

77

"HELP ME PLANT THIS THING," I TOLD THAI DEI AS I SET UP THE STANDARD A few yards downhill from a working party of soldiers. Thai Dei piled rocks around the foot of the lance until it would stand by itself. Then we walked uphill a little farther.

Once upon a time there had been an actual fortress with outbuildings and a genuine gate here. I had not been able to see that in my ghostworld ventures. There were little more than grass-grown foundations left now. Everything had fallen ages ago. But the stone had not been carried away until recently, when some of our bolder soldiers had taken some from the safe side for use in constructing shelters. Which suggested that, chicken-shit as they were about the terrors lurking in the past, they were fearless heroes compared to the people who used to live near the place.

Made me wonder again about how any fear could persist so strongly for so long. And then wonder if maybe Kina was not somehow connected to that effect. Maybe her nightmares leaked over into the dreams of everybody who heard the name Khatovar.

So why was I not dribbling down my leg?

Maybe I am too stupid to be scared about the right things.

The stone that had been used to construct the fortress was not a native rock. It was a greyish sandstone not only foreign to that slope, it was unlike any stone I had seen back in the direction from which we had come. It was not like the stone Longshadow had imported to build Overlook, either.

I glanced back at Overlook. The setting sun was sneaking in under the clouds, firing the south face of the fortress. That was one wall that Longshadow had gotten completed. The metal signs and seals on its face flamed and fairly thundered with power despite the fallen estate of their creator. "Now that's impressive," I said.

"But it doesn't do us any good up here," Isi observed. Glumly, Bucket nodded agreement. Sindawe, I noted, had faded away, gone back to whatever he had been doing before I arrived.

"What are these guys doing?" The working parties were marking the slope and ruins with colored chalk dusts, augmenting similar markings that had suffered from the rain.

"Defining the bounds of the gate. Different colors mean different things. I haven't learned them all myself. I understand the different dusts will glow their particular colors in the dark if they're excited by the proximity of fireballs. Apparently they define areas of threat and the level of danger to be expected in each."

"That what they do?" I asked Bucket.

He shrugged. "Close enough."

I grunted, moved up closer to the workers. As I did I began to feel a vibration or hum that began way down deep inside me. It grew stronger faster. I asked, "Who's the expert here?"

A dirty little man, irritated at being interrupted, unbent his back. I stifled a grin. He was Shadar despite being small and in charge of a Gunni work party. He had a beard big enough for the usual six feet plus of his coreligionists. He was not a Company man. I had noticed that over here pledged brothers all wore something to identify themselves—usually some crude version of the fire-breathing skull we had adopted from Soulcatcher twenty years ago. Maybe they thought that might help protect them from whatever came through the Shadowgate.

"How may I instruct you, Standardbearer?"

Oh, that man was talented. Without venturing one inch from absolute propriety he let me know exactly how he would like to instruct me, right after I bent over and grabbed my ankles.

"I'd like to know what you've determined about the layout here. Especially where the gate itself used to be, if you know, and where the weakest spots are."

"You want to know where the shadows are getting through?"

"Did the man stutter, hairball?" Bucket demanded.

I made a calming gesture. "Easy. Yes. Where they're getting through."

"Everywhere between those two yellow splashes." The little Shadar scowled at Bucket. "The red area is what must have been the actual original gateway."

"Thank you. I'll try not to trouble you much more."

The Shadar muttered, "Will miracles never cease?" as I went to walk over the ground. Bucket thought about adjusting the man's attitude, decided it was not worth the trouble. Not now. But there would be later, when I was not around.

A few rods below the Shadowgate there were torch racks and the remains of bonfires that had been used to produce light the night before. There were crude bunkers where soldiers had lain waiting for the shadows, protected only by repellent candles and their luck with the bamboo poles. There were two rickety ten-foot towers somebody had thrown up to provide plunging fire.

I pushed forward into the buzz until I no longer felt comfortable, which was right at the edge of the red chalk dust. From there I could make out the remains of the fallen gate. It must have been truly substantial in its time. It looked like it had been wide enough to permit passage of four men marching abreast. There was no sign that there had ever been a moat or a ditch or anything such, though. And a ditch is the oldest form of defense work there is. It persists today below every wall that is not some engineering monstrosity like the ramparts surrounding Overlook and Dejagore.

The implication was that the forgotten builders had not been concerned about threats from downhill.

There were still some strong spells on the Shadowgate. You could feel them growl if you pushed against them hard enough.

I did not press my luck.

I mused, "Why is the road in halfway decent shape when everything else here is almost completely gone?" The farther uphill you looked the better preserved the old road was.

Nobody offered an opinion. Chances were nobody gave a rat's ass. It was bad enough they just had to be there.

I strolled back down to the standard. Somehow, vaguely, it seemed to have come alive. I felt a vibration from it, too. That seemed to center on the head of the lance. Which would fit with Croaker's theories about the Lance of Passion.

Thai Dei, Bucket and Isi felt what I felt but did not know what it was. I told Thai Dei, "I want to move the standard up where it'll be the first thing a shadow runs into when it comes through the gate. Let them know the boys are back." I told Isi, "Tonight shouldn't be as rough. Lady thinks she's got Longshadow under control. She might even get the Shadowgate shut down completely before dark." Which I doubted because that was not very far off anymore.

The relief on Isi's face was almost comical.

A couple of soldiers caught part of what I said and scattered to start rumors that, no doubt, would grow fat in the retelling. Bucket grumbled, "I can't wait to see the twist that gets put on that by the time it comes back around."

Hum! We did not want any Taglians still loyal to the Prahbrindrah Drah to become too confident of their safety. "That's only *might*," I said. "And even if she shuts it down tighter than a virgin's twat there's still a shitload of shadows that got out of there last night and are still hiding under rocks and stuff waiting for sunset." *Darkness always comes.* "We're not out of the woods yet. Not by a long way."

I made sure I was overheard saying that, too.

I will teach you to fear the darkness. Who said that? Lady's first husband, maybe, back before my time. Certainly somebody who learned a lesson of his own way back in one of the old Annals.

I added, "We're going to face it every night for a long time to come."

"We're really going up there?" Bucket asked, pointing, when nobody but Thai Dei could hear him. He did not consider the question a major secret, though, or he would have asked in a language unfamiliar to Thai Dei.

"Maybe. I don't know how soon, though. The Old Man keeps talking about getting crops in so we don't need to kill ourselves foraging." While I talked I tried to figure how big a circle of influence the standard would cast. With Thai Dei's help I replanted it an estimated half radius from the Shadowgate, mid-line on the old road. Then I went back down and talked a couple of Vehdna into letting us take over their frontline bunker. Funny. They hardly argued about it.

Lady's horse had followed me around the whole while, staying out of the way but missing nothing. I told him, "Thanks a bunch. You can go back to your boss now." I always talk to mine as an equal. You treat the critters right, they'll do any damned thing. Even run somebody all the way to Taglios. Or back.

The horse argued less than the Vehdna soldiers did. Off he trotted.

I wondered how Sleepy was doing.

He could not have run far yet. It had not been that long since everything turned to shit.

78

CHALK DUST BANDS DEFINED FIELDS OF FIRE FOR THE SOLDIERS, SO THEY could pick off shadows more efficiently. But, though they glowed, the dusts did not betray the shadows perfectly.

Lady had given me some tools and instructions on how to use them. I was supposed to resist any temptation to take shortcuts.

A lot of soldiers came to watch. The Taglians were awed because a man who was neither priest nor sorcerer could read. They made me feel like a freak.

Essentially, Lady's directions had me lay down strips of leather rope in semicircles around the most dangerous passthrough, which was where the original gate had stood. More ropes went down as spokes.

Everything had to be done just so. None of which took into account the presence of the standard. If Lady understood that the standard was special she never made much of it.

I scuttled around inside the bunker we had appropriated. It was barely three feet from floor to ceiling. There was room for four men and a pile of bamboo. The place stank. No one had gone out after dark, no matter how pressing the need. As a shelter it was a feeble improvement over sitting out in the rain.

I told everyone watching, "When a shadow crosses one of the leather ropes it'll make a spark so we'll not only know that one is there, we can follow its movements. As long as we stay calm we can pick them off without wasting any fireballs."

The situation there was grim. A repeat of last night meant not many guys would see another sunrise.

"Not much of a mattress," I told Thai Dei, patting the ground. "Why don't you get some rest?" Whatever happened, I had to sleep later so I could prowl. If that worked for me again.

I crawled outside, settled on a comfortable block from the old wall. I studied the roof of my new home. It had been fashioned from a tent taken from the Shadowlanders. Everywhere around me I saw a wealth of plunder taken from our enemies. So much that in another month we would be as gaunt and disease-ridden as we were when we broke the siege of Dejagore.

The big edge we held over our enemies now was that we were still around. We could pretend to be an army still. Mogaba's band was the best they had left.

What would Mogaba do when he heard about Longshadow's disaster?

"Speaking of disasters." Real bad news was headed my way.

At the bottom of the slope, where the road southward gave up its final pretense and became an eroded dirt track, Uncle Doj stood staring up at the Shadowgate. If he had come any later it would have been too dark to pick him out. Mother Gota was fifty yards behind him, still moving, bitching so loudly that I caught snatches from where I sat. Both carried packs, which suggested that they planned to move in with me again. They had become professional squatters.

I flipped a stone at a crow. It was not a serious effort and the crow showed slight enthusiasm about getting out of the way. He just leaned. There were not a lot of the birds around now that dusk was thickening, though at their most numerous they had remained uncommon all day. Curious. I had seen nothing to explain the absence of the usual flocks. Nobody had started roasting them.

Maybe they were all off taking care of Mom.

I sat by the entrance to the bunker. "Thai Dei. How come your mother and Uncle Doj are over here?"

Thai Dei peeked outside, looked down the long slope, muttered in salty Nyueng Bao, went back in and lay down. You would have thought he had no respect for his elders.

He did not answer my question.

I checked the amulet I had not returned to Croaker. I considered the height of my shadow-repellent candle. We should be all right.

I hoped.

Somebody a lot smarter than me once said, "Put no trust in wizards."

I shut my eyes and waited.

"Murgen, you know a couple guys name of Wobble and Leadbeater?"

I opened my eyes. "Rudy. You ugly son of a bitch. Where'd you come from? I ain't seen you in half a year. How the fuck are you?"

"What is that? It's been so long I forget how. But I still got all my limbs and I'm still breathing."

"Makes you a winner in the soldiering game. Yeah. I remember Wobble. He was Jaicuri. Everybody he ever knew died during the siege of Dejagore. He just stuck with us after we came out of the city. He was a stonemason by trade. He was with us when we caught the Deceivers in the Grove of Doom."

"That's the guy. He made a good showing at Charandaprash, too."

"And the other one? Leadbeater? I didn't know him."

"He was some kind of Shadowlander. A prisoner of war who started out doing scutwork and gradually turned into one of us. Only took the oath maybe a month ago."

I knew but I had to ask. "What about them?"

"They didn't make it last night. I had to tell you. On account of you always want to put all that stuff in the Annals."

"Thank you. Though I don't know if I like this or not."

"What?"

"Only time half you guys talk to me anymore is if somebody gets his ass skragged. Then you come around because you want me to remember them."

"Get away from headquarters, Murgen. Get out here in the field. Stop being one of *them* and turn back into one of *us*."

Damn! Apparently I had crossed over from labor to management without noticing. "You maybe got a point. We're in for some changes now that the Shadowmasters are wrapped up. I'll keep that in mind."

Red Rudy grunted. He was not convinced. He headed back to his command, though, satisfied that he had done his duty.

I scrunched down into myself more tightly, shivering. A cold wind was blowing off the plateau. It was probably my imagination but I thought there was a whiff of Kina in it. It recalled the persistent wind stalking the place of bones. It made the standard sway. I thought about piling more rocks at its foot but could not find the ambition.

I thought about a warm fire, too, but on this side of Overlook, after last night, wood was scarce. Stocks were being used for cooking only. Not that there was much to cook anymore but bitterroot.

You will learn to live without the light. That was in one of the older Annals somewhere, too.

A pair of boots positioned themselves in front of me. Uncle Doj. I knew because Mother Gota was just down the slope, puffing and complaining. She would never catch up unless he waited, wobble-walking the way she did.

"Uncle," I said without looking up. "To what do I owe this dubious pleasure, after all these months?"

"You should plant your standard closer, Soldier of Darkness. You should be able to lay your hand on it at any time. Otherwise you are likely to lose it."

"I don't think so. But one of the Prahbrindrah Drah's loyalists, a Deceiver, hell, maybe even some minor, he-thinks-his-talent-is-a-secret kind of wizard, anybody, can take a crack. And end up in that ditch over there before they know what bit them." I was bullshitting but he would not recognize it. I had not done that in the past. "It knows who the good guys are."

Mother Gota hobbled up. She carried a load as big as she was, everything useful that could be salvaged from our former home and the ruins of Kiaulune. That included an accumulation of firewood.

I decided not to be totally abrasive. While the wood lasted. There are cooks in this world worse than Mother Gota. Among them are her favorite son and son-in-law.

Uncle Doj, being both male and what passes for exalted caste amongst Nyueng Bao, carried Ash Wand and a quite unprepossessing pack.

Mother Gota shed her load, dropped to hands and knees and started to crawl into the bunker. As she met my gaze I could not help grinning. She began muttering curses that, no doubt, were directed at the sort of evil fate that would unleash an earthquake at such an inopportune moment.

The earth moved. One-Eye would hear about that for however many more centuries he hung around.

I said, "Let Thai Dei rest. It's going to be another long night." As I edged over Uncle Doj glimpsed the little bamboo tube I had tucked in my belt behind me.

The cold wind was getting stronger. The cloth of the standard popped and cracked.

Uncle Doj peered up the darkening slope, eyed the bunker, glared at me like he was developing serious reservations about having left his swamp. I said, "Sometimes you have to live like this when you do what we do." Mother Gota crept back outside, still muttering, verbalizing what Uncle Doj was thinking. I reminded them, "You invited yourselves along."

Uncle Doj opened his mouth but overcame the urge to bicker. He settled on the other side of the bunker entrance, Ash Wand across his lap. Gota proceeded to scout the neighborhood, collecting stones. Our neighbors did not object despite rocks beginning to look like the only measure of wealth at this end of the world.

I shut my eyes. Softly, just to be a pain in the ass, I whistled an air Sarie liked to hum when she was happy.

As it always does, darkness came.

79

THEY LET ME SLEEP. AND SLEEP I DID DESPITE THE COLD AND THE WIND, THE cooking smells and my own snoring. As nightfall waxed complete I slipped my moorings to my flesh, slowly. For a while I was like tatters stirring in a ghostly breeze. I made no real effort to go, nor any more to stay. Uncle's Doj's return, with all its unhappy reminders, had inspired a great lethargy.

My heart's inclination was the breeze that carried me north. I loafed over mountains and across wildernesses, past all the conquered cities. I found Sleepy on the road from Taglios to Dejagore. He understood that he would be in no danger if he kept moving. No agent of the Radisha could outrun the steed he rode.

The Radisha remained distraught about his escape. It was critical to the conspiracy that *every* Company brother be caught or killed. If even one escaped the plague would return. Like Narayan Singh, she *knew.* Darkness always comes. She had seen it happen already, after the disaster at Dejagore.

She was terrified. She was convinced that the Year of the Skulls would commence shortly if any part of the grand plan failed. She had a great deal to say about Soulcatcher and none of it was complimentary. To get herself shut of a dreaded ally she might have taken on another who was far worse.

She remembered Catcher's tricks and treats of a few years ago. She knew damned well that Soulcatcher was less predictable than any natural disaster.

The latest quakes had been felt in Taglios though no damage had been done there. Some people were afraid they meant that the gods—or some great power—were displeased by what had been done to the Black Company.

Croaker had mentioned the Company habit of paying back treachery so often that already some people were preparing for the vengeance-storm. Again, that had to do with the terror of the Company name that no one would, or possibly could, explain.

Could that just have stolen into every heart from some shadowy source, never having possessed any substance? Was it a good old-fashioned Kina deceit?

I really needed to get my nose into those old Annals hidden in that room where . . . Oh-oh.

The Radisha had Guards and soldiers searching for Smoke systematically. One-Eye's confusion spells would not withstand so determined an effort. They could not confuse all the senses of that many men all the time.

She could not expect to find Smoke alive. She would just want to know what had become of him. I did not want her looking, though. She might find my books.

Stupid, stupid. I could have had Sleepy collect them while he was up there. If I had invested a little forethought and had done a little planning I could have had him kill several birds. I had to start thinking that way. We had no options to squander anymore.

The Radisha was closeted with the most powerful priests. Each time I visited Taglios, even if only one day had passed, it seemed the priests had gained influence while the wealthy merchants and manufacturers, many of whom owed their fortunes to the existence and efforts of the Company, had faded farther from favor. Unless they were priests clever enough to have used their positions to mercantile advantage during the development of the Taglian armies. It would be interesting to see how well the new bourgeoisie had been able to shed old ways of thinking as the ecclesiastical peril grew. Was there one native-born Taglian with balls big enough to respond?

The Radisha's effort to screw us had put her in bed with men she loathed and at odds with people who thought her way.

The meeting looked like another arm-twisting session. The priests wanted further concessions from the state in return for ecclesiastical support.

You could see the Radisha thinking that Lady had had the right idea when she massacred so many of their predecessors.

I was in a wicked mood. I dropped to a point beside the Woman's ear. "Boo!"

She jumped. She moved away and stared at the empty air, color gone from her face. The room fell silent. The priests looked troubled. They, too, had sensed something. It struck dark sparks of terror inside them. I tried an evil laugh. Some of that got through, too. I felt the black dread fill the room.

The Radisha shivered as if the temperature had dropped to mid-winter.

It was already planting season around Taglios.

I whispered in the Radisha's ear, "Water sleeps." She did not catch that but did not need to to become more frightened.

It is a saying of my people. *Even Water sleeps. But Enemy never rests.*

Sarie was asleep when I reached the temple of Ghanghesha. Just enough light leaked into her room to show that she was there. I floated for a while, enjoying being near her. I did not disturb her. She needed her sleep.

Me, I was immune to that stuff.

Why was there any light at all?

The priests had placed a pair of lanterns outside Sahra's cell. Events the other night must have troubled them.

I had to be getting strong at reaching out of the ghostworld.

Was it a good idea to try? Did I want people all over the place knowing something was going on? It would not hurt to have them scared. Oh, no. But, on the other hand, they would take steps to mask all their deviltry.

I did a tour of the temple, seeking evidence of obvious attitude changes by the priests. I found nothing unusual, although the acolytes handling nighttime ceremonies were abnormally nervous. I went back to hover over my honey.

Damn, she was beautiful! Damn, it was going to be harder and harder not to mention my disappointment to Uncle Doj and Mother Gota. Hell. We might be getting to a time when raising questions would be appropriate. They were a long way from home. They had nowhere to run.

Sarie opened her eyes. My anger melted away. Half a moment later she looked almost directly at me and smiled her wonderful smile. Fish and rice must be good for the teeth because she had the whitest, most perfect teeth I ever saw.

"Are you here, Mur? I feel you very close to me right now."

"I'm here," I said into her ear, with none of the wickedness I had shown the Radisha. Sarie probably did not catch any words but understood that she had gotten a response.

"I miss you a lot, Mur. I don't feel like I'm one of my own people anymore."

Because they will not let you be. Granny Hong Tray did not stay around to manage the results of her sybilline mutterings. Grandpa Ky Dam did not make it clear that Hong Tray's pronouncements were forever.

Of course, the present situation might be exactly what the old lady had had in mind. She never wrote anything down for me, either.

The best of the diviner breed are never wrong because they never set anything in stone.

The moment with Sarie faded without my acquiescence. She looked troubled, as though she sensed me withdrawing. I wriggled but could not hold my position.

Something back in the real world insisted on gaining my attention.

As I drifted out of Sarie's cell several priests invited themselves in. One demanded, "Who are you talking to, woman?"

"Ghosts," my darling replied, showing her sweetest smile.

80

AT FIRST I THOUGHT IT MUST HAVE BEEN JUST THE FLAKE OF FLINT BITING my ass that had brought me back. That bastard hurt. But as I shuffled it out from under me I sensed movement against the starry background south of me. A voice inquired, "Are you awake now, Standard-bearer?"

Sindawe. "No doubt about it. And I was having such a wonderful dream, too."

"Since the Old Man wants you to keep an eye on us I thought it would be useful if you saw what's happening." Unlike most Nar, Sindawe had a sense of humor. It included a major irreverence for authority, though he represented authority himself. He must have driven Mogaba to distraction back when they were best friends. Unless Mogaba started out the same way and grew out of it. A lot of sour old farts start out as all right guys.

I had to roll onto my hands and knees to find the leverage to get up. "Stiff as a log," I grumbled.

"Buy a better mattress."

"What I need is a better body. Like one that's about fifteen years younger. All right. What's going on?"

"Thought you'd want to see what's happening at the Shadowgate."

"Nothing bad, apparently, or you wouldn't be hunking around in the dark." There were no fires tonight. There were no other bold souls wandering around like Sindawe, either. But the most remarkable lack was that of flying fireballs. Over here. There was an occasional pop on the far side of Overlook.

Sindawe headed uphill, though that was not necessary. I could feel the Lance. It seemed to be awakening. I could see the sparks as the shadows tested my leather ropes. I sensed frustrated motion beyond the sparks.

I felt no fear at all.

Always before there had been fear anytime there were shadows near enough to be sensed.

The shadows grew more energetic. So did the sparks. They began to crackle and pop. The soldiers showed remarkable restraint. Not one man went bugfuck and sprayed the hillside with fireballs. They felt no fear, either. Or maybe they were just veteran enough to understand that you can fool yourself. Especially after a trial like last night.

The stupid and the nervous would be over yonder in that trench that the survivors had so grudgingly dug.

"Sky's clearing," I observed, maybe just for something to say. Over the rise ahead that was as clear as it was when my ghostwalks took me up above the clouds.

"Uhm." Sindawe seldom wasted words on small talk.

"Recognize any of those constellations?" I did not. It was like I was looking at a completely foreign sky.

"Too many stars to see any patterns."

"The Noose," said a voice from behind me. I started. I had heard no one come up. And I would not have expected this speaker to move quietly.

"Mother?" The sparks from the Shadowgate generated just enough light to reveal where she stood. A form that may have been Thai Dei loomed behind her, staring into the southern night.

"It was in my mother's book. Part of a fairy tale nobody understood. That nobody knew where it came from anymore. Thirteen stars that form a noose."

I saw nothing of the sort. I said so. Mother Gota must have been stunned into another century, so out of character had she become. She grabbed me by the arm, pulled my head down, made me sight along her pointing arm. Finally, I admitted, "I see something that looks like a bottom-up water ladle right there above what must be the skyline."

"That is it, you fool Stone Soldier. Three stars are hidden by the earth." She remained particularly intense.

"You recognized it, with three stars missing, from a description in a childhood story?"

A particularly brilliant burst amongst the leather ropes revealed the woman staring at me bedecked in an expression of profound bewilderment. It also revealed Uncle Doj behind her. He wore a look of exasperation which vanished the instant he realized I could see him.

"Gota. There you are. Nephew. What is this display?"

From much closer than I would have believed he could be, Thai Dei said, "The Soldiers of Darkness have stopped the leak of death." He spoke in rapid Nyueng Bao. He used several words that were not clear to me. I counted on context to unravel their meanings.

Uncle Doj told Mother Gota, "I have cautioned you about your tongue—"

"I'll caution you, you mountebank." I think "mountebank" is what she meant. Wrapped up in the word she chose was a root meaning "fraud," with a superlative prefix hung out front.

It sounded like a cousin word to "priest." Blade would have been amused. *I* was amused.

Gota had restrained herself with Doj in the past. Compared to how she had berated everyone else. She deferred to Uncle usually, albeit with poor grace. Now they squabbled like children.

I got the impression that their quarrel had nothing to do with what they really wanted to fight about. Even so, the tiff was interesting where I could follow it.

Thai Dei's special mission in life is to poop parties. He embarrassed those two silent long enough to get in the news that they were quarreling amidst all the Bone Warriors in the world, at least one of whom understood their blather.

Doj responded instantly. He shut his mouth and went for a walk. I said, "I hope some nervous type don't pick him off in the dark." Thai Dei went after him.

Gota shut up only because Doj's departure left her to carry both sides of the argument. She considered starting up with me. But she recalled that, whatever I was to her daughter, I was a Soldier of Darkness, too. Anyway, I was not. Nyueng Bao and only the worms of the earth are lower than that.

I was in a peckish mood myself, having been wakened prematurely. I said, "I rather enjoyed that."

Gota made a sputtery noise as she stalked away.

Of the general darkness I asked, "Anybody know anything about a constellation called the Noose? Or any stories about it?"

Nobody knew anything. Naturally.

Over the next several days I asked the question of everybody I ran into and always got a negative answer. Even Narayan Singh, a logical resource for information about nooses, seemed unfamiliar with the constellation. He did not say so in so many words, of course, but Lady was familiar with Deceiver lore and knew nothing, nor was she able to pry anything out of the living saint.

Poor guy seemed destined to be the living martyr Narayan Singh. The heartline of his existence consisted of unrelenting terror.

After assuring myself that the Shadowgate was holding, I ambled back down to my bunker. The standard seemed almost aglow with power. Something noteworthy was going on there. I would have to go see Croaker. If my inner thigh healed enough. If I ever got any sleep.

My in-laws were no problem. None had gone back to our nasty little bunker. I had its stone floor and stink to myself.

I was asleep about the time I chunked my head onto my rock pillow.

81

FOR A WHILE I JUST SLEPT. IN FACT, I AM CONVINCED THAT I DREAMED NORmal dreams, though I cannot recall them now. Then, gradually, my spirit slipped its moorings again, in a kind of tattered, fuzzy way that might have indicated difficulty letting go. I felt no resistance. But I was not trying to go anywhere, I was just drifting.

I floated upward. It did take an effort of will but I faced southward, trying to find the noose of stars that had gotten Mother Gota exercised. Yes. There they were. But I had to climb a thousand feet to see them all and even then they were not easily discerned. They had dropped dramatically in a very short time.

In fact, when I reflected on it, I could not understand how they might have risen high enough for me to see from the Shadowgate.

I did not let that trouble me, though. My attention was caught by something on the plain of stone. For an instant I saw a ghost of pale light out there, about where I glimpsed that lump of darkness sometime before. *Was* there something out there?

I did not go look. It never occurred to me to try. In retrospect I cannot understand why. How could the impulse not arise? How could I not actively engage the choice of investigating or not investigating? I do not know. I just sort of went *hmm* and continued on about my normal ghost-time ratkilling.

I rejected impulses to search for Mogaba and Goblin. I can be lazy even when all the work I have to do is think. Finding them would take a lot of to-ing and fro-ing and calculating. And then I might not accomplish anything. So I decided to spy on Soulcatcher instead. By now she should be recovered enough to be grumbling and scheming and maybe doing something interesting.

Or she might just be laying around sleeping.

Soulcatcher was just laying around sleeping. Surrounded by woods where every branch and twig boasted a complement of crows. It looked like every crow in the world had gathered around her hideout.

It was unlikely they would starve for a while.

They had been living well. Already the earth beneath them was buried under their droppings. Shadows drifted below, whimpering because the crows would not come down to play.

Like a shadow myself I wormed into Catcher's cave. I encountered the spells she had woven to keep the darkness at bay. For a time those resisted me, too, but I was different enough to find a way through.

Catcher was sleeping? How often did that happen?

The Daughter of Night was not asleep. And she was a sensitive child. She felt me arrive. She sat up on her bed of damp pine needles. "Mother?"

Catcher was a light sleeper. She sprang erect, alert, turning as she sought danger. She wore the mask that had been one of her trademarks in the old days. Mostly she had done without it lately, but seldom did I see her in public. And never in the flesh.

She resembled Lady though she had even finer features and a more sensual air. Croaker claims he resisted her seductions. Publicly I believe him. But I do not know how he managed. I would have trouble despite my devotion to Sarie.

Maybe it was just his age.

Catcher's hideout was illuminated by a lamp that hung from the ceiling of the cave. It was a cousin of our shadow-repellent candles. It was not bright but its light left no place for any little death to hide.

"What did you say?" The voice Catcher used was that of a man whose throat had been smashed and could speak in only a hoarse whisper. Except this whisper was heavy with malice, a voice in keeping with the old, dread repute of the Ten Who Were Taken. It contained the compassion of a serpent, the sympathy of a spider.

The Daughter of Night did not react. From her response Soulcatcher might not have been there at all.

Catcher giggled like a girl sharing whispers about boys. "Defiance is pointless. Stubbornness is meaningless. There is no one to help you." That was the voice of despair. It rasped, too, but it was the last speech of an old man dying of cancer. "You are mine to do with as I please. It pleases me that you tell me what you just said."

The child raised her eyes. There was no love for her auntie there.

Soulcatcher laughed.

She was a cruel thing at times.

She made a gesture. The child shrieked, thrashed in agony. She fought her cries, not wanting to give her tormenter the pleasure, but her body could not be controlled by her will, powerful as that was.

"You think your mother was here? You have no mother, neither my sister nor Kina." This voice was that of an accountant reporting the week's profits. "I am your mother now. I am your goddess. I am your only reason for living."

I moved my viewpoint slightly so I could see them better. Maybe my movement disturbed the lamp's flame. Maybe a breath of wind crept in from outside. Whatever, Catcher shut up and gave a lot more attention to her surroundings.

After a minute during which she just turned slowly, in silence, she mused, "There's something here. And you sensed it right away." The girlish giggle returned. "Right away. And you thought it might be Kina. But it isn't, is it?"

Soulcatcher made a sudden gesture with her gloved left hand, fingers dancing too fast to follow. The brat collapsed, unconscious. Catcher settled with her back to the cave wall, dragged a pair of ragged leather sacks closer. I could smell nothing out there but I bet she reeked as bad as Howler. She was vain enough to guarantee herself incredible beauty and sensuality but not vain enough to waste much time on personal hygiene.

Maybe the smell would help me push her away if memories of Sahra did not do the trick.

She almost caught me. It did not look like she was doing anything but stirring through her trash. And my thoughts distracted me. I saved myself because she was used to living alone, or with crows. She reasoned aloud, "If it was the freak goddess I'd smell her. And she'd try to do something stupid. But somebody else has been prowling around, too. Let's find out who. Maybe it's my beloved sister." The voice that spoke those last few words was powerfully vicious.

Her hands sprang out of one leather sack, sudden as a snake's strike, but I was on the move, cleverly not toward the entrance. Her all but invisible net of black thread whooshed past two feet away. As soon as it fell I headed toward the exit. I did not know if she could catch me for real but I had no urge to find out.

Soulcatcher laughed. This was no giggle. This was full-blown, malicious adult amusement. "Whatever you are, I can't fool you. Can I?"

She sure could. That was why I was getting out while I could. Like all the Ten must have been, she was way more scary than would seem at first exposure. The madness leaked through only slowly.

Catcher made a series of gestures employing every finger on each hand. She spoke in one of those tongues sorcerers favor, this one probably that of her childhood. I felt a truly ugly presence approaching as I was about to slip my ghostly nose into the crack that would take me outside.

A shadow wriggled in. It cringed. It shuddered. It responded to Catcher's will. I did not hang around to find out what she wanted it to do.

It was enough to know that Soulcatcher had discovered a way to manipulate shadows. Which meant that with the last Shadowmaster barely finished kicking, a new queen of the darkness was about to rise.

She is the darkness.

82

"WAS I RIGHT?" CROAKER ASKED.

"About the standard?"

"What else?" He seemed exasperated. Maybe it was a strain, sharing quarters with Lady and the loon crew of Smoke, Singh and Longshadow.

"Probably. You could sure feel it. And nothing got by." I was worn out. My inner thigh ached again after the long walk over. "But I can't prove that wasn't because of Lady's gimcrackery."

"The Lance did *something,* though?"

"Oh, yeah. Everybody felt something. Some probably even decided it had something to do with the standard." Thai Dei had remained outside, as he always did when I visited the Old Man, so I was not shy about describing the skirmish between Uncle Doj and Mother Gota.

"Which was about this Noose constellation?"

"That started it. I think that was just an excuse. Their conflict runs a lot deeper."

"And this all just started?" He smiled to himself, like me, probably, jumping straight back to Gota's business with One-Eye.

"And where is our pet hedge wizard?" I asked. He was not out riding Smoke, which is what I had expected him to do while I was away. Lady had the little fire chief all tied up.

Croaker shrugged. "Out of my hair, which is all I want right now."

Probably off tending his distillery, which had not been found in his dugout when the rescue crews turned the place inside out, looking more for that than for poor old One-Eye.

I said, "I had a dream. Or maybe I was out of myself. It almost turned into a nightmare."

"Uhm?"

"Catcher's figured out how to run the shadows. Just like our boy in the cage, there." Longshadow, though, was unconscious. More so than Smoke, who insisted on groaning every few minutes.

Croaker sighed. "I'm disappointed but I'm not surprised. It was a logical step for her. And she's had time to work on it."

"You going to do something about it?"

"Haven't I already?"

"You lost me, boss."

"She's figured out how to manage a few shadows. Close up. But I control the source of the shadows. And I don't have to get near her. Though I'm going to."

"I wouldn't get overconfident where she's concerned. You never know with her. Remember how she planted that demon Frogface on us."

"I take nothing for granted, Murgen." He glanced at his woman, lying motionless beside Smoke. "But I try not to let paranoia cripple me."

He would get an argument on that from a lot of people. On the other hand, though, he had overthrown the Shadowmasters and seemed well positioned to have us survive the perfidy of our allies.

But, Soulcatcher? I did not doubt that Smoke had been right every time he insisted *She is the darkness!*

83

ONE-EYE CAUGHT ME OUTSIDE CROAKER'S PLACE. "HER WORSHIP STILL AT IT?"

"Uh . . . You mean . . . ?" Thai Dei's were only one pair of uninitiated ears nearby.

"You know what I mean, Kid."

"She is."

"Damn! I can't get ten minutes at a time now that she's started playing. Damned woman must be worried about her weight."

Took me a minute to figure that out. Then I laughed, remembering how hungry I used to get. "That could do it. If she gets totally hooked."

One-Eye grumbled something and stomped off. He did not go any farther than his dugout, though. He began fussing around the remains like a dog trying to dig a rabbit out of its warren, killing time while he waited to walk the ghost. I went about the business I had, mostly stalling because I had no desire to go back over to the Shadowgate. After ten minutes of slinging mud and trash One-Eye stomped back to me. "I found that little shit Goblin yesterday. Last night. He was just about to jump on the Prahbrindrah Drah. I want to know how that came out."

"Uhm." Yes. I hoped he took the Prince prisoner if they had them an asskicking contest. I would rather have his sister scared of us than mad at us. Mad she would be if we sent her little brother to his funeral ghat.

She was not the kind to jump into the flames after him.

"That bastard was getting pretty good when he turned on us," One-Eye said. "There's no guarantee the runt can take him."

"You worried about Goblin? *You?*"

"Worried? Me? Hell, no. I don't care what happens to the little shit. But if he croaks the Prahbrindrah Drah we're gonna be in shit so deep we'll have to look up to see the horizon."

"I don't think we can get in much deeper than we already are. They can only kill us once. And they've already let us know they intend to try."

One-Eye snorted. No way would he admit that he was worried about Goblin though Goblin's absence obviously made him crazy. He had not been able to feud with anyone for ages. Nobody else would play.

I asked, "Why don't you play a few tricks on Uncle Doj if you're suffering some compulsion to mess with somebody who can mess right back?"

Thai Dei developed a sudden interest in our banter. One-Eye did not cheer up. He did ask, "You figure Lady was right about him? He don't look the part."

"And you do?" Like a derelict in a slum alley does. "You think she's *ever* been wrong about something like that?"

"She's still healthy," One-Eye grumped.

Thai Dei wanted to know what we were talking about but could see no way to get anything out of us without giving something away himself. If he'd just been the kind who chatters incessantly he could have asked anything and nobody would have thought anything about it.

I chuckled.

Puzzled, One-Eye asked, "You going back over there?"

"Got to. Boss says."

One-Eye glared at the distant plateau. "Damned Tals! Just had to stab us in the back. I was all set to retire as soon as we finished Longshadow. But they just had to fuck me up. And now I got to go on up there. Which I'm looking forward to like I'm looking forward to getting a hot poker shoved up my poop chute. Whoa! Here's my chance." He scampered toward Croaker's dugout.

Lady had come up to the light. She looked more haggard than ever. She must have been walking the ghost for all she was worth. She leaned on a post while she spoke softly to one of the messengers waiting for an assignment. He hurried off toward her camp. She looked at me, frowned as though she was having trouble remembering who I was. Maybe she was. I was supposed to be somewhere else.

I decided to go there even though it was no resort for tired professional soldiers.

84

MOTHER GOTA WOULD NOT TALK TO UNCLE DOJ. MOTHER GOTA WOULD not talk to her darling baby boy. But Mother Gota and silence had been strangers for decades. So Mother Gota talked to me.

She was not happy about the way her life was going, though she refused to get specific in front of a Soldier of Darkness—family or not.

I was in a karma-building cycle, apparently. I endured her crabbing, nodding and grunting in the right places while I made notes concerning recent events. I said, "You could always go home. Just pack up and go back to the swamp. Let Uncle boil his own bitterroot." The root was a recent discovery. Shadowlander fugitives had been caught eating it. It was a common weed that was not completely inedible if you boiled its roots for six or eight hours before you ground them into meal that tasted like soggy white oak sawdust. A lot was getting eaten because there was little else to be found close by. Croaker still had not authorized anyone to begin exploiting Overlook.

Uncle Doj had discovered bitterroot long ago. He had not eaten much else since Charandaprash. How had he found that much time to spend sitting in one place? Maybe he cured twenty pounds of root at a time.

"You, Bone Warrior, you would have me abandon my duty?"

Hell, yes. Anything to get you out of my hair. But I did not say that aloud. I just asked, "What duty is that?"

She opened her mouth to tell me but Nyueng Bao caution took over. She gulped like a fish out of water, then, as always when pressed, told me, "I go get some wood." That in Taglian instead of Nyueng Bao, which was good enough for me as long as I asked no questions.

"Good idea."

Thai Dei came to stand by me as I watched her go. I said, "Soon the Company will return to the road to Khatovar. Your people need to decide what to do when that happens." I reached for a rock.

I thought I made no giveaway motion but the crow was ready. It just hopped over the whistling stone and offered me one mocking caw for my trouble. The black birds remained scarce but there was always one near me and a dozen around Croaker's headquarters. Catcher was lying low but she had not stopped watching.

A nearby Taglian, maybe thinking he could curry favor, aimed a bamboo pole at the crow. "Save that for a shadow!" I snapped. "We're not out of this yet." Interesting. The would-be sniper wore a ragged, crudely drawn Company badge. I saw no one armed with bamboo who did not sport some version of our badge. The management had stopped pretending to be fair.

Red Rudy wandered over, stood leaning on a spear. He stared northward, silently watching something. Nobody else said anything, either. I took advantage of the silence to scribble a few more notes. Finally, Rudy mused, "Ever notice how, when the light is right, you can see where everybody's going over there?"

"No." I looked up.

He was right. Just now the light had every piece of metal beyond Overlook reflecting right at us. And a whole lot of metal was headed up the road I had walked with that useless One-Eye. . . . "Oh, no. Whose bright idea was this?"

Somebody wanted to call on Soulcatcher.

"Thought you'd be interested." Rudy collected his spear and strolled off. Probably to find a deep hole to pull in after him.

"What is happening?" Thai Dei asked.

I shrugged. "Maybe just the end of the world."

Or maybe not. Maybe somebody in the headquarters bunker was playing mind games with her sister.

The sun moved on. Light no longer glimmered off the moving force. Nobody but Rudy seemed to understand what was happening but everybody sensed that something was. It became very quiet on my far hillside.

Nothing happened for a while. I made notes. I watched Mother Gota dwindle into the distance. Looked like she planned to do her wood gleaning farther afield.

Afternoon shadows crept across the far foothills. "That's dark," I said. Especially near where Soulcatcher was last seen. That darkness was swelling. . . .

I gaped. That was no shadow. That was a cloud of darkness. It boiled out of the canyons and forests and masked the foothills. . . .

Crows.

All the crows we had not seen for the past several days!

The darkness rose like a blast from a volcano. It began to spread.

"That's got to be every crow in the world," I breathed. The cloud just kept growing. Part seemed headed my way.

Suddenly, lightning sliced inside it. The wind began to blow. I began to lose track of where and when I was and what I was doing. Somebody asked, "What's happening?"

A second voice asked, "What's that smell?"

Kina. But I could not explain.

More lightnings ripped through the thunderhead of crows. Most of that darkness rushed my way. The stench of Kina became overpowering. There were sounds around me, heard as though from a great distance. They did not include the panic that seemed appropriate.

The darkness bent over and grabbed me, took me up like a mother lifts a frightened infant. The face of Kina was in the darkness but it was not Kina who possessed me. She was angry. Again. She was disoriented.

She was not alone.

Lady was there, maybe riding Smoke, maybe in some other fashion. The lightning was her doing, evidently. She had Kina in one sorcerous hand while trying to spank her sister with the other.

Catcher was there, too. And she seemed amused, not troubled, although she was caught between a devil goddess and a sister who would roast her happily. Soulcatcher would go to the burning stake chuckling at the fire. The woman was completely mad.

The darkness wrapped me up. It devoured me. It tried to chew me up but found me unpalatable. It spit me out.

I staggered like a drunk. A voice in my head said, *There you are, darling. I missed you. You have been away too long.* Moonlight glinted off the corpse-strewn black water lapping at Dejagore's wall. I imagined something stirring in those waters, something that wanted to grab me and pull me deep into the inky darkness, down amongst the naked bones. I looked to my left and there stood the long-dead Speaker of the Nyueng Bao, Ky Dam. His wife Hong Tray was with him. They smiled. The old woman made a finger sign I knew to be a blessing.

Darkness swallowed me.

Darkness had no stomach for me. It puked me up.

I was in a tree. My eyes saw strangely. I had to turn my head this way and that to see out of one or the other. Men of half a dozen races were slaughtering men of several others below me. The trees were repelled. They loved death but hated the shedding of blood.

I was in the Grove of Doom. In a tree?

I raised a hand to feel my eyes. White feathers blocked my vision.

I lost consciousness.

I went a hundred places. A hundred places came to me. I seemed to visit all times and all places of the past several years.

I was on the plain of bones. Darkness had come. A black wind blew the bones about. I tumbled like a leaf. Crows mocked me from the naked trees. I rolled over into a deeper night and in an instant was strolling up the sloped floor of the tunnel where the old men rested in their cocoons of spun ice.

A great deep booming thundered in my head. It was pain incarnate, yet seemed to carry a message. I tried to listen.

Time expanded to encompass the throbbing within me, which became a slow, deep voice that speeded up until it turned into Thai Dei nagging worriedly in Nyueng Bao. "Standardbearer! Speak to me."

I tried but my jaws would not work. I could do nothing but make inarticulate noises.

"He's all right." That was Uncle Doj. I opened my eyes. Doj knelt beside me, fingers against the side of my neck. "What happened, Bone Warrior?"

I sat up. My muscles were watery. I was drained. But it seemed no time had passed. I volleyed the question back. "What happened over there?" Crows still swarmed in the distance, though not in clouds like I had seen.

"Where?" Thai Dei asked.

"There. Where the birds are."

Thai Dei said. "I do not know. I saw nothing unusual."

"No cloud of darkness? No lightning?"

After a pause, "None that I saw."

Uncle Doj considered the distance thoughtfully.

"I need something to eat." Though I had not been ghostwalking, I was that weak.

The event was troubling.

85

THE SUMMONS CAME FROM CROAKER. I WENT ACROSS. ONLY A FEW DAYS had passed but already the world had begun to seem peaceful again. The soldiers looked less haggard.

Shadows were not a problem now. For us.

"I'm here," I told the Old Man. The guard outside had sent me right in.

"Where's your mother-in-law?"

"Good question. The other day she said she was going after firewood. We haven't seen her since."

"One-Eye's gone, too."

I gaped. Then I started to snicker. The snicker turned into a guffaw. Before long I was bent double, unable to regain control. "They eloped? Don't tell me they eloped."

"I wouldn't think of it. Knock off the braying. You sound like a jack-ass giving birth." A stone impossibility. He indicated the alcove where special people were stored. "Use Smoke. Find them."

I headed that way, still shivering with restless giggles. "How come I have to do it? You and Lady were already here."

"We're busy restructuring the force. We don't have time."

"She over being hooked on ghostwalking?"

"She's gonna have to be. Get busy. I don't have time to jack my jaw, either." He pointed. He was not in a playful mood. Must have been getting less sleep than usual.

Smoke was alone behind the curtain. "What happened? You bury the other two?"

"Stashed them in what's left of your dugout. We needed the room. Get to work."

I pulled the curtain. He was the boss. He did not have to be a nice guy all the time.

Smoke did not look the same. Lady had done something to keep him under. He seemed more drugged than comatose.

He smelled, too. Bad. Somebody had been letting their chores slide. "You're the physician, you ought to know about keeping clean. This guy is a mess."

"I'll get you a bucket."

I did not wait for him to tell me. I went to work.

Croaker had made appropriate preparations. There was drinking water and fresh bread. I ate some of the latter immediately. The command types sure lived the good life. I had not had anything but bad bitterroot for the past several days—and not nearly enough of that. A point I ought to make to Rudy.

"Send out for sausages," I muttered. Maybe when we finally found Khatovar it would be like the Vehdna paradise. Hot and hotter running houris driven by an overwhelming passion for smelly old guys with no social skills, houris who spent the rest of their time whipping up lots of freshly cooked food. Good food.

"Quit stalling around," Croaker growled a while later. "That little prick is clean enough."

I was not anxious to go out. "Somebody ought to watch what he eats." Smoke looked like he was suffering the early stages of dietary disease.

Croaker just gave me a dark look. He did not much care, apparently. "You have a problem doing your job?"

"Cranky, cranky."

I had a problem with going out. It had been scary getting batted around between Catcher and Kina and the place of the bones the other day. I had tapped a reservoir of fear I did not know I contained.

I especially did not like being a bird. That part I had not understood at all.

Catcher now knew I could walk the ghostworld without her manipulations. Maybe I could because she had opened the way. Now I feared she could hunt me down and snap me up out there whenever the mood took her. I was not inclined to suffer her torments voluntarily.

"Murgen."

I chomped down a last mouthful of bread, followed it with a slug of water. Bloated, I did what I had to do.

Goblin must have had a notion that he was being watched from afar. Or suspected that he could be. I would not have found him had I had no idea how his mind worked. The clever little shit. The spells he used to camouflage himself and his men were of the simplest sort, almost undetectable. All they did was make the eye wander away from what was probably just a modest boulder lurking in the bushes, gently so as to go unremarked even when you were expecting something. He and his rangers were scattered so no concentration stood out. Mogaba did not appear to be a concern.

I might be wrong but I assumed One-Eye's first move, if he deserted, would be to find Goblin. They had been best friends before anyone else in the Company was born. If you didn't count Lady.

A quick, determined search revealed that One-Eye had not joined Goblin yet. A cruise up and down the road from Kiaulune did not turn him up, either. He must be in hiding for the day.

I did not feel Kina or Soulcatcher. More confident, I found Goblin again, rode Smoke backward in time.

Goblin did a good job ambushing the Prahbrindrah Drah's gang. And no spells concealed the encounter. He'd been too busy with other work.

It was a traditional Black Company–style ambush. The Prince hurried into it at dusk. He was accompanied by several hundred soldiers. They outnumbered Goblin's force heavily. A few arrows wobbled in from the brush south of the road, striking several Taglians. Ululations went up. Brush rustled. More arrows flew.

The Prahbrindrah Drah had no idea who was attacking. Shadowlander partisans probably seemed more likely than the Company. He did not know about Goblin.

We had taught the Taglians to respond to an ambush by counterattacking immediately. That is what the Prince's companions did, though not quite instantly.

Better than half charged into the brush, chasing rustlings. A handful of those rustles were created by Goblin's men but most were contributed by little owls groggily trying to get away from they knew not what without ever rising out of the cover.

Goblin's second attack, from the opposite hillside, was far more vigorous and included illusory people the Taglians would know could not possibly be there if they just thought. I saw my own doppelgänger wading through the brush waving a nicked-up, rusty sword.

A couple of Goblin's men and a gang of ghosts retreated toward Kiaulune, drawing most of the remainder of the Prince's band with them. Then the remainder of Goblin's force jumped in after the Prince. It was a brisk fight. When the dust settled our erstwhile employer was a prisoner, alive but in no shape to trouble anyone. He had collected a dozen wounds.

Goblin faded away. Rangers and illusions harassed and baffled the Taglians till dawn made Goblin's illusions too obviously illusory.

The Taglians made a valiant effort to find their Prince. They had no luck. Soon after the next sunset a brush with a killer shadow panicked them. They fled north with the news that the Prince might be dead.

I could imagine the effect that would have when it reached Taglios. The capital would fall into chaos if the priesthoods rejected the Radisha's right to rule. It could mean civil war. The Woman had noncanonical supporters and there was no alternate heir-apparent. The question of the succession had been around for years but always got pushed aside by more immediate crises.

Hee-hee. She would start paying the price of her perfidy before we ever glanced her way.

One-Eye and Gota must still be on the road. Instead of trying to find them there it seemed easier to go all the way back and pick them up as they began their adventure.

That worked. After a fashion. When Gota caught One-Eye alone they held only a brief discussion before the little wizard grunted, dug a pack out of his ruined bunker and joined her in slipping off into the nearest woods. Obviously the matter had been discussed before. Preparations had been made.

They did not talk much, which was hard to credit. One-Eye was not known for his reticence and Mother Gota was worse. He only grunted occasionally. When she said anything at all it was just to complain about the general unfairness of life.

Total silence descended once they entered the shade of the trees. Light and shadow fluttered about as the wind stirred the branches and leaves. They became increasingly hard to track. . . . Oh, but the little shit was a wizard, wasn't he? And one who damned well knew about Smoke.

He made me work at it but I stayed with him till my world began to shake.

Earthquake? Again?

It dawned on me at last. Somebody outside the ghostworld wanted me. Reluctantly, I returned to flesh. "About damned time!" the Old Man snapped when I opened my eyes. "I really thought we lost you this time."

"Huh?" That came out a dry-throated croak. I tried for a cup but found I had no strength to extend my arm. I was wasted bad. The Captain had to pour water into my mouth for me.

"I really fucked up. How long was I out there?"

"Eleven hours." That was how tough One-Eye had made it to track him.

"I bet there's no finding him at all once it gets dark," I said after I had gotten a little sugar water inside me. I was confused about when I was. I meant after dark the day he fled. He could lose himself thoroughly in the dark.

And darkness always comes.

Croaker wasted a lot of energy cursing.

I said, "I can watch for crows. Wherever there're crows there's something they're watching." Except around Goblin, who had his owls and confusion spells. Unless they never looked because Catcher did not know he was out there. "Mostly they're too dim to be fooled by low-grade glamors." Which had to say something about people and crows both but I am not bright enough to define it.

"I'll just count him gone. For now. I don't want you going out there if you're going to lose track so bad that you forget you've got to come back."

It was my own habit of dreaming that endangered me. I had encountered fewer perils roaming around that way.

Again Croaker said, "I'll just count him gone." He smiled grimly. "He'll be back. Right after he strangles that woman. Which will happen about as soon as the new wears off. You go back over there. Keep a close eye on the standard. And send me whatever writings you've got ready for review."

Ulp. I was not ready for this. He had not shown much interest ever before.

"When are we going to move on? Or are we not going to?"

"Not till we have our crops in. Unless we're under really heavy pressure. Five months minimum. Enjoy the rest."

Enjoy the rest. Like I enjoyed all that loafing around when we were bottled up inside Dejagore. He missed all that because he could not turn down the chance to go off and play games with Soulcatcher.

"When you went after Catcher the other day. . . . Was there a plan? Did you really expect to accomplish anything?" I retained doubts about the depth of their antagonism even now.

"Check with my dearly beloved. That was her scheme. You'll probably see it again. She's got the notion that if she keeps harassing Soulcatcher, Catcher won't be able to concentrate on giving us grief."

"Now there's an idea. Jab sticks into a nest of vipers so they don't have time to come hunt you down. Why not whack on hornets' nests and hibernating bears while we're at it?"

"Find One-Eye or go work on the Annals. I've got all the bitching I can handle right here at home."

"You ought to get some sleep," I said, heading out. "You're way too crabby."

There is color. There is life of a sort. There is light. Without light there can be no darkness.

There is death. The husks of a hundred crows surround the listing throne.

Death will find a way. Darkness will find a way inside.

Darkness always comes.

The thing on the throne sits wide-eyed, blind. Its orbs show no pupils. They are half-fried egg-white blanks, yet the creature does seem to see. Certainly it is aware. Grimacing in agony, its face turns as it tracks each venturesome spy from the world. It concentrates its will on each new-comer, wanting it to land. A twinge of evil humor stirs its features when-ever a weak bird fails to carry out its instructions.

The earth quivers.

The throne slides a foot, tilts another inch. Alarm underscores the refreshed pain on the face of the sleeper.

The crack in the earth opens wider. The color wafting up brightens. A breeze whispers out of the bowels of the earth. It is colder than the heart of a starving spider. It carries a black vapor.

The throne jerks another inch.

Death will find a way.

Even the gods must pass.

86

THINGS WENT TOO WELL FOR TOO LONG. SUMMER WAS AN IDYLL. IT NEVER got too hot. The rains were perfect for the crops we planted. We were threatened with the sort of harvest for which peasants pray. We made sure the peasants we encountered understood that the wonderful weather was all our fault. Our foragers had liberated draft animals enough to support us if we traveled light, leaving the heavy equipment that had followed us down from friendly territory. There were even a few sheep for those not bound by Gunni strictures against eating flesh.

The old saw is true. An army does travel on its stomach. What we accomplished by projecting the Taglian will the distance we did was a tribute to Croaker's planning, preparation and devotion. And psychosis. And, of course, it was founded on the four years given us by Long-shadow's utter failure to interfere. Poor boy. Should have listened to Mogaba. He would not be living in a kennel. Not that he could be faulted for having been deceived by the Mother of Deceivers when Kina could spin webs of deception to warp the eyesight of gods as great as she.

We had not yet fattened up from the winter but we were getting set to take the next leap already.

Neither Soulcatcher nor Mogaba, neither lost Taglian loyalists nor the local population seemed further inclined to make our lives miserable. We were getting along with the latter fairly well, now.

After—apparently at Lady's insistence—finally sending recon forces to winkle out the secrets of Overlook, the Old Man had discovered that the fortress contained several treasures. Half became the Company treasury, something we have not had for a generation. All pledged brothers received equal shares of the rest. Eventually, Croaker ordered a market established where locals could bring anything they cared to sell.

Results were disappointing at first. But once we demonstrated that we would not rob or murder anybody trade picked up. Peasants are resilient. They are realists. These did not see how our yoke could weigh heavier than Longshadow's. They had no problems with old or imagined myths of the Black Company despite existing so much closer to Khatovar.

They did not know the name Khatovar, as such, either. Nor were they concerned about Kina, under any of her names. Their Kina was a creator as well as a destroyer, fierce but no unhallowed queen of darkness. The Year of the Skulls was no terror to them. They could imagine no future more grim than their past.

Nobody hailed us as liberators, however. We were but the shadow that displaced the darkness.

I wandered the market occasionally, accompanied by Thai Dei and an interpreter. Thai Dei objected. He was sure my curiosity would get me killed. He was not shy about advising me that curiosity was a lethal curse.

Uncle Doj usually tagged along. Despite pretenses to the contrary, a lot of strain had developed between us. I could not forgive Sarie's absence, though I controlled my urge to bring my knowledge into the open. What I did to irritate him was ask every southerner I interviewed about the constellation called the Noose.

But nobody knew it.

Except for the devastation that was Kiaulune it would have seemed a good world.

I enjoyed myself, except for missing Sarie. And I saw her in my dreams. There were fewer demands on me lately, though I was in charge at the Shadowgate. Red Rudy and Bucket did most of the real work there, showing me the ropes as they went. Nobody said so but I was getting educated in case I ever had to take over. I did not remind anybody that I managed the Old Crew tolerably during our ordeal in Dejagore. I did not remind them that we had a Lieutenant and she was a whole lot more experienced and hard-edged than me. Anytime you say anything you just get more work piled on.

87

I LOOKED DOWNSLOPE ONE MORNING AND SAW A YOUNG ARMY HEADED MY way, twenty-five men and as many jackasses, loaded down with packs and bamboo. I told Thai Dei, "I don't like the looks of this. That's Loftus, Longinus and Cletus all at the same time." Not to mention Otto and Hagop, whom I had not seen for a while. "When them three all clot up together you can bet something is up."

Thai Dei looked at me like he wondered if I really thought he was dim enough to think they were off for a picnic. He remembered the brothers from Dejagore and probably understood their obsessions better than I did.

Something was in the wind, though.

I went down to meet them.

"Hey!" Clete hollered, waving. "It's the hermit prince."

"What're you guys up to?"

"We heard you set up your own kingdom over here. We come to see its wonders."

"Looks like you're here to invade me. What *is* all this shit?" I couched the question in the language of the Jewel Cities.

"Field trials for a new toy. We been playing with it in the cellars of the castle."

"Hnh?" Could there be a real reason that the Old Man still kept most of Overlook off limits? "I hope it's good to eat."

Longo snickered. "This wouldn't be too tasty, Murgen. But it'll be fun to dish out."

Thai Dei scowled. Left out again. Too bad. He was with the Company but not of the Company. As I lived with Nyueng Bao without being Nyueng Bao.

"The way you guys are grinning I got to figure, whatever it is, it's got a lot of gears and levers and does something entirely decorative with a reliability quotient of ten percent."

"O ye of weak faith. Clete, you ever seen a sourball as negative as this guy?"

"He just don't understand engineering."

"I understand engineering fine. I don't understand engineers. What're we doing?"

"Field tests," Clete reminded me. "We applied a little engineering to Lady's fireball flingers."

"Range, accuracy, power, Murgen," Loftus enthused. "Velocity. All areas where we thought there was room for improvement."

Absolutely. The fireball throwers would do a man a lot of damage but you practically had to stick him with your pole to make sure you hit him.

All this foreign yammer brought Uncle Doj around to poke his nose in. Which did him no good. But he would figure it out quickly enough.

Longo said, "You got a nice field of fire here, Murgen." He waved toward the mountains. Miles of nothing lay between us and the evergreen forest. His arm swung around to indicate Overlook. "And a nice measured range down that way." Men were out there setting some kind of survey stakes already.

Guys up close started working double-time, dragging stuff off the pack animals. Cletus grabbed a bamboo pole. "Your basic bamboo. The kind Lady turned out until we brought our thoughts to the table."

Clete popped off a few fireballs in the general direction of a couple of gossiping crows. The crows laughed. The fireballs wobbled into the distance, ran out of momentum, drifted to the ground, faded away. "Can't hit shit. Except shadows. Unless you walk right up to what you want to burn."

Longo interjected, "We made her believe that since soldiers would be using the bamboo to work *other* targets—whether she liked that or not—they ought to be able to hit whatever they're aiming at."

Loftus said, "She's spent time around soldiers. She understands how they think."

I sneered. "She's been screwing one for five years. She ought to have a clue."

Clete grabbed a bamboo pole with black bands around it. "This's a cute little number." He nodded to his brothers. They picked up similar poles. Each brother pointed his in the general direction of a crow. Clete said, "Do it."

They cranked. Fireballs flew. Black feathers exploded, floated around smoldering. More fireballs darted out. It did not seem to matter whether the guys aimed well or not. The fireballs hunted their targets down however desperately they darted and dodged. Just the way they had hunted down shadows.

Clete leaned on his pole. "That ought to take care of the spy problem." His brothers remained alert. Longo picked off a clever little devil trying to sneak off at low altitude, whipping between boulders in turns so tight it lost wing feathers every time.

A ball of violet fire closed in at four times the crow's best speed.

Poof!

"Now there's a trick I can appreciate," I said.

Likewise Thai Dei and Uncle Doj and the guys of the thin desperate line at the Shadowgate. Jaws dropped. Rudy swore, "Fugginay! I want me one a them mudsuckers."

I asked, "You got a special problem with crows?"

Rudy asked, "It only kills crows?"

Cletus averred, "I suppose we could set them to knock down most anything. But the more targets you want to specify the more complicated your logistics is gonna get."

"That's not why you're here," I guessed.

"That was just to clear the area."

Longo said, "We wanted something guys like us could appreciate."

Loftus added, "Considering that we're not likely to bring in a lot of recruits anytime soon, while Taglios can come up with as many as they want."

There was a growing faction up north, these days, who wanted Taglios to pretend that the Company had gone its way. We were headed for Khatovar when we came to Taglios. There was nothing to keep us from going there, now. If everybody held real still and stayed real quiet we might lose interest and head on down the road.

While I talked to the engineers Otto and Hagop erected several trestle tables. These acquired decorative vises and tool collection place settings. Racks rose behind the tables. Their companions began stacking bamboo tubes in those. "Big bastards," I said. Some were fifteen feet long. Some were four inches in diameter.

Clete said, "Big and brutal. Careful where you point that damned thing!" A soldier was trying to get a bead on a crow speeding south. He was not worried about people dumb enough to get between him and his target. "What we wanted most was increased accuracy and velocity. A little extra oomph at the other end would be a nice plus, too. Hagop."

Hagop took a twelve-footer with a three-inch bore, striped red, locked it into a vise. He sighted down its length. He tapped gently with a hammer, shifting his aim slightly. "That boulder out there that looks like One-Eye's hat." He armed a complicated bamboo spring mechanism.

I did not think the boulder looked much like a hat. It was a good four hundred yards away. Three soldiers with standard bamboo launched a dozen fireballs before one got lucky and painted a lime glow along one edge.

"Usual problem. When you finally do get a hit you don't do much damage. Unless it's people. Go ahead, Hagop."

Hagop triggered his pole. There was a frying-bacon sound. An intense orange ball crossed to the boulder too fast for me to follow. It hit dead center. A lance of fire blew out of the rock for fifteen seconds. I felt the heat.

The boulder shifted position slightly, pointing its tail of fire farther downhill.

The fireball popped out the other side of the rock like a pimple's core squirting.

"Shit!" said I. "And double shit! That fucker must be ten feet thick!"

Clete said, "A three-inch ball will run at least fifteen feet into the kind of stone we have around here. Hagop, see the silver character that looks like the rune for Fate?" He pointed at Overlook. There were thousands of characters on the wall. I did not understand which one he meant. Neither did Hagop.

"Tallest line of characters. Middle of the target. Looks like a flagpole trailing two pennons to the right, next to something like a three-tined pitchfork."

"All right."

I found it, too.

"Go ahead. Snipe away when you're ready."

I protested, "That's over three thousand yards! Closer to four. He'll be lucky to hit the wall."

"Ready."

"Do it."

Bacon fried. An orange ball left the bamboo pole. It took less than three seconds to reach Overlook. I would not have been able to follow it had I not been standing behind Hagop. A flash lit up the whole countryside when the fireball hit the spells protecting the wall. It struck right where Hagop aimed it. The target rune appeared slightly discolored once the glare waned.

"Oh, my!" said I. Thai Dei and Uncle Doj yammered at one another. They had no need to understand our quacking to see the potential.

"We figure a ball will run out at least fourteen miles before it loses all its momentum," Clete said. "By then it won't have much more energy than a regular ball and won't be much good for anything but killing shadows and general destruction anymore." He patted the tube Hagop had used. "This was our prototype. It's sighted in. We got to do all these others now. Which is why we come up here."

Hagop and Otto replaced that pole with another not yet marked. Otto gave the back end a half twist. A complete, traylike section came off. Two guys from Lady's factory packed the tray with something that looked like potter's clay, then seated a big black rubber marble in that. Hagop put the tray back into his toy, fiddled with the triggering mechanism, asked the engineer brothers, "You guys satisfied with the way this thing is laid?"

All three squatted. They bickered. Hammers tapped. They argued. Then they, Otto, Hagop and the factory people all assumed particular positions and stared at Overlook.

Bacon crackled. An orange fireball hit the air. A thousand yards out it began to drift to the left, then downward. It hit ground short of the wall. Fire gouted into the air for fifteen seconds. So did bits of stone and sod.

All seven observers began combining observations on a chart. Bickering steadily. They took the tray off the pole and peered through. More notes went onto the chart. That eventually passed into the hands of a specialist who used some of the arcane tools to machine the interior of the pole.

The brothers moved to another pole. Their accomplices had a dozen set up for testing. They repeated the process over and over. Some poles put their fireballs on target first try. Some missed badly. The worst got discarded right away. No sense wasting time on those. There was still a need for less accurate shadowslappers.

Once a pole went through its rework it got tested for consistency. An alphabet of arcane marks in various paints went on to tell the soldiers what quirks the weapon retained.

Otto seldom says much but during his lunch break he observed, "Lady's really got the power back, now."

Hardly anyone even suspected the truth. Those who did were not prepared to believe it.

"How many of them things you going to work?" My guys had stopped getting any work done. They were hanging around watching the fireworks like a bunch of big kids.

Clete said, "We brought fifty in this batch. We hope we can come up with twenty reliables out of those. Everything goes right, we'll start work on some really *big* stuff. Boy, will the Tals be surprised."

I could imagine what these new fireballs would do to men's bodies. But I suspected that scything through legions was not their purpose. And my suspicion was confirmed next afternoon.

Lady herself came to inspect the twenty-six pieces the brothers had found acceptable.

The woman seemed emotionally drained, yet did show a bounce that said part of her life was going well. She and the Old Man were finding free moments to be something other than Captain and Lieutenant.

I was pleased for them.

"Excellent," she said, after she watched every accepted tube smite Overlook's wall at least once. "What about the crow-specific light arms?"

"You see any crows?" Longo asked. "We got a picket line out. They don't even get close."

"Good. Prime all of these things with full loads. I'm going to try my own experiment."

Hagop told me, "We're in the chips. We done come up with six more than we even hoped. And half the others are good enough we can use them up close, a mile or less. We'll kick us some ass, big time." The whole gang were as thrilled as kids with new toys. And Lady was the worst. She bounced around like she was fifteen again.

The troops shuffled the tables around, began packing tools and loading wagons.

Loftus, Longinus and Otto kept chuckling about something.

I glanced around. I did not like the portents. Even Lady had the look. The look that always showed up on One-Eye and/or Goblin when they were going to pull a stunt the rest of us might regret.

"Just hang on here, everybody!" I yelled, trying to be the responsible one. "I don't know what you're up to, but—" This was *my* fief.

A bunch of them, including Lady, the brothers, Otto and Hagop, all got behind the tables. They started wisecracking as they sighted down the lengths of fully loaded heavyweight poles.

"Don't even think about it!" I growled.

My in-laws hovered behind me, silently, not understanding anything being said but clear on the fact that yesterday and today added up to something significant. Something beyond the obvious.

"Don't do it!" I begged.

Twenty-two bamboo tubes discharged within seconds of one another. The villains all watched the orange fireballs streak north-northwest, straight into the area where that storm of crows had exploded in my imagination.

It was not my imagination this time.

Catcher's hideout had to be more than ten miles away. It did not take the fireballs ten seconds to get there. Maybe not five. I was too shaken to be a good judge of time's passage.

Fire and smoke and shit flew half a mile high.

Now the whole gang went bugfuck. Every one of them—Lady, too— put fireballs into the air in streams of four and five. The distant woods began to boil. Even from so far away I could make out gigantic trees being hurled a thousand feet into the air.

I recalled some trees there being twice as thick as I was tall. They twisted through the sky like scythes of fire.

A firestorm took life below. It hurled flames and smoke heavenward like an angry volcano.

It was a day when a lot of crows died.

I am sure it was a day when Soulcatcher found not one reason to laugh.

88

THERE IS A LOT OF RITUAL IN HUMAN AFFAIRS.

The Old Man started me doing sermons from the Annals, the way he had himself in ancient times. He was a firm believer in every man knowing his exact place in our long history. And then most of the older hands were stuck with teaching Taglian to anyone who did not speak it already. Croaker wanted every brother to have a language in common with every other. Sometimes it seemed we had as many native tongues as we had men to speak them. I recalled no instance in the Annals when the Company had become as polyglot as it was now.

Another burden I bore was keeping in shape by hoofing it across to headquarters for staff meetings every few days.

A wonderful aroma wakened me. I shoved my head out of our oft-improved bunker. "What're you cooking?" I asked Thai Dei.

"Uncle Doj killed a wild pig last night. There will be roast pork today."

"I hope I can keep it down."

"It won't be ready for hours yet. You told me to remind you of your staff meeting this morning."

"Shit." It was supposed to be important, too. I did not dare be late. "Better save me some." I dragged my ass out and made what morning preparations I could. None of us were the sort who spent hours trimming our beards or prettying our hair or taking baths. But you do have to splash a little water in your face sometimes and you do have to get the crud out of your teeth just so you feel like keeping on.

I wondered what would become of our teeth if we did not get One-Eye back. Those tiny little spells he put on them, to protect them, had to be renewed every two years. And we had battalions of new men still lacking their initial exposures.

Thai Dei did not save me diddly. He took the pig off the fire and followed me. There is just no ditching the man.

I was still not riding. Sleepy had not brought my mount back. Sleepy had not come home yet himself, though he had had ample time. He had disappeared while crossing the mountains. No search through the ghost-world nor on site had produced a trace. I feared the worst.

Two sleek crows followed me, gliding from bush to rock to ruin. Otherwise there was no evidence to indicate that Soulcatcher remained alive or was interested in us anymore, despite the vandalism of her home. She was biding her time.

You could say that about the woman. She was crazy but never impatient. Her temper did not control her.

Lady said she had escaped the barrage only because she had taken Howler's carpet north so she could conspire with the Radisha.

I had orders not to look for Soulcatcher. I had orders to run whenever I sensed her presence. The same with Kina. Smoke was next to useless now. I had become too valuable a resource to risk.

Right.

I glanced back before we started up the far slope. Uncle Doj was trailing us, as he did so often. His step suggested he was ready for anything. One hand rested on Ash Wand always.

Thai Dei and I had resumed training with him, want to or not. He would not explain what was going on inside his head. He just kept whacking away, forcing us to defend ourselves or enjoy painful bruises.

He despaired of my ever reaching what he considered minimal proficiency with a sword. He did not understand the difference between a lone wolf warrior and a soldier who is part of a team of mutually supporting fighters. Or he pretended not to understand.

He expected trouble, no doubt about that. But it was too much trouble to explain.

I have been running with Croaker long enough that I should be used to that.

I reminded Thai Dei, "We're mushrooms."

"Huh?"

"Kept in the dark? Fed a diet of horseshit?" You would think that he would remember. But he was not interested in trying. Like most Nyueng Bao attached to the Company. "Never mind."

Uncle Doj tried to invite himself into the meeting. A couple of hard-eyed guards stepped into his path. He chose to go hang around with the other Nyueng Bao. He never did that before. He seemed to be looking for JoJo, One-Eye's erstwhile bodyguard. JoJo was never a gregarious sort, even among other Nyueng Bao.

I ducked inside the Old Man's dugout.

A whole herd of people had gathered in there. They were waiting for me, apparently.

"Let's get started," Croaker said. "First, intelligence received. The rumor is true. Mogaba definitely did sign on with the Radisha. He's started putting together a force somewhere south of Dejagore. The reports didn't explain where but did say his men have begun evicting the locals from the best croplands so they can support themselves. The leadership in

Taglios hasn't decided exactly what to do yet. There's actually a lot of sentiment for forgetting us altogether."

The Captain did not reveal his sources. Some of that came from me and Lady, dreaming and walking the ghost when Smoke was not completely useless. He added, "It seems Mogaba will enjoy the support of several small auxiliary units raised by religious sects with a grudge against us or our friends."

Blade chuckled.

89

SILENCE STRETCHED. I FOUND A BATTERED MUG LEFT OVER FROM Kiaulune's glory days, helped myself to tea from a pot steeping beside Croaker's crude hearth. The stuff was more bitter than medicine. That explained why it was still there. I pretended to enjoy it.

"Clete," Croaker said. "What's the agricultural situation?" Only in the Black Company would a siege engineer be in charge of farming.

Cletus said, "Nothing new to report. Exceptional crops threatening to mature earlier than the locals predicted. We could do worse than to establish ourselves here." Cletus and his brothers centered a faction interested in settling down. They felt their new weapons could discourage our most determined enemies. They made no strong representations, though.

The Company had slogged through hell for an age. Now we possessed a rich province and a fine fortress and our only serious enemies were hundreds of miles away and probably disinclined to come after us anytime soon.

I did not listen to the editorializing following a suggestion that the gods loved us because our crops were doing so well. I paid no attention till Longinus started telling us why we no longer needed to be afraid of anyone.

"If the Radisha really traded away half her power so she could keep her position that means the priests are really in charge. I don't see them, no matter how much they fear us or hate Blade, ever saddling themselves with another real army. The cost and the threat to their power . . ."

I had heard it all before. The priests would not let the Radisha come after us.

I did not believe it. He was whistling in the dark. But I was a ghost-walker. I could go anywhere and see anything. I had to work harder to mislead myself.

"You're wrong, Longo," I said. "We'll have company here eventually. Probably way sooner than any of us would like." I even had the Old Man's attention, suddenly.

"I had a dream." Most everyone knew that I had visions. The mechanics and reliability remained my secret. To avoid troubling people who might worry about me, I blamed it all on the kinds of seizures I had been having since the siege.

Lady clucked her tongue, an irksome habit she did not know she had acquired. She and Croaker were turning into everybody's grandparents. The inner circle needed young blood bad. She asked, "Could you tell us about your dream, Murgen? Or do we have to wait for the book?" She was annoyed with me because I had begun making new revisions to her volume of the Annals. Some of our latest class of enlistees had been around back then. Not all of them recalled events the same as she did.

"The high point, like the boss said, is that our old pal Mogaba isn't unemployed anymore."

A general susurrus. Had they thought that the Old Man was joking?

"I don't get much from my dreams. I have no control over them. I get knocked back in time sometimes but I can't go whenever I want to find out *why* something happened after we find out that it did happen. I have to wait for news from our friends on the scene just like everybody else." We do have friends up north who supply us with reliable intelligence. I check up on them whenever I can.

We did not use Smoke much anymore. He wanted to wake up. He was not really in a coma now, anyway. Lady had to struggle to make him useful. She took advantage of the resulting opportunities herself.

I continued, "But Soulcatcher must have been in touch with Mogaba at some point. She recommended him to the Radisha. Bet you the Woman took him on mostly because she didn't want to get Catcher pissed off at her. Mogaba's already promising the priests that he'll catch Blade and Lady for them." There had been huge bounties on those two from the moment the Radisha turned on the Company.

Mogaba never let failure dent his confidence.

Blade volunteered, "I could go hit them back first. It would be fun to pick them off and watch the live ones squirm . . ."

"No." Croaker was in no mood for flights of fancy. "I know who'd pick off who if you went dancing with Mogaba. Sindawe. Talk to me about this."

"I'm hearing this for the first time. I need to think about it, Captain."

"Think out loud."

"Mogaba is alone." By which Sindawe meant that Mogaba had no Nar adherents anymore. Those who had gone with him when he left the Company were dead. "His sanity will be more strained than ever. He may become obsessed with destroying you, personally, because you took away his birthright."

Croaker grunted, unsurprised. "Murgen. How long before he can get into our hair? It took four years for us to get where we could make it here still in good enough shape to starve. And we wouldn't be as happy as we are now if the Radisha had fooled us and stayed faithful. We didn't lose as many men fighting as I expected and a lot fewer to disease."

He let slide the fact that we had come during the off season, when, normally, moving an army is next to impossible.

"Speaking of numbers," Bucket said. "That last bunch who wanted to go home are long gone."

Lady stated the obvious. "Mogaba won't have to train the way we did. He can round up men we've already trained for him."

The Old Man asked me, "What does the Radisha want from Mogaba?"

"The priests think he should just maintain control of the territories we overran. Some of them are real excited about their chances to make a killing down there. But the Woman just wants to keep us south of the mountains." I chuckled. "His job will be the same as it was when he worked for Longshadow. Only he'll plug the bottle from the other end."

"Mogaba will come someday," Isi observed. "As Sindawe said."

Croaker grunted again.

Bucket said, "If he don't bring half a shitload of timber, kites, and tons of bamboo, and comes in the summer . . ."

Longo cracked, "He could have peasants carry his supplies up, then eat the peasants."

Sindawe, Ochiba and Isi glared.

Croaker said, "Stick to business. There're changes happening in Taglios. Thanks to Murgen's spells we know about some of them."

Everybody waited for him to say something more. He did not. Finally, Lady remarked, "Soulcatcher is still a problem."

Definitely. She had not responded to Lady's barrage. Yet. I was not supposed to look for her but I did know she was still around. She was shielding herself with illusions and moving a lot. I had every confidence that she had lost no interest in causing us misery.

No one ever mentioned the child. I knew she had survived and had been rescued, not by the Kina to whom she wept her appeals but by Catcher, to the accompaniment of merry taunts. Lady and Croaker had hardened their hearts. Which was understandable. They had had scarcely more contact with her than some unknown child born the same day at the far end of the world.

I would not say anything. I was supposed to avoid Catcher until I received specific orders otherwise. The Old Man's tolerance for my improvisations had been exhausted.

Sleepy's loss remained unforgiven.

Croaker asked, "What about your mother-in-law, Murgen? What about Goblin and One-Eye?"

What could I say? "They're still missing." That could not be blamed on me. Not yet. He might find a way.

Our last contact with any of them had come when some of Goblin's rangers had arrived with the Prahbrindrah Drah in manacles, Lisa Bowalk snarling in a cage on a cart, and no word at all about what Goblin was doing or why he was doing it. I did not think his desertion was part of the Old Man's master plan. I refused to believe that Croaker could plan that far ahead. The pasty-faced little wizard was out there somewhere, playing out his own scheme.

I did not get many chances to look for him anymore. The dreams did not come as often now. If they did I visited Sarie first. Sarie and my son, that absolutely beautiful drooling lump she nicknamed Tobo because she did not want to pick a real name without me there to talk it over and find out face-to-face what his name would be and why.

She was determined to join me, though by now even the most remote parts of the swamp had heard about the falling-out between the Radisha and the Black Company. That would put Sahra at greater risk if she left the temple. Almost all the Nyueng Bao who had left their swamps in recent times have been associated with the Company somehow.

Sarie's keepers were alert. They expected her to try something now she was no longer the size of a small house. Clever woman, she was using guerrilla tactics while she regained her strength. Every day in every way she made the priestly population more miserable. That was easy. She just imitated her mother. When the time came they would, probably, lack enthusiasm for the task of her recapture.

Croaker stared at Lady. He was waiting for her to say something else about her sister. The others did the same. Catcher weighed on all our minds. Her luck never stopped running strong. Her grudge list kept getting longer. Though there was no way we could hurt *our* cause any more. She could not do worse than kill us, could she?

Hell, we all take on a death sentence when we join the Company.

Lady said, "Several soldiers have gone missing the last couple of nights. Some probably deserted. But not all of them." She waved. Isi and Ochiba, already cued, brought a bundle to the front of the crowd. They dropped it on the dirt floor.

I did not remind the Old Man that we could enjoy real floors and real furniture if he would just move into Overlook.

Lady said, "This may be a little ripe."

Oh-oh.

Isi and Ochiba spun the dead man out of his wrappings. He did not stink as bad as I expected. He was shriveled like an old mummy. His mouth was open in a scream that would never end. He seemed to have suffered a lot of bruises before he died.

Those would have been self-inflicted during his final struggle. "Shadow got him," I said. Needlessly.

Croaker eyed me. I shrugged. "No shadows have gotten through since I've been on guard." I was sure. There would have been an uproar.

"They're under control, then," he said. "It's her, using Longshadow's leftovers."

Catcher was the new Shadowmaster. Maybe she was honing her skills.

Lady observed, "There's nothing we can do about this kind of attack except never go anywhere alone and never without bamboo. . . . What's the matter with him?"

The "him" she referred to was the Company Annalist, who had started making weird noises. He jerked around, apparently trying to swallow his own tongue. So they told me later. At the time I was out of touch with my body entirely. I was a fly who never saw the swatter coming.

I went to the place of all the bones for a moment and for that whole eternity seemed to be smeared all over the grim landscape. A white crow mocked me. Then I *was* the white crow. Then I was out of there but I did not follow my habitual course. I did not get to see all those grumpy old men glowering from their cocoons of ice. I got to wing my way away through curtains of darkness back to those gaunt and wonderful days when first I met my Sarie, then before that, where I met my own ghost and joined it in a tour of the besieged city. None of the words from my invisible beak were my own but the madwoman who manufactured them did not seem to be paying attention to or really directing what was happening. Poor me. I was like a moth caught in an unexpected squall. The hammer of my desperate wings did nothing to daunt a gale indifferent to my existence.

I saw a lot of death and despair. I learned nothing new and saw nothing I had not had a more intimate relationship with in the past.

Catcher maybe just poked at me in passing, because she was bored, or maybe she was unaware that she had bumped me at all. It did not matter. I could not retaliate. All I could do was flap like a son of a bitch and hope I could survive one more storm.

Darkness came.

90

I WAKENED IN THE ALCOVE WHERE SMOKE USED TO BE STORED. IT WAS DARK. I had no idea how long I had been out. The meeting was over, that was certain. I did not hear a sound.

I started to clamber out of there, found I was incredibly weak. My legs betrayed me when I tried to stand. I pitched forward through the curtain masking the alcove.

There was a sudden mouselike scurry. I lifted my head. The little bit of light betrayed the rodent.

Thai Dei was stuffing papers back into piles while trying to appear innocent. Maybe he was. He could not read.

"There you are. I got worried." He helped me up. "What happened?"

My knees were watery. "I had one of those attacks like I used to have when we were in Dejagore and Taglios."

"Why did they . . . ? They all trooped out of here hours ago. Even the guards went away."

"What time is it?" The meeting had begun early in the morning.

"Be sunset in an hour."

"Shit. A whole day shot, then." Thai Dei helped me stay standing. I did not shake him off. I looked for food. Food always helped after a long ghostwalk with Smoke.

This was not the same. At least cold, tough, burnt mutton did not help. And there was nothing else available.

What I wanted was something alcoholic. A few amateurs had arisen to take One-Eye's place. Best known were Willow Swan and Cordy Mather, who had stayed around despite being free to go back north. Cordy no longer had that fire in his belly where the Radisha was concerned. But their product was no good. And, if I wanted some, I had to acquire it through intermediaries since we all had to pretend to observe the rules.

But I had a suspicion, of late, about where One-Eye could have hidden his manufacturing equipment. There was a small, reinforced cubby in my old dugout where I had kept the Annals and the odd private item. It had survived disasters unscathed. Mother Gota had helped build it.

We climbed up out of Croaker's dugout, me still wobble-kneed and griping. "I wish the hell he'd move into the fucking fortress." The experimentation was all over but our crowd was still scattered through the hills, roughing it. An hour of light remained. "Where *is* everybody?" I did not see a soul closer than the ruins of Kiaulune. That gave me a little shock of fright. Had I returned to the world I left when the seizure took me? Was I caught in another layer of dream?

"They all went away. Even the guards." Thai Dei repeated the news as though he was talking to someone both deaf and dense. "Else I could not have entered the Liberator's shelter."

It had been a while since anybody called the Old Man that. "I take it Uncle Doj went to keep an eye on them."

Thai Dei did not reply.

I headed for my former home. "Compared to the bunker we moved to over there this dump was a palace."

Lady and the Old Man had turned my palace into a prison. The downhill side entrance that we put in for Mother Gota and Uncle Doj now opened into an exercise area fenced with captured spears. Lisa Bowalk lay in a cage there, muzzle on paws, exposed to the elements, dully resigned. The Prahbrindrah Drah paced, avoiding glittering spearpoints and the reach of the shapeshifter's claws. He seemed patient, counting his condition only a temporary setback.

Neither Longshadow, Howler, nor Narayan Singh were outside. Singh's absence was not surprising. He was punished if he ventured into the light. But the former Shadowmaster was not and he hated the darkness inside. He feared what might be lurking there.

The poor old boy had lost all his self-confidence. He spent most of his time shivering, rocking and whimpering to himself. He was losing weight. Which was hard to believe.

The stench was awful. Those people had no friends now. They lived worse than animals in the cruelest zoo or feedlot. Passersby were encouraged to torment Longshadow and the living saint of the Deceivers.

Howler had not earned his final standing on Lady's shitlist. He was treated with indifference yet fed the best table scraps.

Smoke would be inside somewhere, too. He and the prince were treated best. Bowalk was fed and otherwise ignored—as long as she behaved.

A sign that could be read by only a few actually insisted that the Prahbrindrah Drah was an honored guest. Somebody's little joke.

"A good storm would help with the smell," I said. I glanced at the sky. Relief seemed unlikely anytime soon.

Thai Dei grunted. He raised a hand.

Something was up. He was on his toes, nostrils flaring. His head moved in little jerks as he tried to hear something.

I froze. This was his business. His expertise.

I heard it, too, now. Scratching from within the dugout. Months had gone by and still I had no clear idea why Longshadow and Singh remained among the living. They kept farting around, Croaker and Lady would regret not having disposed of them quickly.

Lady thought they might be useful. Someday. Somehow. Somewhere.

"Better find out what it is," I said. With no enthusiasm whatsoever. This kind of thing always meant trouble. "What happened to Uncle Doj?" He might be handy to have around if something happened. I was not carrying anything but a little three-ball bamboo stick.

Thai Dei stepped over to the headquarters company woodpile—now serviced by Shadowlander peasant contractors—and selected a yard of kindling with a burly knot at one end. He gestured me forward.

I slipped down and yanked on the door of my former home.

Narayan Singh, the living saint of the Deceivers, tumbled into the twilight. He had been kept inside for a long time. He was naturally dark-skinned but had acquired a pasty, maggoty coloration. Maybe Lady *was* doing more than just keeping him locked up in his own filth. She *could* be subtle when she wanted. She just did not want that often.

Thai Dei bopped him on the noggin.

Poor old Narayan. His life had not gone well for a long time. And the son of a bitch had earned every second of pain. Bet his goddess snickered whenever she thought about him.

Half of his torment would be the waiting, knowing that someday Lady would take time to offer him some specialized, personalized, unloving attention.

"Let's be real careful," I told Thai Dei.

Thai Dei grunted. He wore the ultimate Nyueng Bao stone face. To Tan had not been forgotten.

"Don't even think about it, Thai Dei. Lady would roast you. Besides, there're more of them inside. And they're all worse than Singh."

I meant worse trouble but it did not turn out that way. Both Longshadow and Howler wore hobbles and metal gags. Longshadow had not eaten well since his capture. A starved sorcerer is a tame sorcerer, I guess. Covered with filth, Howler and the Shadowmaster barely had the strength to crawl into the light after—they thought—Narayan had opened the way.

Even famine had not yet tamed them completely. A point worth keeping in mind.

Thai Dei remarked, "They were supposed to seal off the kennel side."

"Don't look like anybody bothered. Keep an eye on them. Without breaking anything. Or anybody. I'll be right back out."

Thai Dei grunted again. In deep disappointment.

"We'll get our turn," I promised.

Smoke was still inside. He had looked so bad for so long he did not look much worse now. His clothing had decayed into rotten rags. He was chained. One chain trailed back into the darkness.

The others had been chained, too. The guys had shown that much sense before they took off wherever they went. Somehow, the villains managed to get loose. I wondered if they would have dragged Smoke any farther had they had the strength and time to manage a successful getaway.

Might have been amusing to watch them return to a world that had changed completely during their holidays.

I stepped over the little wizard, found a small lamp and got it burning. Except for the stink and mess everything was pretty much as we had left it. A ragged shawl belonging to Ky Gota still lay tangled on a three-legged chair liberated from Kiaulune ages ago. There was no evidence that the prisoners had spent any time in this part of the dugout.

Following Smoke's chain, I discovered that the one side *had* been walled off. But the carpenters had done a poor job using salvage lumber that had not stood up to someone's patient ministrations.

I ducked through the hole.

The stench was a lot thicker on the other side. I had seen less filthy pigsties.

The prisoners had not explored their prison thoroughly. They had not found my little cubby. But someone else had and had decided to take advantage of it.

One-Eye's lost manufacturing equipment and finished product had been stuffed into the hole, along with what looked like a bunch of treasures harvested from the ruined city. Mother Gota had enjoyed collecting junk during her nocturnal rambles.

I dragged out a jug, popped its cork. Damn, that stuff smelled nasty! Some kind of distilled spirits . . . I took a long pull that left my eyes running. The stuff tasted worse than it smelled.

After a second throat-burning draught I raised my lamp high, trying to get some light in there past the clutter. I had left a few treasures of my own, though nothing important enough to have dragged on over to the Shadowgate yet. I did not recall what all I had stashed.

"Ah! What's this?" I snaked an arm in through the junk.

As I closed my fingers on ragged burlap I managed to elbow a stack of earthenware bottles piled on their sides. One-Eye evidently had meant to revisit them long ago because even an ignoramus like me knows you do not leave bottled beer horizontal forever.

It took only that nudge to get the bottles banging against one another, then blasting their contents all over me and the inside of the dugout. I snagged one spewing bottle and got some of its contents inside me. Not bad, but a little yeasty.

"I'm all right!" I shouted in response to Thai Dei's inquiry from out-side. "I found One-Eye's treasure." In more ways than one, I discovered. The object wrapped in burlap was that wonderful wizard-killer spear he had whittled while we were trapped in Dejagore. The gold and silver inlays alone were worth a fortune.

More evidence that the little wizard had not planned to stay away for-ever. He did not know I knew but he had continued working on that spear secretly, always improving it, making it ever more his masterwork.

"And what's this?" There was another object in burlap, behind the spear. Had the little shit been making knockoffs of his own artwork?

No. This was a bow, with arrows. I did not recognize it immediately because I had not seen it in more years than I wanted to count, but it was the weapon Lady had given Croaker way back when she was still The Lady. I thought the boss lost it a long time ago.

Croaker always had another secret.

I had to wonder if he had not had some part in One-Eye's desertion.

It was always possible that he did not know what had become of the bow.

I collected spear and bow and as many stoneware containers as I could lug. I could send Thai Dei in for more beer and . . .

I could not carry my lamp and plunder, too. I used to live here. I could find my way around without a lamp. Besides, there was a glimmer of twilight still leaking in through the doorway.

The alcohol was taking effect. As I stepped over him I told Smoke, "I wouldn't have your luck on a bet, chief."

Smoke opened his eyes.

I jumped. It had been five or six years. . . . And he did not appear to be in a friendly mood.

I discovered that I just wanted to get out and indulge my taste for beer.

Thai Dei helped me with my burdens. Somehow, one bottle of beer stuck to his hand. I noted that his charges were all healthy still, though Narayan Singh might have acquired a fresh crop of bruises.

"Where the hell is everybody?" I grumbled again. "I've got stuff to do. But we can't go off and leave these characters alone. They're bound to get into some kind of mischief." Longshadow, Howler and Singh were not volunteering to go back into captivity.

I took another long drink.

The quiet really bothered me. It might indicate yet another less-than-brilliant attempt to subdue Soulcatcher. She had grudges enough against us as it was.

I had seen the ground that had suffered Lady's barrage. It bore no resemblance to its springtime self. Rocks as big as houses had had holes punched right through them. Most of the busted-up trees had burned. There had been rockslides and cave-ins. In places the rock appeared to have become plastic. It had sagged like candle wax. Catcher's cave could not be found.

The only bodies found so far were those of crows. There was no evidence that Soulcatcher or her prisoner had suffered any serious discomfiture.

Live crows laughed amongst the tortured rocks.

91

THAI DEI GRUNTED. THESE DAYS HE WAS POSITIVELY GARRULOUS, SOMEtimes mouthing as many as two entire sentences in an hour. But this time he needed no words. He just put his beer in his other hand and pointed into the gathering darkness.

The missing folks were returning in a mob, coming from the direction of Catcher's disaster. Why would they all charge off into the foothills? Because the Old Man realized my seizure must have been caused by Lady's rascal sister?

No. He would not bother for something that trivial.

But he would go to all that trouble to round up Sleepy.

"Where did you find him?" I asked Sparkle, who was leading the mule dragging the travois onto which Sleepy was strapped. It was obvious that the kid had had it rough. His weight was down. His wardrobe was not much fresher than Narayan Singh's. Whom I mentioned to the Old Man as soon as I found him. "It was pure luck that we showed up when we did. We got them under control. But you've got to do something. Or they're going to become a major bite in the ass someday. Where did Sleepy come from?"

"A patrol spotted him in the hills not far from Lady's tear-up. He didn't know who he was."

I grunted. I laid a narrow look on the kid as he passed. "It took this whole mob to bring him in?"

"Took them all to hunt him down. You all right now? What happened?"

"I had one of my seizures. Like I used to have when I went back to Dejagore."

He frowned, tossed off orders left and right. Soldiers scattered to resume chores they should not have abandoned.

"Did you know that One-Eye had your bow?"

"My bow? What bow?"

"The one Lady gave you as a present."

"No. I didn't. Though maybe I told him to put it away for me one time. Or something. I haven't seen it in so long I'd forgotten it." He sniffed the air. "What else did you find?" I still smelled of beer.

"All kinds of treasures. And circumstantial evidence that One-Eye wasn't planning to stay away forever."

Croaker grunted. It was getting too dark to read his expressions well. Was he irked because I had figured something out? Or was he considering the possibilities?

I said, "I can't believe that finding Sleepy would cause so much excitement."

"Lady hoped we could catch Catcher all goofed up, too."

"But we already knew she was all right. She was sending shadows down. She was messing with me." Maybe she was just tickling me because I was there when her big sister yanked her pigtails.

"We didn't know. We suspected. If Sleepy had been her prisoner and wandered away, then maybe she wasn't in control after all. There isn't anybody around here who wouldn't love to add Catcher to our zoo. And, too, there was the chance that . . . the girl . . ."

Yeah. There was the chance they could grab their daughter back. Maybe when nobody was looking. "Where's Lady?"

"Still out there." His tone told me I had used my quota of questions in that area.

"Sleepy said anything useful?" I asked.

"He hasn't said anything. He doesn't act like he's all there."

"Just what this outfit needs. Another goofball."

"You finding One-Eye's stash reminds me. You stumbled over either one of our prodigal conjuremen lately?"

"I don't dream that much, boss. When I do, it's always in real time. Which means only after dark, when they can hide a lot better. And they do have to be hiding if they're still in this part of the world. I don't even find campfire traces anymore."

"One-Eye would know who was looking and how," Croaker mused. "Tell you the truth, Murgen, I don't miss them that much nowadays. It was a stroke of genius, if I do say so myself, to split them up. I couldn't have survived the last couple of years, working twenty-hour days, with them squabbling around me all the time."

"You'd think if they'd joined forces there would've been forest fires and avalanches to mark the occasion."

"We do keep having earthquakes."

"I'm worried about them, boss. Because of the spear."

"Spear? What spear?"

"The black spear. I told you I found it. The one One-Eye made while we were in Dejagore. He didn't take it with him. But he hasn't come back for it."

"And?"

"He would. Using some sneak spell if he had to. It was important to him. He didn't brag but he considered it his masterpiece. He wouldn't just throw it away—no matter how many times he's been through the Company having to cut and run."

"You saying he's coming back?"

"I'm saying I think he planned to. He might not have been one hundred percent serious about eloping. Wouldn't be the first time a man wasn't completely honest with a woman."

Croaker looked at me like he was trying to figure out what was really going on inside my head. Then he shrugged, said, "Could be. You men. Take Sleepy into my shelter. Leave him on the examining table."

"Good idea," I said. "See how bad he's been treated."

Croaker grunted. "You stay out here," he told Thai Dei, who was standing over his captives with his beer-drinking hand tucked up behind him. "You come with me, Murgen." Like Thai Dei needed reminding that the Old Man did not want him in his house. "Jamadar Subadir. See that those prisoners are put away properly. And make certain that the rest of our guests haven't exceeded themselves, too."

I said, "The Prince never tried anything." The Prahbrindrah Drah did not have to suffer the indignity of shackles. Our Taglians would not have tolerated that.

I spied Uncle Doj watching from some shadows, arms crossed. I wondered why he stayed with us. Narayan Singh? Hardly. His persistence nudged my paranoia level whenever I thought about him.

Croaker, of course, was more enduringly suspicious than I was.

We descended into the Old Man's dugout.

He told the men carrying Sleepy, "That's good. The Standardbearer and I will take care of him now. Hold on, Sparkle. I want you to double-check on those men I told to deal with the prisoners. We haven't given enough consideration to the possibility of treachery amongst our own people."

Sparkle asked, "You want I should look for anything in particular?"

"Just keep your eyes open." Croaker turned to me. "I agree with you. We need to drown the whole bunch of them."

"But Lady has a use for them."

"Waste not, want not. She says. I keep reminding myself that she's supposed to be smarter and more experienced than me. Let's get him undressed. You start at that end."

Sleepy was awake but showed no interest in conversation. Or in anything else. I asked, "Where's my horse, Sleepy?"

Croaker chuckled. "Good question, Murgen. You might want to pursue it. Unless you prefer to walk to Khatovar."

I asked Sleepy several questions. He answered none of them. His eyes would track me and the Old Man but I could not tell if he understood anything.

Croaker said, "We could use Smoke to backtrack him and find out where he's been and how he lost the beast."

I grunted. We could have Lady sock the little shit with a knockout spell and make him useful for a while. The hard part would be getting her to agree not to hog him all for herself. "He was wide awake today. Smoke was. You might better make sure she knows."

Croaker began poking and prodding Sleepy. "Lot of bruises. Must've gotten pounded around good." Sleepy took it silently, without flinching.

"If he was in Catcher's cave . . . I saw it happen from ten miles away. It was—"

"I saw enough." Something was bothering him. He had that air people get when they have something difficult to say and are not morally convinced of their right to say it. Which troubled me. Croaker had no trouble barking at anybody but his old lady. "Been catching up on your Annals, Murgen."

Oh-oh.

"And I hate to say this, but I don't like them very much."

"As I recall, you weren't going to dictate what I write."

"That's right. I'm not going to now. You got the job. You do it. I'm just saying I don't like what I've been reading. Though you have gotten a lot better in some ways. You seen this man naked before?"

"No. Why? Should I have?" I had a feeling he was harboring a big beef with my Annals. Since he was one of probably no more than three people who would read them during my lifetime I supposed I could get into closer touch with the needs of my audience. Or at least pretend to. He could not fire me. Unless he wanted the job back himself. The only candidate lay before us, still untrained, unpolished, unclothed and quite probably unsane. "So what am I doing wrong?"

"You could start by not being so being polite. *Look* at your pal. What's missing?"

Sleepy was not a boy.

I forgot about the Annals. "I'll be damned."

"You didn't know?"

"Never suspected. I thought he was kind of short and skinny. . . . But he always was. He was barely out of diapers when he latched on to us in Dejagore. I figured him for maybe thirteen. He wasn't as sane as he is now. I remember Bucket throwing one of his uncles off the wall for raping him." I kept right on saying "him" because it was hard to think of Sleepy as anything else despite the lack of evidence right there in front of me.

"Good soldier?"

He knew. "The best. Always makes up for his smallness and lack of strength by using his head." Which was something Croaker particularly appreciated.

"Then let's just forget we didn't see something here. Don't even let Sleepy know you know." He resumed his examination.

It would not be the first time a woman had been with the Company disguised as a man. The Annals recalled several instances where amazing discoveries had been made about one of our forebrethren, usually after they got themselves killed somehow.

Still . . . It would be uncomfortable, knowing.

"What I don't like about your Annals is that they're more about you than they are about the Company."

"What?" I did not understand.

"I mean you focus everything on yourself. Except for a few chapters you adapted from Lady's dispatches or Bucket or One-Eye or somebody, you never report anything that doesn't involve you or that you didn't see yourself. You're too self-absorbed. *Why* should we give a rat's ass about your recurring nightmares? And, except for Dejagore, your sense of place is usually pretty weak. If I weren't here myself I'd have a lot of trouble picturing this whole end of the world."

My first reaction, of course, was to defend my babies from the butcher. But I kept my mouth shut. You gain nothing by arguing with your critics. You get more satisfying results teaching pigs to sing. With fewer ulcers.

You have to trust your own muse. Even if she has a clubfoot and is subject to unpredictable seizures.

I think the Old Man said something like that himself a time or two over the years.

I did not mention it.

"You could work on writing a little more sparely, too."

"Sparely?"

"You tend to go on a lot longer than you need to. At times."

"I'll try to keep that in mind. You think we ought to put something on her?"

It was plain he had plenty more to say about my Annals but was uncomfortable about it. He was willing to accept a change of subject. "Yes. There's no permanent physical damage. Lady's got some old things stored in that black chest. They'll be a little big, probably, but—"

"Thought we weren't going to know anything about Sleepy being a girl."

"When's the last time you saw Lady in a dress?"

"Good point." I opened the chest. "Though there's still never any doubt."

Croaker grunted. He was studying Sleepy intently, frowning.

"New wearing off?" I asked.

He smiled weakly. "Sort of. You'll understand someday."

I picked some things. "Not what I want to hear, boss." Always way back there, however much I loved my wife, was a niggle when I recalled that she was the daughter of Ky Gota.

He chuckled. "Get some pants on her before my dearly beloved walks in."

We finished just in time, too. Lady arrived in a foul humor. "I found nothing useful. Nothing. How is he?"

"Beat up, starved and suffering from extended exposure. Otherwise, he's fine. Physically."

"But absent mentally?" Lady stared at the kid. There was nothing in Sleepy's eyes.

Croaker grunted. "In a coma with his eyes open."

"Speaking of sleepers," I said, "our favorite fireman was wide awake today. And the way he looked at me, he's all home in here."

I swear Sleepy's cheek twitched. But maybe it was just a trick of the lamp.

"Not good," Lady said. "And I was looking forward to a quiet evening at home."

"What're we going to do with Sleepy?"

The Captain had an answer all set. "You're going to take him with you. And get to work teaching him your trade." For an instant a shadow crossed his face, as though all thoughts of the future brought despair.

"I can't—" Move a girl into my bunker?

"Yes you can." Because Sleepy was just one of the guys. Wasn't he? "And keep me posted on his progress."

Lady comes home and he starts to give me the rush. How do you figure that? "Get your ass up," I told Sleepy. "We're going over to my house. We're gonna figure out what you did with my horse."

Sleepy did not respond.

Thai Dei and I ended up lugging him across on a litter, along with the treasures we had exhumed. I would like Sleepy a whole lot less before we got to the other side.

As we passed the prison kennel the shapeshifter began to rumble and growl. She roared a leopardlike challenge as we drew abreast. "Ah, go fuck yourself," I said. Sleepy was getting heavy already.

The big cat howled and tried to push her claws between the cruel spears confining her. "I think maybe she could use a few drinks," I told Thai Dei.

"Perhaps she is coming into her season."

92

THE STARS WERE OUT. THE CAMPFIRE WAS LOW. THAI DEI AND I AND SOME of my pals were mellow on One-Eye's beer and filled to the nostrils with roast pig. I flipped a bone into the fire. It began to crackle. "This is living," Bucket rumbled, punctuating with a belch.

"If you like to camp out," I said. "The weather's right. Me, you give me my druthers, I'd be living like we did in Taglios. Without all the work."

"What work? I never seen you lift a finger."

"I had to keep Sarie smiling."

"Rub it in, shithead."

Rudy asked, "That guy snore like that all the time?"

He meant Thai Dei, who was splashed against the outside wall of our bunker, snorting and roaring, out cold. He had put away a lot, for him. The other Nyueng Bao were shunning him.

"Only when he's had a good time."

"First time, huh?"

"That I know about. But I wasn't there the night he got married."

Somebody said, "You got the Old Man's ear. Whyn't you whisper some sweet nothings about us heading on up the mountain?"

"Why would I want to do that?"

" 'Cause when we get to Khatovar all the traveling and fighting and shit will be over." Pause. "Won't it?"

I did not know. "I don't have a clue. You go twenty feet on up the hill and you've gotten to the limit of what I know."

"I thought everything was in them old books."

Everything was. But I did not have the right old books. I glanced at Thai Dei. It was starting to look like he had the right idea. "I've had all the fun I can stand, guys." I unfolded sore knees, got up, headed for bed. As I stepped over Thai Dei I said, "Don't wake me up for anything less than a shadow breakout. And make sure you leave some pig for Uncle."

It was a good thing the bunker roof was low enough to make me get down on my hands and knees inside. I did not have as far to fall.

I tripped over Sleepy first, then over One-Eye's spear, which I had no idea why we had brought along but we had and which I had left lying in the middle of the rock floor.

I fell onto my pallet without crippling myself.

I know I went dreamwalking but do not remember where I went. I have vague recollections of Sarie and a trivial brush with a Soulcatcher as eager to avoid me as I was to avoid her. I woke up with a headache, a big thirst, a desperate need to hit the latrine and a very short temper.

"Oh, cut the bullshit, you old fraud," I told Uncle Doj after I slithered out of the shack. He was giving an indifferent Thai Dei Nyueng Bao hell, using all the buzzwords that get trotted out when somebody cuts loose and makes an ass of himself. "Damn, it's bright out here. Thai Dei, get your ass up. Drink some water. Shit." I put away some water myself. I was a little green. If it did not rain soon I would have to have some more carried up.

"Standardbearer."

"Uh?" I found myself surrounded by Isi and Ochiba. "You guys pop out of the ground or something?"

"We've been waiting," Isi said.

"Your people are stubborn about protecting your rest," Ochiba added.

Their manner was disturbing, somehow. "Good for them. What's up?" Obviously, they had not trekked over for the exercise.

Isi had more of the Jewel Cities dialect than Ochiba but even he did not speak it well. Still, he got the message through. "The Captain and Lieutenant want you should know that prisoner Smoke is perished."

"Perished? Perished like in dead?"

"As a stone," Ochiba managed.

I recalled some pretty frisky stones, met long before these stiffnecks joined the gang. I did not mention them. Nobody cares about the Plain of Fear nowadays.

"Murdered," Isi added, because he thought I had missed the point.

My mouth hung open. Finally, I said, "Come on over here where we can talk." I grabbed a crow killer and led them across the slope far enough that no one could eavesdrop. "Let's have some details." The weapon proved needless. The black birds were not out.

"His throat was cut," Isi said.

How could that happen? "How could that happen? Somebody would have to climb over Singh and Longshadow and Howler . . . he wasn't out of the kennel somewhere, was he?" I would have been even more shocked if he had been killed in Croaker's dugout.

"He was imprisoned."

"I presume we don't have whoever did it." My first suspect in any sneak killing would be Narayan Singh or some tag-end member of his brotherhood. But the Deceivers did not spill blood. Narayan certainly would not, even in self-defense.

"No."

"Do we know *who* did it?"

"No."

"I'm coming over." I headed back into camp, "Shiner! Rudy! Spiff! Kloo! Bucket!" I bellowed and my officers and sergeants reacted like they thought we were about to suffer an unexpected visit from Mogaba and the entire Taglian army. I was loud. My hangover etched my entire universe in uncompromising blacks and whites.

"Sorry," I said, not meaning it. "It's not as bad as I sound. A minor emergency across the way. I'm going over. Raise the state of alert a notch. Tell them to drop the tonk games till they get their gear in shape." I drank another pint of water, then donated an equal quantity to the earth spirits. "Ochiba. Isi. Let's go."

Thai Dei shook the embrace of gravity, grabbed a bamboo pole he used as a staff. He stumbled after me, stubbornly keeping pace.

Thai Dei defined who and what he was against a bevy of inflexible standards that ignored his own desires, his likes and dislikes, and his pain.

Uncle Doj cancelled the Mother Gota show, straightened his apparel, touched the hilt of Ash Wand to make sure the sword had not deserted him, then trudged along after us. That morning he looked very tired and very old.

"There was no need for you to come over," Croaker grumbled. He looked old and tired himself this morning. "There's nothing you can do."

"I knew Smoke better than anybody. I thought maybe—"

"Wasting time. Unless you were so close you can raise his ghost."

I wondered. "It doesn't make sense."

"Sure it does. Somebody doesn't want us to spy on them."

I started to protest that Smoke was a big secret, thought better of that. The Old Man did not want a debate. Instead, I asked, "What did the others have to say?"

Questions would have been asked, perhaps with great vigor.

"Nobody saw nothing. Nobody knows nothing. But I think Howler has an idea. And I think he's scared somebody might find out and come after him."

"Then the smart thing to do would be for him to tell us what he knows." Torture would not get it out of the little shit. He was older than Lady and had been screaming in pain before she met him.

"So Lady told him. He's considering the angles."

"This might be a chance to get him on our side."

"Like I said, Murgen. You didn't need to come over. We're almost as smart as you. Just takes us a little longer to work these things out."

"No doubt. Did you hear Bowalk carrying on last night?"

"The changer? No. What're you talking about?"

"She went bugfuck when Thai Dei and I went past the cage last night," I told him.

"She does that sometimes. Lady thinks it might be her animal side getting stronger. She might be trying to attract a boyfriend."

Uncle Doj, I noted, had gone to the cage soon after our arrival, independently, after a few words with JoJo. He did not understand anything Croaker and I were saying.

"Thai Dei said that's what it sounded like."

"Guy might not be as dumb as he looks." The Old Man focused on Uncle Doj while he talked. I was not sure who he meant. He asked, "How is our foundling?"

"Sleepy? Sleeping."

"Over here we burn comedians for firewood."

"What? I made a statement. The kid sleeps. He eats if you put stuff in his hands and show him what to do. He stares a lot. But mostly he just sleeps."

"All right. Go back. Get to work. Start thinking uphill a little more. I don't know if it's nerves or premonition or if I'm just getting antsy but I find myself more and more in a mood to travel on whether or not someone pushes us into it."

"The Radisha will be pleased."

"I doubt that. All that paranoia about the Company came from somewhere. She didn't buy it as bad as Smoke did but she bought it and she still believes it. I don't believe the source that sold her has ceased to exist. I don't think she really believes Soulcatcher when Catcher tells her she can weasel out of her infernal bargain without getting hurt." He was thinking of Kina. These days the popular wisdom was that Kina had put the fear of the Company into the minds of the Taglians and their rulers. We always suspected that they did not plan to keep their half of our agreement and help us reach Khatovar once the Shadowmasters had been overcome.

The Kina hypothesis was attractive but I had a nit to pick. If the Mother of Deceptions was determined to bring on the Year of the Skulls why would she keep the Company away? Did she see the Shadowmasters as tools better suited to achieving the necessary level of destruction?

I shrugged, told Thai Dei, "I guess we're just not wanted here."

"What the hell?" Croaker barked.

The shapechanger had begun trying to get to Uncle Doj. Uncle poked her with his swordtip till she settled down.

"Dream for me, Murgen," Croaker said as I started down the hill. "Right now I'm feeling blind and vulnerable. I need to know what's going on out there."

93

THERE WAS SOMETHING GOING AROUND. EVERYONE WE RAN INTO CROSSING to our camp wanted to know what was going on. It was not a matter of rampant rumor. Nobody had heard anything outrageous. But every man had developed an unfocused case of nerves. I felt it myself. Everything seemed portentous, though of what no one could say. As I entered the squalid village that had sprung up below the Shadowgate I noted that most of my men were seeing to their arms and equipment, just in case. I made a mental note to take advantage of their nerves and begin whipping them into more presentable shape.

It was time to take some raggedy-ass volunteers and begin molding them into brothers.

Counting soldiers and officials and camp followers at least a hundred thousand Taglians had been involved in Croaker's last crusade against the Shadowmaster. I have not dwelled on it but death did claim most of those folks, some in the fighting, more by way of disease and accident and hardship. Disease and hardship and Taglians probably accounted for even greater numbers of Shadowlanders. The conflict generated a human disaster far greater than the worst of the earthquakes shaking the region.

Disease remains a problem. Always.

The point is, there has not been a lot of fun and glory down here. The few thousand men who remain with us, many of them permanently crippled in some way, are real nervous sorts. They find signs and portents in everything.

Like most who stumble into the mercenary life they were men their society did not cherish. Maybe they had no families to rejoin. Maybe they had things turned a little sideways inside their heads. Maybe they were criminals or fugitives from enemies or wives or debt collectors. It takes a great deal to bring order and discipline to men of that sort. The Company's concept of itself as home and family had worked pretty well the past few generations but during that time the outfit never got bigger than a few hundred men. Never had it been so big that each man did not know every other.

I realized that I, for one, despite all pretense to the contrary, had not been doing everything I could to pull the family together. I had let a lack of outside pressure lull me into relaxing.

Paranoia is a must. The more so when times seem fat and favorable.

The guys were nervous now. It was time to work them a little harder.

"A reading from the First Book of Croaker," I told the force assembled. I was a bit bemused. There must have been six hundred of them. Even the worst of the halt and lame had come. "In those days the Company was in service to the Syndics of Beryl. . . ." It should be a good reading. Unless Otto and Hagop came over those times would be safely in the past, yet would still be close enough that the men would know that veterans of those events were still amongst them. They would know that there were forces ranged against us that their predecessors first encountered then. The very emblem on their badges had been chosen by the Company then. It was an easy connection to the past, comprehensible, with current relevance. It was a doorway through which they could be led to accept the belief that they were part of something that has survived everything for over four hundred years.

I got no cheers. I did get passionate enough to make even the most cynical member of my audience suspect that there might be something to what I said.

I made my speech and did my reading from the roof of my bunker. Sleepy sat beside the doorway throughout, showing all the ambition of a protective gargoyle. I wondered if some forced exercise might not help bring him back.

The uproar of Bucket arguing with Thai Dei wakened me. "What the hell is going on?" I yelled.

"Get your ass out here, Murgen!"

I slithered across the rocky floor and into a brilliant night.

I did not need to have anything pointed out. The fireworks were self-explanatory.

Lady's weapons plant was burning. Fireballs began to fly. It got worse fast. Fires started in the forest, in the ruins of Kiaulune and amongst the shanties of the camps across the way. A few fireballs even reached my neighborhood, though my guys were heads-up enough to dodge them.

I said, "No way I'm going over there."

"Somebody ain't afraid," Bucket said. A glimmer betrayed Uncle Doj loping away, Ash Wand in hand, colorful reflections setting its edge aglitter.

"Thai Dei!" I barked. "What the hell is he doing?"

"I do not know."

The excitement across the way grew so loud we could make out a general roar of people shouting.

"Shit and double shit," somebody said. "Can you believe that?"

I reiterated, "I'm not going over there."

The fireworks continued. Random balls arced across the night. Sometimes a pole would discharge rapidly, hurling a stream of fiery dots into the darkness. Lady's factory was mostly underground but the earth did not confine the devastation.

For a few minutes the night got lost in the glare.

Back behind me the standard dusk-to-dawn fog of darkness crowding the Shadowgate rippled away uphill, clinging to the deepest washes and gullies. The shadows did not like what was happening.

Neither did I. Again I observed, "I'm not going over there."

Some wiseass remarked, "Any of you other guys think Murgen maybe ain't going over there?"

Shithead.

I held out a few hours. I even got some sleep.

94

THE GROUND STILL BURNED.

The earth had collapsed into Lady's factory, evidently while so much fireball material was ablaze that the dirt itself could not resist ignition. The burning soil glowed various colors. Little flames pranced close to the ground, randomly, like those on the surface of burning sulfur. A smell of sulfur did hang in the air but it was a memory of fireballs past.

There was just enough light to get around by. Consequently the disaster's aftermath was more impressive visually.

Hundreds of soldiers and scores of hastily recruited Shadowlanders carried water in any container available. Water killed these fires not by smothering them but by cooling them down.

A column of steam towered thousands of feet above us.

"I think I'm about to get pissed off."

I glanced back. The Old Man had come up beside me. "This didn't do us much good," I agreed.

"It's maybe not as bad as it looks except for we lost so many of the people who made the poles. The battle-ready pieces were stored somewhere else. Lady didn't want to keep all her peas in one pod."

"Smart girl. Was it an accident?"

"No. The survivors say the lamps down there started going out, then people started screaming. The way they describe that makes me sure shadows got in. Right behind those came something or somebody who couldn't be seen very well. She strolled through the confusion setting off the reactions that caused the blowup."

"Soulcatcher?"

"That's my bet. She's really starting to get up my nose."

I grunted. Starting? Just now? Then he was more patient than I believed possible.

Somebody yelled my name. I made out a crowd gathering downhill. "My public calls," I grumbled. "I wonder what gruesome surprise they have for me this time." "Gruesome" was a weak word to describe what lay scattered around the collapsed area. Mangled, partial, dismembered and thoroughly cooked corpses abounded. Most were not soldiers. Lady's workers had gotten a running start but that had not been good enough for most. "Where's Lady?" I asked as Croaker followed me.

"Trying to get a fix on Catcher. Hoping we can slap back while she's still tired and feeling smug."

"Waste of time."

"Probably. You do any dreaming last night?"

"No. I tossed and turned and tried to talk myself out of coming over here."

"I would've sent for you eventually."

I saw why in a moment.

He had spotted the body first.

Uncle Doj lay sprawled on his back amidst the crowd. One shoulder had been burned by a fireball. A second fireball had burned part of his hair away. Much of what remained had been bleached white. His face was contorted. His right eye was wrinkled shut and buried beneath a crust of dried blood. His left eye was open. It stared at the sky. Ash Wand lay across his chest. He still gripped it with both hands. Its perpetually sharp blade was discolored as though it had been used to stir a fire, as though the temper had been burned out. Uncle Doj's clothing looked as though somebody had sprinkled him with small coals after he went down.

A small white feather was stuck in the blood on his cheek.

He shuddered. A sound like a giant fart came out of him. Thai Dei, who had been standing beside me, staring dumbstruck, dove forward.

Croaker snapped, "You men get back. Give us room. Murgen, bring my medical kit and I'll do what I can."

I took off. To my amazement Thai Dei bounced up and followed me. He did bark orders at other Nyueng Bao as we went, though. Uncle would be watched over by his own kind.

I dove into Croaker's shelter, found his bag and popped back up into the gathering light. I asked Thai Dei, "Could you tell anything from looking at Uncle?"

"He went into the mangrove alone." Which was Nyueng Bao idiom. It derived from the story of an incautious hunter who chased a wild pig into a mangrove stand and ran into a tiger when he got there.

I dropped Croaker's bag beside him. He grunted acknowledgment, then growled at the Nyueng Bao pressing in around us. Not ten minutes had passed but it seemed every Nyueng Bao following the Old Crew had come to see what was happening. Thai Dei whispered angrily at several. The gist seemed to be that they were shirking their duties by straying from those they were supposed to protect. So strong was the Nyueng Bao concept of debt that the whole bunch scattered immediately.

The Nyueng Bao said little. What they did say I understood perfectly. But I learned nothing.

Thai Dei knelt beside Uncle, on his left side. The Old Man knelt opposite him. Croaker gave Thai Dei a wet cloth. "Here. Sponge the crud off his face so I can see how much real damage there is." There was light enough now to see the dried blood and oozings crusted on Uncle's face.

While we were gone Croaker had accumulated several buckets of water and had opened Uncle Doj's clothing. He concentrated on the damaged shoulder, which still trickled blood. Doj's scalp wound had cauterized itself, evidently.

Uncle shuddered again. He could see because he looked up at Thai Dei, recognized him, tried to raise his arm, barely got hold of Thai Dei's right elbow. He whispered, "The Thousand Voices. Watch for the Thousand Voices."

"Rest, Uncle," Thai Dei replied.

"You must . . . I have little time left. The Thousand Voices is among us. I struck her down, thinking to reclaim the Key, but my blow was not lethal." That seemed to amaze him.

Croaker glared at me, silently willing me to listen carefully because it was obvious Uncle was saying something important. I nodded, not only listening and remembering but watching Doj's lips to make sure he *was* saying what I thought I was hearing.

Most of the Nyueng Bao had gone back to their charges. But JoJo had no one to protect anymore. His man had gotten away. He stayed. He stepped forward. "Uncle! Your tongue betrays you."

At least that is what he wanted to say. The instant his mouth opened Croaker made signs to Otto and Hagop, who hovered like angels looking for unbelievers to smite. They wrapped JoJo up, clamped hands over his mouth, carried him away, and managed the whole abduction so slickly that nobody paid any attention.

Uncle Doj thought he was dying. He was trying to stick Thai Dei with some obligation. "Find her before she recovers. Kill her while she is vulnerable. Burn her flesh. Scatter her ashes. Scatter them to the winds."

Thai Dei did not want the obligation. "I am not the one, Uncle. I have a mission already. Rest. Hold your tongue." He knew I was listening.

Uncle's eye shifted my way. He knew I was listening, too, now. But he was convinced he saw Death peering over my shoulder. He kept on talking.

What he said made sense. If you assumed that "the Thousand Voices" was Soulcatcher. That was a good nickname for her—particularly where she had not bothered to introduce herself.

Unfortunately, Uncle and Thai Dei did not make illuminating, "As you know" expository speeches to one another so I could only fill the chasms by guesswork. I did get the impression that this Thousand Voices had stolen something from the Nyueng Bao. Uncle called it the Key. Key to what did not come up. Thai Dei had no need to have it explained.

A quest to recover the item might explain why Uncle had been dogging the Company. It might explain his disappearances, both overnight or for as long as after Charandaprash. I suspected I might have been exposed to earlier hints but had been too dense to catch or record them.

Uncle Doj was getting weaker. For a man as strong physically and mentally as he was that hinted that he might be right about having very little time left. I yielded to temptation and gave pettiness a loose rein. I dropped to my haunches, as near Nyueng Bao style as I could manage. "Is there anything you want me to tell Sahra when she gets here?"

His one eye fixed on mine. He winced as Thai Dei peeled a big hunk of scab off his other eye but his gaze did not waver.

"I've known for a long time. I also know we have a son. And I can find no forgiveness in my heart."

Croaker said, "He's got more wounds than I thought. This arm is broken. His leg might be, too."

I said, "He ran into Catcher. Probably when she was making her get-away. He might have cut her up some."

"That would explain the sword. Also him still being in relatively good health. What's the chatter?" We were, of course, muttering in Jewel Cities dialect.

"He's sure he's dying. He's trying to pass some kind of obligation on to Thai Dei. Thai Dei doesn't want it. I think Catcher visited the swamp between the time when we broke the siege of Dejagore and when my in-laws moved in with me in Taglios. She snatched something really impor-tant to the Nyueng Bao—something apparently considered an object of power in their religion, like a holy relic—and Uncle's quest is to steal it back."

"He ain't ready to check out yet," Croaker told me. "It looks worse than it is. Half this mess isn't his blood. He'll be all right if we can beat the infection. But you don't have to clue him. Let him talk."

I shifted to Nyueng Bao. "Thai Dei, my Captain expresses a regret that your people have not dealt with us frankly. However, in honor of Sahra, and because I asked for it as family, he will do what he can to ease Uncle Doj's passage back to the *cao gnum*." *Cao gnum* could be either a place or a state of being that could be described as the universe's central depository of souls. I was not sure which because the Nyueng Bao did not discuss their religious beliefs. Whatever, *cao gnum* was where souls waited to return to the world if they had not accumulated enough good karma to get off the Wheel of Life. The Gunni call their similar place Swegah, which for them can be several places at once, including Heaven and Hell, with the soul on standby getting doses of each according to the tally sheet that has been kept of his good deeds and bad.

My comments strained Thai Dei's honor and loyalty. He was angry with me. "Too much disrespect, my brother."

I said, "So explain why I should treat him better than some pain-in-the-ass second cousin."

"Ignorance is your shield," Thai Dei advised me. "Grant me a boon."

"Ask away."

"Say nothing more."

I had begun to suspect that I had run my mouth too much already so I had no problem granting his wish. "You got it."

Uncle muttered to Thai Dei several times during the next quarter hour. That was pure delirium. Nothing he said illuminated the situation any better. Then he passed into unconsciousness because Croaker had given him something for his pain. I did not reassure Thai Dei about him waking up. Let him be astounded by the Old Man's medical magic. Let him feel even more obligation than he already did.

Once Uncle was out and unable to fight us we set his bones and cleansed his wounds. Not much flesh had to be abraded. The fireballs had done a great job of cauterization.

Uncle was going to sport some major scars from now on, though.

He might never have complete use of the right side of his body again, either. His right arm was broken in three places. One break was a compound fracture. His right shinbone was broken as well, six inches below the knee.

It never occurred to Thai Dei to ask why he was helping set the bones of a man who was about to die.

He was in another world. He was communing with his soul, with the thing that made him Thai Dei.

After a while, he said, "I argued against it when they sent Sahra away. My voice was too small to carry any weight." He did not look at me when he spoke. His body language told me it was not something he would discuss again, ever.

95

THE FOLLOWING MORNING I TALKED CAUTIOUSLY TO SEVERAL GUNNI ABOUT Nyueng Bao mythology. They were no help. I ran into a slough of contempt. If the Gunni had possessed any grasp of the concept they would have labeled the Nyueng Bao heretics. They did not. Taglian society was too completely pluralistic religiously. Nobody I spoke to had any idea what the Key might be. I suspected it might not be a religious relic even though I had overheard enough to understand that it had been one of the major treasures kept hidden at the temple where Sahra was confined.

I wondered what the connection might be. If there was any.

"I'm getting really tired of this hike," I told Thai Dei as we headed across the valley in response to a summons from our Supreme Commander. Not far away from us Shadowlander volunteers were helping take in a grain that was a cousin of barley, working for a share of the harvest. Croaker had a notion that the locals would resent us less if we helped them out. I had a feeling their own crops were not so bad and we ought to be stashing our surpluses inside Overlook. Sure as winter follows summer the day would come when we would need every kernel of reserve.

The Old Man insisted that I had been scarred too deeply by my past, that I would never outgrow Dejagore. Maybe he was right. We are all the sum total of our pasts, good and evil.

Thai Dei said nothing right away. He was more reticent than ever this morning. A mile down the path he said, "You knew Uncle would not die."

"Yep."

"You meant to manipulate him."

"Yep. So tell me. What's the Key?"

"Something that should have been destroyed long ago."

Did I say he was not talking anymore? I checked to make sure I was with my sidekick of many years. "Big mojo, eh?"

He understood the word in context. "Big trouble. All prophecies, all articles and tools of prophecy, bring nothing but trouble."

"This Key wouldn't tie in to Hong Tray's prophecy, would it?" I had not gotten that pinned down yet, despite being part of it and married to part of it. Sarie always claimed that she did not know, she was just a woman.

Thai Dei had found his center, his silence, again. He refused to say anything more.

"You been talking about me?" I asked when I pushed into Croaker's place and found sudden silence and stares my only greeting.

"Perhaps," Lady said. She eyed me speculatively, evidently wondering what was going on inside me these days.

Otto, Hagop and a couple other Old Crew guys were there. Isi and Sindawe were present. Numerous senior Taglians were noteworthy for their absence, as was Blade. We had not seen much of Blade lately, though he and Lady had worked together for years. There seemed to be a shift in the tides of trust.

"What's up?"

"What's your readiness state?" Croaker asked.

"Not bad, actually. A good blowup like the one last night will make guys want to put an edge on."

"No sign of Catcher?"

"No. You ask me, Uncle got her good and she's somewhere licking her wounds." I had not seen a single crow since before Sleepy returned. Talk about your basic good omens.

"Thai Dei talking any more?"

"No. You haven't said—"

"I'm going to go recon the plain."

"I thought—"

"Now's the time. Catcher is weak. I know how she heals. We'll have a week before she's strong enough to cause us more grief. We need to dive through that window of opportunity. If we put together a balanced force and pack train and push it hard, we should be able to travel seventy or eighty miles before we have to turn back. That ought to give us a good idea where we stand."

I did not like the idea but did not argue. Lady was the Lieutenant. It was her job to expose the flaws in the Captain's reasoning. She said nothing so I supposed their discussion was complete.

"I'm thinking fifty men for the first probe," Croaker said. "All the old guys who followed us here to get to Khatovar. Plus the best new men. All volunteers."

Not many recent recruits wanted to go to Khatovar. The old terror still held some power even though now they were part of the Company.

"What's happening in Taglios?" Croaker asked.

I shrugged. "I'm only having normal dreams these days. In fact, I hardly slept the last couple nights. Sleepy mumbles all night. I tried to get him talking but he didn't seem to hear me."

"We'll take him with us. A good long hike might bring him out of it."

I sighed. "When do you want to do this?"

"As soon as we can get it together. Catcher's already getting better."

I sighed again. "I was getting used to not traveling. I was really getting attached to the idea of staying in one place." And waiting for my wife. Or maybe even going back to meet her if I could get Sleepy to tell me what he had done with my horse.

Croaker harrumphed. Really. The son of a bitch was turning into my grandfather. He said, "You know what this means? Standardbearer?"

"I got a bad feeling it means some dumb fuck name of Murgen is going to have to go be out front again."

"With no Goblin or One-Eye to cover your back."

"Shit. Yeah." But my back *was* covered, for now until forever. "I see a problem, boss. The Nyueng Bao will insist on sticking with their guys from Dejagore."

"I'm counting on it. Every one of them who goes up the mountain is one less Taglian I have to worry about getting behind me and maybe wrapping one of those silk dinguses around my neck."

"What? We haven't had any trouble with those characters since last winter. There aren't any left."

"Ready to bet your life on that? I mean to take the living saint and the rest of our pals along with us."

"Why you want to do that?"

"So we don't get any surprises while our backs are turned. You want Howler getting loose, or Longshadow, when none of us are there to round them up again? You want the Prahbrindrah Drah on the prowl again? Or that panther bitch?"

"No. But if I was running things we'd just kill them and burn their bodies. Then we'd mix what was left up good and throw it all in about six different rivers."

Lady gave me the sort of look that would have made me shit my knickers a few years back. She did not much scare me anymore.

Croaker ignored my opinion. "Once we're up there and see what it's like I might set up staging camps so we can move the whole mob in steps."

"I don't think I'm ready for this, boss."

"Not ready? This is where we've been heading for the last ten years."

"There's a big fucking difference between being on the road and getting there, chief. You go out in the camp and ask, every guy out there will tell you he's perfectly happy to be on his way to Khatovar. But I bet you you won't get the same answer about getting there." I do not believe Croaker ever understood that *nobody* was as enthusiastic about our quest as he was.

"What do I got to do?" I asked.

"Pack up and get ready. Get your protégé whipped into shape because I expect him to trudge right along with the rest of us."

There was something there. . . . Something that left me on the outside. Something, maybe, that had something to do with the sudden silence that had fallen when I walked in.

"Then I'd better go pack up and get ready, hadn't I?"

The Old Man glowered at me as I walked out but did not raise a finger to stop me.

Something was going on.

"Another damned wasted trip," I told Thai Dei. "Only this was the worst one yet." I was getting mad. I was being used somehow.

96

"IT AIN'T MY FUCKING IDEA," I TOLD RUDY. FOR THE THIRD TIME. "YOU don't like it, go join Goblin and One-Eye. Wherever they are."

"I just never thought we'd really do it."

"Nobody but the Old Man did. Me included. But he says we're going, we're going. That's the way it works."

"Never said I wouldn't go," Rudy grumbled, more to himself than to me. He went off to scream at his sergeants. He would need to decide who to leave in charge while we were gone.

I was working on that myself. I had sought recommendations as soon as I got back from the Old Man's place. We would learn a lot about our southern recruits. The Old Man wanted to leave no Old Crew or Nar behind.

Ochiba, Isi and Sindawe were the only surviving Nar.

Bucket came by. In practical terms, he was my assistant. He did most of the work. I did not interfere unless he got headed in a direction I knew would get the Captain after me. He said, "You really squeezed Rudy's nuts."

"The man is driving me bugfuck. What do you want?" More than Rudy was making me cranky. Sleepy was getting worse. Thai Dei was being a pain in the ass because I had not bothered to visit Uncle Doj while we were across the valley.

"Hey, Murgen, it's all right to be scared. But you don't need to make everybody else miserable because you are."

I started to bark but realized that would not change the fact that he was right. I grabbed up a stone and threw it as far as I could, as if the fear would fly away with it. The rock clattered around amongst some boulders. Half a dozen crows flapped into the air, cursing in their native tongue. "Shit."

"Not a good sign," Bucket agreed. "We haven't seen any of those for a while. Want we should take them out?"

"They weren't close enough to hear anything. But have somebody check the area." I considered the sun. There were a few hours of daylight left. I had time to start the recon that needed doing before we took a bigger gang up the mountain.

Bucket sent men to the crow site. One held up what might have been a ground squirrel when it was alive. He held his nose with his free hand. Bucket told me, "Maybe they weren't spying at all."

"All things are possible," I said. "But some are more likely than others. Thai Dei. I know you got some pretty determined ideas about what you owe me but you really don't need to take risks just because I do."

The Nyueng Bao squatted not far away, sword sheathed across his back, waiting, a ragged little man who did not look dangerous at all. He looked me in the eye, grunted his go-ahead-and-explain grunt.

"I'm going through the Shadowgate. Wait! It's all right. I've got the key. The Lance. As long as I've got that I should be all right." If Croaker really had guessed correctly.

I would have felt more confident had I had a chance to study those earliest Annals.

Thai Dei climbed to his feet wearily, like his knees hurt him. He sighed, made a "let's go" gesture.

"Look," I said, "you don't have to."

He gestured again.

I would get nowhere arguing. Thai Dei was two steps beyond being stubborn. All Nyueng Bao are at least one step beyond. My wife . . .

I grabbed the shaft of the standard, started kicking rocks away from its base. It had stood undisturbed, right there, for half a year, becoming a fixture nobody much noticed anymore.

"Wait," Bucket said. "Use your noggin, Murgen. You can't just tighten your jaw and go charging up there. Take some bamboo. Take a canteen. Take a loaf of bread and some jerky. And let me set some guys up to cover your ass."

"All right. You're right." This business had me more rattled and scared than I realized.

I let Bucket take over. He did not have to go through the Shadowgate so he could remain calm and rational.

The Standardbearer is always the first guy into any Company scrape.

I was as far uphill as any of us had gone. The standard shivered in my hands. I leaned on it and stared at the ruins, trying to pick the path I wanted to follow. Bucket stood a few paces behind me, relaying instructions to Rudy. Rudy was posting observers. I did not want to be out of sight for an instant, ever. If the boogies got me the rest needed to know how, when, why and where.

"Anytime you're ready," I growled. I had a feeling I was not going to get less frightened for a while.

"You're set," Bucket yelled. "Tie a rope to your ass and go be a hero."

Be a hero. Not something I ever wanted. I gave him the high sign with both hands, grabbed the standard before it could topple. "See you in hell, mudsucker." I headed up the hill.

Thai Dei shouldered a bundle of bamboo and followed. He did a better job of hiding his fear but he let them tie a rope to his belt, too. In case he had to be hauled back through the gate.

The standard almost hummed in my hands.

I knew the precise instant when I crossed over. It felt like I had fallen into a cold pond that was nothing but surface. The chill ran over me, then was behind me, yet I was in a place where it was cold all the time. You might be able to fry eggs on the rocks but it was cold.

I took only a few steps. I paused. I waited. Minutes passed. The cold did not go away. I stared up the slope. And, gradually, the road became more clear, a thin black line like polished coal meandering up the hill like the trail of a snake just barely not drunk enough to wander off into the

barren wilds. I waited some more. Nothing jumped out at me. No shadows came to wriggle up my legs.

The standard seemed very much at home. It seemed to pull me uphill.

"You all got a good fix on me?" I yelled at Bucket.

"Got ahold of the rope, too, buddy." Bucket's reply and laugh
sounded like they had come to me through a long metal tunnel.

"I got a rope for you, Bucket." I took another three steps. Thai Dei
dragged after me. The man lacked enthusiasm.

Nothing happened. I took a few more steps. The road up the hill
gleamed like polished darkness, calling me onward. The fear began to
drain away. Fast.

Thai Dei said something but I did not catch it.

The rope tautening stopped me.

I had moved farther uphill without realizing it. I had reached the end
of my tether. Bucket gave me a tug. "Far enough for now, Murgen."

Yeah. I was way past where I had intended to go. But there was nothing to be afraid of— Bucket gave me another tug, with greater vigor.

I backed downhill reluctantly. Thai Dei said something again. I
looked back. Then I understood what he wanted.

He pointed northward.

The world looked kind of shimmery, as though we were seeing it
through a curtain of heat.

"Let's go, Murgen!" Bucket yelled. "We want you back and the gateway sealed up before it gets dark." He gave my tether another yank.

The man was getting nervous.

Still reluctant, I stepped across the boundary. This time was like stepping into summer out of winter.

Thai Dei sighed. He was pleased. The hill held no attraction for him.

My world had changed. Just the slightest. I could still see the pen-
stroke of polished darkness meandering down what once had been a road.
Dirt and fallen stone concealed most of it but adequate evidence remained
if one but had the eye.

I felt I was a different man after having crossed that line.

"You all right?" Rudy asked. "You look strange."

"It's strange over there. The same but different."

"Huh?"

"I can't explain. That's the way it feels. You'll understand once you
go up there."

Bucket joined us, wrapping rope into a coil. "You all right? You look
like you saw a ghost."

"It's just weird over there."

"Weird? How? You didn't do anything that strange. Except kind of forget yourself. And your sidekick didn't do that. He just stood there and shivered."

"That's part of it. It feels cold. Only not physically cold. More like the cold Blade would claim you'll find in a priest's heart."

I must have looked puzzled. Bucket said, "You're telling me you had to be there to understand."

I told Thai Dei, "The man acts as dumb as a stump but he'll fool you sometimes. You got it exactly, Bucket. Get some fresh dust up here. And make sure those ropes are all taut and the shadowtraps are all set. I want a full complement of—"

"Calm down," Rudy told me. "You set it all up before. Remember?" Soldiers were at work making sure of our protection already. My fuss was a waste of worry.

"Tell you straight up, that was scary. It's gonna take me a while to wind down. You got a messenger ready to go? I'll jot a report for the Old Man. Then I'm going to crawl into my bunker and get intimately acquainted with my last jug of One-Eye's medicine." I had one jug of the little wizard's most potent distillate squirreled away for use in a medical emergency.

This seemed like an emergency to me.

97

ONE-EYE'S ELIXIR DID NOT KILL THE FEAR, IT ONLY PUSHED IT AWAY briefly.

The fear was amazing. It was not the sort that paralyzes, nor was it strong enough to impair my thinking, but it was there all the time, unfocused, not growing numb the way an ongoing battlefield fear will eventually if nobody pops up to wale away at you with a piece of nicked-up iron. I did not like it. It abraded my temper.

I glared at Sleepy. "You ever going to be good for anything but turning food into shit?"

Sleepy just sat there in the gathering darkness, on what used to be Mother Gota's pallet, staring into infinity. Not only was he not coming back from whatever fairy kingdom had captured his mind, he could hardly move anymore. He did very little of anything. When he did it seemed to hurt him a great deal. If he kept on without exercising he was going to have to hope one of his Company brothers liked him enough to carry him.

I liked him better than anybody but Bucket, but I did not like him that much. See you when we get back, little guy.

We are not a march-or-die outfit. Not quite. We *try* to take care of our own. But there is an underlying assumption that our own will try to manage for themselves first. There are plenty of precedents for ending the misery of a brother who becomes too great a burden or risk to the rest of the Company.

Sleepy did not respond. He never did. I rolled onto my pallet. I tried not to think about having to go up the mountain again tomorrow. The heebie-jeebies got worse if I did.

I felt Soulcatcher somewhere nearby. The darkness was total, though. I could not find her. Maybe it was my good fortune that she was not interested in finding me. Though she did not seem interested in anything at the moment.

I was ghostwalking. I knew it. But in total darkness there were no landmarks. I could not find my way anywhere.

I drifted.

Only gradually did I become aware that I was not alone.

Somebody was watching me. Or something was.

The scrutiny of that other intensified as I became more aware of it. The darkness around me remained total but in some other way I began to fathom it.

Red eyes, yellow fangs, skin so much blacker than the darkness that it seemed to gleam negatively . . . Kina. Destroyer. Queen of Deception. Mother . . . Not exactly evil incarnate—the Shadowlanders insist that one of her avatars is creative—but for goddamn sure she was a power big enough to scare the shit out of me if she took an interest.

She had. Her crimson eyes bored a hole right through my ghostly soul. Her great ugly face shriveled in upon itself like a skinned apple drying out, then in upon itself some more, till there was nothing left but a ruby point. That point began to move. At the same time I had a growing feeling that someone was trying to warn me about something.

Kina? Trying to communicate? With me? But she had her own agents in the world.

Or did she?

Narayan Singh was a prisoner. The Daughter of Night was a prisoner, or maybe dead. There had been no sign of her lately. And Lady had declared her independence long ago. Now she was just a mystic parasite.

Maybe I was the only one out there in the world that the goddess could touch.

I followed the red dot. It led me to the plain of old bones. I spread my wings and braked, settled onto a branch in a leafless tree. Incompletely decomposed corpses lay strewn amongst the bones this time. I took wing again and glided close above them. Scarab beetles scattered, frightened by my shadow. Never before had I seen anything but a few crows out there.

A tower of darkness loomed on the horizon, a tall black thunderstorm filled with muttering blood-colored lightnings. I flapped heavy wings, headed that way. It seemed like the right thing to do.

For a moment the cloud revealed an evil vampire face and lots of arms. Those reached out to welcome me.

After a moment of disorientation I was gliding above a land where only a few sparks of light marked human habitation. I tilted my head. I had very good eyes—even in the dark. But I did not recognize where I was until I dropped low enough to make out Overlook's battlements masking the stars south of me.

I could not have been more than a hundred feet off the unseen ground when the earth began to boil and spawn a thousand minnows of light. The air slammed against me, flipped me over on my back. Then came the roar.

I was really there. I was no imaginary crow. I was the white beast itself.

I righted myself just in time to see a spray of fireballs headed my way. I dodged them.

I was back in the middle of last night.

I got down low where rocks and whatnot would protect me from the growing storm of fireballs. I did not forget what they could do to stone— if they were the new jumped-up variety. And I had several opportunities to see what they could do, up close, like I was some poor sucker on the wrong side of the Company. Every time I found a nice perch, *zow!* Crackling bacon.

The people I saw were all running with tremendous enthusiasm. Most were not fast enough or had gotten too late a start. Some never got up out of the underground at all. Smothering earth did the job on them.

The movement of colorfully glittering steel caught my eye.

Somebody was headed the wrong way.

Uncle Doj had run toward the disaster as soon as it started happening. The old boy had made good time if what I saw was him. Maybe he was more spry than he pretended. I flapped upward, glided toward the reflections off Ash Wand.

A crow is damned ungainly when he is first getting himself airborne.

It was Uncle. And he was not eager to enjoy my company. Ash Wand snapped like a lightning stroke. Doj had more reach than I recalled from our drills. He almost got me. The crow's reflexes saved me. It dodged before the thought even occurred to me.

I got behind him, let the fires show where he was, stayed out of reach. When he found a place from which to watch and knelt there, I found myself a modestly prominent stone and perched, cursing the human plague that had devoured all the trees and other high places hereabouts. I watched the watcher.

Uncle was there just long enough to catch his breath and demonstrate his own fantastic reflexes by dodging a few fireballs before the earth opened and a pillar of dark green light emerged. Fireballs slid off it. Its color was so deep I doubted anyone much farther away could see it. It moved straight toward me. Which meant it would pass right by Uncle Doj.

Once it left the pit the green shielding melted away. The creature within emerged. Lucky me, I was a bird. Lucky Uncle, he was old. Else both of us would have drowned in our own drool. This was one gorgeous woman and she was not wearing a stitch.

Soulcatcher.

Even in a birdly state I did appreciate how long it had been since I had seen my wife.

Catcher began to shimmer, not putting on another shield but taking another face. The effort distracted her from her surroundings. She did not spot Uncle Doj, who had become one with the night as deftly as a Deceiver. I recognized form and face just as Uncle, from behind Catcher, brought Ash Wand whining down in a stroke that should have sliced her to her breastbone.

She was fast. She tried to dodge and throw up some sort of sorcerous defense. The air groaned. She cried out and plunged forward, not killed but certainly cut badly. Uncle jumped in to finish her off. Ash Wand flashed. Blood flew. Catcher bounced around. So did Uncle. Chance interceded. A bamboo pole in the holocaust began popping off. Two fireballs clipped Uncle good. Catcher bounced him around some while he was distracted but did not have the strength to finish him. Anyway, people were responding to the noise, though it would be hours before Doj was found.

Catcher dragged herself away, used her enfeebled power to control her bleeding and change her shape. By the time she reached her hidden clothing she had become Sleepy. Which explained why Sleepy was so useless. As long as he passed for insane he was less likely to endure a scrutiny close enough to reveal the fact that he was not my prodigal assistant.

I was angry in a major way. Where was the real kid?

I flapped down and landed on Uncle's chest. He was drowning in his own blood. I pecked and pulled and forced him to turn his head to the side. Then I went after Soulcatcher.

She had disappeared.

I did not find a trace. But I knew where she was headed. Sleepy would be inside my bunker, never having been missed, when I got up in the morning thinking I had suffered through a sleepless night.

Now I knew what had happened to Smoke, too. That twitch of cheek I had glimpsed on Sleepy had been Catcher realizing she could be found out if anybody took Smoke cruising along her backtrail.

I knew her secret now, anyway, though. Maybe Kina was a more powerful enemy than Catcher suspected. The goddess might even have a sense of irony, using a crow to stalk the mistress of crows.

I settled onto the roof of my bunker. Beneath me Thai Dei snorted and snored as badly as he had the night we decimated One-Eye's trove. Someone else down there was making a racket, too. Since Sleepy was out I figured it had to be me, which meant Sahra was right when she accused me of roaring like a starving bear.

I never believed her before.

Hard to believe we had gone to sleep after watching all the excitement across the way. Catcher must have sent a spell ahead or left a doozie behind.

I had a feeling I would not be comfortable looking at myself from outside so overcame the temptation to flap down and peek through the doorway.

Sleepy came out of the darkness.

For somebody who had been mauled and cut up Soulcatcher could move like a gazelle. No healthy, normal human could run that well. Maybe a little sorcery?

I had wondered how I would get out of the white crow. Catcher's swift approach was the key. The crow took off. I stayed behind. I floated and watched. And as Catcher slowed and had to begin to acknowledge her wounds I floated up and away and in a direction that could only be described as tomorrow. Catcher did not sense my presence even though it was she who had made it easy for me to slip the moorings of my flesh.

Then it was the night I had left. And everybody, including me, was snoring away inside the bunker. And I was still free to wander the ghost-world.

98

SAHRA WAS SLEEPING RESTLESSLY. TOBO LAY BESIDE HER, ONE LITTLE PAW on her bare breast, occasionally sucking at her nipple. I watched for a while. My tension slipped away as I did.

What kind of lunatic was I? This was what I wanted and where I wanted to be but in a few hours I was going to hoist my weary body up and climb the mountain again. And I would keep climbing the mountain even though it might kill me.

Why?

I would. I knew I would. But I did not know what compelled me to do so.

I extended a ghostly hand to Tobo. For a moment it seemed I actually felt his warmth. He stirred as though having a bad dream. I withdrew, tried to stroke Sarie's hair instead.

She smiled.

"Mur. I thought I felt you. It's been so long." She chattered softly. I basked in it, wishing I could talk to her, too. She peeled Tobo off her breast and stood up, bare to the waist, doing a little dance that reminded me just how long it had been. She was recovering her figure already. She flashed me a mocking smile, looking right at me. Maybe she *was* a witch. "Tobo is strong enough to travel. The Water Dragon Festival is coming soon. I will leave then, in the confusion. My preparations are all made."

My wife, the smart, confident, competent woman. I wondered what I had done to deserve so much, other than to tickle her grandmother's fancy.

Sarie danced. I drooled. Tobo began to fuss. I think he sensed my presence easier than Sarie did. I frightened him.

"If you were here . . ." Sarie sighed, stared me in the invisible eye as she offered me an even more lascivious look. "But you aren't." She shrugged. "But it won't be that long." She cradled our son in her arms. He took a nipple immediately, donning a look of smug satisfaction.

I know what you mean, kid.

Tobo's eyes popped open. The one I could see stared right at me where I watched over Sarie's shoulder. He let go, took a deep breath, let out a whopper of a howl. The kid had lungs.

A priest invited himself in almost instantly. "What's going on?" he demanded. "Why is the child screaming? Who were you whispering to?"

"Get out," Sahra told him. "You have no right to come in here."

The priest had trouble dragging his gaze away from her breasts. He began to apologize with not entirely credible sincerity.

Sahra snapped, "The baby has gas tonight. He's having trouble with his digestion. I talk to him. That allows me a chance to have a sensible conversation occasionally."

That's the girl. Get the poor kid dosed with shark's-liver oil or some nasty-tasting powder. That will teach him to yell when his old man comes around.

I drifted in and did my best to plant a kiss on the small of Sarie's neck before I left. I went away as happy as a man could be in my circumstances. I knew my wife and child were well and still loved me. There are plenty of men in today's Company who do not have a clue about their families— although, in truth, not many care. Were they the sort who did care they would have left when the Taglian loyalists were allowed to go home.

The rest of the swamp was a silent, dark place. Which was to be expected at that time of night. I found my way to Taglios though there was no moon and the sky was overcast.

It would not be long before the rainy season began.

I spent hours roaming the Palace and the more important temples but learned very little. Without Smoke I was constrained by real time and it was too late for anybody but the priests of the Night Gods to be stirring and scheming. And those people were not plotting, they were preparing for some minor feast night.

Maybe, if I planned to do much useful ghostwalking, I would have to get to bed early in the evening, while the world was still awake and conspiring. I found no news anywhere unless you count the overwhelming evidence that persecution of friends of the Company had spread throughout most of the territories our efforts had brought under Taglian suzerainty. It did not seem a persecution as vicious as had been ours of the Stranglers. Our friends were surviving it. Mostly they were just losing their appointments. In a few cases where there were personality conflicts some people ended up inside cells. Murder did not appear to be a tool the Radisha cared to employ.

All my assumptions were based on spare, postmidnight evidence.

I could not find Mogaba. I could not find either of our prodigal wizards. No surprise. I did not invest much effort in the hunt. I did put some into trying to locate Croaker's kid.

Wherever she was she would be alone. There might be an opportunity in that.

While I searched I also kept an eye out for some evidence of what had become of the real Sleepy.

I had no luck with those quests, either. But I did stumble on evidence that my blindness might not be entirely accidental.

I was drifting over a slope I knew to be in the mountains not many miles from Catcher's former cave. I was sure Catcher would not have gone far when she moved, despite having Howler's carpet at her disposal. I wandered into an area of small, deep and dark canyons. I flitted up and down those, letting their walls guide me, figuring the kid, or anyone else, would be detectable by the heat or light of a fire. I doubted she could do without.

I found no fire. I did find my horse. I think. I whipped past the beast, catching only a glimpse, an impression that it was confined inescapably, another that it sensed my passage and tried to respond. But when I stopped and turned back I could find nothing. In fact, it seemed that in just a moment that entire corner of the world became a sensory desert.

I had run with Kina once already this trip. I might not be alone now, especially if I was anywhere near the Daughter of Night.

I knew the general area. I would tell Croaker. He could send soldiers out if he wanted.

Catcher would not be getting in our way.

My last action was to check on Uncle Doj where the Nyueng Bao bodyguards were keeping vigil. He was unconscious but alive. I gathered that they were keeping him drugged for his own good, giving him time to heal. Whatever his mission, he did not need to complete it immediately.

I went home to my comfortable flesh and uncomfortable bed.

The guys let me sleep in like it was a holiday. The sun was already up when I crawled out of my bunker, past the vacant-eyed Sleepy doppelgänger sprawled beside the doorway.

99

CROAKER ARRIVED SOON AFTER I FINISHED MY BREAKFAST MUSH. HE HAD not slept in. "You went in yesterday? How was it?"

"Just a few yards. Thai Dei, too. He insisted. We had ropes tied to our butts. Sit down here and check out the view across the way." I had my back to Sleepy. I did not want my lips read. I made gestures like I was talking about something else while I whispered my news.

Croaker chuckled. "Now isn't that interesting. We'll just play along for now. I won't even tell Lady. Though I got to tell you, everybody but you already suspected."

"Shit. That's why you were such a bunch of assholes. You didn't trust me not to give it away. What's the plan for today?"

"Try the road all the way to the top. I'll go with you. Save the talk till we get on the other side."

"Good idea." I let everything wait till later. "You eaten?"

He glanced at my battered tin bowl. "You live like kings over here, don't you?"

"Absolutely. Only the best for the cream of the legion."

"I'll pass. This time." He looked up the mountain and sighed. "One-Eye had the right idea. I'm too old for this shit."

"It's not that bad." It was not. When I call the slope a mountain I mean it metaphorically. The road could be made usable by wagons with very little work and the rim of the plateau could not have been more than a thousand feet higher than the Shadowgate. And probably not that far.

"Let me know when you're ready." The Old Man massaged his right knee. He noticed me noticing. "Little rheumatiz. But it only hurts when I walk on it."

Buy a horse, I thought but did not say. "How old are you really?"

"You're as young as you think you are," he replied, his expression branding that one a load of old manure. "Lady keeps me young."

I wondered if there might not be a touch of truth in that one. She did a great job of keeping herself slim, sleek and fresh.

"Grab the standard and let's go."

"You want to take a couple guys along? Just in case?"

"Your guy will follow us. Want him or not. Grab a couple others. Rudy and Bucket will do."

"You going to ride?" He had ridden over on his big stallion. "I always figured you'd go whole hog when you went up there. The full Widow-maker rig and whatnot."

"Next time. Let's go." He was nervous.

I hollered for Rudy and Bucket. They showed up quickly, like maybe they had been lurking nearby, expecting a summons. Their Nyueng Bao shadows drifted along behind them. The whole bunch were ready to travel.

I said, "Looks like it'll be me holding up the parade." I was pleased the guys had shown some initiative.

I crawled back into my bunker, noting as I went that Thai Dei too was ready to climb the mountain.

I needed only a moment to collect some jerky, roasted oats and a canteen. On my way out I told Sleepy, "Don't go away, pal. I'll be back in time for supper." Gods and devils of the earth willing.

I grabbed the standard. We crossed over the boundary a man at a time. The vibration seemed less dramatic this time. Thai Dei too seemed less touched. But the others turned pale and became very jumpy. The chill was no less strong. I shivered.

In a moment the road was clear before me, the polished jet thread wandering up the slope. "You see the way?" I lowered the head of the standard till the iron head touched that thread. I do not know why I did that.

A vibration went through me that was a dozen times stronger than that coming through the Shadowgate. I gasped. I shuddered. Maybe I sputtered and foamed at the mouth.

"What's wrong with you?" Croaker demanded.

I pushed the standard into his hand. "You just do what I did." I stepped away. Looking up the slope I realized I was seeing it in a different way. I saw the same old dirty, barren slope with its glistening black thread but also saw a ghost of what it must have been like in an age long gone, when the road was new and the slope, while nearly as barren, had not had such a godsforsaken look.

Human ghosts moved there, too, though they were even more insubstantial than the road and slope and unfallen fortifications around us.

Croaker reacted exactly the way I had. But he must have had a clue or two more. As soon as he regained control he passed the standard to Bucket and told him to repeat the process.

The standard passed from Bucket to Rudy and from Rudy to Thai Dei. Thai Dei thought about it for more than a minute before he went ahead. He did so only when the Old Man told him, "You don't follow through, you don't go up the hill." Thai Dei did not want to do that either but had no choice. He was trapped by his own character as well as, I suspected, the task Uncle Doj had laid upon him.

Once Thai Dei made his move the other Nyueng Bao followed. Croaker told them, "It doesn't mean you're committed to the Company, boys."

A moment later I observed, "Now that we've got that out of the way what say we climb the mountain?" Good Standardbearer me, I took up the Lance and started trudging.

It felt good to be headed home.

What?

I looked at the others. Nobody appeared to be having trouble keeping touch with reality. Maybe it was another aspect of the dreaming and falling into nightmares.

Thai Dei hung close to my back. He was not comfortable at all this morning. He had his sword out and ready.

The black ribbon widened as it climbed the slope. It also seemed to take on depth. Its surface, though flat, assumed an appearance of concavity. If you touched it, it felt hard and cold yet seemed almost soft underfoot.

The slope steepened a bit. I huffed and puffed. Then the going became easier, the road less timeworn. The horizon line stopped retreating as fast as I chased it.

"Stop!" Croaker yelled.

I stopped. I looked back. The Old Man was a hundred yards behind me. Even Thai Dei was having trouble keeping up.

I looked across the valley. Already I was high enough to look down on all Overlook but the broken tooth that used to be Longshadow's crystal-capped tower. Men were at work inside the fortress, scurrying little dots. They were Lady's guys, many having been with her since the Company's big disaster outside Dejagore. I guess the Captain finally had something in mind for the old stone shack.

Croaker was puffing badly when he caught up. "Man, I'm really out of shape."

"You're the one wants to take this walk. It'll suck that belly right off you." He was not fat. Yet. But he had not been missing any meals lately. "You see the road clearly?" Just to make sure I was not suffering some vision with my eyes open. I am no longer ever quite sure of my place in reality, never unsuspicious that there might not be an objective reality at all. Everything could be dreams inside of dreams, the illusions of souls rolling forever in a Swegah where now and then a few collided and joined in an almost common fantasy.

You notice, nobody ever sees things exactly the same?

"The black path? I don't remember reading anything about that in the Annals."

"We never read anything by anybody who ever actually saw any of this. We've never read anything by anybody who was closer than two generations to this place. By then the Company had a different set of concerns."

Croaker grunted.

To make sure we held this illusion in common I polled everybody. Even the Nyueng Bao agreed we were following a ribbon of blackness. They did not like that. They were frightened by it but accepted it. The entire world, outside Man's natural swamp realm, was a frightening place.

"Everybody got their breath? Let's trudge on." I really wanted to get to that plain. I tried to remember what it looked like at night, from up high and far away, but the view had been pretty obscure. I wondered why I never tried to go exploring. I wondered what Kina had to do with the plain. Could this be the plain where she fought the great battle of her legend? I wondered if we would find out why no Taglian would talk about the place, why, when it was mentioned, most walked off shaking their heads and muttering, "Glittering stone." I wondered how that phrase could have found its way into a language as an idiom for "madness." Especially inasmuch as we were now certain that the Taglian terror of the Company and the Year of the Skulls had been artificially induced.

There was not that much more to the slope but I was gasping for air, staring down at the dark guide a step in front of me and pushing for that just one more step when the footing suddenly stopped insisting that I keep climbing. I stumbled, got my balance, overcame an urge to run ahead, halted while the others caught up.

I examined the plain while I waited.

"Glittering stone" was apt. The jet path became a wide and perfectly preserved road here and curved gently off into a region of tall, square pillars, each of which glittered as though splattered with polished gold coins. To either side of the road the plain consisted of dark grey basaltic stone cut smooth, showing only the slightest evidence of aging. Nothing grew there. Nothing. Not even a lichen. Not a fly or an ant. The place was unnaturally clean. No dust, no dirt, no leaves.

The morning sun had set the pillars sparkling but clouds were moving in from the west. We would have an overcast sky soon. Maybe rain before the evening.

"Hold up, Murgen!" Croaker yelled. "Goddamnit, if you don't stop charging off I'm going to nail your feet to the ground."

I looked down. My feet were moving again. I stopped. I looked back. The others were a hundred yards behind again, right at the rim. Except for Thai Dei. My brother-in-law was an island in between, drawn by his obligation to me but held back by his reluctance to follow the black road.

"Get your ass back here!" Croaker bellowed. "The fuck you think this is? Some kind of race to the edge of the world?"

I went back. It was like walking against the wind. The vibration of the standard seemed to change, to become almost plaintive. When I got there I told him, "Captain, take this thing for a while. It's going to carry me off."

He felt it right away. But he was stronger than me, I guess. He planted the damned thing and stared ahead. "You bring something to write on?"

"Yes, I did."

"Something to write with, too?" He was reminding me of a time when I had done everything right but remember to bring a pen.

"I'm all set, boss. Long as this wind don't blow me away."

"You still afraid?"

"Huh?"

"You said that before you were afraid all the time after you came back."

I frowned. I felt no fear at all. Now. "Out there, I guess. I'm fine here." I looked back at the world. From where we stood you could see only the mountains beyond the broad valley containing Overlook and the ruins of Kiaulune. Not only did there seem to be a heat shimmer between us and them, there was a haze, too. The world seemed very remote.

I mentioned that to Croaker.

"I don't see it," he said. "There's always a haze over a forest in the summer. Unless it's just rained."

I shrugged. These days I was not as uncomfortable with the fact that I was different. I had suffered various incarnations of weirdness for too long. "You going up the road?" It stretched so invitingly before us.

"Not today. What's that?"

"What?" I saw nothing but the standing stones. They seemed to be arranged in no special order, spaced well apart from one another.

"Past the stones." He pointed. "Let your gaze follow the road. When you can't make it out anymore just lift your eye to the top of the stones. You'll see it. Your eyes are younger than mine."

I saw something. Just a looming something.

"It looks like a fortress," Thai Dei said. The Old Man and I had not been using a secret language. His companions both grunted assent. Rudy and Bucket just looked troubled.

"I'll take your word for it," I said. I recalled having seen what might have been a light out there during one of my ghostwalks. "Reckon that's Khatovar?"

"I couldn't say from here. But if it's a fortress and that's all it is then it stands a good chance of being a big-ass disappointment."

Yeah. If you were counting skipping through the gates of paradise when you got to the end of the road. I did not know anybody who was. Unless it was him.

"How far would you guess that is, Thai Dei?" Croaker asked.

The Nyueng Boa shrugged. "Many miles. Perhaps a walk of days."

Ugh. That gave me a chance to consider what it might mean to spend the night on the plain, inside the Shadowgate, in the land whence the Shadowmasters' deadly pets had come.

The Old Man said, "This is enough for today. We'll go back and set up the major probe."

Thinking about shadows, I found, encouraged me to resist the call of the black road.

I paused on the brink, took one last look at the glittering pillars before I left the mountain.

It is immortality of a sort.

"What?"

"You say something?" Croaker asked. He was fifty feet ahead of me already.

"No. Just thinking out loud. I think."

100

THE OLD MAN DID NOT SLEEP IN. HE AND LADY, OTTO AND HAGOP, SWAN, Mather and Blade, the Nar, Clete, Longo and Loftus and all the rest of the Old Crew and their bodyguards, with some of Lady's longtime followers, were on the road to the Shadowgate when I dragged myself out. It was still dark enough that Croaker's outriders carried torches. "That son of a bitch really wants to get a head start."

Thai Dei was awake already. He was boiling water to make breakfast mush. He looked downhill and grunted.

Big Bucket stumbled up, yawning, rubbing sleep out of his eyes with the back of one hand. "That the Old Man already?"

"Mudsucker's eager, isn't he? Everything set?"

"Completely. I'll go drag Sparkle and Wheezer out of the sack."

"Wheezer? What the hell is he doing up here?"

"Came up during the night. Took off early from over there because he didn't figure he could keep up with the Old Man this morning. Didn't want to get left behind."

"The old boy's got balls," I said. Once again I had underestimated the man. With no direct evidence I had assumed he had passed on during the summer. I should have known better. He had been dying when he latched on seven years ago. Every day seemed like it had to be the one when he coughed up his last lung, but something kept him going. "Where's Red Rudy?"

"Sent him to check the perimeter."

"One more time, eh?" That damned perimeter had been checked and rechecked five hundred times since I had been in charge. It is a military kind of thinking, never trusting anything but the situation right this minute. Time is the implacable eater of all preparations.

"All hands standing by?" I asked.

"Said everything was set." He looked into Thai Dei's pot. "Looks tasty, my man."

Thai Dei had no sense of humor and little ability to recognize sarcasm. He nodded. "A little salt, a little sugar. A handful of *tuloc* grubs or shredded monkey jerky would improve the flavor."

"Twolock grubs?"

I would not have asked myself.

"You find them in rotten logs. In the swamp we fell trees so they will have a place to grow."

I asked, "Are you nervous?"

Thai Dei gave me his hard look, like how on earth could I think he would be bothered by anything?

"You're chattering like a flock of crows."

Thai Dei grunted, recognizing the truth. He went back to being himself.

"Beetle grubs," I grumbled. "Only the Nyueng Bao would think of farming them."

"What's wrong with grubs?" Bucket asked. "You fry them in butter, toss in a couple sliced mushrooms . . . It's time to play the game."

Croaker and Lady were climbing the slope now. I could see them clearly enough to tell that they were dressed in their Widowmaker and Lifetaker costumes with all the showoff spells alive and crawling. They rode the stallions from the stables of the Tower at Charm. Those giants' hooves struck sparks every time they hit the ground. Their eyes shone red. Their nostrils puffed breath that seemed somehow more than just steam in the cool of the morning. Trumpets, cymbals and drums seemed appropriate but Lady and the Old Man never went in for that kind of thing. Those two, and every man behind them except the prisoners, carried a small arsenal of bamboo.

Howler was in a small wheeled wooden cage drawn by a brace of black goats. He and Lady must have reached an accommodation because no obvious control measures had been added to the bars. Although he was surrounded by a half-dozen soldiers who could bathe him in fireballs before he could get off any really ugly spell.

Longshadow endured similar confinement but he and Lady had not reached any agreement. His mouth had been sewn shut. His fingers had been sewn together. If he was going to cast any spells he would have to do so by wiggling his ears. But the nervous soldiers nearby would roast him before he could do much more than twitch.

The guys were rattled because *he* was in such a state. He kept tearing at the bars of his cage while trying to scream incoherently through his sealed lips.

Longshadow did *not* want to go up the mountain.

The Prahbrindrah Drah was being treated well. Willow Swan and

Cordy Mather flanked him, doing their duties as Royal Guards, while Otto, Hagop, the engineer brothers and the Nyueng Bao bodyguards who tagged along after everybody formed a larger diamond around those three. Longinus and Loftus conversed with the Prince as though this venture was nothing remarkable.

I admired the Prahbrindrah Drah. He was a good man and a sound one. It was a pity we could not let him go home. After his years in the field he had the self-confidence and willpower to stand up to his sister and take up the reins of the state. He had learned enough and had developed the strength of character to resist the extortion efforts of the senior priests.

The panther that used to be a woman was in a cage that was more like a coffin. She could not stand up. At no time would she be able to use the full leverage of her powerful muscles. She could do little but lie there and be angry.

The Captain did not believe in taking chances. He had seen what the forvalaka could do ages ago.

All our enemies would share our adventure. And our fate—unless they elected to warn us about something.

Rudy slipped down the slope to meet the Captain, alerted by Bucket's remark about it being game time. I did not look back. I knew he meant that Sleepy had come out of the bunker and was sprawled against the wall by the door again. Just the way we wanted.

Rudy would ask the Old Man to have his crowd make a racket coming into my shanty monarchy.

One of Bucket's favorite Taglian lieutenants, stuck with the name Lhopal Pete to distinguish him from a sergeant everybody called Khusavir Pete (both "Petes" deriving from the center syllable of an eleven-syllable Gunni godname), came to tell his leader he would need to bring up a lot more water if the men were going to take care of all the cleanup I wanted them to do while I explored beyond the Shadowgate. Bucket told him, "Wait till that bunch of aristocratic assholes gets on up here. We don't want anybody to get trampled."

"Yes, sir." Lhopal Pete collected his work party and took them around behind my bunker where they would be out of the way till Croaker arrived and made enough noise to cover the bunch sneaking up on Sleepy.

I started spooning mush into my mouth. "You're right, Thai Dei. Even grubs and bugs couldn't hurt this stuff. Give me a bowl for Sleepy."

I took it over myself. "Here you go, kid."

Sleepy just stared. I moved the bowl up under his nose. "You better get well enough to feed yourself, kid. I'm in no mood to keep doing it for you." I glanced back to see how close Croaker was. There was enough light now that torches were becoming superfluous.

In minutes he was close enough. The racket was loud enough. I dropped the wooden spoon into Sleepy's lap, seized his wrists, clamped down. The guys came out from behind the bunker. One grabbed Sleepy's hair and yanked his head back. Another shoved a wad of dirty rag into the kid's mouth.

Soulcatcher fought. But the surprise was complete. She never had a chance. "All wrapped up," I told the Old Man when he stopped his mount beside us.

"You use every piece of rope you had?"

Catcher did look like a victim of excessive enthusiasm. "Don't want to take any chances, boss. I wish you'd brought another one of those cages."

"Now that would've been a dead giveaway, wouldn't it? Even if I'd known what you planned."

Lady stopped right behind Croaker. She had her Lifetaker helmet on. There was no way to tell what she was thinking. She never said a word, just stared at the sister who had caused her so much trouble for so long.

Catcher did not abandon the Sleepy form. She was not a natural shapeshifter so maybe changing was difficult to do. I did not count on that, though. She had a history of altering her appearance. I asked, "She have to stay this way as long as we've got her tied up?"

Lady did not respond. She just stared.

"I mean, I wouldn't want her turning to jelly and oozing away when I wasn't looking. I guess I could stuff her into a big jar. If I had a jar. If it had a lid that could be sealed."

Croaker said, "I don't think she can do anything as long as she's gagged and her hands are tied."

"Want we should cut off her fingers?"

"I think she'll behave. For now. Won't you?"

Catcher did not respond.

She was over her surprise. Already I could sense calculation and the beginnings of what might be amusement.

Bucket asked, "Any of you geniuses decide what to do with her now that you've caught her?"

I said something real intelligent like, "Huh?"

"Like Murgen said, you should of brung a cage. Or was you just going to let her walk?"

The Old Man's mood blackened. "Make a litter. She always wanted to be treated like a queen. She can even have her own royal guards. Swan! Mather! You guys can carry the lady."

"Aw, go fuck yourself," Swan said.

Cordy said, "Take it easy, Willow."

"What the fuck's he gonna do, Cordy? Drag me off to Khatovar?"

Lady tugged her reins. Her mount turned till she was facing Swan and Mather. After a moment Swan said, "All right. All right." Ten minutes later he was carrying the downhill end of a litter. He never stopped grumbling but he was far enough behind me that I did not have to listen. Hagop let Swan and Mather start rotating with others after a few miles.

I went through the Shadowgate first. Croaker followed. After a few dozen yards, he said, "Stop here. I want to experiment. Lower the Lancehead to the black path." He dismounted as I did that. He took his silver Company badge off his cloak, held it to the Lance for a moment, then knelt and pressed it against the ribbon of black. His knees creaked. He grunted and strained.

I asked, "What's that all about?"

"I'm not sure. Lady thought it couldn't hurt."

So the killer shadows could pick us out of the crowd? Or maybe the other way around. Lady's instincts were sound. She had been around since before the original Company came *down* this mountain.

Croaker told me, "Stay here till everybody goes by. Have all our guys get their badges blessed. And don't forget yourself."

Lady dismounted, followed the Old Man's example. Then she remounted and continued up the slope, following Croaker, single file.

Man by man and animal by animal the column filed past. I got puzzled looks from the Company guys and black looks from everybody else. I checked to see where the Old Man was. In Nyueng Bao I told Thai Dei, "If you want you could touch the Lancehead, then that spot on the ground. The others, too."

He thought about that. "I wish Uncle was here to make a ruling."

"What's it gonna hurt? And it might be some kind of protection. You don't have to count it as some big-ass commitment to Company fortunes."

He thought some more, probably wondering if we were not sucking them in little by little, then he shouted at the other Nyueng Bao. He gathered them round, told them they had the option and that taking the blessing might offer a measure of protection once the sun went down.

Many of the Nyueng Bao did not like the idea.

Sparkle came past leading a string of overburdened but infinitely patient bullocks. "You going to bless the animals, too?" He was being sarcastic but I wondered if it might not be worthwhile. Shadows seldom bothered animals in the world outside—if human prey was available. But we were not in that world anymore.

The Nyueng Bao argued heatedly but so softly I could not make out a word. Thai Dei eventually had enough. "You do as each of you wishes." He stalked over, slapped his palm against the head of the Lance, dropped and slapped the black trail, got up and took his place beside me.

I expected the Old Man to start bellowing any second but he never bothered to look back.

Howler trundled past. When he reached for the Lance I lifted it. "Keep moving. Friends of the Company only." I touched each of his black goats on the noggin with the Lancehead. Longshadow came along. The Shadowmaster seemed to be paralyzed. His eyes stared into infinity. I had seen that stare before, but only from guys who had suffered too much terror on the battlefield.

Fifty people may not sound like a big gang but when you add in all the animals and whatnot necessary to make a long journey it turns into a pretty good parade. Lady and the Old Man were almost to the top when Rudy and Bucket came up as the rearguard. Rudy asked, "You want we should kiss that thing, too?"

"If you think it'll help."

"I'll give it a handjob if that's what it takes to get me through the next three or four nights."

"I'll let you know. I got to get back up front." By now all the Nyueng Bao had made their decisions one way or another and had dealt with the standard according to their choices.

I hurried through the routine myself, with Rudy's help.

As he neared the top Croaker halted but not to give me a chance to catch up. Good old Murgen would get out front, where he could be the first one to get his head kicked in, only because the Captain had to wait for the troops to adjust to the road so the carts and wagons could make the climb. " 'Scuse me. 'Scuse me there," I said as I clambered past the engineer brothers. "Do a good job so you don't have to do it again on the way back."

A lot of people stood around watching. Construction was not what they did. They felt no urge to learn the trade at this late date. Swan told me, "Lugging this stretcher wasn't such a bad idea after all." Mather, though, was working. Cordy Mather was a good man. I wondered how much the Radisha missed him. I wondered if she spent much time trying to figure out why he had not come back.

I do not believe it was for the sake of the Prahbrindrah Drah.

None of my no never mind, though.

Catcher was awake and alert. She looked me in the eye. I think she would have smiled had she had the use of her mouth. I told her, "I want Sleepy back." She did not respond. She just lay there and twinkled.

When I caught up with the Old Man and finished puffing I asked, "Did you send anyone to look around where I thought I saw my horse?"

"Sent a whole company. Left the same time we did." He looked down the road. "What's taking them so long?"

"All generals and no soldiers." Lady, I noted, had turned her mount completely and was surveying the world from our new vantage point. Men were at work in Overlook already. Smoke rose from cookfires scattered everywhere. Most of the more westerly belonged to shadowlanders gradually creeping back into the farmland. The sky was overcast. I wondered if we would have rain.

"What's that?" Croaker asked.

"What's what?"

"Down there. On the road to your camp."

"Your eyes are better . . . I see it. Little bit of dust." Somebody, maybe several somebodies, was headed for my camp. They were too far off to make anything of them. They did seem to be in a hurry.

The carts began to roll. Clete and Longo and Loftus began congratulating themselves loudly. Goats bleated. Bullocks offered bovine complaints. Men cursed. The column began to creak forward.

"Lead on, Standardbearer," Croaker said. "And don't forget that those goats can't run as fast as you can." He put his helmet on. The spells on his armor came alive.

I started walking, standard raised. I knew it would get damned heavy before this was all over.

My pack was heavy already. I wiggled my shoulders, trying to get the straps settled more comfortably.

I stepped up onto the plain and set foot on the road. Ahead the standing stones sparkled even with the sun behind the clouds.

The ground shook just as Croaker and Lady came up behind me. I dropped to one knee but it was not a bad quake. In fact, it was barely perceptible. Embarrassed, I got up and started walking again. "First one of those in a while," I told Thai Dei. "Took me by surprise."

Lady and the Old Man did not seem troubled so I guessed I did not need to be.

101

IT BECAME A QUIET JOURNEY ONCE EVERYBODY GOT UP ONTO THE PLAIN. WE were all too nervous to talk. After a mile or so, though, Lady said, "Warn everyone not to leave the road. As long as we stay on it nothing can touch us."

Croaker raised a hand to signal a halt. I dropped the butt of the Lance to the road surface. Damn, that thing got heavy fast. The Old Man sent

Lady's news back down the column. He did not question her. He did not distract her at all. Which might mean she was concentrating totally.

Soon after we resumed moving we reached a place where the road widened out into a big circle. A campground, I reasoned. Lady, in one of her rare remarks, confirmed my guess. Whoever created the plain understood its dangers.

It was almost noon when we came at last to a standing stone near enough the road to be examined. It was the same kind of rock as the plain's surface off the road. The sparkle came from metal characters set into the stone. They *were* characters, that much was clear, but they were none I or anyone else could read.

It is immortality of a sort.

I jumped.

Lady said, "There is great power in this place."

"No shit."

The earth shivered again, no more strongly than the last time but sufficient to make everyone nervous. These tremors might be harbingers of something worse. Though, I noted, not one of the pillars had been toppled by the vicious quakes of recent years.

Croaker paid the stone little heed. He kept staring ahead. It was now clear that there was, indeed, some massive structure beyond the forest of stones. It had begun to look like it might be of Overlook's magnitude.

The Old Man pushed hard all day, not sparing himself. He spelled me with the standard, setting its butt in his stirrup. Eventually he halted in one of the circles that occurred about each five miles. He stopped only because Lady insisted that it was time. He wanted to keep going. But the column was strung out for miles now and the animals needed rest and water worse than did the men.

I checked the clouds, wondered if there would be rain and if we could collect any of it. We had brought a lot of water but animals consume a lot and I had a feeling we would get thirsty a long time before we started getting hungry.

The Captain shed his helmet and the more cumbersome parts of his armor. He was less intrigued with his Widowmaker avatar than was Lady with hers. She bent the knee to comfort, too, though, divesting herself of her helmet, then shaking out her hair. Croaker stared into the distance. He asked, "You make anything of that place?"

"There is great power there."

"There is great power there," Croaker grumbled. "She's starting to repeat herself."

"That Kina's hideout?" I asked. "Or Khatovar? Or both? Or neither?"

"I'll tell you when we get there."

"Let me hold that for you," Rudy told me, offering to take the standard. He planted its butt and leaned on it.

"Where the hell were you the last fifty miles?"

"Fifty? You're letting your imagination overload your asshole."

"Felt like five hundred, lugging that thing."

Rudy chuckled. "Bet you we didn't do fifteen." He was having fun. At my expense. "Thought you'd be in shape after all those trips over to suck up to the Old Man."

"Rudy, I ain't in the mood for it." I wanted to keep an eye and ear on Lady and the Captain, who had moved away once Rudy intruded.

"Don't let me get to you, son. I'm just thinking about what a wonderful night it's going to be." Behind us the Nyueng Bao had their heads together contemplating those possibilities. A lot of bamboo was in evidence. Sparkle had a team erecting a community cookfire that would be elevated above the surface of the plain. Lady had an idea the road would not like being burned. She had suggested, during the hike, that it might be alive in its own way.

I wished there was a way to look inside her mind. She had been focused completely since coming onto the plain. Her speculations would be interesting. And she was sharing them with the Old Man, now. And Rudy was keeping me away.

"Hold on there," Croaker told Sparkle. "Go ahead and set it up. But don't start a fire. We'll eat cold if we can."

Shit. We had not eaten well since we left Taglios but plain water and jerky were a step beyond bad.

"Rudy. You got work to do?"

"Yes, Captain."

"Let me see you doing it." Croaker turned around, leaned close to Lady again, stared through the stands of pillars. I was willing to bet he was trying to face down his doubts. Right out there might be the culmination of many hellish years that had begun by what, I suspect sometimes, might have been the momentary whim of a man who had had no idea what to do next and who had big trouble changing his mind in public.

I began to prowl the perimeter of the camping circle. Wherever I looked the view was the same. With an overcast sky that was disorienting.

"Standardbearer? You all right?"

"Sindawe. I'm sorry. I guess I'm more distracted than I thought. I never noticed you coming."

"The place has that effect, doesn't it?" I got the impression he would have been ghostly pale had he been capable. "There's something I thought you should see."

"All right." I followed him through the press of animals and men all trying to set up camp without pushing one another out of the circle or damaging the road.

"There," Sindawe told me, indicating the road where it left the circle on the southern side, a fact I determined only because I could see parts of the huge structure down that way.

"A hole?" That was all I saw. A hole in the road, two inches across and a foot deep. Maybe more. The light was not good enough to betray its bottom.

"Yes. A hole. It may be a huge leap of faith, or just my imagination, but it strikes me that it would be a perfect place to set the standard."

"Sure does." Had I been past this point before? Had there been a hole? I could not recall. The opportunity to put the damned pole down for a while sure was attractive, though. And grew more so as I stared.

I dropped the butt of the standard into the hole. It went in a foot and a half. "That's good," I muttered. "Perfect place for it, too. Assuming the Old Man don't have some notion of his own." I stretched. I had not lugged the standard all day but I had carried it more than anybody else.

Sindawe grunted. He sounded nervous.

I felt it, too. Another earth tremor. "Hope it's not building up to a big one."

I looked down at the base of the Lance. The road had hold of it solidly. But when I put it in there, there had been half an inch to spare.

I tried to pull it out.

No go.

It was not vibrating anymore.

"Shit."

Sindawe tried to pull it out. He stopped before he got a hernia.

"No problem," I grouched. "If I have to, I'll just cut it off. Tomorrow."

I checked the Old Man and his woman. They still stood shoulder to shoulder, staring southward, now only exchanging the rare word or two. Even with their helmets off they looked pretty spooky.

Thai Dei materialized to tell me he had our camp set and food prepared. His expression was so bland I knew that he was angry. Here I was out gallivanting around, having a good time, while he was home working his fingers to the bone.

"I wish you'd grow tits and lose the sausage, we're going to be married."

Another feeble tremor stirred the stone beneath us. I murmured, "And the earth shakes when they walk."

"What?" Thai Dei asked.

"Something from a story I heard when I was a kid. About ancient gods called titans. I was just thinking how far I've come since then." And maybe we were giants.

102

I KNEW I WAS DREAMING BECAUSE THERE WAS A FULL MOON AND NO CLOUDS overhead. But there was some sort of haze between me and the world because the moon was just the center of a cloud of light drifting across the sky, never rising directly overhead the way it had in the land of my childhood. The ghostly, bluish light betrayed the restless shadows prowling the bounds of the circle, flowing over and around one another in hundreds. From a thousand miles away, it seemed, I heard Longshadow whimper without respite.

One large shadow pressed against the edge of the circle not far from where I watched. Something kept it from entering. It spread out upon that invisible surface. I remembered the time I touched a shadow while ghostwalking.

I began to find traces of the fear that had been missing since I climbed up onto the plain.

That one shadow seemed to be obsessed with me. I turned away and tried to forget it.

I looked up. Vaguely fishlike silhouettes moved back and forth against the diffuse moonlight. This must be the kind of view you would have if you were a crab on the bottom of the sea.

I do not know if it was a true dream. It felt that way. If it was, it would seem that shadows could rise above the surface.

The schooling shadows suddenly shot off as though impelled by a single will.

The moon was past its zenith. Maybe that was why.

Or maybe they were afraid of the creatures who appeared upon the black road, coming from the direction we were headed. They were the shape of men from the waist down and on their right sides. Their heads and left sides were masked by shawls that looked like they were made of polished brass fish scales. There were three of them. They felt like powerful ghosts.

My big shadow buddy did not run away with the others. I began to have some sense of it, as I had had with that other. It was terrified.

I caught one little flash of an instant in a place of torture, of pain beyond pain, while priests chanted.

I rose from my pallet. I went to stand beneath the standard, facing the ghosts. They let the shawls fall from their faces.

I do not know why. I thought, *You motherfuckers are too ugly. Get the fuck off my road. And quit messing with my sleep.* I had a feeling if they conformed to legend or whatnot they would be something like the Lady's Ten Who Were Taken, demons or sorcerer kings who had been enslaved by some power greater and darker than they. *Go on. Get out of here. You're dead. Stay that way.* I reached for the Lance, felt it come alive in my ghostly hand. *Go on.*

Three ugly beast masks inclined slightly toward the surface of the road. At least I think they were masks. I hope they were. Anybody that ugly for real should not have been allowed to climb out of the cradle.

They folded their hands before them. They began to withdraw. They did so without moving their feet.

Weird.

They flickered into nonexistence as they dwindled into the distance.

I stalked the perimeter of the circle. The shadows began to return. My pet matched my movements, always pressing against the barrier. I sensed a great hunger there.

I was surprised to find four roads leading out of the circle, matching the primary arms of the compass rose.

How come the east and west arms were not visible in the waking world?

The Shapechanger's roar reached into the ghostworld. Goats and bullocks protested. The men on watch, already scared shitless from watching shadows search for a break in the barrier, cursed all the beasts. Some went to beat the panther. Somebody yelled, "What the fuck is that?" and pointed toward the standard. The lack of light made it unclear. I drifted that way swiftly.

A white crow perched on the crosspiece, apparently sleeping. Which brought up a hundred questions immediately.

Was there another me up there watching from a time yet to come? Was the bird Kina's creature? Or Soulcatcher's? How had it gotten here, by night, from the world beyond the Shadowgate? I had seen huge shadows circling above . . . but I saw no such thing when I looked at the moon now. In fact, that untimely moon was no longer there. What I did see was a fingernail clipping of moon just beginning to rise.

More questions.

The panther roared again, this time in startled pain. They were paying her back for scaring the animals.

I drifted past where Croaker and Lady had made their beds. He was snoring. She was wide awake. She sensed my passage somehow. Her gaze followed me inaccurately. I lost her after a few yards. I wriggled between the cages. Longshadow was awake, too. He was sobbing quietly and shaking. I do not think there was anything left of the once dreadful, insane sorcerer.

Howler was awake, too. I realized, belatedly, that he had not been making much noise lately.

As I watched he tried to get off one of his ferocious yowls but nothing came out.

What had Lady done to him?

Soulcatcher was the one I really wanted to examine. And she too was awake when I found her. She was still bundled and gagged to a point that would have driven me over the edge, but she seemed as madly merry as at her best moments. She sensed me as easily as her sister had. Her eyes tracked me. They seemed to laugh, filled with secret knowledge. In fact, I got the distinct feeling that if she wanted to badly enough she could slide out of her flesh and chase me around.

No. But she wanted me to think she could do that. She was messing around with me even in her present circumstances.

That troubled me not nearly so much as her confidence did. She was not at all afraid or even worried.

That had to be passed on to the Captain and Lieutenant.

I drifted near the boundary, wondering if I ought to go see Sarie or engage in any of the hundred tasks I pursued when I walked the ghost-world. I did not really *want* to do anything but sleep. My personal shadow splashed itself against the barrier. There was some emotion there. But I could not tell if the thing wanted to talk to me or to eat me. It made me feel the way I might have, had I acknowledged the existence of a beggar who then refused to let me get away.

I passed a nervous Nyueng Bao prowling on catlike feet, his sword ready. The swamp men were more troubled by our quest than were the few Taglians accompanying us, despite their traditional burden of fear of Khatovar.

Sleeplessness was a common problem. I paused to eavesdrop on the murmurs of Blade, Mather and Willow Swan. No sedition surfaced there,

though. Swan, being Willow Swan, was telling ghost stories. I wish I
could talk about the man more. He was a character.

The Prahbrindrah Drah was awake as well, among them but evidently
not with them. He contributed nothing.

I drifted near the crow. It sensed me. It cawed softly once, opened
one reddish eye momentarily, resumed napping. But it cawed again
sharply when I considered testing the barrier's ability to contain me.

Without knowing how I got the message, I understood that it insisted
I go roaming only by flying above the plain.

The wings were there, available, but I did not choose to don them. I
continued around the camp. No ghosts watched me from any of the roads.
The east and west ways were growing tenuous while the route back north
remained solid, unthreatening, even inviting. My shadow companion
could not reach me there, either. The roads were protected, too.

I raced northward. I am not sure what I meant to do, though I had
some notion of visiting Sarie one more time.

Long before I managed that I got yanked back to my flesh.

I did find something else to intrigue me, though, right in front of the
Shadowgate, before I went.

103

CROAKER WAS OBNOXIOUSLY BRIGHT AND CHEERFUL NEXT MORNING. LADY
wore a secretive smile. They must have invented some kind of privacy for
a few minutes. "Why're you so grim?" Croaker demanded.

"Didn't sleep for shit."

"Nervous?" Half the guys were complaining about not having gotten
any sleep.

"Ghostwalking."

"Ah. And you saw something interesting or you wouldn't be in a foul
temper now."

I talked about everything but the white crow. I underscored my belief
that Catcher was in too good spirits for anybody in her situation. "She's
up to something."

"She was born scheming," Lady said. "She was manipulating people
before she could talk. Don't worry about it."

"You eaten?" Croaker asked.

I nodded.

"Then let's get them up and headed out."

"Hang on while I provide you with one final taste of good cheer from my midnight walkabout. Those people we saw running toward my camp when we were climbing the hill yesterday? Guess who. You say anybody but Goblin, One-Eye and Gota, you're wrong. I can't go back in time to find out but I think it's a safe bet they wanted to catch us before we came up here."

Croaker lost his smile. "You overhear anything?"

"A lot of snoring. They were asleep. Goblin did mumble something but it wasn't in any language I understand."

"The road is open," Lady observed. "You could go collect them."

"Hardly practical," Croaker said. "Even if one of us rode back the rest would have to stay here waiting. Half our supplies would get used just sitting."

"We could all go back."

Neither the Old Man nor I responded but nothing needed saying. She did not mean that, anyway. She was just listing options.

There was light enough to see the standing stones nearest us. The characters on them started to shine. They had not shone during the night. I wondered how they managed with so little light.

"I'm worried," I told Croaker.

"So am I. But we have to make choices. You think we ought to cancel the expedition because the prodigals crawled out of their holes?" He asked Lady. "Do you?"

"No. They'll be there when we get back."

I hoped her confidence was justified. Us being gone was an opportunity for all sorts of mischief to happen back up the road.

"Let's move them out," Croaker said. "Grab your pole and hike, Standardbearer."

When I went and tried lifting the standard it came up as though it never had been stuck.

That place up ahead never seemed to get any closer. I hate open country because of that. You can travel for days with the scenery never changing.

Croaker's mood darkened with time. He grew more impatient to get on. In the afternoon, when he spelled me carrying the standard, he began to pull ahead. After a while I asked Lady, "You figure you better slow him down?"

"What?" She had not noticed, so deep was she into her own interior world.

"Him." I pointed.

She urged her mount forward.

I kept trudging. Maybe I even slowed down a little. There was no drive to rush forward once the standard was out of hand. In fact, the world behind me grew more and more attractive as time passed, the sky darkened and the plain changed not at all. The only color anywhere was inside our party—unless you counted the gold characters on the pillars.

Lady caught the Old Man. I did not overhear their exchange. I suspect she was a bit sharp. He looked back at me, now understanding how come I zoomed ahead before.

He kept watching till I caught up. "You want to take this thing back now?"

"I still haven't got the kinks out from carrying it before. You just got to concentrate."

He grunted. And the next circle we hit turned out to be our campground for the night.

Soon after we settled the men began going to the southern roadhead to study the fortress ahead. And fortress it surely was, partially fallen. Speculation centered on whether or not we would reach it the next day and whether the Old Man would turn back if we did not. There was no reason to be optimistic about that. This close to his goal the Old Man would push on and worry about hunger when the time came.

This time we lighted the communal fires, enjoyed a warm meal. We all needed the morale boost.

There would be fresh meat from now on because we could not feed and water animals doing no useful work.

It is a tough world for livestock.

I asked Thai Dei, "There anything in mythology anywhere that might tell us something about that place up ahead?"

"No. At least in no way we would recognize."

"You sure? Your buddies seem real uncomfortable with it."

"They are uncomfortable with everything, this plain in particular. They can see this is a place that should not be. That this is not natural."

"No shit."

"It would take an entire nation a thousand years to build something this vast. No monument so huge can be a good thing."

"I don't understand."

"Only a very great evil could remain so single of purpose, so uncaring of cost, as to create something so ultimately useless. Consider the evil of the sorcerer Longshadow. He invested a generation in his fortress. It is nothing in comparison to this plain."

He had a point.

I stepped over to the barrier and stared at the countless sparkling standing stones.

A swarm of sudden shadows flickered over our encampment. I jumped. So did everybody else. The flock of crows wheeled, crossed the sun again, flew on to the north. All but one.

The birds were strangely silent. Not one caw trailed behind them.

The straggler settled atop a column almost directly in line with the fortress ahead. He stalked around, stretched his wings, settled down to watch us.

Pthwan! A fireball streaked toward the crow. It missed. It had not come from a dedicated crow-killer.

I leapt, grabbed Wheezer's shoulder, nearly spun him ass over appetite. But I did not get there in time to keep him from loosing another ball.

This one clipped the top of the pillar where the crow perched. It ricocheted slightly left and upward after taking a bite of stone, then caught the squawking, flapping bird squarely. Black feathers exploded.

The earth shook.

This was a big one. I went down. Most of the others did, too. Animals bleated and bellowed. Nyueng Bao yammered at one another. The plain seemed to shimmer and wobble around us.

Lady strode up, balance perfect, to all appearances completely unperturbed. But she kicked old Wheezer so hard he flipped over. "You idiot. You may have just killed us all." She slammed her hands onto her hips, studied the injured pillar. She did not look like a woman who was convinced that she was about to die. Suddenly, she turned and shouted, "Get those animals under control! Whatever you do, don't let them run out of the circle."

A bullock became supper because he was determined to run for it. People took Lady's orders literally.

The plain heaved one more time, then a stillness gathered. For several seconds there were no sounds and nothing moved.

"Look," somebody said, murdering the silence.

Part of the distant fortress appeared to be sliding down. In time a remote rumble reached us, long after a cloud obscured the place.

Wheezer coughed. "Shit. Did I do that?"

104

LADY WAS ALL BUSINESS. SHE SNAPPED ORDERS. MEN SCURRIED OFF IN search of her shopping list of apparently unrelated items.

I strolled around the perimeter while waiting to learn what she was doing. Other than the settling dust in the distance this site was identical to the last. When I got to the road leading south I found a place to set the standard waiting. I took advantage.

I went back to Lady and watched over her shoulder while she concocted a rusty-colored dust that swirled in a small, lazy wind-witch in front of her. She considered it for a moment, then sent it splashing against the invisible barrier protecting us from the plain. It behaved like a liquid then. It ran down the barrier, defining it clearly.

It also defined, as clearly as imminent death, the holes Wheezer's fireballs had opened. And the sun was charging the horizon.

Wheezer garnered some black looks. His hacking got worse but nobody offered any sympathy.

Lady kept everybody too busy to turn ugly.

The flock of crows returned for a second pass, this time laughing all the way. They circled once, then fled northward for good.

Lady's way of dealing with the deadly holes was not dramatic. She employed no great gaudy sorceries. She took Wheezer's ragged leather jacket away from him, cut chunks out of it, wadded them up and plugged the holes. Then she used some minor spell to cement them there.

Even she did not seem sure that her fix was a good answer. She snagged Wheezer's shoulder and dragged him to a particular spot facing the damaged barrier. "Right here. And don't move. All night. If anything gets through your screams will warn the rest of us." *Bam!* She slammed him down.

Not a good idea to get her mad at you.

As I moved back to where Thai Dei had settled I overheard murmured prayers from men who seldom behaved as though gods were anything but nuisances.

There is that about the Company. You see little evidence of religion. For most of us all spirituality resides in a blade. Uncle Doj was right about that. But his approach was just too damned mystical.

Maybe the Lance of Passion was once a tutelary but time has taken that away. Any information would be in the Annals hidden back in Taglios.

We are not really a godless bunch. We are just the sort who ignore the gods—probably in the unconscious hope that the gods will not notice us.

Obviously, in Kina's case, that was not working. It had not worked even before we knew she existed. Half the guys did not believe in Kina even now. That they did not, did not matter. Kina believed in us.

Fresh meat did improve morale dramatically. But darkness coming crushed it right down again. I did not face the night with any eagerness myself. I told Thai Dei, "I just realized something, brother."

He grunted.

"Almost all the important events in my life happen at night. I was even born right about midnight."

Thai Dei grunted again but this time looked at me with some curiosity and maybe a little surprise.

"What? That part of Hong Tray's prophecy or something?"

"No. But it may say something about your ruling stars."

Oh, boy. They let astrology guide them, too? How come I never heard of this before? "I've had a bad day. I'm going to turn in." Maybe I would get a chance to see my Sarie tonight.

105

STARS. I SAW SOME OF THOSE. AFTER I FELL ASLEEP AND WENT OUT OF myself and passed through the same murky world as the previous night, I found myself right there in the circle on the plain, my personal shadow oozing around on the protective barrier while scores of its buddies tried to get through the holes Wheezer had blasted. The old fellow sat where Lady had parked him, staring and shaking.

The stars I saw hung above the loom of the crumbling fortress. They formed the constellation that had been the subject of some discussion with Mother Gota a while back. The complete constellation. I wondered why I had not noticed them the night before. I wondered why I noticed them tonight. The sky was supposed to be heavily overcast.

A lot of seeing and thinking seemed to be very selective lately. That probably deserved some reflection itself.

There seemed to be a glimmer of light down south. Or maybe it was just a star caught between crennels on a battlement. Whatever, it went away. And when I went to the southern roadhead, thinking of charging ahead, I found the way blocked not only by the ghosts I had seen previously but by vaguely perceived scores more hanging back behind them. They were much stronger this time. They would not go away when I commanded them. Not right away. They made gestures and probably tried to mouth words behind their ugly masks. I was confident they were trying to communicate. What was not clear.

A warning, perhaps.

I did not go down the southern road.

I toddled round the perimeter. The east and west roads were open. Daring me, I ran down each a short way. They remained real enough but I did not want them to fade away while I was out there. I went back to the gang, then headed north. I would go see what was happening in the world.

There was a lot of sleeping going on around Overlook. Even quite a few sentries were snoozing. I made mental notes where I recognized faces.

I found Goblin and One-Eye snoring in my own bunker below the Shadowgate. Gota was awake but had her eyes closed as she murmured over a prayer shawl vaguely resembling those some Gunni cults used. But she held hers folded in her lap and ran the tip of her fingers over it lightly, as though reading something by touch. She muttered continuously in Nyueng Bao but I could not follow her even when I got up close.

She jumped, looked around wildly, apparently sensing me. There are elements of ancestor worship connected with Nyueng Bao beliefs. Ghosts are certainly very real to them. Gota started asking the air questions.

She seemed to think I was either the spirit of her mother, Hong Tray, or of her grandfather, Cao Khi, spoken of as a necromancer in family oral histories Sarie had related to me. When he got mentioned at all it was with mild embarrassment. We all have those crooked limbs in our family trees. A necromancer who could raise his own shade would make for a particularly gnarly branch.

I did not pay much attention. I wanted to see if they had done something with Uncle Doj. They must have collected him and gone to work getting him healed up.

I could not find Uncle. I did find a crude sign scratched on a weathered fragment of board, in charcoal, in One-Eye's crude lettering. KID. IT IS A TRAP.

Oh, my.

I wanted to shake the little shit awake and ask him what that meant. I tried. Maybe I gave him bad dreams. He did groan and toss. But he did not do anything else. I raged.

What if it was true?

How could it be? And who?

Catcher? Was that why she seemed happy? Or Kina? Did the goddess not want us running loose in the world, threatening to bring on the Year of the Skulls? But she had interceded before to make sure we stayed in the game.

But was it not Kina who had filled the minds of an entire nation with an overwhelming, irrational fear of the Company?

I was confused. I tried to shake One-Eye again. I had no more luck this time. Still raging, I zipped outside and started southward. And ran into a wall of death stench so powerful I reeled away.

Kina. Up very close.

I caught glimpses of slick ebony skin, a chest with lots of breasts, half a dozen arms paddling the air like the legs of an overturned bug. I got an indistinct impression that she was trying to pull herself through the veil between my ghostworld and hers. She seemed driven to deliver an important message. Or maybe she just wanted to jump over and gobble me up.

I did not learn which. I could not stay there. She brought too much fear with her. I fled. No plan. No thought at all. I just went, fast and frenzied.

I found myself in the mountains north of Kiaulune, running away from the plain with my back toward an unseen destination. From out here the stars of the Noose were invisible. No stars could be seen at all. The overcast masked them. I turned to see where I was headed. The sparkle of campfires away to my left caught my attention. I directed my flight that way. Whoever was over there would be human. I needed to be close to something human.

They were the bunch Croaker had sent after my horse. I recognized many of the restless men. Fear was an animate presence in their camp, and a big one. I got in among them, tried to draw warmth and comfort while I steeled myself for another attempt to get back to my flesh. Nobody sensed my presence.

Once I felt ready I left the circle of light and headed southward slowly, trying hard to sense Kina before Kina sensed me. Would she try to ambush me again?

Who knows? I ran into Uncle Doj first.

Actually, he ran into me. He was making no more sound than I as he scouted the camp. Pretty good for an old boy who ought still to be laid up with his wounds.

I decided to find out what he was up to. It was a good excuse not to fly into the teeth of the demon right now.

Maybe she would be more attractive if she would get rid of the necklaces of severed penises and baby skulls.

Uncle drifted along the edge of the camp, close enough to see anything that happened, far enough away to avoid notice by sentries unless he made a racket falling into a hole. In minutes it was evident that he just wanted to see what was happening, that the camp was not his real interest. He continued on into the night, still creeping northward.

I followed.

He dug something out of his pouch. It gave off a tiny light, less than that of a firefly. He consulted it frequently. I tried to get close enough to see what it was but he kept his back toward me however I maneuvered. He seemed to sense a watcher without being conscious of the fact.

Darkness closed in as the camp fell behind. But we were not alone out there. Time and again I felt Kina's presence, though never very close. For a goddess she did not seem especially omniscient. Or maybe she was not looking for me.

If she was in the mountains she could not block my way back to my body. But I was not scared now. And Uncle had begun moving faster, determined to get somewhere quickly. What would make him come out here in his condition?

It became evident soon enough. He wanted to take advantage of the fact that Soulcatcher was preoccupied.

He found what Croaker's searchers had not, probably because of what he carried in his hand. The hiding place was not obvious because a veil of illusion surrounded it.

The first hint was the snort of a large animal. A moment later I recognized my horse. And he recognized me although I was invisible and he had not seen me for almost a year.

The beast had more talent than Uncle Doj did. Doj thought the animal was excited to see him.

Uncle was more attuned to the waking world than I was, though. Ash Wand leapt into his hand as he reacted to something else before I sensed anything. I caught nothing but a flicker of darkness in the dark. I thought shadow but felt none of the coldness that indicated their proximity.

We were not the only ones out there.

I flitted around trying to find the lurker.

I found Sleepy instead. And the Daughter of Night. They were chained to a tree, each by an ankle, with ten feet of slack. They had no fire. They did have a keg of water that was nearly empty and a stash of hard bread that was down to the crumbs. Catcher had planned to be back sooner. Sleepy was awake but seemed drugged. The child was too small to break away. There was evidence Sleepy had not been able to pull himself together well enough to try.

I heard a choking sound behind me. Metal rattled on stone. A large object crashed through brush.

I found Doj on his knees, Ash Wand two feet from his fingers. His left hand was at his throat, clawing at a piece of black cloth. He was lucky. Few men ever survived such attacks.

All it took was a lifetime of training to hone the reflexes.

There was a Strangler in the darkness. And I could do nothing to help.

Doj's left hand dropped to the ground. With his right he reached for Ash Wand. His wounds forced him to stay put but once he had his sword back nobody would end his tale prematurely.

I went to see if I could keep Sleepy's luck from turning worse than it already was. I found him alert and frightened but unharmed. He was ready to fight. He was alone.

The Daughter of Night was gone.

I scouted around. Child and Deceiver had gotten away clean. I felt no need to hunt them down. Not now. But the task would rise to the top of several to-do lists real soon.

I had a notion this was not part of Soulcatcher's plan. Maybe the lady had been deceived. Kina was slow but she kept on plugging.

For the little it was worth I decided to hang around till Uncle gathered his wits and Sleepy regained his peace of mind. Sleepy recovered first. As soon as he felt safe he decided to take a leak. He did not know that Uncle and I were around.

Well. So Catcher knew what she was doing when she played Sleepy as a slim girl pretending to be a guy. Interesting. Sleepy did a great job fooling everybody.

I needed to have a talk with Bucket. He had to know something, somehow.

I caught a whiff of Kina. She was close and getting closer.

Sleepy jumped up, yanked up her pants, looked around wildly. She sensed the goddess, too. She concentrated visibly, turned slowly, tried to identify the bearing of the source of her discomfort. But the presence faded fast. Kina had no more interest here.

Sleepy stopped turning when she faced me. She jumped. Her chin thrust forward slightly the way people do sometimes when they see something unexpected. She squinted. "Murgen? Are you a ghost or something? Are you dead?"

I tried saying no, but she could not hear me so I shook my head.

"So the rumors were true. You really can leave your body."

I nodded, too amazed to wonder how the kid could take it so calmly. One thing people can always do is surprise you.

If Sleepy could see me that meant I could communicate over a distance. Even if he could not hear me. As long as he remembered the deaf and dumb sign he was supposed to have learned. But, as I recalled, he had had trouble catching on. . . . *She,* Murgen. She.

I had not gotten used to the idea the first time it came around.

I started using finger speech without the slightest idea of what Sleepy could follow. I might be just some shimmering blob of ectoplasm that smelled like Murgen.

No point. As I started Uncle Doj arrived, drawn by Sleepy's voice. His movements were a painful shuffle. "Be calm, young one," he said. "You remember me. I am of the Standardbearer's family. I have been looking for you." Doj was about as alert as any human being could be. He should have been able to hear me breathing. "You called out to the Standardbearer. Why did you do that?"

"I don't know. I'm trapped. A man came. He took the child who was here with me. I was afraid. The Standardbearer is my friend and mentor."

Glib, that kid. And thoroughly loaded up with a healthy dose of Company suspicion.

And I was thoroughly loaded up with a healthy burden of news they needed out on the plain. I had to go. Sleepy would be all right with Doj. I made the sign for horse. After three tries Sleepy nodded. I hoped that was a response.

Doj asked, "You were a captive of she who flies the crows?" He said that last part in Nyueng Bao, as though it was a name like the Thousand Voices, but Sleepy understood anyway. Sharp kid. Must have picked it up following me around.

"Yes."

"Did she leave anything behind? Where did she hide when she was here?" Doj cut Sleepy loose but it was obvious Sleepy's liberty was not his real concern. His behavior confirmed my notion that there had been a clash between Catcher and the Nyueng Bao.

I began to drift away. Sleepy said, "There's a cave. Over there. But we weren't here very long." She whistled a peculiar four note melody. My horse snorted in reply. He could not come, of course, because he was a captive himself.

I headed for the plain.

106

KINA WAS LOOKING FOR ME. OR FOR SOMETHING. WHATEVER DIRECTION I went I sensed her before long, though she never closed in. But if I was not her object, what was?

I fought off the urge to run to Sarie, telling myself to wait the demon out. But the logical side of my mind, logically, told me that Kina had been waiting for ages. She would not get impatient in one night.

But why *would* she want to find me?

I needed to get back to my flesh. The goddess was less a terror when I was not amongst the ghosts.

I wished Thai Dei would waken me. When somebody did that it seemed my spirit did not have to traverse the distance between.

I sneaked around to the camp in front of the Shadowgate. Gods, what squalor! Successful conquerors ought to live better.

One-Eye was stirring. So was Gota. Another terrible breakfast was about to be committed.

It was light out. I was still ghostwalking. I had not done so during daylight since we lost Smoke. I had begun to think that I could not do it during the day.

Got to get back up there, I thought. They need to know. They would not wait around for me. They would not carry me anywhere, either. I was no prisoner.

One-Eye seemed to sense something. He became nervous, snippy. Which was not much of a change, really. Then Goblin sat up and threatened to turn One-Eye into a lizard if he did not quit his bitching. Goblin had not aged well during the campaign and One-Eye did not fail to mention that fact, probably for the thousandth time. The bickering started. Mother Gota was not shy about offering an occasional opinion of her own. One-Eye found time amidst his endless verbal feud to cuss the rest of us for not having hung around till he turned up again before we went up the mountain. "They had to know I'd be back. They know I couldn't stay away. They went just to spite me. It's that fucking woman. Or the kid. They think they're punishing me. They got another think coming. I'm tempted just to walk out on them. That'd show them. They'd miss me if I was gone."

That was One-Eye all wrapped up in one quintessential wad of contradictory nonsense.

His heart would have been broken had he known just how little he had been missed by most of us. Of course, we had not run into many situations where having him around might have been useful. One-Eye—and his pal Goblin—was not much use during peacetime.

Suddenly, I realized we were surrounded by the stench of Kina. It had grown so slowly it had not intruded on my awareness. I squirted through the Shadowgate moaning because I might have missed learning something interesting. When One-Eye got to running his mouth he seldom shut up till he emptied his entire head.

I streaked down the southward road as fast as I could. Which did not seem very swift by daylight. Maybe I was slower with the sun shining. In fact, as the sun rose higher I grew more sluggish. And more easily distracted.

I noticed that every circle showed hints of gates for east and west roads. I became entangled in the puzzle of why they should exist, of what sort of tangle that would make of the face of the plain. If there was only one gate from outside and only one destination to be sought . . . The stones? The pillars. Of course.

The side roads could be used to reach individual stones. Though why anyone would want to do so remained a mystery.

It struck me, suddenly, that I had been in the same place a long time, wandering through the wilderness of my own thoughts.

I sat up. I looked around wildly. "Where is Narayan Singh?" I demanded. I was alone except for Thai Dei. There was no evidence the circle had been visited by anyone else. Where was all the trash?

"You woke up," Thai Dei said. People really sound stupid when they are caught off guard and state the obvious.

"Where is everybody?"

"You would not wake up. They left without you." Which meant without him. "The Liberator said he would collect you on the way back. He seemed troubled."

"I don't blame him. I'm troubled. Help me up here."

My knees were wobbly. That did not last, though.

"Food?" I croaked. Walking the ghostworld alone was less demanding than doing it with Smoke but still it drained me.

"They took everything. Almost. I was able to steal a small amount."

His small amount was actually a fair amount by Nyueng Bao standards. Those people thrived on two grains of rice and a rotten fishhead a day. He said, "They were generous with water." He held up two canteens, explained, "It rained while you were sleeping."

"What?" I muttered around a mouthful. "When?" I had not been conscious of the weather where I was.

"It rained. The water seemed to run into the circle and pool here.

Without harming the protective barriers. Will we wait here?" He sounded hopeful.

"No. I need to see the Captain right away."

Thai Dei grunted one of his expressive grunts. He found me lacking in wisdom.

We two could cover ground faster than the gang up ahead. After a couple hours we could make out a small group in the distance. I asked, "What the hell are they doing?" Thai Dei's eyes were better than mine.

"They appear to be handing things from man to man."

They were, indeed. We saw that when we got closer. One man stood astride something. He accepted an unhappy goat from a man nearer us on the road and passed it to a man beyond him. That goat appeared to be the last thing needing to be passed over. The man on our side hopped across while the fellow on the far side helped the man standing astraddle.

I hollered and waved. Somebody hollered and waved back but nobody waited up.

"Fucker is *big*," I said, meaning the fortress. Now we were close it seemed to swell with every step. It was built of a blackish basaltic stone darker than the surrounding plain. It was in a bad state of repair. "It wasn't immune to the earthquakes."

Thai Dei grunted. He was nervous again.

"There's what they were crossing." It was a crack in the plain. It extended both directions as far as I could see. Nowhere did it appear to be very wide though it was narrowest where our guys had crossed. It was about three feet wide there. They had even taken the carts and wagons over.

Farther away part of the fortress wall had collapsed and poured into the gap. The stone looked freshly fallen so I presumed this was the collapse we had witnessed. There were a couple of older falls evident, too. At a guess I would say the oldest occurred the day we felt the quake all the way off in Taglios.

Thai Dei and I were too old to run except when we had to. But we wasted no time. We hopped the crack before the goat guys moved out of sight around the curve of the wall. One was Sparkle, another Wheezer. Wheezer would be getting a lot of shit details for a while.

I huffed and puffed and hurried on. My pack seemed to be putting on weight. I panted, "It feel like we've gained some altitude since we've been up here?"

Thai Dei offered an affirmative grunt. He said nothing else. He was puffing himself.

I looked back. It did seem I could see more plain from here than I had seen from back up the road.

Thai Dei wondered, "Have the earthquakes broken the road's protection?" He must have been worrying for a while.

I thought as we walked. "Couldn't have. The shadows would have gotten us." There was still road surface underfoot but it was not as clear here. I wondered if the entire fortress was encased in protection and, if so, how elastic that could be. I was still alive but it seemed unlikely the fortress could fall down again and again without overstressing the barrier somewhere.

Once across the crack we were soon under the wall's loom. I ran my fingers over the dark stone. "Huh?" It was crumbly. "That look like sandstone to you?"

Thai Dei grunted negatively, followed that with an interrogative noise. "Seems like a lot of little tiny crystals. Like salt. But it is not sandstone."

Something had been done to it. Something not natural. That kind of stone stood up to everything forever—like the rest of the stone on the plain.

Thai Dei muttered, "I smell sorcery."

"You have a fine nose, my brother."

The guys we were following were in a hurry themselves, also following the curve of the wall and whoever was ahead of them. They refused to wait but we continued to gain ground.

We rounded a knee of wall and found many of the animals and much of the equipment crowded into a shady patch in front of what once must have been the main gate. I glanced upward. The clever builders ran the only protected approach where it could be bombarded at will for a great distance. I wondered if I went up there with a big enough rock could I squash the forvalaka. The black leopard was in a foul mood. She roared and snarled and chewed at the bars of her cage. She was being ignored because of her bad attitude.

I wondered if we ought not just leave her behind when we turned back. The shadows would find a way.

The other animals had been left to supervise themselves, too.

Sparkle and Wheezer, only twenty yards ahead now, were squeezing through the gateway. The gate itself was broken and twisted and hung on a single huge lower hinge. A big crack in the masonry indicated that this damage had been caused by earthquakes, too.

There was a large open space immediately behind the gate. Most fortifications have them. They are where you put the people the place was built to protect. A lot of the guys were there. A debate was running about whether or not the broken gate should be busted down so the animals and wagons could be brought inside. Concurrently, an argument raged amongst the Nyueng Bao about whether or not they were obligated to follow the Company deeper into the fortress.

"Shit. I thought you died," Willow Swan said when he saw me. "Thought we were gonna pick up the stiff on the way back. If you didn't start smelling too bad."

"Thoughtful of you. Where's the Old Man?" Mather and Blade, I noted, were not among those in the courtyard. I peered around.

Every vertical surface consisted of the same decomposed basalt. The inner fortress was so huge its magnitude would have stricken me numb had I not experienced Overlook and the Palace in Taglios. Though still standing, it had been cracked a hundred ways. Thousands of chunks great and small had fallen from its face and lay in heaps at the base of the wall.

"They went inside. Ten minutes ago, maybe. Shouldn't take long to catch up." Swan winced as he started toward the steps rising to the skinny door of the inner fortress. I suspected that, as he had a habit of doing, he had begged off earlier and had changed his mind since.

Thai Dei clumped after me, every slamming step an indictment. Because he joined me several other Nyueng Bao peeled off the debating party and followed.

The doorway seemed like a veil of darkness. It *felt* like a veil of darkness when I stepped through it. Like what I thought a veil of darkness ought to feel like, anyway.

There was little light inside. That little seemed to seep through unseen cracks above and ahead and got all the life sucked out before it reached me. "Quit shoving back there!" I snapped. Thai Dei's cousins were pushing me forward as they came through the doorway. "And be quiet. I'm trying to listen." Sounds were coming from somewhere. They were ricocheting around inside a vast empty space, though, which made it impossible to guess where they originated.

Willow Swan muttered, "I was right the first time. I got no business being in here." And he *was* right, for sure, as I would learn before much time passed.

"Quiet." In a moment I set off in the apparent direction of the voices.

107

I HEARD LADY AND CROAKER, BUCKET, HAGOP, OTTO, LOFTUS, LONGO AND Clete all cheerfully engaged in a vulgar debate. There was not one high-brow among them. When I caught up I found the whole Old Crew in one ugly clump. They had even brought Howler, Longshadow and Catcher along. Howler and Longshadow were out of their cages. Longshadow was presided over by Blade and Cordy Mather. Howler was alert but Longshadow was little more than a drooling cabbage. The Prahbrindrah Drah had gotten stuck with watching and helping Howler.

No matter. I approached the Old Man where he and Lady were crouched, peering through a break in a wall at something that was, I guessed, never meant to be seen. Croaker looked back to see who was crowding him. I demanded, "Where's Narayan Singh?"

"He's . . ." A bewildered, blank look captured his face. It was hard to make out, though. His whole crowd had only one torch burning for light. Longinus held that and he was about twenty feet away. Still, I could see Croaker well enough to see that, suddenly, he looked like he had been hit over the head with an axe handle.

I turned to Lady. "You tell me. Where's Narayan Singh? Wasn't he one of your favorite prisoners?" Was he not somebody who would have been killed a long time ago if a fool name of Murgen was in charge?

Lady just stared at me. I got the feeling she wanted to put her Life-taker helmet back on and kick me in the head. But she remained strong. She continued to avoid old habits.

Croaker said, "I forgot he even existed. How could that happen?"

Lady went on from there. "What happened? What did Singh do?"

I ticked fingers. "He escaped. He attacked Uncle Doj. Using a black rumel. He found Catcher's hideout and freed the Daughter of Night. They're on the run, probably already plotting how to get back in business."

Lady's fingers probed her waistline, then felt for a left sleeve that did not exist. She had no place to hide a strangling cloth while wearing armor. Her expression of surprise left her looking totally goofy. This sort of thing did not happen to her!

Soulcatcher, although farther away than Longo and his torch, heard me just fine. She made an inarticulate sound that had to be rage, began to flop on her litter. She seemed to be in awfully good shape for somebody who had been tied and gagged for three days.

I said, "I think the Mother of Deceivers pulled a fast one." I thought I would shut my mouth for a while. Croaker was so angry he was shaking.

Lady handled it better. After a long, exasperated sigh directed at no one in particular she crouched and peered through the crack again. I bent over. There was a hint of reddish light beyond her. She said, "He's marked now. He can be found. I'll handle that when we get back to camp. This time I'll take your advice." She shook her head suddenly, violently, as though trying to clear it. "She *is* insidious. I didn't think she could do that to *me*. Come on." She ducked through the gap in the wall.

"Here. Take this." Bucket shoved the standard into my hands. I had sort of pretended not to notice him carrying it. "Where the hell have you been, anyway?"

"I overslept."

Croaker went through behind Lady. A couple other guys were thinking about going. Nobody was in a hurry, though, so I shoved the head of the standard into the hole and started after it.

Croaker had a little trouble. He was a big man. I had more trouble than he did because I went into the crack with a long pole.

Thai Dei grabbed the standard from behind about the same time Croaker got ahold of the other end. One pulled one way and the other pushed the other and I got squished in the middle. After I yelled some and dragged my ass on through and got the damned standard back under control I took the opportunity to look around.

It was very dark in there. Except for the glow from a crack in the floor about a half mile away. . . .

Death is eternity. Eternity is stone.

"Stone is silent," Lady said.

It is immortality of a sort.

The earth twitched. From up ahead came the scream of stone moving on stone. A hulking darkness above the reddish lightleak heaved.

Men coming through the crack behind us forced us first three forward. Longo finally arrived with the torch. It did not do much to relieve the darkness but did show us where we were putting our feet. "One-Eye says we're walking into a trap, boss." I began telling him and Lady about my latest night of ghostwalking.

"Whose trap is it?" Croaker demanded after a while. "That might be critical."

I said, "I didn't have a chance to talk it over with the little shit."

Lady said, "It's my sister's trap. Have the men drag her in here. I'll stop listening to me and start taking your advice. She can stay right here when we go back."

I nodded as though that plan excited me. Far be it from me to remind her that she had killed Soulcatcher before.

Croaker raised an eyebrow in my direction but said nothing otherwise. He had a peace to maintain.

"Get them all in here," Lady ordered. There were times when she was something more than the Lieutenant.

They banged Catcher around good dragging her through the crack. But the bitch kept right on smiling behind her gag. That was unnerving. Which is why she did it, I guess. Logically, she ought to be starved, thirsty, littersore and very depressed. Few of the men were gutsy enough to stand guard over her while she was allowed to eat or relieve herself. Usually the job went to Swan or Mather or the Prince—if anybody bothered to remember her at all. Blade, though, would have nothing to do with Catcher. I think he hated her because Lady did and his regard for Lady was well inside the realm of obsession.

Catcher had a really dark and promising look for good old Murgen, happy or not otherwise.

"Start exploring," Lady snapped. She knelt over Catcher but looked up at Croaker. "You're here. What are you going to do about it?" It was obvious that she was suffering one of her mood swings.

I knew Croaker wanted to tell her that this was not Khatovar, to insist that we had not traveled halfway across the earth and had not hacked our ways through hell only for the sake of finding an abandoned rockpile already fallen into ruin. But he could not claim that because he did not know the truth.

He said nothing.

Croaker was becoming more taciturn all the time.

Lady muttered under her breath, grabbed Soulcatcher's chin and forced her sister to look her in the eye. "You have anything you want to share with us, dear? Is there any little secret about this place that you'd trade for not getting left behind when we leave?"

Catcher winked at me. Lady did not have a hope.

I got the impression that she was willing to haul out of there right now and to hell with puttering around the rockpile trying to get the angle on everybody else.

Catcher really was in a bad mood. And Lady, too. Lucky for Kina she was divine.

Catcher smiled and smiled but never volunteered anything. She would not, not to save her own ass. Which was what I expected. All the Ten Who Were Taken were vulnerable only through their obsessions.

"Shee-it!" echoed through the darkness. "What the fuck was that? Captain! Murgen. You got to see this."

Croaker shrugged and nodded. It did not matter what it was. It was an excuse to get away from the old lady for a minute.

I shuffled out onto a floor I could sense only by feeling it under my feet. Croaker shuffled behind me. He was muttering like an old madman, shaking his head, wanting to know what the hell he was doing here. This was not the place he had been going for the last thirty years. This was somebody's cruel joke. This was somebody's nightmare. This could not be the birthplace of the Free Companies of Khatovar. There was nothing here.

I felt his despair grow. And knew it would swell till it became deep and black. And then, in all likelihood, it would take a sideways turn when he convinced himself that it had all come to this because he had let himself get distracted. I had no trouble seeing the future, no sheep's guts needed. Sometime not long after we returned to Kiaulune he would decide we went wrong because we moved before we studied those early Annals. He would decide we had to go get them. And doing that just might generate the bloodshed needed to give Kina her Year of the Skulls.

She is the darkness, all right.

I was surrounded by females, human, divine and demigod, every one of whom could drape herself in that cloak. But right now lumbering, dull old Kina seemed to have all her many sets of claws firmly locked on the title.

"Yah!" The Old Man grabbed my shoulder, stopped me just a few steps short of daydreaming my way into an unscheduled dive into an abyss with no bottom. The weak scarlet light came up from that. So did a trailer of mist. But that gap got only a glance before our attention became fixed on the cause of the recent outburst.

Now I could get a fair look at what had heaved following that last little tickle of an earth tremor. "Torches!" I bellowed. "Get some light over here. Get some more torches lit." They did have plenty more, the brothers, but they were being frugal. "It's a big-ass old wooden throne." What I could not bring myself to add was that that big-ass old wooden throne had a big-ass old humanoid body nailed to it with silver knives. Throne and body were poised above the abyss, painted cruelly by the red light. I wanted torches so I could see the body better. I thought its eyes were open and I did not want that to be true.

"What the fuck is it?" somebody asked. "A giant?"

Thai Dei, lurking in my shadow as always, offered one quick phrase in Nyueng Bao. I did not understand anything but the accusation "Bone Warrior." "What was that?"

"It might be the golem Shivetya, Stone Soldier." Why was he dragging that old stuff out now?

"Shivetya?" I knew what a golem was. An artificial man, commonly created from clay. In some mythologies all of us descend from such divine knickknacks.

"It is Gunni myth, Soldier of Darkness. Khadi, or Kina, when she was young, warred with everyone. She so weakened the Lords of Light that the Lords of Darkness thought to see a chance to conquer them and sent an army of demons to attack them. The fighting went so poorly for the Lords of Light that the god Fretinyahl, who is sometimes said to be Kina's father, begged Kina for help. She agreed, but for reasons of her own. In the final battle on the stone plain Khadi grew bigger and stronger every time she devoured one of the demons."

This much of the mythology I knew. Among other versions. Some witnesses claimed Kina was created specially for the last great battle with the demon host sent up by the Lords of Darkness. According to others she was sired by the devil Ranashya who disguised himself in the aspect of Fretinyahl and had his way with Mata, one of the forms the mother goddess takes in Gunni myth. Still others insist Kina is not native to Gunni myth at all but is a powerful outside intruder whose presence was so wicked it had to be accepted even while mostly ignored.

The key story was pretty basic. Desperate gods chose to battle evil with evil and ended up having their weapon turn and chomp on their fingers. Kina's creator, or father, eventually tricked her into falling asleep, after which she was imprisoned until her worshippers could spring her with the Year of the Skulls. The Year of the Skulls was something that *was* going to come. There was no preventing it. Even though Kina was asleep and imprisoned a tiny wisp of her essence had escaped and remained in the world guiding those who would bring on the end of the age. But it could be thwarted indefinitely by the efforts of good and righteous men.

"Once they understood how they had damned themselves the other Lords of Light directed Fretinyahl to make a demon out of clay and animate it with a shard of his own soul so he would never lose control. This golem was given the name Shivetya, which means Deathless. Shivetya is supposed to guard the gateway to Khadi's resting place forever. I never heard anything about Shivetya being nailed into place but even the gods are cruel and unforgiving, Bone Warrior."

"No shit. And can that crap. I didn't like it from Gota and Doj and I sure don't like it from you." I looked at Croaker. "You follow that? You ever heard any of that before?"

"Some. A friendly old scholar in Taglios did tell me that while the exact meaning of Khatovar has been lost, similarities with modern dialect suggested something like 'Place from which Khadi went forth,' or simply 'Khadi's gate.' "

"And you wanted to go there anyway?" Were we walking into the realities behind the dark heart of southern myth? I did not want that. I wanted to be on my way to paradise. We were supposed to be on the road to paradise.

Croaker did not answer me.

"Tell me more," I said to the air. A bunch of torches were burning now. Most of the gang were ranged behind me and the Old Man. More light did not stop me having to see what I did not want to see. The thing pinned to the throne had open eyes.

It did not move, though. "Shit," Longinus said. "It's just some kind of goddamn idol. Don't let's get all spooked out."

I began to inch forward, lowering the standard so I could use it like a pike. I have no clue why I thought that might do me some good against some divine toss-off.

Croaker came with me.

We halved the distance to the throne. The engineer brothers stuck close with torches. Everybody else seemed less inclined to look at anything up close. I saw no evidence that the thing on the throne was anything but a carving. At closer view it did begin to look a little crudely made.

We halved the distance again. I could now inhale the thin vapors from the crack in the floor. They were very cold and smelled faintly of old death.

For an instant I had a sense of coming home.

It is immortality of a sort.

I jumped, looked around. Only Lady seemed to have sensed something, too.

When I looked back at the toppled throne I saw the hall as it may have appeared a thousand years ago. Or more. When a band of cruel priests were making the original shadows from prisoners of war. It was there for just an instant but that moment was long enough to tell me that this had been a very ugly place once upon a time, long before the advent of the twelve Free Companies.

"Stop right there," Croaker whispered.

I stopped. His tone was urgent. "What?"

"Look down."

I looked. Before us lay the desiccated remains of a crow. Just the way it lay struck terror right down to the bones of my toes. "A shadow got it. We're not safe here."

"We still have the standard." He did not sound completely confident, though.

I used my toe to flip the dead bird into the crack in the floor, which was just a few feet away. The effort was pointless. Some of the men had seen the dead bird. They understood its significance.

I understood that it meant a lot more than just that shadows roamed this part of the fortress. It meant that Soulcatcher knew the place well. It meant. . . .

Mad laughter came from back where we had entered. Soulcatcher's laughter. Lady spun, sorceries forming around her already.

108

THE EARTH SHOOK.

This was a bad one. The worst since we had come up onto the plain. Possibly the worst since the terrible one that destroyed whole cities and killed thousands before we ever left Taglios. I hit the floor and began to slide toward the abyss. Croaker grabbed me and Lady hung on to him. Everybody else fell down, too. Catcher stopped cackling in mid-laugh. Torches scattered around, dropped. There was nothing for them to set on fire.

Something fell from above. Something like little balls of glass or clear hailstones. Some shattered on impact, some bounced. They seemed to have nothing to do with anything. At first.

The throne with the golem aboard shifted, tilted forward until it was almost bottom up, a mouse's breath short of plunging into the red abyss.

There was an incredible flash of white light. It blinded me momentarily. While I hugged the floor Soulcatcher cursed someone in three voices and as many languages. Rips and cracks and barks tore the air as sorceries flew. More marbles pattered around me. I began to feel weak and sleepy. It occurred to me that shiny bits of glass were exactly what crows liked to carry around and maybe hoard up someplace so their boss could have them rain down when the passion took her.

Soulcatcher had sprung her trap despite all.

I grasped the standard and went fearlessly to sleep, happily sure there was no way Catcher could get off the plain. The shadows would get her. They would get everybody as soon as the sun went down.

I could not sleep without ghostwalking. The moment I slipped loose from my flesh I ran out to try to tell One-Eye or Sleepy or somebody what had

happened. When I reached the Shadowgate I found everyone shaken by
the earthquake and One-Eye already having worked out a pretty good
idea of what had happened. He had the troops packing to run for Overlook. In fact, that was going on everywhere, as though every man out
there had had the same notion at the same time. Nobody was in a positive
frame of mind.

It took hours to find Sleepy even though Uncle Doj had taken her
directly to the company he had circled during the night. She was asleep
when I found her, her disguise still good. I poked and prodded and
nagged the best a ghost could do and finally drew a response.

I spent much of the day slowly getting a brief message across.

It was nearly sunset when I passed through the Shadowgate headed
south. I was wrestling the temptation to run to Sarie. I did not want to be
around her when the shadows discovered my flesh.

I do not know what bizarre reasoning moved me. I was convinced
that I needed to be inside my body when I died. I might become an eternally wandering spook if I did not.

I met Soulcatcher halfway down the road. She was headed north
aboard Lady's horse at a hell-bent pace. Croaker's steed galloped a length
behind, running just as hard. Its rider had his face buried in the stallion's
mane but trailed wild golden hair that betrayed him. You cannot have the
woman you want, go for her little sister? Willow, Willow, you let yourself
be damned over some pussy?

I jumped in front of the lead horse, sure I would be seen. My own
horse had been able to see me. I would spook these guys.

It saw me fine. And ran right through me. Evidently ghosts did not
scare the critters. I jumped up and tried to swat Willow as he charged
past. *You treacherous asshole.*

Somebody had to let her loose.

How did she get to him?

I continued southward, mood bleak because of my failure. The entire
plain seemed to reverberate with Soulcatcher's laughter.

She had won. After an age, she had won. She had put her sister down.
The world was her toy at last.

Darkness gathered. I hurried. I passed a ragtag bunch of men and animals
in vain flight northward. They numbered fewer than half our recon company. Sindawe and Bucket were the only noteworthy names among them.
I did not see the panther. When I reached that crack into the innermost
room I found it blocked. Somebody had stuffed it with rags and rocks and
broken masonry, I suppose so the shadows could not loose. Must have

been Swan. Catcher knew shadows can slither through the tiniest pinhole. She was the new Shadowmaster.

What a shadow could snake through so could I. And Swan had not done that good a job.

The golem, or whatever it was, still hung above the glowing abyss. I ignored it. I had something to panic about. My body was not where I had left it. There were no bodies around. I had to close my astral eyes and let my flesh draw me to it.

I should have seen it coming. I should have known. I had been only loosely anchored in time for years. And so many of the faces had seemed to be those of men I knew.

My return to awareness, though not actually in flesh yet, took place in the caverns of the old men and the ice cocoons. And I found myself there, at the end of the line, sitting against the cavern wall with the standard across my lap. The Lancehead seemed to whisper and murmur to itself. The rest were everybody who had clambered through that final crack, Old Crew guys, Nyueng Bao, Cordy Mather, Blade, the Prahbrindrah Drah, Isi and Ochiba. Every last fool, including Lady and the Old Man. Little sister and woman scorned had invested the extra minutes to arrange those two, holding hands, heads leaning together, in mockery. Lady radiated rage. This was the second time she had been buried alive, the second husband with whom she had shared a grave.

The Old Man radiated despair.

So did the rest. This was the end of the dream, little as it had been.

I fluttered on up the cavern, between stalactites and stalagmites, webs and lacy structures of ice, to where, an age before the appearance of the Free Companies, desperate, hunted followers of Kina had hidden her holy Books of the Dead from the murderous warlord Rhaydreynak. Rhaydreynak had not found the books nor had Kina's children survived to return to them.

It could be worse than it was already. Soulcatcher could have found and taken those grim books.

She had not. They remained safe upon their lecterns, open to early passages.

I hustled back to the gang.

Some of them sensed me moving. They focused their anger upon me. Which was maybe good. *Water sleeps,* I thought at them. They were locked in some sorcerous stasis. I was trapped only in my flesh, presumably because I had been away at a convenient time.

Water sleeps. Catcher might be the darkness but she would learn. *Water sleeps, but Enemy never rests.*

*   *   *

In the night, when the wind no longer whines through a fortress that was there before the plain that was there before the first Free Company marched, stone whispers. Stone sprouts. Stone grows. Stone buds and stone flowers. A thousand pillars rise where no pillar has stood before. Moonlight sweeps the plain, setting aglitter the characters taking form, remembering a few of the fallen.

It is immortality of a sort.